For Paul + Frances + Joe + Audrey —
Thank you for the "Right to know!"
With respect and love,

D

**THIS BOOK BELONGS IN THE
TERRACE ALCOVE**

THE SPYMASTER

A Novel of America
by Donald Freed THE

SPYMASTER

ARBOR HOUSE
NEW YORK

For P.E. and H.M.F.

Then everything includes itself in power,
Power into will, will into appetite;
And appetite, an universal wolf,
So doubly seconded with will and power,
Must make, perforce, an universal prey,
And, last, eat up himself.
—WILLIAM SHAKESPEARE

Acknowledgments

Researchers from the Citizens Commission of Inquiry have been of long-standing help in securing and analyzing the voluminous and necessary Freedom of Information Act documents that this novel required. Jean Anderson, Dorothy Sinclair, Walter H. King and Eileen McGuire spent valuable time in both editorial and verbal help with the far-ranging time span of the book. Rita Levin's preparation of the manuscript over several drafts maintained the necessary momentum. My widely respected literary representative, Jo Stewart, was, as always, always there. Donald Fine, of Arbor House, gave generously of his enthusiasm and vivid imagination from the beginning. But it was my full-time editor and friend, Patty Ezor, who made all the difference.

A word beyond the usual acknowledgments is, I think, required because of the "amphibious" nature of the kind of novel of which

The Spymaster is an example. Like the ancient myths this kind of work constructs connecting links between actual events.

Readers are sometimes hard put to distinguish fact from fiction in the modern "novel of fact." The most unlikely or incredible events described are frequently factual as well as poetically "true." For instance, I am indebted to a number of former intelligence officers and analysts for material used that is both anecdotal and of historical magnitude. Thus, the reader can be assured of some new "hard" information in the Kissinger passages, as well as in the sections bearing on Senator Joseph McCarthy, the Rosenberg case, the Khrushchev speech, the Kennedy and King assassinations, the Black Panther party and the early days of what would later be called "Watergate."

In the record of the old hearings before the McCormack-Dickstein Committee can be found the traces of the plot by the "junta" to overthrow the Roosevelt presidency from within. In our own day the Senate Select Hearings (of the Church Committee) tell a story of abuses by the intelligence establishment, including thought control, character assassination and actual assassination. The record of former Nazis and present-day gangsters working side by side with officers of the Central Intelligence Agency now lies open before us.

The reader is also recommended to the study of documents newly disclosed under the Freedom of Information Act.

Langley, Virginia, 1970

"I DON'T see why we have to stand by and watch a country go Communist due to the irresponsibility of its own people. I am referring of course to Chile, gentlemen."

Henry Kissinger's mouth closed like a rosebud, or so it seemed to the Director of Central Intelligence, Vivian T. J. Prescott. Out of the corner of his eye, the Director took note of the tiny, angry doodles his deputy was carving into the yellow legal pad.

Vivian Prescott had been the Director of Central Intelligence ("DCI" in the vocabulary of Washington's power elite) since 1964.

1

During the six years of his reign he had attended perhaps two hundred and fifty of these top secret "40 Committee" meetings. Until Richard Nixon appointed Henry Kissinger—as his Special Assistant for National Security Affairs—Vivian Prescott's voice had carried some weight in this room where the fate of smaller nations was voted up or down.

So sensitive was this secret decision-making body that it did not include a single elected official. All members served at the discretion of the executive branch. When over the years since 1950 the public had chanced to learn, through the media, of the existence of this mysterious circle of power, then even the name itself had been changed: from Special Group, to 54–12 Group, to the 303 Committee to, in Prescott's time as DCI, the 40 Committee.

Except for Vivian Prescott, the committee had slowly but surely since 1968 become a rubber stamp in the hand of Henry Kissinger. In Washington's inner circles it was common knowledge that Kissinger's long knives were looking for the World War II hero, Prescott, where he had gone to ground in his CIA lair in Langley, Virginia.

Kissinger's guttural voice began to boom again. "The election of Dr. Allende poses the most profound threat to democratic forces in Latin America and to our own hemispheric . . ." The DCI's eyes flinched away from the perpetually moving mouth.

Today's White House meeting included General George S. Brown, Chairman of the Joint Chiefs of Staff, an ultra-conservative and hard-liner. Prescott's gaze continued to pan the table. Next to Brown was the Deputy Secretary of Defense, a man whose dossier at CIA made him vulnerable any time that Prescott decided to leak his defense contract overrun—more than nine hundred million dollars according to WALNUT, the CIA's most sophisticated computer. Kissinger's unreconstructed German accent rasped against Prescott's hearing ". . . of course there is absolutely nothing that the United States government can do against a legally elected administration of another country . . ."

The only other man sitting in at today's extraordinary Saturday meeting was an old friend of the Director's that he had met through his father many years before. Morgan Lowry, at seventy, was almost fifteen years younger than the distinguished father of the DCI, but his good, gray air of rectitude and tradition reminded

Vivian of his father, Samuel Adams Prescott, whose advanced age, together with the election of his ancient enemy, Richard Nixon, had forced him, finally, into retirement from the political wars.

The Ambassador to Chile, the Honorable Morgan Lowry, was the particular object, this day, of Kissinger's verbal *blitz-krieg:* ". . . the President is seriously disappointed that the embassy in Santiago remained silent after the death of General Schneider . . ."

The month before, in October, General René Schneider, head of Chile's armed forces, had been assassinated by Cuban exile contract agents of the Central Intelligence Agency. Vivian Prescott had been ordered by White House authorities to set the action in motion. In so doing, also on orders, he had circumvented the American ambassador in Santiago and violated the tradition, since the Kennedy administration, of ambassadorial oversight of foreign covert actions.

Ambassador Lowry's outrage at the execution of the leader of Chile's traditionally nonpolitical military had infuriated Nixon and Kissinger. Lowry's silence, his refusal to join the chorus of the administration's cover story (a jealous husband) had brought him to the 40 Committee and put him under the lash of Henry Kissinger's tongue.

". . . a Marxist government, elected or not, in our hemisphere, just when we are on the verge of victory in Southeast Asia, is absolutely . . ."

The Ambassador's gray head sank lower on his chest. That could be my father, thought Vivian Prescott. Suddenly he realized that Kissinger had paused, was staring owlishly at him. He repeated the question: "Mr. Prescott, does Central Intelligence agree that the Agency's hands are absolutely tied in this Allende matter?"

"Yes," replied the DCI.

Vivian sat across the heavy oak table from Dr. Kissinger. The two men were in dramatic contrast. Haldeman had summed up the power struggle between Kissinger and Prescott as the war of the Gai-Gai toad against the Siberian tiger. The Gai-Gai genus is a deadly poison toad. The world view of the Nixon White House displayed a rigid tendency toward seeing powerful men as paired combatants in the Washington wars of all against all.

The comparison of Vivian T. J. Prescott to a tiger was, the secret

3

services of the world would agree, fairly apt. At fifty years of age Prescott, a former collegiate tennis champion, was as lean and hard as he had been on that day at Forest Hills when, with the young Jack Kramer, the two American whiz kids had humbled the great Australian Davis Cup doubles team in a five-set match. If anything, Viv Prescott was a bit leaner now, the bone structure, especially at the shoulders, more prominent. You had to notice his long powerful hands with which, according to insiders, he had personally disposed of antagonists in a series of confrontations during the wars, hot and cold. His face and head were classic, with short curly chestnut hair, strong symmetrical features, very large smoky gray eyes. Richard B. Kenner, the current historian of the American power elite, had described the Director of Central Intelligence as the "DCI with the head of Moray's 'Head of Cronus Wounded'." Prescott's wife, in her down-to-earth style, had once commented that her husband "looked like Cro-Magnon man on a good day."

Henry Kissinger was round. His expensive suit did not really fit; it bulged and, somehow, sitting opposite the grace and potency of Prescott in the Brooks charcoal, seemed to make him look even more round and fat. But it was Kissinger who had more power, and since 1968 the 40 Committee had known that the Nixon-Kissinger entry would slowly but surely bring down the tiger. Already several "Special Task Force" teams had been organized by the Nixon men and the director had been excluded. He was not trusted to investigate the "bombing-in-Asia leaks" to the media. Instead, an ancient enemy and CIA super hawk, Francis Sherman Scott, had been appointed. Insiders gave Prescott six more months at the outside.

Nixon's master plan was simplicity itself. Henry Kissinger had been made nothing less than the czar of a vast intelligence network whose hidden budget was some twenty-five *billion* dollars and whose personnel numbered more than one hundred thousand agents. Kissinger's secret army included Military Intelligence, the Defense Intelligence Agency, the National Security Agency, the Central Intelligence Agency, the State Department Bureau of Intelligence, the Drug Enforcement Administration and, of course, the Federal Bureau of Investigation. Besides these, the Nixon-Kissinger group maintained close ties to multinational private security forces including Howard Hughes' organization.

Hughes was so closely connected to Central Intelligence that

4

many of the Agency's "supergrades," or generals, owed their first loyalty to the billionaire and functioned at Langley as double agents in a covert, ongoing power struggle against Vivian Prescott and his loyal forces. Like a tiger at bay, Prescott fought back with cunning and ferocity in the unequal struggle against the Nixon-Kissinger-Hughes forces.

The Prescott circle of power at CIA had been stunned the year before, in 1969, to learn that the Nixon-Kissinger White House had begun to put together its own secret intelligence agency. Presidential aides John Erlichman and Charles "Tex" Colson had initiated the recruitment of former police, FBI, CIA and, some said, beyond-the-law clandestine operatives. In charge of the entire array was F. Sherman Scott, Prescott's long-time enemy and rival at Central Intelligence. But Prescott, the spymaster, had counterattacked.

In 1968, the Agency—through its conduit the Pappas Foundation—had brought ten million dollars to Nixon in an effort to manage the vice-presidential nod for Spiro Agnew. So Agnew, repellent in style though he was to Vivian Prescott, was the Agency's man—in case of a crunch. Besides, the Director had infiltrated his own operatives into Scott's covert team, and through "assets" in the Secret Service, set up a tape recording system in Nixon's Oval Office and Kissinger's executive suite as well. CIA spies in the offices of the Joint Chiefs of Staff had been employed to steal Kissinger's closely guarded Department of State memoranda and deliver the documents to Langley. Thus, in a finish fight Prescott was confident that the Nixon-Kissinger forces could be mortally wounded from within. . . .

Sitting now watching Kissinger move mechanically through the agenda, DCI Prescott smiled inwardly at the thought of the document that he had two days before leaked—through a third party—to the New York *Times*. The memo was from Hughes to a high ranking executive in CIA's clandestine section: ". . . that we must exert more influence to continue the Vietnam war in order to recoup losses on the L.O. (light observationary) helicopter program. Order 'Ball Player' to approach 'Bismark's' brother and . . ." The identity of the cryptonyms would be revealed in the next leak. He would not, the director decided, go down alone. But, in the institutional sense, he *was* alone. Great generals who had been

5

his friends and World War II comrades—like Ridgeway and Gavin —had been driven out by the hawks among the Joint Chiefs.

The man's mouth kept moving. He was on to the U.S. "commitment" to the Greek colonels and "the lesson that teaches us for Chile." Prescott's teeth clenched at the professorial style. Greek colonels, South Korean despots, Iranian megalomaniacs, Latin American gangster premiers: an old professor of the DCI's had once said, simply, "Whoever fights monsters should see to it that in the process he does not become a monster." Vivian's eyes shifted. He was looking into the lined face of Ambassador Lowry. An unspoken message passed between the two men before they both turned their attention back to the talking face and the vibrating vocal chords.

. . . and this bloody Chile business, thought Ambassador Lowry, will be Vivian's downfall, I know it. They will order him to assassinate Allende and he will not do it and that will be the end of perhaps the greatest American secret agent in the history of the republic.

It had not been all that one-sided. The Estimates at CIA, under Prescott, had warned Nixon and his national security adviser that Vietnam was lost and that Africa would follow. When, despite these firm predictions, Nixon and the secretary ordered escalation, Vivian through his father had leaked information concerning the illegal and secret bombing of Cambodia and Laos to the New York *Times.* These stories in the press of the administration's duplicity had drawn blood and had put Prescott's name at the top of the White House enemy list.

Prescott, for his part, had powerful connections and a base of armed men loyal to him at Langley and in addition his estimates about the war abroad and the dissent at home, if made completely public, might wreck the Nixon-Agnew team's chances in 1972. Added to which there was what the DCI knew about Dr. Kissinger's private life.

When the Professor was not moving and shaking the world, he could be found involved in tapes of telephone calls of his aides and colleagues, secretly recorded for him. When he was not listening in on his employees, he was often busy with certain Hollywood stars and starlets.

The CIA had a number of contacts inside the Secret Service

responsible for the protection of the White House staff—indeed, they were not so much double agents as they were straight CIA penetrations. These men had provided the Director with a minute-by-minute account of a number of the Professor's enchanted evenings. "Fullback's" file (the Secret Service code name for Kissinger was "Fullback") was running over with what Vivian told his top aides were " 'factoids' that can be used if we have to go to the mat with our homegrown Dr. Strangelove and the rest of the Nixon mob.

"Let's see," the DCI would say, and begin the day's reading in his resonant New England diction.

"Item: Nan Marks. According to SL/TOR Miss Marks is to be noted because Fullback did *not,* repeat *not,* meet her through Mr. Frank Sinatra. There is no link between Miss Marks and organized crime, repeat no link, as is the case of . . .

"Fullback called Marks and introduced himself on . . . Fullback planed to West Coast for private dinner on . . . Fullback spent evening at dinner table talking about his career and future books he would write. At 2 A.M. Fullback accepted invitation to stay the night in Mark's pool house. At 3 A.M. Marks joined Fullback in pool house."

This sort of caper was child's play to the Agency, but the potential for compromise by organized crime was not. This was Vivian Prescott's most closely guarded material. His sources included former agents of the FBI, the CIA and the Los Angeles Police Department's Criminal Conspiracy Section.

The stage for the Kissinger set-up was said to be the posh Beverly Hills club, Le Bistro. An important investor in Le Bistro was said to be one Stanley Silverman, the attorney for and, some believed, the brains of organized crime and crime unions. It was Silverman who, at the club, arranged a meeting between Kissinger and the movie star Heather Court. Ms. Court had long been close to Silverman and his Associated Booking Corporation. Both Silverman and the actress had been indicted in 1969 along with a Cuban crime operative Estaban Oguvire in a federal action involving a $13.2 million SEC fraud case. Kissinger was introduced to a table in a private room for VIP's at Le Bistro. The party included Ms. Court.

The LAPD's Criminal Conspiracy Section (CCS) was thoroughly

penetrated by CIA-trained police officers monitoring telephonic communication between Beverly Hills and Palm Springs and Meyer Lansky in Israel, where the aging vice lord was fighting expulsion. According to Vivian Prescott's sources, the telephone contacts were routed through a conference line in a mob-owned Miami hotel. In taped conversations, the plan unfolded: To play on the well-known vanity of Nixon's gray eminence; to involve him with a beautiful woman; then to involve him in a scheme to use his influence to secure Israeli citizenship for the fugitive Lansky as an element in his agenda for Mid-East negotiations. According to the director's secret report, the final message from Israel to Beverly Hills was, "The patient is very ill. Find a Doctor immediately."

The Kissinger set-up had, somehow, misfired as Lansky was forced to return to the United States, though he was never jailed, while the doctor enjoyed a well-publicized friendship with Ms. Court. In Chicago in the 1950s, Silverman had used exactly the same methods to stop Senator Kefauver from any further crime exposure. But media sophisticates such as Prescott or Kissinger knew that this kind of story could be played two ways.

The President's man did not know that the DCI would not leak and use such information against him, did not know that the Director's image of a carefully married man was only a corner of the canvas of Vivian Prescott's own life. Because he could not be sure, he did not bully the Director or jump down his throat when he disagreed, as he did with almost everyone else.

As if tuning in again, Prescott was aware that the Professor's guttural disquisition had ceased. What had he just intoned?— ". . . the President's stricture is that the United States government not be compromised in any way should Dr. Allende's regime become unstable." The faces of the Nixon men in the room were perfectly blank. Ambassador Lowry stared at his liver-spotted hands, as if looking for traces of blood.

The meeting broke up quickly. Vivian rose first, leaving his deputy, Vic Korcuska, to gather up the charts. He pressed the ambassador's elbow.

"Give my love to your father," said the old man.

The streets around the Capitol were not crowded on this gray November Saturday. The Director's official, bulletproof limousine was waiting. T. T. Provosty, the man who had driven for the Director since 1964, wheeled away from the curb expertly, waving to the Capitol cop.

Vivian slipped his hands into the pockets of the oxford gray cashmere topcoat and hoped that no one would talk to him during the twenty-minute ride to Langley. But Vic Korcuska was upset.

"Mr. Prescott, I've sat in on some weasel-worded conferences, but this one was too deep for me."

The Director's deputy was ordinarily a very quiet man. He had grown up in coal-mining country poverty before winning a football scholarship to Notre Dame, where he had majored in languages. Discreet, dedicated and blessedly efficient, but difficult to read was Victor Francis Korcuska. He would rise no higher in the Agency, lacking as he did the Eastern Establishment lineage, the Ivy League credentials, the white Anglo-Saxon Protestant patrimony required in the world of Yankee power. "Someday," Vivian had once told his wife, "the Soviets will have a super mole in place. And he will be a second-generation Catholic from a state college who has just cracked his head on the low Establishment ceiling."

". . . I mean exactly what are we being asked to *do?*"

Korcuska also had a knack for sensing trouble, and he'd been sensing it for one full year now. Since 1969 he had been a regular, silent observer at the meetings of the 40 Committee and his suspicions had crystallized. The committee was a sort of fig leaf of legitimacy that could not cover the secret agenda of sabotage and assassination that Nixon's top aides and the Clandestine Section at CIA had concocted. His boss, the DCI, Vivian T. J. Prescott, looked like the other Old Boys at the top of covert actions, talked like them, but in his fashion was actually at war with them. Korcuska respected the DCI, admired the losing battle he was fighting against his own—the adenoidal supergrades from Groton and St. Mark's and Andover—and all the breeding grounds of the killer hawks with the perfect manners that he despised and feared. He wished that the DCI would confide in him more. Prescott was a man caught in the middle, between Nixon heavies led by "Fullback," and the hawks at his own Central Intelligence. But who was

9

watching the watchers? Korcuska planned to quit if . . . as soon as
. . . his boss got the ax, which at least would please his wife and
kids, not to mention Dr. Stein, the ulcer man.

"Later," said the Director. He looked out the window at the
historic architecture of the republic sliding by as T. T. picked up
speed. He was not inclined to tell his deputy that he read Dr.
Kissinger's message loud and clear . . . Since the U.S. overthrow
of the duly elected government of Chile would shock an already
war-torn America, he, as DCI, was instructed by the President to
go, laterally, outside the Agency to a private corporation with vital
interests in Chile, such as Anaconda or ITT, and to use that corporation's Latin American assets as cover for your overthrow. A
former DCI now on the board of ITT would probably be waiting
for his call . . . How long is the list of those who must be "terminated," the Director wondered as the automobile picked up
speed.

The black limousine was heading west toward the Potomac
under a leaden sky. Through a short tunnel, across the Roosevelt
bridge and over to the Virginia side, then onto the parkway heading north toward Langley. How many times had Vivian Prescott
passed the sign—FAIRBANK HIGHWAY RESEARCH STATION—known to
the secret services of all the world as the cover sign for the United
States Central Intelligence Agency.

The long Cadillac sped through the wire-mesh fence and past
the heavily armed guard gate, the man with the automatic weapon
waving the DCI on. The asphalt drive turned into a thickly wooded
compound in the middle of which was a huge parking area. On a
Saturday, only a small fraction of the Agency's 18,000 employees
were parked, and the limousine swung directly toward the gray
stone mass of the seven-storied building. "We'll go in black," the
Director told the driver, meaning through a secret entrance.

Vivian had always intensely disliked the aesthetics of the regular
entrance at Central Intelligence. The first story of the building
curved deeply in and out around a series of rectangular sections.
A concrete canopy loomed over the double row of glass doors.
Every building material chosen seemed to consist of some mixture
of the properties of glass, stone and marble. Modern with narrow
windows and plastic guard disks set in a frozen sea of marble. In

10

the center of the polished entrance sat the insignia: a sixteen-point compass rose, squared into the great eagle-headed shield of the United States. Just to the left of the shield, on the wall, in flowing script was the official inscription:

And ye shall know the truth and the truth shall make you free.
John 8:32

The inscription had always seemed gallows humor to Viv Prescott, coming upon it, as the visitor did, after driving through the electrified fence and past the attack dogs, into the eerie silence of the wooded redoubt in which the gray-white concrete modern fortress was set. This was the castle of secrecy, not truth; they all knew that, from the trainees who signed a series of secrecy oaths to the DCI who presided over the unremitting intramural spying between competitive branches of the agency. Here each intelligence officer with his laminated badge was a separate bundle of secrets. Here medals, even sports trophies, were awarded in secret. So DCI Prescott very seldom walked past the barred ground floor windows into "Moby Dick," as he often referred to the massive structure, and the cult of the clandestine of which he was the current high priest. He preferred to go in "black."

The Agency had dug a tunnel a quarter-mile long under its own grounds to provide a secret entrance for the supergrades, the Agency's highest officials—civilian equivalent of generals.

The DCI and his deputy walked into the private foyer, across the thick carpet, past the armed agents in gray flannels and through the open mahogany doors of the elevator. The elevator rose soundlessly to an unnumbered floor and they emerged, turning toward the executive diningroom.

The DCI was drained, as always, by the 40 meeting and needed something to drink. The corridor appeared to be totally empty and silent. As they passed an office suite marked "Project Records," the Director paused and inclined his head. He motioned to his deputy with long, tapered fingers. Behind the meaningless sign was a replica—not a stage set—an exact simulacrum of the interior of a miniature Swiss hunting lodge: high, slanted ceiling, exposed beam rafters, German water paintings. Here, behind these doors, the Director's enemies, the "animals," as he called them, could be

11

found—day or night, Saturday or Sunday, Christmas Day and Easter Sunday—planning and plotting against him, at least that's how it appeared to Vic Korcuska as he paused dutifully while the Director angled his head toward what might have been the low sound of voices within.

The executive diningroom was white linen and sparkling Lenox china and black waiters in starched white coats. Here one could order an alcoholic beverage. Here, both waiters and gourmet chefs were regular CIA employees. Their service was impeccable, their lips sealed. This was the dark marble tower of secrecy for those scions of Yankee power and great wealth who commanded the heights of America's invisible power structure. The Ivy League Brahmins, the supergrades who saw themselves proudly serving the nation as field marshals on the ramparts of Freedom in the cold and secret and endless war against the Communist conspiracy.

"Scotch," said the Director. "Tea, please" murmured his deputy.

"Vic, will you please call *Newsweek* and ask them to reschedule the interview for Tuesday?" CIA had "assets" swimming all through the major media, and it was time, now, for the periodic magazine layout of the "New Central Intelligence Agency." The process disgusted Director Prescott, who, the press always pointed out, was considered an accomplished author in his own right. The aim was always the same: no more "dirty tricks"—technology and surveillance overflights, the better to achieve disarmament, Mr. and Mrs. America. "Better yet," the DCI added in a low voice, "we'll do the damn boiler-plate and send it over. Spare me the boozers and spies masquerading as members of the Fourth Estate." Korcuska nodded. It worried him that the DCI seemed, these days, to be functioning in a constant state of low-grade fury, like a man who suffers from a virus for which there is no vaccine.

After a moment, an aide entered. The signal, "The DCI is in the building," had been flashed through the complex the moment the limousine had sped by the outer guard gate. The Director studied the message sheet: "Please call: your wife; your father; Miss Buchanan."

"Vic, go on home. You can still catch the last half of the USC game. Regards to Hilda and the family. Oh, have a very pleasant Thanksgiving, won't you?"

The Director then walked alone from the executive elevator

toward his seventh floor suite, past the always manned glass room where agents with snub-nosed .38 revolvers under their conservative flannels scrutinized all those who passed.

The Director strode through the cluster of empty secretarial desks and into his office. Fifty feet long, with a desk at the far end, expensive decorator furniture, the walls studded with framed photographs, the office could have belonged to the chairman of the board of any giant corporation.

The light was failing. Soon it would be night. The Director sat at the oversized desk that had been cleared on the previous day of all current work. On the empty smooth mahogany surface he placed the message list so that it sat there in isolation, fading into the thickening November light. Vivian forced himself to try to unwind and sit back in the reclining chair.

Out of the dimness the photographs on the walls stared down at him. Even in the dark, especially in the dark, he knew them all by heart. By *heart.*

Presidents and shahs, generals and war heroes from all the wars of his time. Faces that he knew were there in the dark: "Wild Bill" Donovan, Intrepid ("Little Bill" Stephenson), Leopold Trepper (the "Big Chief"), General Gehlen (the "Gray Fox"), H. A. R. "Kim" Philby, Allen Dulles . . . the pantheon of legends. These were the almost mythic secret warriors and master spies of the armies of the night. This was the iconography of Vivian T. J. Prescott, the spymaster.

The Director's wide gray eyes sank from the dim penumbra of the perimeter where the old photographs seemed to hang, disembodied and timeless. His gaze rested with something approaching pain—was it from pity or terror?—on a connecting set of four photos framed in silver at the top of his desk.

The first pictured a tall young man with the brow and head of one of Michelangelo's godlike youths. The supple, lean figure stood posed in the photograph against the ground of what could have been a park—or a cemetery, since the stone arch under which the young man stood bore the legend, "THE DEAD SHALL RISE."

The young man was, of course, himself, Vivian Prescott at age twenty.

But he did not recognize him.

BOOK I

CHAPTER 1

New Haven, 1939

Asleep on the Back of a Tiger

" 'WHY SHOULD I go down there and risk my life just to put up a flag in the Sudanese desert?' " Henry Harrison Hewes was eighty-three years old but the quaver in the old voice tensed, and the question of the tortured British subaltern to his fiancée rang out with all the callow intensity of youth and empire that the Liston Professor of Literature had brought to this moment for over fifty years. "Gentlemen, how is that question resolved by the end of *The Four Feathers,* this classic piece of nineteenth-century literature?"

The quarter hour was tolling in the distance from the churches on the Green. Henry Hewes stood in a natural spotlight of late morning April sun. Professor Hewes was Yale '76 and he could remember whole decades of upper classmen who would have tossed their hands into the air like caps to answer the obvious question posed in the story; but now some eighteen young men, connected to many of the first families in the nation, stared up at the old English master and only one hand was raised. "Mr. Prescott?"

He had hoped that someone besides the editor of the Yale literary magazine would venture a response. He did not completely trust Vivian Thomas Jefferson Prescott any more than he had trusted the boy's father, Samuel Adams Prescott, in 1904 when he, Hewes, had been Sam Prescott's master at Trumbull College at Yale; he did not trust people who were what Europeans called Social Democrats and what the press now called New Dealers but what he called Socialists. Especially when they used names like Thomas Jefferson and Sam Adams to add some luster and credibility to their crackpot internationalist ideology.

"Mr. Prescott will now, I believe, plunge *The Four Feathers* into the crucible of the 'New Criticism,' as I hear it is called in certain New York circles." Two football players snickered softly and three other seniors smiled.

H. H. Hewes could remember vividly when such a comment, delivered with flared lips on a background of teeth both yellow and green, would have produced a comforting yelp of student approval and all heads would have turned toward the red-faced dissident who had somehow dared to challenge the magisterial Aristotelian authority of Henry Harrison Hewes. But now these specimens of the class of 1939 waited and watched the old man instead, to see how *he* would take the answer from Vivian T. J. Prescott.

All of the other members of the senior honors seminar, "English and American Classics," respected Viv Prescott and most of them liked him too. Even the athletes had to recognize that Prescott was the best tennis player in the history of the university, a Davis Cup member if he chose to make the commitment.

Lean and graceful, rubbing an old blister scar on his racket hand, young Prescott turned his deep gray eyes toward the imitation eighteenth-century window and the clean blue New Haven sky beyond, and began to talk in a light, resonant voice, focusing thoughts and choosing words as if mentally dictating an essay for the literary magazine. He did not rush, though aware that the noon bells would strike before the discussion could be joined.

"Traditionally, the four white feathers of the story have signified, simply, cowardice, because of the attempt by the protagonist to avoid fighting for God, country and the monarch in the North African desert . . ." Hewes could not abide the way in which Prescott had inflected that word "traditionally"; the world had become hateful, full of tennis players and poets whose mission in life seemed to be to torment his last years—no, not years, *year;* this would be his last. With Prescott and his gang (Whitney III, Booth, Stimson IV, Coffin) in control of the university newspaper, the literary magazine *Furioso* and the other poetry journals at New Haven (and with Cambridge and Cambridge in England all under the control of Socialists and pacifists like Prescott), he, Yale's most distinguished and oldest scholar, would simply retire and die at once, he had decided. Prescott's strong, quiet voice flicked at Hewes's nerves like a thong's tip.

"Why indeed should he risk his life in the Sudan to raise the Union Jack? There was no threat to the mother country . . . 'Patriotism' is the euphemism of the Raj and the colonial office for the extraction of minerals and resources from the colonies. And the myth of the mother country and the White Man's Burden was spread like compost on the weeds by every element of the superstructure: the church, the schools, the charities and certainly the popular authors of the day."

The bell tolled noon; there would be no time now for the old professor or any of his loyalists to charge Prescott with alien and seditious motives and literary terminology. The old man opened his eyes, then closed them again against the bright spring sunlight. "Good morning, gentlemen."

Hungry students filed out. Viv Prescott was last; he paused to nod to the famous man.

"Prescott, when did your grandfather pass?"

"Three years ago, sir."

"Nineteen thirty-six? That's right. He and I went up to the Yard together, you know."

"Yes, sir, he often spoke of you and those years with the greatest warmth and enthusiasm."

"His reading of the Gospels was very radical for that day, but he was a very good man, your grandfather, very good . . ."

"He often said the same of you, Professor Hewes."

The old man's eyes were misted over as his Harvard postgraduate days of sixty years ago rose up for a moment in his mind's eye. The watery brown eyes behind the pince-nez tried to focus on the face before him. It, the face, was not overbred—the jaw was too square, the white teeth too regular—and the large gray eyes glinted with real intelligence. Young Prescott stood there, easy and light, the expensive gray cashmere sweater molding his long supple muscles, the blue-and-red striped tie slightly flared, the white shirt collar, soft and fine, rounding the tanned throat and the acute angle of the Adam's apple; stood there poised and alert, trying to leave his grandfather's old classmate spared of further embarrassment. Thinking, Professor Einstein writes that "anything that tells time is a clock." To Professor Hewes I'm a clock, and a calendar, and a gravestone too—he has to despise me as he despises the grave; my politics have nothing to do with it, or theories of literary criticism, or anything except that he and my grandfather were young then and I'm young now. That's all. . . .

Vivian was hungry too, so he cut through the law school quad, passing the cemetery, hardly looking up at the legend wrought over the gate: "THE DEAD SHALL RISE." He was thinking forward to midnight tonight and his meeting in the graveyard with Janet Hammersmith, the luminous young woman that the news magazines called the "ultimate deb." His thoughts were interrupted by Guy Standish, the photographer for the Yale *Daily News*. "Hey Viv, Mr. Editor, hold it right there in front of the gate. I want a photograph for the silly section of the last issue—you know, 'ELI tennis ace communing with defeated opponents,' et cetera." He raised his German Graflex. Vivian paused, struck a suitably mock-serious pose, then started walking again, even faster.

He came out of the law school, turned left, long-striding the half block to Trumbull and into the diningroom and the Friday filet of fish with au gratin potatoes. He sat by himself so he could look over copy for the literary magazine and waved to Arthur Gould III, signaling that their tennis game for four that afternoon was still on.

20

Then he turned to the copy. The tightly reasoned essay was the work of James Jesus Angleton, who had matriculated from Malvern College in England to Yale, where he had organized a brilliant coterie of writers and poets, including Archibald MacLeish, E. E. Cummings, Richard Eberhart, William Carlos Williams and Ezra Pound. Angleton, lean-jawed with Byronic looks and manner, and a poet in his own right, was Vivian T. J. Prescott's only serious competitor for the most respected man on campus. Included also was Angleton's poem, "The Immaculate Conversion":

> I murmur to see the sun and rain
> Quicken to dust the flowers again
> Quicken to flowers the dust again
> Quicken to dust

Vivian turned over the pages as the church bells tolled quarter of one, one hour until his philosophy tutorial. Angleton's copy concluded with the note: "Communications should be addressed to, and left at, George and Harry's until called for by my messenger." Vivian smiled slightly and sipped his cold coffee. "My messenger"; who would that be, he wondered, some Caliban of an undergraduate, an acned hack of a freshman writhing under the literary and critical tyranny of James Jesus Angleton? And yet Angleton seemed to know what he wanted and where he was going and that was more than Vivian could say for himself. He got up for hot coffee; the commons was empty except for two young history instructors agreeing with each other that the fall of Madrid was a curse on the houses of both Berlin and Washington. One of the instructors, Fithian, was an aggressive left-handed tennis player who could occasionally badger Vivian into a few sets. Now Fithian challenged him from what he believed to be his strength.

"What do you say, Vivian? Do you agree with your father's statement to the New York *Times* that he agrees with General Rojo and that he has so told President Roosevelt?" The stubby red-bearded Fithian crooked and waggled his first and index fingers to indicate that he was quoting Vivian's father. "Sit down," said the formal-sounding first generation academic from Boston's tough South Ward.

21

"I can't. I have a tutorial. What did General Rojo say that my father agreed with?"

Fithian flushed with eloquence as he gave a Boston-accented version of the Spanish Loyalist leader's statement: " 'You can conquer more ground, but you cannot conquer the people. Even if you succeed in crushing us, you could be sure that from the ruins of our cities and the bones of our dead there would rise the ideal of liberty and independence.' " Vivian, sipping coffee, cut in, "Oh, yes, yes, I read it in a wire story at the paper."

"Well?"

"Well what? You know my position: Berlin supported the fascists, Moscow destroyed the antifascist volunteer force, and Washington played both ends against the middle."

"I was referring to your—"

"Mr. Fithian, if you mean do I think the actual statement is high rhetoric, no, I don't. I mean great rhetoric is *Pasionaria* saying, *'no pasaran'* at the barricades in Madrid, or that fascist general calling out, 'Long live death!' He had a black patch over his missing eye and a steel claw for one hand, and that's my idea of rhetoric, Mr. Fithian."

Fithian turned puce, and as he was a Marxist, he bowed his head at what he hoped was an ironic angle and ordered Vivian back to his "ivory tower." Vivian smiled, eyebrows up, and walked back to his table. Actually, the week before he had written to his father that America's nonintervention posture doomed Spain to tyranny. In an unsigned editorial opinion piece in the Yale *Daily News,* he had written of how "the snow and blood ran together on frozen ground as Madrid fell"; how the "great city lay prostrate without fuel, food, medicine or hope." He had concluded with an invocation of Cervantes and the murdered poet García Lorca. If those references weren't enough to tip off a news hound like Fithian as to where he stood on Spain, then the hell with it.

There were some who considered Prescott a tennis natural and a scribbler of some glibness, another rich man's son with grace and magnetism enough to seduce a covey of waitresses and debutantes, but in no way a serious thinker of the first rank or sufficiently socially responsible. Vivian knew this and that he was envied as well for his physical and athletic image, his literary activity, even his father's close relationship with President Roosevelt. In matters of food, drink and the flesh he was considered only a moderate hedonist; the only exception to this being his relationship to girls. With them his reputation, like that of his Harvard friend Jack Kennedy, fell somewhere between a legend and a scandal.

He had just time to scan the *Daily*'s sports notes before leaving for his tutorial. American champion Don Budge was considering a professional career. The big redhead was debating when he should begin hitting those steaming backhands for money. Vivian looked up at the empty dining commons. Fithian, all of them, would shake their heads when they read that Vivian T. J. Prescott had declined to play for the United States Davis Cup squad in order to study abroad and work with the ambassador, his father, in the event of war. His father had asked him to come to London in September and he had agreed for two reasons. He loved and respected his father; besides, there was that other matter, a certain "debt." And then, too, he did not believe that he could become the best tennis player in the world, so he saw no purpose in devoting his time exclusively to match play as he would have to do if he hoped to rise to the top of the championship class. And that was the only class that interested Vivian Thomas Jefferson Prescott.

Vivian did not believe in being late. He swung around the corner of William Street and up to the sagging, weather-worn, wooden two-story house of Professor Rudolph Mann. Professor Mann was a distant cousin of the author Thomas Mann and Vivian had arranged to read Nietzsche and Heidegger with the white-haired exile from Nazi Germany.

Sitting in the plainly furnished kitchen that winter and spring exploring time and will with Rudolph Mann had been a memorable experience. Yale had taken in the distinguished refugee but had then given him little to do. The philosophy department was not at ease with the fierce, gaunt humanist, and neither was the German department; Mann was deep, abrasive, ironic and no great admirer of Ivy League scholarship. His tremendous erudition was intimidating to the campus community and he had no wife to pave the way socially for him, so except for three tutorial students, including Vivian, and one small honors seminar that met on an irregular basis, he read and wrote in German in his unfashionable, lopsided William Street house.

Vivian knocked on the screen door, breathing in the fresh April air. He could see the shining white mane of hair as Dr. Mann materialized in the shadowy hall, shuffling swiftly toward the door to let him in. Over cups of tea they discussed Vivian's term paper on Nietzsche's *Beyond Good and Evil.* It was a continuing tragedy in the life of Rudolph Mann that Friedrich Nietzsche's name was coupled in the popular—even the academic—imagination with Adolph Hitler's. Over and over again Mann hissed at Vivian that the blame belonged to "that bitch, his sister, that filthy anti-Semite of a sister," cursing her in German, and telling Vivian something he had not known: that Nietzsche's fatal syphilitic episode and madness had commenced on that day the philosopher had chanced to pass a drover beating his old horse unmercifully, at which the genius had intervened, throwing himself over the horse and taking the crushing blows on his own back. *"There* is your Superman," rasped Dr. Mann, looking out the kitchen window onto the pocked, weed-ridden backyard. Then, in German, softly quoting Nietzsche's, and his own, motto: "I love the great despisers for they are the great adorers, and arrows of longing for another shore." Rudolph Mann was that, a great despiser, a great adorer. At that moment Vivian felt love for the fierce, unbending European. Now, in the silence, Vivian, as had become his custom, poured them both fresh cups of the strong black tea that the old man seemed to live on. . . .

Just before dismissing him early from this, their last meeting together, Dr. Mann read him his own translation of a passage beyond pessimism or cynicism, fear or hope:

> Does not nature keep secret things, even about this body, e.g., the convolutions of the intestines, the quick flow of the blood currents, the intricate vibrations of the fibres, so as to banish and lock us up in proud, delusive knowledge? Nature threw away the key; and woe to the fateful curiosity which might be able for a moment to look out and down through a crevice in the chamber of consciousness, and discover that man, indifferent to his own ignorance, is resting on the pitiless, the greedy, the insatiable, the murderous, and, as it were, hanging in dreams on the back of a tiger. . . .

He was early, so Vivian sat down to think about what he had just heard from Professor Mann. The New Haven Green, from his bench, faced three churches and, beyond, the campus. As always after leaving Dr. Mann, he felt the stimulation of the philosophical grand tour give way to anxiety, even a slight sense of nausea, that led him to consider canceling his four o'clock tennis appointment with Art Gould, who in any case would be fortunate to win one game in a set and offered little challenge.

Just a week ago, here on the Green, Vivian had lingered at the edge of a gathering of more than 400 students, younger faculty, and local political activists to listen to Earl Browder. Browder, the premier Communist in the United States, had been barred from speaking at Harvard, Princeton, Dartmouth and numerous lesser institutions, but the American Civil Liberties Union had prevailed upon Yale President Charles to permit the Communist leader to invade New Haven with a broadside attack on "America and the Imperialist War." The audience was polite, apathetic, with only an occasional "Prove it!" interrupting the steady flow of agit-prop invective. There were mocking cheers and some sincere applause when Browder announced that if the United States would only follow the Russian system, "by 1950 every man, woman and child could receive a bonus of twenty-five thousand dollars."

Though Vivian's father was bitterly critical of the Hitler-Stalin nonaggression pact, and Viv tended to agree that it was the "vilest kind of opportunism," still he voted with the majority of the university newspaper's editorial board to have Browder on campus. There was some heat from Yale alumni after the New York *Daily News* bannered, "3,000 BOOLA BOO BROWDER AT YALE" and the *World-Telegram* opined acidly that "Liberalism has its sophomore class. . . ."

He felt a slight stirring in his loins, thought of the cemetery where he would meet Janet that night, quickly touched his crotch, tried to clear his mind. He decided that he would play tennis after all; politics made him sick. He thought of Nietzsche again and his contempt for *Zoon Politikin*, the political animal. Up at Cambridge the previous year, visiting his friend Jack Kennedy, he had sought out the poet Robert Frost's seminar. They had gone to Frost's popular Thursday night meeting in the comfortable Upper Common Room at Harvard's Adams House. Frost sat there cross-legged, talking with a New England music in his voice, telling the students, "Don't work—worry!" and "I save my scorn for the people who say what everybody else says. If you repeat a thing three times, it isn't true any more."

That's politics, Vivian thought, automatic lying. What had stayed with him most clearly, though, was the poet's injunction, "Don't write for A's, write for blood. Writing for A's is just practice. Athletics are more terribly real than anything else in education. It's because athletics are for blood, for keeps. . . ."

He would play one hard set of tennis today, for keeps, smash Art Gould off the court. The sun was moving across the Green and the sky was still hot. New Haven was flanked by mill and manufacturing towns crushed flat by the depression and he had heard the authentic voice of revolution or nihilism once on this same Green when a dispossessed farmer had screamed hoarsely at a few curious passersby: "If they come to take my farm, I'm going to fight. I'd rather be killed outright than die by starvation. But before I die I'm going to set fire to my crops, I'm going to burn my house, I'm going to p'izen my cattle!" Who would speak for these men, the Communists or the poets? Who would write—would he?—the tragedy without God that Rudolph Mann had spread before his eyes?

He sat there, staring at the churches on the Green and the college beyond, the School of Churches as it had once been called. On this very Green he had sat as a boy while his old grandfather, the Right Reverend W. W. Prescott, had fascinated him with fairy tales from the Industrial Age, of how the slave Cinque had, in 1835, been held captive. A linguist from the college had been able to establish communication with the fugitive and after twelve years John Quincy Adams had won his freedom. On this Green had been the first court and schoolhouse side by side with the jail, the stocks and the whipping post.

Bells were ringing from the churches over Vivian's hearing as they had rung there a century before, and the same sky, the delicate elms around this Green, where as his grandfather told it, "bound and corseted white women and black-coated, pale men had walked and stared for a moment at the slaves. There were ox carts, then, and the oyster booths and the farm wagons filled with fruit and vegetables . . ." Suffering and plenty on the nineteenth-

26

century Green, within the old man's and now the boy, Vivian's, remembering. The same state flag then, too, and the motto: *"Qui Transtulit Sustinet,"* "He who transplanted continues to sustain," *Psalms,* Chapter 79, Verse 3. His grandfather, the tall Episcopalian minister, had first told him that and much more, his grandfather William Warren Prescott, who had resided in New Haven within the living memory of the time of Cinque and the slaves.

Vivian could see it all again as he fixed his wide eyes on the old Center Church on the Green, the Church of the Regicides in the century before the revolution; the church where the news of John Brown's agony was told to New Haven. Before the churches had been the seventeenth-century meeting house, where those who had some affluence were called "Mister" and occupied the first pews; then came the "Brothers and Sisters"; then "Goodman and Goody." There were no seats for the servants and slaves. That was after 1630, when the rebels against King Charles I's taxation policy had "bought" the land from the Indians for a few knives and bolts of cloth. Quinnipiac, a "fair haven" indeed for the first families, who in 1776 chose Benedict Arnold as their leader. Theirs had been the "Fundamental Agreement," a shrewd blend of theocracy and mercantilism that made the New Haven First Church of Christ the ruling council of the New Haven Company. Vivian's father and grandfather had talked of this Fundamental Agreement to him while he was a new boy at Groton, impressing on him the responsibility, and guilt, of wealth and education.

Telling him, each in his own style, of how after 1643 New Haven's Fundamental Agreement had been "extended to the neighboring towns of Branford, Milford, Guilford, Stanford, now peopled by working-class and unemployed Irish and Italians." Then his grandfather's deep, pulpit-trained voice sliding in to steer the talk . . . "These immigrant offspring do not attend the churches of the Green, Christ's and Trinity, United or Center; instead they troop into St. Anne's or Holy Name of the Virgin, and they hate the Yalies whom they fought on Chapel Street with guns and knives in my time."

"Tell me about it, grandfather?"

"The ruined mill towns of the Naugatuck Valley are arrayed against the fiefdom of New Haven and its fortress, Yale. And your father sits as a trustee on the board of the Yale Corporation along

27

with the noble names of government and finance. But like Franklin Roosevelt, whom he admires above all men, Samuel Adams Prescott is not happy with any of this received position and latter-day version of the Fundamental Agreement."

Sam Prescott, it was true, mistrusted it and had passed on that mistrust to his son, who sat now trying to decide whether or not to go and change into his tennis costume as the churches all began, at once, to toll the hour.

Arthur Gould III's tennis shorts were too small for him. He was a descendant of Gould the Robber Baron and his socks collapsed around his ankles. Vivian was immaculate in his traditional whites; he moved, they said, like Frank Perry, with a kind of leashed-in passion. Bowing, sweeping, stroking, spinning, slicing; people stopped to watch when Vivian Prescott played. His long, tapered fingers gripped the finely balanced racket in the eastern grip, the better to take the low bounce off the clay court.

Gould was drenched, rushing back and forth as Vivian fed him long underspin drives to the corners, drives that skimmed the top of the net, rising into long flat angles, then hanging at the corners of the base lines. Gould cursed steadily under his breath as he scrambled up and down the court after Prescott's angular drives and smashes.

At five-love in the third set it occurred to Vivian that perhaps it was a mistake to so ruthlessly punish a fellow Skull and Bones Society member. But that twinge of protocol passed almost at once. Tonight would be his last regular session at the secret society and he was glad as he snap-sliced a drop-shot. So short and so exquisitely backspun a shot that it launched Arthur Gould III into a long scraping slide and left him face-down on the clay at the net, cursing the cruelty of Vivian, who was already trotting toward the showerroom, three rackets under his long muscled right arm. He did not look back.

He washed his brown sun-bleached hair, then soaped his lean, long body. The soap was slippery on his skin, stirring his impulses and thoughts up and out toward a woman, then away to that "ultimate deb" Janet Hammersmith, who would be waiting for him at the cemetery after his secret session at Skull and Bones this night.

Back at Trumbull in his single room, he lay down to nap before dinner. The late spring afternoon weather continued to hold fine and sweet. The only disturbing sensation was Skull and Bones.

The most powerful secret society of all Yale's secret societies was housed on campus in a squat, windowless pile of marble and stone with massive doors, clanking padlocks, and rigid security and code words. Into this tomb of a structure twice a week the "spooks" (for so the secret membership of Skull and Bones and the other secret groups called themselves) gave the password, entered and there carried out certain practices and rituals. So esoteric, so arcane were these rituals that they weighed on the imagination of the balance of the college community—those uninitiated and forever banned from the inner sanctum of Skull and Bones and the life of power and election to come for all those who had been "tapped."

There was a kind of continued clandestine warfare between Skull and Bones and the less important but competing secret societies. Scroll and Key, Book and Snake, Wolf's Head, the chief rivals to Bones's preeminence, all carried out yearly covert forays against Bones that included the offer of bribes to its building employees, or resorted to spying at midnight from the height of adjoining Weir Tower. In 1927 a member of Scroll and Key was discovered to have proposed marriage to the middle-aged cook at Bones, and only the intervention of his family forestalled this heroic espionage effort.

Vivian's father had been Bones, but not his grandfather, who considered the elitism and secrecy to be silly, if not wicked, and Vivian had realistically discussed the advantages of going Bones with Sam Prescott. "If one is going to work from within the 'club' to change the state of the union for the better," Prescott elder had said, "then clearly Bones is the royal road to that change." Among the dozen men chosen—"tapped"—along with Vivian for Skull and Bones were future bankers, high elected officials, newspaper publishers, and so forth. Which was why $10,000 was made payable to each new man upon being "tapped," and this draft, drawn on the Conrad Trust, was to be matched by an equal amount in the form of bank credits upon graduation. This was a lot of money for a young man who intended not to be a banker or a captain of industry, but rather to write and to edit a literary magazine in New

York or Paris, a magazine bound to need almost constant infusions of cash and credit.

And so, in his junior year, a loud pounding had startled Vivian awake in the middle of the night. As he opened his door, a Bonesman whacked him on both shoulders, demanding in the most self-conscious of late adolescent tones, "Skull and Bones: do you accept?" Then a black-bordered missive sealed with black wax was slapped into his hand and on the cover was written the number 322, which signified a centrally located room inside the tomb of the Bones building where the initiate would complete his rite of passage.

Vivian had resigned himself to the obligatory ritual, knowing from his father in advance the general scenario: he would be led blindfolded to an off-campus house, confronted there by Bonesmen costumed as skeletons who swore him to secrecy now and forevermore. Then on to the sepulcher itself, more passwords and then into the parlor: "Tonight you die to the world as you have known it and as it has known you. You will be born again into the order." The voice was not that of a student; obviously Bones alumni took part in these rites. "The vows you take tonight will bind you for life." The deep voice intoned an ancient-sounding contract to the blindfolded candidates, all aware of others watching them. The voice droned, "Good men are rare. Of all societies, none is more glorious nor of greater strength than when good men of similar morals are joined in intimacy."

Stumbling, those tapped were led into a smaller room and the eye covering was removed. The room was velvet, deep red—floor, walls and ceiling. Then the voice again from behind them: "Strip your bodies now as presently you must strip your souls. To the outside world everything that happens here tonight and henceforth must be kept in total secrecy, but here in the inner sanctum we Brothers in Bones have no secrets from each other. Strip, now!"

As an athlete accustomed to the locker room, Vivian was at ease with male nakedness, but some of the others shivered though it was an unusually mild September evening. To him their buttocks seemed to protrude and quiver and he felt somehow sorrow for them, and at the same time hostility for the unidentified voice booming behind him. They all stood there looking at the red walls or the red-carpeted floor. "As you are tapped you will be led to a new life."

In the gloomy light, one by one the neophytes were led to their coffins, the voice chanting over them of death, rebirth and loyalty to the Bone. Then the disembodied voice ordered them to get out, and their nakedness was covered by Bonesmen who draped them in red velvet robes cut after the old Athenian model. Now they were all chanting "Reborn! Reborn!" until the marble lobby reverberated. As they draped Vivian's long frame in red he could not help noticing how happily the initiates wrapped themselves in the velvet togas. The Attic theme of room 322 was now intoned as they gathered there; 322 B.C. dated the death of the Athenian genius Demosthenes. Three hundred twenty-two was a vault of a room in the center of the building. Spread across one arched wall was a painting in the Romantic style of a skull surrounded by whitened thigh bones and over the mass, in German, the legend read: *"Wer war der Tor, wer Weiser, Bettler, oder Kaiser? Ob arm, ob reich, im Tode gleich."* "Who was the fool, who was the wise man, beggar or king? Whether poor or rich, in death it is the same." Each man was given a bone with his name inscribed upon it, then ordered to disrobe again. The new men looked more miserable than ever; their bodies seemed to be turning in on themselves, their private vulnerability unprepared for the mud tank awaiting them in the bowels of the tomb, in the basement.

When Vivian later reported this to his amused father, the older man gave that long-faced chuckle and reported that, "In my day it was dung. What? Yes, you heard me—dung. Oh, yes, you *would* have . . ."

Then came the slipping and clinging in the mud as they were ordered by the voice to "Grapple with Evil; these are the birth pangs of your new life. You are born amongst urine and feces." As they were pushed and shoved into each other, Vivian took a nasty scratch when Arthur Gould III fell clutching at him. Vivian retreated to the edge of the 15-by-15-foot square filled with liquid mud to the depth of just under thirty-six inches, cupping his groin, waiting for it to end. Around him others grappled; some went under and came up vomiting, screaming, sobbing.

Lying on his bed, now, near sleep, the events of the night he had been tapped flowed across his screen of memory. The wrestling in the mud had been the low point; after that he had used tennis tournament trips to cover his absence from various functions, but he could not avoid the two mandatory confrontations of all Bonesmen in April.

He could hear Trumbull students talking as they passed his room on their way to the common for supper and he decided that he would not eat, just lie here with the warm breeze playing on him. It had been one week ago that night that the first of the obligatory two nights of confession had claimed him. The tradition was simple: on the first night you recounted your own biography, leaving out no failure, trauma, shame or guilt; on the second night, one week later, you divulged the peak experiences of your sexual history. In Vivian's case there was a connecting link between his public and private, social and sexual histories, a link that he had not and did not intend to reveal to Bones or anyone else tonight . . . or ever.

Except for that he had given a straightforward accounting of his twenty years. Born in Manhattan on December 17, 1919, the freezing winter of '19, to Samuel Adams Prescott and Jeanette Hurley Prescott. Her people had been Scottish and Scandivanian, Presbyterian and Lutheran, pastors and professors. She was a young poet with an interest in new directions in education and the radical depth psychology that she had come to London to study with a protégé of Sigmund Freud, Ernest Jones. There, in 1910 she had met and married Sam Prescott, who had gone to the London School of Economics after graduating from Yale in '08. He, Samuel Adams Prescott, the only son of the Reverend W. W. Prescott, had been all-league crew at New Haven, majoring in economics and theology, one foot in his father's world and one in commerce.

New Haven was the place that the Prescotts had called home since 1751 when Eli Massingdale Prescott had arrived at Philadelphia to represent the Crown's interests in that difficult day, and had by 1770 become a secret revolutionist, under the influence of Tom Paine and Sam Adams. Almost two hundred years later the two traditions, Tory and revolutionist, still bumped and bruised each other, especially in the Prescott men, many of whom still carried radical appellations like Samuel Adams Prescott and the son he would name Thomas Jefferson, much to his wife's amused concern and then insistence that the echo of the founding fathers be preceded by Vivian, a name enjoying some small vogue in the London of 1919.

The young couple traveled to Switzerland in 1911 to pursue their studies. Both of them met and talked with Carl Jung, whose theories were more appealing than Freud's to the poet and the economist still in their twenties, with everything good ahead of them. The world war, of course, brought them home, Sam to go to work for President Wilson, his father's co-religionist and old friend, and Jeanette to write poetry, sell Liberty Bonds and try to conceive a child. There were complications but finally, in December of 1919, while on a long visit with her family, she was brought to term, giving birth at 11:55 P.M. to Vivian Thomas Jefferson Prescott, and at 12:01 A.M. hemorrhaging to death.

In the hospital corridor Sam Prescott shocked the doctors by what appeared to be a wholly inappropriate reaction—he looked carefully at his watch and announced to the circle of anxious staff and doctors that "God is dead" and walked out, never looking back. But he took the baby and raised him, together with nurses and nannies and maternal aunts, and sent him off to Groton and Yale as he had been sent off. "And that," said Vivian to the room full of Bonesmen, "brings us up to the present."

A fact Vivian did *not* share with his fellow spooks was the occasion of the second Prescott fortune. The first money had pretty much petered out by his grandfather's day . . . "We were down to our last quarter of a million," is how Sam liked to put it. "Then President Wilson sent me as a troubleshooter to the Persian Gulf negotiations and I struck oil," he told his son. By the time he was ten Vivian knew the story by heart. Sam Prescott told it like an adventure story. Boys like Vivian were reared, literally, on the romance of money.

"During the first world war Britain was, on another economic front, fighting for the rich and strategic oil resources of the Middle East. It had been discovered that vast reserves of the precious commodity were contained not only in Persia, but in Turkish controlled territories as well. As soon as Turkey entered the war on the side of the Germans, Britain sent a message to Hussein, spiritual leader of the Arabs, saying that it would recognize him as the head of an independent Arab nation if his people would aid the

Allied cause by revolting against the Turks . . ." By this time his father would be smoking matches in his old pipe . . . "In 1916 Hussein launched that revolt with the help of T. E. Lawrence ('of Arabia') who had been dispatched by the British to advise Prince Faisal, Hussein's son. After a series of campaigns that yielded a stunning set of victories, the Arabs emerged as solid winners at Damascus. . . . It soon became clear, however, that the British had no intention of honoring their promise to Lawrence, of recognizing an independent Arab nation. What came out of the Turkish defeat, in fact, was simply an agreement between France and Britain to divide the Arab territories between themselves. I'll never forget Lawrence telling me that. . . ."

And this is where the unofficial diplomatic genius of young Samuel Adams Prescott came into play. Sent to these crucial negotiations by President Wilson to represent American interests, the quiet, alert young Prescott patiently kept the Arabs from walking out. His low-keyed but tireless resolve helped to hold the lid on the volatile temperaments of all sides at the negotiating table. His mere presence was soothing, especially to Faisal and the Arab League. He had won the respect of all sides.

Young Sam Prescott had ridden the crest of World War I and diplomacy. The magisterial Woodrow Wilson included Sam in the presidential decision-making process—to the envy of Colonel House and the cabinet.

While home from the Mid-East, the President asked Sam to represent him in New York at the legendary Round Table Dining Club where the diplomatic news of the world was regular fare along with the oysters and port. It was at the Knickerbocker Club that Sam was introduced to the American Brahmins: Elihu Root and Joseph H. Choate, Nicholas Murray Butler of Columbia and a complement of bankers, bishops, magnates and diplomats. After the likes of the Arabian potentates he had come to know, the Round Table was like a class reunion, and he was made to feel at home. Vivian loved to hear stories of this Round Table and wished that more of the lions of his father's day were still alive so that perhaps Sam would go back and take him along. But he had never returned, he said, after the outbreak of war when Wilson had severed relations with the Round Table because of what he considered their pacifist and isolationist views. In truth, Sam shared their horror of war and was just as glad to be posted back to the timeless desert and the oil underneath it.

The agreement had to be renegotiated again in 1918, once again with Sam Prescott playing the vital role of conciliator. There was considerable shuffling around of land and oil rights within the Arab world, but it all fell once more into British and French hands. Sam Prescott was particularly instrumental in getting the French premier, Clemenceau, to agree to cede control over all of Palestine to Britain.

Finally, in 1920 at the Peace Conference at San Remo, Prince Faisal stood silently by as he witnessed the dispersion of Arab territories between Britain and France, those territories for which he had fought so dearly. Behind the scenes, young Sam Prescott carried information, even "secrets," to all parties in exchange for Allied victory in the matter.

All sides were nominally happy and remunerated Sam handsomely for his efforts in the form of shares representing considerable portions of Arab soil and the black gold it contained beneath its surface. And, thereby, the emergence of the second and much larger Prescott fortune, its origin sprung from the earth on which he was to walk handsomely for many years to come.

Vivian would not open up this subject at Bones, especially now that in latter years he knew his father had soured bitterly on Anglo-American policy in the Middle East. Instead, he told them, "I never knew my mother, so her death was a historical rather than a personal loss, and thanks to my father my own life has been smooth and predictable." In the silence, the Bonesmen looked at him with a slight puzzlement; the articulate, clipped account had been like one of his critical essays in the literary magazine: cool and coherent but somehow elliptical and too understated, as if it belonged to someone else.

"Uh, I believe your father married again later?"

"That is correct. Three years ago, and his wife's son by her first marriage, Woody Cameron, is, as you know, a heavyweight in a certain rival secret society better left unmentioned." They chuckled at that.

"And the tennis and—"

"Oh, yes, the tennis." And that was the end of his autobiography. (They would have to wait until the next week for a summary

35

of his young if much speculated-about sex life.) That was the version of his life that he was prepared to make available for public consumption. For Vivian secrecy was simply a synonym for either discretion or privacy, and he did not intend to put himself at the mercy of his fellow Bonesmen now or in the future.

In point of fact, his life until prep school had been as empty as it had been smooth. From his father and aunts he had learned the facts of his life, had read his mother's poems and stared at photographs of the young couple in London, Geneva, Paris, Rome. Lithe and handsome, he had always been given special treatment by nurses, teachers, athletic coaches. His father, in the formative years, was a kindly but distant presence whose wealth permitted him to accept executive assignments with the International Red Cross and Herbert Hoover's European Aid Program. The relationship of father and son only really solidified after Vivian finished at Groton and was invited to accompany his father to London for a world peace conference in 1936.

What the Prescott scion saw in London that summer was a conspicuous absence of the climate of fear and foreboding that was building on the Continent. A few voices, like that of Winston Churchill, broke the calm progression of British life—the seaside bank holidays of August, the Bournemouth Open Bowls Tournament, the polo games at Le Tourquet—to warn of the "ferocious passions" stirring across the Channel, where the man Parliament was calling "Herr Hitler" played a much deadlier game.

A call from Jack Kennedy, who with his father and brother Joe, Jr., was a guest of the U.S. Ambassador, Robert Worth Bingham, began a congenial series of afternoon chatter and card games for the two boys at the thirty-six-room embassy in Grosvenor Square. Within two years Bingham's illness would force him to retire and the new ambassador, Joseph P. Kennedy, would be back to stay, bringing with him his wife Rose and what the London papers dubbed "The U.S.A.'s Nine-Child Envoy." While the head of the clan might shock the protocol-conscious British with his refusal to wear knee-britches in court, his elegant wife and handsome offspring would make a favorable impression in print as well as in the high circles of London society.

The London of '36 was ablaze with politics, and it was here that Vivian realized that his father was more than a dedicated antifascist but, indeed, an exponent of the philosophy exemplified by the British Labor Party. Despite his wide travels Sam Prescott believed passionately in an American dream a good deal more radical than his much admired friend, Franklin Roosevelt, for whose second term Sam Prescott had worked long and hard. Vivian discovered that his father was not afraid of the Marxists, but followed instead the concepts of social justice identified with such American philosophers as Horace Greeley, Edward Bellamy, Henry George, Gaylord Wilshire of California and, most of all, Eugene V. Debs. The wealth of the Prescott family had not blinded him, he told his son quietly, "to the thousand million men, women and children of this world whose lives are stunted, brutish and short—blighted by the unrestrained greed of monopoly capitalism worldwide. Viv," he said, "I believe there is under heaven such a thing as capitalism with a human face, and if we are to avoid another world war we must find it or, rather, create it."

The sixteen-year-old tennis prodigy had just returned from a session on the famous Wimbledon grass courts when the conversation took place as the two sat drinking tea at Harwood House at Bletchley, outside London, where they were guests for the summer. The economist and amateur statesman looked closely at his tall, bronzed son. "I think if your mother had lived, I *know* that she would have felt that we have to do everything, give everything we've got to stop another war."

After that they had had a number of talks, sometimes with other guests, peers of the English nobility, some of whom were prepared to see in their time the class of the big capitalists reduced to a managerial role in a planned and democratic society of the future. In any case, they always said, the alternatives were Hitler's fascism or Stalin's communism. That summer, too, Vivian realized that though a widower, his father was a much sought-after single man whose companions at the theater or symphony were not so matronly as to exclude them from Vivian's by now rich sexual fantasy life.

None of this would he ever reveal at Bones, or that his first full sexual experience had been with his father's new wife the following year. . . .

At Christmas, after the London visit, Sam Prescott had married a tall, strikingly beautiful woman of thirty-seven. Nancy Jones-

Moreland Cameron had been the young wife of H. H. "Bull" Cameron, the Union Oil scion. After his alcoholic suicide, she had put her young son in a series of European boarding schools and followed her bent for travel, culture and powerful men. Now in her late thirties, her beauty at its ripest, she considered making another match as a hedge against the years to come. Sam Prescott was of the correct class but what was rare was his character and integrity. This tall, straight man with the sad, strong, long face and the quiet voice was a husband who would not rot with age. She knew that in his seventies, as in his fifties, he would still be upright in Brooks Brothers grays and blues. The truth was that she had a horror of aging and losing that elasticity of body and face that had taken her to the salons of New York to model styles for the Four Hundred when she was only an eighteen-year-old New Jersey high school graduate from a home of old English stock.

Except that nothing about her official background was true. Her mother was Hungarian, and Nancy Jones-Moreland, as she called herself, reflected her eastern European heritage in her rich dark hair, and the olive skin, red and caramel lit with subtle and cunning texture. Her home had been brutal and her introduction to the flesh had come at the hands of "Uncle Al" when she was fourteen. When she left at seventeen her beauty was extraordinary and she had the instincts of a consummate actress who no doubt could have been a star had she not chosen the feature role in her own romance. She was a mythomaniac, believed her own self-started legend and would have insisted on it under torture, but at the same time she knew her years as an international symbol were numbered, and so she came to marry a good man.

That first summer the four of them—Sam and Nancy, Vivian and Nancy's son Woodrow—settled in for a vacation on Deer Island, a part of the Thousand Islands in the St. Lawrence River and a holding of the Conrad Trust, available to Skull and Bonesmen and their families. Here the gene pool of the ruling class met and mingled. Bonesmen of all ages repaired here for holidays, bringing their daughters with them so that the rate of intermarriage bordered statistically on incest. And it was here that Vivian fell into the trap of technical incest . . .

On the fourth of August Sam Prescott received an urgent request to join the President at his Hyde Park estate in New York.

Vivian had never seen his father so agitated. The man who had come for his father was retired early in the guest room, exhausted from the ferryboat ride to the island after a long train trip. Sam signaled his son to join him on a walk to the end of the big white pier that fronted their guest house. There he smoked a pipe until most of the visitors had turned back toward the beach, leaving the two of them in the shadows, the lapping water covering the murmur of their voices.

"Son, that man, Mr. Gristeide, is a Secret Service agent. He was authorized to tell me why I'm required on short notice in New York State. What I'm going to tell you please treat in complete confidence unless some incident should occur that you would consider, ah, catastrophic. I don't mean to be an alarmist, but the situation is absolutely urgent . . . Where to begin? Well, you know that some very important industrial figures in this country are not only sympathetic to Germany and Italy, politically I mean, and of course are linked together in cartels such as the I. G. Farben network and— am I making sense to you, Viv? Good. Now, I learned today that a group of these men—the President calls them the *'Junta'*—led by agents of the House of Morgan and the Henry Ford America First circle, with their insane hatred for the President, this Junta has attempted to recruit a high-ranking Marine Corps general named Smedley Butler—you've heard of him—to lead a veterans' march on Washington. And this time they would not be driven out by General MacArthur but instead would remain until their leader, General Butler, was given a seat in FDR's cabinet. In reality, however, the Morgan-Ford interests would control the government and move at once toward an industrial fascist state, *here* in America . . ."

Vivian stared at his father in the dark moonlit shadow; behind him the lapping water reflected more moon. He couldn't believe his ears. This was America.

His father's voice was unsteady . . . "This army of veterans, bankrolled by big business, would save the nation, according to these plotters—save it from unemployment, for example, by putting those out of work into forced labor camps, by registering every man, woman and child in the country to guard against dissent." . . . Sam Prescott filled his pipe but didn't light it; he was too upset. "I'll leave first thing in the morning—Woody will go in with me then instead of next week for his dental work. You and Nancy stand by here. The Secret Service man says that the Chief is confident about the outcome because General Butler had just been leading the Junta conspirators along the entire time and reporting to the Justice Department. He's a great man. So, as I understand it, if all is well the brain trust and a few amateurs like myself will brief the press and others so that these bastards are on the spot, and if war *does* come this can always be used to remind the press just *who* is *who.*"

Vivian had never seen his father so exercised, or felt so close to him. They walked back to the house and sat down around the kitchen table with Woody and Nancy. Cupping the cocoa mugs and talking quietly so as not to disturb Mr. Gristeide, the Secret Service man, they looked and sounded like any family on holiday who wouldn't know what the words "fascist *putsch*" meant if they heard them in reference to *America . . .*

Vivian and Nancy were separately occupied the next day. She was at a neighbor's for a facial massage while he stayed in despite the bright weather, reading an anthology and restlessly waiting for the word from his father, though he knew it must be another twenty-four hours at least before the situation was clarified.

It was still quite light when they sat down to eat the rare steak and salad that Nancy had organized. As a cook, she was quick and talented, with an eye for color as well as taste. They each had a glass of wine. He noticed that Nancy, like some others, at times seemed intoxicated by even the smallest consumption of alcohol —not always, but sometimes, like tonight.

"Oh, I have no head for wine tonight, maybe because it's not dark yet. Will you excuse me if I step out for some air?"

"Sure. I'll do the dishes."

"You are a sweet boy—even if I am just your stepmother." She laughed, slurring the words just a shade, handed him her light cashmere sweater and stood so that he could help her on with it. Her white cotton skirt and blouse set off the gleaming dark color of her long legs. She was slim but with full breasts thrust forward by her model's posture. He took a step closer to slip the sweater over her shoulders and in so doing his fingers barely grazed her exposed flesh. Later he knew that that moment was chemically or psychologically or somehow singled out, and that everything that happened later was not only inevitable but willful, in the true sense of that word. As if the touch had somehow abstracted and codified fugitive impulses never before admitted and imprinted them like a blueprint on their bodies. She never turned, but walked quickly out into the first twilight.

Vivian walked straight into his bedroom, undressed and lay down on his stomach with a book of short stories. He was tumescent, larger than he had ever been, his groin contracted; he clenched the book and tried with all his might to focus on tennis. After a moment he knew that the crisis had passed, and that he could now turn over and masturbate with the secure image in his mind of the young prostitute that he and Jack Kennedy had shared the summer before in London. He closed his eyes and began to stroke the sheath of flesh with one hand while fingering his nipples lightly as the Cockney girl had done in London.

Whatever it was that made him open his eyes, it was not any noise that Nancy had made. She stood in the bedroom door as if mesmerized. He did not blush; his gray eyes were huge and dark as he watched her, his hand on his groin not frozen, just still for a moment. Her eyes never left his body.

"Did you want me?" she asked directly. "I want you." She shook the sweater from her shoulders with an imperceptible twitch, the way a cat ripples its surface musculature. His breathing was shallow but steady—still no fear, like an actor in a moment of public solitude, an actor who has played the role before and will play it again. But he could not speak. The spill from the bedside reading lamp fell across his body, leaving only his eyes in shadow.

Slowly, her dark eyes never wavering, she began to unbutton her blouse, then shook it back and off, arching her shoulders, the V of the white brassiere thrusting upward, then rounding her shoulders and reaching up and behind to unsnap the elastic and then bringing her arms and hands forward, hooking the brassiere with her thumbs so that it dropped lightly to the floor in front of her. The white cotton and the white sweater were like a pool of moonlight around her feet. As she stepped out of the white Swedish sandals he blinked, but no other move disturbed the perfect vulnerability of his distended body.

He did not shift his gaze, her breasts filled his vision. Somewhere out on the pier someone laughed sharply once as his stepmother's hands moved slowly, as if under water, toward the button that alone held her linen skirt in place. Up and down in his sight the dark roses of her nipples shone in the gloom, the aureoles rust red and spreading outward on the surface of her firm breasts. Her skirt crumpled soundlessly at her feet. The brief white panties clung to her. Instead of slipping them off she cupped her mound of Venus from outside the panties with her left hand and began gently to tense and relax her palm while with the fingers of her right hand she stroked the tip of her right breast. Her lips appeared slightly swollen.

He just watched, his left hand still lying on his chest, his right hand extended around the base of his swollen phallus. As if on cue, she removed the last covering from her hips and down her long legs and stepped out free. The symmetrical bush of dark curly hair covered her entire mound. It was she who finally moved his hand away as she folded herself down alongside him and put her hand where his had been and began to explore the full circumference of him, the other hand raking his thighs and buttocks lightly with her nails so that he arched up as if she had touched a nerve. And when he did she swooped down with infinite tenderness to take him in her mouth. Her tongue and lips glided slowly down the shaft, working toward the base, angling herself to get it all. Holding him in her mouth and throat, then up and down and up and down and around to his testicles, legs, knees, feet, toes, then up again by another route to his nipples, then his lips, with her tongue curling into him. As if from a trance, he stirred now, returning her kisses, shifting to get at her breasts, she holding them up for him as he slipped and bit, then arching her head down and meeting his lips at her nipple, both of them kissing her breast at the same time. Then she lowered herself so slowly down onto him, placing his hand in her too so that he could touch and feel her throbbing clitoris as his shaft disappeared and appeared into the dark hair on her loins, both of them watching the arching and the merging and the mingling.

"I'm going to scream," she panted, then, "Oh, my God, oh, Jesus, Jesus, Jesus—*Vivian!*"

He went into his own spasms then, his body springing.

Then he blacked out.

His body would remember that night.

In all his sorties of the flesh in the years to follow, those few minutes with his father's wife would remain the center, the paradigm of erotic passion.

The uncomplicated love for his father that had been growing in him since their journey to London seemed to swell and diversify after that night. When Sam returned from his emergency meeting with the President at Hyde Park, he filled in the details for his son, dwelling with relish on how FDR, Harry Hopkins, Judge Rosenman and others of the brain trust had confronted the agents of J. P. Morgan with General Butler's information, and how Henry Luce of *Time-Life* and his group had had to swallow the facts of where these attacks on Roosevelt were leading. It had been Sam Prescott's task to talk to Henry Luce because their fathers had served together on church missions in China, and Sam and Luce had been Bones in the same year at Yale. Then he asked his son if he would come to London to study after college so that they could be together in the event of a war, and from what the President had told them it was inevitable . . . "coming on like a juggernaut." Joe Kennedy was now even advising that England could never stand up to Hitler, and that the fall of the United Kingdom was a certainty in the next eighteen months. Tears came into his father's eyes at this and when he saw that his son's eyes were red as well, Sam put his arm around his shoulders and hugged him in a way that the boy had almost forgotten.

Then, to change the mood, he told about who else had been at the President's estate. Stopping at Hyde Park for the weekend during a state visit, their majesties George VI and Elizabeth of England had encountered what Eleanor Roosevelt called a "jinx." During dinner the Roosevelt family dining table, unused to such a show of epicurean bounty and overstacked on one side by a hurried staff, teetered over, crashing china and cutlery to the floor. As if that were not enough to ruffle a pair of visiting royalty, the senior Prescott added with a laugh, a waiter slid into the library later in the evening, baptizing the carpet with ginger ale. "Everyone was acting too refined to laugh, I hear," he concluded, and the Prescott family laughed and chatted just as if nothing had happened: no would-be fascist *putsch,* no consummated technical incest. . . .

43

Never for a moment had Vivian considered revealing one detail of that night during the Bones ritual confession. He had contrived to never again really be alone with Nancy Prescott and she, for her part, he was convinced, was innocent of both responsibility and memory, as if her coming to him had been a dream or the act of a hypnotic fugue. He rose now to dress, choosing his clothes carefully, a quiet glen plaid lounge suit and subdued tie, deciding that he would give them an account of one of his adventures in London or Boston with Jack Kennedy and an assorted cast of female characters.

And that is what he did. The crowded parlor of the old Bones tomb was silent, waiting for him to begin his recital. Did they sense, Vivian wondered, that he did not hold them or their mysteries in awe or even in much respect? He knew that they did not want to hear any shaggy dog Boston stories of how he and Jack Kennedy had had to jump out the back window of a whorehouse during a raid. What they did want to hear was the chapter and verse of his fabled nights with the glamorous Janet Hammersmith. If they had known that he was going directly from this secret meeting to an even more secret rendezvous with Janet inside the very graveyard where new Bonesmen had been led on initiation night for decades, it would have been raw meat to them. He carefully recrossed his long legs and began to talk quietly so that the Bonesmen had to lean forward, almost, to read his lips.

He could feel their disappointment and frustration. "Well, there was a little party out in Brookline one night and Joe Kennedy, Jr., some of you may know, is a rather notorious practical joker. Joe knew that his brother Jack and I were intending to pay a little visit to a certain house in a certain section out there . . ." The senior Bonesmen seemed to know that they were being led down the garden path and besides, most of them had heard the story before from friends of the Kennedy brothers in Cambridge.

". . . so the other young lady threw Jack's clothes out the window and Mrs. Olsen, the madam, right on cue, knocks on the door and calls out in her very fake and very refined voice, 'Oh, Mr. Fritz, there's a *man* downstairs with a *detective* who says he's your *father* and that his name is Joseph Patrick *Kennedy* and I'm asked to slip his card under the *door* so that you'll know that it is *he* . . .'" The new Bonesmen could not help laughing though being only juniors they were, if anything, even more thwarted at being denied the concupiscent minutiae of the great Prescott-Hammersmith romance.

Vivian was able to get away by a few minutes after eleven. He was sick of Yale and its new, faked Gothic architecture that had been constructed by the WPA as part of the New Deal's attempt to provide some work for the Irish and Italian proles who lived on the outskirts of the castle that the university was. He would be early for the tryst with Janet, but the air was sweet and pleasant and once sure that there were no heavy-footed Bonesmen on his trail, he slowed down and opened his coat jacket. Then he saw that Janet was already standing under the arch of the entrance to the graveyard. He waved to her, signaling that she should step out of the street light and back into the shadows of the arch.

Janet Hammersmith "is the most democratic person, bar none, I've ever known," snapped Mrs. Hoit, her mother, to a columnist after stories dwelling on the "decadence" of her daughter's coming-out ball had appeared. She had begun her public career at sixteen when she set in motion a trend by wearing a strapless evening gown as she led the grand march at the famed Velvet Ball, and later in Florida was photographed in something called "crazyjamas." Even at fourteen, men had considered her ravishing and at that tender age her clothing allowance had been close to $6,000 a year. When she came out, the press reports bordered on hysteria concerning the food, music, guest list and the cost of over $70,000 (denied by Mrs. Hoit, who pointed out that non-vintage champagne had been served as an "economy measure"). Elsa Maxwell, New York's lioness of café society, placed her stamp of approval on the affair, which treated 2,000 guests to food, champagne, music and dance until dawn, prompting a tabloid to headline, "Bow's a Wow!" Mrs. Hoit had apparently no argument with that review.

It would have much surprised the readers of the popular press if they had known that this American princess was, in actual fact, an honest, kind and very intelligent young woman who wrote poetry under a *nom de plume*. Or that the bond between herself and Vivian was not that mad adventure of lust on the full lips of young and old in the high society of Manhattan, Boston, San Francisco and Palm Beach, where the topic of the Yale tennis champion and

45

the "No. 1 Glamor Girl" (as the magazines always described her) and their fantasized affair was the subject of incessant discussion.

Janet gestured melodramatically to Vivian as he turned into the graveyard. In her low, resonant voice she began quoting W. B. Yeats:

> Nor dread nor hope attend
> A dying animal
> A man awaits his end
> Dreading and hoping all . . .
> He knows death to the bone—
> Man has created death.

Her penciled eyebrows arched dramatically and her vermilion-painted lips pursed in mock alarm when Vivian began to tiptoe toward her, planting a loud kiss on the pale forehead. "Hi, kid," he whispered.

"Were you followed by any of those spooks and sex maniacs from Bones? Most of them wouldn't know what to do if it were served up to them on a hot plate."

Vivian laughed silently; this profane national goddess with her sharp tongue was a source of constant delight. "Why, Miss Hammersmith, how you talk, like a regular democrat with a small *d.*" They walked hand in hand deeper into the cemetery grounds. "No farther, fine lady, the Whitney tomb is surely far enough. Should you go farther, say as far as the Gorman crypt, I tremble to think of how your reputation—"

"Are you afraid for your body or your soul, Thomas Jefferson?"

He smiled and squeezed her hand, thinking of their actual sexual relationship. Just once they had been naked together in a suite at New York's Plaza Hotel, and that interlude had turned an almost programmed flirtation between two darlings of the press into a life-long relationship. He had raised himself up on one elbow to look down on her pale body stretched stiffly beside him and the tears making their way down her white cheeks. The beautifully proportioned form was not only stiff but shivering; her breasts were not large but rounded with pointed and now erect nipples; a thatch of jet black hair curled up from the V of her tightly closed legs, now clamped together and trembling slightly.

46

She had told him then, softly, that she loved him and had invited him to her mother's suite in order that they could become lovers, but that whether he believed it or not she was a virgin and not only that, she was so paralyzed with conflicts that she literally could not open her legs, though this was the third time since her coming out that she had tried. He could see that, for once, she was deadly serious, this least serious of young women. He had been led to believe by rumors that she possessed an insatiable erotic appetite and a world view cut directly from the bittersweet years of the flapper decade just past. That night he learned that there was a real, anguished person with courage and intelligence behind the picture in the press.

She told him at length about the pressures forced on her by her driven mother, the stark emptiness of her mindless debutante regime and of her thoughts of suicide four years before when her mother had taken her away from her friends at school to begin preparation for the coming-out. She asked him to help her, but every time he touched her legs or stomach she flinched as if from an electric shock, so he kissed her breasts, her neck and her earlobes. Pink welts began to rise across her alabaster skin and the breath to tear from her throat. Gasping, "Vivian, don't hate me, I can't, but soon . . . we will . . . you're kind, not what I thought you'd be like . . . so kind . . . let me touch you—you're so hard. Tell me what to do for you."

"Do you want to . . . ?"

"Down there?"

"Only if you want to."

"Vivian, I can't. I want to but I just can't . . . Can I . . . touch you . . . ?"

"Sure . . . I'll help." But so timidly had they joined the issue that both of them dozed off after several moments of what more closely resembled an act of friendship than a sexual transaction. They had never tried since, but instead had managed to devise a plan whereby Janet could talk with a psychotherapist without her mother finding out. An eminent man from Vienna, who had fled at the same time his mentor Sigmund Freud removed to London, had taken up residence in New Haven and through the good offices of Professor Mann, Vivian had been able to arrange a weekly meeting for Janet with Dr. Grotjohn. The pretext for coming up to New Haven being a series of dates and parties that would satisfy the maternal concern of Mrs. Hoit.

They paused and sat on an ivy-covered stone bench. "How did Bones go tonight?"

"Waste of time. Except for Rudolph Mann—and not seeing you —I'll be glad to get to London."

"Do you mind if I smoke? What would you say if I suddenly turned up in London next year?"

"I'd say, 'Well, if it isn't the number one democrat come to the sceptered isle to do her bit against the fascists.' "

"You tennis bum. You, you—intellectual!"

"You—*critic!*"

"Seriously, Viv, I mean what if it works out with Dr. Grotjohn and the famous legs swing open?"

"Do you want to talk about it?"

"Not really, he says it's best if I don't. But I'll give you a clue— 'Between you und your muzzer, Chanet, zer iss a dess vish.' "

"Do you think your mother suspects anything? She wouldn't hire private detectives or anything again, would she?"

"She is perfectly satisfied that I am up here performing gymnastic sexual feats with the entire class of thirty-nine. It's so obvious when she questions me that behind her air of worried concern is an absolutely steaming vicarious fantasy about my so-called sex life. I don't need a psychoanalyst to tell me that."

"What do you need one for, then?"

"To help me grow up so that I can love you the way I want and should—Oh, Viv . . ." Her straight-backed posture softened as she put her head on his shoulder and curved her arms around his waist. Her hair was warm and sweet-smelling as he kissed and touched it lightly. She rubbed his crotch. "What does the inscription outside the cemetery read?"

" 'The Dead Shall Rise'—you devil."

"No, no,"—her laughter was clear and open—"that's *my* motto; it was in one of my crazy dreams." She lit another cigarette.

"If it works out for you to come to London, you know I'll be glad to see you. We're best friends, aren't we?"

"You're the only one I trust . . . as much as I *can* trust."

They sat without speaking for a while, then walked again and talked about whether war would come, or rather, when, and whether Viv would work with his father or at the American embassy with the Kennedys and how Jack Kennedy was a terrible wolf whose fear of her tart tongue alone kept him at a distance.

She asked him whether he was happy and he quoted Nietzsche and the "great despiser" to her, and she said that she wanted to be a "great adorer." "So do I," he said. "Tell Dr. Grotjohn that maybe I'll drop in on him before I leave for London."

It was nearly four in the morning before he left her at the Orange Street guest house. Later, in bed, when he masturbated, he attempted to fasten his imagination on her body, but when he couldn't control his thoughts he tried to stop and think about his father and everyone's responsibility to save Europe from a new dark age, but at last he could no longer contain the compulsion in his groin.

He would not want anyone to know that behind this tennis-champion, playboy, cocksman image was the remnant of the lonely little boy who could feel for the "No. 1 deb" in her emotional and cultural isolation. He would be a little ashamed to reveal a tenderness that would go so far as to picture him as the platonic protector of a poor little rich girl.

Just before sleep, in his half dream, he saw the stern face of Professor Mann, heard the words again: "The tragedy without God," and thought how that described both his own life and the coming world war. The same was true of Rudolph Mann's description of King Oedipus, the holy sinner—"The seed, the sower and the sown." It was all commingled: he, his father, and the war . . .

CHAPTER 2

London, 1940
The Phony War

A LITTLE more than one year to the day later, on May 3, 1940, Janet Hammersmith did arrive in London, by clipper. Vivian was at Croyden Airport, waiting. As he motored toward the 10 A.M. arrival in the Packard limousine, it occurred to Vivian that more than thirty years ago his mother, like Janet, had come to London too, by boat train from Paris; that she too was a poet and perhaps, as well, marked by tragedy. How and why had Janet come, after all? And what road lay ahead in their relationship?

At 11 A.M. precisely he stood up as she emerged from customs.

The dark hair framing the ivory face, the broad sensuous mouth, lips vermilion, the erect, thrusting figure as she quickened her pace, then ran to greet him. In the embrace he felt her thighs close against him and almost interrupted the kiss to propose a toast to Dr. Grotjohn.

"The No. 1 democrat deb, I believe. Hello, Janet. Let me look at you." He stepped back, admiring her silhouette in the cool shantung silk spring suit, a color that *Vogue* had dubbed "pink lemonade." A foamy white crepe de chine blouse softened the line of the crisply tailored jacket, flared at the hips and fitted at the waist. Dove gray doeskin gloves matched the witty grosgrain and straw hat; the calfskin bag and pumps were in a darker gray.

Her eyes looked somehow different, sadder, wiser, he couldn't tell, or perhaps she was simply fatigued from the transatlantic flight.

Looking at him, she also saw some differences. He was not nearly as tanned as at Yale (that must mean he was not playing tennis daily or that the weather was poor), neither was his hair streaked with sun as it had always appeared to her during the springs and summers she had known him. The eyes were the same, huge and smoky gray, vulnerable, but the jawline looked a bit leaner and the cheek and nose bones more prominent. The double-breasted, brown spring wool suit was crisp, the light blue linen of the small-collared shirt and the gray-and-brown Granedy necktie focused his head and face. They soon became aware that passersby were looking with interest at them. She brushed at his tie as if to straighten it, managing to touch the bulge of his Adam's apple, her eyes narrowing as the spasm of yearning gripped her. Breathing slowly, she said, "Vivian, you know that you are going to be a very distinguished-looking middle-aged man, like your father—how is Uncle Sam? What's he actually doing here?"

"Very well, and he's meeting us for lunch at the Carlton Grill— good food—and he may be bringing your friend Jack Kennedy with him. Well, he's at the embassy this morning and he thinks Jack is a responsible young man. Which, by the way, he is. Let me tell you about what's happening here, with me and Jack—no, first, tell *me*, how did you get away? What are *you* doing here? Come on, I have a limousine courtesy of the embassy. This will be your first and last real food; we're under serious rationing now, so I hope you're

51

hungry. After lunch, something very important—you are being taken to the House of Commons to watch the oldest parliament in the world at a moment of crisis."

"What?"

"Oh, did I forget to mention it? Mr. Chamberlain's government is going to fall today. But first things first—what's the latest bulletin in the war with your mother? We can talk about Hitler and the other war later."

"How's your tennis? Oh, there's the baggage . . ."

"I play a little doubles with American visitors my father wants to persuade to work for the war effort . . . not *all* those are yours, are they? The No. 1 democrat with a small *d?*"

The ruse to escape the mother—Mrs. di Longo, the former Mrs. Hoit, the former Mrs. Hammersmith, née Jinks—was simplicity itself, given Janet's painfully garnered psychological insights into the springs of the No. 1 mother's motivation.

"I told her that Lyman Wolverton Edgar wanted me to come over in order to meet his family, who, I stressed, had been of the nobility, living here in the West Riding for ten generations."

"Lyman Wolverton—is there such a person? Didn't she insist on coming along to—"

"There is. A dear boy—completely homosexual—studying ballet in New York, off and on, and cooperating completely. He told my mother that *his* mother had insisted—*Lady Poole, herself*—on taking charge of the entire visit for the months of May and June, and Lyman got her to write to that effect—"

"Fantastic. You are *something.* That's called a beard. That's the way Victorians referred to a friend who escorted a lady, posing as her lover, so that she could keep secret the important man with whom she was really, uh, having a liaison."

They talked about where she should stay and agreed on the Prescotts' rented manor in Bletchley, there being many empty rooms as his father's wife and her son were living in New York. "No problem, but London isn't really safe now." That's what she wanted—news. Her mother's circle was profascist, which Dr. Grotjohn explained to her was typical of rigid, sexually repressed people who lived in fear of "ze return of ze repressed."

So he told her about the S.S. *Athenia,* the liner filled with American and Canadian passengers that had been torpedoed by the Germans off the Hebrides the previous September. All but a hundred passengers and crew survived, scrambling over the dead to lifeboats and finally being rescued by a Norwegian vessel and the private yacht of Swedish tycoon Axel Wenner-Gren. Ambassador Joseph Kennedy had sent son Jack, accompanied by Vivian, to Glasgow to assure the American survivors that an American ship was on its way to return them home, but when Jack could not assure them that the U.S. Navy would accompany them on their crossing he had his first encounter with the problems of diplomacy. The angry survivors refused to budge from Glasgow's Beresford Hotel without protection from the German navy, and this included a young coed whose wrath had been defused by a little after-hours diplomacy at the Beresford—or so the young Kennedy told Vivian when he arrived back in their room that evening.

"And who did *you* sleep with? With whom are you sleeping?"

"I'll tell you later. I wouldn't want to spoil your lunch. And we only have two hours before the great debate in the Houses of Parliament."

As it worked out, Sam Prescott came alone and Jack joined them for a sweet after they had eaten. Janet was somewhat startled at the proportions of a proper London lunch in a famous restaurant. As a small musical group played "The Poet and Peasant Overture" in the background, the Prescotts and Janet sampled the Carlton Grill's tomato soup with cream Chantilly, roast duck à l'orange, accompanied by fine champagne. Italian ice followed, then fruit and cheese, savory and Napoleon brandy.

Jack and Vivian smiled at Janet's reaction to the savory, her near-translucent skin reddening as she excused herself, framing the word "bastards" with her lips, standing behind Prescott, Sr.

They left the limousine and took a cab instead to the House. At the gate of the House of Commons they passed crowds of people standing patiently in the sunshine, getting as close as they could to the historic event that was to take place inside. The oratory began with Prime Minister Arthur Neville Chamberlain's appearance at 3:30 P.M., looking drawn with the pressure of the previous week, during which an expeditionary force from Britain had met failure in Norway. During his hour-long plea for "the cooperation of members of all parties," the man seemed rattled even to lay observers like Janet and Vivian. They would watch his agitation grow as opposition members heckled and booed his conciliatory message, which was followed by a series of attacks on his government, each more defiant and drawing more cheers from the body.

"Chamberlain's desperate," Sam Prescott whispered to his son and Janet under the hubbub. "He's holding to a margin that's less than half what the Conservative party counts on here. He's going to appeal to the liberals and labor, but it's too late for that now. They want Churchill in—and they're going to get him."

The speeches would go on into the night, when, long after the Prescotts and Janet had departed, Winston Churchill would take the floor. At the end of the week he would hold the offices of Prime Minister and Defense Minister, offering England nothing but "blood, toil, tears and sweat."

Afterward, with Kennedy driving, Janet fell asleep on Vivian's shoulder. Jack turned his wiry neck around to make what he supposed was a serious leer at Vivian and the sleeping princess. Vivian whispered, "Keep your eyes on the road and your hands on the wheel, you ridiculous lounge lizard." "And you," whispered the freckled John F. Kennedy, "keep your hands *off* the wheel. . . ."

The sun was almost down when they arrived at the Bletchley Park house. Vivian led Janet in to find her quarters, leaving the second Kennedy son to lug the baggage all the while taking the Lord's name in vain.

Bletchley Park, some sixty miles outside London, had once been an ancient Roman encampment in that distant time when the fierce islanders had painted their bodies blue and driven Roman generals to distraction with what in 1940 was being called "guerrilla warfare."

"Now once again," Sam Prescott had explained to his son, "Britons are engaged in a kind of secret guerrilla warfare. Just five miles away from this house is the Duke of Bedford's estate." Built in the nineteenth century, the duke's manor was a red brick Victorian "hideosity," as Sam called it. "But here," he had informed his son, "on the site of the former Roman encampment that had been granted to the Church by William the Conqueror after the Battle of Hastings, here, Vivian, is concealed what may be Western civilization's last hope for survival."

Then, in complete trust, he told his son the secret. In August of 1939 Sir William Stephenson and others in British intelligence, including Chief of Intelligence Admiral Sir Hugh Sinclair, or "C," convinced of the ill-preparedness of their nation in the event of a

German attack, took upon themselves, without the full knowledge of the Chamberlain government, a mission that would pit the best brains in England against the so-called foolproof Nazi code machine: Enigma. The cipher-producing mechanism was patterned on a commercial secret-writing machine invented by a Dutchman in 1919, and its existence had been known in intelligence circles for years. Hitler's staff had pounced on the fairly unsuccessful contraption in their search for a light, easily reproduced device that would enable them to constantly change their transmission codes. With a few modifications, Enigma was born. While the Chamberlain government showed little or no interest in cracking the ciphers of Enigma, Stephenson and the growing Government Code and Cipher School were hard at work.

Overcrowded in London, and seeking the security and anonymity of a small town, they chose landlocked Bletchley—noted for little more than its drizzle and brickyards—for their secret headquarters. A motley group of mental giants—acrostics workers, linguists, mathematicians, Oxford and Cambridge dons, young scientists in their twenties—descended on quiet Bletchley under the guise of the "Golf, Cheese and Chess Society," settling at the Duke of Bedford's estate. A network of aerials set up in the rolling hills of Bletchley Park brought the faint signals of enemy transmissions to the ears of the crack radio operators on Stephenson's staff; security men dressed as gamekeepers guarded the footpaths. After Polish intelligence, cooperating with Colonel Colin Gubbins, managed to capture intact a functioning Enigma and smuggle it to Bletchley in the hands of cryptographer Alistair Denniston, the British had a chance to study the device. Without German service manuals and schedules of cipher key changes, however, the code could not be cracked.

So the "priesthood of cipherers" went to work, day and night, in Quonset huts constructed in Bletchley Park, attempting to recreate mechanically the circuits of Enigma, and figure at a speed much greater than that of the human mind which of its seemingly infinite code patterns was being transmitted at any one time.

What the British brains came up with was a device unlike anything intelligence had seen before. Called "the bomb," or by some the "oracle at Bletchley," the machine mimicked the circuitry of Hitler's trusted Enigma, producing in April 1940 the first decoded transmission of Luftwaffe messages as Hitler prepared for his invasion of the Low Countries and France. "Ultra," the top-secret intelligence material that would provide an edge for the British throughout the war, had just come into being a few miles from where Vivian now stayed. His father's confidence sobered him.

After the heavy lunch, no one seemed to mind the plain, rationed fare served up to them by Mrs. McGowan and her husband Laurence. Janet appeared rested, fresh and cool in a shirtwaist dinner dress of beige silk marquisette, delicately smocked at the shoulders, full-skirted and clasped at the throat with a simple brooch.

Jack and Vivian watched with admiration as Janet drew out Sam Prescott on the situation in England during these dark days. Sam Prescott was not a loquacious man, but he responded at length to this obviously intelligent and lovely young woman, so unexpectedly quick and perceptive, just as his son had assured him she would be.

His enormous respect for the British people was clear as he inventoried their sacrifice and spirit. He spoke of the "rationing of the basics of everyday English life—tea, sugar, butter, eggs—accepted with a shrug of the shoulders by the population of the island." When the evacuation of children had begun, women in country villages had gone home in tears when they found out that a child would not be assigned to their homes; in other towns potential hosts fought over evacuee children at train stations, and housewives rushed out their front gates to carry the luggage of the East End mothers and children walking to their new homes. Husbands and wives working at different companies or branches of the government separated without complaint when they were relocated in distant parts of the country. Families opened their homes to servicemen for meals, baths, mending and sewing—"especially the poor," Prescott Sr. said. By that spring of 1940 the Women's Voluntary Service for Civil Defense, or WVS, had swelled its ranks to 350,000 volunteers from all classes of society, only 200 of them receiving any compensation for their work in organizing billeting and first aid. Shop girls and typists from the cities answered the call of the Women's Land Army, enduring rough winters, poorly equipped, on farms in the Midlands and Wales. "The English," he concluded, had "done themselves proud."

A telephone call for Sam Prescott brought to a close his recital of the war situation. When he returned to the table he looked serious. "Vivian, it seems I'm wanted at a meeting at eight-thirty at the Duke of Bedford's and they would like you to be there too. Janet, would you forgive us if we left you and Jack to your own devices for a few hours?" Almost simultaneously Vivian and Janet laughed out loud, to the puzzlement of the senior Prescott and the junior Kennedy.

On the way Sam told his son that the call had been from one of the special operations people headquartered at Bletchley and that the man, Sir Harley Crawford, had been very upset to learn that Ambassador Kennedy's son was a visitor at the Prescotts' and that under no condition could young Jack be allowed to accompany the Prescotts to the meeting. That the ambassador was disliked and distrusted in certain quarters was no news to Vivian, but neither he nor his father was prepared for what they would hear at Bletchley that evening about a German agent in the American embassy, directly under the nose of Ambassador Kennedy.

Ambassador Joseph Patrick Kennedy's popularity in England had declined dramatically in the two years of his tenure at the Court of St. James. The outspoken Irish-American had received British reporters after his arrival at the palatial London embassy with his feet propped up on the desk, charming them with a candid confession, "You can't expect me to develop into a statesman overnight." Some of his more caustic critics were now wisecracking that he'd never become one. From behind the polished desk in his blue-walled office, the unostentatious furnishings of which included two radio sets, Kennedy ran an efficient operation, but his support of the appeasement policies of the Chamberlain government, his weekend socializing at the Clivedon estate of American-born hostess Nancy Astor, where German diplomats toasted British government officials, his insistence that England hadn't the military strength "to defend itself against Hitler," created enemies among the men who were convinced that Britain must engage the support of the United States if fascism was to be stopped.

While his exquisitely dressed wife Rose and eighteen-year-old daughter Kathleen, or "Kick," became the toast of London and the younger children attended school—Bobby, Jean and Teddy in London; Eunice and Patricia at a Sacred Heart Convent School in Roehampton; Joe, Jr., and Jack at Harvard—the head of the clan was sending his candid comments on the unpreparedness of Britain to newsmen in Washington, D.C., a move that some saw as a ploy to keep the Kennedy name fresh in the mind of the American public, with an eye to unseating Roosevelt in 1940.

As the voraciousness of Hitler's armies became more apparent, and criticism of the Chamberlain policies grew in Britain, Ambassador Kennedy's remarks angered the swelling ranks of Churchill supporters, even prompting intelligence officers to "bug" the embassy at Grosvenor Square. Kennedy spoke freely to German Ambassador Herbert von Dirksen, who relayed the comments to Berlin, that the fault of Germany's anti-Semitic policy was in the extremity of the methods the Germans used to execute it; back home in Boston, he confided, there were clubs to which Jews had not been admitted for fifty years and everyone just kept quiet about it. On a trip to America that many believed to be the prelude to a presidential campaign—but that Kennedy insisted was simply to attend his son's Harvard graduation—the ambassador made public statements to the effect that Hitler would win a war against England and that Britain's growing "warmongerism" was mere self-interest, a desire to protect her empire, and not a moral stance against fascism. Stories circulated that Kennedy had toasted Hitler at a dinner at the embassy and tried to undercut Churchill's influence with President Roosevelt by reporting that the British statesman "is loaded with brandy from ten in the morning." "My God," was Churchill's response. "You make me feel I should go around in sackcloth and ashes." Kennedy, the Irish Catholic, was never at ease with the English, confessing to an associate that the memory of the British Black and Tans suppressing the Irish rebels was still fresh in his heart. . . .

As the Prescott men drove into the grounds of the estate they could not help noticing uniformed guards patrolling the entire area. A heavyset man who looked like no butler the Prescotts had ever seen ushered Sam and Vivian into a small den on the second floor. While they waited, a tray containing scotch and soda was brought in. Vivian declined a drink and sat there, trying to picture what Janet and Jack might be doing back at the house. About ten minutes had passed when a tall, young man in rumpled tweeds entered quietly.

After a brusque introduction the man, whose name, he said, was H. A. R. Philby, plunged into his narrative. "I take it that your son's

58

guest, Mr. Kennedy, has no inkling of what Bletchley is? Good. Let me put you in the picture. We have a very urgent situation, and I have been asked to be completely frank with you and your son and to thank you in advance for coming over, as you have done in the past, on such short n-notice . . ."

Motor vehicles could be heard leaving and arriving on the drive below. The representative of Special Operations who called himself Philby had oversized nicotine-stained fingers, and as he talked he nudged a series of cigarettes out of a packet and inhaled one after the other. Smoke poured out of his nose and mouth in such continuous volume that Vivian would not have been much taken aback to see jets of it shoot out of his pointed, hairy ears as well. By this time Sam was puffing on a battered briar and the small room was awash in smoke. In the close air Vivian had to strain to keep from coughing.

"Gentlemen, I am asked to inform you that there is a G-German agent working for Ambassador Kennedy in the American embassy. As you may know, secret information intended for Washington is often handed in for transmission to the embassy, in code of course. Just a few weeks ago we began to hear significant portions of those most secret messages on the wireless from Berlin in various broadcasts, including those of the traitor Lord Haw-Haw. You will be glad to know that Scotland Yard has identified the leak—he is one Lyman G. Hyatt, a twenty-eight-year-old American code clerk." The yellow smoke hung in the air as the implications of what had just been said reverberated.

Philby lit another cigarette from the splayed butt of his previous one and told them all the details that they were allowed. . . . The deciphered German transmissions containing the secret British-American exchanges had come from the German ambassador to Rome; the German diplomat was, in turn, receiving his information from an Italian attaché stationed in London. "The Italian's trail led agents to a tearoom owned by the family of a White Russian fascist sympathizer, one Anna Wolkoff." The woman made no secret of her anti-Semitism, and was a member of the "Right Club," which disseminated Nazi literature. "When she was put under surveillance, our agents noted nightly visits to her apartment by the young American code clerk from Grosvenor Square. That was Hyatt. And he was not the only one this Anna Wolkoff had been in contact with. Let me just say that information passing through her hands has been sent to Hitler through Rumania, and that this woman has a history of fifth-column activity with pro-Nazi diplomats.

"Gentlemen, we need a way into the embassy—quite obviously not a clandestine entry—and a way to get close to Mr. Hyatt so that when we act we can roll up what is obviously a Nazi network here in London." Philby began massaging a fresh packet of cigarettes. "It is your son's friendship with young Kennedy that interests us, Mr. Prescott. We would like to have your son contrive somehow to have the ambassador's son introduce your son to Hyatt." Vivian blinked in the smoke, not certain that all of the pronouns and circumlocutions added up to what he thought he had heard. His father said nothing.

"There is another young American, a veteran of the Spanish Civil War, who is willing to help us in this matter—we feel that we must work *with* and *through* American nationals in bringing this dangerous situation to a satisfactory conclusion. It must appear, in the end, that Ambassador Kennedy himself provided the leadership for exposing and bringing to justice Hyatt and the woman; after that our Special Operations will be able to make a decision as to how best to handle Hyatt's contacts, who are all citizens of the U.K. The plan is, then, for us to put your son together with the American who fought in Spain in the Abraham Lincoln Brigade and have them, through young Kennedy, become somewhat friendly with Hyatt—friendly enough to win his confidence. The details of what will be required at that point will be provided by the other American."

At this point Philby paused at last, spurted smoke through his nostrils, heaved himself to his feet and excused himself "for a m-moment." Sam Prescott half stood to push his chair closer to Vivian's, then sat again and spoke in a low tone to his son. "Were you able to follow that?"

"No. The man both stutters and slurs, mumbles—"

"Well, you followed the thrust—"

"But what am I supposed to do, tell Jack Kennedy that his father is a fool? Or a traitor? Why doesn't Scotland Yard just—"

"That's the point of this entire meeting. Special Operations, which is to say Winston Churchill, wants Kennedy *out* as American ambassador and so does President Roosevelt—you must have guessed that. So they obviously want Americans to compromise the embassy, leaving Joe Kennedy with no choice but to play the hero *and* make a farewell speech that will carry enormous impact in the States and hit the isolationists and "America First" people. Also, they want one of the Americans to be someone closely connected to FDR, and because of my relationship to the President and as I'm your father, you're the logical candidate."

"But what do I know about this kind of thing?"

"Unless I miss my guess, you won't have to know much. This other American, whoever he really is, is obviously trusted by the British."

Vivian studied his father's intense expression, his stiff, taut figure. The gentle man he had come increasingly to respect and love was, clearly, hoping that his son would agree to act. "What do you think, dad?"

"The President wants it done and while I—Viv, you know that I consider you an unusual young man, and I say that with some objectivity even though I am your father—and while I in no sense would want you to interrupt your courses at the London School or to infringe on your friendship with Jack Kennedy, or to do anything irregular such as opening anyone's mail . . . But still, if you think that you can in good faith be of some help, then I feel that if any of the terrible suffering that lies ahead can be mitigated, if somehow the United States can be brought to her senses, if the President's hand can be strengthened, then—"

"All *right*, dad, but can I ask Janet to help?"

"Janet?"

"I trust her—I've seen her in action against her mother. No mean adversary, I assure you . . . How would they feel—?"

"I think it's your decision completely. The responsibility—"

"I'll take the responsibility and so will she, I think . . ."

It was after eleven when the limousine pulled into the curving drive of the Prescott house. The long floor-length windows were opened to the warm evening air and the strains of a Noel Coward phonograph record could be heard clearly as they approached the wide stone doorway. Inside, in the long rectangle of the formal diningroom, at the far end, Jack and Janet were dancing. Vivian stood in the entrance watching the effortless grace of his two friends as they bent to the syncopation. "I'll see you again . . ."

Though all three of them were the same age, twenty-one, somehow Vivian felt older and not wiser but sadder, less innocent, than the stunning couple swaying into a dip and bow as he applauded, more sincerely than they knew.

Vivian and Janet's midnight walk took them down an old, rough-hewn country road. "Well, how did it go?"

"How did it go with you and Jack?" Fog was starting to roll.

"He made one quick, obligatory pass, but after I told him that you and I were secretly married and swore *him* to secrecy, he was a perfect gentleman for the rest of the evening."

"Ha! No . . ."

"Oh, yes, we had a good talk about the causes of World War I. He's much more intelligent and informed than his father, he's almost an FDR Democrat. So, you see, beware the green-eyed monster of jealousy . . . And what were *you* doing?"

He told her how British Intelligence's Special Operations branch had tried to recruit him. Janet listened closely, asking an occasional question, then giving her own summary . . . "They want to use this traitor in the embassy to knock old Joe Kennedy out of the presidential primaries this summer, either as a candidate or as an anti-FDR organizer, and they want respectable American citizens, like us, to do the dirty work so it doesn't look like FDR and the British are stage-managing the whole thing just to destroy old Joe . . . did I tell you that he once made a much cruder pass than his son's at me?"

It pleased her to see Vivian's warm reaction to her analysis; he was quite clearly impressed with her quick appraisal of both the British and American motives in the Hyatt affair, quite a bit shrewder, he realized, than his own had been. As he hoped and suspected, Janet agreed enthusiastically to the entire adventure, whatever it might be. The plan would depend on what the other American had to say. The time of the meeting would be given to Vivian over the weekend; he already had been told the place. But what weighed on him and the problem that he wanted Janet's comment on was, what to say to Jack? "What do we say to him? Your—"

"Tell him everything. He'll understand. Jack is really very decent and sweet, underneath . . ."

"He passed the acid test tonight. I agree with you, otherwise we won't go through with it. Agreed?"

"Agreed."

They had walked over a mile by this time, and the dark, deserted hollow of the Bletchley Park basin seemed to have swallowed up the couple.

"Vivian, where do you think we'll end? *Will* you marry me?"

"Are you serious?" He laughed, but knew that she was. If they did would the evil spirit clutching at her sex be exorcised, would the heavy memory of himself and his father's wife be exorcised too . . .? Out loud he said, " 'Pluck from the memory a rooted sorrow . . . and with some sweet oblivious antidote, cleanse the stuffed bosom . . .' That's where I'm meeting the other American, at the theater."

"Macbeth? Is that what marriage is? A 'sweet oblivious antidote'? Not the ones I've seen. I don't know about you. Dr. Grotjohn thinks it would be crazy at this stage for me. He even accused me of coming here as part of a 'dess vish.' I told him that was oversimplified, like saying he had left Europe *only* because he was afraid."

"Brilliant. Anyway, it was my idea to meet in the graveyard at Yale . . . How is it going?"

The long yellow gorse that lined the road broke to reveal a large boulder, which they made for. Crickets pulsated as they talked under rather than over the night sounds. "Well . . . I can masturbate now, quite freely. Was that your cap you just threw up in the air? Or your dinner? Will you, for Jesus' sake, say something to me? Do you think it's easy?" She stalked away. In one long stride he was after her, turning and leading her back to the rock, as if that were their safe place.

"Janet, sweet girl. Do you know how much I respect and admire you? You don't know that I made your participation in this crazy spy affair at the embassy a precondition of my participation." He kissed her hands and held them.

"I'm so sick of my stupid goddamned neurosis, of being a virgin. Christ, I don't want to die with the goddamned thing. Why don't you just rape me, Viv, and *then* marry me? I'll never tell. Or I'll rape you, whichever . . ."

"You were about to masturbate, or rather tell me about—"

"Ja, ja, ve komm to dat. Is this going to make you never want to make love to me? Viv—talk! Or I turn you ofer to Dr. Greatman of ze Gestapo!"

With the necessary concessions to self-consciousness the conversation, under cover of darkness and fog, proceeded with considerable courage on her part. "The doctor believes that if I can masturbate and fantasize without panic, then I'll be able to take the next step with—you."

He leaned forward to kiss her full, luscious vermilion lips.

"Mmm . . . So I've been, uh, practicing."

"Perfect practice makes—"

"Exactly. But there's another catch. You see, I had masturbated before, but not, uh, digitally, manually, oh, uh, well . . . oh God, this is painful—only love, believe me . . . kiss me again. Mmm, that helps. Well, up until a few months ago what I would do, ah, was to touch myself *only* around the breasts, never my . . . you understand? Never *there* . . . 'downstairs,' as my rotten mother refers to *it. But*—on my birthday, in March—oh, thanks again for the wonderful autographed T. S. Eliot first edition, I *adore* it—that night I got thoroughly drunk and I *did it!*"

"How was it?" His voice was serious.

"Pretty good—for a minute or two, then the anxiety caught up with me." In the silence the crickets throbbed, there was a slight breeze rising. Finally she continued, "Well, what should we do now?"

"Do you know that why I, well, almost love you is because of your sense of humor?"

"You *almost* love me? That must be why I'm falling in *like* with you."

He grabbed her. The warmth of their kiss began to radiate through them. Her tongue tickled at the corners of his lips and she unbuttoned her blouse for him so that he could touch her breasts through her bra while her fingers walked up his leg to the bulge of his crotch and she whispered into his mouth, "How's the old backhand?" And then he was rocking with laughter. "How's *your* Australian twist?" Chasing up to the road, holding her against him, brushing her raven hair with his lips. "Let's go back and masturbate or whatever and talk about the rest of it after we've smashed the great fascist spy ring . . . sweet girl . . ." kissing her as gently as he could, his hands placed lightly on her full, woman's hips.

64

"I assure you, Vivian, that I know a good deal more about my father's politics and problems than you or British intelligence does. He was wrong, as thousands were wrong about Germany's intentions and England's courage and capacity to resist tyranny. No one knows this, but I'm already writing a long paper for a course assignment at Harvard on the misconceptions that led well-meaning men, like my father, to underestimate the threat, and my father is *helping* me. Does that shock you? My father is simply not the mean, hard-hearted, grasping son-of-a-bitch that you progressives accept as an article of faith as the truth about him—let me finish . . . I'll help you get this little creep who's selling secrets to the Nazis, but there's no need to play all these games. You tell me what you need from the embassy and I'll go to my father and it'll be done without all this other horseshit. Come on, let's go pub crawling and get laid before the bombing starts."

It was beyond Vivian how, on the following Tuesday, he was to engage in a melodramatic spy-type caper during a production of Shakespeare's *Macbeth.* His father had been unable to shed any light at all on his son's questions as to why on earth he was to pretend to strike up a conversation with the young man who would be sitting next to him in seat G17 during a performance of Donald Wolfit's highly admired production of "The Tragedy of Macbeth" and his "fiend-like queen."

Wolfit, like the great Edmund Kean, was a short, powerfully built man with a face and voice of kinetic power. Planted like an oak tree at center stage, he roared and whispered his reading of "bloody Macbeth" to deliciously shivering audiences. Despite his mystification as to what he was supposed to be doing, Vivian watched with eerie pleasure as the Thane of Cawdor marched inexorably deeper and deeper through a sea of blood until to go back "were as tedious as go o'er." He was relieved that the only empty seat in the Duke of York Theater seemed to be one immediately on his left side. When, later in the first act, just as Wolfit was hoarsely confiding to the audience that, "Come what come may, time and the hour runs through the roughest day," someone sat down next to him.

Not until the first interval was he able to get a good look at the latecomer. As the house lights went up, he turned to his left to look at the man, who had half risen to allow spectators to file out into the aisle. Moments later they were alone at their end of Row G, and

Vivian had an unobstructed view of a well-built man in his early twenties, dressed inexpensively but very neatly in a blue light-weight Palm Beach suit. Starched white shirt and a rather bright blue-and-white tie and carefully trimmed hair completed the impression of a military officer dressed in mufti for the evening. "Very impressive, isn't it?" The man smiled. His features were regular, slightly fleshy, and he reminded Vivian of the actor Robert Montgomery except that his eyes were rather small and a very dark brown. The shoulders, too, and the chest were powerfully cast and more distinctive. "Very impressive, indeed," replied Vivian automatically. At that, the other man beamed and said, "You're American, huh?" and stuck out a flat hand.

As Vivian gripped it he realized that the American theme of the plan, first explained by the Special Operations man at Bletchley, was now to be acted out. "Well, almost—Yale, thirty-nine." The other gave a short, infectious bark of a laugh and squeezed harder. "The name's Michael Howard, University of Illinois, the real America," he said in a flat midwestern accent. Vivian waited for his next cue, but Howard continued to chat pleasantly about the play and the reason for being in England—a theater arts teaching grant-in-aid from the university—and discussion in general about how to make ends meet in London on a few dollars a day. At the second intermission there was more of the same and the suggestion that the two of them stop in the theater pub after the performance, to all of which Vivian responded with a sort of wooden complicity.

Later, as soon as they were seated at a corner table, he said, *sotto voce*, "Mr. Howard, I'm not cut out for this sort of thing, I'm afraid." The other man smiled slightly as he insisted on paying for the ale that the barmaid delivered. When they were alone again, he spoke in normal tones and Vivian was aware that the flat midwestern twang had disappeared from the now more neutral diction.

"I think you're doing well. We're all amateurs at this stage of the game, except of course the British, who've been at it full time since before Shakespeare's day; what's Macbeth say . . . 'Not a one of them but in his house I keep a spy' . . ."

". . . 'But in whose house I keep a servant fee'd.' "

"That's it. Drink up. My name is Marshall Hollander and I'm called Mush as in Moosh you huskies, hi, ho, heave, et cetera."

66

Vivian had to laugh. Shaking his head, he asked why this meeting had been arranged in such an artificial fashion. "Why not just come out to Bletchley or I could—"

"No, the British are convinced that I'm under German surveillance and they wanted a natural scene of two Americans meeting at the theater by accident. I was in Spain and—they told you?—and I worked for the British there. They asked me to come here afterward to help with a few Anglo-American chores. My contact is a man named Philby. You've met him. I'm a Communist, you might as well know that now, and Philby, for one, didn't let that fact get in the way of working together against the fascists, though he's a regular Tory himself. Anyway, the guidelines for this thing come through him. Shall I lay them out?"

Over a second round of ale Vivian realized that Hollander had been thoroughly briefed about the Prescott biography but that *he* knew nothing about the young Communist. Hollander was not reluctant to tell him about his family (small diamond merchants who migrated from Holland to America in the nineteenth century), his degree in social studies, his marriage before volunteering to go to Spain as a member of the International Brigade, his divorce afterward "because the Hitler-Stalin pact tore people on the Left apart."

"Then," Vivian pointed out, "you must take issue with it if you're working against the Germans."

"That pact is doomed. I understand why Stalin signed it, after what the western powers have done to the Soviets ever since the revolution; I understand it, but I can't *work* for it. If that makes me a heretic, so be it."

Then he laid out the plot as it had been told to him. Vivian was to arrange for Jack Kennedy to give a small party at the embassy for several visiting American "friends," including Mush Hollander, under the cover of "Michael Howard." After the party he and Vivian were to invite the spy Hyatt on to another gathering at Hollander's hotel. There, in the hotel room, liquor would flow and hashish would be provided since, Hollander assured the wide-eyed Vivian, both Hyatt and the German woman spy who would be with him, were users. There would be at least two other women there as well, he said, posing as the companions of Hollander and Prescott. "Then, at the appropriate moment, these women—who will

67

actually be call girls—will suggest some sort of group sex—hold *on*, take it easy, let's have another round . . ."

Vivian was not so much scandalized as incredulous. "Why? What does that have to do with—"

"Hold it. Hyatt and his pal Wolkoff are more than a little kinky, as the English say, and talk of an orgy is unavoidable, especially with Wolkoff. Now, somehow, Philby didn't spell this out, the bastard, somehow you and I are supposed to hold back while the girls and Hyatt go to it. We're supposed to stay dressed or at least out of camera range."

"*Camera* range!"

"Hold it. Special Operations men will have been in the closet—"

"The closet!"

They were both shaking now with suppressed laughter. Slowly they settled down sufficiently so that Hollander could explain the logic of Philby and the British to Vivian: Since Hyatt and Wolkoff were hardcore Nazis being run by the Abwehr, German intelligence, simply catching them spying would not induce them to talk and expose the rest of their ring. So it was mandatory to *embarrass* them, not politically, since that was impossible, but *personally* so that they could, to put it bluntly, be blackmailed into naming their confederates. When the British agents stepped out of the closet, cameras flashing, that would be the signal for the Americans and the call girls to exit quickly, leaving Hyatt and Wolkoff in the professional hands of Special Operations.

"If *they* don't know what they're doing," Hollander concluded seriously, "then no one does. These people are recognized all over the world as the best in the business, and they always use sex when the targets are vulnerable. They claim that Hyatt and Wolkoff can't allow their private peccadillos to be made public and since they will be confronted with absolute proof of their spy activities, their only choice will be to talk and get a lighter sentence and no scandal, or to be exposed as perverts *and* spies *and* have a much longer sentence thrown at them. I think they feel that Hyatt would avoid his mother finding out about his sex life at *any cost,* whereas la Wolkoff would be *proud* of him for helping the Germans. Oh, I guess they know their people, all right."

That was when Vivian told him that they would need only one phony lady of the evening, that Janet Hammersmith, whom Hollander could meet tomorrow, would play the role of the other. "Now, of course, Janet is a terrific actress but of course you wouldn't want her to disrobe or anything." He still found it difficult to take the whole thing seriously.

Hollander agreed to take Vivian's recruit back to Philby for approval, provided Vivian found out if Miss Hammersmith really wanted to go through with it . . .

Late that night Vivian reported to his father and Janet that he was quite impressed with Hollander, even if he was a Communist, or rather a militant antifascist, or independent Marxist, or whatever. He was impressed that Mush Hollander had fought in Spain, showed conspicuous bravery, was trusted by the British, supported FDR and would agree to Janet's participation. Not one word, to his father, did Vivian reveal about the sexual aspect of the plan, only saying that when the spies were drunk, then Scotland Yard would enter, take over, confront them with the purloined cable and code traffic, while the amateurs walked away. It all sounded harmless enough, Senior said.

In Janet's bedroom—it was now close to four in the morning—he told her about the sex and blackmail aspects and tried to convince her to take a role only at the party at the embassy, before the later gathering at the hotel.

"I should say *not*. I'll have photographs blown up and we'll blackmail my mother. Oh, I love you, you tennis bum o'mine. Here, get in with me. Shhh! It's late, get in, we don't have to do anything. Get in, you smell of ale, you terrible man. How was the play? 'Come you spirits that tend on mortal thought—unsex me *here*, and fill me from the crown to the toe top full of direst cruelty' . . . uh, 'come to my woman's breasts and take my milk for gall, you murdering ministers—' Oh, yes, Vivian . . . Do you like to kiss them, Viv? Kiss them, they've been lonely so long . . .'"

Lyman G. Hyatt and his great friend Anna Wolkoff were flattered and honored to be the guests of the ambassador's son John at a select reception and soiree. The guest list was American and so was the motif of the gathering. Before dinner Wisconsin cheeses were featured with the drinks, then Kansas City T-bone steaks, Iowa corn, Idaho potatoes, ending with apple pie and ice cream. Throughout the evening toasts were proposed by Jack Kennedy to America and the various homes states of the guests.

There was "Michael Howard" from Illinois and Chicago—that rated two toasts—and of course there was John Kennedy's friend Vivian Prescott and his father, Samuel Adams Prescott, who stopped by for just one drink; then there was Howard's companion, a petite English girl of provocative dimensions, named Lucy Manners, who proudly claimed that since her father was American she had the right to propose several toasts to New York City, his home; Mr. Prescott's guest was the noted American heiress and socialite Janet Hammersmith, whom, of course, they recognized at once from the newspapers. The ambassador himself dropped in to receive a toast. After a brief tour of the public sections of the thirty-six-room ambassadorial mansion, which had been a gift of J. P. Morgan, all repaired to the Blue Room for more libations. Watching Anna Wolkoff slither along and noting the hungry look on her face, Vivian was struck by her resemblance to a cunning street dog. Hyatt was pudgy with thick glasses, unruly hair and a child's face.

Janet's act was dazzling; racial slurs dripped from her painted lips, as planned. Her costume, too, was memorable: a French gown with a slinky "needle-narrow" sheath of black crepe that had open-work at the hip and neck, offering glimpses of orange satin slip and sash. A stack of onyx bracelets, jet earrings and the merest of open-toed, ankle-strapped evening slippers completed the ensemble. Her perfume: Suivez-Moi, new that year. She thought it a neat touch.

The young man, "Howard," who said he was scraping along in London on a scholarship, supported Janet's anti-Semitic vituperation. So did Miss Manners of the American father and the thrusting bosom and rounded buttocks. In this atmosphere the Wolkoff woman began to bloom, speaking for young Hyatt, who was constrained to be discreet within the embassy itself.

Chilled California champagne and sparkling burgundy graced the meal, followed by brandy and liqueurs. At the introduction of the scotch and soda Jack Kennedy made his exit, saying that he would join them later after fetching his date for the evening. "Meet us at my place," called out the gregarious Howard, "Room three fourteen, Saint Ermin's Hotel, just down from Victoria Station. Come on, you comedians, let's go to my place. It's too formal here, no offense meant. I've got some good hooch straight from the good old U.S.A. *plus* some *very* interesting photographs taken *secretly* at one of those plush camps in the Catskills in New York State."

"Oh, yes, please—*everybody?*" begged Miss Manners.

"Lead on, Mr. Howard, if you please," sang out Janet Hammersmith.

Half staggering, dancing and skipping, they set out for the St. Ermin's Hotel, located between the House of Commons and Victoria Station. The bluff American, Howard, regaled the high-spirited company with Jewish and Negro dialect jokes.

Vivian's role for the evening was that of a quiet, shy young tennis lion who, unaccustomed to alcoholic beverages, was soon too affected to do much more than watch with a silly grin spread half across his handsome face. As they walked, Wolkoff kept trying to include him in the persiflage, touching him as often and as intimately as possible. Londoners passing in the street looked with grim tolerance at the celebrating party of rich foreigners.

The St. Ermin's best and only days of status were *circa* 1901 when old man Ormsby, riding on the prevailing wave of optimism, had redecorated it in what would later be termed the "Victorian" style. The elevator creaked and groaned to the third floor; the happy group trooped down to room 314. There they found liquor enough to float a party three times as large. "All my savings, the hell with it," sang out the genial host.

By midnight the clamor to see the promised "secret" Jewish resort photographs had peaked. Howard had teased for over an hour about whether or not those present were sophisticated and experienced enough to view such shocking images. Vivian had no idea what these photos were or even if there were any, and he retreated further behind his grin and pretended to doze. The sound level kept rising and the dog-like Wolkoff especially took the offensive in insisting on a viewing of the photographs, threatening or *promising* a striptease as proof of her readiness to participate in any adventure. Mrs. Wolkoff was in her early forties, her face was hard and though her body was somewhat tubular there was a kind of eroticism that seemed to radiate from her jerky, stabbing movements. She kept trying to dance with Janet, who cleverly avoided the embraces by tipsily launching into a risqué Cole Porter song:

Birds do it, bees do it,
Even educated fleas do it,
Let's do it, let's fall in love . . .

After three more stiff rounds of assorted libations, their host opened the rickety old bureau in the bedroom and whispered stagily for those who were "game" to "come into the inner sanctum." Vivian, whose eyes were closed, managed to watch from under his lids as the last phase of the charade began to unfold. He squinted at the closed closet door adjacent to the little suite's entrance. Were the Special Operations men actually there; would there really be violence? He felt as foolish as he had at Skull and Bones, and he worried about Janet as he heard her retreat into a slightly more nervous reprise of:

The Dutch in old Amsterdam do it,
Not to mention the Finns,
Folks in Siam do it,
Think of Siamese twins . . .

In the bedroom, the purveyor of the pictures had flopped down on the bed; spread out before him were some twenty photos. The first to join him on the bed was Wolkoff, the dog woman. Crowding in and joining the two on the bed was Miss Manners, with the now giggling code clerk Hyatt in tow. Vivian hoped Janet's sense of irony, of the absurd, would keep her detached from the whole business. He worried if she wasn't overdoing it, though, when she started to sing again, much to the delight of the others:

Some Argentines without means do it,
People say in Boston even beans do it,
Let's do it, let's fall in love.

Sponges, they say, do it,
Oysters down in Oyster Bay do it,
Let's do it, let's fall in love . . .

At that moment Janet, moving away from the Wolkoff woman, who was whispering in her ear, noted the very drunken code clerk's hand under Miss Manners's skirt.

72

Vivian, from his more removed post, had time to wonder how the British government could set up such an adventure, because there was no question that Mush Hollander was following orders every step of the way. His father must never know, and he would beg Janet's forgiveness for involving her at all . . . at the time he just hadn't thought any of it would really come off . . .

"All right, you comedians," Hollander was saying, "I'm going to show you what we call Living Pictures at the state fairs where I come from. Come on, get up, you comedians, get up; it's daylight in the swamps. Get up!"

"Tableaux vivant, liffing pickers, ja, kom on," and Wolkoff began to throw off her clothes. Pretending hysterical mirth at the spectacle, Janet stumbled back into the sittingroom to bend over Vivian, whispering, "What do we do, Viv, I—" just as Wolkoff leaped on her back. "Your turn, beautiful vun—leaf dat drunk man alone, who *needs* him?" and attempted to pull her back toward the bedroom.

Vivian could see Hollander promptly signal to the little prostitute Miss Manners, who swung into the German, waltzing her out and away from Janet. He wondered what the signal was for the authorities to make their entrance . . . how long could this go on? And then he saw Hollander dragging the near-comatose code clerk to his feet and pushing him toward Miss Manners and her nude partner, who picked him up and proceeded to tear the clothes off him. After which, with one push Hollander sent the clerk, the Wolkoff woman and Miss Manners spinning onto the bed, where Miss Manners headed for Wolkoff's crotch, at the same time going into a variation of the Australian press that reminded Vivian of the great Strangler Lewis, whom he had seen wrestle once at New Haven, and caught the code clerk's head up and between her legs as in a vise. Hyatt gave out a blat like a man who has opened his mouth under water, then fought for air.

Janet was rushing out of the room, laughing and crying, as Hollander began to signal at Vivian, then ran to the closet door and threw it open. Two middle-aged men in short-sleeved white shirts with large revolvers strapped over their shoulders and cameras at the ready charged out and rounded the corner into the bedroom. Inside only Miss Manners was aware of their presence, and like the considerable athlete that she was, coordinated her lips and her hips so as to draw the two spies into orbit as if they were

73

mere extensions of her acrobatic vortex. Hollander was pushing Janet and Vivian out into the hall. "Get out, keep going, go home . . . meet me here tomorrow at ten A.M. to swear out statements. Get going, you did fine." . . .

In a state of semi-shock they went downstairs and asked for a room for the night, saying that one of them was ill. The manager assumed that it was the gentleman whose health was in question. Somehow Janet had come through it better. After they had wept with laughter, they stared at each other and shook their heads.

"Janet, my God, I had no idea—but I must say you were perfect." He could see that she was almost manic with excitement. They talked for more than an hour before falling asleep in their clothes.

In the morning they walked up to Hollander's room from the lobby, and he told them to wait for him back in their room. A few minutes after eleven he knocked. He told them that he had not yet been to bed and that he would try to answer their questions, adding, "Philby and the Special Operations people are very pleased. After you left we put the Hobson's choice to them and they both signed statements, but we're keeping the pictures just in case. And you won't need to give any statements for a few days. They've been detained and both the ambassador and Washington are preparing a very strong statement, so there will be a big propaganda yield. Thank you and well done . . ." He was waiting for their attack, if one was coming.

Vivian and Janet had pounding headaches, so for several moments they just stared at Hollander, who looked to Vivian more than ever like the actor Robert Montgomery. Vivian broke the silence. "Mush, you said 'we,' 'we're' keeping the pictures—who *are* you?"

His answer was not exactly a response to the question. "I kept it as clean for you as I could. The Wolkoff woman and Hyatt have a much stranger relationship than anything you saw last night. Look, you know the score . . . If the United States doesn't come into this thing—and that means turning around Joe Kennedy and the Standard Oil boys and ITT and a lot of others—then you're going to be fighting Nazis on the beaches of New Jersey. I'm not exaggerating, and I'll be with the rest of my family in a concentration camp in England or Spain or Chicago. Vivian, the British are fighting for their lives, and the rules are not the ones you're used to on center court at Wimbledon. I mean, don't you know who your father is? He's one of the key liaison men between Special Operations and Washington."

No, he didn't know, but he was hardly surprised. It was through his father, after all, that he'd met Philby and learned about Hyatt . . . Janet's eyes showed her surprise, and her question. She was asking Vivian if it were true that Sam Prescott was some sort of important secret agent. And his son didn't know? It also made Vivian feel disoriented to think that his father was not really just the respected friend of Presidents and diplomats . . . He had hidden certain facts from his father, it seemed the opposite was also true.

They talked for almost an hour. Mush Hollander had deep circles under his eyes and his voice was taut, passionate. Vivian and Janet said hardly a word. Hollander concluded, ". . . so it's up to you. If you don't want to get your hands dirty then walk away, if you think you can. But if you feel that you have any-thing to contribute to this struggle with—there's no other word for it—'evil,' then go downstairs, book this room for another day, get cleaned up and some rest and be ready for a meeting at eight o'clock tonight."

"What kind of meeting?" Janet asked quietly.

"It will include Mr. Prescott, Senior, and someone else very important who can speak for himself, and then you can speak for *yourselves.* Anyway, I'll be here at eight if you want to hear more."

After they were alone again, Vivian wondered aloud if this meant that his father knew about the previous night . . . The No. 1 deb didn't answer, just disrobed and started to draw the bath water. Vivian continued to sit there on the frumpy, cramped settee, finally getting serious. These people were at war, in the real world. Even Janet—sweet, crazy Janet—had apparently made her choice be-tween the people like her mother and the real people like Mush Hollander, or his father. I'm farting around at the London School of Economics and playing tennis and writing literary essays about dead poets while western civilization is about to be sold out to the Wolkoffs, for God's sake. He could hear her splashing in the bath and singing to herself:

In shallow shoals, English soles do it,
Goldfish in the privacy of bowls do it,
Let's do it, let's fall in love . . .

"Yes," he said out loud, but not so that Janet could hear him, "let's *do* it." Then singing out to her, "Even Ernest Hemingway can *just* do it" . . .

When they opened the door for Mush at eight sharp he looked fresh, dressed again in his pressed Palm Beach suit but tonight wearing a clip-on bow tie and carrying a new straw hat, the kind worn turned down all around in the Panama style.

"You're coming to the meeting." He said it as a statement of fact.

"Who are we going to meet, Lord Haw-Haw?" Janet pursed her lips.

Mush touched her nose with the broad tip of a strong finger. "You are going to meet the greatest spy in the world." . . .

Sir William Stephenson, code named Intrepid, was a Canadian who had become master of Great Britain's secret war. He held no military rank and had worn no uniform since World War I, and wore no medals, though he was the most highly decorated man in the British Isles. Trim, short, erect, a millionaire before he was fifty, Intrepid took the long way to the St. Ermin's Hotel. He wanted to walk, he had much to think about. As he strolled by the sandbagged perimeter of the huge BBC complex he paused. It was here that he had conceived of using the opening bars of Beethoven's Fifth Symphony, in Morse code—dot-dot-dot-dash—the letter *V*—and that became the signature of the Allied secret armies of Europe. At the BBC an American-British collaboration was covering London's war effort live in "London after Dark," broadcast simultaneously with portable mikes from locations around the city. Stephenson had to give credit to the Yankee correspondents, but the voice he was partial to was that of J. B. Priestley:

> I'm sitting at an open window in Whitehall. Henry VIII married Anne Boleyn near here. Elizabeth saw Shakespeare's plays here. Charles I was executed a few yards from where I'm sitting. It's historic ground, and the very center of the hopes of free

76

men everywhere. It's the heart of this great rock that's defying the dark tide of invasion that has destroyed freedom all over Western Europe.

It was a fine evening, the sky washed and pale. What troubled Stephenson was more than the Hyatt-Wolkoff affair. He had hoped that Ambassador Kennedy and others at the embassy would not be implicated in Hyatt's treachery, and was now certain that the code clerk's leak had been plugged. The final transmission smuggled to the German ambassador in Rome had been a plea to FDR from Winston Churchill for the use of obsolete American warships, desperately needed by the weakened British fleet, and Roosevelt's answer, explaining his problems in justifying compliance with Churchill's request. Hitler must have smiled when the ciphered intelligence reached Berlin. Now the ambassador, Kennedy, had been told of his employee's treason, and in a call to Roosevelt the same night the Irish-American diplomat had professed to his boss that if the United States had been in a state of war he would have had Hyatt before a firing squad.

Stephenson knew the trial of Hyatt and Wolkoff must proceed in obscurity; the young clerk was insisting his actions were motivated by love of country, and a wish to avoid involvement in an "unconstitutional" war. These "America First" sentiments would, Stephenson would make sure, receive no publicity. He would take no chances, the network of intelligence-sharing that he had set up with Roosevelt in Washington would from this point exclude Ambassador Kennedy's office; although Neville Chamberlain had been forced out of office, his insidious foreign secretary, Lord Halifax, said to be a crony of Joe Kennedy's, was still talking about deals with Hitler and Mussolini.

He smiled at the familiar sign on the Yorkshire Grey pub, a hangout for Yankee newsmen: "Please understand there is no pessimism in this house and we are not interested in the possibilities of defeat. They do not exist." He'd thought to himself that the exigencies of war were the native element of the British, or so it seemed by the look of dutiful contentment on the faces of the scouts who bicycled messages between police stations as the barrage balloons rose up from the trees of Regent's Park, limp harbingers of an impending air raid.

When "Little Bill," as he was sometimes called behind his back, arrived at the hotel, he found his way to the fourth floor, though the lift listed only three floors. The fourth floor of the St. Ermin's was the secret headquarters of Special Operations Executive (SOE), known familiarly as the "Baker Street Irregulars." Here Noel Coward, Leslie Howard, Graham Greene and much of the flower of the British cultural establishment rallied to the magnetic message of Intrepid—who all knew spoke for Sir Winston Churchill himself—*"Set Europe ablaze!"* . . .

Janet sat between Mush and Vivian on the dumpy sofa, the two men laughing over their exertions of the previous night, when the door swung open to admit Kim Philby and another man.

"Hello, k-kids," mumbled Philby, "I'd like you to meet Tony Blunt." Blunt was a tall man of almost spectral leanness. "How do you do?" The voice was velvet, not unlike John Gielgud, the actor, Vivian noted. Anthony Blunt was, they learned, a colleague of Philby's from Cambridge and considered one of the most brilliant students and young teaching dons of his generation. The look he directed at Vivian was clearly erotic. "All the public school boys but Philby are raging fags," Mush had told them that morning. Blunt rested his weight on one foot like an actor in a drawingroom comedy, and shot his impeccable cuffs.

At exactly 8 P.M., Intrepid strode into the small conference room, his compact body cutting through the cigarette smoke and Tony Blunt's amusing monologue at Philby's expense. He began to talk quietly to Vivian and Janet without preamble, his hooded eyes holding them as if in a grip.

"Mr. Prescott, Miss Hammersmith, in the name of His Majesty's government I wish to thank you for your contribution yesterday, however bizarre the circumstances." He told them then what the outcome of the case would be. He paused to take out a cigarette, Philby leaning over with a match. "Within thirty days certain events will have taken place that may lead you to want to join Mr. Hollander in Canada as part of a special mission." His voice was dry and slightly musical. "When this, uh, event takes place next month, amateurs like yourselves from all over the English-speaking world will come forward, I believe, to volunteer for secret service." He asked them to inform Hollander of their decision no later than June 30th.

Actually the fall of Dunkirk had been anticipated by knowledgeable military analysts in Europe. But when it came, Vivian and Janet were as unprepared for the raw spectacle of suffering as any other young couple that summer.

Most days and evenings they spent alone, listening on the radio to the catastrophe as it unfolded. Sam Prescott had returned to Washington for urgent conferences with the President; the Bletchley house was silent except for the everlasting radio, the nervous system of Europe. Each night the young couple sat there just listening, and occasionally touching each other, more out of a need for reassurance than sexual desire.

After the Belgian surrender, 600,000 Allied soldiers retreated toward the sea, pursued by German tanks and bombers. Warships from France and England, assisted by every manner of vessel that could be enlisted in the effort, managed to evacuate over 300,000 ragged, wounded men who had crawled over the carnage to the port of Dunkirk. Within the week the Nazis had claimed Paris, Le Havre, and Montmédy; Marshal Pétain admitted defeat. Hitler sealed his conquest in the forest of Compiègne, in the same railway car in which Germany had surrendered in 1918. The radio told it all.

By June, Vivian and Janet knew that Intrepid's prescience had been based on hard fact and that, before the month was out, one way or another, their youth would be gone forever.

There was almost no static on the radio that evening that the Prime Minister announced the start of a new era:

"What General Weygand called the Battle of France is over. The Battle of Britain is about to begin. The whole fury and might of the enemy must very soon be turned upon us. Hitler knows he must break us in this island or lose the war. If we fail, the whole world, including the United States, and all that we have known and cared for, will sink into the abyss of a new dark age. Let us therefore brace ourselves to our duty and so bear ourselves that if the British Commonwealth and Empire last for a thousand years, men will still say, 'This was their finest hour.'"

At the close of the lifting Churchillian challenge, Vivian turned to look at Janet, sitting rapt at the far end of the Bletchley drawing-room. He snapped off the radio. The old house was deathly quiet in the close June evening. After a while he raised his voice to call out to her, "Will you marry me?"

"Yes. If we can honeymoon in Canada."

CHAPTER 3

Camp X, Canada, 1941
Love and Death

IT WAS called Camp X. The secret nerve center of the "other" war against fascism, organized by British Security Coordination (BSC). To these most closely guarded northern American farmlands came Vivian and Janet Prescott on October 3, 1940. Here, between the United States and Canada, was lake water as black and cold as anywhere in the world. When the young couple crossed in 1940, posing as walking tourists, they were innocent, unsophisticated in the arts of espionage and counterespionage. When the Prescotts would cross back over the icy depths, separately, in 1941, they would still be young and beautiful people, but as highly trained in the ways of secret war as any agents in the world, Janet considered by her teachers to be one of the most promising operatives that they had ever trained, Vivian a bit slower in learning the tricks of deception but physically fearless and strategically audacious.

Camp X was located along the northern shore of Lake Ontario some 300 miles west of New York City, making the site available to nearby FBI special agents from Manhattan. Varied lots of equipment also made their way along the Toronto–Kingston highway disguised as farm machinery. Forty miles of dark lake water formed a protective moat to the south; to the north was heavy forestation. Armed commandoes guarded the approaches from the east and west. Janet and Vivian were not aware of these commandoes when they debarked from Roosevelt Beach, near Niagara Falls, to cross the cold expanse, could not see blackened faces and camouflage uniforms of men trained to kill with wire, pin and scarf. Local townspeople in Oahawa were assured by Canadian Broadcasting Corporation spokesmen that the eruption of aerials throughout the vicinity was all part of the CBC program to bring its signal to all Canadians. To escape attention, the land for Camp X had been purchased in small lots with money supplied by the Canadian millionaire spymaster Intrepid.

When the Prescotts arrived the northern autumn was in full splendor. Their first days were spent in taking medical tests, filling out questionnaires and helping to put the finishing touches on a series of Quonset huts, within one of which they slept. The air was invigorating, carrying the cold news of winter as it rose to a light wind, tugging at the couple as they stepped into the close periphery of the surrounding woods, which they did at every opportunity. They were as happy as they had ever been in their lives. The plain, nutritious food, cooked Canadian style, agreed with them; the still deep nights were restful in themselves and the early morning calisthenics shaped their lean bodies into ever finer tune. They knew who they were, they knew who the enemy was: the enemy was inhuman and evil, while they and all allies of the Allies were "good, beautiful and true," as Vivian had actually put it to his wife. They were collecting pinecones one lunch period during the "honeymoon" that their London contact Kim

Philby had promised them. "And when we have a child, one of these days," she said, "and he asks what—"

"What his parents were doing during the late, great war, we will have to lie because not even a child would believe Camp X. Now, do you care to discuss the issue of immaculate conception?" He pulled her down on the leafy carpet, her pale skin was rosy with health, her unmade-up lips ripe-colored, her jet hair caught simply by a plaid headband. They both wore low boots, corduroy slacks and plaid shirts. They hugged, rubbed together, laughing, looking at each other with loving eyes.

"I thought Dr. Grotjohn's letter really saw between the lines of yours to him and was very positive, didn't you?"

"I did, Viv, but—"

"But what?"

"How do I conceive? *Per os.*"

"*Os . . . ?*"

"*Per os,* by ear."

"I can see you as the Virgin Mary—if you watch your language —but I'm not really cut out to play the Lord who comes and puts the word in your ear . . ."

"Who says you're not cut out?" She was zipping down and fingering in to hold him before he could give a full laugh. "You're beautifully cut out, my sweet, and you haven't said a word about how frustrated you must be . . . don't say it, I know you are because I am too and I want to tell you what I've decided: there are, as you know, several well-known English-speaking psychoanalysts here at the camp. I'm going to arrange for some time with one of them. Supposedly we're going to be here a year, that should be enough time to make some progress, because I want to have a child with you, very much. In the meantime, let's approach the problem scientifically. I possess the standard and requisite body orifices available for gratification to a human male who takes a broad view, as they say. Now, your view is pretty broad so—wait, now, be serious—so tonight I am going to kiss and suck your beautiful cock and if your sperm doesn't take root like a watermelon seed in my belly then bye and bye I will have to burn my psychological bridges and let you into the holy of holies if you will permit a mixed metaphor, as an ex-literary critic—"

He put his hand over her mouth, smiled deep into her eyes. In her slim hand he was hard and pulsing. "I love you," he said. There was no need to say anything else. . . .

Farm-style barns and houses were located over the cleared acreage. During the Prescotts' stay a number of temporary domiciles were erected to house the growing population of the clandestine base. As Vivian and Janet both had literary and journalistic experience, their first assignment was at Station M of the camp.

"M" stood for Magic, and for the popular British illusionist Jasper Maskelyne, who was now putting his sleight-of-hand expertise to work for the toughest audience he'd ever had to face: the fascists. Under the tutelage of Maskelyne and the technicians and forgers of Camp X's "Magic Group," recruits like Janet and Viv learned to simulate documents, which might be slipped without a trace into a Europe-bound package or diplomatic pouch.

Into this station, operating undercover as a radio relay transmitter, flowed information and material from BSC so-called censorship teams. Innocuous-looking people who haunted ports of entry to find in the baggage or on the persons of European refugees the minutiae of authenticity—the contemporary German stamps, gloves with a Berlin label—that would complete the illusion for a Camp X operative who was to be dropped behind enemy lines. When new arrivals in New York from Vienna or occupied France searched their bags for a missing box of stationery, a tailored shirt, a watch, there was a good chance the items were on their way to Station M. Other recruits from special segments of society—and not always on the right side of the law—counterfeited European currency, duplicated typewriters and faked identification. Maskelyne's talent for abracadabra was demonstrated once and for all at the Ontario camp when he rigged up an illusion for J. Edgar Hoover with a few toy warships and mirrors. The visiting FBI director "saw," to his utter amazement, a fleet of battleships apparently moving on the lake.

On the fourth and final night of their honeymoon Vivian and Janet were moved to a comfortable bedroom in a sturdy wood farmhouse-style building. They ate a solid boardinghouse meal of goulash at a long table with ten others from all over Europe, and a bottle of champagne was served in honor of the handsome newlyweds. After their day in the woods Janet and Vivian were positively glowing with vigor; and the spirits at the table were high. Janet, flushed from the wine, was a radiant bride. None would ever have guessed the Prescotts' secret, or the scene that would be played out in the back hall bedroom that night.

Downstairs, a gramophone was in use and Vivian and Janet could clearly hear the swing beat of a big band and her favorite, Helen O'Connell's lilting, whiskey-voiced version of "Six Lessons from Madam LaZonga." By the time Viv returned from the hall bathroom, the music had turned sweet with Artie Shaw's "Begin the Beguine." He was undressed and in bed when Janet came. She shut the door and returned his smile, swaying a bit to the music. "Do you want to dance?"

"I'll watch you—'NO. 1 DEB BRIGHTENS CAMP X BALL—HUSBAND PLEDGES UNDYING LOVE.' "

Her grace as she moved to the music in the dim, warm room was, indeed, a rare sight. Now she began to disrobe. Downstairs someone turned the volume lower, creating gaps in the orchestration that reached up to them behind their closed door. Janet was naked, dancing slowly with no apparent self-consciousness. Her hands seemed to be talking to him as she touched at her breasts, belly and hips. Her fingers fluttered down to her thighs, walking through the curly raven hair there, swaying closer to him in the bed, her eyes half shut and her skin touched with rose from arousal and the champagne. Half-sitting, he reached out as she neared the bed and cupped her buttock, stroking as she continued to sway in place. She did not even see him lean forward and very tenderly place his tongue in her, lightly but firmly moving her closer, but she felt it, "oh yes," and gave out a deep sigh, raising her pink, soft lips of her vagina to meet his mouth.

As if awakened from a trance, she stopped all movement and opened her eyes to look down at him. His eyes searched up the length of her to find her face. Her gaze was solemn as she dropped to her knees at bedside. "Oh, Viv, that's so wonderful, can we try it a little more each night?" He kissed her lips, his tongue at the corners and around her teeth as if still caressing her clitoris. She spread back the coverlet as they kissed and found him. "So big, my God."

As if gliding to the music, she kissed down his chest, bit in passing at the lush pubic hair, then paused at the base of his shaft until he lay flat again and guided her head up and over and down on his erection. Slowly her tongue began to explore and discover

84

him, then her soft lips went their way. He knew that this was the first time and was prepared to stop at any point that her tolerance was reached. But she continued. Downstairs the music had stopped and night sounds filled the room. He put both his hands on her neck now, no longer guiding her but holding on hoping to be able to stop, joyful that no intruding image of his father's wife had come.

He heard her say, "Viv, please come in my mouth." Holding her head, his fingers caught in her full black hair, his hips began to jerk with a life of their own and for the second time that day he breathed out the simple truth, "I love you." But now repeating it like a caress, over and over.

On the November day in 1940 that the first snow drifted down on the humming activity of Camp X, Mush Hollander arrived, greeting them with a shout, bear-hugging them both in his powerful arms. From Chicago he had brought a college classmate named Tim Donahue. Tim was a slight, wiry redhead from one of Chicago's Catholic wards on the West Side, where the priests and nuns are demanding schoolmasters and the school of the streets is even more demanding. On scholarship to the school of architecture at the University of Illinois, he had lived in the same residence hall with Mush and had actually introduced him to his future wife. Tim was much less radical in his politics than Mush. There was such a clear, sensitive and loyal presence coming through his quiet, freckled face that people trusted him at once, whatever their politics.

The next day Mush came for Tim and Vivian to start them in the cross-training of survival skills. Janet had a few words to say about the theory of "male dominance." She was to wait for Major Spinks, a middle-aged woman in charge of the FANY brigade.

Under the aegis of the old-fashioned, volunteer First Aid Nursing Yeomanry, the major quickly transformed her young female recruits into crack radio operators. For weeks they would eat, sleep and breathe in Morse code, preparing for the days ahead when the communications links they would set up between London and operatives in enemy territory might save lives and salvage missions. The young male recruits' jibes that FANY had a "cushy" assignment were taken with good-natured retorts; the importance of the role these women were to play was recognized and—behind the jokes—respected at Camp X.

Tim and Vivian spent the next weeks in the division known as Travelers Censorship. Janet, too, was posted there several hours a week. The three witnessed one of the division's most miraculous finds when port-watchers in New York confiscated and sent to the secret camp a complete woman's wardrobe, custom-tailored in Berlin. The clothing, with minor alterations at Camp X, would be rerouted to outfit a newly trained female agent, ready to assume a new identity in German society. The fashion-conscious Janet was fascinated by the details of the transformation. She learned the ways a button could be sewn on a garment to indicate regional tailoring, the telltale messages that could be read in the wrong cut of a jacket, the finishing touches on a hem or a lining.

The Canadian winter was long and cold and the work of the new spies intense, and harrowing. New recruits continued to arrive, and Vivian, Tim and Janet now began to teach a part of the time.

As the snows melted in the spring of 1941, the Prescotts and Tim Donahue accompanied Mush to a meeting of those agents who were now considered trained for action. To their surprise two dozen young "veterans" were greeted by the short, elegant figure of Intrepid himself, who had arrived at Camp X in secrecy. Over tea, he addressed them with the particular intensity for which William Stephenson was known:

"The prime minister, you may be interested to know, refers to you all as 'leopards,' that's a term from the last war referring to Canadian commando operations." Intrepid did not waste words, talking just enough to put them at their ease.

Basically, Intrepid's message was that the United States would in all probability soon be in the war. British and American recruits and experts in their fields would be arriving in increasing numbers. These newcomers would include authors, professors, professional men and women from every discipline, "people of the highest ideals to pit against the Nazis." To illustrate the combination of principles and skills that Camp X was attempting to create, Sir William recounted to them the story of Ian Fleming, a talented young author:

"Fleming was one of the first to train here and made a brilliant showing in most areas—as a frogman, for example. It was during a practice mission in which I played a small part that he discovered that one of his best qualities as an agent—imagination—could also work against him. It was a little assignment called 'disposal of the tail'—yes, I can see on some of your faces that you've heard of it, but for the benefit of the others I will describe it as . . . an assertion of one's privacy, shall we say?"

As a soft laugh ran through the audience he continued: "Fleming and I stood in the hallway of a deserted hotel we were using near Toronto, just outside the room of the tail we had following him throughout the exercise. The shadow was, of course, one of our own men, a trainer. I handed Fleming a forty-five caliber revolver and nodded toward the door, which he was to throw open, shooting immediately, before his opponent had time to react. I can still see the look on Fleming's face as he said, 'Bill, how can I kill in cold blood?' His total belief in this little exercise of ours, that he'd be spilling real blood when he opened that door, stopped him cold."

Intrepid then came to the reason for the meeting. "You will need, in the next few months, to study the art of violent survival. The probability that you will meet with accidental death in training is one of three chances in a hundred; the same ratio holds for your chances of being captured during a mission. Once in enemy hands, however, one out of three will be interrogated by the Gestapo. The 'pianists,' or radio operators, can expect, according to statistical predictions, to live only six months behind enemy lines."

Janet laced her fingers through Vivian's and squeezed. Hard.

Almost a year had passed now, and both Vivian and Janet had won respect from the chief Camp X advisers. Mush Hollander was back and forth across the border bringing in personnel, and Tim Donahue had fallen in love with a slim and very bright nurse that he had known almost all his life in Chicago. Pat McGuire was a clutch of auburn-haired energy enclosed in a petite dancer's body. Her eyes were a laughing green, her mouth was hungry and sensuous and toothy; her wit was understated and telling. The two couples, Janet and Vivian and Tim and Patricia, played bridge, read to each other, occasionally danced together through the long winter.

The love affair between Tim and Patricia seemed to sadden Janet slightly, driving her to steal time for intense talks with a dry, very bright psychiatrist from New York State, Walter R. Ruhl. She knew that she and Viv could at any time be assigned to an active area and that the probabilities were heavily weighted against their being sent to the same place . . . husband and wife were much too vulnerable to Nazi torture if captured together.

Walter Ruhl was one of four depth psychologists working on profiles of men like Hitler, Göring, Hess and Heydrich. He was especially interested in Hitler's psychosexual motives and tendencies: his loathing for his old father, fixation on his young mother, abuse of his adolescent niece, sadomasochistic and death wishes. This psychological profile was all drawn to the end of provoking the führer into a serious, perhaps even fatal, mistake.

Mush Hollander and Dr. Ruhl carried on a series of discussions, often after dinner around the fire, on the primary motivation of the fascist personality. Mush was critical of the Camp X assessments because they neglected, in his opinion, the economic underpinnings of National Socialism. The discussions were challenging, with light and perhaps more heat.

"Doc, doc. I'm not disagreeing that Hitler's fear of his own Jewish blood has helped to drive him nuts or that he has a deep 'homosexual panic,' but my quarrel with you people is that you're conducting your analysis in a vacuum—not you so much, but the others. Just let me—'Jew' is a code word. To me anti-Semitism equals anti-Communism. Hitler's backing comes from Farben and Krupp and the big industrialists. *Why?* Because Hitler pledged to stamp out Communism. Krupp doesn't hate Jews, some of his top managers are Jews. Jews were decorated in high numbers in the first war; I. G. Farben's niece is married to Henri Blum, the great cellist. The point is that Adolph Hitler's hatred for Jews is irrelevant to understanding him—the big money and the political muscle came from monopoly capital and it occurred to Hitler and his people to stop Communism and socialism, and if he wanted to use 'anti-Semitism' as a cover for anti-Communism—to the working class—and wipe out Jews, so what? As long as the workers can be racially provoked against their own best interests—socialism—under the disguise of race hatred—"

"Yes, but Mush, race hatred begins inside the . . ." and the issue would be joined.

After one of their sessions Dr. Ruhl told Janet about BSC's astrological scheme. "You might see some headlines in the months to come, something like 'Hitler's Star Sinking; Roosevelt Towers over World Horoscope;' and an 'eminent' astrologer from Eastern Europe will be quoted as saying that his interpretation of the movement of the stars and planets shows the inevitable decline of the führer. That man will be a British officer, with his horoscopes supplied by the New York office. We know that Hitler believes in this mumbo jumbo and hope that these reports in the press will be enough to send him into a fit of anger. That's when he makes his mistakes."

Dr. Ruhl was winning her confidence, encouraging her in her nocturnal experiments, matching her sarcastic self-criticism with a warm sense of irony . . . "When you *do* do it, let me assure you that your mother will not die. She finally accepted your marriage despite the fact that you robbed her of a headline wedding, didn't she? Then she must assume that you're having intercourse, doesn't she? And while the birth of a child would make her a *grandmother*, it still wouldn't *kill* her. *You cannot kill anyone, Janet,* in absentia *or in effigy."* That sank in, then, "Your training here underscores *that* —doesn't it?"

Nights with Vivian had become adventures in joy, and fear. After long hard workdays, they would bathe in the house bathtub then snuggle into bed. By spring Janet was able to let Vivian kiss her breasts and clitoris to the point of climax, while at the same time she would wind herself around to his groin and kiss and suck him to orgasm. Sometimes she would dance for him and once, after wine with Tim and Patricia, she had flung herself on him pretending to be a mad rapist. Then, in a whispered shout, she cried, "Lay on, Macduff, and damned be him who first cries hold, enough!" His hips jerked and involuntarily the big head of his penis drove into her opening. Janet froze in her striation like a rider caught forever on a Grecian urn, then rolled off with her back to him, refusing to speak. . . .

During all this time their team of Mush, Tim and Patricia was functioning like the fingers of one hand: codes and guns, surveillance and surprise, interrogation and cover stories. He did not need an absolute sexual bond with Janet but his celibacy, in the sense of intercourse, with his wife, was like a loophole in the skein of their relationship, as full and mutual as it was in the other areas of work and belief.

Which is why, he told himself, the incident with Pat McGuire had come to pass. During a parachute and infiltration exercise in the thick forest, he and Pat had been teamed. The training required them to bury their clothes, dress as French peasants and in this case, find temporary shelter for the night. They had improvised a covering of branches and dirt. Sometime during the night, as they lay cramped close together, Vivian woke up in the act of actually thrusting himself on top of his companion. She was fully awake and before he could apologize, she embraced him and he could feel the heat through her wool skirt. They coupled with the intensity of animals, wordless; her lithe almost boyish form cleaving to his priapic thrusting. In the morning he said to her, "Pat, there's nothing I can say to you that doesn't sound fatuous, but I'll say it anyway. I respect you as a friend and colleague, and I love my wife very much—"

"I know that. And I love Tim, you know that. Let's put it down to the war and being behind the lines." And she kissed him, this time like a sister. . . .

Otherwise, he had worked and waited patiently with Janet. She would open, he knew, like a slow-blooming but fecund flower. What weighed on them was the possibility of imminent separation. Mush tried to prepare them on the day that Janet and Pat McGuire were moved to a training area several miles away from Station M, to a project code-named PROSPER.

Pat and Janet were required to sleep at PROSPER, only able to exchange information with Tim and Vivian every five to seven days. Because the young women both spoke French and were being given intensive language seminars in various dialects of the provinces of the French countryside, Tim and Vivian agreed with Mush that the PROSPER team was being groomed for an operation in occupied France. The pattern of separation was hardening into a scar across their minds.

PROSPER, as Janet and Pat would learn in the weeks to follow, was the largest and strategically the most precarious of the BSC's agent networks in occupied France. And their jobs within this network would be among the most dangerous, if their minds and bodies withstood the rigors of preparation at the hands of Vera Atkins, the service's head of the Paris division. Atkins was not looking for idealists or martyrs as she scanned the new recruits; Janet's intelligence and tough-mindedness and Pat's balance and

90

pragmatism recommended them immediately for the hazardous positions their instructor intended to fill.

What PROSPER needed most were "pianists," the priceless radio transmitters who could keep the operatives in the field in daily contact with Bletchley, ensuring the network's lifeline of ammunition, explosives and agents. The last radio operator's tour of duty had been ominously short, Atkins knew, so she drilled the two young women mercilessly for what lay ahead. Between French dialect instruction and physical workouts, classes in self-defense, weaponry and basic radio electronics, Pat and Janet memorized the initials and codes that would make their transmissions from France more concise and more difficult to crack: "QRM" would signal to their paired FANY telegraphists in England that interference was bad; "QUO" meant they were forced to stop broadcasting at the risk of their lives.

Both realized that it was more than possible that they would be interrogated by the Gestapo and learned the system of nonsense-phrase safety checks with which they indicated to their "fairy godmothers" at Bletchley that they were transmitting freely and not under enemy control. They joked between themselves over their training in the use of the suicide, or "L", pill—what else could they do? They were also issued pills to induce sleep and illness, knives to be wielded "delicately" and revolvers for use in case of ambush when they debarked from their low-flying, nearly invisible "moon" planes. The future pianists became adept in the arts, while Station M's experts produced their new identities—French-made clothing and the European luggage that would contain their lightweight transmitters.

As they neared the end of their training a mock "Gestapo interrogation" session was set up to test their stamina. Isolated from her friend Pat, Janet faced the blazing lights and the commands of her "Nazi" torturers with clenched teeth and stony silence, while in the shadows her instructor watched for a crack in the facade. The former debutante took the threats and jeers with the same show with which she'd faced the raised eyebrows of the dowagers at her first, bare-shouldered cotillion grand march (at the time they were formidable indeed). She even withstood very personal attacks when pieces of her private life, known only to herself and Dr. Ruhl, were thrown at her. If she was shocked at the breach of confidence,

91

at the necessity of testing her in so brutal a manner, she didn't let it show. She hated it, though, and it worried her.

In August they were separated. Mush, Tim and Vivian were to be transferred to New York City to become part of a project called SATAN. Vivian could not understand why his oral order from Kim Philby stressed that he was being assigned to SATAN as an auditor. "SATAN will be a classic military-political operation. Because of your literary background we would like you to keep a complete log of every phase of the preparation. When the SATAN team leaves for Europe you will work up your notes into a 'book.' The SATAN book will never be published, of course, but will be used in training for similar future operations and for our files." Vivian, however, was not persuaded that his theoretical role was not determined by the importance of his father.

New York was sweltering. Mush, Tim and Vivian were domiciled in the Henry Hotel in Greenwich Village, where struggling authors had lived on and off since it was built in the 1910s. The separation was especially difficult for Vivian and Tim, thinking of Janet and Pat in the woods near the cold lakes of Camp X. But the SATAN assignment soon absorbed their imaginations.

The object of SATAN's interest was Reinhard Tristram Eugen Heydrich, Reich Protector of Bohemia-Moravia, head of the Nazi Intelligence and Security Service, "the butcher of Prague." From the sketchy details known to the world about the man whom Hitler described as being "führer material," the specialists assigned to SATAN built a "proso-Profile"—a picture of the history, psychology and character of an individual.

The facts known about Heydrich's meteoric rise in the Third Reich showed him to be power-hungry and viciously anti-Semitic. His early career had been overseen by Heinrich Minnler, Reich Commissioner for Consolidation of German Racial Stock. British intelligence had learned that Heydrich was part Jewish, which he compensated for by out-hating his Nazi colleagues, on whom he also kept files of real or manufactured evidence that could be used to blackmail those whom he felt stood in his way. It was a way that led straight to the führer himself. Heydrich was known to exploit Hitler's sexual fantasies by accusing political enemies within the Nazi hierarchy of "perversion"; for this reason no one dared produce charges of Heydrich's own homosexual tendencies or his paternity hearing as a young naval officer.

Vowing to "exterminate the strain" of Jewry in Europe, Heydrich had brought to bear his organizational brilliance and imagination on a purge of 20,000 Jews throughout Germany in 1938. At that time he issued memoranda to local police on the conditions under which synagogues could be torched as well as the urgency with which arrested Jews should be sent to concentration camps. In 1939, he arranged the fraudulent "attack" on German positions by Polish partisans—in actuality German prisoners—boasting that he had thereby "started the second world war." In September of 1941 Hitler rewarded him with control over the entire Czech nation, and Heydrich moved with his wife Lina and their three children into the Castle Hradcany in Prague.

A model of Hradcany Castle and a duplicate of his green Mercedes became some of the props of the SATAN team's preparation, which included scrutiny of Heydrich's personal habits, his route to his office and the topography of the Prague area.

Hollywood scenarist Zoltan Korda worked at Camp X and produced sets to simulate Heydrich's surroundings at Hradcany. The medieval fortress sat on top of Prague's highest hill overlooking the Vltava. Access to the looming concrete castle could be gained only by climbing upward along narrow, winding ramplike roads. The vine-covered and crumbling walls which surrounded it were set into the steep hillside and were unscalable by all except the most agile of animals—or perhaps secret agents . . . No matter how inaccessible, the next move on the SATAN agenda—as Vivian recorded in his "book"—would be the murder of Heydrich. "The exterminator exterminated," Vivian wrote with a flourish.

He and Tim were told only that after Labor Day there would be no more communication from Camp X. Later, just after Pearl Harbor, they would hear the awful news . . . Mush sat clenching his big hands as he sat on the bed in Vivian's hotel room, unable to look his listeners in the eyes, his voice a bit too loud and his delivery rushed, as if to hide the pain he felt at bearing horrible news to his friends.

"We didn't know how close the Germans were to cracking PROSPER when the girls were dropped in. Nazi intelligence spared no expense in breaking it; to them it was the whole secret

93

war rolled into one operation. They finally made a deal with some farmers, said they would treat the resistance fighters they captured as soldiers, which meant they couldn't be killed, and the peasants bought it. Two Canadians who went in around the same time as Janet and Pat were the first to be arrested. They got Janet's contact in Paris, a professor. She kept on transmitting until the last minute and then they came for her too. Pat was in the countryside when she was taken."

Mush continued in a low voice. "They were interrogated in Paris first and made an escape over the rooftops. Janet didn't make it. All we know is that she spent her last few weeks at Pforzheim in the Black Forest. The underground got Pat to England. I don't know any more."

After Tim had left, Vivian quietly shut the hotel room door and locked it. "What did they do to her, Mush? Did they . . . did they abuse her?"

"No, I don't think—no, there's no evidence of—"

"Don't lie."

"Viv, I don't *know*. I'm sorry. I just don't *know*—where're you going? Viv?"

"To get some *answers*—from Philby."

Kim Philby was waiting in his room as if he had known that Vivian would come. He was already on his feet offering scotch to the man whose body and face were still recognizably those of the boy he had first met in Bletchley, so long ago, it seemed now ". . . but that's the point, we have to wait until . . . *listen* to me, Vivian, of course we'll do everything possible to find out but—"

"You smug son-of-a-bitch, you knew she wasn't ready . . ." gray eyes dark, his breathing ragged, knuckles bleeding from hitting them against the hotel corridor walls ". . . Listen, Philby. I'll be back at SATAN on Monday—as a *participant*. You understand me? I am going in with Hollander and Donahue and the SATAN team.". . .

Sam Prescott was waiting for him at the Boston railroad terminal, looking as stricken as if it had been his own wife who had been murdered. He reminded his son that he *could* understand what it was to lose an irreplaceable person and relationship.

"But you never knew how . . . vulnerable she was . . ." he said in the taxi driving them out to Cambridge. Tears were not hidden.

In the silence Sam Prescott was thinking that he knew more than his son about what had happened to Janet, though not too much more. The reports from France were contradictory. An informer in the Vichy government reported to London that the Canadians, captured first, had talked immediately but that the major PROS-PER contact, the professor, had died under torture without betraying either Janet or Pat, thereby giving the two American women time to get away into the underground railroad and clear of the Gestapo. Pat and two Resistance women had made it as far as the Belgian border before they were stopped. But Janet, according to London's source, had frozen, then shot herself in the head the next day before the Germans could find her. It seemed the Camp X graduates had done poorly—except for Pat's remarkable resourcefulness—and Washington had asked London to cover over their operatives' panic.

Sam Prescott found all of this extremely depressing, but agreed to go along with the story of heroism—true for Pat and adapted some to include Janet. Then, six months later, Little Bill Donovan confided to Sam in Washington at the OSS offices on E Street that the Vichy informer had just been revealed as a double agent who had been planting false information on SOE agents since 1939.

"Well, Bill, what *actually* happened?"

"We know that the McGuire girl did escape as reported; was also captured, tortured and escaped again. But she was *alone.* We have a new source that claims that your daughter-in-law was taken to Pforzheim. What happened there—whether she was tortured to death, cooperated, or went out of her mind—we have no way of knowing . . ."

"Is there a chance we ever *will* know? Vivian—"

"Sam . . . forget it. Why break his heart? I strongly suspect there's no way we'll ever know for sure . . ."

As they walked through the almost deserted Harvard Yard his father asked softly, "What will you do now, Viv?"

"Find Jack Kennedy and get stupid drunk and then *you're* going to talk to Sir William Stephenson about my going over with the rest of the SATAN team."

He finally found Jack Kennedy in the home-going crowd after the Boston College-Lehigh football game. It was the jejeune habit of some Harvard men to descend one rung on the collegiate ladder, the better to meet and "make out" with young women whose families they were unlikely ever to have to explain themselves to. Now, home on a visit, Jack had paid hasty respects to the extended Irish clans from which he sprang and set out in hot pursuit of the leader of the Boston College cheerleading squad.

It was near dark and the late November cold was settling in. Kennedy was with a cheery cheerleader and they were laughing when Vivian came up suddenly in front of him at the corner. "Vivian Prescott . . . where the hell have you been hiding? Vivian, meet the pride of victorious B.C. . . . ." The astringent Back Bay accent sounded somehow comforting to Vivian . . . "Viv, what is it? Is it your father?" The cheer died on the cheerleader's round red lips.

He didn't really care that Mary Agnes Nash heard their conversation as they sat in Kennedy's Buick roadster. She sat helplessly in the front seat while Jack sat with him in the back among the overdue library books, holding his hands and listening with open compassion as Vivian told him just enough for him to understand in a general way what it was that Vivian and Janet had been doing in the secret war since their sudden disappearance from London the year before. There was so much that Vivian could not say, either privately or publicly, to his friend—or to his father, for that matter —that each time he reached a censored area of his grief his outpouring was transformed into silent, unspeakable grief.

After an hour it was dark, and the excited crowd dispersed to victory celebrations. When Jack's cheerleader friend hopped out to get coffee, he said, "Viv, I'll take Mary Agnes home and you'll come with me out to—"

"No. I'll just go with you wherever. I want to get blind, get laid . . . oh, Christ . . ."

"All right. Look, we're meeting people at the Lagoon, there'll be extra girls there. I'm not drinking tonight so you go ahead, don't worry . . . Jesus, Viv, I'm so very sorry . . ."

A press of drunken revelers from the game that night had turned the Sleepy Lagoon's two garishly decorated floors into a standing-room-only victory party, sweeping up the rest of the Saturday night crowd into its high spirits. Downstairs in "the Cove," a ragtime piano was drowned out by the cheers and shouts for the bartender, while the swing band upstairs in the Moonlight Ballroom picked up the fever and put some real energy into their versions of the current Harry James hits. Jack Kennedy pulled rank on some former Harvard teammates of his and cleared a table for the three of them; Vivian followed Jack and Mary Agnes to his seat like a sleepwalker. Jack ordered him an Irish whisky. "Better make that two—doubles," he shouted after the waiter. Jack and Mary Agnes danced as Vivian downed his third and fourth drinks, the noise and heat of the crowd washing over him.

Sometime after midnight, as the press of people reached a peak, a scream cut through Viv's drunken haze: "Fire!" The band stopped playing and the dancers staggered back against each other as a young woman ran screaming into their midst, her hair in flames. Paper palm fronds over the bandstand and the bar seemed to ignite in an instant, and the mass of people pushed in panic toward the one revolving door to the street. Jack and Mary Agnes fought their way toward the table. Vivian sat staring, aimlessly quoting *"Perduta Gente"* from Dante's *Inferno*. A pillar near the table had caught fire and a paper frond flapped loose and blazed over Vivian's head. Behind him a woman screamed; he said out loud to no one . . . "The Gestapo tore her body apart." At that moment Kennedy made his way through the crush and tried to lift Vivian up by the arms.

"She was a virgin . . ." Vivian mumbled.

"What?" Kennedy pulled him forward.

"No, leave me alone," Vivian mumbled, shaking himself free of his friend's grip. "Leave me here . . ."

"You're full of it, Prescott," Kennedy yelled at him, hoisting him to his feet and dragging him back toward the bandstand. They followed a stream of choking people to a basement stage door. A stampede from the downstairs bar had turned the narrow staircase in the front of the nightclub into a mass of suffocating bodies. People pushing both ways in the revolving door had sealed the main entrance. Employees and chorines jumped from the windows of the private quarters upstairs into the locked arms of rescuers on the streets. . . .

The next morning at the Kennedy breakfast table Vivian and Jack read the death toll in the newspapers. Four hundred fifty had perished. The headline bannered: BUSBOY BLAMED.

Vivian felt that the blazing carnage had, in a terrible way, been his own baptism of fire. He was more than ready for Europe.

Karl Joachim Stohr shivered as he fumbled through the folds of his long heavy overcoat. He was having difficulty finding his penis, his "member" as he called it, like his father the pastor before him. As he urinated he concentrated on keeping the stiff, heavy folds of the overcoat free of the stream of his micturation (which was his father's word too). All of the Gestapo major's words descended from his father's catechism. The major sometimes almost believed that his very dreams and thoughts as well as his peculiar pastoral vocabulary were generally inherited from his father just as his flat face and inadequate body had been, along with what he believed was "a less than normative member." He now carefully shook the offending member, which was being further contracted by the slicing chill of the late April night. He shook and jerked it with precision, which served to cancel, as it were, the slight but continual trembling of his right hand.

The major cocked his head, listening. The enemy should be close. He shifted from one foot to the other for warmth. No moon, of course, at between three and four in the morning, in the "stygian darkness" (his father the pastor's image). The major felt himself potent, a man of destiny. In the pitch darkness, height did not matter, short or tall was a trick of the light, the caprice of the diurnal, the stupid sun of the daytime. In dark night no one could ever mistake you for a child. The major licked his lips and stamped the iron-hard earth that no Slovak peasants would work this year. Fifty yards away his squad waited in their black overcoats, though he could not see them.

The Gestapo had requisitioned a medium-sized estate as headquarters and driven away the servants and "freedmen" who planted and harvested the fields. Now the smaller house of the eldest son was where the major conducted his interrogations. In that comfortable old-fashioned country house one of the Americans' Czech agents had screamed out of his intolerable pain that London was sending a radio team that would be parachuting in sometime during the week of April 26.

The major did not believe that the trembling—or "innervation," as the pastor would have diagnosed it—was connected in any way to the late-night torture sessions that animated the comfortable old house. It was the major's experience that near-pulling out of the prisoner's tongue by the roots was a near infallible method for extracting information. "Let us see if one can loosen his tongue" was the only small joke that the major permitted himself to address to his young and stalwart aide Captain Hamburger. It was not such a bad existence, he thought. Someone had to do it, and he was at home with military men, and Hamburger, though a good five inches taller, somehow contrived to give the impression of looking up to and at his commander by inclining his attitude as much as his body. No, not a bad life.

In the dark you literally could not see your hand, innervated or not, in front of your face. Just as the major was rubbing his right arm across his waist, so as to feel the bulge of his Luger, he heard the drone of the oncoming enemy plane.

In the cold, dark cargo plane before the jump, before that in New York as X-day approached, during the long transatlantic flight, at BSC London during final briefings, numb drunk in the pubs, the memory of Janet was a red scar across Vivian's nervous system, along his life . . . a scar that like a demarcation left his youth and innocence in a far country he'd never return to. . . . "Tim—" He would lean across the table and repeat the question for the twentieth time. "When you visit Pat does she tell you what really happened? Why can't I see her? Does she know that we're going to get some back for them . . . ?" Until Mush and Tim would drag him away from the public place, and public display of grief so foreign to the British.

Pat was in the countryside, near Bletchley, too weak to be allowed to meet with Vivian in *his* condition. The plan was to drill the U.S. team for long hours during the day, then allow them several hours to let go at night. Philby, watching Vivian closely, felt confident that he was primed for any contingency but kept Mush with Vivian when he went looking for prostitutes.

Mush reported to Philby Vivian's pitable routine with the prostitutes . . . He would look for a younger woman and though very drunk would invite her to a hotel with a courtliness totally absent of any hint of condescension. Mush, waiting outside the room in the corridor, could not help being aware of the ritual inside. In his drunkenness Vivian would almost always leave the door ajar, or Mush would have been forced to descend to the keyhole. When he had protested to Philby ("out of common decency") the British control agent had stuttered, "And if young Mr. P–P . . . Prescott should do anything rash, then what do you think w–w–w—" and Mush muttering, "Yes, all *right,* for God's sake."

Slowly, tenderly, Vivian would disrobe the street girl, who for her part would be half caught up in or at least bemused by the mysterious inner drama of the chestnut-haired American, handsome as a film star, who appeared to be in some romantic tradition that she had only dimly dreamed of before starting out in Birmingham or the coal towns of the North.

He would call her "Janet" as he draped her body back onto the squeaking hotel bed. She could not help regarding him with curious wonder as he slowly stripped his clothes, revealing a powerful erection. Some of them were actually moved as with tenderness he knelt to lubricate them with his tongue, whispering absurd poetry they had never heard. Then he would lift his head and swing his large gray eyes up to the rapt or bored or confused face of Gert or Betty or Stella, the deep circles under his eyes accentuating their intensity, and slowly turn them over.

These tarts were, though, properly astonished when this fine young man began with effortless intimacy to kiss calf and buttock, finding their orifices with his tongue—as if paying homage. Mush, in the corridor with fists clenched, thought, "The opposite of death is desire," and at last, turning them over again as if to prove Mush's dictum, repeating the magical word "Janet," Vivian would mount the girl and, as if penetrating a frightened virgin, ever so slowly, apply the pressure of his taut hips to her entrance, calling "Janet" in a tone strangled so that as often as not the whore would not even make it out as he came down in slow motion on her, like a body in a dream. . . . Standing in the corridor Mush covered his face as the tears came to his eyes. It was his job—Philby's orders —to usher the streetwalkers to the elevator and push too much money into their hands.

Their last few nights in London, Vivian had abruptly stopped drinking and looking for women, retiring after supper and reappearing hollow-eyed for the early morning briefings, hardly saying a word for the last forty-eight hours.

He was ready.

100

As Vivian stretched motionless on the icy sod of Czecho-slovakia, somehow it seemed to be his grave, and he thought, This is how it must have been for Janet. . . . The drone of the departing carrier plane was replaced by silence, broken only by the cold whistle of the winter wind. He could just make out the approaching silhouettes of Mush and Tim. Now they bent over him to help gather up the parachute as he rose to one knee and began hacking at the frozen earth with the hand shovel so that the chute could be buried. Mush was the first to see the intermittent glow of the lantern signaling to them from some fifty yards away. There was almost no moon, a necessary fact in BSC planning. They stumbled over the uneven frozen field toward the occasional gleam of lantern, unaware that they had been compromised until at point-blank range the Gestapo agents jammed Lugers into their necks.

They froze then on command, raised their hands high in the air, suffering themselves to be disarmed, then pushed and shoved toward two waiting automobiles. Vivian found himself monitoring his reactions as if he were two people. He felt lucid, in control as when in his intercollegiate championship tennis matches he had found himself in the hush of a match point, beyond any region of fear or tension, a functional network of stimulus and response. From the corner of his eye he could sense and see the dizzying shock that sent Mush and Tim tripping and falling in front of the long-overcoated Gestapo men. By contrast he was sure-footed and light, aware that his two escorts were eyeing him with some curios-ity and tension of their own.

Ahead of him the three Gestapo men kneed, pushed Mush and Tim into one of the autos, leaving Vivian and his guards to enter the second black sedan. The headlights knifed into the cold dark as the vehicles began to lurch across the field toward the dirt road. . . . Who had betrayed them? Vivian forced the question from his mind. Don't think about it, or about who had betrayed Janet. Concentrate on now, sound confident . . .

Riding alone with his Nazi contingent, Vivian had spoken only once in clear German. "I want to talk to the official in charge, *alone*, when we reach our destination." Silence. His German was much better than Tim's but not as good as Mush's with his German-Jewish background. Still, there could be no doubt they had understood him. But not enough, he hoped, to sense his obsessive determination to find some way to kill them.

The farmhouse had been carefully converted into an interrogation center and holding jail for just such a contingency. It was here that so many other BSC parachute agents had been taken, and where at least some had been tortured into working for the Germans at what the Nazis called the *Funkspiel*, the radio game; sending back "disinformation" to the BSC center in London, luring to their death new Anglo-American resistance teams. And it was to cope with such an emergency that London had drilled their group for months: if captured they were not to reveal, at any cost, their real mission—the assassination of Reinhard Heydrich—but to confess, after torture, the cover story that they were radio operators on their way to link up with Czech partisans outside Prague in the Central Bohemia area near Sadska. They were to agree to work for the Germans and play the radio game. London would then realize at once that they were in German hands, since their actual mission called for no radio communication until after Heydrich was disposed of and then *only* if they were trapped and in terminal danger.

At the farmhouse the three Americans were locked into a room that was empty except for an unpainted wooden chair and a naked light bulb. Tim's heavy farmer's work pants were soaked with the sweat of his tension. Mush was squint-eyed with barely suppressed anger. They stared at Vivian as he sat slumped down on the chair.

None was so foolish as to say a word, in any language. As if concretized, they remained in their original postures for nearly five minutes. Then there were footsteps along the wooden hallway. The lock turned. The door swung open, and the ranking Gestapo agent was framed there, speaking in a monotone. "You two, out," indicating Mush and Tim, then stepping in and aside so that the two other Germans, still wearing their long coats and hats despite the warmth of the house, could push Tim and Mush out and down the uncarpeted hall.

The Gestapo officer closed the door quietly, opened his coat, revealing a gun, found his cigarettes and buttoned the coat again. He lit a cigarette, offering one to Vivian, who took it, though he was not a smoker. . . .

Was the German's dirty hand trembling ever so slightly? Yes, Vivian decided in that split second. It was, and perhaps not only from the cold . . .? The man seemed unimpressive except for his

102

eyes. He stood no more than five feet four inches, was thin with a caved-in chest, a face that seemed to have descended in folds around his blot of a nose and oversized teeth. Only his eyes sparkled with a kind of preternatural energy. He stood there smoking, and staring at Vivian, who continued to remain almost in a lounging position on the hard chair. Finally the man dropped the cigarette to the hard wood floor, stood and stared, the sleeves of his ill-fitting heavy coat hanging down almost to his fingertips.

Vivian spoke first, violating London's orders or the canons for such a situation. "My name is Vivian T. J. Prescott. Are you in charge here?"

"Yes."

Vivian kept his tone flexible, but that of one accustomed to being obeyed. He had damn little hope, which made his show of bravado in a sense easier. In fact, part of him wanted to die like Janet, the rest was committed to murder. He spoke as if following a rehearsed scenario, with the assumption that the other man would also read his role as if it too had been well-learned—actors whose stage was this "boundary situation," as Professor Mann had called moments of radical existence.

"Do you know who my father is?" Silence (as expected). "He is an American multimillionaire who is prepared to meet any price for my release or safekeeping for the duration of these stupid hostilities." Vivian treated the silences of the man as if they were expected cues in the dialogue. "I am prepared to tell you London's radio code and routine and to act as your agent, but of course the other two prisoners must never learn or even guess what I have just told you, or what kind of understanding we work out between us."

"Why are you telling me all this?"

"Because I do not intend to play games or offer stupid cover stories or submit to torture." The Nazi studied him. Vivian tried a wide grin, at the same time shifted the long grace of his body, unbuttoned the bottom button of his short peasant's jacket and fingered his crotch, as if unconsciously. "May I have another cigarette, *Herr Kommandant?*"

The German felt feverish in the heavy coat in the close room. This time, as he fished out the crumpled packet of French cigarettes, he let his great coat hang open, aware that the handsome American's eyes had lowered to the level of his crotch. His arm felt heavy, trembling slightly as he held out the crooked cigarette. Vivian's glance shifted to the bright and now watering eyes, holding them as he inclined forward to reach for the cigarette.

The two men were motionless as a tableau; then the German shuffled a stiff step toward Vivian. Vivian's long forward leg arced up at an acute angle from the knee, his heavy peasant's boot driving the man's testicles up into his groin, shattering his pelvic plate. The German pitched forward, his head cracking into the chair between Vivian's legs. Lifting himself, Vivian landed on the man's head, hearing teeth crack and the snub nose break as he drove his entire weight into the man's buttocks, smashing his head and face into the wooden chair, then reaching down and under the coat and dragging the Luger loose in almost the same motion.

The German's knees were wobbling on the floor, his arms flapping feebly at his sides. Vivian confided, "I won't kill you, you miserable little shit, if you do exactly as I tell you. Clear? In fact I'll allow you to save what little face you have left by not telling the others what a filthy pervert you really are." The German continued to choke and suck air as Vivian ground his hips down on the man's neck and head.

"Now, I'm going to let you up and take you to the door. You will call for your aides. The gun will be in your ear. Not a sound or it's all over." Slowly Vivian shifted and uncoiled, swung his right leg up and over the height of the back of the chair and put the tip of the Luger in the man's ear.

The German officer sprawled on his knees, his head crushed into the prongs that constituted the back of the chair. Blood spread across its seat. The man's rimless spectacles were ground into his nose and forehead. His bright eyes had been hammered shut into bloody congealing packets.

Vivian lifted him by the straggly hair at the back of his neck, then shifted his grip to the thick collar of the coat, lifted him off his feet, then tucked his head and shoulder under the Gestapo agent's armpit, and stood there to collect his strength, never lowering the gun arm from its upward loop into the German's ear. Vivian's only concern was whether this human remnant would be able to call out to lure the other Germans.

At the door now, Vivian braced the man against the wall with his shoulder, turned the knob tentatively, cracked the door. The dim hall was empty and silent, but straining, he could hear voices somewhere, distinguishing at least two groups emanating from separate locations. He turned back, the man's blood was running down the wall now, streaking the chalky board. "What's the name of the next in command?" Vivian demanded from the ruined creature he now held up by the scruff of his overcoat.

"Dieter Hamburger."

Inching into the hall, the gun still poking into the Gestapo officer's ear, holding him so that only his toes touched the floor . . . "Call Dieter, in a *routine* manner." Vivian dug the sharp nozzle of the Luger into the ear; "If you don't get him here, you're of no further use to me."

"Dieter. Come."

Vivian backed crabwise into the room, dropped the Gestapo agent behind the door, left the door ajar and positioned himself opposite the opening with his gun at head level.

Had the buzz of voices ceased for a moment, was that a step on the stairs? Vivian's breathing was shorter now, his pulse partly blunting his hearing, but not the weight of Janet's unforgivable death—the sound of footsteps broke into his murderous fugue.

The approaching Gestapo aide was young and wiry. *"Ja, Karl?"* He was within twelve yards. Vivian forced himself to breathe. Dieter Hamburger was three and a half steps into the room before he turned. Vivian had the Luger on him, feeling for and closing the door with his left hand. Crouching as if the pistol were a knife. He gestured to Hamburger to keep his distance. "Your superior is not dead, I will let you both live if you do exactly as I say. If you open your mouth I will put a bullet through it." Vivian knew he had to break the German's will before the unexpected happened—such as the arrival of another German agent. "If you have any doubts let me tell you that the Gestapo tortured and murdered my wife. I'm ready to die right now and take you with me. Fact is, I'd prefer it . . . If you hand me your pistol I will tell you how you may get credit for breaking a British spy operation, where twenty thousand British pounds are buried within an hour of this house and, best of all, how you can save your skin. If you do not turn the pistol over I'm going to shoot you where you stand. I'll count to five. One—two —three"—there was no way Vivian could predict, he got ready to pull the trigger—"four—five—" As if a spring had been released, the German shot his hands high in the air.

"Good. Now lie down. On your face." Vivian's knee went into

105

the small of the man's back, the Luger into his neck, his left hand into the suit jacket to find the pistol. Holding both guns, he stood up and behind Hamburger. "I mean it, there is a lot of money, and honor for you if you do exactly as I say." On the floor the senior officer tried to breathe through a froth of blood. Vivian could not kill him without killing his aide too, nor could he leave him alone. "Are there regular Wehrmacht guards here?"

"Yes."

"How many?"

"Six."

"Where is the nearest group?"

"There is a single guard on the first landing of the stairs."

"Good, call him now in a perfectly normal voice. But don't let him get closer to this room than six feet. Stick your head into the hall and tell him to bring the other two Americans down here. Get up on your feet and do it. I will kill you if you so much as cough."

Vivian stood behind him, out of the sight lines of anyone approaching from the stairs. "Wait." At the door, Vivian reached around and unbuckled the German's trousers, letting them fall about his ankles. "Keep your rear in, only your head out." He shoved the Luger through the man's undershorts. "Now, call the guard."

Vivian crouched, with the other gun free to shoot it out if necessary. Hamburger called in a clear voice for the approaching guard to bring down the other Americans; Vivian jerked him back and waited, the guard's footsteps had stopped midway, then could be heard retreating and climbing the stairs. "Back on the floor, over there next to Karl."

Clumping on the stairs announced a party of guards with, Vivian supposed, Mush and Tim. If he waited for them to enter one was bound to get away using Mush or Tim as a shield. The clatter of steps on wood was loud and close now. Vivian went for the door, which opened outward toward the hall, then sank almost to one knee like a runner poised.

The guard party reached the door and paused—so that one of them could come around in front of the Americans to swing open the almost closed room door. Vivian pressed both Lugers in and tight to his chest like crossed swords, arched his spine. As the door began to swing open, he drove down and forward, sliding to his

106

right as he hit the wall, caromed off in a forty-five degree arc, both guns close together in front of him.

"Freeze. Hands up." His voice was a lash. The three uniformed men were young, and in a state of shock. Mush's reaction was fastest. "Up, *up,* damn it, if you want to live." Their hands went up; Mush and Tim unsnapped their service revolvers and pushed them in, Vivian swooping up behind them, shutting the door. "Down on the floor—move."

Mush held on to two of the guns, his keen small eyes alive with the intensity of the moment. Tim was smiling, and the evident vulnerability of him slowed Vivian down enough to avoid making an irreparable mistake. He knelt next to a guard and whispered, "How many more Wehrmacht are there?" poking a barrel into him.

"Four."

"Four? Hamburger said six in all. Who's lying?"

Mush broke the silence. "We can assume—"

"I'm not assuming, Mush" (speaking in English). He moved to another soldier. "How many more of you are there?"

"Three Wehrmacht, two Gestapo." Vivian stepped over the prostrate mass to kneel next to Hamburger. "Is that correct? Three and two, five? Remember what I said."

"Yes. I forgot. Five in all."

"Where are they?"

"The guards are on sentry. My men are asleep."

Only five, that was crucial. He wouldn't need the "L" pill now, he thought, as Janet *had* needed it. Had no chance to use it . . .

"Can they hear you from here?"

"I don't know."

"What time do the guards rotate?"

"Midnight."

"Move your arm. It's now twenty-three nineteen hours. Tim, you and Mush go with this man and bring back the other Gestapo. Kill him if he hesitates." He straddled the chair, keeping the guns leveled at the prisoners on the floor, not looking at Mush and Tim as they moved out, flanking Hamburger.

When they heard the shots from upstairs, the three army men clenched their bodies involuntarily. Vivian spun low to the doorway, one gun hand in the hall outside the door frame, one inside trained on the prisoners. The Gestapo senior officer had not moved, he was slowly choking to death on his own blood. Vivian spoke only to the enlisted man. "You will be released within the hour if you keep quiet." He braced himself on the doorjamb, elbows tight to his hips, guns fanning, his mind free and clear, mercifully purged by action of the memory of his tortured Janet.

Within moments of the pistol reports, Mush and Tim came noisily down the stairs, Mush placing Hamburger in front of them. As they reached the landing and turned into the hall Tim called out, "Viv, they went for their guns. We had to shoot them. This guy may or may not have known that they were washing up for their shift, *not* sleeping." Vivian gestured them to come back into the room, kneeling as they approached to question one of the soldiers. "Did the sentries hear those shots?"

"Yes."

"Have you shot prisoners here before?"

"Yes."

"How often?"

"Two, three times that I know of."

Turning now to Mush and Tim to direct them to the back and front entrances to intercept the sentries if they were coming in, Vivian said "We'll know in a few seconds. Move." He snapped his fingers in Hamburger's face and pointed sharply toward the floor. Mush's face was red with resentment, but both men turned and ran to their assignments. Within thirty seconds Vivian knew that the sentries were not breaking their rounds, apparently assuming that it was the Americans who had been shot. He figured that the guards would expect their relief in another twenty minutes . . .

"Strip." Without hesitation Mush and Tim put on the Wehrmacht grays and ran to find overcoats and helmets. In their underwear the three Germans were fish white as they lay down again in front of Vivian. The leader's breathing was very shallow by this time, and he weakly stared up at Vivian with one hazel eye.

It had not been more than thirty minutes since they had arrived, and within fifteen more it would be over—one way or the other. Two shots now from in front of the house, then Mush's voice shouting in German. The front door almost jumped off its hinges as they shoved in with a thin corporal wedged between them.

There was no longer any room left on the floor for the new prisoner. "Step over the others and stand at attention in that corner." Tim and Mush went to drag in the guard Tim had shot, now moaning on the cold ground. As they were lugging the guard they heard four shots from inside and as they ran to help Vivian they heard four more, then three again. They came to a halt at the bedroom door and saw Vivian pumping bullets into the men who lay on the floor. The naked soldiers were red with blood, Hamburger's hazel eyes were frozen in a stare, the Gestapo leader had finally choked to death on his own blood. Vivian shot him anyway. Then, looking like Prud'hon's *Head of Vengeance,* he turned to Mush and Tim who were panting, frozen in the doorway. What they saw in Vivian Prescott's eyes was a sadness and rage, without hope, without fear. It was a look that would linger in the depths of his wide gray eyes for the rest of his life.

"If the other one is still alive, kill him. We'll take one of the cars, you two dressed as soldiers, me in civvies as a Gestapo officer. Much better cover than London's damned peasants' so-called disguise."

Everything had changed for them in that half hour: three men who had never killed men at close hand—including Mush in Spain—had now gunned to death nine human beings. Vivian had prevailed over the odds, had turned almost certain suicide into the basis for his future legend. As he stood there with the empty guns dangling, it was plain to the other two that the old Vivian had been swallowed up in love and death, that what had emerged out of this blood ritual in the old farmhouse was a new, cross-grained creature. If Vivian was mad, they could also see that there was a method to it—to exhaust his grief by killing the killers, as if in so doing he could kill war itself.

He stood there like death itself, telling them what they would do before burning the house; thinking of everything from identification papers, food, items to trade, handguns, to the message in Czech to be carved on a tree as if left by a group of Catholic partisans, and finally enlisting Tim's vote against Mush that the Communists not get credit "for obvious reasons."

Rushing along the road to Pilsen, Vivian spoke into the darkness, "We had no choice. We never will . . ." They drove southwest out of the hot glow of the fire and into the dark toward Jablonec. Their orders were to pick up the ordinance from the underground at Rakovnik, then deliver it to the Czech team waiting in the crypt of the church at Pilsen, all the while posing as peasants. Now they would drive openly as a Gestapo oberst and his two guards.

"Are you sure," Mush was starting to recover, "that you don't want to change that too and use poison darts and send up a balloon to take credit for killing Heydrich by Mahatma Gandhi?" Tim laughed too loud, but Vivian wasn't bothered. They were brave men, they had their own strong motives pushing them to fight, and if he was the one to take them where they wanted to go, well, they would accept his authority. Besides, neither of them really wanted the responsibility of life and death over other people. Because of Spain, Mush had been the nominal leader of the team, but that had shifted at the farmhouse. Vivian knew it, they knew it. Vivian felt light, cool. The night air was cold as it worked its way into the staff car. He drank in the air as if it were an elixir that would preserve the economy of his thoughts . . . he felt as if he had grown another skin, as if the cold air and his merciless thoughts had covered him with a magical membrane.

As they drove through the Czechoslovakian night they apprehended something in the darkness that all those who choose war come to know: the dead have nothing to say; only those who speak *for* death have a voice. Vivian pushed his perceptions into the spongy core of his being. It was why, he knew, Hitler had chosen the skull and crossbones for his elite Death's-head Battalion, and why the Nazi flags were mostly black and white. Hitler had tried to become death in order to escape it. The Spanish fascist general had called out, "Long live death!" The skull and bones! *Skull and Bones:* Vivian himself had been initiated into that society by others dressed as death. So the privileged and powerful knew about it too. Kill the rat behind the curtain before it dies. Glamorous death, seductive death, whose bargain beautiful women cannot refuse, merciful death, which at last concludes the organized killing before it destroys everyone to the last man, woman and child . . . Vivian's thoughts raced ahead into the dark landscape as the car sped into the night.

In fact, their disguise as Nazis was extremely effective. The Germans were on the hunt for Czech partisans, scrutinizing everyone they could, but yielding to the authoritarian image of an official black Gestapo car with a lean man slumped in the back, hat turned down and the driver and guard in the front seat blowing the horn to force an opening through the crowded streets of Rakovnik.

As if conducting a raid, Vivian's team stormed into a partisan basement hideout. The underground fighters had been prepared to fight and die when they saw the Gestapo vehicle pulling to the curb above their window. It was Mush who went in first, risking his life to warn them . . . "Comrades—Americans, we are Americans. . . ." Minutes later they dragged out two young men and a large bulky bag of what the gathered knot of onlookers assumed was contraband of some kind. The black vehicle went honking through the town and proceeded with official ease toward Pilsen, ready to shoot it out if discovered.

They timed their entrance for after midnight. In the darkness of the cold night they stepped into the church of St. Stephen the Martyr. There, in the crypt, waited the Czech nationals with whom they had trained at Camp X and Manhattan. There was quiet talk and real kümmel schnapps to warm them, and two courageous priests with whom to work out the details for after the assassination. One element of the plan would have to be changed, Vivian told them. "We'll maintain this German cover and so be able to mingle with searchers and reconnoiter instead of being forced to hole up here."

One of the priests pointed out that that would cut down the fire strength of the team in case of a confrontation. However, he had to admit that as Germans rather than peasants they could much better cover the Czech team that would actually strike at Heydrich. As they talked it happened, quite naturally, that Vivian was looked up to as the spokesman for the Americans. The waiting began.

Reinhard Heydrich rode in the front seat of his Mercedes that late May morning, studying intelligence reports as his chauffeur, a new man, maneuvered the big car at a brisk speed down the Dresden–Prague road from Heydrich's villa in Panenske-Breschen.

A Czech partisan, in the Protector's employ as a domestic servant, had chanced on the intelligence chief's itinerary for this, the twenty-seventh of the month. Waiting at a point up ahead, where the chauffeur would need to slow down to negotiate a sharp bend in the road, was the SATAN team at this chosen assassination site.

Word of Heydrich's plans to leave Prague that day had hastened the preparations: in the "contraband" that Viv and his disguised team had "seized" in Pilsen were the machine gun and British-made explosives that were to execute the death sentence. The official car driven by Tim mingled easily with the military vehicles and trams on the suburban street at the bottom of the curve; the Americans watched at a distance as three of the Czechs spaced themselves along the bend, one to watch for the green Mercedes, the others to go into action when it cruised into range.

At nine-thirty the car slowed and the Butcher of Prague narrowed his piercing eyes in the sunlight as he looked up from his official papers. A gleam of metal across the road caught his glance, and he turned to see an agent running at the car with a machine gun. The gun was jammed. In panic the chauffeur pulled the car over and Heydrich struggled to get out as a bomb rolled into the side of the Mercedes.

Viv, Mush and Tim heard the explosion and saw their Czech teammates running. From the smoke on Heydrich's side of the auto a figure emerged, lurching after the three attackers with pistol in hand; shots rang out and the figure collapsed.

The Americans escaped northwest, across the windswept, rolling hills of the Czech countryside. Enormous fields of bright yellow "Raps" covered the landscape between great clumps of forest until the road opened upon the small village of Lidice, each of whose snug wooden houses sat behind its own rose garden.

The Czechs rendezvoused in the crypt of the same church in Prague, a place priests had used to smuggle scores of Resistance fighters into hiding.

The Reich Protector, thought at first to be not seriously wounded, was taken to Bulovka Hospital, where pieces of explosive and clothing were found to have riddled his internal organs; he succumbed to gangrene after a week of the best medical care Hitler could provide. Before he died, partisans informed the Prescott OSS team, Heydrich had screamed out his guilt and begged God for forgiveness. This, more than the assassination itself, truly shocked the Butcher's high aides.

The führer, however, would provide his dead "hangman" with revenge as horrible as anything Heydrich himself could have devised. Hundreds of Czechs were arrested daily in Prague. The partisans in hiding could hear the recurring sounds of execution. When an informer greedy for the reward offered by Heydrich's appointed avenger, Dr. Karl Frank, tipped off the Gestapo about the Resistance fighters' hiding place, the Nazis stormed the church, trapping the Czechs in their ancient crypts by setting the building ablaze. The Resisters shot each other before the flames could reach them; the last man turned the revolver on himself. It was in this basement that London as well as Washington had ordered Vivian's team to hide out after the assassination. . . .

Heydrich's body rode on a funeral train to Berlin in a gunmetal and silver coffin, where it lay for two days in the Palais on Wilhelmstrasse, where he had once had his sumptuous offices. He was eulogized by Hitler at a grandiose state funeral, attended by the top of the Nazi hierarchy.

Hitler had promised Heydrich *Rache*—revenge, which Vivian and his companions would witness firsthand in Lidice. Word of the interrogation of townspeople by Karl Frank's troops reached the American OSS team through the rural partisans who met them outside the village. Frank was convinced that the assassins had been parachuted into Lidice and was ready to make a lesson of it to the rest of the world.

Within days the seven hundred residents of the town were dragged from their homes, the men lined up solemnly in the basement of the town's largest farmhouse and shot down without a word of explanation. The reports rang out above the wails of the kerchiefed women and children who stood huddled together awaiting their own fate to be carried out at Terezin, where they would be "experimented" on in Nazi "hospitals."

Before they set out for Switzerland, the Americans had watched the flames fan and consume the tiny hillside village, a blaze that Hitler ordered filmed in vengeful triumph.

Vivian coaxed the big military vehicle through the smoldering ruins of Lidice the next day, as the three faced in silence this awful consequence of the act they had helped perform in Prague.

They went to ground in a village in the Bohemian Highlands. After Lidice, nothing in the countryside moved. They slept in the cramped cellar under the mayor's house. In their nightmares the ranks of mothers and children in the barn seemed to fall in slow motion forever before their eyes. They had all three seen the slaying of the innocents, the crimes against children, the gratuitous suffering that Churchill had called a crime without a name. But London had played some part in the endless and infernal machine of action and reaction that had produced the decision to execute Heydrich, which in turn had produced the Nazi reaction and retaliation. The only law of war was the law of the talon. To the Nazis, Heydrich was an inestimable loss.

"Mush"—Vivian's voice was a dull monotone—"did London expect anything like Lidice?"

"Yes."

"No one ever mentioned it to me—"

"Who the fuck are you?" They were drinking the mayor's vodka, so strong that they had to shove chunks of black bread into their mouths to keep from gagging. Mush had been in a dark mood even before Lidice. Vivian, warming himself near the stove, spoke slowly, almost didactically.

"Mush, we—I'm glad this came up—we are the people who gather the information on which the decisions are made, which decisions are acted on by us, again, back in the field. In other words, we are the beginning and the end, the alpha and omega, first and last in the ranks of death. We're the grunts and the heroes, the cannon fodder and the cortex, the survivors, maybe, and the inheritors of the war. If we can get to London, if the worst is behind us, then *we* will have to be dealt with . . . We are the survivors of the team that killed Heydrich, for God's sake. We survived only because we *violated* London's orders. London *had* to be wrong because they were *there* and we had to be right because we're *here*. Of course they knew the Nazis would go wild with slaughter after the fact, and of course they did not consult us. As you say so wittily, Mush, 'Who the fuck are we?' I have another quote for you, Mush, from your Internationale—'We who have been naught, we shall be all.' I'm aware of the different meaning of those lyrics. In our terms it means that if we're given the responsibility of this kind of endless bloodshed that we've, uh, done and seen, then we must also have the *power*. 'No power, no responsibility,' that's our new motto. And they'll swallow it. Who else are they going to get to go in to kidnap Hitler?"

114

CHAPTER 4

Paris, 1943
The Red Orchestra

MUSH HOLLANDER was first to be debriefed by the combined BSC-SOE (Special Operation Executive) Center at Bletchley. Across the hard white fields, Vivian was secluded with his father at the Prescott manor; Tim Donahue was sleeping at the hospital in Hampstead so that he could personally help nurse Pat back to health.

When Mush had finished, the executive intelligence officers knew that in Vivian T. J. Prescott they had an extremely valuable if unpredictable "asset," and their concern was how they might make Prescott and the other Americans on his team, including

Patricia McGuire, the exception to the new rule that all American operatives with BSC were to be transferred to the jurisdiction of the new American secret service, the OSS (Office of Special Services). . . .

At Bletchley Sam Prescott and his son began a long tramp across frozen hills. Both were bundled warmly, the older man holding a curved briar with windscreen stuck into his mouth. They were clearly father and son. The elder at six feet was just a shade under his son's height and their weight of one-seventy was exactly the same. Sam Prescott did not have the physique of a championship athlete as his son did, nor did he look like one of Maxfield Parrish's young gods, but he had a hard, gnarled body with a lean face, full of wit and intelligence. Some of his friends insisted that he was the image of Walter Huston when that Canadian actor had played Sinclair Lewis's *Dodsworth* a few years before on the New York stage. This resemblance, including a slightly bowlegged walk, pleased Sam because he knew and respected "Red" Lewis and his wife Dorothy Parker and in fact they had done some "brain trust" work together for the last FDR presidential campaign. They would all have been Social Democrats if there had been such a political party in America. But what worried Sam Prescott now was his son, about whom the entire Anglo-American service was talking.

The sky was leaden, clouds driving from the west across the dimmed sun. The bare trees against the gray-white fields of Bletchley were black on white. He did not know how to make contact with this boy of his at the level of what his father, the High Church man of God, would have called his "essential soul." The death of Vivian's wife, he knew, was different in quality from the death of his own wife, Viv's mother, and so he had only half a vocabulary to speak to the hidden self locked up in the lean frame of the youth who strode wordlessly beside him. "I suppose they've told you that both you and Janet are to receive the Saint George Cross from BSC?" Vivian nodded, the eyes fixed in a bruised stare, as if at an image in the chiaroscuro of the middle distance. "You're to meet with Wild Bill Donovan before Christmas? And Mush and Tim as well, and Pat, too, if she's going to go on with it?"

"Yes. I'll be seeing her on Monday."

"I met with Donovan and the President just before I left, when you went into Czechoslovakia." He had decided to respond to his son's silence as if it was an invitation to continue. He knocked the wasted ash from the pipe against the cup of his gloved hand and tried to involve his son in a discussion of Colonel Donovan and the new OSS.

"Wild Bill" Donovan, as a staunch Republican and Wall Street lawyer, might have seemed an unlikely ally to President Roosevelt in the years he traveled in Europe as the chief executive's eyes and ears, but the passionate conviction and resourcefulness he shared with his British counterpart "Little Bill" Stephenson had made him the inevitable choice to head the Office of the Coordinator of Information (COI), which became the Office of Strategic Services six months after America's involvement in the war. The millionaire Irishman and World War I hero had an unconventional mind that found no plan too farfetched if it had a chance of undermining Nazi strength, no recruit too unstable or undisciplined if the man came through when it counted—in the field. It was taking all of Donovan's charm, Sam Prescott told his son, to hold together the Olympian aggregation of intellectual and business talent he had recruited for the OSS, where classicist Norman O. Brown, Hollywood screenwriter Abraham Polonsky and various Morgans, Mellons and Vanderbilts were among those plotting and executing Wild Bill's notions . . . "There are more than a few in the military, and at home in the cabinet, who'd like to see some reins put on Donovan's dragons. He's a sky's-the-limit man. And from what I hear the BSC hasn't looked too kindly on the wet-behind-the-ears Yankees who've been trying to tell them how to run a secret service. The British are about to give up control of their operations on the Continent. . . . I would be interested to hear you compare Donovan to Intrepid." Their footsteps were soundless on the frozen earth. The younger man had nodded his head from time to time, no more.

Three crows winged over, high and calling, as they completed the long oval of their walk and turned into the manor grounds. It was then that Vivian broke his silence, speaking in a voice flat but resonant. "It's power politics—as usual."

"Well, in—"

"It's *politics*. Mush and Kim Philby have the same story from the Russian side—although Mush is still some kind of a hybrid Marxist and Philby . . ."

"A Tory, perhaps, but certainly no fascist. I must admit that Philby is a mystery to me." He was glad that Vivian was opening up, trying to draw him out.

"Dad, I know how much you admire the British, but I want you to understand that I consider these secret service rivalries a damned scandal. I saw it in Czechoslovakia—it's got to be ended. Our team is going back in after the New Year—I know this in advance from OSS through Philby, who knows everything—to establish liaison with the resistance networks in France. Then, although they don't know it, we make for Geneva and convince Allen Dulles, the OSS chief there, that it can be done."

"What can be done?"

"Adolph Hitler can, must, be assassinated."

Two more crows broke the silence with their calls. Sam Prescott was already cold, and as he stared at his twenty-three-year-old son, standing there on the hard ground as cold and drawn as an unsheathed dagger, he shivered from an inner chill. Vivian seemed to be staring straight through him. Then, turning, he broke away and stalked up the rise toward the manor.

Tim Donahue did not really object to his fiancée spending long afternoons over the Christmas holiday with Vivian. He knew that it was important for both of them to face the shock of what had happened to Janet. Vivian's pain might call out to Pat, Vivian might need to hold onto Pat, to assuage his loss in her . . . Tim also felt somehow ashamed to begrudge his friend the time alone with her. After all, she had been a nurse, had studied psychotherapy . . . she would respond to Vivian as she would to a wounded man, which he was. He trusted them, he instructed himself, and would not, damn it, allow himself to resent that Pat was probably able to confide in Vivian more of what had happened to her and Janet than she had to him. . . .

Tim had loved Pat McGuire, without saying a word, for as long as he could remember, at least as early as Corvallis and Sacred Heart back in Chicago. They had both lived in tenements way out on West Van Buren. The Irish Catholic culture of Chicago was a bag of shifting values. The nuns and priests ran a rhetorical curriculum through the minds of generations of children of the Catholic working class. But at the same time the downtown political ma-

118

chine taught the offspring of the wards a different lesson. Under Boss Kelly and his immediate predecessors in political plunder, both Tim's and Pat's families had enjoyed appointments from downtown. Tim's old grandfather sat next to a round-bellied stove, pipe in gums, telling the younger Park District men that they "had it very good in this country," and eating his big sandwich lunches by eleven in the morning. Pat's father was dead but her brother was a machine appointee in the county assessor's office; the assessor, a gentleman of Polish extraction, had only recently been hauled into a courtroom in handcuffs to answer charges. When Pat described that scene to him, in the nasal Irish idiom of Chicago, Vivian laughed out loud for the first time since Janet's death, or rather Janet's "murder," as he persisted in calling it.

Irish wards were tough and cohesive, striped with the faith of the Sacred Heart and downtown; God, his archangels, Hizzoner and the boys of the commission; the Virgin Mary and the whores of Division Street. Future priests, labor leaders, politicians, gangsters, and some Communists would spring from these slums and streets. Sometimes the younger children in the family, Pat and Tim, for example, could break away to a teachers' college or nursing school, as Pat had, or engineering trade school or even the University of Illinois School of Architecture, where Tim's brilliance and meticulous draftsmanship had come to the attention of a worker priest who brought his Jesuitical skills into play in order to secure a scholarship for Tim, and Tim's grandfather had driven the ward committeeman from the district almost mad on Tim's behalf.

So Tim and Pat had both been favored younger children of the ward. Favored to the extent that their parents were much older than when the first brothers and sisters were born in the coal towns of Pennsylvania and Ohio before the move west to Chicago, the refuge and the rock of the machine. The youngest McGuire and the youngest of the Donahues began doing homework together in grammar school, by high school they were going steady, by the time they reached twenty they were engaged.

Tim was still a virgin; technically, Pat was not. A good-looking Italian intern at County Hospital, where she was studying nursing, became almost obsessed with her neat boyish figure, glossy auburn hair streaked with red, freckled face and round green eyes, full lips and slight overbite, which somehow lent a hungry sexuality to her mouth. The green eyes reflected the wisdom, tough good humor and sensitivity to hurt of the youngest of a large, poor working-class family. Pat's secret was a grandmother who, before she lost her leg, had stopped traffic with her umbrella so that she and the little girl, whom she called Trish, could cross the street at leisure as they proceeded toward the Rivoli and the Saturday movies, carrying a large bag of oranges and snacks to be consumed over the long, image-filled afternoon. In later years, by fighting with "Trish" over everything, she had taught her how to stand up and defend herself. Yet she was also tender . . . "Does the dog have water?" she would ask a dozen times a day in her tense County Mayo tones, and when she wasn't inquiring after the state of health of the latest street dog, she was announcing the time of day, like a town crier on the eve of doom. When she died, Pat took it hard.

Tim was accustomed to strong women. In the dry, radiator-knocking flats of their adjacent buildings, under runny colored tintypes of the Sacred Heart and the Archangel Michael (after whom both of them had had fathers and older brothers named), Tim fell in love with the bright, slightly brash tomboy and pixie Pat resembled in the years before her small, neatly proportioned breasts made their appearance, pushing up at her tight cotton sweaters. One day she had said to him, "I've never seen a fifteen-year-old boy in the nude," frowning slightly and wiggling her nose rabbitlike. His freckles flamed scarlet. He had been too shy, but another time on the stairs, after a thrilling evening ushering at the Chicago Opera House, she had brushed her hand against his crotch as their braces collided, whispering, "Is that a carrot?" and he had pressed her hand back on the bulge and this time he knew, despite the dark, that *her* cheeks had turned a flaming color as well.

It was natural, then, when Father O'Connor, who had helped Tim break away to the university, talked with him about the "calling in Canada to defeat the tyrant," that Tim should have asked Pat to marry him and to join in the action. She had then told him about her defloration at the heavy hands of young Doctor Delgado, whose father, he had assured her, could fix it so that she could expect an immediate teaching appointment at County . . . "He looked like Victor Mature," she confided to a very sober-faced Tim, "completely self-centered. He got me drunk at an expensive

120

place way out north past Highland Park, his uncle owned it so we had champagne. He had this big Buick . . . are you *sure* you want to hear the details? All right, so on the ride back I fell asleep and he parked down at the lakefront somewhere around Howard Street, and I woke up to find him, well, doing something to me, let's just leave it at that. Then he proceeds to tell me of his mad passion for me, how he can't sleep or eat—he's a huge eater—et cetera, et cetera. Tim, he's a big handsome dumb wolf whom I never believed for a second, but I pretended to because . . . because I guess I just had hot pants. So you can fill in the rest, we got into the back seat and he—believe it or not—had a tube of K-Y lubricating jelly back there on the floor, with the prophylactics, which was just as well . . . It all lasted about forty-five seconds . . . but the *answer* is *yes,* I'll marry you, gladly, and it will be *much* better with us. And Canada, even in the middle of Hudson Bay, will be an improvement over Chicago County Hospital where the young nurses look for husbands and the young doctors look for you know what.". . .

The plan now, at last, was for them to be married privately on New Year's Day 1944 at the Prescott manor with just the team and a few BSC people present. Pat was spending a part of every day with Vivian, often talking at the flat BSC had found for her after she came out of the hospital. Her supple young body had managed a very good recovery from the shock it had undergone, and her intimate knowledge of hospital life allowed her to make the most of the still adequate facilities at the small clinic in Harley Street that BSC used.

Though he had taken her—almost convulsively—in the woods at Camp X that time, it was only on these long, cold London afternoons that Vivian began to understand Patricia McGuire . . . to begin to admire the wit, and the warmth, and find that he was transferring some of his anguish for Janet into affection for this girl —woman—with the rugged tongue and so tender eyes. He realized that this wit must have made a bond between the two women, but unlike Janet, Pat was not haunted. Sometimes, as they sipped tea at Pat's flat, memories of Janet, like pieces from a puzzle, would be superimposed in his mind's eye over the freckled reality seated across the narrow table from him; watching her lips move as she talked and nibbled at a biscuit, so different from the vermilion that

121

had been Janet's lips in the graveyard at Yale a lifetime ago, or so it seemed to him now.

Pat was constantly a discovery to Vivian; large family, working class, Catholic, midwest, a different world, and yet she was—to use her own phrase in describing her rather eccentric grandmother— she was "a good soul," and a first rate intelligence that had abstracted from the parochial education the mental discipline while jettisoning the cant.

She told him what parts she knew of Janet's agony, censoring what she could that was still too terrible for her to remember. Then the talk would veer away and they would compare the disparate stories of their backgrounds. They would become silent finally, then bundle up and walk out into the dreary weather of wartime London at the Yule season.

There would be few Christmas puddings that year and the stockings that hung over the hearth would be well-darned. "Shabby" was the latest style of dress for the populace, which seemed to spend its time in queues for everything it consumed or wore.

Once they went tea dancing. Holding each other lightly, eyes closed and their thoughts far away:

> *A cigarette that bears the lipstick traces,*
> *An airline ticket to romantic places . . .*

And twice they sat through matinee showings of *Casablanca:*

> *You must remember this,*
> *A kiss is still a kiss,*
> *A sigh is still a sigh . . .*

But they would always return to the talk of the war, the common denominator that had first brought them together. "It's a funny old world, isn't it?" she said. "In order to be able to have babies I'll have to kill men, and maybe mothers and children too before it's over." She never doubted that she would go back in behind the lines with Mush and Tim and Vivian . . . As the lights went out in the late afternoons they would meet Mush and Tim at the St.

122

Ermin's for a meager dinner and a few rubbers of bridge before the engaged couple left to walk back to Pat's place. . . .

Two days before Pat's marriage to Tim, Vivian talked to her about his secret agenda for the team: the execution of Adolph Hitler. She did not laugh, did not, in fact, speak. "Don't tell the others yet," he said, and as though it had been planned, stood up to walk slowly around the table to stoop and pick her up in his arms and carry her into the bedroom. Outside a cold sleet had begun.

Her eyes and lips were full with her desire, her voice was rich with the resonance of Irish lilt, a sharp departure from the public sharpness of her midwestern tone . . . "Vivian, you and I both loved Janet, in our own ways, and we both love Tim in our different ways . . . and so I suppose it's only natural that we love each other. Would you understand if I said that I intend to keep faith with all of you?"

He nodded.

"You would? Maybe you can explain it to me then."

"Well, you're a saint and I'm the devil and—"

"Oh, sure you're a terrible man," and then continuing to quote her grandmother, but pronouncing the word as if it were "satin" . . . "Satan, get thee behind me."

"All right," he said, and helped her slip off the plaid skirt and schoolgirl blouse, and then they both stood to finish their undressing. They were looking at each other. He stood almost a head taller. As she turned to draw the curtain his eyes focused on her high, firm buttocks. The room was dim in the winter light. She turned back. The bush of hair curling up toward her flat belly was a shade darker than the red-brown pageboy cut that framed her fine-boned face. Her body was honed fine, a gymnast's body. His eyes riveted on the Gestapo burn-scar she still carried high up on her thigh.

They walked toward each other to embrace, and he had to cup his hard member in his hand in order to hold her against him.

"Will it fit?" she mocked him slightly with her brogue. Kissing, her teeth nipping, nibbling at the corners of his mouth, she traced the line of his jaw with her fingers.

He sank down to one knee, his head just below her breasts, stretching to kiss and suck, her fingers twined in his hair as he teased her nipples with his tongue and lips. Softly he then kissed

123

the scars the Nazis had left on her. Someday at least they would heal on the outside. His hair was only slightly darker than hers, so that when he sank back onto his haunches and moved her pelvis forward to his mouth, his chestnut hair seemed to intermingle with her pubic curls as she looked down on his head between her legs. His fingers pressed into her buttocks, hard, as her slim muscled legs and thighs went hard. "Ah, Viv," she crooned, arching her hips to give him more of herself.

Then he picked her up again and put her on the bed, standing over her. "Get thee behind me?"

"Oh, you devil," she smiled, and turned over and raised herself up on all fours. He stroked her, starting from the crown. Down the firm back, across the perfect buttocks and around the thighs, then running his fingers between her legs. He lifted her up by the breasts so that her head was thrown back against his shoulder, her hands reaching back to grasp his buttocks to bring him forward, then sloping down again with athletic grace, her arms still extended behind her like a ballerina in her art, her neck drooping, head in profile. He could see an expression of pleasure spread across the half of her face visible to him, and as he positioned himself to enter her he saw her bite into the pillow's corner.

". . . Ahh" was her cry as he penetrated, and he felt happiness without guilt, the greatest yet, he thought, of his life. His tempo steadily increased until he too was panting and calling her name. His climax drove her down flat and they finished prostrate, saying each other's names into the thick mattress. . . .

Forty-eight hours later, at the wedding, everyone noticed that Vivian Prescott's eyes had returned to the land of the living.

Kim Philby had requested a meeting with Vivian before the Americans reported to Colonel Donovan at the American Embassy to put themselves under OSS control.

Philby was in charge of counterespionage at Section Six of British intelligence, where as the head of the Spain-Portugal division he had impressed his superiors with the thoroughness with which he pieced together snippets of information to block virtually all Nazi espionage efforts originating in that area. As a young journalist just down from Cambridge Philby had covered Franco's army for the (London) *Times,* later had parlayed his flair for propaganda

124

into a secret service post. His meticulous mind was hidden by an air of slurred superciliousness.

Philby sat now in his St. Ermin's cubbyhole in the BSC fourth floor headquarters, sipping tea. Both he and Vivian compensated for the fuel rationing by keeping on thick overcoats, scarfs and gloves.

"Viv, there's a split in Special Operations Executive as to whether you rescued the Heydrich plan or whether you're a romantic damned fool. Personally, I agree with Mush Hollander and Tim Donahue, who were, after all, on the scene, that you saved the entire bloody operation. But I daresay you're going to find the chaps at E Street in Washington's OSS shop a good deal more conservative than ours, for all our faults. Mush, for one, I happen to know, is quite wary of some of the people that you'll be working with. It's all very well to say that Mush is a leftist but I mean, look at the record: Greece, France, Italy, the Balkans, Yugoslavia. Very, very strange bedfellows."

He sketched out for Vivian a few of the political contradictions emerging from OSS activities in Europe. Plans to provide supplies for the Yugoslavian royalist Mihajlović and his chetniks while Tito's partisans were kept dangling with vague hopes of future American support; the interest the OSS's Algerian operatives were showing in rightist French General Henri Giraud; the sympathy with which Greek-American officers worked with the leftist EAM-ELAS in the Balkans while socialist antifascists in Italy were considered too Red. An imminent invasion of North Africa by an American expeditionary force, he continued, was being plotted with the help of ultra-right French businessmen and colonials with histories of collaboration with the Nazis.

"Mr. Philby," Vivian said, "for some reason there are some people who do not totally trust you. I don't know why, you've just made me a completely straightforward proposition. I know all about the mixture of Communists and Wall Street capitalists in OSS, the Mush Hollanders and the James Hewitt the Fourth crowd. But how different is SOE, except that you've been in it forever. Look at the Heydrich business, you had *everything* wrong. Look, Philby, I don't trust anybody at *all* in this war—I mean, after all, that's the *essence* of war, isn't it? The politicization of resentment and mistrust. I don't trust *war*. Those are *my* politics. So what

I do to try to bring the war to an end is not particularly the business of SOE *or* OSS." He rose to leave when Philby, bunched in his heavy coat and hat like a toad, hit him with the truth—

"What did you say, Philby?"

"I said Ultra knew where the Gestapo was holding your wife. Both BSC, and OSS *through* Ultra."

Vivian stood there shivering while Philby drawled in swallowed syllables what Ultra knew . . . The true nature of secret warfare had been brought home to Ultra's guardians when in early November, 1940, they decoded Hitler's order to bomb the defenseless city of Coventry. Any last minute mobilization to save its residents would have alerted the Germans to the fact that their code had been cracked, so Churchill was left with the decision to keep silent and save the code. On November 14 over three hundred bombers rained death and destruction on Coventry for eleven hours, killing more than five hundred people. The world had a new word for devastation as a result of this raid: the city, the Nazi propaganda machine boasted, had been "Coventryized."

"And Lidice too. And your wife, old boy. Even if Janet had been betrayed, London could have saved her. Ultra had the Nazi code and so knew where Janet was being held. But the code meant more to London and Washington than Janet, meant more than a thousand, ten thousand Janets."

Vivian felt himself going cold.

"So you see, I'm supporting *your* argument. *It has to stop.* If you'll sit down, dear boy, I'll tell you what some of us—nothing to do with SOE or OSS—what *some* of us have in mind and if you are not interested I hope that you will forget this communication entirely."

Vivian sat down, his face pale with shock. Philby stiffly removed one glove in order to light another cigarette, then went to urinate; when he returned Vivian had not moved from staring at his own reflection in the green mirror hanging behind the chair, where Philby again sat.

"Okay, OSS is sending your team to France to try to marry the rightists to the Gaullists. I know that and you know that. Okay. And if you don't get yourself killed in the crossfire, then it'll be on to Italy for you, then the Low Countries and so forth for the greater glory of *Pax Americana* and tough titty to the Ruskies and the

Limeys. Okay. But you're Captain America, a bright young hero—you've told me so yourself—and you see through the machinations of all these dirty old men—Intrepid, Donovan, the lot—and you and your freelance team want to go for the jugular, because why? Because you are not interested in *power. You* are interested in *peace* . . . Okay . . ." Philby slurred and swallowed the stream of words in his fashion that was, actually, extremely effective. Philby was, as they said, good.

"There are other men besides you and Mush and Tim and myself. Many others, actually, and you can link up with them, if you like, while you're in France. That's it. The Nazis call them the *Rote Kapelle,* the Red Orchestra. They're the best spies in the world, maybe the best in history. I mean it quite seriously and it is not, at all, a Red Communist organization. Communists were instrumental in starting up the orchestra, but now the net of antifascist agents reaches right up into Adolf Hitler's palace guard. Okay?"

Philby was stretching the story of the *Rote Kapelle* to the breaking point—Vivian's eyes were fathomless—but still there was a hard kernel of truth in the account.

The secret music of the *Rote Kapelle* had spread throughout occupied Europe between 1939 and 1941 when the Nazis detected a transmitter operating right under the noses of the Gestapo in the heart of Berlin. The elusive instrument enraged and demoralized Nazi intelligence. Meanwhile in Brussels and Paris the other sections of the orchestra played variations on the theme under the capable hand of *Le Grand Chef,* the mastermind of the group: Leopold Trepper. Trepper's network, begun in Brussels in 1939 under the cover of the "Foreign Excellent Trench Coat Company," was a tight system of antifascists—under the control of Moscow Center—each knowing his job and that job only. The existence and placement of other agents was Trepper's closely guarded secret, a precaution that proved to be essential to the survival of the orchestra when one of its number was captured. From 1940 on, Trepper had worked out of a plush Paris apartment that he shared with the elegant Belgian-American socialite Georgie de Winter, a striking brunette almost twenty years his junior.

From the Berlin section led by Harro Schulze-Boysen, Trepper had information flowing from within the Nazi raciopolitical office, from the ministries of economics and propaganda, as well as the

127

operational staff of the Luftwaffe itself. The fortune-teller to whom a Nazi colonel confided his secrets was a *Rote Kapelle* informer. The dedicated wife of a highly placed agent in the Berlin group became the lover of a lieutenant in Abwehr to obtain his secrets. And all the while a special Nazi intelligence team worked desperately to root out the "cancer" that was the Red Orchestra. . . .

By three in the morning Philby had drawn for Vivian the extraordinary history of the "antifascist" spy ring, always stressing its connections in Berlin. As he talked, Vivian had the uncanny feeling that somehow Philby knew about his secret Hitler plan. When there was nothing more to say they both stood, the British agent's knees popping loudly.

"The ball's in your court, Viv. If you decide to make contact with Trepper, Mush Hollander has the drill. Cheers."

Paris in early 1944 reeked of bad faith. In the black market restaurants and hidden nightclubs the only ones who could afford to eat were collaborators, spies and Nazi officers, paying more for one meal than a Parisian family would spend in a week. For the working people food was a constant worry—especially, would the ration card be honored?

OSS in London had provided the Americans with forged documents that described them as three Belgian engineers and their female secretary on a mission to Paris to arrange subcontracting for a Brussels park project. Tim Donahue's special talents as an architect and engineer lent some credibility to their pose, but the group was, in general, so young in appearance and their French, except for Pat's, so halting that London had ordered them to operate underground for as long as possible. Their assignment was to represent American interests in the ongoing meetings of the resistance organizations as General de Gaulle and General Giraud prepared for a showdown. Their orders focused on the development of partisans sympathetic to the United States in both camps who were prepared to work with the United States right up to the coming invasion and afterward.

In preparation for the across-channel landings, code-named Overlord and directed by General Dwight Eisenhower, French agents had been dropped into northern France to gather military intelligence. Overlord's planners were counting on teams like

Vivian's to link splintered French partisan groups in a political truce until the Allies landed successfully.

The Americans went to ground at Suresnes, outside Paris, in a large stone cottage that had belonged to the W. A. Must family before the war. Bill Must, Jr.—Skull and Bones '34, now OSS London—had briefed them as intensively as time allowed in "manners and customs" during their stay at the St. Ermin's. The married couple, Tim and Pat, shared a large room, Mush and Vivian another, a third was reserved for use as a parlor or meetingroom. There was also a kitchen and a small basement.

Vivian and Pat had not made love since before her wedding and had left the affair unresolved. Vivian felt suspended between the memory of Janet and the reality of Pat, suspended but not tortured, rather like a moratorium between loves, was the way he put it to himself. He felt light, lucid, "a great despiser," in Professor Mann's phrase, very ready to kill or be killed.

Their first evening in Suresnes they ate stew—Pat and Mush were adept at something they called Irish stew cum tzimmes—and drank a good wine purchased by Vivian, who had brought a large sum of money despite Bill Must's orders to the contrary. The decision made that night was that Tim and Pat would function as a team—again, contrary to orders—and make contact with the two French General G's, while Mush and Viv approached the Red Orchestra. The Donahues would keep a careful record in code of their meetings, which would then be given to London, while the meetings with the Red Orchestra would be kept secret from OSS.

"We are antifascists," said Mush, and all raised their glasses. "No more—no less." Vivian insisted that each one, seriously or otherwise, express his or her feelings about why they felt that neither SOE or OSS was effective or committed sufficiently in its methods and philosophy to the soonest possible termination of the war. When they finished the wine and rose to retire Pat kissed them all good night and Vivian felt a short, sharp pang. He slept heavily, dreaming of a faceless man who cried out to him for help in a foreign language, a language that Vivian had never heard before. . . .

Within forty-eight hours Mush and Vivian, following Philby's suggestions, had made contact with the Red Orchestra through its Simexco export-import front. It was a sleeting, nasty Thursday morning, an hour after the lifting of curfew, when Vivian and Mush pedaled their bicycles into the Rue de Beaujolais and toward the apartment house that hid the man considered by many veterans of the covert war to be the greatest secret agent of the century. A slender, slightly Semitic woman of great beauty in her early twenties ushered them into a pleasant sittingroom where they were greeted by a man in his forties with a presence of tremendous energy and intelligence and a face that was at the same time fierce and creased with kindness. As the woman served coffee the Americans took the occasion to compare this man, known as "the Chief," to the top British and American spymasters with whom they had had contact—Intrepid and Colonel Donovan. He had the same penetrating eyes as they, but there was a quality somehow fiercer, more finely drawn about this man. He could sense the curiosity of the young Americans and at once, and this was different, began in accented English a frank and spirited résumé of his career.

What Leopold Trepper—alias Otto, Eddy, René, Domb, Henri, General, Georges, Uncle, Bauer, Gilbert, Herbert, and Sommer—chose to regale the young men with could be called an essentially factual précis of the life and times and even loves of a premier *Kapellmeister,* or *chef d'orchestre,* the prime mover of the fabled Red Orchestra . . . The oldest son of a dirt-poor Polish family, Trepper had been forced by poverty to drop out of the university in Kraków to seek work. At twenty-two he joined in a riot and foundry strike at Dombrau and was jailed. The town's first four letters would give him his first code name: Domb. At twenty-four, when a Zionist group arranged his passage, Trepper emigrated to Palestine, where he labored in a kibbutz and helped form an outlawed socialist group, among whose members he would find his future wife, Luba, and some of his most trusted agents. His work under another ex-Palestinian espionage agent, Isaia Bir, in the Paris of the late 1920s taught him the spy's art; Bir, known as "Fantomas" to the gendarmes, rivaled Houdini in his talent for disappearances. When the ring was cracked, Trepper proved himself an observant pupil of Fantomas and escaped to Berlin. After espionage training in Moscow, he returned to Paris in 1936. Brussels and the Foreign Excellent Trench Coat Company followed . . .

Two hours vanished under the spell of the rich, musical voice, and before they were aware of the shift in emphasis, the Chief had

130

changed from the past to the future tense . . . "But it will all come to a *temporary* end any day now. Georgie knows this, don't you, sweet one? The center in Moscow chooses to believe members of the network who have fallen into the hands of the Gestapo and are presently playing back false information to them at the direction of the Germans—what is one to do with such idiocy?" Trepper shrugged his muscular shoulders and turned toward the young woman. "I know from sources in London what your assignment here is and I can help you. I will furnish you with a list of names of informers who have infiltrated both the Gaullists and Giraudists. This list will establish at one stroke your *bona fides* and both camps will take into consideration the wishes of London and Washington. But of course de Gaulle will win out in the coming months and you must make this absolutely clear to your superiors. And you must also tilt all of your reports in that direction so that Washington can, as quickly as possible, throw its weight behind General de Gaulle. We must not meet again, so let me sum up . . ."

The most precious possession of the Orchestra was its Berlin network, within the Third Reich itself. This cell of anti-Nazi German officers was in imminent danger of discovery, he told them quietly, his eyes especially intense now. He spoke to them from the heart. For Trepper, his career in espionage had always been part of the struggle against the fascists, as much a part of the fabric of his life as his Jewishness, as his support of the workers so many years before at Dombrau, his socialist work in Palestine. He might be capable of as cold an analysis of strategy as any of the Abwehr's best agents, but he felt deeply for the men and women who served him, and his cause. He knew that the time was approaching when their courage would be tested at the hands of the Gestapo.

Trepper and his "old guard" had retreated into hiding; he no longer played the businessman's role in Paris and his escape plan was ready to be put into action. He worried especially about the others in his "orchestra," mostly ideologically motivated people, not hardened spies. One route to safety he had planned for them —through Algiers—had been closed by the Allied invasion. He knew to what lengths Nazi torture had driven men in the past; "interrogation techniques" such as burning with ultraviolet rays, or "the boot," which slowly crushed a person's arms and legs with wood blocks. To escape such monstrosities men had smashed their eyeglasses to swallow the glass, jumped out of windows, cut themselves and infected the wounds. Could he expect his Berlin group to withstand such torture?

". . . So they will talk and Berlin will be compromised. Your principals in London and Washington are committed to Germany's unconditional surrender. Let the Russian people die by the millions but Mr. Churchill will teach the Germans a history lesson. I am going to tell you something you don't know now . . ." And he told how after it had become apparent to the Nazis that their campaign in Russia would be longer and harder than they had anticipated, Heinrich Himmler had begun to put out feelers to British and American officials in Scandinavia through a lawyer friend of his: would the western powers consider "a separate peace" with Germany, on the condition that a new leadership take over the reins of government? Himmler, smelling defeat in a two-front war, was playing a complex survival game, even, it was said, to the point of meeting with German resistance leaders plotting the assassination of Adolf Hitler.

"You look as if you've seen a ghost. I'm telling you that our agents in Berlin are ready to act. *But* dissident elements on the general staff must be convinced that the Allies will then treat with them—*after Hitler is gone.*" Vivian got to his feet. Suddenly they were all standing. The Chief stepped around the coffee table and took hold of the lapels of Vivian's cheap suit-coat jacket. "I will give you documents. Go directly from Paris to Geneva. Report there to the OSS chief Allen Dulles. If he *could* he would not let you go into Berlin for any direct action. But he is no fool and if you have contacts in Germany who are willing to talk treason then he will send you in for that reason alone. Once you are inside you will contact our agents, give them Dulles's offer, which will not satisfy anybody, and then give them *my* orders. And my orders are: *Force the hand of the general staff and the allies—execute Adolf Hitler.*"

Mush and Vivian listened solemnly to these final instructions. If the Chief were to be taken by the Gestapo before they left Paris, then they were to kill a number of ranking officers from Gestapo headquarters, and he would tell them how.

"And why? To force the hand of the Resistance *and* the SOE *and* Washington, *and* the center in Moscow. You see, since the Heydrich affair they have *all* been playing their little power games as if the war were already won, and they have chosen to ignore the fact that the Nazis are not yet beaten materially *or,* most important, psychologically."

Trepper was taken two days after his extraordinary interview with Vivian and Mush. In a late night meeting in the basement of a small *pension* at Bourg-la-Reine, Georgie de Winter told them how it had happened. Bundled in a luxurious plaid coat she sipped brandy, trembling and talking.

The Chief, whom she called "Eddy," had been ready to take his escape route within days of his capture, Georgie told them. He had written in his last transmission that "the situation is worsening hour by hour. Simex has been liquidated." According to Trepper's plan, the Gestapo would be looking at his gravestone within the week, his death certificate, provided by a cooperative physician in their hands, while he, the "corpse," would be safely in the mountains of Auvergne. Georgie's son Patrick had been placed with a family in the suburbs. Before he disappeared, however, Trepper wished to complete the dental work being done for him by a Dr. Maleplate . . . "The Gestapo had interrogated the dentist that morning," Georgie said. "They forced him to cooperate in the trap. He sent his assistant out and when Eddy sat down in the chair at two o'clock they came out of a side room with their Lugers. They tell me he remained still and said, 'I'm unarmed.' He even offered to pay the dentist what he owed and when the frightened man apologized to him he said, 'As if I'd dream of bearing you a grudge, even for a moment.' That's the kind of man he is. He'll get out of it somehow," she added passionately. "You'll see."

In the first hour Vivian stood alone in his determination to carry out the Chief's plan. "But what's the point?" Tim kept demanding and Pat and Mush would turn their heads to look at Vivian. He was adamant, as if the spirit of Trepper had entered into his arguments. Combing passion and logic he returned again and again to the blindness of Moscow, London, Washington ". . . *before* they were attacked and *today,* and *tomorrow* . . ." The Allies were in murderous competition with each other in *every* occupied country; Moscow had been completely taken in by German counterintelligence and Stalin's paranoia; Hitler would *never* give up, and he had secret weapons near completion . . . "There's only one answer—

action and terror. Set Europe ablaze . . . I thought that was what they told us at Camp X. Well, they were right—*before* they lost their nerve . . ."

The Foreign Excellent Trench Coat Company provided Vivian with a perfectly fitting lieutenant colonel's S.S. uniform. This company had been one of the Chief's earliest and most successful fronts and had made a fortune selling uniforms to the Germans.

Striding like the Nazi superman he pretended to be, the tall blond (dyed) "S.S. officer" headed through Monmartre toward the House of Aphrodite, the most famous whorehouse in Paris. It had not yet opened for business as Vivian pounded imperiously on the high double door. The polished stone town house etched in black grillwork was the preferred public arena of erotica for important Nazis and rich collaborators in occupied Paris. Nightly the supermen of the Third Reich acted out their psychosexual scenarios on the hard and soft bodies of French girls and women and boys at the One Two Two, the *Chabanais,* the *Panier Fleuri* and the *Abbaye.* But it was at the Aphrodite that the most bizarre scenes were played out.

Vivian brushed past the sullen black maid with the heavy Martinique accent, swaying as if already drunk before he tossed a thick roll of notes in her face. "Nana," he ordered, and pushed past her toward the stairs. In the oversized public room the maids were still cleaning and polishing. At the first landing, to cover his ignorance of the layout, he shouted, "Nana!"

Three women in various states of undress peered down at him from the floor above, their painted faces hanging like masks in the dim light. "Good evening, Herr Oberst."

She was in her late twenties, standing almost six feet in her bare feet, dwarfing the other three dark-haired mignonettes. Her hair was honey-colored, unusual for Paris, and her physique, covered carelessly in a cherry red Japanese kimono, was Junoesque. "Nana," he mumbled and swung up the stairs to follow her down the hall to her room. The arch of her back and deep curves of her buttocks as she walked in front of him registered on Vivian despite the tension of his masquerade, and his mission.

Once inside the whitewashed room he gestured to her to remain silent. "Champagne," he said loudly, then, "come here." She

134

stared at him with large green eyes. Her proportions were the talk of the Paris demimonde, and she was known to have a caustic tongue if insulted beyond the bounds of the trade. He gestured to her to come over, his look now sober and polite. He whispered in her ear that he came from the Chief with special orders. She looked seriously at him, then took the risk, "Is he alive?"

He gave her enough money to ensure from the madam an undisturbed night of champagne and sex. Moving into the act with easy skill, she gave a long, throaty laugh, then went out into the corridor to find a maid. Before the knock at the door signaled that the watered champagne had arrived, he was able to whisper the entire plan into her ear, holding the grand mane of hair away with his hand so that his lips barely had to move. She did not at all smell like a perfumed whore but fresh as if from a subtly scented bath, and she wore no jewelry.

"Nana" was in fact Gabrielle Hoffman; her *nom de guerre* had been selected for her from a novel by Emile Zola, whose works were banned by the Nazis. Trepper had enjoyed this little joke and so had Gabrielle, who had read Zola and Dostoyevsky and Balzac as well. The Chief had brought her from Brussels, where she had been born to a French mother during the first world war. Her father had been a German deserter who remained true to form by walking out on his young wife and blonde infant daughter after the armistice. For two years she had been the Chief's agent at the House of Aphrodite. Madame Louise tolerated her moody work habits because her beauty was so striking that she brought a fortune from German officers of the highest rank. She picked and chose, ruling out native collaborators, catering to Gestapo big shots, one of whom was Joseph Erik Fortner, a wiry runt of a man whom even his underlings at headquarters referred to as a "butcher." It was the habit of this professional torturer to demand of Nana that she strike him with a leather thong. This she did with whistling strokes whose smacking could be heard across the hall, but only *after* much champagne and talk . . . talk that often yielded rich lodes of information for the Chief's ring, and since Fortner would have his orgasm from the beating, Nana rarely even was required to disrobe on those nights when he paid a small fortune to Madame Louise for her time.

When Vivian whispered the plan to her, her bright green eyes

135

glistened as they never had for any of Madame Louise's customers. So, this would be her last night in this sty. Thank God. The plan was that early the next morning Gabrielle and Vivian would blow up the House of Aphrodite and the Gestapo officers who would be inside it. In the early morning, as the last of the customers was leaving, Nana would emerge and confide to Madame Louise that the important colonel had killed himself while she slept. If Madame Louise would only contain herself she, Nana, would run out and claim a favor from Fortner, her best customer. She would then leave, returning with two Gestapo men in long overcoats—Mush and Tim—who would discreetly carry the "body" out through the alley to a waiting van, driven by Pat in a trench coat and a man's hat pulled low—she handled a car better than any of the men, with a cold audacity. Gabrielle would go with them as far as Suresnes and from there into the underground. The Aphrodite, of course, would be leveled by the high explosives brought in inside the stretcher and oversized medical bag intended for the dead German customer. And all the Gestapo who would have been called in by Fortner after he had received an urgent early morning telephone message from Nana would then be destroyed, "and with any luck," she whispered, "the little worm will come himself and get the thrill of his life—his death."

"The others, too," he said, looking at her.

"Oh, yes, Madame Louise and all the collaborators, too." And then, "Let me make love to you, you are a very beautiful man."

They had twelve hours to wait, time enough for their three-part swan song to the Aphrodite, temple of love. The first time she said, "No, you rest, save your strength," then straddled him, the thrusts of her sculptured body driving him into the soft mattress. The second time was at midnight. Below, the evening's orgy . . . girls and women in tennis costumes, evening gowns, *apache* jerseys, Nazi uniforms, jockeys' silks; a piano player making the Germans weep with his rendition of "Lilli Marlene"; Madame Louise collecting her money without letup . . . Upstairs Gabrielle hooked her long muscled legs over Vivian's shoulders and rose up at near-right angles, her vagina a soft, wet fulcrum of pleasure extending him fully.

Finally, just after cold daylight, she sponged him all over, then knelt and took his cooling flesh in her warm mouth, and as he grew

136

she seemed to open her throat wider and wider, reaching down to touch herself as he ejaculated.

They dressed and she left, kissing him, saying, "I'm going to tell the piano player to get out. I know him.". . .

The explosion at the notorious House of Aphrodite killed fifteen women and seven Gestapo officers, including Group Leader Fortner; three others were badly burned. Soviet agents were blamed. The Chief, Trepper, cooperated by feeding the Gestapo the names of half a dozen informers and *agents-provocateurs.* The Germans did not believe him but they rounded up and executed his candidates because Berlin had demanded immediate results. In a sense, they were grateful to the Chief for his suggestions.

CHAPTER 5

Berlin, 1944
The End of the Beginning

IN BERNE, Vivian Prescott swore to Allen Dulles that his team had had absolutely nothing to do with the terror in Paris. Tim Donahue presented a ten thousand word report on the Free French and Resistance forces, the followers of General de Gaulle and General Giraud.

The confidential position papers of the French Communist party —supplied courtesy of the Red Orchestra—all were meticulously organized, indexed and printed in the basement of the Foreign Excellent Trench Coat Company and bound in heavy paper. They

138

made a lasting impression on Geneva and at E Street in Washington. It was said that these Americans were capable of the most sophisticated propaganda and political estimates as well as fearless and violent action. "Donovan's Dreamers," as SOE was referring to the OSS, would become a great secret service "with more agents like the Prescott, Hollander, Donahue, McGuire team". . . so Dulles reported to Washington. The report concluded:

"The Gaullist movement is unquestionably the most powerful in France. Further, de Gaulle has become *the* symbol of French Resistance. This situation has thereby created the following serious risk: the leaders of Resistance groups would look upon any movement led by Giraud or others who have ridden along with Vichy as merely representing the Vichy ideology and as an attempt to save the regime in order to maintain its power.

"The OSS should therefore begin actively to support and supply the Gaullists, and seek to reconcile the Fighting French with Giraud's following . . ."

Allen Dulles was, in turn, a different man from the other spymasters that Vivian had encountered since he had first looked into Intrepid's hooded eyes that day in 1940. In robust middle years, bespectacled and pipe-smoking, his sedate exterior concealed a wide-ranging appetite for intrigue and manipulation of events. Dulles sensed the tremendous potential of young Turks like Prescott and his team and spoke to them in their own language, representing himself and Wild Bill Donovan as young rebels at heart.

Dulles heartily took up the "field viewpoint" as further evidence of his flexible outlook. Always wary of working too close to Washington, he stressed the importance of "the man on the spot"; only *he* could really pass judgment on details, as contrasted with policy decisions made at headquarters. Almost without exception, Dulles feared the burden of high-level policy-making that might cramp freedom of choice. In fact, both his heart and Bill Donovan's belonged only to the people on the firing line. . . .

It was partly true. During World War I as a young foreign service officer Dulles had come to Berne as a neophyte to practice diplomacy (and espionage). His first great lesson in this field came when he passed up the opportunity to meet with an obscure Russian visitor who was staying in the Swiss capital. This "visitor" turned out to be none other than the revolutionary, Nikolai Lenin. Dulles resolved then and there never again to disregard *any* source of intelligence. After the German defeat in 1918 he was transferred to Berlin, where he made the acquaintance of many important people. From Berlin he went to Constantinople, then returned to Washington, where he first became the friend of William J. Donovan. While he was decidedly on his way to a brilliant diplomatic career, its minimal financial rewards sent him back to the private practice of law with his brother's international law firm. He kept his hand in public affairs, though, and it was during this period that he was first exposed to what he recognized as the threat of Nazism. From the beginning he had no sympathy for the Nazi cause, and if at first he appeared to some to have isolationist sympathies, he soon had other thoughts. He acknowledged himself as an interventionist and stated publicly that the United States must not allow a defeated England. Soon after he made these remarks the country entered the war and he was quickly recruited by Donovan for his new intelligence organization.

Later, the now middle-aged spy had been sent to Berne for the second time in his career. He went to great pains to cultivate his reputation as an apolitical pragmatist. Above all he wanted to avoid the inheritance of the British stalemate with the Free French forces, but it was indeed a narrow line to walk. Important elements on the British side wanted to work with General Giraud and other rightists, while Dulles could see the emerging strength of the Gaullists. Nobody but the Gestapo benefited from this high-level infighting.

He managed to move brilliantly through the maze of plots and counterplots and eventually won the confidence of the Gaullists (despite his conservative Wall Street background, he knew a winner when he saw one and wanted to go with him even if he did see the drawbacks of de Gaulle's tremendous independence of spirit). Finally, conflict was temporarily set aside when de Gaulle accepted a political marriage to Giraud and they formed an apparently united French Committee of National Liberation. . . .

Their morning discussions in the comfortable club room of Dulles's Herrengasse flat turned on whether Vivian's team was to be sent into Germany as a unit of SI or SO. To enhance the discussions there were tea and hot chocolate and delicious kuchen prepared by a pleasant, purse-lipped woman named Elizabeth.

Dulles would puff away and play the game of pitting SI against SO. These two organizational divisions were established by General Donovan and approached operational problems from two entirely different perspectives. SI was charged with espionage—the secret collection of intelligence information; SO was given responsibility for sabotage and liaison activities with underground movements. The two, not surprisingly, were not always compatible. Dulles favored the SI position, saying that "an intelligence officer should be free to talk to the devil himself if he could gain any useful knowledge for the conduct or termination of the war."

Of course, Trepper's introductions to the German network were of great importance to Dulles's own calculations. He had been in contact with the Nazis and had received various offers of peace . . . especially with regard to the Italian front. He paid little attention to these overtures, though, because he saw them as emanating directly from the Gestapo hierarchy.

Dulles was an artist at intrigue, and he literally salivated at the thought of the daring Prescott team as front-line pawns in the heart of the enemy. He had already dabbled, himself, in a rightist plot to eliminate Hitler.

Actually he had become an expert on German infighting as he watched first from his window in room 3663 at Rockefeller Plaza in New York City. There he and his staff launched intelligence projects that reflected his personal interest in German operations. The creation of a committee of anti-Hitler German emigrés was proposed with the intention that these people would act as a front for American support of a German resistance organization.

Indeed, he had been conspiring ever since the Roosevelt-Churchill meeting in Casablanca proclaimed the policy of unconditional surrender—a doctrine that when translated meant that any German government, even if headed by anti-Hitler insurgents, could bring an end to the war by declaring unequivocal loyalty to the Allies. In short, there was to be no distinction made between those who defied the führer and those who remained loyal.

Dulles's attempt to provoke Himmler into an assassination plot against Hitler failed, but this was not the only coup d'état planned and participated in by the OSS in Washington at the old Gas Works on E Street. Some quite inane schemes were being tried on for size by the various OSS sections around the world. OSS had decided that the only way to topple fascism was to undermine its chief exponent and symbol. They employed a group of psychoanalysts who determined from the führer's personality profile that he could be dragged to his fall by exposure to massive quantities of pornography! The OSS then proceeded to put together the largest and most "in-depth" assemblage of German smut ever to be seen, and intended to drop it by plane around the führer's headquarters. Apparently it was hoped that Hitler would be curious about the objects falling from the sky, would step outside, pick up some bit of it and promptly lapse into a state of porn-induced madness. In still another OSS section there were propaganda stickers printed to be distributed among chilly German laboratories. They read, "Make the führer cold, and this room will be warm again!". . .

Dulles found this young Prescott shrewd far beyond his years, but Hollander was a Red and couldn't be trusted. He must proceed cautiously. Perhaps the one link that might be tugged open was Tim Donahue. Tim seemed to Dulles to be slightly depressed as he reported each day to the flat to prepare reports on Free French Forces Estimates and drink cups of rich Swiss chocolate. The OSS chief began to put a word, or moment of silence, here and there together until, from Donahue, he began to realize that there was more to Vivian Prescott than that so winning all-American boy was volunteering . . . Dulles fancied himself a natural psychologist, not to mention sexologist, and he was, after a fashion. His own personal life had always been abstemious and constrained as any in that long line of Presbyterian missionaries of which he was the secular descendant. Now he watched Tim Donahue through a cloud of pipe smoke and decided that that quiet, shy young man might suspect his wife with the all-American Prescott but say nothing out of fear of forcing the issue, and so losing his attractive spouse. If, he reasoned, Donahue felt inadequate in comparison to Prescott, then he might well do the pragmatic thing and keep quiet. Yes, that was it, Dulles decided, and if there was any doubt over Prescott's extramarital affair it would be resolved by assigning surveillance to Prescott and Mrs. Donahue. . . .

"How's married life?" Vivian and Pat had recourse to a ski lodge unused since the late thirties. On their outings to the slopes on the outskirts of the city they did ski, occasionally, after fierce, hungry coupling in front of the low fire that they managed to start in the lodge fireplace. This was their first time together since London. They had worked silently building the fire before Vivian spread the lap robe from the car and started to unbutton her blue wool ski suit.

Her nipples stood up hard to his touch. "Tim is uneasy. About Berlin and . . . things in general."

He stopped at the bottom button. "Is there a problem?"

"You know the Catholic church has an historical position on tyrannicide; Thomas Aquinas on 'The Death of Tyrants,' and others too. I *think* this will convince Tim, but he's true blue, in every way . . . So far as we're concerned, you and I, I have to make a decision." She touched his lips with her fingertips.

"Could he handle the truth?"

"I don't know. Could you? Or I?"

" 'What is truth?' asked Pontius Pilate."

"That's very literary. No, the truth is that I need you both."

"Enough to sneak and lie?"

"I don't know. What about you?

"Me? I've been trained by experts."

She stepped back, naked, to look at him as he stripped off his togs. "Vivian, who are you? What do you want me for?"

"Because you're a good soul who believes in the Sacred Heart of Jesus *and* the death of tyrants. Because you can drive like Damon O'Dell, because you, ah, know your Shakespeare, and last but not least you have a figure that will always look sixteen and the sweetest, most perfect little rear end I ever—"

She was full of laughter as she threw her arms around his neck. "What a line. But, seriously, there's no sense in my talking to Tim if this is all just a passing . . ."

"Pat, if we come out of Germany in one piece—if we don't have to swallow the 'L' pills—*then* talk to him. You know me better than you think. There's less here than meets the eye, I hate all this secrecy business. Sounds odd for me to say but it's true. People know what they know. I don't believe in a category called faithfulness. I believe you can invent rules if you're willing to take the responsibility, the heat. I'm willing to face Tim, or lie like a bastard . . . No one owns anybody. I won't lie to you, *ever,* even if the truth kills you—no, not the truth, the facts, that's all we're talking about, the *facts*. The *fact* is that I think you're a wonderful, sexy, good soul. From that follows everything, and nothing."

She had taken hold and seemed to be studying his broad phallus. "And when it's over?" she asked quietly.

"When it's over—it won't be over. I'll never help to bring a child into this world until there's a force organized to make war on war itself. We've been there, we *will* have been there, in the belly of the war. We'll have to write and talk and organize—"

"What? Organize what?"

"The *peace*. Organize the *peace*. Are we going to talk all afternoon?"

"Vivian Prescott, are you a good man or a prick?" She smiled and squeezed his testicles. "Talk, *Amerikaner!*" At the same moment the torture of Janet entered both their thoughts like a bolt. Her knees buckled and recovered and she flung herself against his chest, her tears running down his chest. "Oh, Viv, Viv, poor Vivian —much more, so much more than meets the eye."

Vivian's team went in with Swiss passports, dressed as wealthy graduate students, with letters from the School of History at the University of Basel. They arrived in Berlin on the night train.

Germany's railroad system was run-down, irregular and crowded—the cars needed paint and the broken windows had been replaced with wooden boards.

As soon as they disembarked they made directly for the Haupstadl, a poor working-class district. Their headquarters was a freezing basement flat in an ugly dilapidated tenement. Twice during the first night they were awakened as they slept wrapped in their overcoats and forced to hurry a hundred yards to the nearest air raid shelter. The missiles screamed as they ran, and they had to dodge sharply to keep from being hit by the debris that hurtled through the air from a not too distant blast.

There were two things they would constantly be aware of during their short stay in that Berlin flat: the ever present, pungent odor of chemical smoke, and the thick dust that hung in the unsettled air and that seemed to have been accumulating for half a century.

In the morning Pat went to queue up in front of the corner delicatessen, and Mush left for the underground to meet the contact that would put them in touch with the Berlin section of the Red

Orchestra. After eating the bread and wurst that Pat had purchased, they wrapped up in their dirty blankets to try to keep warm. There was nothing to do but wait for Mush and news of the S-B group.

S-B stood for Harro Schulze-Boysen, the charismatic leader of what German intelligence insisted was a Communist spy ring of almost supernatural power. As the group emerged, it became clear that it all centered around the vivid figure of the man from whom it took its name . . . Harro Schulze-Boysen had been known to the Gestapo since 1933 as someone with "extreme Communist tendencies." It was learned also from the tapping of his telephone that he was the driving force behind the Berlin end of the *Rote Kapelle*. But it was the romantic stature of the man himself that created the real threat. There was no middle ground in the way one reacted to his cold, icy, blue-eyed stare. The tension and energy that worked constantly in his face reflected both what his supporters saw as intelligence and his enemies as recklessness. With the air of a religious fanatic he carried the banner of his group with the controversial figure of his wife Libertas at his side. . . .

The steel gray Berlin sky was already fading into twilight when Mush finally returned. He had had to wait for hours for the contact. The underground station had been filled by a troop team of wounded. Near hysterical wives and mothers had battered at the wooden protective fencing that separated them from their loved ones. Their curses and cries mingled with the screams of the wounded begging for morphine. The station guards had been forced to use their clubs during the near riot. The smell was appalling despite the bitter cold.

The Chief, Trepper, in Paris had been correct, Mush reported. The S-B ring's days were numbered. An informer had been placed next to Schulze-Boysen's wife, Libertas, and the arrests could come at any time. All their plans would have to be changed. Mush concluded his pessimistic inventory and looked inquiringly at Vivian. "Let's get out," Tim said; "they'll just wrap us up with them and we'll all be wiped out." Vivian held up a gloved hand and began to ask Mush a series of questions. At length he summarized their position as he saw it, ". . . so we can leave tomorrow, *or* . . . we can take the informer hostage, buy a few days' time for the S-B group, and, with their help, still make an attempt on Hitler. We

145

know that they've been talking about killing him for years, have all the plans and routes worked out. We can look them over, pick and choose and then decide . . ."

They temporized by deciding to send Mush out again in the morning to get details on the feasibility of taking the informer and to verify if, in the contact's opinion, the disappearance of the informer would stop the Gestapo's hand, and, if so, for how long.

The facts, as they found out the following afternoon, were that Libertas had met, and was attracted to, the shorthand-typist Gertrud Breiter, who worked at the Gestapo interrogation offices where Libertas had been frequently questioned. In her anxiety she sought a friend, and during the conversations that followed she confessed the secrets of her husband's group to this anxious-to-please, politically zealous young woman. Gertrud Breiter reported to her superiors the secrets that Libertas confessed during their first exchange, and they, at first with some reluctance but eventually with great enthusiasm, listened to her and recognized her potential value. Finally the Gestapo ordered Breiter to begin a lesbian relationship with Libertas. And, now, many people would go to the gallows because of this lonely young woman's hunger for life and her need to appease it by reaching out and touching what she believed was a kindred soul.

Schulze-Boysen had been warned repeatedly, but his reaction was to discount talk critical of Libertas as characteristic old-line German bourgeois prudery. As a follower of Wilhelm Reich, he devoutly believed that fascism had a core of repressed sexuality . . . "Why have the German people chosen fascism and dancing lessons and torchlight parades instead of a life of productive work and intimate relationships? Because deep down we all have drab little souls and we want to rouge them up a bit. And for those who have had the will to live beaten out of them as children, this absurd gang of pornographers and perverts has come to represent the German people. So to escape perversion, sadism, death, we must have the courage to smash every rotten taboo . . ." And the others would lift their champagne goblets to toast their leader and his, fatefully, beautiful wife. No question . . . Schulze-Boysen believed devoutly that the antidote to sadism and war was love, albeit carnal love. This belief formed a bond among the entire S-B group and for that reason none of them would even consider interfering with

146

Libertas's affair with Gertrud Breiter. The Gestapo, for their part, were driven to a frenzy by what they referred to as the scandalous "endorsement of sex" of the leading members of the ring. They had arranged with Fraulein Breiter to take moving pictures of one of her trysts with Frau Schulze-Boysen, and the secret police were dumbfounded to discover that their home movie contained an affair between three—none other than Schulze-Boysen himself had accompanied his wife to that particular filmed meeting.

So *Sturmbannführer* Kolan and his deputies, plus no less a personage than Gustave Roeder of the Reich Ministry of Justice, together with his legal aides and visitors from Göring's staff, were found at any hour of the day or night at the Gestapo safe house on Wilhelmstrasse watching the edifying spectacle of the Schulze-Boysens making love to Gertrud Breiter and vice versa. Harro and Lib Schulze-Boysen were a slim handsome German couple, blond and aristocratic, while the Breiter woman, the Gestapo, was a healthy looking young specimen of the working class. The film was grainy and without sound, but the technician operating the camera from outside the window had not shirked his duty. There was almost thirty minutes of the threesome, stopping only for occasional refreshment from a large bottle of liebfraumilch.

The Nazis, to cover any betrayal of prurient fascination, maintained a steady stream of insults and moralizing epithets at the "shocking" spectacle as they ran and reran their favorite sections. What particularly offended the ever larger group of viewers, apparently, was the long sequence in which the Schulze-Boysens made the Gestapo informer into a sex sandwich. With Fraulein Breiter between them, Lib and Harro ate her from head to toe, all the while calling out, though none of this could be heard since there was no sound track. Eventually the Schulze-Boysens met at Fraulein Breiter's plump private parts, whereupon they fell to gratifying each other, leaving the fraulein to make do for herself. The film was played so often that it began to fall apart, and the consensus was that when it wore out altogether they would round up the ring, starting with the "depraved" Libertas.

All of this Mush recounted to the group, and a plan based on what they learned emerged: Mush's contact would meet with and detain Libertas, preventing her from keeping her appointment the next day with Gertrud Breiter—of which they had been informed

—while Tim and Pat would pick up Breiter where she waited for Libertas.

Pat, emphasizing her lean body image, had no trouble attracting the informer within fifteen minutes of Breiter's proposed meeting time with Libertas. The place was the lobby of the Kaiser Wilhelm Institute, paid for with Rockefeller money, according to Mush. Within a block the two women had "run into" Vivian, and the new threesome walked arm in arm into the Café Geiser, where they indulged in hot chocolate with real whipped cream. They then repaired to a small hotel. Their false identity as students was easily believable, even if one was not lost in a genital fugue, as Fraulein Breiter most assuredly was, brought on by the presence of this delectable student couple. At the Hotel Rittner Vivian and Pat gagged and bound her. At least the OSS team no longer needed to worry about Libertas inadvertently compromising them with the Breiter woman. Pat stayed to guard, Vivian left at once for the tenement where Tim and Mush would be waiting with the dossier marked "A. H."

It was snowing hard, big flakes pouring out of a gunmetal sky. For three freezing mornings Vivian, Tim and Mush had waited; they could push their luck no farther. It was a little colder each day, but the Nazi uniforms were as warm as anything else they could possibly have worn. They looked every inch the part of a Leibstandarte motorized unit as it patrolled, with other identical vehicles, the circumference of Adolf Hitler's new chancellery, a vast pile of stone and granite shaped like a mammoth stable or barrack. The floors were mosaic in the lobbies, red marble in the giant corridor at the end of which was the double door with the bronze initials "A. H." The paneled private offices of the führer opened onto a garden, at one end of which stood an enormous block of concrete the size of a small house. From the S-B reports they had learned that behind the small steel door, cut into the block, was a descending flight of stairs. Bombproof under eighteen feet of concrete was the wolf's lair. Down that flight of stairs lay the eerie refuge of Adolf Hitler. There he lived with his Bavarian lady friend, Eva Braun, and entertained those who came to pay, or pretended to pay, homage; there too he waited out the air raids. The stairs emptied into a central hall, evidently a guard room, and beyond, behind the creaking steel door, lay the private apartments of the

148

führer. Deep pile carpets, paneled walls, overstuffed furniture and cherished paintings all fought against rot and decay in the damp, hostile darkness.

It was the security of this central redoubt, not mundane affairs of state, that would draw Hitler to the chancellery. Only here could he feel completely safe. But would he come today, in this gathering storm?

As warned, it happened fast. The OSS team had just completed a slow round of the stone and marble edifices, snowflakes falling, when they heard the grenades. They had been thrown by a team of two agents—professionals run directly by the Chief in Paris . . . Trepper's arrest had not stopped a flow of orders to the Red Orchestra from Gestapo headquarters itself, where Trepper was now ensconced, having managed to convince his captors that he was working for them . . . These two from the S-B group were dressed as street cleaners. Their grenades were meant to kill or maim the führer, with the OSS team speeding into the confusion to finish the job, at the same time providing cover for the S-B men to make their escape. It was such a backup team as had been lacking in the Heydrich operation. It had taken only one such event for Vivian to learn that there had to be *both* diversion and cover for a murder in the streets. . . .

The disguised OSS team was in the first vehicle to approach the smoking official limousine. The assassins were nowhere to be seen. Snow was falling and the street was silent. Where was the chosen Leibstandarte? Could the snow be muffling and camouflaging the tyrannicide from the elite guard pledged to die for the führer? The gray Wehrmacht sedan, with the OSS team inside, braked and slid on the fresh snow ending up exactly next to the bombed limousine. The three occupants—including the führer, the driver, and a general staff officer, all seemed to be dead or unconscious. "Something's wrong," Vivian said tightly as they all ducked and drew machine pistols. "Let's make it quick."

Tim stayed at the wheel covering them as they slipped out and moved, low and ready, toward the other vehicle. Without warning the slumped-over figure of the führer sat bolt upright, staring at the OSS men, and began to curse in a flat nasal voice. Was he raving? The words made no sense. "That's it! No more! I quit!" Mush's bullet went into his mouth and tore the back of his head

149

out, covering the staff officer next to him with blood and brain matter. This same officer, who had appeared dead, now flinched out of his moribund pose, calling to the OSS men, "Don't shoot, I'm with *you*. . . . You're Bormann's men, yes? Don't waste time, you only killed his *double* . . ."

Before Mush could put a bullet into that red face, Vivian got into the back seat through the sprung door. He crouched, staring down into the face of the impostor. He could not be sure—heavier, younger?—he leaned across and raked the barrel of the heavy pistol across the other man's face. "Get in the other car now, before I kill you."

"My God," the round-faced man managed to get out, "you're not even Germans!"

No more than two and a half minutes had elapsed before Tim gunned them out and into the broad street. The sound of sirens wailed through the heavy falling snow—it was the storm that had given cover to both the assassins and the OSS team. They passed traffic slowed by the slippery slush, as well as frightened young faces of the elite guards looking for the smoke that was already misting into the white curtain of snow. No one noted the two "officers" driving in the opposite direction or knew that on the floor of the back seat a Jewish OSS agent lay on top of Lieutenant Colonel Hermann Paul Herre, one of the most important intelligence officers in the Third Reich. The OSS team was not aware yet, either, of their hostage's identity.

They went to ground in a Red Orchestra safe house outside the city in Bernau. The message was passed for Pat to leave the Breiter woman. If the S-B group was to be arrested, it was better that it "happen right now," Vivian pointed out. It was clear that it was not Adolf Hitler they had killed . . . there was not a word on the radio of any trouble in front of the chancellery. Libertas and the S-B group scattered, but arrests came almost at once—Breiter had done her work well; Libertas and the S-B had been destroyed by Libertas's foolish, if consuming, passion. . . .

Inside the cottage Colonel Herre pleaded for his life. His face was caked with blood. He stunned the team with his offer: Germany was finished; Martin Bormann was a Soviet agent—Mush told him he was a liar; Colonel Herre was Reinhard Gehlen's right hand; General Gehlen was prepared to conclude a separate arrangement with the Americans *before* the Soviets arrived; General Gehlen's Eastern European spy network held "the key to postwar power," insisted Colonel Herre, chain-smoking as he talked.

"Who in the world is General Gehlen?" Pat whispered at their first break from the interrogation. The team was divided, with Vivian leaning toward believing the Nazi, Mush and Tim wanting nothing to do with him, and Pat undecided.

A plan, though, began to shape up in Vivian's mind. "Could you bring me face to face with the General?"

"I don't know. Who knows what the Gestapo thinks I had to do with the killing of the double?"

"If we cannot hear from the General's own lips what he is prepared to offer then we have no choice but to eliminate you, Colonel. If, on the other hand, you and the general are willing to make a contract in good faith, I can start the negotiations with Washington at once for a postwar arrangement at the highest level."

They listened in as Herre made call after call, and just before midnight, Reinhard Gehlen's private automobile emerged at the little house out of the still falling sheet of snow.

The "Gray Fox" was alone. He was of sturdy build and middle height, handsome with lustrous black eyes and slick black hair. He arrived in a perfectly tailored overcoat and dark gray suit. Herre was a forceful talker, but the general was a virtuoso. He crossed his legs, straightened the flawless crease in his trouser, and lifted a corner of the curtain . . .

General Gehlen's biography did not actually exist, any more than did his photographs—he had been known to go to fantastic lengths to retrieve and destroy any photos that inadvertently might have been made. The Fox had also caused to be planted several conflicting biographical dossiers. Vivian had come to recognize the pattern of a master spy and Gehlen, like the others, spent a large amount of time in constructing his personal myth and mystique. Also like his brothers-in-covert, Vivian guessed, Gehlen came from a statistically typical middle-class home. There was, though, one rather remarkable aspect of the Gehlen family tradition: the general's maternal grandfather, a Lutheran pastor named Stryker, had been accused of "devil possession and child molestation in 1867. The charge was half true. A year later the young religious man had been found hanging from a beam in the chan-

151

cery. Despite this unfortunate episode, or because of it, the immediate background of young Reinhard had been relentlessly ordinary . . . so much so that the bright student had gone fishing in troubled waters during his years at the state university. His worried mother never mentioned how much her restless son reminded her of her tragic father, the pastor. . . .

Vivian had to admire the man's style; it caused him to play brilliantly, over his head.

"Here is what I want—" the General said, but Vivian interrupted.

"No, Herr General, let me tell you what we have been asked to require of *you*—and, parenthetically, I must tell you that the possibility of this meeting was one of the factors in the OSS decision to come into Berlin. I have pen and paper for your convenience, colonel, in making notes." Now lying with eloquence, Vivian began to dictate a fabricated list of "American demands" from what his friends knew must be a blank piece of paper in his student notebook. . . . at times he even sounded a bit like Dulles himself . . . "In conclusion, I, Reinhard Gehlen, will deliver to the relevant American intelligence officers the secret files of my entire eastern network and, further, I will, myself, put my services under American control together with the services of those of my subordinates as shall have access to them. In exchange for these services I will expect the American authorities to make every effort to ensure that I and my subordinates will be guaranteed the same rank, position and control of the eastern network, if and when said network comes under complete American command."

Outside the snow had finally stopped. Colonel Herre scribbled furiously to the conclusion. Vivian closed the notebook on the blank paper from which he had been pretending to read. The General started as his forgotten cigarette burned his fingers. Mush Hollander was so upset that he left the room. Finally Tim and Pat stood up, as a sign that they wanted Vivian to join them in the kitchen for a conference, but he refused, saying to the general, "Shall we type it up?"

The Fox lit a fresh cigarette. "My dear sir, I cannot, of course, sign such a document. But I will tell you this. I will, in the presence of Colonel Herre, give you my word that I am prepared to negotiate terms based closely on your *official* offer." The tension was too much for Tim, who sneezed.

It was cold, deadly still.

"Very well, Herr General, I will so report. Now, if you will be kind enough to drive us past any roadblocks as far as . . . well, we can discuss the actual destination en route . . . Colonel, may I have your notes, please, and would you make yourself comfortable, here? Since people may be looking for you it would not be safe for you to travel with us.". . .

So it was not until dawn as the train crossed over into Switzerland that the others were able to demand an accounting of Vivian. Mush was in a cold rage and had been since the dictation seven hours before. "The man is a war criminal, a butcher, and you have the colossal nerve to speak for OSS and the American authorities —who the hell are you? That was total bullshit. Who in the hell do you think you are to pull a stunt like that? That's it—you play your Skull and Bones games with someone else, I want *no* part of them. You may be an in-house legend with the oh-so-sophisticated OSS, but, old buddy, as a human being you stink . . ."

Vivian sighed and looked at the others. Then instead of directly challenging Mush he explained that he had improvised for several reasons. He talked slowly, waiting for the anger to settle. First, to get them transportation out of Germany during the combination of a paralyzing winter storm and the general alert because of the shooting and Colonel Herre's disappearance, but mostly because they now had a trump card to play with Dulles and Donovan . . . "Look, Mush, the unconditional surrender position of Britain and the United States comes, as we know, as much from competition with the Soviet Union as it does from fear of Germany—maybe more, and this Gehlen so-called understanding is a symbol of German readiness to negotiate at the *highest* level. The Nazis will fall all over themselves to spy on Russia for the victors. Gehlen's a policeman, for Christ's sake, do you think the Soviets wouldn't use him? Don't be naive, Mush. It was perfectly obvious that he wouldn't sign *anything,* much less what I dictated, but it's also obvious that Gehlen and Herre and others like them are ready to roll over, and Washington has to *know* that. We're in a position now to demand serious secret negotiations with the Gehlens and the Herres. I mean, what's *your* alternative? Fight to the last man?

153

Does your honor demand another, let's say, ten million Russian lives, not to mention the lives of British and Americans—I apologize, that was uncalled for, all *right*, Pat, I *said* I'm sorry. Look, talk it over with Philby . . . you trust *him* . . . unless all of you agree, I won't say anything to Dulles or anyone else. I suggest, though, that you come up with a good story of just what the hell we were doing in Berlin."

The train rattled at high speed. Outside their compartment window the snow-covered foothills of the Swiss mountains threw the gray rocks and clear blue sky into bright relief.

Allen Dulles had been called back to Washington, so after a day and a half of rest the team started out for London, where Kim Philby and Sam Prescott convinced Mush, and the Donahues went along, that the Gehlen "contract" was a major intelligence coup. Mush said he guessed that he "saw the logic," but he shook his head and said softly that it was beyond him how "any of us can ever consider honoring such an agreement with a man like Gehlen." Vivian felt considerably older than his twenty-four years as he looked at Mush. They were all bone weary but Mush seemed almost wounded, his powerful physique slack in an armchair of the Prescott Bletchley manor. The Spanish Civil War veteran, of the Abe Lincoln Brigade, the man who had introduced Vivian to the craft of intelligence right here in London, and had been one of his mentors at Camp X, was now somehow—the phrase "burnt out" flashed across his mind. He had heard some of the veteran agents use the idiom "a burnt out case." But not Mush . . . God, he was only twenty-eight years old . . .

Philby was sniffing his brandy and drinking quantities of it while the elder Prescott urged them all not to be too depressed by the seemingly endless war. It would all be over soon, Roosevelt had assured him, and every one of them was going to be needed to help build a lasting peace. He was the only one in the room who did not have dirty hands from the war, and so although older than any of them his hopeful sentiments had, ironically, a ring of youthful idealism that caused Philby to smile into his brandy. Vivian saw the Englishman's lips curl up slightly and once again felt mistrust for the SOE veteran. If his father and the President and the others of their generation and clan were feeding an illusion, then what was

154

there to believe in? What was the use of anything if all the bloodshed had no meaning? He thought back across to Professor Mann
and his grandfather, and even old Hewes, he of *The Four Feathers*,
and, always, Janet—all had been, in their fashion, idealists, "arrows
of longing for another shore." Especially his father, whom he'd
betrayed that once, that night—but that was past, he would not
again. If Sam Prescott was an idealist, then so be it. Sam was *his*
father's son, and Vivian his—they were all their fathers' sons.
Weren't they . . . ?

Within a week they had their orders. The team was to report to
General Eisenhower at SHAEF and establish liaison with Ike's
deputy for intelligence, General W. Bedell Smith, and help to
coordinate the interrogation of captured German officers. This
assignment had grown out of the Gehlen deal. According to Sam
Prescott, Vivian's contact had caused shock waves in Washington
on E Street in the old Gas Works that housed OSS and, the story
went, Dulles himself had taken part of the credit.

As it turned out only Vivian and Patricia went. Tim's father was
dying of the miner's lung that had been killing him slowly for thirty
years. Mush embraced him, and couldn't resist the heartfelt rhetoric . . . "A million men have died in the mines from accidents, and
from black lung. No one can count them. You tell me there's no
class war in America? Those are real casualty figures." The words,
though, were directed less at Tim than at Vivian. Afterward Mush
reported to OSS control at the embassy that he was too emotionally involved because of what had happened to his relatives in the
Nazi death camps to be effective in communicating on *any* level
with German officers. He was at once reassigned to Washington,
to train new recruits.

Their last dinner together was Vivian's treat at the Spanish Inn.
Tim would, he promised, be back with the team after his father's
funeral. Tim was so much younger than the other children that his
father had been an old man for as long as he could remember: mug
of tea, caked pipe, slippers, Chicago *Journal*, miner's cough. . . .

The beef was thin and the Yorkshire pudding flaky but there was
wine and for once Tim talked, about his father and Pat's family too,
and Vivian could see the richness of the bond between them. For
the first time he felt real envy, not for the sexual part of their
married life—how could he?—but for their shared memories, their

155

mutual journey, those hours, days, years when he had floated, baseless, from governess to schoolmaster to summer camp, from surrogate to surrogate. And then he found the envy gave way to a kind of love for them both . . . he fancied that he could see their faces as they must have looked when they were children . . . he often indulged in this habit of regressing people as he looked at them until they seemed to become softened, early models of themselves. "A couple of redheads," he said, and Tim laughed and drank more wine as Pat stroked his red hair.

Mush Hollander was making an effort to be cheerful for Tim's sake, but Vivian was well aware of how much Mush had aged and changed since their first meeting. Somehow his face was more ethnic, as if the Eastern European genes had begun to dominate the neat, regular American features. His eyes seemed smaller and darker, his nose rounder, his forehead larger—his hair was thinning—and his muscular physique was starting to slump from the shoulders, as if some intangible burden weighed down on him. But he did talk about Trepper and Schulze-Boysen with more animation than they had seen him display since Paris, when he had been so inspired by the meeting with the Chief.

Indeed, when Mush talked about Leopold Trepper it was as though he were speaking about his father. "He was the best they had." His ability intellectually and emotionally to dodge his captors especially showed itself in his skill at pretending to cooperate. . . . The Chief was a real "pro," a true revolutionary, said Mush, "by definition someone who has dirty hands." He was a Marxist and agreed with his mentor that the only truly revolutionary emotion was shame . . . not guilt but shame. When the Chief reached his decision to try to escape from the Gestapo, it was after a considerable period of weighing his chances. He had, after all, no more marginal information to divulge, and with the dearth of it at last about to become obvious, the end had to come to the special treatment he had been receiving as a prisoner. Soon he would be entitled only to the same horrors as the others: torture and death. Mush leaned into the table . . . "As he plotted his escape he realized that conditions were about as favorable as he could hope for. The tight security that had surrounded him at first had relaxed considerably and his relationship with his personal guard, Berg, had developed to the extent that he had learned to exploit the man's

156

alcoholic propensities." Trepper had calculatedly shown deep concern for Berg's health problems and promised someday to take him to a pharmacy where he could find the remedy that would once and for all relieve his pains. It was not by coincidence that this particular pharmacy had two doors. When the day of the planned escape arrived, Berg was feeling especially bad, making a stop at the providential Pharmacie Bailly almost inevitable. When they pulled up in front Berg was in an almost stuporous doze and Trepper was obliged to nudge him into wakefulness.

"We're here. Are you coming in?"

The incredible answer came: "No. Go upstairs and buy the medicine and come right back."

Trepper looked him in the eye. "But Berg, this pharmacy has another exit."

"I have complete confidence in you," the Nazi replied. "And besides, you know I'm too tired to climb the stairs."

And so, near-miraculously, he was free, but only someone running from the Gestapo knew how precarious such freedom was. ". . . So later, to throw the Gestapo off the track, the Chief sent a letter to Berg. He wrote that two men had approached him in the pharmacy and by their gestures he thought he was being rearrested by the Gestapo and being taken to a safe place . . . Listen to this, the Chief added that he would write in the future and keep his old friend informed as to the course of events. And *that* is what he did and will continue to do until the end of the war!"

They all felt some of the Camp X élan return, felt less old for the moment, though at twenty-eight Mush was the oldest of the group. Then, as if he were group historian, he told them about the death of Schulze-Boysen. Handsome Harro was no Trepper, his maneuvers had been merely gestures. But those gestures had been sincere, even elegant, and although he was an amateur he met his execution with dignity, in itself no small feat since the manner in which he was to be exterminated was the most humiliating possible: death by hanging. Mush's voice was low, and Vivian felt as if he were listening to his own story . . . Schulze-Boysen wrote a farewell letter to his parents acknowledging the inevitability of the kind of end ahead. "To live by the sword is to die by it, someone said, and such a fate is especially destined to be if one is thoroughly convinced of the necessity of its use," he wrote his family.

Harro, until the end, called the verdict of his judges unjust, and when he was bound, handcuffed, and the noose placed around his neck, he let life slip away calmly and without struggle.

"First as farce, then as tragedy, if I may reverse Marx's suggested order of history," Mush concluded. The others were not familiar with the quotation but it was clear that Mush intended they not forget the people whose lives they had crossed, saying, in effect, you, Vivian, may not choose to look back, but I do, I choose to remember . . .

There was no fruit but the sweet was not half bad and Vivian even managed to divert the talk away from the past. "Jack Kennedy is supposed to be in sometime next month. Let's see . . . well, Pat, you can meet him. He's a droll sort of guy. Likes a good time. Just won a navy-marine medal for something heroic in the South Pacific. But let him know you're married, first thing." Tim did not laugh, or smile.

At last there was nothing much more to say so Vivian said, "Well, Mush, old *comrade,* we met at *Macbeth,* didn't we, so it's only natural for me to ask 'When shall we three meet again?' "

"You mean *four,* don't you?" Pat said.

"Ah, aren't *you* forgetting that' . . . husband and wife are one flesh and therefore, farewell my—' "

"What in hell is that?" Tim asked.

"*Hamlet.* You know these Yalies," she said. They got up to put on coats and hats and never did actually discuss any details beyond what had already been established; that Mush and Tim would go home and report to the Gas Works in Washington and then, perhaps, all be together again by summer, but where they would all be in a year's turning no one could or would try to say.

Outside in the protective dark, between raids, the cold winter wind was blowing as Big Ben tolled.

Vivian was careful to keep his father from knowing that he was virtually living with Patricia McGuire Donahue, though she was a frequent guest at Bletchley. And when in early February, 1945, six weeks after Tim and Mush had left for the States, Sam Prescott set off for the conference at Yalta, Vivian and Pat had the house to themselves. FDR was not well and his adviser and friend Samuel Adams Prescott was upset on his return from the Crimean conference with Roosevelt, Churchill and Stalin . . . "He can't live another year." Sam's long, sensitive face was drawn. He was becoming something of an abstraction of himself. . . .

Pat and Vivian waited for their orders by walking the low hills of Bletchley for hours, then back to the manor to make love and sleep, then read at night or, occasionally, dance to the old Noel Coward phonograph records. *I'll see you again* . . . he remembered Janet and Jack Kennedy that night when they were still innocent, had not yet shed blood . . . and he gripped Pat close, kissed her bruisingly, pulled her down to the rug in front of the fireplace, almost tearing at her clothes and she, catching his furious passion, was naked in moments, her nipples hard before he even put his tongue, and teeth, to them, and she was moist, throbbing—"Viv, kiss my pussy." It was the first time she had ever asked, much less used such a graphic term. Minutes later she gave a low cry, her body arched like a gymnast's as he lifted her toward him to enter her, to consume himself in her, and find release from the past.

After that night she told him something about her intimate life with Tim. Before they had simply not spoken of it . . . "He is not a great lover, like you, but he *is* tender and thoughtful—not to say that you aren't—and he can, well, last a long time, you know?" Vivian didn't, he said, feel threatened and there was no sense of gossip as they talked. In fact, the talk made him feel, somehow, more like her husband and less like a mere lover . . . .

Tim's father could not last much longer, he wrote, and he and Mush were both staying in Chicago and working there with Bill Must on a history of OSS decision-making, focusing on Tim's report on the Free French.

On the first day of the last week of February the word came into the embassy from France: "GEHLEN LOCATED. REQUEST PRESCOTT UNIT."

Five days later the briefing included: Vivian, Pat, Sam Prescott auditing for the President, Allen Dulles in from Berne for OSS, and Kim Philby as SOE liaison. Dulles was in charge, as he "put them in the picture," to use Philby's swallowed idiom, and Dulles was generous in his credit given to Vivian for having "started the old Fox in our direction."

By March 10 Vivian and Pat were in temporary army officers' uniforms en route to meet with Bedell Smith, Eisenhower's intelli-

159

gence aide, at SHAEF—Supreme Headquarters, Allied Expeditionary Forces—in Paris. Once together, Viv's main objective was to convince General Smith to exclude the army intelligence G_2 members from any interviews with Gehlen and keep it only between themselves as to how important the general really was. He found that interservice rivalries and intelligence establishment politics were a terrain of battle like any other. Intrigue within OSS had at first disgusted him. Now he saw that he could deal and deceive with the virtuosity of any desk officer back in the E Street Gas Works.

The pretense for the private interview would be to question Gehlen about war crimes; Vivian, however, saw it as a golden opportunity to put to rest once and for all the suspicions engendered by the still, to some, notorious bombing incident in Paris carried out by the Prescott team. Certain OSS circles had jealously condemned it as reckless, and also were annoyed that such a spectacular success should have been linked to the Red Chief Trepper. Vivian would now prove his competence, not allow his detractors to act out their jealousy toward him and his family connections, and perhaps even secure himself a high-level job in the government after the close of the war. All of this he would accomplish, he told Pat, if he were only allowed to penetrate the mind of the Gray Fox and win his confidence.

When the OSS party, including Pat, Vivian and Dulles's men Dick Helms and Tracy Barnes, searched the POW camp at Oberursae, Vivian tried and failed to convince Barnes and Helms to let him see Gehlen alone. When the OSS agents entered the general's windowless holding room he yelled at them to *get out*.

The next morning Vivian went in alone, bringing cups of real coffee. "Herr General, greetings. Military stupidity has reached new heights in the way you have been treated. I want you to know that my father is taking up this entire matter with the President himself. He wants you to know that the highest circles of our government are concerned." There was an orderly named Phillips who anticipated their need for coffee and cigarettes very nicely and who later provided them with a very decent omelet. The Fox purred under Vivian's deft touch, and because under the velvet glove the general sensed an iron fist, he talked. He even consented to pose with Vivian for Pat's "official" photograph.

Gehlen had a cunning mind, was a dynamic talker and used his body to add force to his words. His concern was not only for the past—that, after all, was over, but for the future as well. Diplomats, embassies, what did they know? Vivian was believable as a convinced anti-Communist and lent a sympathetic ear to Gehlen's explanation of the aims of the Soviet Union: the Fox forecast that Stalin would not allow independence to Poland, Czechoslovakia, Bulgaria or Rumania, would subject Finland to control from the Kremlin and probably wished to impose Communism on the whole of Germany, including the U.S. zone.

He also talked of the time Neville Chamberlain flew to Berchtesgaden to placate Adolf Hitler. "He upset our plans," Gehlen said. "We had planned our own coup against the regime of the führer, but when they found out about the British prime minister's impending visit we had to call it off and go along with Hitler's line. Later Chamberlain's policy was defended as giving the British time to prepare. Ha! It was Germany that actually won the time . . ."

Gehlen had poured forth the hard facts in order to save himself; Vivian proved his worth as an interrogator. "I will go with you to Washington, Herr General, to personally represent your interests. You may want to insist on that point when drawing up your preliminary understanding."

Gehlen responded with equal courtesy and indicated to Viv that he was indeed counting on his help in setting up a life-style which would be in accordance with what he had known in Germany.

The next day there was more coffee and Pat was brought in as a secretary to take notes. The Fox smoothed his mustache and bowed to the petite "WAC" and took in at a glance the athletic grace coiled inside the khaki.

On day three Barnes and Helms took over. They were polite and correct and the Fox was now in too deep to complain about the absence of Mr. Prescott. Mr. Prescott and Mrs. Donahue had been called back to Paris, he was told.

It was then that the Fox told them that Allen Dulles's Swiss maid was a German agent.

Gehlen's interrogators were stunned. This would be a more cutting wound to the vanity of American intelligence than Dulles's missed opportunity with Lenin during the first war. The general noted with pleasure the look on the faces of the OSS Ivy Leaguers.

These men, he thought, were not Prescott's equals; they could be manipulated, they would be afraid to tell Dulles that his own home had been penetrated. He would tell them more—secrets both true and false about his penetration of the OSS—and they would slowly but surely become addicted to the fruits of his forbidden information. And then they would belong to him. The general called for real coffee.

At SHAEF Vivian briefed General Smith and secured his agreement not to take Gehlen to Washington without him. "Beetle" Smith was a bright-eyed, ambitious little man whose thoughts were fixed tightly on the future. It would take several months to prepare the case, he said, and he would contact Prescott in London in about sixty days. And, yes, he could arrange for a pool car . . . .

The sky had cleared as Vivian and Pat drove into the countryside. "How would you like a breather in Cannes? We won't tell anyone where we are. Well?"

"OSS TEAM LOST IN FRANCE. Can you see the headlines?"

"No . . . and I can't believe that you're hesitating."

"What's in it for me?"

"This," he said, reaching over to find her hand and put it on his bulging crotch.

"What's this? Hadn't you better see a doctor? How long have you had this growth?"

"Off and on for years. But it's a damn sight worse lately, nurse. Can't you help me?"

"You drive carefully toward Cannes, mister, and I'll try."

She addressed herself to his zipper, working his erection free. "Try to avoid sudden stops, please." He did his best to cruise at around thirty as she began to kiss and tickle with her tongue, her head nestling, somehow, between the wheel of the G2-issue Ford and his fullness. Sucking, then stopping, prolonging it, while he slipped his right hand down to try to find her nipples through the stiff uniform blouse. Finally he did and squeezed gently as he came into her throat, her auburn cap of hair rising and falling with his convulsions.

From a hay wagon an old farmer waved as they passed, calling out something into the wind as the car picked up speed, heading down the southern route past the Burgundy Canal and the Yonne,

162

on to the wide delta of the Rhone and Avignon—toward the high sun of constant noon . . . .

Under the warmth of the Midi—literally the midday of a sky and sun not torn by war—their bodies turned golden and the sun streaks appeared again in Vivian's hair for the first time since his last year at New Haven and the Ivy League tennis championship. And as if the sun could cleanse and bleach the mind and memory, too, he thought again of the old ideals and dreams of creativity that had been stirred in him at New Haven by Rudolph Mann. Bleached, too, was the memory of Janet, deeper into the bone of the past. For the first time he could not immediately recall her face —though always her body—and it terrified him.

As if by contract neither of them mentioned a word of what their relationship would be after they returned to London. Instead they talked about the azure sky and what effect it must have had on the lucidity and audacity of the heroic Greeks of the fifth century before Christ. They were filled with a strange joy, away from the war and its secrets. They opened themselves to each other with a rare intimacy of thought and sensation.

"I guess happiness is inevitable, too," he told her.

They were almost alone there in the last spring of the war. Gone now were the fortunate survivors of the post-World War I era, those who had come to the harbors of Cannes and Nice with no submarines to challenge their crossing. They had found a land still plentiful with arbors, laurel and myrtle; found also that they could freely roam the battlefields and gather trench helmets or shell cases from the last war to take home and use as book ends.

The Côte d'Azur itself remained unscarred then, its rocky shores and cliffs as innocent as a young Vivian Prescott had been when he came to see them for the first time in the summer of '35, just before he was about to enter Yale.

It was a new landscape now, and he was a different man. . . .

Before they could no longer avoid contacting London, the waiter at the *pension* where they had been taking breakfast rushed up to inform them that President Roosevelt was dead.

The two Prescott men walked slowly through London's Hyde Park. The ever-present flower beds were bursting with blooms that no man's war, at least up to that point, had ever been able to stifle.

163

And something else was here that no one could suppress—a man's right to exercise free speech.

Today Vivian and Sam walked through this famed place where on Sunday afternoons you could take your choice of a dozen different social doctrines and as many religious ones. Even if someone called for murder of the king not much attention was paid . . . the British were convinced that the reason they had never had assassinations was that they let everyone come here to Hyde Park and blow off steam.

Sam Prescott had been shaken by the "governor's" (he used the old familiar term for his friend) passing. He was still haunted by that warm spring afternoon in New York City when he had been summoned to Warm Springs, Georgia. He'd arrived by mid-afternoon, in time to witness the last hour of life slipping away from the great man.

Franklin Roosevelt had spent his final morning in the company of his mistress, Sam Prescott informed his son. She had in fact rushed to his aid only moments after he slumped sideways in his chair. She heard him murmur, "I have a terrific headache," and then watched him lapse into unconsciousness.

Sam would always rationalize her presence by saying, if only to himself, "His greatest love affair was with his country . . . to *that* he was never unfaithful . . ."

Apart now from his grief, Sam also had an overwhelming sense of fear for the country that Roosevelt had been, in his view, so faithful to. For the man had, after all, staved off revolution during a time when it had seemed almost inevitable. Now that he was gone, Sam felt deep concern about where this energy, this headlong course toward change, which the President had only temporarily diverted, would be directed.

After a while they sat on one of the wide benches near a looming bronze steed and rider that had been cast in the imperial style of the Victorian age. Vivian stared at the long forgotten general of empire and his rearing mount. "Two feet in the air. Did you ever hear that there's a strict code for their heroic statues? If the horse has both feet on the ground then it means the hero died in battle; one foot raised, he died of wounds *received* in battle; both front feet raised, he died in bed."

"No. I never heard that."

"I believe it. Are these the types that are going to set up a United Nations to ensure world peace?" Vivian's voice was low and harsh, his face tanned but drawn slightly.

His father was pale, looking his age. "I don't know, Viv. I'll let you know . . . Better yet why don't you come with me? I can get you into the American delegation. I'm sure Jack Kennedy'll be around and some old pals of yours. Laurence III and Chip Richardson from Bones and some of the OSS boys like Cord Meyer and—"

"How can I? We're taking General Gehlen to Washington any week now."

"I know, but you could join us. Viv, you have to get the poison of this war out of your system, somehow. Mush is going to teach, you say, and Patricia and Tim are going to work in the Chicago area. What about you?"

"Is there any hope? They're already choosing up sides while the corpses rot on the fields—"

"But, son, remember, 'Man is great in his ashes.' If young people like you don't pitch in now, then who *will* help? You haven't written anything in five years, why don't you put your thoughts on war and peace down in—"

"I started, on the Riviera, on furlough."

"You have! Splendid."

"We'll see. I'm calling the book—if it *is* a book—*War against War.*"

"That's very strong. *War against War?* . . . *War against War.* Not *Peace?*"

"No."

"Well, write it . . ." The oversized bronze war-horse and rider cast a shadow over father and son as the afternoon drew to its close.

That night they dined late at Claridge's. Neither was very hungry and the production of *Hamlet* that they attended had failed to move them. The older man, speaking quietly, said he suspected that Churchill was through, and with the "governor" gone that left only Stalin. " 'Woe to the conquered,' that's Joe Stalin's plan now while we're tied down in the Pacific." He leaned forward. "But the OSS boys at the Gas Works in Washington—when I was back for the funeral—some of them just *mentioned* some kind of surprise super-weapon that might be used against Japan . . ."

"I know, Kim Philby knows something. He says that nothing will ever be the same again if we employ whatever it is that we're supposed to have."

"What is it?"

"I don't know. I don't think he does either. Just keeps repeating that nothing will ever be the same again."

"There's a conference in a few weeks at Potsdam, maybe I'll hear something."

They walked toward the embassy, no sign of rain yet. "Well, back to work tomorrow for me," his father said, puffing away on the thick-bowled briar that his son had bought for him at the Duke of Buckingham's Tobacco Shop. "And you are, in a way, in Hamlet's dilemma, aren't you? 'To be or not to be, that is the question.'"

They turned into the embassy walk. Vivian stopped. His eyes seemed very dark as the soft light from the street lamp fell across his hair and bronzed face.

"Tell them I'll join you in San Francisco, at the new United Nations, this summer."

BOOK II

Chicago, 1950

The Time of the Toad

VIVIAN FOLDED his newspaper carefully to avoid printer's ink staining his light brown worsted, rose and walked into the coffee shop of the Blackstone Hotel as soon as the doors were opened at eight o'clock. The lobby and restaurant were quiet, Chicago was in the third day of a paralyzing heat wave and Vivian was grateful for the cool emptiness of the restaurant. He ordered tea, still loyal to his London days, and tapped the tobacco firm in his Lucky Strike, spun the flat Ronson to flame, checked his hands to see if they had been smudged by the moist front page of the Chicago *Tribune*. The smoke stung his throat and he stubbed the fresh cigarette out, deciding, on the instant, to give up the new habit.

His hands were clean, lean and tanned like the rest of him, honed fine by weekends of tennis in Georgetown and Virginia. In fact, he had brought a racket with him in the DC-7 from Washington on the off chance of a game out at Northwestern with some of the old gang. He opened the paper again as the tea cooled, hot tea on a hot day his father had always urged—his father whom he had not spoken to in two years.

LAKE MICHIGAN CRASH OF DC-4/NO LIFE-SAVING GEAR. If all fifty-eight aboard were lost, this would be the worst air disaster in the history of commercial aviation. Vivian could not really fault the *Tribune* for playing the crash story more prominently in the right center of the page above the fold, than the news that REDS CROSS SOUTH KOREAN BORDER.

The killing in Europe had been over for him for five years now and yet there was still no clarity on this matter of death—in a plane by accident or in a military battle or in a crime of passion—which the press *and* the public insisted on treating separately and differently. He had been an editor at Yale and knew that he too would have handled the story of unearned suffering (the plane crash) more prominently than the major casualty figures in Korea, figures that could be the start of the countdown for World War III. He glanced at his watch, fifteen minutes before Mush Hollander or the Donahues would be here, if they were on time, as they would be. He scanned the balance of the front page:

SENATOR GRAHAM BEATEN
IN NORTH CAROLINA:
REBUFF TO TRUMAN

MAN PROTECTS BOMB
SHELTER WITH RIFLE

1500 EAST GERMAN SPIES
INFILTRATE BONN

And then, boldly dominating the upper right hand corner of the page . . .

He folded the paper and laid it under the table. There was a blackish residue on the white cloth left from the print. Vivian looked away from the dirty streak toward the long curtained windows glowing with the first yellow heat of the scorching day to come. His soft off-white cotton shirt was still dry and the neat patterned Sulka bow tie firm and straight, but everything would wilt before the onslaught of the midwestern heat wave. His head throbbed as he massaged his eyes gently with his fingertips. He had not slept well in the hotel and had awakened at seven with a mild headache that the hot and cold shower had not totally relieved. He was irritated for not having booked a room at the Drake, on the lakefront, but the agency had insisted that he stay at the old Blackstone, in room 712 to be exact.

Salesmen were beginning to straggle into the coffee shop as he contemplated the dirty tablecloth, the yellow glare heating up the curtains, the corkscrew English of the *Tribune* headline editors, the scare-word salad of so much of the American mass-media language at mid-century. Every morning the bad news was fed into the nation's nervous system with breakfast, with a second edition to be digested with dinner at night. He looked about the room—at men who were overdrawn on their commissions for books or beer or refrigerators or hotel supplies or any of the spreading new "leisure industries." Newspapers were being riffled and thrown up for protective cover. Vivian had to shut his deep gray eyes, otherwise with his acute vision he could not help collecting the tom-tom beat of the headlines as they flashed behind his eyes:

REDS EXPLODE "A" BOMB

HOUSE UNIT CHARGES
REDS IN UNIVERSITIES

WARNER, HUGHES LEAD FIGHT
AGAINST REDS IN HOLLYWOOD

FUCHS GIVES
"A" SECRET
TO SOVIETS

GIRL SCOUTS HELD
INFILTRATED—MCCARTHY

PHILLY CHEMIST FUCHS
SPY CONTACT IN U.S.

HOOVER PROMISES
MORE ARRESTS

NEW YORKER SEIZED
AS ATOM SPY

PLOT TO HAVE GI
GIVE BOMB DATA
TO SOVIETS
LAID TO SISTER

MCCARTHY CHARGES
20 YEARS OF TREASON

MCCARTHY HINTS MARSHALL
SOFT ON REDS
IN STATE DEPARTMENT

"WE NEED MORE KILLERS"
ASSERTS GENERAL HERSHEY

GOOKS MACHINE-GUNNED
WHILE TRYING TO
RESCUE FAMILIES

MCCLELLAN ADVOCATES
FIRING FIRST SHOT

THE SENATOR STATES WAR IS INEVITABLE IF
MOSCOW DOES NOT COOPERATE
ON AMERICAN TERMS

He opened his eyes to see Patricia Donahue standing in the entrance to the coffee shop. She had not yet spotted him, her back was partly turned as she waited for someone, but his memory boiled over at the sight of the slim, supple legs flowing up into the symmetry of hips and buttocks, the straight back, the auburn hair

. . . she wore a subtle floral print which clung and moved discreetly with her dancer's body as she walked. It wrapped around her small full breasts, stretched gently across her backside and tied neatly at the nipped-in waist. Her rust-brown hair was swirled and fastened in a neat chignon at the back of her head.

Now she turned into the coffee shop and saw him. Their eyes held across the room, and his throat went tight as he stood to greet her. She did not move, then her husband Tim entered and waved. The three embraced and touched each other as people who have been close together will after a separation of years. Before they could sit Mush Hollander was on top of them for more embraces and laughter . . . .

Vivian had not been alone with Pat since London in '45, but all three of them had met for dinner once in 1947 and again in 1948 when Vivian came through Chicago with his father on a university tour for the United World Federalist peace mission. He knew that Tim was with a small Chicago architectural firm and that Pat was teaching in the County Hospital school for nurses and that they had a small, old house in Oak Park. Mush, he assumed, was still lecturing in sociology at Roosevelt College near downtown and living alone on the near North Side.

As they ordered, the talk was obligatorily about the developing Korean situation. The scattered salesmen were already removing themselves to begin a day in the steaming Loop of downtown Chicago, to slip, as soon as possible, into air-conditioned newsreel theaters; to wait for nightfall and the bars to fill up, to fill their trembling hands with cold glasses of beer and bourbon and ginger ale. With relief.

Tim looked the same, more so than the others, his red hair short, almost crew-cut, his Botany suit crumpling already in the humidity. He lifted up a slim volume and grinned. "Your autograph please, Mr. Prescott." They all congratulated Vivian on his book, *War against War,* published since they had last seen him.

"The second page," Mush put in, "read that, Tim. I thought it was first-rate."

Tim's voice was flat but clear, like the good Catholic schoolboy he had once, long ago, been:

... today our choice is, simply, between worldwide cooperation or world war: all scientists agree that the human race is at the crossroad of its history. We can make the desert bloom or we can make of the earth a desert. Our historical struggle now must be against war itself. No ideology—left or right—can be allowed to detour us from our mission. World peace stands on the far side of ideology. Waiting.

Vivian turned to the facing page to write, avoiding the dedication . . . "THIS WORK IS DEDICATED TO THE MEMORY OF MY WIFE JANET HAMMERSMITH PRESCOTT, KILLED IN ACTION SOMEWHERE IN FRANCE, 1943" . . . And wrote, "For Tim and Pat—and a world at peace, V. P. 6/26/50."

"My copy's in my office," Mush said. Vivian smiled noticing that his first teacher in the secret war looked almost a decade older than his thirty-three years. His old-fashioned prewar blue gabardine suit was tight for Mush's two hundred pounds, his frayed collar and wrinkled tie could not enclose his heavy neck, his face seemed rounder with shadows under the eyes and in the hollows of the cheeks, his hair neatly cut but much thinner than years ago.

"Your office? That's no excuse." Vivian's tone was warm. Tim and Pat looked down, Mush blushed. "What is it, Mush?"

"At the moment I'm locked out of my so-called office."

"What? Why?"

"The latest purge at Roosevelt. My luck ran out."

"Jesus Christ"—Vivian's face showed disgust—"this McCarthy thing is turning into gallows humor."

"I see where your friend Jack Kennedy supports him," Pat said.

"Jack's a congressman now and his father is a big McCarthy supporter so . . ." Vivian broke up the silence as the others finished their eggs with what he hoped were amusing stories—because they were so damned farfetched—about the junior senator from Wisconsin and his fellow travelers on the low road . . . "Have you been following Liebling's articles on Elizabeth Bentley's testimony? What a wit that man has! Did you read the *New Yorker* series? 'Miss Bentley has handed over to the Russians the secret formula for making synthetic rubber out of garbage . . .' And later, after the New York *World-Telegram* stopped calling her a Red spy queen and

174

began describing her as striking and blonde Liebling took to referring to her as 'the Red blond spy queen.'"

And suddenly they were all young and innocent, rebellious and immortal again, as if seven years had never passed . . . Vivian told them it was rumored around the Agency that McCarthy was holding secret the name of a man now connected with the State Department who was the "top Russian espionage agent in the U.S." He lowered his voice. "Every cab driver in town knows who it's supposed to be—Owen J. Lattimore, director of Johns Hopkins School of International Relations. Good God. He just won't stay down. He's a master at making headlines. He's already backed off on the business about fifty-seven card-carrying Communists in the State Department, he hasn't named *one,* but he goes rushing on. He's even going after General Marshall himself, for God's sake . . ."

Washington, too, according to Vivian's father, he told them, had surely none of the charm of the age of FDR. He told them about a party that he and his father had attended at the home of the famed "hostess with the mostest," Perle Mesta. They could picture Sam Prescott shuddering when he received a noisy and robust greeting from the lady bedecked in black lace and blinding diamonds. Sam and Vivian were the guests of a woman who had made a science of flattery and spectacle, used all her money and brains to pull off the biggest social coups that Washington had ever seen. The bigger the better was her credo. Vivian went on about the enormous Black Sea sturgeon that was flown in especially for dinner the evening the Prescotts were invited. "It had been prepared in the largest oven in Washington and brought in whole on a silver platter that required four men to carry it." Several salesmen glared at the animated group before sneaking out into the humidity. Vivian finally brought his news of the rialto to a conclusion, and they waited, knowing that he had a purpose behind this rendezvous. "In Washington the word is that McCarthy's for Saint Elizabeths," he said, referring to the mental institution that served the nation's capital.

Mush seemed to be embarrassed at having been fired so Vivian drew out the Donahues, neither of whom seemed particularly enthusiastic about their work. They wanted, instead, to talk about Vivian's "adventures." Pat said, half seriously, "After all, you're still our hero." So he told them of the road he had traveled since London that had led him to his new role as an assistant to the Deputy Director of Plans—their OSS colleague Frank Wisner—of the new Central Intelligence Agency.

"And Dulles is coming on to head up the Clandestine Section, Plans, after Labor Day and he wanted me to talk to you about reenlisting." They were impressed when he told them that Plans had given the Joint Chiefs a clear warning that the Korean situation was about to erupt. "But the mean old Joint Cheats wouldn't listen," said Pat, "and the Republic desperately needs to stem the tide . . . ?"

"Something like that," said Vivian. Five years had added poise and authority to Pat's air of sensuousness.

"Is your father involved too?" Tim had said almost nothing up to now.

Vivian stared down at the table. His tea was cold. "No," he said, and changed the subject, mentioning instead old OSS friends who had come on board, and launching into "the opportunity for people with your background."

"What can *we* do?" asked Pat, catching Vivian's enthusiasm but still uncertain about where she and the others would fit in.

"We need the best we can get," he answered, his eyes meeting theirs and pausing separately on each of them, "and you're it. We've got to take the lies that Stalin is circulating and smash them . . . smash them with information, circulate the truth in every known language!" His fist came down hard on the table and he startled even himself with his passionate tone, but he decided not to spell out to them the blank check that the Hoover Commission had written for Dulles and the Directorate of Plans:

> There are no rules in such a game. Hitherto acceptable norms of human conduct do not apply. If the U.S. is to survive, long-standing American concepts of "fair play" must be reconsidered. We must develop effective espionage and counterespionage services. We must learn to subvert, sabotage and destroy our enemies by more clever, more sophisticated and more effective methods than those used against us. It may become necessary that the American people be acquainted with, understand and support this fundamentally repugnant philosophy.

176

Instead, he said, "This is war," and then more calmly, "and you're needed in Washington . . ."

He realized that he was grateful to have had a subject to divert the conversation from his father . . . Vivian had not spoken to his father, or rather Samuel Adams Prescott had refused to speak to his son, since the summer of 1948. Vivian had been so bitter about the Truman Doctrine and its implication of nuclear blackmail that he had agreed with his father that to work for World Federalism and world peace and then turn around and support an atomic saber rattler like that "processed puppet of the Pendergast machine" was, in Senior's words, "ambulatory political schizophrenia." Vivian shared his father's concern that men Sam had known and respected for years were being fired, hounded, red-baited into desperation while the little man from Missouri seemed to be loading up Washington with party wheelhorses, but when Sam said that he intended to work quietly for Henry Wallace, Vivian told him that he was a fool, that the Wallace insurgency was doomed to failure—the fate of every American third party. To be successful, Wallace was dependent on the forces of the labor and liberal communities, but they had already, in fact, departed to do battle in the Cold War. They did this, he felt, with the same enthusiasm that a former zealot who has become an atheist turns on the church . . . and this left only the Communists and a few irreconcilable pacifists like Sam Prescott clearly in the Wallace camp. With great sadness Sam stood by and saw, one by one, his friends in the intellectual community embrace the cause of the Cold War. The only leftovers were a few like himself, militant Negroes and diehard intellectuals who risked much in that McCarthy era by voicing their support of Wallace.

When Vivian informed his father that he intended to work for Dewey, Sam's jaw fell slack, and when he heard the explanation of Vivian's intended "work" he nearly wept . . . Vivian had met with a number of Colonel Donovan's veterans from OSS who had been organized as a continuing discussion group by Allen Dulles. By the spring of 1948 Dulles, Wisner, Chase Harvey and other senior men were openly expressing their fear that Truman was becoming a captive of the military, that Dewey was being perceived as a war hawk when in fact he was not. Dulles's point was that Dewey, with whom he had worked in OSS, believed in paramilitary and political approaches to the Soviet as against Truman's atomic bomb tactics which would soon blow them all to hell. In response to Vivian's skeptical questions Dulles came down hard: "You have several choices. One, pack up and leave the country; two, go round the bend and vote for Wallace; three, vote for the mad bomber himself; four, support a man who worked with *us* all during the war."

"When, where?" Vivian had demanded. "I never met him."

Dulles puffed away and let those who didn't know in on Operation Underworld, the marriage of convenience made in Washington . . . Roosevelt had been having trouble getting U.S. merchant ships loaded on the New York docks. At the same time organized crime was having its own troubles. Its titular head since the arrest of Lucky Luciano, Meyer Lansky, was trying to unite the Italian Mafia under his Jewish leadership. Lansky acknowledged the teachings of the Harvard School of Business and insisted that the sons of his "associates" learn the lessons of monopoly capitalism by actually attending the most prestigious colleges of the Ivy League. All of which was the genesis of that new super-corporate organization, "the Syndicate," that changed every area of American business and politics as well as crime. Its members owned the controlling interests in new resorts and leisure industries across the land, and the common benefit to everyone involved became apparent over the issue of the docks. To solve the problem of Fascist sabotage against U.S. ships and to complete the formation of the Syndicate, there was only one solution—Roosevelt's pardon, through Dewey, for Luciano in exchange for the help of the mafiosi in getting the ships loaded . . .

So Dewey had been their man, Dulles stressed, and if he became President it would mean that the intelligence people would replace the Joint Chiefs at the doorway to the atomic arsenal. Dewey was obviously going to win anyway so that their little planning group would have to move early, fast and provide impressive funds. At least one million dollars . . .

"And where will you get that much?" Sam Prescott demanded.

"We already have it. It came from a group of hotel owners who—"

"It came from organized crime." Vivian had never heard his father raise his voice in such fashion before. They were in Sam's Central Park South suite in Manhattan. A bachelor again, he had discov-

ered the late Mrs. Samuel Prescott on the rug in front of the fireplace, *en flagrante,* with the young couple she had hired as butler and maid. Vivian had not seen her since 1946, had not returned several telephone calls.

He had met Nancy once for lunch at Schrafft's after she telephoned. She seemed concerned that he not think badly of her, but there was no hint in her gestures or words that she even remembered the night on Deer Island. She also looked much older. Vivian decided that Nancy was one of those women who do not age well, as if the reality of time had taken its revenge. The old, inexorable equalizer. He did not guess that she was already dying of cancer.

"Vivian, you intend going to this gopher-faced automaton as the Dulles brothers' errand boy, carrying a paper bag full of thousand dollar bills fresh from the brothels and narcotic parlors of America? Are you crazy? The Dulleses are the agents of the Rockefeller family; Allen is out of Cromwell and Sullivan, for God's sake, the Rockefeller law firm. What are you getting yourself into?"

"Well, who's backing Henry Wallace? The Boy Scouts of America? Dad, aren't you forgetting the rats of your own father's generation? Except for grandpa . . . look at his contemporaries . . . Vanderbilts, Morgans, Goulds . . . pirates all, I don't have to tell you . . . Someday there'll be a Lansky Library in downtown Wilmington . . ."

Sam slumped in his chair, closed his eyes and mumbled what Vivian thought was ". . . God help us all . . ." Then suddenly he sat upright. "You red-bait *me?*" He was nearly trembling with anger. "Vivian, why do you have to do *anything* more than working for the Federated Peace Program?"

"Look, dad, if you have actually seen and done what I—let me finish, please—you would not be so outraged at what comes down to an ordinary political ploy to influence a candidate who as President will have the power to choose strategies that involve selective and surgical responses to aggression rather than nuclear holocaust. Munich. Can't you remember *Munich?*" It was then that Sam Prescott nearly wept in frustration as Vivian walked out.

Weeks later Vivian had received a short note from Rudolph Mann from Yale telling him that the "lesser of two evils was still evil." . . .

"I have to get to work," Tim's voice interrupted Vivian's reverie. "I have to see my lawyer." Mush pushed back his chair.

Vivian looked at his former comrades in arms. I need them, he thought . . . "Mush, can you have dinner? I'd like to help with this mess you're in."

"I have a meeting with a doctoral candidate out at the university —eight dollars an hour, don't scoff—but I could meet you here around ten. How long are you in for?"

"Probably till Wednesday. I thought maybe Pat would give me a tennis lesson. Ten's fine."

"It's too hot to play tennis but we could talk awhile. I don't go in until four today."

"Fine. Well, Tim, I'll bring Pat a little more up to date and you two can discuss the options. I may say that trained personnel like yourselves would come in at around G13, the equivalent of a major in the service.

"Well, I don't know, Viv. But it's great to see you. I'll see you later, honey. Mush, I'll walk you to the el," Tim said.

And Vivian and Pat were left alone in the almost deserted coffee shop.

Pat sipped ice water. "Have you read the Kinsey report?" Her green eyes couldn't hide their twinkle. The freckles across her lovely Irish face were suntanned into a sheen of health.

"No, tell me about it. As if I could stop you."

"Well . . . first of all men really start early . . . especially among the so-called lower classes. By the time they're in their mid-teens most of them have had a lot of experience . . . And it's not true what the middle class says . . . they talk about not engaging in premarital sex but do it as much as all the others. Oh! And most men have affairs outside their marriages . . . let's see . . . masturbation and homosexual activities are much more common than you'd expect . . . and though I never had a head for figures it seems that an awful lot of people are, uh, doing it . . . "

It made him feel good just looking at her. "How about you? Do you swell the statistics?"

"Oh, I'm a swell statistic, for sure." She paused, a faint smile pulling at the corners of her full lips, her slightly buck teeth glistening. "No, I've been faithful all these years. Make love two and a half

180

times every week." She stopped again and her voice was slow. "Also masturbate occasionally, remembering you and us . . ." He reached under the table for her, and she gripped his hand. "Can we get out of here?" she said.

"Yes. Let me take another room. I'm pretty sure that good old seven-twelve has a hidden microphone. The agency likes a record of these job interviews.

"Is it bugged?"

"Yes."

"Why don't you ask for the honeymoon suite?" . . .

In the new room she undressed him. "Let me. You know, our statistics are pretty sad . . . every five years." There were tears in her eyes. He felt a rush of tenderness and helped her with the shirt buttons, then began to disrobe her. She was tanned except for her breasts and buttocks and lower abdomen. For a moment they just hungrily took in the sight of each other. Then he brushed the wiry red hair curling up from between her legs, his fingers touched the moisture from the lips of her vagina. As always with him, her nipples were instantly hard.

They could not wait. She wrapped her arms around his neck and he gripped her buttocks, picking her up and slipping her down onto him. His long, muscular legs braced as he arched his pelvis. She clung to him, making low sounds . . . half of passion, half of grief . . . "Oh, Viv, please, please don't leave me again," and his response was strangled as he came into her, then carried her to the bed and lay down, still inside her. In the air-conditioned room the perspiration poured off them as they continued to stroke and feel, then slowly touched each other as they made love again, side by side, both of them watching each other's hair and flesh merge and return like two parts of the same living organism.

Toward evening they lay quietly and talked, and the plan seemed to evolve itself as a fire engine going west shrieked somewhere in the streets and out in the killing heat of the Loop the representatives of Schenley and Pabst now began to sneak into Harvey's and the Blackhawk and the Rail and Henrice's and Maurici's and all the other entrances into private worlds where a salesman could find some refuge from the city and the heat . . . Vivian was saying, "These are bad times, and they're going to get worse. There's a shit storm coming"—he rarely used such language—"you'll come soon . . ."

Yes, she would come to Washington to look for a house while Tim finished the contract he was working on for the Chicago Park District. As they talked she held onto his sex, an exterior muscle or a heart at rest sleeping in her hand, but when she told him that she loved him and would come to Washington soon, it stirred like a beast rousing. She climbed on top. "*À la mama* is good, no?"

"Oh, yes. And *à la papa,* too. No?"

"I love you."

"I love *you.*"

The bed began to creak again, as outside in the melting streets the whores were appearing, spotting their salesman customers, bringing on the night.

After Pat left, Vivian showered, walked around the corner from the hotel to Moore's and ordered farmer's chop suey, their specialty of a big bowl of cottage cheese and sour cream dotted with fresh green onions and radishes. From there he strolled across the street past the guarding lions and into the Art Institute.

In the Niessen Wing was a small showing of ancient Grecian pottery. Here was clarity and action, no subjectivity or arcane psychology, only frugal speed and motion. The riders seemed to grow out of their horses as they raced forever around the circumference of the clay. Circles, Vivian thought, staring as if mesmerized at the earth-colored imitations of action of twenty-five hundred years ago . . . circles, the eternal return, the cycles of finitude that Professor Mann had talked about. Mann, whom he had not seen since the break with his father. Somehow, he did not know how, like the Attic jockey he would return, round the shape of his life, back to everyone he had passed. Which was why he felt that Mush Hollander, along with Tim and Pat, would come to Washington? . . .

Later Vivian told Mush outright that if he would come in as his aide in the Directorate of Plans that he would insulate him from the domestic witch hunt that was going to get worse, and he repeated his words to Pat, "There's a shit storm coming, Mush." And went on, "I mean, between people who look toward the Atlantic and the neo-imperialists, as you'd call them, who say that somehow

182

we lost China and want a preemptive strike and I strongly suspect they're going to get it unless people like you come back in. Philby's there, you know. He said to tell you that it's 1938 again . . . I see him for lunch occasionally, snide bastard, but he's helpful. We're working together with MI6 on some behind-the-line operations in Albania and other Soviet bloc countries. Philby says that it's your cup of tea. But you need to come right now, Mush, so the Company can surround you with the whole Dulles iron guard . . ."

Mush listened. He looked drained, almost wasted. But there was still a certain strength and intensity in his eyes, power and endurance in his square, flexed hands. He said that he had broken up a relationship with another teacher after he was suspended . . . "Lucky in politics I've always been . . ." and so there was really nothing holding him to Chicago except a few remaining aunts and uncles . . . "Jews without money, Viv, all over, from Dempster Avenue to Howard Street. The Negroes are starting to migrate west now so the Jews are moving north and the mayor's machine plays the marching music. The whole system—no news—is rotten to the core, just like Stalinism is rotten to the core . . ." He would not let Vivian interrupt, insisted on spelling out his world view for the record, which was the tip-off to Vivian that Mush would be joining the company. He talked about the Marshall Plan as a form of disguised imperialism, a cover by American Intelligence to buy European politicians to fight the socialist parties in their own countries . . . "Okay, maybe it's doing some good, but how much can it really do when it's so loaded down with those damned Madison Avenue plastic types?" As for labor, unions were much more powerful than they had been prior to the war, so their fight centered on preserving wartime gains and not just on fighting for their right to exist. But there was no party responsive to their needs, and Mush talked with intensity about the necessity for them to regard themselves as a major political power.

"The Marshall Plan is politically shortsighted. What we should be encouraging is the development of *independent* parties and unions in Europe, let the Russians be the bad guys trying to set up puppets. Oh, hell . . ." Mush got up and started nervously pacing the room . . . "Capitalist ideology . . . Stalinist method, a deadly combination, and confrontation. And the CIA is spreading over Europe, doing the very thing they and the liberals blame Stalin for

... And while we're on the subject, I'm still not happy about your meal ticket, Gehlen. You took care of him, all right, definitely in the style to which he was accustomed . . ."

Gehlen, accompanied by Vivian, had arrived in Washington August 22, 1945, attired in the uniform of a general of the United States Army. In a series of meetings that took place among himself, Dulles and Donovan, he had laid out the surrender conditions he was offering the Americans.

Vivian as translator became the necessary third man. Now he tried to explain the deal to Mush . . . "Gehlen's proposal was for us to pick up his organization and incorporate it into our own intelligence system. He would personally guarantee loyalty to the cause of anti-Communism, and he held up his store of secret information as proof of his present and future power . . . He set up four conditions in exchange for his cooperation. First he was to have control and autonomy within his organization. Second we had to agree to use his talents only against the USSR and the East European satellites. Third, when a new German government was set up the Americans would install him and his ORG as its official central intelligence agency and cancel all his commitments to the United States. Fourth, he would never be asked to do anything he considered to be against the interests of Germany. That's it."

"Not quite." Mush's laugh was dry. "I know for a fact that the Gehlen ORG is dependent on the White Russian counterrevolutionary Andrei Vlassov. The logic of the situation is foolproof—in the time of Trotsky there's General Vlassov and his anti-Bolshevist army and spy ring. Later this apparatus is assimilated into the Gehlen organization. Then when both the Russian and the Nazi armies of spies go down together, they both jump to the Americans. Vlassov first belongs to Gehlen, then Gehlen belongs to Dulles! So we have a czarist spy ring inside a Nazi spy ring inside the American Central Intelligence Agency. And this is how, I presume, we're to get knowledge about our enemies—the Soviet Union and East Europe . . . on the impeccable authority of the czarists and the Nazis who are installed at the center of our *own* intelligence system. Jesus, Viv . . ."

Mush sat down and went on more calmly. "It still could happen here, you know . . . The big question is whether or not we have an overwhelming stake in the perpetuation of military power, and is this vested interest being given more and more of a voice in our government? The elite of this country have become militarized civilians who favor the military establishment because they see it as invaluable to the objectives of the cold war. And while their own careers may not directly be tied to any of this, their law firms, banks and corporations *are.*" Mush sounded like Sam Prescott, Vivian realized . . . "One last point, Viv. Bernard Baruch's plan for atom bomb control is guaranteed to provoke a Russian refusal and we're going to go on being petrified of the shadow of our own bomb . . ."

Vivian stopped trying to answer or comment. Mush was up again and pacing, sweating through his shirt, growing more angry the longer he soliloquized. The country seemed to be going into a nervous breakdown. Fathers were being torn apart from sons, people were flushing letters down the toilets. Paranoia was rampant on both sides of the iron curtain as people who had been involved in controversial activities were disappearing or mysteriously dying and/or killing themselves in shocking numbers. Newspaper headlines glared:

HISS CIRCLE DOUBLE SPY DISAPPEARS
WITHOUT A TRACE
HUNGARIAN MINISTER RAJAK EXECUTED FOR SO-CALLED TREASON

And so while "Russian-style" justice was being reported here, America was also busy with its own purge: Defense Secretary Forrestal, while staying with the Harrimans in Florida, had a nocturnal hallucination that he was being chased by Russian invaders. . . . A short time later he was found dead beneath the window of a Washington hospital . . . A State Department employee slit his throat after J. Edgar Hoover started to come after him . . . MANGLED BODY OF STATE DEPARTMENT EMPLOYEE LAURENCE DUGGAN FOUND IN MANHATTAN SNOWBANK . . .

Mental wards were filled with paranoid cases who had in common three fantasies—they were being chased by "the Russians," "the bomb" and "the FBI."

When Mush had subsided there was silence until Vivian said, "Mush, there's only one thing worse in America right now than a Communist, and that's an *ex*-Communist." Mush, in spite of himself, broke out laughing. "That's the first time I've heard you really laugh in five years," Vivian said. "We have got to hang together —no, seriously, there can be an alternative to the extremists on both sides, a third force. That's why *I'm* in it—"

"Yeah, war against peace?" They both laughed again.

"No, war against *war*. That's the third force. Colored neither red nor brown, as in Nazi Brown Shirts."

"Neither red nor dead?"

"That's right. Somewhere between the Roundheads and the Cavaliers, the Atlanticists and the Orientalists, the Communist Manifesto and the Truman Doctrine—"

"Is that what you call a third force? Well, it's an idea."

In the streets the sirens knifed through the sweltering night.

"Mush, will you join the Agency?"

". . . Okay."

Pat arrived in Washington on August 1. Vivian had taken a furnished single-room apartment for her down the block from the Supreme Court on Second Street, N.E. But her nights were spent in Georgetown, in his apartment. There, on good clay courts, they played their tennis, becoming the most sought-after doubles team in that posh suburb. In the evening they had quiet dinners with discreet friends, and made love as if they would never again be together after January when Tim was scheduled to arrive.

"Face it," Pat said one day on the courts, "there are problems. I mean, Tim's not here now and you're officially supervising my training, but what about after January? Besides, Tim isn't stupid, in fact in some ways he's brighter than either of us. Suppose he finds out?"

"Suppose he doesn't?"

Vivian turned a tennis ball under his foot. They sat alone between sets, sipping orange drinks.

"That's worse . . . because then the choice for . . . this is ours."

"Pat, sometimes I think you want to be found out . . . no matter what the pain for, among others, Tim . . ."

"You know, Vivian, sometimes you're a little too clever . . . you do remember what love is, don't you? I assume that my husband loves me as much as you loved your wife—oh, Jesus, I'm sorry."

Vivian closed his eyes and tilted his face up toward the sun.

"Okay, I'm a kind of son-of-a-bitch, didn't you know that?"

"You used to—"

"A real son-of-a-bitch. With a few redeeming qualities, maybe, but still a not altogether nice guy. So be warned."

"Now he tells me. I don't believe this I'm-a-bastard pose of yours any more than I do the golden hero who was born full-grown behind the lines in Europe. You're a man . . . like Tim. I'm a woman. We all have feelings, and needs. So let's cut down a little on the rhetoric and try to—"

"Look, Pat, I don't know. Maybe it *would* be better if Tim found out and there was a showdown. I don't know. Whatever happens, happens. I'll go on loving you or needing you—if you like that word better—whether we're together or not . . . Enough . . . let's play tennis. Some good clean sport . . . ."

They found an inexpensive house for her and Tim just over the Virginia line. While discussing the desirable number of bedrooms she told Vivian, "Viv, I plan to have a child in the next few years." He nodded, gray eyes smoky and distant.

Her days Pat spent in orientation at Central Intelligence, where her past training and quick grasp soon gave her an overview of the blueprint of America's new secret service. Mush Hollander arrived in mid-August and the two spent their time together mastering the map of secrecy. In the Plans division of the Clandestine Section, Pat and Mush, and later Tim, were to work with Vivian on the covert action staff.

The Agency was cramped into and spilling out of the old OSS complex on E Street. The building itself was really a group of four old structures known as "the hill" that bordered on an unused brewery and sat almost unseen because of the cover of dead weeds and underbrush, enclosed by a barbed wire fence.

Within, however, it was alive with the buzz of reunited friends, the élan and excitement of World War II awakened once again in the nervous systems of the new Cold Warriors. . . .

The other recruits seemed decades—though they were only a very few years—younger than Pat and Mush. The strain that appeared around the students' eyes was not the result of the private and public battles one fights in a world war, but of the rigid screening and training process they had recently passed through as new members of the Company . . . First, a rigorous battery of tests, academic and behavioral, had to be passed; then, for many, the Russian language had to be learned, hours and hours of sitting inside a cubicle listening to tapes; next, they were submitted to a series of questions while hooked to a polygraph, or lie detector . . . "Have you ever had any homosexual relations?" . . . and finally, physical training that made a marine combat course look like lawn bowling.

Vivian personally introduced them, when it was in order, to the other ten slash two (10/2) people. The date, October 2, referred to the formation of what had become Covert Action by Dulles and his team, out of which had also grown the Dewey discussion group in 1948, when Vivian had first been invited to participate. The corridors were full of people who because of secrecy and compartmentalization not only did not speak to but usually did not look at each other.

"A nightmare," Mush complained, but there was no doubt that he was glad to be active and working again. He had looked up several old friends in the D.C. area and, whether or not he suspected that Vivian and Pat were lovers, on occasion the three of them did go out together after work and then, usually, to Vivian's large flat, where Vivian enjoyed preparing delicious meals.

On Thanksgiving Tim flew in for a visit and Vivian played host. He roasted a carefully chosen turkey stuffed with walnuts and wild rice. The sweet potatoes were whipped to a soufflelike consistency and just barely topped with brown sugar and spice. He cooked his own cranberries and painstakingly strained them through cheesecloth. Pat's pumpkin pie sat in a flaky crust that she had labored over, rolling pin in hand, for hours. "Let somebody else do *something*," she had ordered him finally.

By Christmas, because of their war record in Europe, Mush and Pat were considered fully briefed and ready to work. Even Mush was impressed with what he had seen of the Agency's third force. Besides its stated objective of protecting freedom in general and young people in particular from the other forces of fascism and Communism, Mush was most impressed with its operational efficiency . . . First, all employees were divided into two categories— the "Whites" and the "Blacks." The Whites worked openly, maintained their true identities and engaged primarily in research activities. They took specialized postgraduate courses, read reports

188

of professional groups or scientific organizations and, in fact, virtually every Communist publication available. What characterized their work was its compartmentalization and the expert attention afforded to the most minor, seemingly innocuous detail. One White rarely knew what another White was working on, even in the adjoining office. Secrecy was the ultimate byword—the whole and the sum of the parts known only to the Director himself. The technical facilities available to help the researchers Mush found overwhelmingly sophisticated. Photographic equipment and computers as well as human technicians who possessed the finest expertise in the world were all at their disposal.

In the Black division were the cloak and dagger people who in order to become agents had first to acquire an entirely new identity. If one was sent abroad, he took on his new personality and country as if it were a second skin, and never had far from his reach those little white pills that carried within them the seeds of destruction for either the old or the new identity, in case either should be threatened.

Vivian and Mush, the Donahues and their friends would have to walk a tightrope, because Plans itself was a world divided. Plans was the Black side of the Agency but within this clandestine twilight zone there were those, like the Prescott group, who were willing to use illegal operations *abroad* to stop tyranny. But there were others—perhaps the majority of the OSS Old Boy team—who believed that the war had never ended, only that the enemy had changed. These officers—the hawks, the hard-liners, the "Animals," Mush would later call them—were dedicated to the blackest operations abroad *and* at home. Theirs was an almost desperate pride. They were self-styled men of *action,* and they peddled their powerful narcotic all over the Agency and the rest of the government.

Covert briefings began in earnest in December and Mush was surprised and pleased to learn that what he called the Dulles-Prescott elements of maturity in Plans were looking for a way to stop General MacArthur from starting a world war. To the hawks, these elements were traitors. But in this case Dulles backed them.

The CIA had played the part of the scapegoat in the battle between MacArthur and Truman. The imperious general launched his ill-fated home-by-Christmas offensive, ignoring the information he was provided by CIA about the Red Chinese buildup of troops, thereby placing in peril the UN forces. Mush saw this as pure racism on MacArthur's part . . . he refused to see the Chinese as anything other than opium addicts and houseboys, Mush felt. "They say that orientals think life is cheap . . . MacArthur makes Churchill look like a piker, sending those guys in there to be slaughtered . . ." his self-righteous rage continuing in the way it had in the old days when the OSS cause had been primary.

The massive Chinese buildup was continuing and a secret war was in progress against them. Agents were being air-dropped within their borders in order to train the "natives" in the refinements of "secret codes, forging documents, psychological warfare, guerrilla tactics and demolition." Formosa too was providing access to the mainland, from which the CIA could launch attacks; there they operated under a thin cover organization called Western Enterprises, Inc.

Mush became aware that the CIA was less meaningfully busy in other parts of the world as well, engaging itself in various actions such as trapping King Farouk's urine as it flowed through the pipes in the men's room of a Monte Carlo casino . . . "To know the exact state of his health is for some reason important to them, and a complete urinalysis will no doubt provide the clues." Mush paced about Vivian's apartment, dodging Pat's well-aimed pillows. "Damn it, we've got to stop that MacArthur," Mush intoned. "If they'll let us play tricks with Farouk's urine they'll certainly let Scott, and Hunt and your friend James Jesus Angleton . . . every one of your fellow Bonesmen in fact . . . make all the dirty movies they want."

Vivian laughed. By "dirty movies" he knew that Mush meant the number of cases in which the Agency had wanted to bring down an official or two of a third world country. Simple blackmail was all that was required: a few out-of-work Hollywood actors, some old intelligence pros with propensities for theatrics . . . a prostitute or two . . . Makeup was especially important, the new techniques could make anyone look like the man whose head was wanted. That, and a carefully angled camera shot of the fake notable at play was all it usually took to bring down a high official.

"Gathering intelligence is one thing," Mush went on, "but

sometimes, Viv, goddamn it, provocation is another—torture another still."

It didn't take Mush long to understand that if the Agency, under "Beetle" Smith's direction, was supposedly divided into two sections—Intelligence and Plans—it was also true that Plans itself was divided, its Black operations at times as innocuous as the Farouk caper, at other times far less so when in the hands of the assassins called the Animals, who in deadly seriousness were engaged in trying to start World War III, which they considered a most noble objective. Mush had heard also that the Animals had their friends and protectors at the highest political and corporate levels, and even though most of his friends scoffed at anything quite so melodramatic, Vivian (while he too pretended to scoff) knew otherwise. He remembered his father and FDR, and the last-minute suppression of the junta that had almost come to power. . . .

Tim was expected to arrive during the first week of the new year of 1951. On Christmas Eve Pat told Vivian that she was pregnant. On Christmas day Mush told Vivian that he had discovered the answer to the major question confronting CIA: whether or not the Soviet Union had an espionage ring in the United States capable of stealing the secret of the atom bomb.

"I *am* Catholic, you know."
"I know."
"I'm carrying *your* baby, as Miss Marsh used to say."
"Who?"
"Oh, shut up, Viv. I can't divorce Tim and I can't abort a baby and I can't have it, either. Oh, my God—"
"In point of actual fact, as Philby says, you could do any of the above. You *could* divorce, abort, or bear it—"
"Let's talk about what *you* could do. You could—"
"I'll tell you what I can do. I'm prepared to stand by—well, what word would you prefer?—I'll support *whatever* decision you make. I love you, Pat."
"That's all I wanted to hear . . . I slept with Tim at Thanksgiving, so it's at least *possible* . . . just give me a few days to think about it . . . you *do* love me?"

"There isn't any atom spy ring." Since coming to Washington Mush Hollander seemed to have regained the concentrated intensity that had so impressed Vivian in their beginning years in London. He was down to 188 pounds, decisive, focused, a different man from the hounded and failed Communist in Chicago. As promised, Dulles and Wisner had pledged to protect Mush from any McCarthy attempts to smear the Agency through him. It was no secret that Allen Dulles would soon replace General Smith as Director of Central Intelligence, to be the new DCI. Dulles was going up and "McCarthy," promised Frank Wisner, Vivian's boss, "McCarthy is going down."

"What do you mean?" Vivian stared at Mush.

"First of all," Mush said, "there isn't any secret *to* steal. Next, there isn't any ring as identified by the FBI. I mean there are KGB people all over the country, but there isn't any *American* atom spy ring of Rosenberg, Gold, et cetera."

"There isn't any ring?"

"Viv, listen, there *is* no ring. This so-called ring is the FBI's Reichstag fire. It's the opening gun of a rightist *putsch.*"

Mush expected Vivian to take him seriously and to hear him out not only because, technically, Vivian was his immediate superior, but also because of their shared experiences in London, Paris, Berlin, Czechoslovakia and all those days at Camp X with Janet. Vivian did listen, and remembered again the junta that had moved against FDR and how his father had been called to join the brain-trust—that was the summer at Deer Island when his stepmother . . . yes, he knew that it could happen in America, so he listened well into the night and no one seemed uncomfortable about Pat being there too.

"No one but you is to know that Philby will be working with us on this. He's my source for Henry Jacks, Hy Jacobson. He says that Jacks is ready to swear that he was coached by the bureau to fabricate the same atom spy ring story that Hoover later put together using Gold, Greenglass and so forth . . ."

On the spot, Vivian made the commitment—without yet telling anyone—to go with Mush to see Jacks. Despite the fact that he did not trust Philby—and that this man Jacks was no more credible than any other police informant—Vivian sensed a potential coup for his people in the agency if he could document that the FBI had put together the atom spy story as if it were a well-made melo-drama . . .

Mush was armed with a series of flow charts covering his major points. "Look at these, all the research is verified in-house at CIA by Science and Technology. The bomb is an *industry,* not a secret. Skip all these tables and charts. Here, I jotted down a sort of free-style capsule."

Vivian scanned the hastily typed slogans . . . "$E=mc^2$ . . . All matter is a dormant form of energy. For decades all over the world scientific imaginations have been centered on splitting the atom. Free exchange of information, one scientist to another. Americans and Soviets *together* thriving on this lifeblood of science, a cosmo-politan community, international. Articles translated into *all* lan-guages . . . EINSTEIN WARNS PRESIDENT of potential to create power-ful new bombs. Japan taking steps. Germany not. Hitler had counted on a short war . . . Soviets going faster . . . NONE OF THIS WAS SECRET . . . the British surged ahead . . . *they* inspired us. Roosevelt gave go-ahead—five million dollars available. PEARL HARBOR! We became the only nation with the resources to make the bomb . . . the world's great scientists at our disposal . . . secret cities built. Six thousand people to design the bomb. A scientific Shangri-La. Politicians started to distrust the scientists. They were given false names, bodyguards, politics investigated, SHADOWED by INTELLIGENCE AGENTS, mail censored, phones tapped . . . no travel. Scientists *knew* the Soviets could make one too . . . *knew* the historic peril . . . TRUMAN BECOMES PRESIDENT—no knowledge of the bomb . . . slowly learned. GERMANY SURRENDERS. BOMB TO BE DROPPED—NOT ONLY TO DEFEAT JAPAN BUT TO TERRORIZE SOVIET. What is more important, the scientists asked, the start of an arms race or knock-ing out Japan? THE LATTER WOULD START THE FORMER.

"The world is raining radioactive particles . . . AMERICAN ATOM BOMB MONOPOLY ENDED . . . 1949 . . . USSR EXPLODES . . .

"NO ONE HAD LISTENED. The traitors must be found. FBI DISCOV-ERS SOVIET SPY RING. ROSENBERGS ARRESTED AS ATOM SPIES."

Mush leaned over Vivian's shoulder. "When you're finished with that—here, Pat, here's the bibliography for my actual report, in cold sober bureaucratese."

"Mush"—Vivian shook his head—"this may be history as poetry or poetry as history, but as blank verse . . ."

Pat squeezed Mush's big hand. She was, Vivian noticed, excited. What was it, he thought, that made life take on its special meaning only in the presence of death? *Memento mori,* Professor Hewes used to intone at Yale. Poor old Hewes, dead now, and Professor Mann had already left America because of what he called "a familiar stench in the air."

Vivian leafed quickly through the summary. No spy ring! If the FBI was bluffing, the brass at Central Intelligence would be delighted to pull the rug out from under Hoover and company. The FBI had fought the CIA from the first day. Each secret service had planted agents on the other. The CIA by hindsight blamed Hoover for the nation's unpreparedness at Pearl Harbor. Hoover let it be known that CIA, like the OSS before it, was "ridden with Reds." If this Rosenberg case was made up out of the whole cloth, then Hoover could be toppled. But the Philby connection bothered him. Why was the aging Tory agent so concerned with helping the CIA?

"Mush, why is Kim fishing around in troubled waters?"

"He can tell you himself. We're supposed to see him at his place after we meet with Jacks. But old Philby's okay. Fuchs was arrested first in England so that's how he got onto it. Here's my report on Kim's information."

KLAUS FUCHS
arrested May 20, 1950:

> MI5 GIVES FBI PERMISSION
> TO INTERRO FUCHS RE:
> ATOMIC ESPIONAGE.

> ACCORDING TO PHILBY'S MI5 SOURCES
> FUCHS *CANNOT* IDENTIFY ANY AMERICAN
> CONTACTS.

> FBI CONVINCES FUCHS
> THAT HIS AMERICAN CONTACT
> IS HARRY GOLD, A PHILADELPHIA
> CHEMIST GOLD IS 5'6" TALL
> WOULD HAVE BEEN 33 YEARS
> OLD AT THE TIME FUCHS WAS

IN U.S. FUCHS HAD ACTUALLY
UP UNTIL THIS TIME IDENTIFIED
U.S. CONTACT AS 45 YEARS OF
AGE, 5'10" TALL.

HARRY GOLD
arrested May 23, 1950

GOLD IS PROBABLY PSYCHOPATHIC
PERSONALITY INFORMED JUDGE—"I MUST
BE ALLOWED TO COOPERATE WITH FBI."
GOLD WAS AND IS ANTI-COMMUNIST.

DAVID GREENGLASS
arrested June 15, 1950

GREENGLASS STATIONED AT LOS ALAMOS
ATOM BOMB PLANT DURING WW II.
ILLITERATE ENLISTED MAN, GREEN-
GLASS STOLE TOOLS AND PETTY CASH
THERE. DISCOVERED BY FBI AND
HAS BEEN THEIR INFORMANT SINCE
1945.

JULIUS ROSENBERG
arrested July 17, 1950

GREENGLASS NAMES HIS BROTHER-IN-
LAW AS MASTER ATOM SPY. GREENGLASS
AND GOLD MEET ON A REGULAR BASIS IN
INFORMANT'S WING OF N.Y.'S TOMBS
CITY JAIL TO BE COACHED BY FBI.
NAMING OF ROSENBERG AND HIS WIFE ETHEL
ON AUG. 11, 1950, IS RESULT OF
THESE COACHING SESSIONS WITH FBI AND
U.S. ATTORNEYS.

"Right," Mush said, "now Kim has much more to give you but here's what I personally have decided. Let's see . . .

One: Fuchs denies he ever identified Gold. The FBI *told him* that Gold was his American contact.

195

Two: Gold was an *anti*-Communist.
Three: Greenglass was an *anti*-Communist.

"That much we know. Is tomorrow night all right for the tref with Jacks?" . . . The term "tref," for a clandestine assignation, had not been used by any of them since the war; now they had slipped into a wartime vocabulary without even noticing. After Mush left, Pat and Vivian discussed the implications of a Reichstag fire kind of propaganda blitzkrieg by the FBI. The subject of Pat's pregnancy never came up.

The wind drove against them as they pushed down M Street, behind the Capitol at the edge of what native Washingtonians called "the colored quarter." Mush's face was set against more than the chill and the dark. Vivian knew that Mush considered the nation's capital to be a sort of colonial city. White men in charge of a "native" population—white southern men at that—no vote or redress for the citizens of the district, "colored" people waiting on tables and serving as butlers and maids, darker Negroes digging ditches and washing windows: white, colored, black, the declension of position and privilege in the District of Columbia . . .

They turned into the vestibule of a decaying brownstone. It was after 10 P.M. and the cold streets were almost deserted. They wore lumber jackets and old corduroys so that the black men they did pass assumed that they were no more than off-duty policemen looking for an informer or some "poontang."

The bell did not work on the second floor back, Jacks's apartment, so Mush knocked. They could hear a radio from inside playing Beethoven.

The man who answered the door was short and sickly looking, with heavy glasses. He wore a food-stained and out-of-fashion sweater and slacks, and was barefooted in his shrunken slippers. The apartment was a kitchen and sitting room combination with a greasy green couch that pulled out into a bed. Behind a curtain, they assumed, was the bathroom and clothes space. In the one soft chair, reading under a torn lampshade, sat a thin black woman who had obviously once been a beauty. She was missing one stem of her glasses and an absent button provided a glimpse through her faded housecoat of one shrunken breast. She was high cheek-

196

boned, perhaps some American Indian blood, Vivian thought, and her hands were claw-stiff from arthritis.

Jacks did not introduce either himself or the woman, who was in fact his legal wife, and did not invite them to sit.

"Mr. Jacks, my name is Horwitz, this is Mr. Paul. We are private citizens. Thank you for seeing us. Mr. English said that you would be kind enough to tell us a little bit about your experiences as an FBI informant for the book that we're writing. Your name, of course, will never be used and we are prepared to pay you for your time this evening."

The little man was breathing noisily through his mouth. His eyes did not seem to coordinate so that he appeared to be studying each of them simultaneously with separate eyes, though that might have been an effect created by the powerful refraction of the smeared lenses of his glasses. The woman did not look up at them; they stood no more than eight feet from her in the open kitchen area. Vivian wished someone would turn down the radio but they had agreed that Mush would do the talking. "What are you talking about?" Jacks said.

Mush looked at his note pad. "I believe you are acquainted with Mr. English?"

"Who?"

The woman dropped the book to the floor. The three men's heads turned toward her. Her glasses were at a crazy angle but they could see that her eyes were large, intelligent and full of hostility. Her voice was pure "white" with a slight Philadelphia nasality.

"You've got five minutes. Fantomas, here, is the hero of the story. I'll give you the narration, *I'll* take the money. Five hundred dollars. Now."

No one spoke as Mush counted it out on the red-and-white linoleum table top.

"Here, Dick Tracy, bring it over here."

Mush, bowing slightly, carried the bills over to her. She reached up with her arthritic claws, finger-tipped them, reached down for the heavy book and slammed the money inside it. When she did Vivian saw enough of the binding to be almost sure that it was Jean-Paul Sartre's *Being and Nothingness*. "Hyman," she said flatly, "turn off that goddamn radio." Then she said to Mush, "Let's go, Sherlock."

"Thank you, Mrs. Jacks"—she did not blink.

"You see, Albert Einstein, Jr., here, decided to change his luck some years ago. He's a great believer in change. So comrade Jacobson, himself, decided that as his contribution to the world revolution he would marry himself some sweet black pussy." The words, in her cultivated delivery, sounded especially brutal. Jacks didn't move, just stood there in the kitchen at right angles to them, breathing heavily through his mouth. The ritual proceeded.

"But, as I said, he does like a nice change. So after he lied his way into Oak Ridge he decided to start informing for the G-men. Naturally, he had committed perjury when he signed the loyalty oath and then, too, being married to a nigger, in Tennessee, put even his great powers at a slight disadvantage. So, two fine gentlemen from the FBI began to drop around every week until I informed them that they were no longer welcome. It was just after that candid conversation that little Hymie, here, was laid off from his important position as tenth assistant engineer of blueprints. So that was it until about a year ago some more fine G-men paid a call with their photographs and lists of names and tried to talk Hy, here, into playing some role in their caper about stealing the atom bomb for the Russians. But Henry couldn't quite remember giving the blueprints to Dr. Fuchs and as he's not working anyway, and not getting that good black pussy anymore, there was nothing that they could threaten to take away from him, that and the fact that Mr. Jacobsen, here, knew that if he let himself get involved I would personally have cut his asshole out with my butcher knife. Good night, gentlemen." . . .

In the vestibule a man in an old army overcoat shuffled from foot to foot to escape the cold. As they passed they saw that he was no older than they were, though at first they had thought him to be at least middleage. His black face was gray.

"Can you mens help me out? I'se a veteran. I fought at the Bulge. I ate human flesh at the Bulge . . ." Mush slapped five dollars into his hand. Back in the street they walked with the wind at their backs.

"Mush, where did Philby ever meet—"

"She works for him."

"You're not serious. As an agent?"

"No, she's temporary cleaning crew at the British embassy. They had a few belts together—she liked him, don't ask me why, he's as miserable as she is and that's—"

"But is it *true?* Was Jacks slated to play the role of Harry Gold in the Rosenberg case?"

"Kim says yes. You know he has a line into the bureau. He says he's going to give you hard evidence tonight."

"But why do we have to meet at midnight, for God's sake?"

"You know Philby. Mr. Top Secret."

Kim Philby kept an expensive duplex apartment in Georgetown near the embassy. He greeted them, cognac in hand, almost before they could knock. "I say, you chaps look cold. Here, have something." His wool cardigan was a beige sweater of beauty, his slippers were wool-lined, his silk shirt was open at the neck revealing a gray silk handkerchief tie. A lock of hair hung over his wide pale forehead and his eyes were, as always, a mixture of mockery and sadness.

They followed him with their snifters of Courvoisier into the cluttered library. The carved oak desk had been cleared—the books and papers having been expediently shoved to the four corners. A heavy wire recorder sat in the middle. Whatever Philby was saying was so swallowed as he puttered about with the spool of wire that Mush and Vivian made no attempt to clarify. It sounded as if he mumbled something about "Mrs. Hoover and her kinky waifes," whatever that meant.

But the three electronic wire recordings he played for them were clear enough. They were obviously a product of FBI wiretaps and hidden recorders. The first one was an interview with Harry Gold by two FBI special agents. Philby kept skipping the wire forward, looking for one section. At one point Gold seemed to be talking to an attorney.

HARRY GOLD: I first got involved in spying through Tom Black of Jersey City. He was a fantastic man. He coiled a pet black snake around his neck and he had a trained crow that he used to pitch marbles to. I got involved in order to get Black off my neck about joining the Communist party. I didn't want to. I didn't like *(unclear)*

FBI: Mr. Gold, could we please not—

199

HG: First I created a wife I did not have. Then there had to be children to go along with the wife, and they had to grow old—it's a wonder steam didn't come out of my ears sometimes. When I went on a mission for the Russians, I immediately turned a switch in my mind; and when I was done, I turned the switch again and I was once again Harry Gold—just a chemist. I *(unclear)*

FBI: You say you met Fuchs—can we go over it again?

HG: While riding in a trolley car one day in Philadelphia I met and fell in love with a beautiful girl named Helen, who had one brown eye and one blue eye. I tried to court her but a wealthy rival named Frank, whose uncle manufactured peanut-chew candy, beat me out.

FBI: You never told us you were married. Where *(unclear)*

HG: She felt that I was too cold *(unclear)* What she didn't know was that what made me cold all over and especially down here was the thought that if we were married and this thing came to light, what then? But I lost her anyway to someone called Nigger Nate. Later I lost my wife to an *(unclear)* elderly, rich real estate broker. I actually had no wife and twin children. I was a bachelor and had always been one— *(unclear)*

FBI: Lower your voice, Mr.—.

HG: It was my mother I lived with. My father's name was Sam and so was my Soviet spymaster. I *(unclear)* always lent other people money. Even when I didn't know them or *(unclear)* even if I had to borrow to do it.

FBI: Mr. Gold! Here, have some gum *(unclear)* We have to tie up the Greenglass thing.

HG: Yeah, yeah. Here—here's the list of twenty names you gave me. Now, first, I eliminated the least likely ten. Then I cut the list further. Finally that leaves a group of the three most likely, and lo, Greenglass is at the top. For his wife's name I *(unclear)*

"Here we go," Philby said. "Hear this."

FBI: Didn't you have some recognition sign between the two of you? Some sign?

HG: Yes, we did. I believe that it *(unclear)* involved the name of a man and was something on the order of "Bob sent me" or "Benny sent me" or "John sent me" or something like that.

FBI: Then in this case you would've had to say "Julius sent me," huh?

HG: Who's Julius?

"Who, indeed, is Julius?" Philby's tone was pure Oxford. And pure venom. "This terrible little man was chosen after the formidable Mrs. Jacks terminated her dear husband's acting career with the FBI repertory company . . . Now, here we have Mr. David Greenglass with two special agents." Philby fumbled with the machine and cursed. Finally . . .

FBI: Let's have this again. *(unclear)* You say you met Harry Gold where? Let's look at the picture again. You know he was arrested last month and confessed? *(unclear)* There's no need to protect him. He came to see you in Albuquerque in 1945, didn't he?

DAVID GREENGLASS: Albuquerque, New Mexico.

FBI: Now, do you remember when? I said, do you remember when?

DG: Not too well.

FBI: In June?

DG: Okay. *(unclear)*

FBI: Shall I put that in?

DG: Put it in.

FBI: So he came to your place in Albuquerque in June of '45. But then you told him to come back later. Because you weren't ready yet, isn't that right?

DG: All right. Put that in. But, listen, my wife wasn't in the room when this guy came to see me. She *(unclear)*

FBI: What did Gold say about who sent him? "Julius sent me"—was it something like that? Shall I put that in?

DG: Put it in. *(unclear)*

FBI: Now back to the Jell-O box. Do you remember where Gold said he got his half of the Jell-O box or where you got yours?

Philby savored more cognac. "This little pile right here is recordings the FBI made in the informer wing of the New York City jail in what they call 'Singers' Heaven.' I will give you copies to play at your leisure and you will enjoy hearing Mr. Gold and Mr. Greenglass literally being rehearsed by agents and one of the attorneys currently involved in the actual atom spy trial in New York."

Philby refreshed his snifter and commenced moving his lips again as he pushed about the desk looking for another spool of wire.

"Oh, yes. Here we have a selection from the FBI's bug in the prison visiting room where Mrs. Rosenberg is allowed to meet with

201

her psychotherapist, the gentleman with the rather heavy Viennese accent. This bloody wire is . . . ah, here now is that desperate saboteur Ethel Rosenberg." It seemed to Vivian that Philby and the black woman, Mrs. Jacks, both talked in the same style.

ETHEL ROSENBERG: . . . but I'm not crying so much now. I still have that dream though.

DOCTOR: Of the boy?

ER: The scream on the phone when I told him *(unclear)*. I'm dreaming about my mother lately, too.

D: What are your feelings?

ER: None. That's the point. *(unclear)* What's wrong with me that I still think of my mother and Davey as family? Why shouldn't I hate them?

D: Why not?

ER: Why shouldn't I hate them and love the people who've been more than a family to me? Wait a minute. I have a funny feeling right now. I feel *(unclear)*

D: Go ahead.

ER: I feel frightened, as if my mother could come right here into the prison and get me. Why can't I tell the truth about my feelings?

D: Try.

ER: What is there to be afraid of? It's the government, not my mother, that's killing me. *(unclear)*

D: Ethel, can't you let them go?

ER: I've got to. Who am I to judge anyone? I could save my children if I did what my mother says, "So what would be so bad, what would be so bad?" And Ruthie, my brother's wife? So now she's just like my mother. That's what terrifies me—that I'm just like her too. There's only one choice when the government picks your family out. Maybe if they'd come to us first I'd be Ruth Greenglass and Ruthie would have been Ethel Rosenberg. Listen, I know, I know *(unclear)*

D: So, can you let them go?

ER: Well, what difference does it make now? Who I hate, who I love? But I know that I would have made it. That's true, isn't it? . . .

D: Before you were—

ER: Before I was arrested, this summer, there was a real difference. I would have graduated, wouldn't I?

D: *Ja. (unclear)*

ER: I haven't mentioned Julius. I remember him as he looked when he was in college. And I love him truly. But the past is really gone, isn't it? Why should I hate anyone?

Philby fiddled with an ivory cigarette holder. "And that completes the performance. Quite poignant, isn't it—except for a recording here of Mr. Hoover himself, but it's of poor quality and I will spare you the longish pauses."

"Hoover himself?" Vivian was half sick from the cognac and the recording he had just overheard. Mush sat with his eyes closed. Philby's murmur surfaced to the level of audible speech.

"Oh, yes, dear boy. You see my man is one of those favored few who are allowed to go into Mr. Hoover's private home to oversee various repairs at government expense that the Director orders quite regularly. Availing himself of this privilege he managed to install a device of which *this* is the fruit, so to speak. The thrust of the recording is that Mr. Hoover and his great friend Mr. Tolson seem to be closeted with a prostitute. There is almost no sound or talking but I believe it is a fair reconstruction to say that Mr. Tolson and the prostitute are seated, fully clothed, while the Director goes about the room in his, ah, his undergarments. I believe that as he does this it is his habit to flex his muscles, because suddenly we hear the little lady begin to praise what she refers to as his physique in *the* most lavish terms. This panegyric is punctuated periodically by Mr. Tolson's much quieter but, one has no doubt, equally sincere compliments . . . But enough of such trivia. The point is, Vivian, that unless you people can stop this travesty in New York the Rosenberg couple will be sentenced to death. It's all arranged. And then, innocent or not, framed or not, they will in all probability be persuaded by Mr. Hoover to name everyone from Alger Hiss back to Franklin Roosevelt. Then, my young friends, you and all of us will be in for it. Of course my name mustn't come into it, but Allen Dulles is no fool. He *has* to say stop when he hears this . . ."

"*Stop.*" Allen Dulles banged his pipe on the heavy ashtray. He had heard no more than half of the recordings when he signaled for Mush and Vivian to draw their chairs close to the desk. Allen Dulles was, indeed, no fool. The atom spy case, he told them, had to be put into perspective. There were, he insisted, several varia-

203

bles. First, the frightening deterioration of the Korean police action. Second, the actual outcome of the trial (they were not convicted yet). Third, the upcoming presidential election. If his friend Dwight Eisenhower was elected then he and his brother Foster and their friends would be right next to the President and anything was possible, "including proving, once and for all, that that little emperor John Edgar Hoover has no clothes at all." At this figure of speech Mush and Vivian exchanged quick glances . . . impossible that Dulles should know about the other so-called Hoover sex recording, which, of course, neither of them had mentioned because they had only Philby's mumbled word for it.

"In short, we have to wait for the verdict, the election and the war. The war, gentlemen, watch the war, that's the key."

"You're going to have it?"

"Genes for red hair are recessive. There's a fifty-fifty chance that the child will have red hair. So, yes."

"What language are you speaking? What red hair?"

"Viv, what difference does the reason make? You love me. I love you. Tim and I will have *our* baby and you will be the godfather. Any questions?"

"Yes, what if it has your recessive red-headed gene *and* your *mind?*"

"Put your hand here."

"Pat—no regrets?"

"Nothing *but,* my love, nothing but."

In the spring Pat had to take temporary leave. By then Tim was a functioning member of Section C, of the Covert Action staff, and all of them had been posted on emergency basis to the Korean desk. Dulles and Wisner had put the entire staff on a war footing. The short goal was to staunch the hemorrhaging until Eisenhower could be elected and some way, any way, get General MacArthur out before he went over Truman's head to the country.

MacArthur had been vociferously calling upon the administration to recognize a state of war with the Chinese and recommended the "dropping of from thirty to fifty atomic bombs on Manchuria." He also called for a gigantic attack manned by Chinese Nationalist troops and U.S. Marines aimed at the border areas. He stated one addition to this plan. To prevent once and for all any further Communist incursions into Korea, we "should lay a belt of radioactive cobalt all along the Yalu."

Vivian and his father had long gloomy talks all during the bloody months that seemed to be leading, inexorably, to a total war. Vivian agreed with most of the elder Prescott's sad analysis . . . their reconciliation had been more or less forced on them by a shared dread of the unfolding events. It was not a happy reunion. Sam Prescott spoke for a diminishing minority:

"MacArthur and his call for unrestrained intervention are definitely a product of the cold war ideology. It has mass support because of the policies that so recently were vindicated in the big war with Hitler. We have now made Stalin . . . any Russian leader . . . the new Hitler and the official line is that we must not make the same mistake twice, never mind a slight difference between then and now—the atom bomb. When the Joint Chiefs issued the order against bombing within five miles of Manchuria MacArthur rebelled and held over the heads of his superiors the threat of the destruction of his troops in order to secure a change of orders . . ."

As they talked, father and son paced around each other in concentric circles—a practice from years of dialogue. In fact the circling was the very pattern of their relationship. Suddenly Sam stopped and stared into the fireplace.

"How the egos take over . . . MacArthur now searches publicly for a person or group to project the blame for his failure on. He's finally settled on administration policy as the scapegoat. And the President, himself, has added to the tension by telling the media that we are seriously considering the use of the atom bomb."

It was then that Vivian dropped his own small bombshell into the conversation. The CIA had been embarrassed by a number of stories in the press concerning their attempt to "get" MacArthur. According to these accounts General Walter Bedell Smith, the CIA director, tried to enlist the aid of another general, Del Valle, to downgrade MacArthur but Del Valle double-crossed the CIA and in an exclusive interview with the Washington *Times-Herald* said that he was a good American and that he could never be party to a plan to bring down "the best soldier-statesman we had ever produced." Vivian then told his father of Dulles's fury and of how

205

he had sent agents into the field actually to undercut MacArthur, whom he viewed as a dangerous threat to the United States and a man out of control. Vivian and Mush Hollander had been sent under U.S. Army cover to Burma via Nationalist China. Their mission was a high-risk ploy in the Agency's war against MacArthur, and their job was to explore whether or not the Nationalist Chinese troops were likely candidates to replace American boys in Korea . . . "You see," he told his amazed father, "the Agency hoped to be able to recommend phasing out the MacArthur army and turning the Korean police action into an all-Asian contest. When we arrived in our well-tailored tropical khakis, we found ourselves sitting in a pressure cooker of a Quonset hut engaged in a hopeless discussion with a Nationalist Chinese general, himself attired in splendid white mufti. After two hours of playing cat and mouse in broken English I finally said, 'General, exactly where is your army? This place looks like a plantation to me . . .'

"He smiled warmly at us and actually said, 'Oh, they're workin' in the fields. You know it takes money to run an operation like this and so we've gone into agriculture to make some . . . we're growing opium.' You see, the Nationalist Chinese in Burma had quickly gotten tired of fighting and settled in, almost from the start, to grow opium. They began by chasing the native Burmese off their own land, cultivated it with opium and supplemented the fortune they made by selling American arms and ammunition to the Chinese Communist guerrillas who operated in the area . . ."

Vivian and Mush had returned from Burma impressed by the hopelessness of the situation there. The Agency quickly picked up on their gloomy spirits, the general political climate reflecting the dreadful winter that had befallen Korea with large masses of cold air from Siberia sweeping over that embattled country and armies doing battle in sub-zero cold . . . "As the end approached," Vivian summed up, "The agency signed off with a curt damage report to the White House. MacArthur tried his so-called massive compression envelopment against the superior forces of the Chinese. The strength and vigor of the Chinese apparently surprised him completely. They've now broken through envelopment so that our center is being wiped out and our flanks pushed back toward the sea. It was MacArthur's intelligence people who had failed not only in estimating the numbers of Chinese troops involved but in their quality and discipline as well."

206

"And so," intoned his father, "finally it was once again a failure of intelligence that lost another battle for the United States."

Not until General Eisenhower became the thirty-fourth President of the United States were the shackles cut off the Dulles team at Covert Action.

By that time Vivian and Pat's child—Terence Michael Donahue, after both Tim's and Pat's fathers—was almost two years old and Pat was now returning to the CIA as Vivian's aide. They had not made love since Tim's arrival, but both now knew that their affair would resume. That January Vivian had an operation performed guaranteed to prevent him from ever again impregnating a woman.

Pat was upset when he told her . . . "You're a reverse Catholic. 'Anything absolute belongs to pathology.' Who said that?"

"Nietzsche," he brightly responded. It didn't solve a thing.

They noted, as did everyone, how much the child Terry looked like Pat. He was a happy, beautifully formed boy with "the map of Ireland on his face," as Tim liked to say proudly. On weekends Mush and Vivian almost always came out to the Donahues' Virginia house and frequently shared the guest room, staying over both Friday and Saturday night. Vivian cooked delicious feasts ranging from stuffed duck to venison. On occasion Mush would invite one of the secretaries from the Agency out for dinner, but usually they worked part of the time and played doubles in fine weather for exercise. That was all it was, since Vivian and Pat made a most formidable team. Vivian did not invite women out for these weekend activities for several reasons. Many of the subjects under discussion were secret and even under the best of circumstances people in the world of intelligence tended to socialize among themselves. Then too Vivian's relationship with women had taken on a pattern that was more easily followed alone on weeknights in Washington. In the time since Tim's arrival and Pat's pregnancy he had reduced his relationships to ones of sexual convenience. There were any number of bright, attractive young women in the capital—a city famous for its disproportionately high ratio of women to men—and Vivian was an extremely desirable young man. In his early thirties now, he looked less the Maxfield Parrish faun-God of his twenties and more the mature Michelangelo man. At six feet one and one hundred seventy-five pounds on a lean

207

frame, with chestnut hair and a quiet but impeccable wardrobe, he had his pick of an impressively large population of young nubile women.

Indeed, so full was the agenda at Covert Action and so many were the women that Vivian fell into the practice of frequently sharing himself with two at the same time. Besides, though he didn't always acknowledge it, there was a certain blessed escape in numbers. If it couldn't be Pat . . .

Erika Swearingen, manager of the East/West Travel Agency, was a Scandinavian beauty in her late twenties. Slim, honey-haired and fine featured, she also was a contract agent for Vivian's section at Covert Action and she was an eager recruiter of young women to complete a threesome.

Sometimes Vivian was totally exhausted from overwork, especially during the hot summer of the 1952 election year. He and a staff of eight, including Mush and Tim and Pat, on weekends had had to work overtime and in strictest secrecy to undercut General MacArthur's potential for stampeding the GOP convention to the extreme right. The responsibility of Vivian's special team—they referred to themselves as the "115" group, the number of the conference room where their meetings were held—was to plant a wide range of stories, all somehow making invidious comparisons between the two generals, MacArthur and Eisenhower, in the conservative media . . .

Often during that summer, when he took no holidays, Vivian would not arrive back in Georgetown until nine or ten at night. Erika would be there waiting for him, sometimes alone, sometimes with another. With three people there was no need for possessive intimacy; no secrets, no pressure of commitment. And no guilt, no envy . . . no future.

Vivian was working day and night at the agency to invent history, with the collaboration of "elite assets" in the media and elsewhere. At night, after the relief of impersonal sex, he could find oblivion in sleep, with only the nagging fear of blackmail by the KGB. Or the FBI.

All during the presidential election Vivian and Mush were building a file on the Rosenberg atom spy case as time began to run out on appeals for a new trial, and after the couple's conviction and sentence of death. They were also laboring with Kim Philby on more Anglo-American operations behind the lines in Communist Albania, similar to the ones being run with parachute agents in China. Counterinsurgency training for foreign nationals had to be run out at the "Farm," so Tim and Vivian commuted to Camp Peary, Virginia, at least once a week, and on weekends they all were often needed to provide leadership to recruits from the Philippines, Iran, Guatemala, the Congo and some two dozen other countries, all at one time.

The "Farm" was the CIA's West Point and operated under the cover name of Camp Peary. Most of the methods taught there applied to covert action, and to a great extent training was oriented toward paramilitary activity. Graduates of the Farm found that the most coveted job openings were in the emerging nations, especially in the Far East. The countries making up the underdeveloped world offered far more tempting targets for covert action than those in Europe.

Regular members of urban police forces were trained at the Farm; probably no other program of the CIA was handled with greater secrecy than this one because of the Agency's particular sensitivity about the subject of illegal domestic operations.

One of Mush's specialties was tipping off the new recruits about the rivalries they would encounter during training. He warned them good-humoredly that their stint would be a "mixture of common sense, insanity, old-time religion, and some of the weirdest lectures you can imagine." But especially it was the cliques and infighting the trainees should be aware of; Sinophiles wouldn't be caught dead having lunch with an expert on the Soviet Union, and even at weekend parties the Russian analysts congregated only with the Eastern European analysts, and so it went. Another status conflict grew from the fact that the CIA was the last solid WASP bulwark in government. Blatant discrimination was something, Mush warned, they all must look out for. Finally, in sardonic, tongue-in-cheek fashion, Mush told the men of the long-standing CIA dress code. "We dress like Harvard men . . . regimental ties, our tweeds and flannels are worn with distinction. We wear vests beginning in October, never take our jackets off in the office and never roll up our sleeves. We don't go in for rings on our little

209

fingers either, *that* has certain overtones . . . and our cuff links must be small and simple."

During this time Vivian received regular briefings on the operations of the Fox, General Gehlen . . . The lid had to be left on so that no one could smear or blackmail the agency with charges of neo-Nazi activity, so Vivian kept these developments even from Mush, who still completely mistrusted, morally and politically, working with "former" fascists. It was a damn sensitive matter, no question.

Mush did know, though, that German industrial scions as well as Nazi military leaders had seen the handwriting on the wall clearly by '44 . . . saw too the necessity to go underground for a while and place their interests abroad in Nazi-financed firms, especially in the United States. The little German town of Altaissee was to be a jumping-off point for this operation, the point of debarkation for Nazis and their worldly goods, among which was the gold taken from the teeth of six million concentration camp victims. To leave, though, several preconditions were necessary, and one of these was the helping hand of the U. S. A. . . . .

Yes, Mush knew all of this, although he didn't let on to Viv . . . the rage was too close to the surface and even *he* was afraid to let it out to his friend . . . knew all of this and more: for example, Richard Helms, formerly with the OSS, now with the CIA and a superior of both Mush and Vivian, passively turned the teeth-gold back to Germany as soon as the war was over.

Vivian had become the major troubleshooter for Covert Action. In Dulles's eyes he could do no wrong; he was a champion and a man of action, much more so, the DCI would say, than his old man, Sam Prescott.

Though he was now the DCI, Dulles kept to his first love—"Ops," Operations Gray and Black. He knew that Vivian would be a superb recruiter for the Agency, which was why he sent him up to New Haven to talk to Bonesmen about joining. Dulles had been taken aback when Vivian, almost humorously, suggested that the old Bones mausoleum be bugged so that the recruits coming in could later be told that their errant behavior would, if necessary, be used against them. Besides, the whole idea seemed a sort of ironic change-of-pace to Vivian, a sort of comic relief. Dulles gave his consent, and was duly, if humorouslessly, impressed. Mush and Tim were included in the bugging and break-in plans.

The three of them personally went in on the July Fourth holiday. In the near dark Vivian gave his colleagues a brief tour based on humorous memories of his own "rebirth" at Bones. When they walked away in the dark, past the graveyard and the looming inscription—"The dead shall rise"—he turned away and silently said to hell with this school where he had been young, a champion who could never lose or die . . . now Janet was dead, Professor Mann had left the country in protest . . . They turned into the Law School quad, walking quietly, and Vivian mouthed the words "Bulldog, bulldog . . ." and the other two formed with their lips, "Bow-wow-wow."

The new President had felt no apprehension about moving into Washington's historic Blair House while the White House was being renovated. His move did, however, wreak havoc with the Secret Service, which saw the grand old place as possessing about the same security as a shooting gallery. Guards and agents armed with submachine guns swarmed all over the house and its grounds, but until that lazy unseasonably hot afternoon, all was quiet.

The tip-off of a Puerto Rican nationalist attempt on Eisenhower had come to Mush by way of Kim Philby. *His* source was Rob Garabedian, a stolid Armenian FBI special agent assigned to Chicago who had trained at Camp X with Mush and Vivian and had known and worked for Philby at the same time. After a meeting in Chicago, Vivian had been convinced enough to go to the DCI with the information.

Dulles, of course, had leaped at the opportunity to show up the Secret Service *and* the FBI. Later he would make certain to let the President know that Hoover's reaction to the plot had been to triple his *own* bodyguard and *not* to tell the Secret Service.

Garabedian had his informant placed high up in the mad conspiracy and was able to tell Vivian the exact time the shooting was to take place.

On the day, Vivian and Mush appeared at Blair House with only minutes to spare. Irritated Secret Service men were arguing loudly with them about the irregularity of the CIA officers being there when Vivian suddenly shouted, *"Get down!"* . . .

And then it happened. A fat White House cop found himself

nearly face-to-face with a neatly dressed man in a pinstriped suit wielding a German P-38 automatic pistol. The guard jumped out of range, already hit. Vivian and Mush started firing at the gunman and at a second man who had appeared with a Luger.

When the din subsided, one guard was dead, two injured, only one of the two Puerto Rican assassins surviving the exchange.

The foolishness of the attempt was exemplified by the fact that the two men did not even know if the President was at home that afternoon, and that he, a few hours later, would have made an easy target as he left to attend a public dedication at Arlington. The Secret Service and the FBI were wild with rage and jealousy, insisting that such a crazy scheme could easily have been disrupted long before the gunplay erupted at Blair House. But Dulles was delighted, and both Vivian and Mush were rewarded with secret medals and promotions.

The President had indeed been at home that day, peacefully napping in his upstairs bedroom. When he heard the shots, he moved swiftly and peered out a window. Mush had shouted, "Get back, get back!" The President dutifully obeyed but seemed later to be truly unconcerned by the incident. "A President has to expect those things," he said. "The only thing you have to worry about is bad luck. I never have bad luck."

After that Garabedian considered himself the Agency's man inside the Bureau.

Mush had admired Adlai Stevenson, as had the Donahues. He had been their governor in Illinois, and Vivian had met him through his father and thought him bright and wonderfully articulate. It simply made Vivian more taut to know that his father was working full-time for Stevenson's election while he, under orders, was working for a general whom he did not particularly believe in, except that Dulles and Wisner had convinced him, because the evidence was overwhelming, that Eisenhower alone was beyond the reach of MacArthur and McCarthy. What had been done to General Marshall would not be done to Ike, and Ike would stop the war in Korea and be able to negotiate with the Soviets from *strength.* "It's Ike or war," Dulles warned them. They had made themselves like Ike.

212

Allen Dulles was surely right about one thing—Eisenhower was unbeatable—and he, Dulles, was appointed Director of Central Intelligence a month after the inauguration. "And he was wrong about one thing," Mush reminded Vivian—the Rosenbergs *had* been convicted. If the new President was going to intervene then it should be done "right now." They all agreed.

On December 30 Emmanual Block appeared before Judge Irving Kaufman and pleaded with him to commute his clients' death sentences, to be carried out only two weeks hence. Much of the world had been aroused on behalf of the Rosenbergs, who still firmly insisted on their innocence, and his burden as their attorney was to introduce into the conscience of the judge the possibility that there was at least some small iota of uncertainty regarding their guilt.

Speaking for the government now was Myles J. Lane, who insisted that the alleged information the Rosenbergs had given the Soviets had indeed hastened their ability to master the secrets of atomic weapons construction, that this in itself accounted for the strong stand the Russians had taken in Korea against the United States, which in turn resulted in the killing and injuring of thousands of American boys.

The judge held firm, stating that the defendants' insistence on their innocence was indeed the most incriminating stance they could take. They obviously preferred the glory of martyrdom to naming the names of their fellow conspirators, he said. Now, with the executions a week away, the judge granted time for the condemned couple to apply to the President for executive clemency.

In a plea for her life, Ethel Rosenberg summarized her need and her husband's to hold to their declaration of innocence: "To forsake this truth is to pay too high a price even for the priceless gift of life—for life thus purchased we could not live out in dignity and self-respect."

Thousands throughout the world wrote or cabled the White House urging that the Rosenbergs' lives be spared. U.S. diplomats in Europe were so harried that the State Department was forced to prepare a special bulletin on the case to aid them in dealing with Rosenberg sympathizers. In the United States as well, support for the couple was gathering force and becoming increasingly vocal. Most of it was not based on the question of guilt or innocence but the necessity to commute the death sentence. However, the overwhelming majority of Americans continued to hold firmly to their conviction of the magnitude of the crime, and felt the only strong posture to take was that of execution.

Truman had willed the Rosenberg clemency appeal to his successor, so it was up to Dwight D. Eisenhower to act on a solution to this emotionally charged problem.

By the end of February, Dulles sent his plan, through Frank Wisner, Tracy Barnes and Desmond FitzGerald, to Vivian's section. The plan contained two dimensions of power politics: one, derail the FBI's self-serving propaganda express; two, score a worldwide CIA propaganda coup in the process of saving their lives. Dulles's emissaries made it clear that the DCI knew that the Cominform had not been running a spy ring of native Americans during the war. The Soviet agents in the United States were deep-cover penetrations, not middle-class ex-Communists. There was no "secret" to be stolen and no homegrown "ring."

First they gamed out the FBI's position for Vivian and Mush, the conversation taking place at FitzGerald's Connecticut country estate on a particularly clear winter night. Des FitzGerald was a sandy-haired, patrician-looking man about a decade older than Vivian. Skull and Bones Old Boy mold, Vivian thought to himself, wondering if in ten years he would have moved up to a decision-making level as had these senior OSS men. FitzGerald closed the library door and Wisner nodded to Barnes to fill them in . . . "The Bureau is acting on the assumption that the Rosenbergs or Sobell will panic and name big names—Communist party, U.S.A. leadership, and *then* some *dead* FDR Democrats like Harry Dexter White or living ones like Alger Hiss and Henry Wallace. Always moving toward compromising what they believe to be an exclusive club or as the British say, the Establishment."

As a former Marxist, Mush knew the ruling circle struggle being hinted at. Vivian, for his part, understood that the FBI was perceived by the leadership of the Agency to constitute something akin to a goon squad, state college graduates on the make, in short, the shock troops for new money generated by the war machine of the 1940s and again by Korea. The FBI's particular brand of snake oil patriotism and rhetoric, Dulles was fond of telling his aides over afternoon tea, was especially suited to war and rumor of wartime.

Moreover, Hoover's stripe of blunderbuss anti-Communism whipped people up so that they were incapable of focusing on the actual geopolitical threats to American interests, which were certainly dangerous enough. Now, the Bureau was reaping a propaganda bonanza from one long front-page poem of praise that drowned out all other voices. The "Old Lady," as Agency executives frequently referred to Hoover, was a past master at the game of power and image, and the threat of a fast-expanding Central Intelligence Agency was a nightmare to him.

Through his father Vivian had learned that General Bedell Smith, when he was DCI several years before, had commissioned several of the men in this room as well as others like C. D. Jackson of *Time* to approach some of America's oldest money and invite them to a carefully unadvertised meeting at the Bilderberg Hotel's grand conference center in the Netherlands. There they were to parley with their opposite numbers in industry and government from Western Europe and Japan . . . "This self-appointed group sees itself as the spirit and the conscience of monopoly capital," Vivian's father had commented, "and they see the United States as their private public relations firm and the big New York bond houses as their piggy banks." Vivian had not particularly disagreed with his father but, again, he found Samuel Adams Prescott measuring entities like the "Bilderberg group," as it was now known to insiders, against some Utopian model of capital that did not yet exist . . .

Desmond FitzGerald was summing up now, poking the low fire awake. ". . . so the Bureau figures they'll make up any names they have to in order to save their skins. I promise you that the great search for the traitors will lead home to our shop, and I'm not just referring to old Lincoln *Brigadistas* like Mush. I mean Hoover and Joe McCarthy will walk right up our spine like a ladder. The OSS boys will be turned into a roster of reds. It will go to J. Robert Oppenheimer, it will even go to Eleanor Roosevelt. So far the Rosenbergs have refused to join the chorus . . . the question is, will they hold out? Mush?"

"I don't think there's much question that they will. And if it's now possible to get permission to see them—"

"Everything's possible now," FitzGerald said. "What we propose to do is approach the Rosenbergs . . . through third parties, of course . . . with a counteroffer to the effect that, well . . . let me tell you about the third party. Through Arthur Goldberg and others we can put together a group of Jewish labor leaders, add to that several highly intelligent rabbis who have a labor or socialist background. These emissaries would inform the prisoners that they could, through Attorney General Brownell, convince Eisenhower to grant clemency and to commute the death sentence."

The fire crackled in the pause as they digested what was being suggested. "What's the catch?" Mush asked. "What do they have to do, if not confess and name names?"

"One, publicly appeal to Jews in all countries to get out of the Communist movement. Two, they would denounce the treatment of Jews in the Soviet Union." FitzGerald turned to the last page of a document that was placed in the middle of the top of a meticulously clean and clear desk. "This is the conclusion from the proposed action memo to the White House. . . . 'Date of execution should be stayed until commissioner ascertains whether or not the Rosenbergs are interested in entering into such protracted negotiations. If they are not' . . . I'm still quoting . . . 'the executions should proceed and the emissaries should observe total silence.' "

The fire snapped the edges of the logs, the house was asleep, an aging golden retriever snuffled where he lay near the warmth. After nightcaps Mush and Vivian knew that they were free to retire, to consider the Dulles-Wisner plans. Then, for the rest of their weekend stay they were to draw up operational plans for implementing what could turn out to be one of the great propaganda coups of modern history.

Such a statement from the Rosenbergs charging Russia with anti-Semitism would have the Western European Communist parties erupting in political civil war, because the anti-Stalinist sentiment on the left needed only a catalyst to explode it . . . so the Company reasoning went.

Vivian's feet stretched slightly over the scout bed against the cold wall of the small guest room. Through the lace curtains the moon shone full in the dark blue sky . . . It was nearly ten years now since his wife's death. In some ways he could hardly recognize himself as the green young man of the halcyon days at New Haven and London and Camp X. Janet was his youth, and it, like Janet, was dead. The moratorium during which he'd preached the gospel of World Federation and peace had been shot down in Korea. He felt suspended. The Agency was, perhaps, the lesser evil, and soon he would have time again with Pat, and somehow he would get the Donahues some money for the best education for the child . . . He could try to recruit better people for the Agency to do meaningful battle with J. Edgar Hoover, Joe McCarthy and the armies of the night, but there were too many senior men above for him to rise fast or far. The Wisners, Barneses, FitzGeralds, Blacks, Bissells were older and much better Company men than he. Though none of them could match his record, still they were not behind the lines now, so the premium would be on their game, theory—not practice. Vivian stared deep into the midnight sky feeling as if a piece of the armor inside him was wearing a bit thinner every day. Before sleep he saw Janet's face as it had looked at Camp X, minus makeup or falseness of any kind, and tried to remember. What had Janet whispered to him in the graveyard?

> Cast a cold eye on life, on death,
> Horseman! Pass by . . .

In the next room, a twin of Vivian's, Mush sat in the white wicker chair and stared into the winter sky at the pale, full moon. His heavily muscled frame was starting to sag, he was feeling much too old for thirty-four. In his fantasy he was physically assaulting the senior agents, Barnes, Wisner, FitzGerald. These Agency supergrade scions of the Ivy League were depending on him, Marshall Hollander, failed Communist, and failed Jew, to turn the last turn of the screw on the Rosenbergs. He hoped Vivian was different, but right now he was not sure . . . He had been a Communist, then an ex-Communist, now an anti-Communist. So who *was* he? His ex-wife was not an ex-Communist, she did not, she had said, cut and run every time the party line deviated from her particular preference. She knew who she was . . . His loins stirred as the warm ambience of her body returned to him in the clinical cold Connecticut whiteness of the country house guest room. Carmen was living with a black man now, near the University of Chicago. She was a

217

leader in the Chicago mobilization to save the Rosenbergs. She was four years older than he and looked more. She was big-boned and strong and try as he might he could not find another woman who could move him sexually in the same way. Again he thought of quitting, but where could he go? There was no Abraham Lincoln Brigade to join now, and burgling the Skull and Bones crypt at Yale was hardly behind the lines. He shivered in the cold light. I need someone to love and someone to hate, he thought, and then —well, okay, I'll be their goddamn courier but you damn well know whose interests I'm really going to represent . . . Except, of course, that was precisely the problem. Whose interests, in the end, *did* he represent? Certainly not the false god that had failed in Moscow, and not the game plan of the Agency Old Boys. Vivian's growing circle in the intelligence establishment? He guessed that was close to it, but right now his head ached too much to think on it any longer . . .

By Sunday afternoon they were pretty well set on their course. Vivian was to try to recruit his father, and together with men like the writer Sidney Hook organize a prestigious front group. These distinguished liberal and conservative leaders from the academy, labor, the clergy would announce their presence with a full-page ad in the New York *Times.* Famous scientists would be quoted to the effect that *there was no secret to steal.* Leading rabbis would be quoted on their death-house interview with the Rosenbergs and the details of their protests of anti-Communism and innocence.

"The *Times* ad," Barnes said, "will *follow* . . . this is the *point,* Mush . . . the Rosenbergs' statement about Communist anti-Semitism." Leaders of the Jewish community would be alerted to the coming news bombshell from Sing Sing and could prepare to galvanize the frightened Jewish majority into action to save the Rosenbergs. Vivian and Jim Angleton would brief the new government of Israel on the development and encourage the Israelis to appeal to the United States for commutation. "The Israelis owe us one," Barnes pointed out. "Jim Angleton gave them the information on a shipment of arms from us to Yugoslavia, and lo and behold, the boat was hijacked on the high seas by guess who . . . ? The Israelis will go along."

FitzGerald and Vivian, Barnes was saying, would bring Cardinal Spellman into the picture, and he in turn would advise the Vatican

218

that a major propaganda defeat for the Soviet was in the offing and that His Holiness should pull out the stops by putting the Vatican secret service, the Society of Jesus, into action worldwide. In coordination, Time Inc.'s C. D. Jackson would unleash the Bilderberg group's network of influence, including the CIA's potent Time-Life "assets."

At the same time Mush would be permitted into Death Row. He would represent himself as a researcher for the Committee against the Death Penalty, "if that's the name we settle on," and would "prepare the prisoners for the secret meeting with the rabbis and the others," Wisner said, adding that, naturally, the rabbis would have no idea that the Agency was in charge of the operation. "But if we don't move like lightning Hoover will put two and two together and take it like red meat to his press wolves like Winchell, Considine, Sokolsky, and who knows where the charges would stop? That's the risk we're running on this operation. So we start tomorrow and if there's any hitch we wash our hands. Mush, you have the ball. We need a winner."

Everyone in the room knew the pressure that the DCI was under. The Rosenberg case was the perfect vehicle to provide the CIA with a much needed victory. If the couple could somehow be convinced to act as rallying points around which American Jewry could gather to attack the Soviets for their hostile treatment of their people, then Hoover and the FBI could finally be revealed as the bullyboy fools they were. The Agency needed to change its image inside the Anglo-American spy empire—Kim Philby and MI6 had found them wanting.

Philby had been welcomed to the United States by both the CIA and the FBI as a top expert in "Black" activities against the left. He was meticulous, beyond reproach, and in the United States to aid in a string of Anglo-American operations aimed at Albania, which included air-dropping agents, sending them over the Greek border and landing them from submarines. Once in, however, they were only to find the police there waiting to welcome them.

Philby himself never received the blame for this costly fiasco, which left some three hundred trained men dead before it was over. It was the CIA that was accused of being too inexperienced, its former OSS luck gone bad as operation after operation failed dismally.

Yes, the Agency definitely needed a winner. How ironic that a relative outsider like Mush should have been picked for the kick-off.

Sam Prescott needed to talk to his son. The estrangement from Vivian had left him more alone than he had ever been. Nancy's death had stunned him . . . could she have known somewhere in that insatiable body that the cancer was claiming her? Now he saw her compulsive sexual frenzy of their last year together as a symptom of anguish and he blamed himself for judging her. He wanted, he needed, to talk to someone, to Vivian, about his unhappy wife who had run like a fox with her tail on fire. Apparently she had sought sex as an anodyne, or pawn to play against the White Queen of death. She'd had a rage just to live, stay alive, while he was already living in the future, in a time after his own death and even after Vivian's, and if he had no heirs, then after the demise of the Prescott line itself. The old cabinet clock by Furnish of London ticked away as Sam half listened to his son's story and remembered his two dead wives. There would be only one more woman in his life . . . mother earth . . . Increasingly, now, he found himself talking with men and women who were no longer as respectable as before under the accommodating umbrella of the United Front against fascism. He had not yet recovered from his shattering experience the month before involving the Cultural and Scientific Conference for World Peace endowed by Nobel Prize winner Albert Einstein. He had worked long and hard for a successful event, had been one of the prime movers in getting some five hundred fifty sponsors together representing every area of professional and artistic expertise in America. To him they were the best, and the bravest—they at least did not fear living in the same world with *socialists*. Or perhaps, he thought, they were at last ready to face the consequences. But the conference turned into a circus when what some felt was a State Department-created meeting was set up at the same hotel to compete for public and media attention. Outside, delegates were barraged by picketers hurling treasonous accusations at them. Inside former friends turned against each other. The fight between the intensely anti-Communist liberals and the leftists became even more bitter for taking place between old friends—it turned out to be anything but a

220

conference for peace. Lillian Hellman tried to keep faith with its original purpose when she said, "It no longer matters whose fault it is [the cold war]. It matters only that this game be stopped."

Mostly, though, the conference rooms were buzzing with the CIA personnel Vivian knew were stationed there (and his father did not), and with those who wanted to bring the conference down to what concerned them most: an attack against the Stalinist inquisition.

The conference also provided an up-to-date guide of people for the secret police—people who had not yet learned that to sit in the same room with Communists meant, in that day, to be one. Presence at the Waldorf-Astoria that March guaranteed a black mark prominently placed on all FBI files of those who attended . . . .

Now his son was asking him to engage in another version of this kind of affair with the Rosenbergs. He focused on the handsome man in front of him speaking so articulately about how this time the Agency could turn such a conference into a victory.

Sam felt his age. The Central Park South suite was decorated with taste and warmth, but it was still no good living alone here with no wife and no son. This morning's paper had been no help:

DETROIT FORBIDS VENDORS
TO SELL SUBVERSIVE LITERATURE

HOUSTON GANG HURLS ROCKS
AT COMMUNIST PARTY STATE SECRETARY

A headline on the same page with a photo of Julius Rosenberg stated:

MEMBERS OF L.A. "CRUSADE
AGAINST COMMUNISM" BEAT
(SURPRISED) INDUSTRIAL WORKERS

And finally:

BIRMINGHAM ORDINANCE SAYS
NO TALKING TO COMMUNISTS
IN NON-PUBLIC PLACES

221

Vivian nodded wearily as Sam quoted James Madison: "The means of defense against foreign danger historically have become the instruments of tyranny here at home." His pipe had gone out again: "Viv, Albert Einstein says that they couldn't be guilty. That's good enough for me." The founding fathers, and Einstein, Vivian reflected . . . the Agency would know just how to lay it all out for the newspaper ads.

As they talked it became clear to Sam Prescott that while the old relationship of father and son had fallen victim, as had so many others, to the cold war, still there might be left the basis for working together on certain issues of peace and conscience. So, as much as anything else, in the hope of maintaining some connection with his son he'd agreed to try to save the Rosenbergs because, on the key issue of guilt or innocence, not to mention the death penalty, he agreed completely with Vivian.

By the week's end the operation was well under way. Mush returned from the Ossining, New York, federal prison on Thursday night. On Friday he brought Vivian, Tim and Pat to his bachelor flat in one of Washington's unfashionable districts.

They sat around the spare dinette unit. "Julius Rosenberg just smiled and told me to save my breath. He says they haven't been active leftists for years but they aren't political cravens either. I guess we must have been crazy to think that they'd go along with this . . . but I talked to Philby last night. He had one or two ideas. There's an ex-Nazi angle to get to Dulles but that would hurt your deal with General Gehlen. But the other involves one of the government prosecutors Philby says is a pederast—"

Vivian stood, scraping back the chipped wooden chair. "Mush, Mush, just stop right there. This thing at best was a high-risk operation. Either the Rosenbergs cooperate with a full-dress statement or they go to the chair. Don't even mention Kim Philby's name to me in this affair. The Albanian situation has MI6 and our people at each other's throats, you know that. Come on, let's go back to work. I'll speak to Wisner and tell him it's off."

Mush continued to sit as the others rose. He was pale, and his lips were twisted in a grimace of suppressed pain. He felt very cold.

Later, alone in his office, Vivian and Pat planned to begin playing indoor tennis once or twice a week—after hours—as soon as the press of events permitted. (Vivian had been unfailingly kind to her boy, Terry, but no more, she was positive, than if he were only his godfather.)

They stood now, gazing at each other as if there were no such thing as clothing. She looked more attractive to him than ever. Her breasts seemed fuller under the pale green knit sweater, the slim strong legs and thighs drew him as always and, of course, the sweet symmetry of her buttocks. For the moment they were alone. He reached and found her nipples through the sweater, she cupped his groin with her hand and squeezed him with pressure. "Hi," she whispered . . . "I want to eat your pussy" . . .

"Not today, sir . . . Viv, you sit over there—*Viv,* I'm afraid for Mush. I'm going to have a drink with him after we're through here today."

"Pat, don't discuss any of Philby's crackpot schemes with him, promise me that."

'Promises, promises," she said and twitched her sweet symmetry at him as she left. . . .

She went back to Mush's place; Tim agreed that she should, that their friend was in a bad way. Mush had some sweet wine left over from some holiday and they drank a water glass of the stuff. He was pushing the wine down and talking freely. Pat had never seen him so at odds, cursing the Agency one minute and the Russians the next, and then he started in on the Communist party, U.S.A., which hadn't "lifted a fucking finger for the Rosenbergs until it was too late." He had never used such language in front of her. Mush Hollander was in great pain.

He was disgusted with Philby's plan but he told her anyway. "Martin Kahn, one of Roy Cohn's assistants in the U.S. Attorney's office, is the guy. Philby knows who his doctor is and that he was treated for rectal gonorrhea within the last sixty days. I can get or make copies of the test. We confront Kahn, with you as the lab technician—you *were* a nurse—and we . . ."

Soon, in spite of themselves, they were laughing, it was obviously so hopeless, so ridiculous. The wine was sweet and they were feeling it. Mush was still angry but tender, too, praising her as a mother and a person. Several times she almost hinted at her double life, could it be that Mush suspected? Could it be that he did not? He was like a big bear, hurt and fierce. He was suddenly very

223

drunk, talking about his wife and hitting the wall with his heavy fist. He stood there with bloody knuckles, his shirt pulled loose, his hair falling over his forehead. "Pat, they're innocent . . . It could be me . . . Julius Rosenberg told me that he and his wife are being killed by *American* fascism . . . God help us, Pat, sweet Patricia . . ."

She knew that he needed her but it was more than pity that led her to the cramped bedroom with him. Somehow she was angry at Vivian for not trying hard enough, for being so sure of her, and at herself and her own ambiguity. And she was thinking. Soon he will be in me and then I will have had all of them in me . . . Viv, Tim and Mush will have all *known* me . . . and that's good and right, because *they* are my life . . .

Mush stood swaying. He was still muscular, like an aging fullback, and he was covered by a fine mat of wiry black hair. He seemed to her a bear tied to a stake, she would not have been shocked to find wounds across his flesh. The ghosts of Spain and Buchenwald and Treblinka and the rest were all still unburied, all looming, she knew, in Mush's mind, over the Rosenbergs, and over their two young sons. And he would feel guilty about this one time with her too—what he remembered of it. "Arise, ye prisoner of starvation, arise, ye wretched of the earth . . ." He was croaking the Communist international anthem, his fist uplifted.

"Pray for us sinners now and at the hour of our death," she said, smiling crookedly at him across the room. Poor tormented beast, she thought, stepping out of her clothes. "Wait," he said. She paused, naked except for her stockings and garter belt. "My God, let me look at you. Jesus Christ, let me love you. I have to love someone."

He sank to his knees in front of her. When he looked up the tears were running down his face. Tenderly he kissed the old, faded scar the Gestapo had left on her thigh. And drunk as he was, he made love to her with a slow fierceness, converting her early pity into honest passion.

The crowd had already started to gather in New York's Union Square by the time the early morning summer glare began to pop out from behind the tall buildings. By mid-afternoon it was scorching and thousands were milling about in anticipation. The death wait had begun for this mass that had now swollen to ten thousand.

At seven-fifteen Mush hurried into the crowd. The tension in his clenched body served to blend him completely into the mood and structure of the deathwatch. His powerful frame thrust forward to get close to the makeshift podium that had been set up to allow the final pleas to be spoken and to narrate the progress of the execution. He touched lightly the shoulders of men and women in the crowd to gently move them aside. His sense of affiliation with this throbbing clot of wounded humanity was obvious: he was, after all, one of them.

Vivian also pushed his way through the throng, calling Mush's name. At the speakers' stand the microphone squawked, "Your country is sick with fear, you are afraid of the shadow of your own bomb, do not be astonished if we cry out from one end of Europe to the other . . ." The anger and grief in the familiar voice of the actor Sam Jaffe fell on Vivian like a judgment. He winced, felt as if he would suffocate. The crowd listened to the warning that had been sent by Jean-Paul Sartre from Paris. A female relative of the condemned couple was near collapse as she read a final letter to their lawyer:

"Dear Manny. Never let them change the truth of our innocence. For peace, bread and roses in simple dignity we face the executioner with courage, confidence and perspective, never losing faith . . .

"P.S. All my personal effects are in three cartons and you can get them from the warden. Ethel wants it known that we are the first victims of American fascism. All my love, Julie."

A black minister took the stand to say, "Police have opened fire on mass protests in Paris and London . . ."

Paul Robeson towered over them from the platform. He tried to lift his magnificent voice but could not control it . . . "Going home . . ."

Vivian was dripping wet now, dizzy, shouting in Mush's ear. "Stalin's dead, it's over . . ." Then, trying to steer Mush away, he shouted, "There's nothing we can do here . . . come on, let's get a drink . . ."

A gaunt man, a lawyer, was at the microphone: "Dearest sweethearts, my most precious children . . . I want so much for you to know all that I have come to know . . . Always remember that we were innocent . . ."

225

The woman standing next to Mush started to sink to the pavement. The screams were starting . . . "The children, those children . . ." The woman would not be comforted by her husband, who himself was in an agitated state. They were, inevitably, all thinking of their own young children left behind that day and allowed the illusions of the innocence of childhood and a safe home.

Mush wrenched his arm away from Vivian. "I'm quitting . . ."

"Get out of here, damn it," Vivian hissed between clenched teeth. "This thing could turn into a riot any minute—"

"Your daddy, who is with me in these last momentous hours, sends his heart and all the love . . ."

Mush's face collapsed in grief. "In five minutes those two people are going to be dragged into that room and murdered . . . do you hear me? And the FBI'll hold that goddamn phone up until the last minute, waiting for them to confess to a crime they never committed . . ."

The crowd was going out of control now. Vivian heard a shout, then a massive outbreak of groans. "It is ending." The speaker chocked on his words. The Rosenbergs were the first Americans ever to be put to death for such a charge in time of peace . . .

Vivian elbowed to get out of the suffocating riot. As if in slow motion he ran, leaping over falling bodies. Desperate hands seemed to reach up from the pavement to claw at his high-stepping legs. He stumbled and nearly fell over two women who had gone down locked in each other's arms. Mounted police rode into the chaos. For some of these people, it was as though the cossacks had come again.

At Sing Sing orderlies hurriedly mop the floor around the electric chair. Julius Rosenberg is wheeled out in a gurney.

Ethel Rosenberg is led forward, the rabbi begins the Hebrew lament for the dead. The marshal steps near, the unhooked telephone with the open line to Washington in his hand, still waiting for the confession.

Ethel Rosenberg turns and embraces the prison matron. The heavyset woman begins to shake with sobs. The rabbi continues: ". . . for I have heard the slander of many: fear was on every side: while they took counsel together against me, they devised to take away my life."

She is strapped down. The guard adjusts the cathode. The helmet is lowered over her head where the hair is shaved. The mask is fixed on. The first jolt dims the lights. The chair shudders. Yellow smoke puffs up from her head. The second and third electrical charges last exactly fifty-seven seconds each.

In Union Square the cries, screams hit Vivian with the force of a solid wave.

The plainclothesmen from the New York Police Department "red squad" and the group of watching FBI special agents glanced curiously at Vivian as he ran out from the hysteria—then exchanged slow, dubious looks among themselves.

The tall athletic man now striding away from the scene of suffering did not look at them, or back. His deep gray eyes were wide, his nostrils dilated, breathing slowly. He kept walking uptown toward his father's place at Fifty-ninth Street and the park.

His thoughts were a whispering credo inside him . . . "I am a white male Anglo-Saxon Protestant. I am not and I must not become a victim of this witchhunt. I am a human being, not a human sacrifice. Mush Hollander may choose to go down with the losers but I do not. I am not a victim and I am not an executioner. Not a Communist and not a fascist. I am not a great despiser and therefore not a great adorer. Not God and not the devil, goddamn it."

At Fifty-first and Fifth Avenue he noticed that the expensively dressed shoppers coming and going in and out of the shops seemed to be members of a different race from those he had left in Union Square. Including the Jews here on Fifth Avenue, who were smooth-skinned and well tailored, just like the Christians. Just like me, he thought . . .

Newsboys were already on the street with extras:

SPIES DIE
HE GOES FIRST
EXTRA SHOCKS FOR HER

CHAPTER 2

Fire Island, 1955
The Coldness of the War

THE JULY Fourth weekend was the unofficial commencement of the season at New York's nearby Fire Island. The island—with its wide clean beach and clustered resort villages, no automobiles and sea breezes—was a refuge not only from the broiling claustrophobia of the Manhattan summer but also from the confining, intimidating climate of an America still in the depths of the cold war, a giant tragically afraid of its shadow.

Cherry Grove, the homosexual community, rivaled the legendary isle of Lesbos on weekends, from the hysteria of the Fourth

228

through the operatic finale at Labor Day. Young "trade" from the hinterlands rubbed shoulders with some of Broadway's grandest and gayest eminences. Famous names lay down or danced beside putative chorus boys and impoverished ribbon clerks with the democracy of damned souls, as if to betray the interconnected nature of both the sexual and political taboos from which the gay weekend refugees had fled. The uncrowned queen of this frantic sex cult was known to all as "Red Russian Rose."

The Prescott summer house was in the more traditional resort community of Ocean Beach several miles down the strand from Cherry Grove. But Rose and others of the Cherry Grove vanguard led an existence of seeming perpetual motion. Through the long sun-drenched days and misty nights, Rose and her legions walked, as if condemned, along the whole length of the island's one street, or what Rose called the Main Drag, in search of whatever dream it was that had lured them from Dayton or Muncie or the Bronx —or all the other places of their nomadic existence.

Vivian Prescott seemed to them precisely the fixed image so many of them envied and sought. On the island, tanned golden, long and strong, strolling in Brooks Brothers soft-colored cotton shorts and shirts, he was the image of summer proper—of all things right and proper.

Rose, and consequently everyone else, knew that Viv Prescott was a ranking member of the American mission to the United Nations, as well as the possessor of impeccable heterosexual credentials. Actually Rose, who owned an extremely successful beauty parlor on Manhattan's East Side, was Vivian's agent, in areas both Black and White. Rose's performance, in private with Vivian, was modeled on an improbable vamp from an ancient W. C. Fields film —"Hello, Viv, dis iss Mata . . ."

Rose, whose real name was Isador Fratkin, was an orange-haired ball of libidinous energy who had been born fifty years before in 1905 into an Orthodox Jewish family. In his unbounded revenge on all tradition Rose now cited Fire Island's generous Jewish representation in the summer crowds as evidence that "the Island is becoming so Jewish that on Fridays they're coming in on racks." Rose was referring to the ferry from Long Island and the racks of Manhattan's garment district, from which the generations of lawyers, doctors and producers were descended—several nose and name changes later, according to Rose. Not that the content of Russian Rose's wit was impressive in the literary sense, but almost no one could resist the high camp or the inflamed style of delivery. The accent was a variation of Greta Garbo's morose manner of diction while the timbre of Rose's voice seemed to be a cross between that of Tallulah Bankhead and Nelson Eddy, though with *Weltschmerz* and a dying fall. For emphasis the steady stream of sibilance could rise to gale force, driving all combatants before it.

Rose was so open and so outrageous that no one suspected that he was an invaluable operative, enabling Vivian to build sexual dossiers of truly international scope based on Rose's U. N. contacts. This material was not turned over wholesale to the Agency but used at Vivian's own discretion . . . he would not allow himself to indulge in the practices that he so condemned in the FBI. Besides the carnal cornucopia provided by Rose, there was his inestimable aid in Vivian's major new assignment of recruitment.

After the FBI's atom spy ring coup—which the Agency had been powerless to prevent short of exposure of the hoax, and that could not be done without mortally compromising Agency contacts and key personnel—Vivian's team had been broken up by Frank Wisner, the chief of clandestine operations. Past heroics notwithstanding, the Rosenberg operation had been counted a serious failure for Mush Hollander, and therefore for Vivian.

Mush had actually threatened to go public if the Agency let the Rosenbergs go to the electric chair. During the showdown in Wisner's neat cold office cubicle in the cramped E Street quarters there had hardly been room for the participants even to gesture. There was Mush, Vivian, Wisner and his Ivy League guard of Des FitzGerald, Dick Helms and Dick Bissell. This crowded confrontation forced the debaters to stand at tortured angles to answer the cross-cutting charges. Wisner had finally shouted at Mush that if he thought Allen Dulles was going to bring down the government to save two little New York Commies who refused to cooperate with the Agency, then Mush was so deluded as to be on his way to Saint Elizabeths, and the way he said it made it sound exactly like the threat that it was intended to be. Mush with his Communist party background was in an untenable position, his only ally being the Clandestine Section's hatred of the FBI. *After* the execution, Wisner had said, he'd give Mush a file to hand over to the U. S.

Attorney in Manhattan guaranteed to bring an indictment of one of the prosecutors of the Rosenbergs . . . in the following silence Mush's heavy shoulders sagged. FitzGerald's pipe smoke slowly filled the room; outside, the dull drilling of the street-repair crew measured the pause. Mush, when he finally spoke, sounded far away. "Frank, I speak three Eastern European languages. I want a transfer to the Soviet Russian or Eastern Desk."

"Out of Ops?"

"That's right. Out from under the rock." He walked out stiffly, so as not to brush against any of them.

Tim and Pat had left in August of 1953 for Division 10, Western Europe, Psychological Warfare/Paramilitary. Pat's duties included organizing youth festivals, youth seminars, trips, conferences, press conferences and an entire range of related activities. All had a single purpose—to provide a rallying point for well-educated liberal young people other than the Socialist or Communist parties. Pat, whose sense of justice burned bright at all times and who still looked like a cheerleader—which she had been at Chicago's St. Catherine's High School—was an immediate success. Tim had been assigned to liaison with "the Circus," British intelligence's M16 covert operations. His job was to build the experimental statistical model, with flow charts and oral histories, of the Agency's new directions in psychological warfare. The centers of these ultra-secret programs were some of the oldest universities in England and America.

Tim preferred screening, removed as it was from any covert "wet stuff." On occasion, though, he reluctantly took part with Vivian in, for instance, the recruiting of one Melville Winston Wachs, the distinguished president of Brown University, as an Agency employee. The Agency had long secretly used the services of academics at more than one hundred colleges and universities across the country, and there had been a "revolving door" between the Ivy League and the CIA for some time. Tim and Vivian placed their man at the head of a cover organization called the Human Environment Fund, a front for perhaps the most controversial domestic project in CIA history. This "foundation" was one of many that the Agency was using in order to channel millions of dollars into the study of mind-control research, including LSD

231

testing of human subjects. While Wachs was told only the official purpose of the research—to develop a strategy to counter Soviet and Chinese brainwashing techniques—its real purpose was to study the drug's use as a behavioral-control agent. When during a weekend experiment a group of students was gathered and administered the drug (one result of which was a double suicide), Wachs flew directly to Washington and insisted on confronting Vivian and Tim immediately.

Vivian, acting more angry than he felt and running out of rationalizations, sounded like a stranger to himself as he said, "Don't worry, we'll take care of it."

"But what if the information becomes public?"

Vivian's stare was ice-cold. "Why, then you will be killed, of course." . . .

Pat's letters and family photographs from London, in her warm and ironic style, served only to increase Vivian's sense of isolation.

He had been assigned, again, to teach at "the Farm," one of the Agency's career dumping grounds, and in 1955 had been given his State Department cover at the United Nations. From this vantage he was expected to recruit from the rich pool of talent living and working in and around the Rockefeller-donated U. N. complex that towered above the ground on Manhattan's East Side. He had been rushed to the Indian Ocean when Iran erupted and broke away—temporarily—from American control. Though he had played a key role in bailing the Agency out of a fiasco, there was much bad blood still flowing between competing clandestine teams.

At the Farm Vivian's days were spent in a series of seminars on the "Theory and Practice of Intelligence." Nights he sometimes socialized with other instructors or even drove into the capital to see Erika Swearingen. He no longer found the prospect of two women palatable, even tolerable . . . He missed Pat, damn it, and he had caught a dose of Mush's depression.

He and Mush talked by telephone. The Farm was a dead end. Somebody up there definitely did not like him. Who? Dulles's Old Boys—Helms, Bissell, Barnes, et al.—were moving ever deeper into the Agency infrastructure. They were desk men, suspicious of Vivian's proved virtuosity in action. He was forced now once again, as after the Rosenbergs' execution, to begin to think about his career options. The prospect of following his father's suggestion

232

of joining a university or foundation was equally unappetizing, as well as dull.

What he did was to bide his time and go through the motions of teaching all the young agents to believe the Company version of organized illusion called intelligence. His teaching style was ironic and, therefore, much admired, especially since all the new boys knew he had been an authentic hero in the war. He would walk briskly into the classroom, always dressed and groomed immaculately, almost gratuitously adding to his natural good looks and charm. His lectures on the historical setting of intelligence operations were often witty and alive (his style just a little resembling that of his old Professor Hewes), the mystique of his personal legend adding to the students' receptivity. He would always begin his first lecture with the words of the Chinese sage Sun Tzu on the value of foreknowledge: ". . . the reason the enlightened prince and the wise general conquer the enemy whenever they move." And so he would proceed to talk about intelligence work as the creative art he believed—if only for that moment on the podium standing before such eager faces—it was . . .

"The earliest sources of intelligence, in the age of a belief in supernatural intervention . . . were prophets, seers, oracles, soothsayers and astrologers . . ." His voice would rise to the impressive proportions of, perhaps, an angry Hamlet or even an Anglo-Saxon Jeremiah . . . "When Moses was in the wilderness he was directed by the Lord to send a ruler of each of the tribes of Israel to spy out the Land of Canaan . . ." And, "We all know what Cassandra did . . ." followed by titters from the more literary in the audience, who knew the story of this first "deception" operation. Continuing with the saga of the Greeks, he would tell the story of how they sent three spies to Persia before the great invasion of 480 B.C. to see how large the enemy forces were. Then there was "Mithridates, who brought the power of Rome to its knees because he had become an outstanding intelligence officer in his own right . . ."

As if the mere presence before them of the mythical Vivian Prescott were not enough, he continued through history, touching all corners of the world and pointing out the heroics of intelligence teams past . . . "In the fifteenth century, it was the Italians who made the most important contribution to intelligence collection by establishing permanent embassies abroad." On through the six-

233

teenth and seventeenth centuries he raced, keeping his audience spellbound . . . "It was during this time that the first specialists in intelligence appeared on the western scene . . . and the greatest of the spymasters to appear during this time was Sir Francis Walsingham . . ." Vivian did not examine the great men of the past uncritically, however. Looking back with the wisdom of historical perspective, he spoke of "Cromwell's intelligence chief, John Thurloe. *He* certainly did not possess ingenuity, inventiveness, daring . . ." But he fired their fantasies with stories of Joseph Fouché and Colonel Savary, who served under Napoleon as chiefs of a political secret police and counterespionage organization. On to the nineteenth century, which marked the beginning of great intelligence services maintained not by government but by private firms such as the house of Rothschild . . .

"Gentlemen, spying is not only the oldest profession (discounting you know which), it is as old as time itself . . . as old also as the attempt to *control* time. And, after all, time is history. When the great powers of Europe entered World War II their intelligence services were in no way equipped to cope with the battle they were about to face . . . but their efforts were both tireless and valiant . . .

"And that, gentlemen, brings us to our own country, our own history of official intelligence activity that was, to say the least, rather sketchy until World War II. To be sure, Boudinot and Tallmadge wrote their memoirs recounting their intrigues during the American Revolution, but they were very, very discreet. As well known as the assassination of President Lincoln is, few know about what occasioned the necessity for a really efficient secret intelligence service in this country. Thanks to the efforts of Allan Pinkerton and Timothy Webster, a conspiracy by a group of hotheads to assassinate the President on his way to his first inauguration was defeated. And of course every schoolboy knows about Nathan Hale and Benedict Arnold. Perhaps the best thing to come out of their experience was a model for an intelligence brief written by Washington himself for agent Peter Townsend late in 1778: 'Mix as much as possible among the officers . . . visit the Coffee Houses and all public places . . .' Washington went on to list specific targets and information he wanted, and he even told the agent how to go about getting it. In the 1880s came the creation of the first perma-

234

nent peacetime military and naval intelligence organization in the United States, but this early G-2 dwindled almost immediately from lack of interest.

"So it was only with World War II and Pearl Harbor in particular that the stimulation came for the rapid growth of the OSS and its intelligence operations. By this time the OSS was already deep into the task of special services, using especially the support of various antifascist underground groups behind the enemy lines. During 1943 elements of OSS were at work all over the world, except Latin America, where the FBI had a stronghold . . .

"And so this, gentlemen, brings us down to you, the class of fifty-four. In contrast with our policy of the past of limiting the functions of intelligence to time of war, we are looking to you to help it flourish and grow to meet the ever-broadening needs of *peace* . . ."

Vivian was in the worst funk of his life. Not since Janet's death had he been so sore inside. That time he had reached out for the little whores of London to lead him through his rituals of mourning, then later he and Pat had found their private, sensual relief. Now he felt himself withdrawing, backing toward some invisible wall. And then came the orders from Washington to report to New York.

At first this post promised both a cultural and personal awakening. He liked living on Sutton Place with its nearby tennis courts. For the first few weeks he simply established his cover as a sportsman-playboy whose father had wangled him a minor sinecure with the State Department. Observers at the American Mission to the United Nations would notice him strolling away after lunch to play tennis for drinks and money at Rip's.

Nights were beginning to be interesting again too. The theater had always been a place where he could lose himself for a few hours. Now for the first time in years he found himself at the center of this world and voraciously indulged his appetite for its stimulation and escape.

When he went to see *Fallen Angels* it reminded him of his London days when Noel Coward had used his wit to help the OSS cause, no one ever dreaming that someone with such aristocratic airs could possibly act as a secret agent. It reminded Vivian too—and with great relief—that he had not lost his capacity for laughter, and as he watched Nancy Walker use her cigarette holder like a wind instrument, he roared along with the rest of the audience.

He did not limit himself, however, to just comedy; his first passion had always been the literary and tragic. When *Long Day's Journey into Night* finally arrived on Broadway he was there opening night and sat spellbound through its four-and-a-half hours of harshness and pain. Once again it took him back, this time to Deer Island; it was genius when someone like Eugene O'Neill could make poetry out of human degradation.

But his favorite was *Waiting for Godot.* Many nights he found himself returning to the performance. He had known Samuel Beckett in the OSS days, and it amused him to read the existential and theological discussions the play was eliciting from the critics. Privately he knew of another interpretation that no critic could possibly guess at, and that was based on his knowledge that Beckett himself had fought in the Resistance. Vivian's first-hand knowledge of the underground made him recall the tedium felt by its members, the majority of their time spent in agonized *waiting* . . . waiting for London to deliver the tools of war, *waiting* for the OSS and SOE factions to solve their internal struggles and choose between Giraud and de Gaulle, and most painful of all . . . *waiting* for comrades to return from their missions. Beckett had removed from his play all references to a specific Nazi-Allied conflict. It was as if the piece had been written a thousand years after World War II, and time had abstracted everything except the quality of waiting. . . .

By the early spring of '55 he was ready to start his recruiting. He began by focusing on the recruitment of a certain African diplomat named Edward Obale. Their common ground was the tennis court, although they were by no means evenly matched. They met on a Saturday in the clubhouse, where Obale had retreated to salve his feelings of defeat. Edward Obale was a mediocre player, but tennis provided him with not only exercise but an excuse to sit around afterward and lick his wounds with something a bit stronger than orange juice and strike up friendships with wealthy white western diplomats.

It was after one of Obale's bouts with defeat that he found himself seated next to Vivian, who had just lost his tennis partner

236

to an urgent call from the office. Vivian turned to the young black diplomat and casually suggested a set. Afterward as they sat sipping drinks Vivian told him a few superficial details about his "work," then politely excused himself and left.

The first CIA contact had been made. Of course, everything had been thought out in detail long in advance of the first meeting. Edward had been selected for recruitment, and all of the relevant facts about his life sat neatly in a file that had been provided to Vivian weeks before. Preliminary analysis had shown that they had good potential in Obale. Besides, they thought, they had a hold on him.

As if by coincidence, the following Saturday Vivian and his friends turned up on a court adjacent to Edward's. "We need a fourth for doubles," Vivian said, flashing the charming smile, "and afterward I'll take you to lunch. I did enjoy our conversation last week . . . we'll continue it."

And so everything was proceeding according to plan. At lunch Vivian talked mostly about China. "We're about to investigate a potential defector from the Chinese government." Now that he was finally into it, he made his next move. "If an independent party, like yourself, for example, were to help us out in this matter, I would see to it, of course, that you would be very well compensated for your services. In more ways than money . . ."

Vivian let the silence hang as he lifted his brandy and watched it swirl around in the glass. The fact that he had now arrived at the most critical point in the recruitment process did not show at all in Vivian's near-casual manner. Times before at such a moment the person on the other side of the table had simply downed the brandy and left. Edward Obale stayed. The whole affair had gone easily . . . almost too easily.

Some days later Vivian telephoned Edward and invited him to a second lunch. Obale accepted and this time the two men met in the company of a couple of Vivian's associates. By now the recruitment process had advanced to the point where the case officer (Vivian) engaged the help of colleagues to assess his potential agent and above all to find the means by which he could be bought or threatened into service. Did he drink? Was money or ambition the more important? "What does he like to eat or fuck?" is how

237

the questions were put at the Farm during training. And how did he feel about Communism?

At a dinner meeting at a small and very good east side French restaurant, Vivian commenced telling Obale just how much the Company knew about him, especially in regard to both family and finances.

"How did you find out so much about me?"

Vivian responded by saying that the Company left no stone unturned. He spoke about those relatives of Edward's that the Agency had located in Africa, casually slipping in the fact that his cousin "C" had been arrested only a few days before by a small East African country.

"You know how things are with those people," Vivian said. "He's probably being tortured at this very minute. So you see, Edward, here is an example of how we can help each other. If you join me and the Company, I'll see that your cousin is safely released."

In short order Edward agreed. He secretly, however, only intended to play the game as long as his cousin's life was at stake. As soon as his cousin was out of danger, Obale planned to withdraw. Even if he had known this intent, it would scarcely have mattered to Vivian; he, for one, knew that leaving the Company was never easy.

Once Edward agreed to cooperate, Vivian began the training process. From his briefcase he produced a set of photos that showed all the most important KGB members of the Russian embassy in New York. Vivian explained that from then on Edward would be spending a good deal of time among Communist-country diplomats, and that it was best that he knew who the KGB were as they, too, were good recruiters. "You see, we don't want any shuffling back and forth between us, so stay away from them from now on." The charming smile had vanished.

And so Vivian completed his first successful recruitment. For future rendezvous, Vivian informed Edward of four select locations at which they would meet. He told him as well that lying was never tolerated within the Company . . . "That could result in your unfortunate death," Vivian said. "Besides, we offer, just as a check, a lie detector test. A routine for all CIA agents."

In mid-June Vivian was instructed to turn Edward Obale over to

238

a new control. Vivian would then be free to go on to fresh pickings. Russian Rose alone had half a dozen U. N. men lined up for him to scrutinize, "all of dem gorgeous," he lisped to Vivian over cold drinks at Rip's. Rose took tennis lessons three times a week at Rip's from Al Doyle, the best of the pressure money-players. On occasion Vivian and Doyle would transfix the tyros and business executives with a display of big-time tennis with Rose screaming a grand opera commentary from the sidelines, basking in the reflected glory of his two friends . . . "It's not *tennisss,* it's *ballet,*" Rose would hiss, writhing on his pudgy bottom. . . .

Obale drank so much after their last treff that Vivian had to take him home, where, for the first time, he met Mrs. Obale. Together they put Edward to bed. On the balcony overlooking the U. N. apartment complex she—he never used her first name—asked him to leave her husband alone. She was over five feet eight, jet black, of the Masai royal family. She was a striking African beauty with long legs; when she arched her back pointed breasts thrust against the soft cotton of her lime and azure dashiki. Her buttocks were beautifully molded, sloping out and down with an abrupt sensuousness.

"Good night, Mrs. Obale, I hope—"

"Leave my husband alone."

"I beg your pardon?"

"I know that you have entrapped my husband."

"But I—"

"What do you want me to do?"

And there on the balcony on a fine New York June night this proud African woman knelt at super-Wasp Vivian Prescott's feet. He tried to lift her but her body was rigid, as though leashed. Vivian moved to turn and leave but her hands on his groin held him rooted. Slowly her tightly braided, beautifully rounded head moved back and forth over the swollen length of his erection. He did not touch her head or shoulders. After he exploded into her throat, the long arching neck turned her face up to him.

"Leave him alone, now, for God's sake."

Vivian did not look back. Thinking as he closed the outer door, "What is happening, what is happening to my life?" And then he cursed the woman. She had made him feel terrible guilt, and *that* was the one unforgivable, intolerable act.

Senator Kennedy did not bring his wife with him to Fire Island that year of 1955 for his July visit at the Prescott summer house for two reasons: his wife, Jacqueline, once an admirer of Vivian, now could not abide him. Further, Jack's visit was really not for pleasure.

Once, before her marriage, Jacqueline Bouvier had had a crush on Viv Prescott. Vivian, handsome and vital in appearance and intelligence, was from the same mold as Congressman John F. Kennedy, whom the striking heiress had also admired with considerable intensity. As for Vivian, he saw in the vivid Miss Bouvier a reminder in type and looks of his murdered wife. Not surprising then that at first they had clung together, though still strangers, reacting to one another as fellow travelers in a world of wealth and privilege. There was about men like Kennedy and Prescott the cut and thrust of the adventurer or pirate-hero that had defined her dashing and seductive father, "Black Jack" Bouvier, whom she had adored.

In Vivian's opinion Jacqueline Bouvier had all of Janet Hammersmith's curses with none of her blessings. He had, he realized, simply tried to recapture Janet by pursuing her shadow. He found painful inhibition without any of Janet's courage or wit or compassion.

He had never understood how Jack could marry her, but then he and Jack were not as nearly alike as they appeared to casual observers. They had met for lunch on a regular basis, and occasionally for tennis, until Vivian's posting to New York. This visit to the island would be their first extended time together in years. Vivian was looking forward to a proper talk . . . Jack was the man to whom he could confide that he had just about made up his mind to leave the Agency. . . .

By July, Vivian had commitments from the Donahues, in the States for their summer leave, and from his father to spend the July Fourth holidays with him at Fire Island. He did not care that he was being robbed by the owner of the white two-story beach house because he had rented at the last minute before the season began. He knew that one way or another he could not continue in New York. When the call came from Jack Kennedy's Senate office,

Vivian felt intuitively that there might be a way out. There had been rumors for months that the senator was preparing for a major effort at the Democratic National Convention scheduled for that summer in Chicago.

Vivian was also hungry to spend time with Pat, to cancel the searing curse of guilt with which the African woman had branded him. He had met the Donahue family on their arrival in New York. His son-godchild, Terry, was a limber, outgoing redhead of four, who, Vivian could see, was coming to resemble increasingly his own childhood snapshots of thirty years before. "These are Woody's crumbs," Terry piped, holding up an oblong package for Vivian to see.

Pat put in, "Woody was our dog in London. She was run over just before we left, and these are her *'crumbs.'*" He had not expected tears to come to his eyes, but they did when his son added, "Woody's in heaven with John Henderson's poor cat."

"John Henderson is—"

"I get it," Vivian nodded, turning away. . . .

Sam Prescott and the Donahues were not expected until the third so the house was empty when Vivian walked down to the pier to meet Jack Kennedy's ferry in the late afternoon of the first.

Perhaps a bit heavier around the jawline, Jack had aged very little, the shock of hair and teasing eyes the same as always. The big teeth clipped the words in that distinctive pattern, the smile absolutely infectious . . . "Vivian, ah, where are the girls?" A strong handclasp and the two men made for the house to change for a swim. Later, Vivian broiled pepper steaks, delicious with fresh corn, tossed salad and caterers' chocolate ice cream with their freshly brewed coffee.

As was his style, Kennedy laid what he had to say on the line. " . . . so we were just worms over in the House, nobody knew we existed. And you know I didn't exactly come up through the ranks with the party wheelhorses. After I got out of the service I just sort of slipped in sideways." He talked easily about his "altogether unremarkable career in the Senate" and his father's "private scenario, now that Joe's gone, to get me into the White House— through the front door . . ."

Continuing as they walked along the beach, Jack smoked a short Havana cigar, Vivian listening carefully for his opening. "The plan, Viv, is to let loose a little trial balloon in a few weeks in Chicago.

241

The word is that Adlai will throw the convention open for the choice of vice-president. He's a damn fine man. He can't beat Eisenhower—no one can—but he's . . . so, I don't have a chance in hell, of course, but it's—"

"The first step toward 1960."

"That's right . . . now, since you refuse to tell me where the young ladies are and we have the entire goddamn evening before us, suppose you tell me what your plans are for the next four years."

"Funny that you should mention it."

"Funny ha-ha or funny strange?"

Vivian briefly described the dead end he had reached at the Agency. ". . . so, as they say in the Company, my options are open."

"I'm building a team of men—our age, Viv. People still young enough to believe in the future, not burned out yet. We'll start working for 1960 during *this* election. You know, as Bobby says, building up the IOUs—I'll campaign for the ticket every place I can. In three years we'll be ready for the primaries. But it's a long road, and even if we don't crash, Richard Nixon'll be waiting for me at the end of the tunnel . . . that's if Ike lives. If he doesn't, then that's it. We'll have Nixon for plus eight years . . ." They turned back toward the house as they contemplated the prospect of a President Nixon.

Both men knew what the country did not—Dwight Eisenhower had an unstable heart and Richard Nixon knew it too, knew that he was literally just a heartbeat away.

The Dulles brothers—John Foster and Allen—had discovered that Nixon and a few of his friends had set up a secret contingency plan to take over the presidency when and if Ike's heart condition warranted. Something about the specificity of the Nixon secret scenario sent bells ringing all along the corridors of Allen Dulles's canny old mind. Especially the leaks to the press concerning the President's health—already begun through Sherman Scott at CIA, a longtime Nixon loyalist—were calculated to drive Ike's blood pressure up past the danger level. It was John Foster Dulles, as Secretary of State, who let the vice-president know that in the event of a catastrophe the cabinet as a whole—not he—would pick up the reins of power. . . .

Back at the house they sat talking in the moonlight without turning on any lamps. Vivian had begun to understand, he thought, why his old friend had come out to the island to talk to him about 1960. He was sure of it when Jack asked him about how Joe McCarthy had actually been stopped.

Now it was Kennedy's turn to listen closely to the story of the Agency's role in stopping the junior senator from Wisconsin—a man whom he had not openly opposed, for whom his brother Bobby had worked as an assistant counsel and to whom his father had made large contributions. In 1954 Joe McCarthy had gone too far by attacking the army, the Ivy League, the Protestant church and, fatally, the CIA. Kennedy laughed, demanded details.

Dr. Horace Wexler, who had been at Camp X with Vivian, had led a team of behavioral scientists to produce a psychological profile on McCarthy—

"Viv, give me a few *details.*"

"Dr. Wexler's analysis went like this . . . Republicans feel there is no other way to 'get' Democrats. McCarthy has built a coalition of the dissatisfied. These people are angry about internationalism, elitism, the welfare state . . . they are also heavily of the Roman Catholic faith, particularly of Irish descent. They see in McCarthy's aggressivity an evangelical avenger of the past wrongs inflicted upon them. He symbolizes them with pathological fervor . . . he convinces them of his honesty. How could he *not* be? Men and women not abnormally disposed to suasion become fixated by his intensity, his aura of conviction and power . . . ."

Mush, whom Jack remembered from London, had been especially threatened by the vehemence with which McCarthy spoke of the "serious situation" within the CIA. The junior senator had said he had in his possession information leading to more than one hundred Communists within the Agency and was going to "root them out" at any cost.

But as Dr. Wexler aptly put it in his profile: "McCarthy possesses a delicate sensitivity to the costliness of certain acts. The expending of great psychic energy without valid expectation of equally great rewards results in his withdrawal from the situation."

"Viv, what price did CIA make him pay?"

"Gory details?"

"Yeah."

"In a minute. 'Anyway, I guess I'll skip it,' McCarthy finally said about his impending investigation of CIA members, and Mush and others breathed at least a tentative sigh of relief. There was also a thick dossier on financial irregularities. We have him, he's finished," Vivian added . . . down the footpath they could hear a woman's laughter.

"So you had him, but what did the agency actually *do*, based on the *information?*"

"I don't know exactly. Seriously, Jack, I think it was his dependence on Hoover and the Bureau that we attacked. The profile indicated that if we could break the link to Hoover—*psychologically* as well as his access to information or help from agents—McCarthy would revert to his . . . I think they called it his underlying outlaw identity. In other words Hoover not only gave him political and intelligence credibility—such as it was—but validated McCarthy's own credibility to *himself.*"

"Viv, what did you guys *do?*"

"Jack, I don't know the details. I believe it involved the use of a friendly priest to get him drunk and get him on tape making fun of the Hoover-Tolson relationship. Or at least that was the plan but I think that, in the end, we had to edit the tape because Joe got sloppy and actually defended homosexuals, referring to them as 'these young men, these *fine* young men.' And he became completely incoherent, weeping and . . . I don't know, Jack, it's like ninety-nine percent of everything we do. It's all crackpot covert ops, none of it really works, not like—"

"Not like such sober little projects as kidnapping Hitler or—"

"Or blowing up the entire Japanese navy."

Laughing, kidding and feeling good in the easy and partial intimacy of the remembering, Vivian did not feel it was absolutely necessary to inform his friend that the Agency's knowledge of McCarthy's drug dependency, and their covert encouragement of it, had provided the blueprint for the destruction of the senator, in which, God knew, he had collaborated with his disastrous performance during the army hearing, leaving himself an open target to defense counsel Welch, ending up nearly incoherent.

They talked until after one. It was left that Vivian would let Kennedy know within six months whether or not he would accept a position as chief of research for the senator's expanded staff to

244

help chart John Fitzgerald Kennedy's course to the White House in 1960. Vivian's job description was a general cover for what would be his single and exclusive project: to defeat Richard Milhous Nixon by every means necessary.

"No girls, huh, Viv?"

"No, no girls, Jack. Good night."

The ferries were jammed with upper-middle-class emigrants fleeing from the pitiless pavement of the city. Vivian spread his arms when he saw that both his father and Mush Hollander were disembarking with the Donahues.

The crowds on the dock and walks were so dense that the Prescott group tried as much as possible to alternate between the house and the beach. Parties originated in so many adjacent houses that the footpaths were a stream of drink-carrying, sunburned weekend Sybarites. Under the general hilarity there were persistent notes of hysteria especially disturbing to Sam Prescott. Twice over the weekend, while the others were playing volleyball on the sand, Sam had to help young women who had drunk too much into the house to the bathroom. He gave them tea, and one, a secretary at a large theatrical agency, acquired one of Pat's blouses, her own having been ripped away in the good fellowship of a nearby holiday celebration. Two executives and a lawyer from a recording company had raped her, serially as well as simultaneously, upstairs, while downstairs her screams finally caused two celebrants to shout up to her to *shut up.* Fire Island, Sam Prescott reflected, was too much a "part of the main."

Everybody took part in the cooking of dinner, Sam and the boy, Terry, peeling potatoes. During the preparation of the food, Sam told them about the wounded young woman who seemed to be wandering about the island. Pat, who knew her Shakespeare, quoted *The Tempest*... "O brave new world that has such creatures in't," and Mush parried her ironic thrust in the direction of real bitterness. He had just spent his three-week holiday in the South, choosing the site of tense, chaotic clashes to spend his "vacation," and as was typical of him, emerged emotionally swayed and battle weary.

"The fight between the segregationists and the civil rights groups is really off and running," Mush was saying, "and we haven't begun to see the beginning of the grief that's bound to come."

He said he felt the 1954 Supreme Court decision directing the integration of schools had "put the South in the vanguard of a struggle that could bring this country to its knees if we aren't careful. Martin Luther King and his bus boycott forced people really to look at themselves and their motives . . . he's a giant of a man and probably the only one who can save the situation . . ."

The child sat quietly in the corner. He was accustomed to listening to intense adult voices rise and fall in conversational exchange and had long ago given up trying to distract them with his innocent concerns. He was getting old enough now, though, to have some understanding of what was being discussed, and when he heard words like "school bus" and "guns" his interest perked up, straining to understand where in this world the two could possibly go together. He looked up at his mother and asked, "But why do the soldiers with guns bring the children to school like I saw on TV?" While Pat was debating whether to answer, Mush took her off the hook by going on with the story of how he could not stand by while . . .

While he was in Birmingham he had gone to see a Nat King Cole concert. "During the second set," he said, "I heard a wolf howl and all of a sudden there were five thugs on the stage beating the hell out of Cole. Police appeared from nowhere and there was a pitched battle on stage right in front of our eyes. You know I can't control myself . . . I was up there before I knew what was happening, trying to pry loose the guy who had a death grip on Cole. It was all over in a matter of minutes but the evening was ruined. Cole was really shattered, he couldn't go on, and I've come back from my so-called vacation with a sore wrist and having seen another battle I know I ought to be part of . . ."

Sam Prescott asked for all of them, "Will it come north and east, Mush?"

"Mr. Prescott, you know the history of this country probably better than any of us. I've heard you talk about the New Haven Agreements. Let me ask *you*. Will it come?" They all looked at the gray man with the cold pipe in his hand.

"Well, I think the country may well be broken on the color line unless we can reconstitute and reorganize the old FDR coalition,"

246

he said, and stroked Terry's red hair, thinking how much this child reminded him of Viv when he was this age. They talked until the boy fell asleep. Tomorrow, they told each other, there would be time to find out what each intended doing about assignments and callings, old and new. Long after they had retired to beds, couches, and sleeping bag for Terry, Vivian could still hear, outside, the shrill laughter of the escapees from the city.

"You've done a magnificent job, Pat, with the boy." The two of them had volunteered to go back to the house for a thermos of lemonade while Tim and Mush hiked down the beach with Terry. "What was the dog's name?"

"Woody."

"Woody's crumbs . . ."

"He's something. Turned out to have my intelligence, after all, I guess."

That made Vivian laugh. "I've missed you," he said.

"I know." She smiled. "London wasn't the same."

"How's it going?" he asked.

"Okay. I don't know. Students of the world, unite! I'd like to come home."

A young woman with dark circles under her eyes and a big older man passed, forcing them to step aside. The man appeared to be crying.

The house was cool inside, they could feel the difference as soon as they entered. She told him that Tim expected to be put under cover at an eastern university where he would function as comptroller of an ambitious psychological warfare program. His meticulous records and accounting had endeared Tim to the budget office of the Agency . . . "And I," she said as she spread more lotion on her fair, freckled skin, "will also get an assignment in the States, or retire again. I'll tell them that I'm having another baby."

"Are you?"

"I don't know. Maybe, if I had this one with Tim and then another one with Mush we could all be assured that there would be a second generation of Prescott's heroes to stand there at the ramparts of the free world."

"Sort of a red-headed league."

"Yes, with my militant recessive genes."

"God, Pat, you look wonderful. Like the sweetheart of Sigma Chi, but you sound tired."

"I suppose I am . . . of leading armies of adolescents around by my apron strings. What do you think, Viv? Don't you sense a change since Stalin's death? The summit meeting with Khrushchev in two weeks . . . ?"

"I *don't* think. That's the problem, since you left." He told her something of his disgust with the U. N. assignment. He could see that she disapproved of recruiting under cover from what was supposed to be the nucleus for a future world government. "Do you still think we can do some good, *inside?*" she asked.

"Yes, I do, *if* we could get anywhere near the levers of decision-making power . . . how would you like to work for Jack Kennedy until 1960 and then join his White House staff? You wouldn't hold the fact that he's Irish against him, would you?"

She didn't know the senator well but it did sound interesting and Tim, she thought, would very much like helping run a political campaign. "He knows Chicago and—"

"How are you two doing?"

". . . We, ahh, respect each other . . . and he is a tremendous father to . . . *our* son."

"Pat, do you . . . do you hold it against me?"

"Why? I made my bed."

"Is it too late?" He reached for her.

The slamming of the screen door made them flinch apart. Sam Prescott was ushering another distraught and drunken young woman toward the downstairs bathroom. "Put on the kettle," he called to them as he passed the kitchen, his charge already starting to vomit. . . .

That evening after Mush and Pat's potluck Irish-Jewish Great Depression Chicago stew they all discussed the coming convention in Chicago and agreed with Sam that there would not be another Adlai Stevenson for a long time to come. Vivian steered the conversation beyond to 1960 and tried to convince the elder Prescott that "young Jack Kennedy," as Sam still insisted on calling him, was aging well and growing into presidential timber.

From the beach the steady exploding of fireworks punctuated the night. The boy was asleep despite the racket, and the others talked over it but each of them could not help remembering other nights during the war. Then, too, there had been the reports of gunpowder igniting, hoarse shouts and women's screams. Once long ago, gunshots had sounded to civilian ears like firecrackers but now in the age of war the crackers reminded them only of gunfire.

"Well," said Vivian, "one Dulles may be all right but the two brothers together represent just too much concentrated power. I like Adlai but I think you may be underestimating Eisenhower. Believe me when I tell you that it was not Allen Dulles—and certainly not Foster Dulles—who stopped the United States of America from using tactical nuclear weapons to bail the French out at Dien Bien Phu. The Nixon gang, and that includes plenty of Agency people, was ready to go. I'm afraid a President Stevenson couldn't have prevented a nuclear strike. But Eisenhower is a bigger general than any of them and he woke up long enough to say no. And now he's gone to the summit virtually on his own. It was a close call and Foster Dulles just squelched Allen completely . . . now, Jack Kennedy *might* just be able to stand up to the war hawks and bring off a real summit . . . you think you hate Nixon now. Wait . . ." Then he decided to come out with it. "I'm seriously thinking of leaving the Agency to help Jack . . . and I wish you would all consider the possibility, too."

But Vivian Thomas Jefferson Prescott did not resign from the Central Intelligence Agency to officially help his friend Jack Kennedy. Premier Nikita Khrushchev made a speech six months later and a series of events was set in train that was to catapult Vivian out of the dead end of his career and change all of their lives.

The "speech," as Dulles and everybody else at Central Intelligence called it, was made in secret. CIA officers had been sobered to learn that the chief of the Soviet secret police, Lavrenti Beria, had been shot at point-blank range by Khrushchev, in person. Beria had not gone down by himself, he took all of his staff, both top and middle levels, down with him. But there had been no retribution wreaked upon the hard-line rank and file apparatchiks of Soviet intelligence.

Vivian and Mush had carefully studied and debated how Khrushchev was gradually losing his grip within the central committee. The premier did, though, maintain an outward mask of enthusiasm in spite of the threat of another poor harvest—the Russians had suffered one the previous year—which would make his removal from office inevitable. Ironically, the unexpectedly bountiful harvest that came created its own unique set of problems.

Now everyone, East and West, was waiting for Khrushchev to drop his other shoe, and gradually he did just that. In order to perform a thorough examination of Stalin's role and the true extent of his repressive measures, Khrushchev and his colleagues on the Central Committee formed a special commission to prepare a report and make recommendations. P. N. Passelov was appointed as the commission's head but he had personally participated in many acts of mass repression himself and was in no way suited to supervise an exposé of terror. But even under the chairmanship of such a man, the Passelov Report revealed with chilling realism the horrors of Stalinism. The report itself had immediate effect, and Presidium members vowed publicly to criticize the abuses it uncovered at the Twentieth Party Congress, which was approaching.

The official agenda of the Congress did not, however, include a specific speech to be delivered by Khrushchev, but because of a temporary lapse in the leadership of the Congress, the Premier came forward with his dramatic move. He called together the delegates to return to Kremlin Hall for a "closed" meeting shortly before midnight on February 24. No foreign delegations, not even from other Socialist countries, were invited. By about midnight he began what was to be, according to varying reports, a speech that lasted anywhere from three to seven hours. Mush's hands shook a bit as he quoted to Vivian. In a straightforward if emotional manner Khrushev began to talk of the horrors of Stalinism, stories that included massive evidence of terror, torture and death. There was no discussion afterward; the stunned delegates simply were overwhelmed; they listened in silence and returned home.

Khrushchev, throughout the speech, spoke on the brink of tears. While he started out in praise of Stalin, he soon got to the fact that during the previous nineteen years of his life the dictator had done enormous harm. Stalin had, during this time, falsified evidence against old and loyal party members, had murdered a virtual army of old Bolshevists, and tortured hundreds more in order to get confessions out of them. Tears were said to have run down Khrushchev's face as he talked about abuses committed upon even

250

small children. Mush was moved as he paraphrased. "Stalin fled to Moscow when Hitler was about to attack Russia. He had erected statues to himself and finally, toward the end, as his paranoia grew to gigantic proportions—"We never knew . . . when we entered his presence . . . whether we would come out alive." . . .

Then they would argue, Mush saying that the denunciation of the tyrant "proves that Stalin was an aberration, not typical. Khrushchev is so much more real—"

"Well, then, where was he all those years?"

"What?"

"All those years when you . . . when he knew and was silent."

Mush stared at him red-eyed. Vivian had turned the knife, now he felt a surge of pity, affection, for the . . . well, failed secular saint was one way to put it . . . "Mush, the speech is going to make history. Everybody knows that."

The word went out in the CIA . . . whoever could deliver a transcript of the speech would be entrenched forever in the Agency hierarchy. At first the analysis of how to approach this problem centered upon which Communist nations had been given copies.

And Vivian was designated the man to do it. . . .

Paris was in the false spring weather of March as Vivian and Mush prepared to leave. The Director himself had given permission for Vivian to draw $100,000 in expense money and to recruit Mush from the Soviet Desk in order to pursue what Vivian had represented as the single best line to a bona fide copy of the speech.

The line began in Paris, he had explained, with certain former Resistance fighters whom he and Mush had contacted in 1944 through Leopold Trepper, the chief of the Red Orchestra. Dulles and Wisner had refused, however, to allow Tim and Pat to leave with them unless the Paris leads all held up. Vivian's standing in the Agency was very much on the line with this operation and, for reasons not quite clear to him, it was apparent that the Company Old Boy elite no longer considered him a totally safe member of the club. Despite Mush's formidable presentation of his French Communist contacts and their access to Soviet intelligence circles, all that Vivian had actually been granted was a working leave and the right to open negotiations. The leash was very

251

short, and the $100,000 was only enough to bait the trap. . . .

Mush had been caustic as they picked up guns and tapes at the Technical Services Division. "In private the limit is not quite as high as the sky, is it? I think Philby's right about them—"

"Please leave Philby out this time, Mush. He destroyed our Rosenberg-Hoover operation." Except, of course, that was not really true . . . The Agency had vetoed public exposure of the FBI . . . and Mush did have a point in his insistence that Vivian at least *talk* with the British master spy before they took off for Paris. Mush seemed to have shaken off his depression. This was a historic assignment even if the brass pretended to be humoring them. Vivian, too, felt on edge, combative. His revulsion with the New York recruitment scene had led him to almost six months of total abstinence from cigarettes, alcohol and, for the first time in his life, sex. Not since the night when the African princess had knelt before him had he been with a woman, though he knew that had Pat been available he would have resumed, perhaps even deepened, their relationship.

Philby still occupied the same old expensive but sloppy George-town flat, still appeared at the door in his pre-World War II Saville Row burgundy dressing gown, and still, in every way possible, managed to provoke and confuse whomever he might have happened to summon to a mysterious midnight treff.

Tonight he opened his cognac-laced monologue with "Watch your back, Viv, on this one, the stakes are very high." Satisfied that he had their undivided attention the MI6 man proceeded to present his thesis. It was simplicity itself: Cain versus Abel . . . "Though he is terribly overrated, at least Allen understands that whichever western intelligence chap comes up first with a transcript of the speech will get all the credit, from the headlines to the history books. At least he's sincere in wanting to protect his somewhat uneven image."

It really was too much. Here lounged Philby alternately sniffing expensive cognac and sneering through both nose and mouth at the whole dirty world in general and the pathetic, benighted farce of U. S. intelligence in particular. How the British must hate us since the war, Vivian thought, to keep this obvious Americaphobe in Washington year after year. Now he was orchestrating his slurred nasal whine through his fleshy nose as if that purplish organ were a priceless musical instrument.

". . . simply shocking that Allen should allow his brother to pull the wool over poor old Ike's eyes by telling him that the cold war thaw is a Red trick. Foster Fulles is quite mad, you know. Reads his Bible the entire night long, then sets out for a brisk constitutional to the *brink* bright and early in the morning." By straining most of the nerves in his body Vivian was finally able to decipher what the aging Tory spy was selling. Allen Dulles wanted the Khrushchev speech for a feather in the Agency's cap, but in subservience to his brother, the Secretary of State, the speech would then be discounted at the same time it was released so that the Pentagon would not miss a beat in its preparations for a hotter war.

This was too much for Mush, who ordinarily indulged his old Spanish Civil War spymaster's xenophobic mutterings. "Kim, you're amazing. You're the most anti-anti-Communist I know. You head up the Circus pack of hard-line anti-Soviet ops and yet you insist that *our* State Department is scheming night and day to plunge the world into nuclear war. I mean, I happen to think you're half right, but all the more reason to get the speech out so that people can see documentary proof that Khrushchev—"

"But, dear boy, of course the Soviet war hawks *also* want to discount the speech *and* bring down the Khrushchev circle as a gang of capitalist capitulationists, as they say . . . but you're not working for them—are you?—tut, tut, easy, old boy. What I'm trying to impress upon you and Captain America, here, is that you two dear boys are going into Paris with strong factions on *both* sides trying to bury that speech before it can be used to pave the road to a bigger and better summit. And I want to give you the names of some of our chaps on the Continent in case the weather gets a bit wet." Philby snuffled and subsided, tried to wipe off the smudges his fingers had made on the oversized snifter. His wicked, tiny red eyes sparkled with happy malevolence, a distant rumble sounded somewhere in the depths of his burgundy-covered paunch. Vivian stood and put his hand out for the list of contacts. You might despise but you did not ignore Kim Philby's oracular word salads. "Here, Ian Burton's your chap in Paris. Drinks the Baltic but an absolute first rater, mmm . . . ."

That first day in Paris Viv and Mush joined one Harold Spare for a stroll around the Left Bank, preferring to exchange information while moving through the late afternoon lull in the open market. Somehow the sight of Spare's road map of a face, lined as it was not only with signs of laughter and pain but with evidence of a creative mind as well, was uplifting to his two younger companions. Three perfectly parallel engravings shot up and outward from the corners of his left eye, splaying into his receding hairline. They could picture him, lost in concentration, sitting for hours on end behind his desk, head propped on a clenched fist forcing the skin up into folds that would leave forever signs of a thoughtful man.

His sense of humor and rumbling laugh made the three men appear to be on holiday as they wound through the deserted stalls, some hung with cheeses, others displaying their wares of plump grapes and graying hens. The fish now lay limp on melting ice, the morning's frigid efficiency long since past. Whoever came to gather the stuff of an evening meal at this hour had to contend with the smell of ripening Roquefort and poultry hung out too long.

To Viv and Mush, however, the odors were delicious. Spare's lively talk was about the state of the Communist party in Paris, and as he eyed the delicacies laid and withering before them, he would make an occasional jibe about his robust weight since his move to Paris not long before. Often, as he held court with the two Americans on the French political *zeitgeist,* his hand would shoot up and pat his more than ample belly, which stood out even under the loosely fitting V-neck sweater.

"The Communist daily here, *L'Humanité,* is now running one of those American-style circulation-boosting contests—the first prize a one-week all-expense-paid trip to Moscow, for *two*—based on the old true-or-false game. Last week *Figaro* ran its own set of questions aimed at goading its rival . . . Stalin was a tyrannical maniac: true or false . . . Stalin was wrong for twenty-five years: true or false . . . the blow really fell hard on the wounded ears of the French Communists here who are still reeling from the attack on Stalin made at the Twentieth Communist Party Congress."

"Are the French Communists still so pro-Stalin?" Vivian asked.

"You bet," answered Spare, plucking a grape while the proprietor of a fruit stall sat napping in a darkened corner under an awning. "Why, those two French delegates to the Moscow Congress were so unaware of the change in the direction of Stalinist sympathies they even made a rousing pro-Stalin speech before they realized this view had become obsolete and was now opposed to official Soviet policy. If they had made such a blunder while Stalin was alive they surely would have been eliminated on the spot."

"But what about the party rank and file here? How do they feel about things?" Mush, as always, was concerned about the people.

"They feel that they've been ignored by Moscow for years in favor of the Italian Communist party. And now they're beginning to say so. Out loud. But they're going to have their troubles de-Stalinizing the Italians . . . what with their history of canons and saints, you mark my words. And setting up the idol of Stalin in the mind of the independent-thinking French worker was no easy task either, but they did it. All that's gone now."

"When did this swing actually become official?" Vivian asked.

"Just last week *L'Humanité* made it so by disclaiming Stalin's theories as erroneous. A violation of what Lenin stood for . . . you know the rest."

"I do know the French really made a personal cult out of Stalin as well as their own man of the people, Thorez. He was the real idol of the French comrades." Mush still knew the workings of his former party.

"This is a real first in the annals of Paris history. What would have been blasphemy in January became holy writ in March, and now five million French workers supposedly have bought it."

They sat at last sipping *café au lait* at one of the outside tables of the Café Select. The squall of the morning had blown itself out against a bright blue sky so their raincoats hung over the two extra chairs at their table.

Vivian felt as if their luck had changed now that they were once again in Europe, the scene of youthful triumphs, and he knew that given half a chance they would pull off a coup. He felt it. The blacklisted screenwriter, Spare, was a find. He had the kind of imagination and perspective that would have made him, had he so chosen, a top agent. Spare was not helping them for money. Both Vivian and Mush agreed that when the independent Marxist with the jolly eyes promised that he would use every contact he had to reach a certain man in the Soviet Union who might help them, he was absolutely as good as his word.

They relaxed in the fine false spring weather as if it were authentic April and took note of the young women passing. Vivian felt a stirring for the first time in months. Their mission was much too sensitive to allow for womanizing—that was surely the easiest way to find yourself set up by any secret service—but when this op was over, with or without the speech, Vivian told himself that he would do something definitive about himself and Pat. If they managed to come out *with* the speech he would tell Allen Dulles what *he,* Vivian, wanted as his next assignment and with *whom* he wanted to work. If they did not get their hands on the speech then he and the Donahues could exercise the option of leaving to join the Kennedy-for-President machine that was even now being tuned up for the run in 1960 . . .

Chicago had followed the format exactly as laid down that night at Fire Island by Jack. Vivian had watched the whole thing on TV with fascination as he sat high above New York City in his Sutton Place apartment. Mostly what had impressed him was the style and grace of Adlai Stevenson. Yes, the candidate certainly did deserve Vivian's father's unqualified admiration. When the Democratic presidential choice had calmly stepped forward and thrown the option of a running mate entirely into the laps of the delegates, Vivian couldn't help being impressed. He'd sat on the edge of his chair as the balloting began, and as he considered the energy with which the Kennedy team must have swung into motion trying to gather votes, he experienced more than a few pangs of regret that he wasn't there to be part of it. For a while, during the second ballot, it had looked as if Kennedy was actually going to make it (in fact, Jack told him later, he had already begun dressing to make his triumphal appearance before the convention as their choice for vice-president). But Vivian, of course, had seen only what was before him on the TV screen:

755½ KEFAUVER
589 KENNEDY

and it was all over for another four years. . . .

At exactly noon the turtle-necked figure of Harold Spare pushed through the promenade and made toward the Select. He slid his barrel chest close to the table and waved the waiter away.

"You haven't by any chance had me followed? . . . Okay, I was sure you hadn't. Well, since I left you, two for real gorillas have been with me everywhere I've gone. I thought that I had lost them last night but this morning they were waiting for me at the metro. Who would they be, do you suppose? They must weigh six hundred pounds between them."

"Do you think it could be the DST?" Vivian asked.

In Paris the DST, counterespionage, installed wiretaps on telephones and other electronic devices in the American embassy for the purpose of detecting suspicious contacts and specifically to monitor visiting agents like Vivian and Mush. Recently, the Americans knew, there had been a growing distrust between the DST and the CIA as the result of a deep rift that had developed between a DST man in Washington and his superiors in Paris, in which the man in Washington was accused by his superiors in Paris of having been turned by the CIA. Naturally, the CIA denied the charge, which didn't convince anybody. The relationship between counterespionage in Paris and the CIA had continued to disintegrate since this incident, which was why Vivian thought Spare's shadows might have been DST.

Spare shrugged his shoulders and went to the matter they were most concerned about.

"You know the Russian poet and novelist, Osip Lieberman?"

They certainly knew *of* him. He had just been forced by the regime to refuse the Nobel Prize for literature. Vivian remembered with what relish he had plunged into his Russian literature honors seminar at Yale, and how he was especially inspired by the works of Lieberman. Now he summoned up the rest of what he knew about this giant of a man, his information gleaned subsequent to his Yale days by flipping through Agency files labeled: P. D.— Potential Defector.

Spare was talking very quietly. "He's a saint to an entire generation of Russian authors. A great poet in Russia is something quite different from America—you know this, of course—but you cannot overestimate the veneration in which this man is held by most writers in the Soviet Union. Here's the point . . . Yuri Kirilov is a minor Russian poet, and secretary, off and on over the years, to

Lieberman. He's in Paris with a Soviet cultural delegation. I talked to him last night and—he says Lieberman has a copy of Khrushchev's speech, smuggled to him by one of the actual *researchers* who helped put it together."

Vivian could have leaned over and kissed Harold Spare on his big round forehead. Instead he stuck his arm straight out and gripped the writer's shoulder. "Wait, you haven't heard my price yet." Spare's perfect potato nose twitched. "Lieberman's autograph—on a first edition." Two women stopped to look at the three men laughing with such voluble gusto.

They left Spare at the Café Select and headed for the American embassy to contact Washington with the news. As they turned down the Avenue Ternes Mush nodded toward two men crossing in front of them to the east side of the avenue. Both were squat and powerfully built, could have been brothers—dark, southern Europeans. Something clicked in unison in Mush's and Vivian's apprehensions. Sherman Scott's goon squad . . .

They had bumped into Sherman Scott in *Le Drugstore* the day before while looking for a hemorrhoid salve for Mush. Scott, in his usual heavy, confidential manner, had side-mouthed, "I'm in deep cover. Contact you later." Sherman Scott was the kind of man who in the opinion of Mush and the Donahues was surely and not too slowly taking over the middle-level control of the Agency. Vivian, though, felt the Scott types could still be stopped. "Scott . . ." Vivian intoned as they entered the embassy gate.

Sherman Scott was a thin, light-haired man of thirty-eight. Above his receding chin the face was thin, too, and the eyes hooded. He affected a pipe and tweeds in order to fit himself into his private image of a well-born intelligence agent. He had been recruited at Dartmouth for OSS. In the Far East he had worked with and grown very close to Chiang Kai-shek's Nationalist ruling circle. After the war he had written several anti-Communist spy novels whose obligatory recipe seemed to depend upon: Red Commie rat killers, practitioners of various devilish cults who worked for the Commie killers, and a series of ripe virgins who fell into the clutches of the cult and/or the killers only to be rescued by the omnipresent American hero-agent "Steve Sargent," who always deceived the killer-cultists, to say nothing of the virgins, by disguising himself as one of the devils. These pulps were churned out under the name Eric St. Paul and caused a good deal of amused disapproval around the Agency.

Scott had joined in 1948 and had begun at once to act out his most lurid fantasies, and Scott was not alone, which was what frightened Mush and other people. A growing number of OSS hard-liners were able to inflame the imagination of hot recruits. This extremist element of veteran agent-handlers combined with idealistic amateurs was spreading through the Agency. Agents who had lived the glamorous life of World War II behind-the-lines glory in a world of Good and Evil longed to recreate the epic of Freedom against Tyranny. Sherman Scott and his ilk lived in the past, in a Homeric golden age of war, and they affected the younger men coming in with their extremist passions. The new recruits from Notre Dame and Michigan State had missed the glory and the combat, they were searching for a rite of passage into manhood and they found it at Central Intelligence under super hawks like Scott. During their first training at the Farm and from there on, the word "clandestine" carried for the new generation of spies the promise of manhood and becoming.

"They think they'll find their balls, excuse the expression, in Latin America or Africa," Mush had once said to Pat. The young agents affected the drinking, dressing, speech and violent tastes of their hero-handlers, who had had the good fortune to have been born early enough to fight, kill and *almost* die in World War II. The booze, the women, the hairbreadth escapes in the deadly breach —the legends of these heroes, of the weak-chinned, knobby-kneed men like Sherman Scott were, Mush was convinced, undermining the Agency and slowly driving it mad.

Scott and the "Animals," as the Prescott group called them, had set out to create a postwar saga. This time the enemy hordes would be members of the worldwide Communist conspiracy and the devil would be Joseph Stalin and if he died, no matter, the conspiracy would generate a fresh incubus of evil to tilt against on the atomic stage. The Khrushchev speech was heresy and deception to the hard-lining Animals on E Street and in American embassies all over the world. They had become the spear carriers in the new secret war that Vivian had joined the Agency, in the first place, to end.

Vivian and Sherman Scott had been sworn enemies since Iran. The Prescott team had been able to create a spectacular eleventh hour turnaround to rescue the situation in Iran from the miscalculations of Sherman Scott and his Animals. Scott had sold Dulles on using General Fazollah Zahedi as the Agency stalking horse to overthrow the government. Dulles, acting for the American powers, said later that he had had no choice.

General Zahedi was indeed a bizarre choice even for the CIA. A six-foot-tall ladies' man with a background in intrigue that paled those of most men in the Agency, he had been Minister of Interior back in 1951 when Premier Mossadegh had nationalized the British-owned Anglo-Iranian Oil Company. The refinery immediately shut down, leaving thousands out of work and forcing financial crisis upon the country. The British then boycotted Iran's oil and consequently left the natives without the resources to run their refineries, so dependent were they on the expertise of British technicians.

Mossadegh then began negotiating with Iran's Communist party. London and Washington had become fearful that Iran's vast oil reserves would end up in the hands of the Soviet Union which, after all, shared a common border with Iran. Mossadegh, at this time, broke with Zahedi who had said that he could not tolerate Communists.

The Anglo-American oil cartel had grown so big and powerful that not even the governments that supplied it with most of its crude oil could defy it. Finally, Iran's largest single industry was forced to close down. The first country Mossadegh went to for help was the United States, but, as in the case of Vietnam, the State Department tactfully refused, not wanting to go against its British ally.

It was at this time that Dulles went on "holiday" to Switzerland and met with the U. S. ambassador to Iran, an Iranian princess and Kermit Roosevelt, a specialist in clandestine activities for the CIA. During these secret meetings a plan was worked out for the overthrow of the government in Teheran. The CIA intended that the coup be bloodless, but General Zahedi, with Scott's hard-liners behind the scenes cheering him on, had a real bloodbath in mind. And if the result was to bring the Soviet Union into the fray, that was so much the better for the Animals, whose philosophy, in any case, was "sooner rather than later."

Meanwhile, General Zahedi was becoming uncontrollable, and the danger of the Soviet Union entering was rising by the moment. The CIA was on the verge of another major disaster. Dulles, in desperation, turned to Kim Roosevelt, who in turn chose the relatively young OSS hero (very much Scott's junior in the Agency), Vivian Prescott, as his aide. It was too late to get rid of Zahedi, and the only alternative left was to make him a figurehead instead of the Shah . . . the real power to go to the Shah anyway.

Roosevelt entered Iran legally, but immediately upon his arrival went under cover. Moving around constantly to keep ahead of Mossadegh's agents, he operated only with the help of Vivian and three men stationed in the American embassy. On August 13 the Shah signed a proclamation dismissing Mossadegh as premier and naming Zahedi as his replacement. This action provoked rioting in the streets and forced the young Shah and his wife to escape to Baghdad and then, ultimately, to Rome. Meanwhile the riots continued, Communists controlling the streets and celebrating the exit of the Shah. Suddenly, though, the opposition to Mossadegh consolidated, and the army, with Roosevelt and Vivian directing from their hiding place, began rounding up demonstrators. Soon it was clear that the tone of the uprising had reversed, and there was nothing anyone could do to change it. (One myth that grew around the coup had it that Roosevelt, in the tradition of his grandfather Teddy, and young Prescott had led the uprising against the tearful Mossadegh with a gun at the head of an Iranian tank commander as the procession rolled through the streets of the capital.) After the smoke had cleared, Zahedi came out of hiding and took up his post as premier; the Shah returned from Rome; and Mossadegh went to jail. But the original Agency mishandling of the situation made the overthrow of a democratically elected government something less than the triumph Dulles liked to claim it was, and although Iran remained faithful to her western ties, little was done to aid the terrible poverty of that land. Somehow the great oil resources never benefited the people, and the vast number of U. S. aid dollars that poured into the country never seemed to get by the sticky fingers of its officials. And even though the overthrow planned in Switzerland was achieved without the bloodbath the Animals had wanted, the restoration of the Shah did nothing to nullify the nationalization of Iran's oil. The Shah was no more about to do that than was his predecessor Mossadegh.

The "American solution" eventually came when a consortium of international companies was worked out to operate Iran's oil industry and turn over to Iran a share of the profits. After some hesitancy, the Shah agreed to this solution, mostly as a result of the desperate straits he found himself in economically. The consortium, however, contained one last hitch unbeknown to the Shah— its secret "clause 28" allowed cartel members to limit or reduce Iranian production to maintain prices or relative market shares. So despite nationalization the cartel managed to sustain its control over Iran. Vivian and his father had argued long and hard over what Sam called "another Pyrrhic victory." How right he was to be proved to be.

Roosevelt and Prescott had saved the skins of the original team of Scott and his hawks and, in particular, had pulled Scott's chestnuts out of the fire at the last possible moment. Scott's response to this, quite naturally, as Vivian knew only too well, was undying and lifelong hatred. . . .

The reason that the two heavyset men crossing the street in front of them had made Mush and Vivian think particularly of Sherman Scott was the Agency's use of Corsican gangsters in Western Europe to break up leftist labor unions. Scott had been notorious for organizing Marseilles dock violence under Marshall Plan cover. Scott had also developed quite a reputation through his activities with the National Student Association's Supervisory Board (NSA). During his involvement with this organization, it was a well-known fact that he would select, on behalf of the Agency, one or two association officers as contacts. At first Scott would tell the young men that they should be aware of certain secrets and asked them to sign an oath of silence. Only after the students signed the pledge of secrecy did he then tell them, "You are now working for the CIA," and from this relationship there was no way out.

But mostly Scott the spook was known for his use of strong-arm tactics in Mediterranean ports. Dulles had tried to interest Vivian and Mush in these plans but they had declined. That would have been even worse than his U. N. nightmare, Vivian felt. The AFL-CIA, they called the leadership of the American labor movement around the Agency . . . the sin of sins in Mush's proletarian perspective—the corruption of the working class.

Scott's history with labor unions went as far back as World War II when American unions had raised large sums to rescue their European counterparts from Nazism. This had also brought them into a close working relationship with the OSS, especially in the person of Sherman Scott, who was at that time the principal U. S. liaison official in these secret commando operations. As the war finally drew to a close Scott and his men followed the soldiers and made sure that as liberated members of the European working class they toed the line with trade unions and political leaders who were acceptable to Washington. All of this was funded by those who wanted to take the wind out of the sails of the political left wing in Europe. The latter-day Scott, more brutally, was still involved in these operations.

Vivian and his team had always worked at the political level, and the thought of getting down in the gutter with Scott was almost more than he wanted to think of on this day. Agency liberals like Tom Braden and Vivian's fellow Yale man, Cord Meyer, Jr., were supposed to muzzle the Scotts, but in fact they depended on them to do the dirty field work while the executives sat high up in the ivory tower of the local American embassy and manicured their consciences. . . .

"Let's go back to the hotel." Mush understood, without words, that if the Corsican strong-arm squad *did* belong to Sherman Scott, then one of Scott's men in the embassy would leak their message to E Street about the Lieberman development. Scott was quite capable, as well, of tipping off the KGB—as the Soviet secret police had recently been renamed since Stalin's death—about Vivian's and Mush's plans to go into Russia to see Lieberman.

They entered the Regents Garden Hotel restaurant and ordered the omelet-with-herbs specialty. "Let's talk here, our room must be wired by the Animals," Vivian continued, covering his mouth with his hand so that the man wearing the thick mustache and sitting near the window could not read his lips—if the man was a spy. Vivian reasoned that if he was not one, someone else was.

"They let us see the Corsicans on purpose," he muttered.

"Who do they think they're trying to scare?"

"Mush, cover your mouth, please. We want to dictate the time

263

and place of any confrontation. Scott's a moral idiot but he's not stupid, and after running into us, which had to be a mistake, he has to cut out completely. So that leaves us the Corsicans to deal with. We have to file false information of some sort to E Street and let it leak to Scott. Then Scott unleashes the Corsicans, for whom we're ready and waiting. Scott gets the message and so do the people protecting him in the Company. Yes?"

"Yes. He's tight with Nixon, you know, Viv."

"I know all about that operation. That's why we're going to work for Jack Kennedy and help him clean house."

"One thing at a time. Let's take care of the Corsicans and then, maybe, we can deal with the Irish."

Vivian's fear was that Scott's cold warrior protectors in the embassy or even in Washington would sell them out to the KGB if they lost sight of him or Mush or suspected that they were going to suddenly produce the speech. It was, therefore, necessary to cover the tracks to Lieberman in Russia and, at the same time, flood E Street with false information so that the hawks did not become unstable and "go critical," as their jargon had it.

The first thing to do was to get Harold Spare some protection, but they couldn't locate him that afternoon or evening.

That afternoon they cabled the first message from the embassy:

BERLIN CONTACT POSSIBLE SOURCE FOR ML/APRIL. REQUEST PERMISSION TO CONTACT EMBASSY BERLIN SOONEST.

The weather was turning sour again but they still sat outside at the Café Select on the chance that Hal Spare would trudge by as he did almost every evening. While they waited they plotted quietly how they might disappear into the Soviet Union.

Washington's answer was waiting in the code room for them the next morning:

YOUR CONTACT BERLIN ML/APRIL IS ER/RAIL.

ER/RAIL, they had learned by noon, was none other than "Tank" Murdoch—Scott's agent-handler in Iran. "That psychopath is supposed to be *our* contact, I mean if we *were* going to Berlin? Viv, Philby was right."

"Mush, don't let Philby's fantasies carry you away. The way I read it is that E Street wants to get onto our leads so that *they* can reach the target by another route and bring in the bacon directly through the DCI staff."

"All right, then where do the Animals come in?"

"They've hated me since Iran, so who better to put on our trail? They're just running errands for E Street, with, maybe, a little Corsicaning on the side for fun and games."

That night Vivian realized that he had analyzed the relationship of forces incorrectly. After dinner they walked over to the Left Bank and around to Hal Spare's converted garden flat.

Spare lay on the bedroom floor. A cooking fork had been driven into his eye sockets with such force that nothing of the tines showed above the congealed and bloody orbs. They stayed long enough to discover that he had been tortured—water and fire—somewhere else, since there was no sign of struggle or blood beyond the Chinese throw rug on which the corpse lay. So that meant that the fork had been driven in as a message to Vivian and Mush when they eventually came around to see the writer. They wiped away any possible fingerprints and left.

As they walked out into the dark night, they began to tremble not only from the blustery wind and rain that had come up but from the horror they had just witnessed. As they proceeded down the barely lit street that contained no sign of life, it was a sad irony that this was the city that symbolized the very essence of vivacity and life to most of the world. The only sounds were the eerie echo of their footsteps on the wet pavement and those of their voices as they bounced off the crumbling yet elegant stone blocks that composed the texture of most Paris residences.

"Mush, did he talk? . . . I don't think he did."

"I don't either. If he had they wouldn't have returned the body for us to see. Also the flat wasn't torn apart so everything must have been put back in place to hide motive from the police when *they* eventually get there." A newspaper began to blow by, a page or two at a time. Mush shivered. "The poor guy." The rage began to shake him.

"Mush, I know . . . they're going to pay. But first we have to come

265

to a decision. I was wrong. Whatever the DCI believes, the Agency is *not* in control of Scott or his people, plus the embassy is full of leaks. I can only figure that as soon as Hal Spare's body is found by the Paris authorities Scott will cable the DCI that we blew the op and that the KGB liquidated Spare after *we* had inadvertently, or purposefully, exposed him to the other side.''

"Unless it *was* the KGB."

"No. For them to do it would *ensure* that we followed up Spare's leads. To kill him like that and leave him to be found—never. He's not unknown, this is going to cause a sensation . . . so, I'm sorry to say that we have to get rid of Hal's body right now. Then—'' A student in a raincoat hurried past. They turned and began to walk against the rising wind.

The priorities were to dispose of the body and then—they had no choice—to go to ground at a safe house provided by Philby's friends. Then let Murdoch in Berlin know that they were en route to meet him and he, naturally, would contact Scott, and Scott would cable E Street. Finally, if Philby's people could be trusted, Mush and he would ask *them* for the documents and disguises that they might need to get to Lieberman at his provincial house out-side Moscow. "Oh, and of course," Vivian concluded, "settle with the Corsicans."

They did not check out of the hotel or even collect their luggage. They buried Harold Karl Spare in his little back garden in the pitch black of the night. The drizzle had let up. Mush Hollander looked for a few words to say over Hal Spare. They crouched on the wet earth of the weedy garden, their clothes and shoes removed and placed on the entrance step. They breathed in the earth's loamy odor rising up to them. "What do you say, Viv, when all your gods are dead?" It was much too dark for Vivian to be able to make out whether or not Mush was crying. Then, as if in embarrassment, he heard him mumble . . . " 'In the coarse yellow grass the poet prepares for the coming of the harvest . . .' "

"Mush? What's that?"

"Something Lieberman wrote in the twenties."

By dawn they were knocking on the caretaker's door at Putney and Sons Ltd. Export—Antiques.

The "caretaker," in his small but comfortable quarters, turned

266

out to be Ian "Skip" Burton, an MI6 man who had worked in Spain in the late thirties with both Mush and Philby. He gave them hot tea and scotch and let them lie down to sleep on quilts on the floor.

Putney and Sons was exclusively an MI6 operation. Within thirty-six hours Mush and Vivian had been provided with the "shoes" (false documents) they needed. Vivian and Mush would go into Moscow as two UCLA professors of world literature on sabbatical in search of scenes portrayed in the novels of Feodor Dostoyevsky. The documents and other props were done in such rich detail that the Americans had to admire the work and once again realize that MI6 was the old master in the world of political illusion, still far ahead of CIA. This was music to the ears of Skip Burton, a cheerful Welshman, completely bald, who could talk about Spain and youth for hours with Mush.

By the weekend they were ready to send the false information to Berlin. After their departure Skip Burton would continue to play messages in Vivian's name to Murdoch at the U. S. embassy in Berlin, from different locations, as if Vivian and Mush were in trouble and on the run. This ploy would give them time and cover to go in the opposite direction and find Lieberman—and, they hoped, the speech.

The matter of the Corsicans was delicate. Since killing them was not absolutely essential to their plan it might be considered a breach of faith, as far as Philby was concerned, to in any way compromise the Paris MI6 operation. They broached the subject obliquely two days before they were scheduled to fly out of Orly for Moscow.

"I know them, all right." Burton nodded. They were, he informed them, strong-arm soldiers of a Corsican family that was involved in the world heroin traffic out of Marseilles and Paris and they were, as well, "CIA contract agents. Strictly Black stuff. *Very* wet." So they *were* Agency contract hit men. Vivian and Mush nodded at one another.

Burton studied their reactions, then he made it clear that as far as MI6 was concerned using killers like the Corsicans was really "terribly bad form."

They had not said a word to Burton about the murder of Hal Spare but he was too seasoned an operative not to intuit that Vivian and Mush would not have come to him by way of Philby unless they were in some sort of trouble with their own "shop." He did not know, either, why the Americans needed to go into the Soviet Union, but he hoped that it had to do with the Khrushchev speech. Philby had certainly not discouraged that notion in their coded communications since his old friend Mush had appeared on the rainy Saturday morning six days before. . . .

They crawled now, in Burton's nondescript Renault, through the crazy twisting turns of *Saint Ouen, Levallois-Perret, Clichy, Asnières, Issy-les-Moulineaux* and *Boulognes-Billancourt.* The heroin cutting factory was in the depths of the Place des Voges warehouse district. Skip Burton drove them, in person, through the ancient alleys just after three of a Thursday morning. All three were in dark seamen's clothing, hands and faces blackened. The plastique was locked in the Renault trunk, wrapped in old painting canvas. According to Burton's detailed file the factory was closed and opened six days and nights a week by a team of four Corsican enforcers, two of whom remained all night to guard the premises.

The car crept along the alley with its lights out. They parked behind what appeared to be an abandoned warehouse. Burton pointed to a gray hulk some fifty yards south on the other side of the alleyway. And at that moment Vivian knew where Scott's thugs had tortured and murdered Harold Spare.

Burton, as arranged, stayed in the automobile. In case of a hitch he was to drive past, lights out, and keep going if they were not there waiting.

Vivian and Mush saw the dim light glowing from the basement window when they were no more than ten yards away. They stopped their low, stalking approach to let two rats scurry past, then went down on their stomachs to crawl away from each other until they were some fifteen yards apart. The explosives were in canvas sacks strapped to their backs. Underneath heavy sweaters each was armed with two snub-nosed police-special automatics.

They began crawling again, inclining toward the dirty glow of illumination, from their acute angles until they reached the basement stairs. Down a flight of five steps was the window. By dropping their heads over the cement structure of the stairwell they could each make out one corner of the room. Mush's angle of vision provided only a square of the room, filled by a table and four chairs. But Vivian, from the opposite point of view, could

268

see the guards. He gestured to Mush to crawl over toward him.

Now they could both make out the scene. Two naked men as powerfully bursting with muscled fat as Japanese wrestlers appeared to be in the process of taking, by turns, a skinny girl who could not have been more than thirteen years old. One of the squat characters pulled the girl up by her hair until she knelt in front of him on all fours. The other one then seized her head and forced his blunt, thick organ down her throat. The first man now left their field of vision momentarily. Within seconds he shuffled back, carrying a squirter can of oil. He pushed the nozzle of the can between the girl's buttocks. As he squirted she left the floor as if the pointed end were an electric prod. All the while his partner held her by the head. Then the man with the oil can tossed it aside and threw himself on her pathetically thin shanks, penetrating her and almost breaking her back with the force of his dead weight.

These were the men who had followed Hal Spare, and murdered him, very likely in this very room. Vivian's imagination erupted . . . Janet . . . it was what the Gestapo had done to his wife . . .

Vivian put his lips to Mush's ear and whispered. They began to crawl toward the stairs. They went down on their stomachs below the level of the window, close enough now to hear the girl's strangled cries.

At the bottom Vivian turned away from Mush so that Mush could reach into Vivian's shoulder sack and remove the smoke grenade. They each extracted one automatic from their safety belts and inserted silencers. Finally they wrapped chemically treated face cloth masks over their eyes and nose.

The glass made a modest tinkling sound as Mush cracked the window open with the butt of his gun and Vivian angled the smoke grenade toward the section of the room where the assassins were with the girl. Moments later Mush vaulted through the opening, taking the rest of the glass and part of the sash with him. The room was half-filled with yellow teargas and smoke.

Mush hugged the floor, taking shallow breaths through the treated cloth of the face mask. Vivian, on one knee, shouted in French, *"Freeze. Police. Don't move or we shoot."*

The girl and one of the men had fallen to the floor, the other man stumbled forward and gasped for air, stepped on the girl's head and lost his footing, crashing to the cement floor.

269

Vivian went in in one long motion. Mush dragged the girl toward the door. Vivian kicked the head of the Corsican who had fallen first, but as he turned to kill the other man a blow to his kneecap sent him staggering and he crashed against the wall. Before he could turn or recover he was pulled down.

Now the immense expanse of sweaty flesh was on top of Vivian, pressing the breath out of his collapsed lungs. The muscle and sheer weight of the Corsican held him splayed on the floor. He began to lose consciousness.

The man loomed above him in the yellow choking smoke. One strike from those huge arms, Vivian knew, would kill him. The Corsican raised himself to smash down. Vivian barely heard the dull ring of the silencer. Mush had shoved the barrel into the Corsican's ear and pulled the trigger. The Corsican fell sideways across Vivian. Pinned, he still could not move until Mush, using himself as a wedge, raised enough of the Corsican's dead weight to allow Vivian to slide out.

The exertion had weakened their resistance to the smoke. Vivian pumped a bullet into the other Corsican's ear. Outside, the girl lay in the stairwell, gasping.

"Mush, let's forget the—let's go, this is enough." Their eyes were watering, the tears streaking the sooty cork covering their faces. Mush took off his sweater and wrapped it around the prostrate girl, lifted her in his arms and led the way up the stairs and out toward the alley. As they staggered through the rubbish-strewn lot they could hear Burton's ignition turn over.

Mush put the girl in the back seat. She was lost in the clothes they put on her, not functioning, disoriented. Burton sped back to the safe house, let Mush and Vivian out and drove on to deposit the girl at an emergency clinic. They hoped that she would remember nothing.

Vivian and Mush stumbled into the house. Mush was in his underwear, having put his other garments on and around the child. They looked as if they had been in a war. They had, Vivian reflected in his exhaustion, they *were*. "Harold Spare . . ." Mush muttered, their mouths and throats were raw from the smoke.

"I know," Vivian got out, "he's still dead."

And so was Janet Hammersmith.

April in Moscow was ominous, with sudden cold spells and ice in the street. Winter was making an obstinate, angry leavetaking, as if cursing the golden domes of the city, fitfully illuminated into a glow by the gestating sun of spring.

Vivian and Mush, as, respectively, Professors Kent and Stern, were slightly alarmed at how smoothly they were able to pass through the in-tourist area at the large airport at the western edge of the city. On two separate occasions, as they took the air in Red Square that first day, Vivian was convinced that they were being followed.

They would entrain from the Kursk station for Osip Lieberman's country home the next morning—was he not *the* great authority and, some said, heir to Dostoyevsky? Their documents, furnished by Burton, stated they had come to Russia to research him and his works. The light had begun to fail, but they quickly realized where they were and turned back from the huge complex of buildings that they had seen photographs of so many times in the laboratories and situation rooms of E Street . . .

So here it stood before them, KGB headquarters, the castle of the bad king. The huge stone facade could have faced any square in Paris or Vienna, so meshed architecturally was it with the style of Western Europe. There, however, it would not have inspired the same awe in the two present onlookers. Night was falling softly on Moscow. Without having to verbalize the notion Vivian and Mush knew that, however their scheme worked out or didn't, Paris and now Russia were fateful signposts on their way. In fact, Russia was their crossroad.

Anyone following them would have overheard two Americans engrossed in a discussion of Dostoyevsky's Moscow, the city into which Osip Lieberman had been born in 1880 . . . When Osip Lieberman was born, Moscow was a study in contrasts. Lavish, golden-domed churches, rich palaces, wide boulevards and very close by, tucked away between the folds of the grandeur, the alleyways and hovels. And always in the background of it all was the presence of the black earth. For Moscow was dependent on the moods of season, not so much a city but a vast feudal town. The king's castle was the Kremlin, while his knights inhabited the palaces around him; between these, in the squalor, lived the serfs.

271

Muscovites had remained insulated from western influence, retaining their earthy sense of life and color, priding themselves above all on an ability to survive the vicissitudes of history. The people of Moscow were the blessed who resided in "the third Rome," and they sat patiently waiting for the rest of Russia to restore them to their proper standing as the capital city.

When the Czar came to visit he stayed at the Kremlin and ate off gold plates studded with emeralds. Wealth and luxury ran rampant through the city's streets side-by-side with dire poverty. Osip Lieberman was born at the edge of this poverty in a once palatial dwelling that had been cut up into apartments. It was called Arsenal Street, and the huge old houses still possessed an aura of a not forgotten, aristocratic past. Like all slums, it was alive and sweating, crowded with hordes of people from one end of Russia to the other yelling in their native dialects. Beggars, wife-beaters and drunks were everywhere, as well as a theological school across the street from Lieberman's window, where he stood as a child, never tiring of watching the divinity students praying in their garden courtyard.

Here in 1905, as a young man, he had watched and listened as the Russian earth trembled. His first book of poems was entitled, simply, *1905*. In that year Russia began to fall apart, not gradually, but abruptly after centuries of abuse and corruption. Nineteen hundred and five: In January the priest Gapon led a protest march of some 200,000 people through St. Petersburg. While they were presenting a petition to the czar they carried portraits of him and his family, all the while singing religious hymns. As they moved through the streets, the air was laced with flecks of ice, brittle snow lay on the ground. When the procession reached the palace, the czar's cossacks opened fire, leaving one hundred and fifty dead and more than three hundred wounded.

The snow lay mingling with the blood of the people, a revolution had begun. Gapon, who later became a double agent, began to preach violence as the only way to get rid of the czar and his family. Less than a month later a young student named Kaliayev threw a bomb at the Czar's uncle, killing him instantly. The assassin calmly gave himself up for hanging, but the violent battle to destroy czarism had begun . . . .

Now, Lieberman was an old man, frail, with deep brown eyes and soft white hair. His neck was thin, his shoulders bony and high, his whole body reduced to its essence of energy and spirit. This very frailness and vulnerability was, of course, his strength in his unequal struggle with the power of the state. He had lived for years in near-total isolation, and even though he was a legend to the world, he was most comfortable blending into the landscape of his homeland, becoming one with the domes of Moscow or the flowing trees of the countryside. He was the last of the line of Russian literary giants, and for those who loved poetry he was the only worthy successor to Pushkin left on earth.

But while all the world knew of his existence, he chose to live out his last years in the obscurity of the countryside, walking its roads, digging in its fields, working only late at night on his poetry. As the drawers filled with manuscripts, so did his old but strangely boyish face fill with the expressive signs of the internal struggles a man has with his soul. He had weathered the worst of the storm. The move inward had begun during the thirties, Lieberman drawing more and more away from the official policies of state and turning toward a world of his own, where the rewards were only of the spirit and the only external signposts, fields and forests, were set in a landscape of changing seasons.

It was this aspect of Lieberman's existence that was new to Vivian: a man's private examination of the universe was not contained in his dossier. All that was provided at E Street was that there were no more poems in praise of socialism or Stalinism, no more verse extolling the Five-Year Plan. Occasionally there would be a brief poem or a fragment of a story that would appear in a literary journal, but since no line he ever wrote was short of being memorable, it soon became obvious that his beliefs were not coincident with those of the state and its rulers.

What was especially amazing was his capacity for survival in a totally hostile atmosphere. One after another of the prominent Soviet literary figures committed suicide, vanished or were shot. They quickly joined the ranks of those who were sacrificed to the cause of unquestioned faith in the regime, which Stalin dominated. Lieberman himself said that he managed to survive only "by a series of miracles," and although he was many times close to suicide, he never really learned why he was spared. Later, sitting and gazing into his extraordinary face, Vivian would somehow come to

273

feel that Stalin had let him be because even he saw in Lieberman the awesome, almost superhuman qualities.

Lieberman would soon provide Vivian with more of the data left out of his Agency file. During the thirties he "lay like a dead man on furlough," never hoping to survive and perfectly ready to die. There was, after all, nothing left to live for; no source of poetry, nothing over which men or God had any say whatsoever. And so he sat by as if in a trance, making a meager living by translating the literary greats of other countries. . . .

The train arrived in the *mir* of Deshkino shortly after noon. The stationmaster was proud to direct them to Comrade Lieberman's house on the outskirts of the little farming town. Mush's Russian had been more than adequate for their needs so far. Lieberman, they knew, spoke six languages, including English.

When no transportation appeared readily available the station-master himself offered to drive them. Within a minute the road broke out into the open. Fields and forests rose up. The country-side was bathed in the fresh spring. Here was the timeless land-scape that surrounded, protected, nourished the *mir*. *Mir*, the word for village, was also the Russian word for world, and in that immense cold world the saying sprang up, "Even death is good if you are in the *mir*." It was here where one found primal peace, the animistic tie to the earth of Mother Russia.

Vivian, unlike the cult of Soviet specialists at the Agency, had come to view the Russians through his exposure to their literature. At New Haven he had learned the world view of the *mir* and its origins in the Russian tradition of infant-nurturing. The long peri-ods of tight swaddling alternated with moments of affectionate interchange at the time of "unswaddling." The Slavic tradition of wooden endurance and apathetic serfdom was, for Vivian, con-trasted with a periodic emotional catharsis achieved by explosive and effusive soulbaring. Now as he looked out over the immense vista of fields and trees he wished that he were still a literary man come to this country in pursuit of what Dostoyesvky and Tolstoy called "the reason beneath the reasons."

Vivian knew that not far from here, in a field cut from the same earth on which they were now riding, the Count Leo Tolstoy had written . . . "The limitless, brilliantly yellow field . . . bounded only on one side by the tall, bluish forest, which then seemed to me a

274

most distant, mysterious place beyond which either the world came to an end or uninhabited countries began . . . The peasants' voices, the tramp of horses and creaking of carts, the merry whistle of quail, the hum of insects hovering in the air . . . the thousands of different colors and shadows with which the burning sun flooded the light yellow stubble . . . all this I saw, heard, felt."

An hour later they were thanking the poet for his hospitality. Lieberman had greeted them as visiting professors—of which, they knew, there was a steady stream to the old white house from all over the world—and offered them strong tea, cold fish and dark bread. The combination was delicious, and the poet was almost effervescent with energy, chatting in the most animated manner about his three children and their lives, asking questions about America. Vivian began to suspect that perhaps the great man was feeling them out to learn whether or not they could be trusted to take the copy of the Khrushchev speech and broadcast it to America and the world. Mush thought so too. After luncheon they retired to a guest room for a rest and in low tones quickly decided not to make an overture that evening but to wait and see if the old man would take the lead.

At four they gathered on the small front porch. Lieberman wore a sort of brown corduroy smock over cotton trousers and shirt, adapted for the spring weather. The planes and bones of his face were a map of his life and character. It was a face warm with wrinkles and skin of a light nut color. His hair was wiry and thick, disarranged from scratching, which he did when he became engaged in a deep conversation.

"Greetings, professors. Now we have low tea. You see no one works. Tolstoy, my master, made a good joke in a diary entry from 1883. I'm paraphrasing, but it was, oh, 'Timetable for the day at Yasnaya Polyana: 10:00 to 11:00 A.M.—coffee indoors; 11:00 to noon, tea on the lawn; noon to 1:00 P.M., lunch; 1:00 to 2:00 P.M., tea on the lawn . . . again; 2:00 to 3:00 P.M., study; 3:00 to 5:00 P.M., swimming; 5:00 to 7:00 P.M., dinner' . . . and so on."

Laughing, passing biscuits that an old woman brought in on a striking blue-and-white plate that had been presented to the poet by his Danish colleagues . . . Vivian had never seen Mush so alive, roaring with laughter one minute, his eyes filling with tears the next as Lieberman spoke on and on in searing bursts of ideas and images. How Russian Mush is, Vivian thought, no wonder he seems more at home here than in America. "Where shall I find my home?" . . . Nietzsche's cry rang in his memory just as Rudolph Mann had phrased it—was it only seventeen years ago?—at Yale. Men like Mann and Lieberman, surely they dwarfed all of the great spymasters that he had encountered, except perhaps for Trepper, the big Chief . . . too late, he thought, for me to find or invent a new set of gods. I'm stuck with the old ones—and the old devils?

The old man was laughing and shaking his finger. He was ready to take on any or all government boards of censors. The river of his life flowed through his words. If the poet was under virtual house arrest then he had, Vivian thought, like the old King Lear, taken upon him "the mystery of things as if he were God's spy."

The controversy that surrounded his nomination for the Nobel Prize did shake him. It differed from the general trauma of war, provoking as it did an intense personal crisis, a conflict whose pains he could share with no one else.

The personal assaults that came about because of his refusal had shaken him, and those who saw him before and after the prize observed a profound change in his demeanor. Before, he had seemed poised for a good fight; afterward, he looked shocked and somewhat defeated. Finally in the late autumn he became ill, and when he recovered he looked more aged, the skin pulled tightly across his protruding bones. He emerged, then, with an inner glow; he was dying, he knew it, and was once again prepared to go. . . .

They could see workers coming in from the fields now, black against the yellow orange of the sinking sun. Vivian felt an inner peace so unique that at first he perceived it only as the relaxation of his interior armor. Mush was hanging on the poet's words, almost breathing them in.

". . . young men, teachers like yourself, have but one lesson to give to youth . . . We are not free and the sky can still fall on our heads, and . . ."

Vivian read another meaning. Was this a veiled reference to the need to circulate the speech in order to move the extremists back from the atomic brink?

". . . poetry consoles us, interprets for us. We cling to ignorance.

To think ahead is terrifying, in the personal sense, yet not to imagine the future—*without ourselves*—is to commit *race* suicide."

The poet's eyes seemed to shine in the gathering twilight, his body one thin tendon of concentration. Mush leaned the whole weight of his head on his hand. This was no pamphleteer talking. This man was purging them of the poison generated at E Street and the U.N. and the KGB. Vivian had had his first love affair with language, but in these last years of war and cold war the words of the humanist vocabulary had been discounted, their meanings slipping or wearing away like old silver. Now it was as if the language center in his cortex were being revived by the thin, unbroken resonance of Osip Lieberman's voice.

". . . what we know in advance terrifies us. For a moment our conscious lives roll along in the wake of time. At first the downward grade is exhilarating, then we see the bend toward which the gathering momentum of the great wheel is turning. It is then that we reach out desperately, clutching at weeds, rocks, nails digging into the earth to stop the downward slide. This needing passion, as we cling to each other, helps make us human . . ."

The old woman servant had come out to join them, leaning now in the doorway, listening. Just beyond this vision, in the gloom, two voices, much too young to have lived in the old Russia, lifted in the prerevolutionary song of lament:

> *The sun rises and sets*
> *but in my prison cell it's dark . . .*

Lieberman's song, too, rose and fell in counterpoint to that of the young workers, and Vivian marveled at the life urge spilling out of this hungry body, remembering descriptions of Tolstoy that he was like "yesterday's east wind," which brought tears when you faced it and numbed you meanwhile.

". . . art is not for everybody, but it is for *anybody*. The only question about a work of art is out of how deep a life it springs. So Dostoyevsky was a vicious reactionary anti-Semite, yet his *moral* genius, not his politics, ignited the revolution once and for all . . ."

A thin trickle of saliva was making its way from the corner of

Mush's stretched-open mouth down along to the palm of his hand. The thought of having to tell the poet that they were spies filled Vivian with shame . . . spies who had not merely come just to compromise his life but to ask him, in a way, to commit treason.

". . . I lay the blame on German poets. They invented a toothache of the heart. Ha! . . ."

Could they turn around and go back to E Street with some cock-and-bull story about what, why and where? Yes, we can, he thought, if we bring the speech with us. We can tell them a space capsule descended with it . . .

". . . my master used to say that his existence had been torn into rags. He was a prophet. This is us, today. Terror—red, white and square. Science—pray to the bomb? Pray with what? The brain? 'Ah,' you say, 'but the mind—' No, no. The mind, too, is flesh and blood, after all. That is why God and man need art. It is art that lays on the souls of men the rails along which they must pass on their way to destiny. There is a direction—I don't mean hateful progress, of course. At the same time I spit on your *Geworfenheit ins Dasein* . . ."

"Thrownness into being . . ." Professor Mann had translated it years ago to Vivian when he also spit on bourgeois existentialism. Who were the realists? The crackpot covert ops in the woodwork at E Street—like Scott and the Animals—or the great adorer in front of him, translating his substance into concepts that had life on their side? At E Street they were lost in dreams on the back of a tiger. Men like Lieberman, they knew a hawk from a handsaw. They were not mad.

". . . and if you clung to the truth, even against the whole world, you were not mad. So you see I *am* a fool. I love in spite of the fact that it is a losing wager. It is the death of passion that the individual must steel himself for, and for which he is no more prepared than he is for his actual death."

Lieberman stood up, unsteady from his exertions. Vivian felt a compulsion to confide in him the story of Janet, his dead virgin wife. To confess something, anything. To have the old man put his thin trembling hands over him in blessing . . .

The woman turned back to prepare the supper. It was now dark. The three stood in a blur on the small porch. Inside, the woman turned on a light in the kitchen at the back of the house. Lieberman stood blocking the doorway, not looking at them. "If I give to you the speech of Chairman Khrushchev, will you put it on the front page of this world?"

Vivian and Mush were walking toward the copse of birch trees. The moon was up now, throwing the white wood into relief. The dinner had been simple and silent. Fish cakes and lemonade and not a word, on any subject, from the poet. Afterward, "Wait," and then he reappeared with a canvas sack. Inside was the original transcript of the speech. "The regime is going to release a softer version very soon. But this is the thing itself." . . .

They had walked almost as far as the approach to the forest proper before Mush spoke. Vivian stopped dead in his tracks. It was not that he was overwhelmed with surprise; it was the shock of recognition that rooted him to the forest floor . . . Mush was not going to return to the United States. Vivian was to take the speech in and cover their tracks by providing a Berlin story of some kind and a series of adventures leading up to the discovery of the speech and the *death* of Mush Hollander. Mush would, he promised, look after himself and make a decision about how he would live before the summer was out. Meanwhile, he would keep the better share of the $100,000.

"Vivian, I know I'll soon be in trouble here just like Lieberman. I know *that*. And I could not work for the KGB. I'm through with this madness—or at least until the next round of the Spanish Civil War breaks out." He was smiling, trying to make it easy for Vivian, the darkness hiding the naked awareness in their eyes and faces.

Mush stooped to pick up a sun-bleached stick of wood, working it in his hands as he talked . . . "There's more. I really believe America is moving toward war, and its own brand of fascism. Scott and the Animals in Paris weren't just an aberration. You and I are the freaks and the aberration. We can't beat them and I can't join them . . ."

Vivian studied the canopy of the forest and the stars and sky beyond. Mush worked the stick smooth in his large square hands. ". . . Kim Philby is a Russian agent. He's been trying to recruit me for years. I would never do it, Viv. But now if I go back I'll have no choice—"

"What?" Losing the thread, his eyes closed in stunned reaction against what he should have seen all along.

"Look, Viv, the only reason we have the speech is because Philby's people bailed us out in Paris and, I think, protected us in Moscow from *their* Animals. I owe him—because I knew. You're safe because you didn't, and besides if he threatens you then you can blow his cover a mile high . . . you don't need them, you can live anywhere in Europe you want. You have money, you have Jack Kennedy waiting for you . . ."

When Vivian opened his eyes Mush had seemingly melted away, walking ahead in the moonlight toward the patient, timeless trees. . . .

The Director took it like a man. Dulles was much too shrewd not to recognize that Vivian Prescott had a formidable and even audacious will . . . an Old Boy who did not play the game, a superagent with the savage reflex strike-potential of one of the Animals, yet with a rigorously independent mind.

Vivian delivered his terms right through the smoke that billowed out around Dulles's furious pipe.

". . . the KGB held us in Berlin for seventy-two hours. I had no way to contact Murdoch or the embassy. Mush made a break for it and they shot him in the head, but it gave me enough time to take a gun away from one of them—"

"And you shot them."

"That's it."

"And the speech?" Knowing it was all a lie.

"The speech was the real thing. They could never have set us up that way, lured us into the countryside if we had not seen their *bona fides.* We held out for a look at the speech. When they showed it to us and set a price of five million dollars, we made the deal. We covered ourselves the best we could. Gave them $90,000 in exchange for fifty pages of text. Then met them at the lake cottage for the balance—and you know the rest." Dulles puffed and puffed, waiting for the other shoe to drop.

". . . it's completely up to you, Allen. I have some very interesting and challenging offers—from outside the agency. And then there's bound to be considerable publishing interest in the whole . . . saga. I *am* still a writer, you know."

The speech in the hands of CIA would cause a worldwide sensation. Dulles knew that it would be the capstone of his career. If Prescott were to quit—and who could doubt him now?—and take the speech to the New York *Times,* then Dulles would be humiliated, *and* who knew what Prescott might know about the Animals —about whom he himself was careful not to know too much—and certain of their methods and sources and so forth . . .

"Well, Vivian, what would you say to Deputy Director of Plans?"

"Operation 'Race Car.' "

"You know about that, do you?"

"I do. And that the overflights could convince your brother that it was safe to take a disarmament plan to the summit." He had called him Allen and had dared to mention his brother in that tone. The stem of the pipe was beginning to crumble under the pressure of the striated jaws. So Prescott knew about Race Car. How?

Vivian had made it his business to know about the U-2 spy plane that had been turned down by the Pentagon. Later, the Defense Department had approved it and the ultra-secret espionage project had, since August of 1955, been flying missions over Russia and bringing back vital information on "airfields, aircraft, missiles, missile testing and training and special aircraft deployments." The secret of its success was the height at which it flew—well over 80,000 feet, so high that the Russians could not shoot it down.

The so-called doves inside the Agency had passed the word that the needle-nosed silver plane was the scientific breakthrough that now made it possible for the United States to negotiate disarmament with the Soviets from strength. Helms, Barnes, Sherman Scott and the hawks were determined to use the overflights as a constant and humiliating reminder to the Russians that they were under surveillance. Once again the issue was joined between the contending factions of the directorate of Black operations . . . between Vivian and those in the gray area of ops and the Bissell-Scott faction, the black of the Black. "In the darkness of blackness," Mush used to quote Melville to make the distinction between "the spies and the spooks, the flawed humans and the Animals." Vivian's eyes on Dulles were cold gray as he tried to bury Mush deep in his memory.

"I'll take it," said Vivian. "Let Frank and his people handle Cuba and the Western Hemisphere. I'll put together my own team to coordinate the overflight intelligence with the nuclear estimates

281

people and take responsibility for working it up for your delivery to the White House . . ." Which he felt was what Mush would have wanted.

All that remained were the details. It was actually a perfect solution—for the time being—Dulles realized. He knew that Prescott would put Tim Donahue in charge of drawing up the master plan and that it would be a superb estimates study and even well written when it was ready. Then, too, Prescott's final demand made the results of the overflights, whatever they showed, failsafe. Vivian had insisted that the project "be covered on the ground," that the U2-op have agents on the ground in the Soviet Union, close up, to verify and amplify the high-resolution photography of the spy satellites. Vivian would run a new program of infiltrating agents into Russia. Recruiting would be handled by the Tokyo station. Servicemen, primarily sailors and marines, would be housed and trained at Atsugi right next to the satellite installation. The whole operation would be under Vivian's control.

As the door closed behind Vivian, Dulles threw his cold pipe into the wastebasket and picked up the black telephone to call his brother.

Vivian had one stop to make before his appointment with Kim Philby. He beckoned to Jack Kennedy and the two strolled out and into the wide marble corridor of the Senate Office Building. By the time they had reached the water fountain and returned Vivian had told the senator that there was no reason, now, to leave the Agency. From his new post at the executive level he could do far more for the Kennedy presidential campaign organization than as a freelance, dependent on worn-out contacts at lower levels of CIA.

"I promise you, Jack, that Richard Nixon will be an open book that you will be able to read long before New Hampshire."

"Viv, I think it only appropriate, don't you, that the youngest President in the history of the United States appoint the youngest Director of Central Intelligence—circa 1961." They laughed and shook hands as if it were Cambridge or London sixteen years ago and they had just concluded nothing weightier than making their amorous plans for the evening.

Walking into the warm air, Vivian debated what and how to tell

Tim and Pat Donahue. He couldn't tell *them* that Mush was dead, but at the same time he couldn't tell them the truth about Philby. Not even them, because if Philby went down, so very well might they, as well as himself. Scott and the Animals would see to that. A series of press leaks would link the Prescott unit to Philby—and the Soviets—over the years since London-Paris-Berlin. The half-truths would be enough to ruin them all, force them to retire in disgrace—disastrously compromised. He grimaced. This would be the first time that he would actually lie to them . . . to Pat. To relieve the ache he would tell her with his body instead of words . . . (In his mind's eye he saw her as she arched her perfect red-headed pussy—it excited him when she talked to him in bed about her pussy—up toward his thrusting organ, her balletic body straining, and he, on his knees, gripping her buttocks and driving his hips back and forth into her soft-hardness . . .)

He would have to tell her part of the truth. . . .

Philby was not wearing the shapeless silk dressing gown and he had not yet switched from martinis to cognac. Otherwise he seemed to be his usual fleshy package of malice and intrigue.

"Not indulging this evening? Wine? No."

"We delivered the speech. Mush is gone and—"

"Gone? You mean—"

"Shut up, Philby. I know everything."

"You—"

"I said, *shut up. You're* answering the questions tonight."

Philby's eyes were black with animal apprehension, his nose puce against the drained pallor of the soft face. He played for time.

Vivian's voice was the slow switching of a big cat's tail. "First, was your Rosenberg caper a set-up?"

"No. They never worked for . . . us."

"Then why in hell didn't your government do something?"

"We did, dear boy. Behind the scenes."

"Shit!"

"I say. Who would have believed us? Think of that. I did put you onto the informer and I offered Mush a—"

"All right, that's your story. Second, in London, the Red Orchestra connection . . . were you—"

"But Vivian, we were *allies.* Be fair. I've always tried to help you.

283

It's your own bloody ten slash two boys who tried to do you in in Paris. Let's not rewrite history." Philby was not slurring or swallowing his words tonight.

"No, let's not. Third, all the Anglo-American operations in Albania and Hungary and the bloc countries . . . you sold them out?"

"Listen to me, Prescott." Every word was a tiny dagger. "The Central Intelligence Agency had lost control of its bloc ops. Those dreadful thirdraters and playboys in your shop were right on the brink, so to say, of *World War III*. That's the truth and you know it. Sold *who* out?"

They stared at each other.

"Philby, I want you to know that I hold you personally responsible for whatever has happened or happens to Mush Hollander. A tremendously decent human being whom you have betrayed, *criminally,* has become a nonentity, and that is unforgivable. I never want to see or talk to you again."

Both were now up and walking fast to the front door. Both possessed of the same grace and authority of their "background," both locked in a life-long ambivalence with their "breeding," both, in their way, traitors to their "class." The difference between them was half a generation of time, and chance. The secret society of Skull and Bones had simply not called out Vivian's loyalty the way the young Communist club at Cambridge had captured Kim Philby's.

The Soviet masterspy's face was drawn and white, Vivian's flushed. The door was about to be slammed on a relationship born in those simple, good and glamorous days of World War II. Philby reached for the door, Vivian stared through it into the moonlit forest, where a part of him had wanted to follow Mush that night at Lieberman's country retreat. It was over. They would never, he thought, any of them, ever meet each other again. . . .

Not until the spring of 1963, when Philby would inform Vivian that a conspiracy to assassinate President John F. Kennedy was approaching its final stage.

BOOK III

Dallas, 1963

The Death of Lancer

VIVIAN STEPPED out of the shower into the steam. The green-and-white tiled floor between the rugs was cool under his feet. He rubbed his head vigorously, then mopped the mirror clean. The ivory shaving mug and badger brush he set out were from his London days and would have appeared old-fashioned to most Americans. He toweled himself slowly . . . he had more than two hours before his surprise appointment with Kim Philby, whom he had once told he never wanted to see again—and had meant it.

Vivian brought a dry green towel into play, looking into the mirror as he rubbed himself dry. At forty-three years of age the body and skin tone of the former Yale intercollegiate tennis champion were those of a man a decade younger. As he wrapped the towel around his tapered waist before shaving, the muscles of the torso and arms rippled back to him from the mirror, making him think, ironically, of a phrase from Hemingway . . . "We are young and we will never die." Young or old, he reflected as he looked at his face, depended on when you lived and when you died. The rich chestnut hair was flecked at the sideburns with brushes of gray, the temples becoming more prominent as the hairline had receded slightly, the wide-set eyes large and blue-gray as ever. Looking into his eyes, the resemblance to both his father and his son rooted him in time and generation. Neither that father nor son really knew their own flesh and blood—Vivian Thomas Jefferson Prescott, the Deputy Director of Plans of the Central Intelligence Agency. Neither did they—he would indulge himself with the rather pompous thought—know his soul. If he had lived in the period before the writing of history he would be, after four decades, considered a very old man; his father, at seventy-three, would certainly be dead, while his son, Terry Donahue, just thirteen, would be entering the rite of passage to join the adult members and warriors of the tribe. In fact, his father Samuel Adams Prescott was in New York City alive, well and almost fanatically involved in the search for world peace. Vivian's son by Patricia Donahue, Terence Michael Donahue, was entering not the *Gemeinschaft* of the primitive warrior class but rather the Greeley Junior High School of Hamilton County, Virginia.

Vivian lathered up the light growth of red beard. He did not hurry; he had chosen to take the day for his personal use rather than attend a series of office parties out at the huge Langley, Virginia, facilities of Central Intelligence. He also wanted time before his appointment with Philby to think things through . . . he could only assume that Philby had reappeared from out of the blue in order to bring him news of Mush Hollander from the Soviet Union, the news of his death. He scraped the lather clean from his prominent Adam's apple with the long, old-fashioned straight razor and stared deep into his own eyes in search of guilt.

Face it, he *had* profited from Mush's defection, or disappearance . . . or death. He had gotten the full credit for bringing in the

Khrushchev speech, and he had vaulted high over the heads of Agency hawks and hard-liners to his present role as DDP. His special relationship to President Kennedy was well known. Widespread speculation had it that Vivian T. J. Prescott was slated to become the next and youngest Director of Central Intelligence in the short history of the Agency. The hand of those favoring limited action against the Soviets had been strengthened immeasurably by the elevation of a man with Prescott's outlook to the second highest position in Section C, or Plans, the division of clandestine operations. Those like-minded who had not been purged during the McCarthy witchhunts quickly coalesced around Vivian, the better to cling to what they felt to be the diminishing edge of sanity within the Agency. This group was referred to bitterly by William Must, Sherman Scott, James Angleton, Helms, Barnes, FitzGerald and others as the "doves" or the "bleeding hearts." The Prescott critics were, in turn, still described by Vivian's faction as the "hawks" and the "Animals."

The small but extremely effective Prescott fraction in Central Intelligence made themselves into a constant stumbling block to the hard-liners who awaited with apocalyptic certainty the opening atomic salvos of World War III. The deep respect accorded the Donahues, Tim and Patricia, and their subordinates for their work in the Psychological Warfare section of Plans was an important buffer for the Prescott forces. . . .

Vivian completed his toilet and walked naked down the hall to his bachelor bedroom and switched his radio on to the music station. Gershwin. From 1956 Tim had been the complete deputy to Vivian in everything from the U2 agent program—BR/RAZE— to the 1960 Kennedy campaign for the presidency.

Tim had, if anything, grown more quiet with the years. Most of his free time was spent working around his Virginia house with his "son," Terry, or taking the boy out for a round of golf on the public links. And still on Sunday mornings the two would go to early mass and then to a coffee shop for pancakes. Tim was thinner, more drawn, his short-cut red hair dotted with pure white. Often Vivian would spend the weekend and the four of them, in fine weather, would play doubles. Under Vivian's expert tutelage the boy had achieved an all-state ranking in the junior tennis division.

289

Terry was slim, very tall for his age, red-headed and, like Tim, quiet, with flashes of his mother's wit.

Vivian's relationship with Pat had gone a difficult course. As if by tacit agreement both of them shied away from extended personal deception of Tim. Their daily work in Section C was in itself so disingenuous that they each sought constantly to maintain a stance of good faith in the no-man's-land of their affair. When travel did not provide an opportunity for intimacy they would avail themselves of a safe house under Vivian's control near the Farm.

Much of Tim's time was spent in the most sensitive top secret area of the Pentagon, where under cover of Military Estimates he controlled the budgets and planning for a series of behavior modification experiments conducted by the Agency at medical and military installations all across the country. In San Diego, for instance, perhaps the Company's most sensitive project was run under cover of the Office of Naval Intelligence. Tim carried this blackest of Black ops in his classified records as "The Use of a Symbolic Model and Verbal Intervention in Inducing and Reducing Stress." The euphemistic subheading read "Special Programs for Servicemen Not Naturally Inclined to Kill." Tim made it his business never actually to observe any of the experiments conducted by the Agency's psychiatrist, Dr. Marion East, and his staff. Vivian, however, as the Director of Plans, had no choice. He had to be familiar with what the Agency liked to label "anti-brainwashing techniques."

For this so-called stress-reduction training the subjects were taken either to the navy's neuropsychiatric laboratory in San Diego or to another one in Naples, Italy. There they were first taught to shoot, and then they began their strict regimen of "Clockwork Orange"—Dr. East's term—desensitization, finally purging themselves of any qualms about "extreme prejudice."

According to the doctor the level of shock contained in the films grew in severity as the training proceeded, until the content became more and more gruesome. "In this way," said Dr. East, "the trainees learn to cope with the most terrifying aspects of life with complete detachment. As soon as the physiological monitoring of vital signs such as heart and breathing rate show normal patterns during the most bloodthirsty scenes, the men are judged to have completed this stage of training. Those who do not are presumed

290

to have failed." East was holding forth on his work to Vivian in his Brentwood home, less than a mile from UCLA. Vivian was always the genial doctor's houseguest when Agency matters brought him to Los Angeles, a city that Vivian had never trusted. East was an expansive host, a gourmet cook, and loved to expatiate on the wonders of the behavorial sciences. He made Vivian sick to his stomach.

Vivian tuned him out, hearing only "the last phase of the entire procedure is known as . . ." MK-Ultra was so classified that even the President had little knowledge of it.

Still, Vivian knew that as far back as 1943 the Office of Strategic Services had sought to develop a truth serum for use against enemy agents. The OSS agent who had played the key role in this project was none other than Sherman Scott, who had become involved in drug experiments as early as the 1940s.

A derivative of marijuana was being used in the search for a truth serum in 1943, and after Scott tried it out on himself he traveled from Washington to New York, where he checked into a hotel and used it on unsuspecting guests he lured into his room. All the while he was guarded by armed intelligence agents protecting this wartime weapon.

Although by 1953 Allen Dulles was admitting the unethical nature of MK-Ultra, he justified it in the name of urgent need, stating that it was necessary to find "effective and practical techniques to render an individual subservient to an imposed will or control." Though warnings did come from within the Agency, they were aimed more at keeping these activities concealed from the American public than at the nature of the activities themselves.

The urgent search for a wonder drug soon passed from marijuana to LSD, the magic substance that would enable the Agency to control human behavior. Scott's memo to Helms states its uses: "Disturbance of memory, discrediting by aberrant behavior, alterations of sex patterns, eliciting of information, suggestibility, creation of dependence."

CIA also sought to discover drugs that would confuse thinking and create impulsive behavior to the point where the recipient would be made to look foolish in public. A knockout drug that could be secretly administered in food, drinks, cigarettes and aerosol was highly sought after as well. One more was wanted: a drug that would make it impossible for a man to perform any physical activity whatsoever.

The Agency wanted to create pain, produce headaches and render the subject susceptible so that he might be manipulated. "Amnesia is another major goal, and by extension, control over people's memories in general. To wipe out certain areas of experience and leave intact only what the Agency wants, this is indeed an objective to strive for," read one of Scott's flow of memos to Helms and Dulles.

Murder was also on the agenda. In the past it had been too messy an affair. In order to neaten it up the Agency set about learning how to kill without leaving any ugly residue. Much neater to drive the target to suicide.

Scott was dedicated to the MK-Ultra project. He began his duties by setting up a "safe house" in which to conduct experiments. First he put himself up in a Greenwich Village apartment that he completely wiretapped, and then took up the profession of pimp, in the interests of national security. He then proceeded to hire prostitutes in order to lure men from the neighborhood bars to the bugged apartment, where the drinks were spiked with LSD and the conversations recorded. Scott had a number of methods to get the drug into the unsuspecting consciousness of his guests: coated swizzle sticks, injections through wine bottle corks—he even tried to spray it in the air. His operation in New York was so successful that he was sent to San Francisco to open a West Coast extension.

Vivian understood that the number of people involved in these experiments probably numbered into the thousands over the years. But many university scientists participated and took money, believing their studies to be entirely independent, since at no time did any of the foundations reveal their link with the CIA.

In 1963 Vivian and Tim Donahue wrote a report stating that "the concepts involved in manipulating human behavior are found by many people both within and outside the Agency to be distasteful and unethical. Since the United States is a signatory to the international standards formulated at the Nuremberg war crimes trials, which assert that medical experiments on humans are to be undertaken only for the good of mankind and with the full, informed consent of the subjects, it is not rhetorical to state that the CIA in the MK-Ultra case is actually guilty of war crimes, with the unusual twist that they were conducted mainly against Americans.''

Despite this warning, Scott and his men at the Agency continued their gambles with the human nervous system, and it was during the San Diego experiments that Tim was called to San Francisco to set up the books and covers for a scheme hatched in Section C by an in-house team. He informed Vivian that he was disgusted to learn that the Agency was to set up a whole series of plush houses of prostitution in order to administer mind-altering drugs to unsuspecting customers. He hated to be involved, even from a distance, with a project about which he was ashamed to tell his wife.

Vivian, for his part, would not have told his father about such creative projects as the use of cobra venom and shellfish-toxin-tipped poison darts that had been perfected in the Technical Services Division. These "micro-bio-inoculators" were so tiny that the victim felt nothing when penetrated, and no trace of the dart or the poison could be found later on his clothing or skin.

This was Project Naomi. Naomi's most ominous achievement involved a simulated biological warfare attack on the subway system of New York City. Bulbs loaded with a nontoxic substance were placed on the tracks; when the bulbs were broken, the substance spread through the air over forty-three blocks of tracks. Vivian himself had been obliged to test poison-dart launchers concealed in fountain pens, umbrellas, walking canes, and a light bulb that spread death when turned on by the victim. He felt like a fool, and worse, and tried to remind himself again about staying the course, working from the inside. By now, though, reason was not enough. Rationalization was the only device left; A covert process that even the subject was not altogether aware of.

Tim was frequently required to collect data from San Diego and then fly or drive up to the University of California at Los Angeles. There, under Department of Zoology cover, experiments with apes were conducted—the objective being to program the chimpanzees and orangutans into a capability for wartime close combat encounters with a PE, potential enemy—"Tarzan and the British Foreign Office," according to Pat's mordant estimate of the relevance of this twenty million dollar covert op. She was no less caustic in relating to Vivian and Tim her own "hush-hush science fiction" at the Farm. ". . . a 'psychic shield' we're calling it. Not to be outdone by the two of you, *I'm* going to prevent the Soviets from infiltrating the subconscious minds of our leaders while they sleep. Really, Viv, they say it can be done. And what we're doing is trying to jam the waves so that mind-reading experts from enemy countries can't use their extrasensory powers to spy on us. Go ahead . . . laugh . . . It really is a major threat to our national security, you know. *Mind Fucking as a Political Weapon* . . . now how do the two of you like *that* for the title of my next book? . . ."

Vivian opened the bedroom heating grate a bit wider and began to look for a favorite pair of old gray slacks in the recesses of his walk-in closet. He thought now of Pat and the safe house and of their ritual of lathering each other and showering together before making love. . . .

The safe house was actually an apartment near Gaithersburg, Maryland, in an old red brick building cleverly designed to suggest the Colonial period. Whenever possible they would leave the Farm early, drive to Gaithersburg and enter the apartment through a private entrance.

Vivian, trained in the analysis of patterns, had come to recognize his own with Pat. It was her almost athletic physical assertiveness that most excited him. Often she would begin to fling off her clothes before he had even shut the outside door. He would hear the water spattering against the glass door of the shower and hurry to join her. Inside she would soap him all over, slipping her hands around his groin until he was erect, then handing him the bar to do her; turning her strong, straight back to him and slightly arching her firm small buttocks so that he could slip his soapy hand between her legs. Sometimes she would kneel there, under the spray, to suck him almost to the point of climax.

In the bedroom they would towel each other. The current of Vivians's urge would sometimes swell to such a level that he would grasp her by the buttocks and lift her up and onto him. And she, the gymnast, would lock her slim legs around his waist and thrust the erect nipples of her still-firm breasts close enough for him to nip and kiss. He would hold her, balanced and notched around his long still-lean body . . . pumping with such force that her hands eventually had to lose their grip from around his neck and let her body fall away, he catching her just above the swell of her hips and

294

holding her extended in the air, his powerful fingers sinking into her back, almost slamming her hips back and forth as they approached mutual orgasm, both of them in rising crescendo, calling out each other's names, then falling sideways onto the until now untouched double bed. . . .

Those were the best times. There were others. Not that the other times were bad. Pat kept a few old Benny Goodman and Stan Kenton albums from Chicago at the safe house and liked to put them on if they had a glass of wine and time for a talk. "I'll subvert you to my middle-brow ideology," she told Vivian, and he admitted that the big bands were indeed seductive and compelling in their innocence.

Many times they would talk without making love . . . about innocence and evil and whether they had known what they knew. Pat considered her *un*official role in the Agency to be of some importance—running interference and generally watching out for the interests of the Prescott group, "not 'doves,' *'eagles'*—if *they're* 'hawks' then we're 'eagles'," and her jargon was picked up and circulated: hawks versus eagles. But her assigned work, she told Vivian, was only marginally redeemable or relevant and she intended to quit for good after the 1964 election and do some teaching in the school of social sciences at Catholic University in Washington.

"What are *you* going to do, my love?" she had asked Vivian two weeks before.

"Funny you should ask . . . well, we have to reelect Jack with a big enough majority so that he can maneuver with Congress and the Russians."

"When will he appoint you DCI?"

"I think in 1965, when he doesn't have to worry about reelection."

"Why, do you expect a congressional fight?"

"And how . . . the FBI, the Animals in our shop, the entire Right —these people own a lot of elected representatives. They'll come after me in the open through their media assets . . . and *behind* the scenes, well, love, they'll probably circulate pictures of us, you know, of—"

"You eating my pussy!" And the two rolling around on the bed with

laughter . . . "Oh, God, all you fine gentlemen are such little boys. I can see Sherman Scott or Des FitzGerald lurking around the Capitol in long raincoats, flashing dirty pictures. It's too funny, Viv. Where are they hiding? I'm ready for my close-up!" Then wiping away tears, "Seriously, Viv, do you think they will?"

"Of course. That's why they have to be stopped now, before they manage to unhorse us *and* provoke another missile crisis . . . and how many brinks do you think we both can go out on before one of us idiotically falls off . . . ?"

The talk turned to Kennedy's covert campaign to stamp out the cells of the secret army that had been recruited and then cut up at the Bay of Pigs but that, like a serpent, was slowly reconstituting itself into an even more dangerous organism than before. "We've scotched the snake, not killed it," quoted Pat from *Macbeth*. "She'll close and be herself again."

Except that they knew it would be worse, and that was why Vivian talked with her about the leaking of Cuban exile operations to Bobby Kennedy so that he could put the FBI, Treasury, Coast Guard, customs and local police into action against covert ops, including those involved from Vivian's *own* directorate.

"If the hard-liners ever learned that we're blowing Company personnel and operations to other agencies of our government they would react exactly as if I'd given the information to the Soviets. I'd be a candidate for termination with extreme prejudice."

"And they've degraded and discounted the English language to the point where it would take another Shakespeare to purge it . . . but you know . . . all these years, Viv, and I don't think that I really know you very well. It just seems to me that the built-in secrecy of the decision-making process at the Agency has reduced you to . . . well, literally, now don't get mad, whistling in the dark. The man I've loved, off and on, since 1942 . . . God, Viv, do you realize that it's going on twenty years? . . . In a way you've sort of traded off autonomy for power . . . Do you know what I'm saying? I mean—"

"I hear you. You expected, so did I, that I would have sufficiently violated the rules of their insane game long since and been fired. I think if you hadn't believed so in my rebelling that neither you all . . . nor Mush . . . would ever have joined in the first place."

"I think that's true. I think we gave ourselves about two years.

Of course, Mush didn't have much choice in that period . . ." For a moment the memory of Mush leaped between them like electricity. Mush, stubborn and outraged . . . "I've dreamed about him so often," she said. Vivian said nothing, but he could see the hunched shoulders retreating across the harvested field toward the birch forest waiting in the dark . . . Because he had never detailed what had happened in Russia, she and Tim had assumed that Mush was dead. It was what Viv had counted on, and he was at once grateful for that, and yet somehow ashamed.

"If Mush were here," she said after a silence, "he would tell us to expose the whole Agency murder incorporated, if the President is afraid of an open confrontation. Mush would have no time for the Kennedy brothers. It was their idea to adopt your idea of substituting surgical clandestine war games for Dulles's nuclear brinksmanship. You *know* what Mush would say, after the Bay of Pigs . . . What are you thinking?"

"Mush's 'crumbs'."

"What?"

"Mush's crumbs. Don't you remember—"

"My *God!*" Remembering with a chill their son's description of the cremated remains of the dog. "Mush's crumbs. What made you think of that? . . . What about *our* crumbs, our ghosts and memories . . . where've the years gone, Viv?"

" 'The body remembers.' Professor Mann used to say that the mind was flesh and that it is the *body*, not the mind, that remembers."

"What does that splendid tennis champion body of yours remember? Does it remember me?"

Her question stirred more than he could tell her . . . His body could still remember the descent out of the night on Deer Island of his outrageously young stepmother, dead now, savaged by cancer, yet along the rivers and valleys of his body, across the expanses of erectile tissue, her impression lingered like the image on a photographic plate.

"Janet?" Pat asked softly.

"Janet . . . Pat, the Germans abused her sexually, didn't they? You can tell me."

"I think so . . . because after they killed her they stopped their, uh, foreplay with me . . . Do you *remember* Janet?"

"Pat, Janet was a virgin until they killed her." The old wound

297

opened up as he talked. The light was fading, the swing records were long since over, Pat came over to sit on his lap as, his head back against the chair, he searched through his memory for Janet. ". . . the most courageous and the most frightened person I think I've ever known . . ."

After a while he picked Pat up and carried her back to the bed. "Do I remember you?" He nuzzled along her shoulder. "Let's take inventory . . ." touching and talking as he undressed her . . . "hair, color of elm leaves just before they fall—you're partial to poetry, ain't you? . . . hazel eyes, sometimes green, that *almost* see through me . . . two lips, indifferent red, and sharp little teeth that can kiss and bite . . . one neck and two shoulders, smooth with crowds of freckles . . . two alert perky breasts . . . one belly button and belly, curving toward the horizon, covered with auburn colored down, sloping down to the mouth of desire . . . all warm and moist as memory, and ready, thank God, for me."

It was time to leave for the meeting alone with Philby. Vivian slipped on a fur-lined Swedish half-coat and started for the door, then returned to his bedroom to tuck a hand-sized Astra .22 automatic into his coat pocket. He had not, for many reasons, including self-interest, turned Philby in, but he sure as hell was not about to trust him.

He drove out over the Key Bridge from Georgetown toward the Virginia motel Philby had specified in his abrupt telephone call, the voice as condescending as ever, a sound from out of the past that filled Vivian with apprehension. This was the last workday before the Christmas holiday of this year of 1962 for government employees, but the highway would not be clogged with home-going traffic for another hour. The weather was overcast and in the low 50s. Within fifteen minutes he had passed the highway research station sign that every secret service in the world knew indicated the turn-off to the new Central Intelligence Agency facilities.

At least, Vivian thought, as he sped west into Virginia, Philby had not had the run of the new plant. At least the KGB did not have an exact blueprint of the Agency, which unquestionably they would have had had not CIA suspicions forced Philby, the supera-

298

gent, to leave Washington in the 1950s. Or did they? Was it not probable that Philby, in turn, reported to a control in the United States? And who could be over Philby if not some "mole" in the Agency itself? These questions haunted the executive cadre at CIA, especially Vivian and his Yale classmate James Angleton and Angleton's hard-liners in the counterintelligence section.

After all, Philby had seemed the quintessential Tory. An anti-Communist so militant that he had risen to the head of the MI6 anti-Soviet section. By the same token that meant that a hawk like Wisner or Barnes or FitzGerald, or *even* Scott, *could* be a classic penetration agent, recruited back in OSS days in Europe or Asia. It was crazy, of course, but it would also explain, rationally, the string of disasters that had become so obvious since Philby's sudden departure in the mid-1950s. What if a fiasco like the U2 or even Bay of Pigs could not be laid so simply to blind hawk mentality or suicidal provocation? Vivian knew only too well how MI6, the greatest secret service in the world, had been compromised, as well as CIA at the highest level, by H. A. R. "Kim" Philby.

Duplicity was, after all, almost an inherent part of Kim Philby's nature. Kim was the offspring of a powerful father; St. John Philby did not hide from his son the contempt and cynicism with which he viewed his countrymen. A person of many contradictions, on the one hand an Empire man and a collector of intelligence, an Arabist raising a son within a desert palace; on the other, a wheeler-dealer in consumer goods, the person responsible for bringing fancy American cars to the sheiks. Occasionally he switched roles and sold oil concessions to the United States, all the while repenting, with a self-righteousness that survived in his son, the morally questionable quality of his enterprises. Kim Philby's inheritance from his father was rich indeed: from him he acquired the neofascist manner of a slightly deranged English gentleman, the Establishment's way of rationalizing brutally self-centered decisions and masking them under the name of a high-flown cause. When Philby was old enough to be placed in the hands of the English Establishment for his education, he had assimilated enough of his heritage to fool even the most astute of his enemies. Like Kipling's boy, "he had known all evil since he could speak—but what he loved was the game for its own sake—the stealthy prowl though the dark gullies and lanes . . ."

Vivian knew that the British and the Americans would be lucky to find out even a fraction of the damage Philby had wrought: the plans betrayed, agents blown and sent to perdition, codes leaked, master strategies shredded. He had got through on class, style, vanity, and played up to the snobbism and self-styled aristocratic pretensions of the Anglophiles in the Agency. In the world of the Raj, the Empire and the white man's burden, Kim Philby walked like a ghost of Britain's imperial past, and none quite dared to challenge his credentials. Vivian himself had barely escaped becoming a permanent member of that club, the world of Skull and Bones and everything else they had tried so hard to inculcate in him at Yale . . . .

He slowed his Buick sedan now and pulled off the highway, coasting around behind the cluster of bungalows to park. Philby would be in number 4. He touched the outline of the gun in his coat pocket, took a deep breath and climbed out for the meeting with one of history's most amazing secret agents. . . .

"Hello, Viv."

"Hello, Kim."

"Viv, you look fantastic. James Bond himself." They had both worked with Ian Fleming, the creator of the James Bond books, in Canada at Camp X.

Philby looked terrible. The bloodshot eyes and broken capillaries told the story all too clearly of a famous drinker whose luck has run out. The sick-sweet smell of gin was on his breath as he leaned past Vivian to shut the cabin door, and a half-empty bottle sat on the rickety nightstand next to the rumpled, sagging double bed. Philby turned and surveyed the room with Vivian. "So typically American, isn't it? The setting for a thousand guilty couplings. It is clandestineness itself, and so very fitting for my last treff in the United States."

"How long are you staying?"

"Until tonight. Then, home." It might have been in this very motel cabin that Philby had met with his Soviet control for countless debriefings in the days when he rode so high in Anglo-American secret circles. The motor hotel was no more than fifteen minutes from the Agency grounds.

As if reading his mind, Philby mumbled, "I assure you, old chap, that this place is clean—if you will permit that word *here*—you'll

300

believe me when you hear what I have to say . . . Gin? . . . take off your coat."

"That's all right. It's cold as hell in here." Philby, of course, would know that he was armed. Philby was attired in a baggy tropical suit with no sign of an overcoat in the two-wire-hanger closet alcove.

"Right with you." Philby shuffled into the lavatory. Vivian sat gingerly in the single wooden chair after moving it away from the broken, shade-drawn window. The Soviet spy's small suitcase sat at the foot of the bed.

The toilet pipes protested and Philby emerged, propped up the pillows and lounged on the bed, sinking deep into the valley of the splayed mattress. "Ahh, if this old bed could talk, hey, Viv?" Philby reached for his water glass of gin on the nightstand. "What tales we would hear of salesmen and spies, concupiscent college students, and gay G6 clerks in search of the passing moment to which they might say, 'Linger awhile, so fair thou art.' "

Vivian nodded noncommittally. How suitable, he thought, for a devil like Philby to quote Faust . . . "Well, Kim, what can I do for you?"

"Right. Down to business. Viv, I haven't come back *just* to see you, but I do appreciate your coming out here, if even just for old times' sake."

Was the man going to ask for money? Vivian waited. The rising noise level of the traffic on the highway penetrated the thin walls of the cabin.

Philby drained his glass and rapped it down. "Viv, I'm blown, dear boy. I tell you this because I happen to know that in all these years you have never, ah, betrayed my little secret. But this is it. I'm through. In a few weeks I'll be in Moscow and CIA will be in a state of terminal shock. The damage is obviously so great that the Agency, like the British, will have to play the story way, way down. So I don't expect any important purges in London or Washington. If all goes well in the next few days, I'll be in Moscow and I can promise you that I will look for Mush Hollander. By the way, do you have any message for him? If he's alive?"

"Not that I'd care to give you." The unlit room was darkening. Horns blared out on the highway.

"No, I quite understand . . . you think very badly of me, don't you?"

Vivian studied the pattern of flaking paint on the far wall next to the window.

Philby sighed. Then, though he had not intended to—and this Vivian knew—Philby put him into the picture one last time. Vivian listened, knowing that whatever it was that Philby had come here to disclose would have to wait until he had made his confession. The story took exactly four Gauloise cigarettes to tell . . . .

"Jim Angleton and your counterintelligence sleuths have actually been slinking about Beirut with their dreadful poison darts looking for me. You know the routine, disrupting perfectly quiet little bars and terrorizing quite harmless street people. It's enough to drive a man to drink."

Vivian could picture Philby staggering along the alleys of Beirut, dressed in native garb, speaking fluent Arabic to prostitutes and pimps in his fine and nasty style. In his last months in Beirut, Philby's colorful collection of friends and sources would have begun to notice that his periods of drunkenness had become more frequent. In fact, he was physically ill and had been found rolling in the gutter on several occasions. His family life was a shambles, his cover had become transparent, and he caused any number of scandals in the English-speaking community by his bizarre behavior at polite parties. Gossip had it that he was collapsing under emotional and financial stress. Which was indeed true, and due to the fact that the British had caught a major Russian spy. Philby, with his built-in sensitivity to danger, knew he was in mortal jeopardy himself. The agent the British had uncovered was George Blake, a man who had been aligned with the Soviets for almost ten years and who was betrayed by the chief of Polish intelligence. This same informant was capable of exposing Philby as well, and while he waited to see if the ax would fall on his own neck, Philby activated a plan for his own escape.

The superagent was finally faced in Beirut with a direct accusation by an SIS interrogator sent from London to confront him with the truth (which was that the British now *knew* he had been working for the Russians for some time). Philby took the news quietly, simply shrugging and mouthing a reply that he was to use many times in the future: "Knowing what I did, I could not have done anything else."

"Kim, don't you think that I'd better know who the other man is? We know there has to have been one."

"Oh, dear, *that* old bromide . . . other man, third man . . . come off it, dear boy—"

"No, you come off it. You damn well know what I mean. Now let's have it or I walk out of here without your precious information and call the FBI . . ."

"But it's out of the question, d-d-dear boy."

"No, it isn't. And it's important to all of us . . . I mean, if you're gone and there's a catastrophe . . . you know, actual war or peace . . . and I have to get a signal to you—"

"Yes . . . well, I see . . . quite . . . all right then, Vivian, if it gets to be eleven-fifty-nine, then you go right to Tony Blunt."

(Just like that.) "Christ!"

"But only in an emergency. Jim Angleton, Mother, and his counterintelligence people have known about him for years. So they'll know that you . . ."

The smoke-filled little conference room at the St. Ermin's; the tall, lucid aesthete Tony, now Sir Anthony Blunt: how he had made Janet and Mush laugh with his imitation of Philby. It all came back to Vivian like a yellowed photograph. Sir Anthony Blunt, the Queen of England's personal adviser, now the most celebrated art expert in the English-speaking world . . . there was nothing to say. Vivian knew well enough what had motivated the brilliant young men from Oxford and Cambridge, "Oxbridge," in the late thirties. He had seen the same thing at Yale. And as for after, well there was the old school tie; one did not betray one's friends. Especially if Moscow Center had the sexual information to destroy you and any good memory of you forever.

The cigarette smoke hung heavy in the cold air. It was dark now but neither man made a move to turn on the harsh overhead bulb. Rooms like this seemed designed for darkness.

"Well, Kim—"

"Don't say a word, old boy. Nothing to be said. I'm going . . . home, that's all." He pulled himself to a sitting position. In the dark, he was a shapeless mass on the edge of the bed. His voice came out of the gloom disembodied and clear, not slurred for once . . . "There is a plan, and it's rather far along the road, to murder the President."

"Whose president?"

"Yours, old boy. Jack Kennedy." In the bathroom, water dripped. Bursts of sound from the passing traffic cut into the cabin. Philby cleared his throat . . . "I have *some* information. Not too much. But it may be enough for you to intervene. I may be able to be of some help from where I'll be and, in turn, I may need some assistance from you." He fumbled in the near dark for a Gauloise, then gave it up. Vivian bit his upper lip into silence.

"One of the Agency's teams that's been hunting Castro has gone critical. Some group in the Agency—large or small I don't know —has turned an assassination team of organized crime and Cuban killers around, with the goal of eliminating Kennedy. You—"

"Back up, Philby. Give me sources." Vivian's voice was hoarse with tension. He bit into his upper lip again.

"The source is firm. You know I don't work without tapes. His name is De Mohrenschildt. He's been doubling for years, for everybody . . . Nazis, French, British, ourselves, and for your shop, including the Cuban invasion. I first ran into him in '42."

"Tell me about him."

"You know the type . . . born of White Russian petty nobility, grew up in the nostalgia and neurosis of the exiles and pretenders in their Parisian retreats. In the thirties he took his doctorate in economic theory at the Sorbonne, where he was recruited by French intelligence. Eventually he was assigned to the United States, and here our prodigy earnestly penetrated the Establishment. It was all so simple then—he was merely a double agent.

"After he was around for a while he became a troubleshooter for petroleum interests all over the world, helped organize their private diplomatic and secret services. He speaks fifteen languages, you know, and is a genuine cultural anthropologist. When you can do all that, old man, you can live, love and kill on every continent . . . and that he has.

"After World War II, when they started calling him the Chinaman because of his oil intelligence work over there, he was ready to move into the bedrooms and boardrooms of America's so-called military-industrial complex.

"Dallas is really the center of all this, as you know, and so he's comfortably down there with his fifth wife, a mistress, and a young lover boy. Sounds like a good life, wouldn't you say so, Vivian?

Organizing the eastern European intelligence community for the CIA, all the while doubling for the French Secret Service and South African industrial intelligence as well? . . . Yes, he's a very smooth operator in a White Russian sort of way, but he's not the control for this. He's good, not of the first rank, but good enough to make a high-class cutout."

The motel cabin was now in utter darkness. Cold. The traffic sound was slacking off. Vivian went into the lavatory and turned the light on so that he could see to urinate, then turned it off again. He was afraid to look at himself in the mirror.

Back with Philby, he said, "Who's De Mohrenschildt working for now?"

"CIA, MI6, and the Texas International Petroleum Institute. That's a partial list."

"What do you mean you have tapes that back up this so-called source?" Knowing that if Philby said he had tapes, then he had them. Remembering the Rosenberg case and *those* tapes. That operation had failed, but Philby's information had passed the acid test at every miserable step of the way.

As Philby fumbled at the foot of the bed to open the suitcase, Vivian stepped to the bathroom and snapped the switch. In the half light Philby found the box with the reel of tape and tossed it up to Vivian. They resumed their positions on bed and chair, the spill from the laboratory light cutting their bodies in half. As Philby spoke, one half of his round, red face was in light, the other half in darkness, and Vivian sat chewing on his lip in the darkness.

". . . This is a tape, in Spanish, that includes two or three Cubans, De Mohrenschildt, and an old friend of yours from dear old Section C. None other than Mr. F. Sherman Scott, who has, if I'm not mistaken, been trying, along with the rest of the ultras and primitives, to kill *you* since Iran in 1953."

"Scott?"

"Scott."

"Could it be a provocation of some sort?"

"No. Listen to it—tonight."

"Scott . . . Scott and who else?"

"I don't know. The Central Intelligence Agency? I mean he does work for you. In fact, he's technically just under *you* in Section C, isn't he?"

305

"Are you serious? Director McCone will drop dead when he hears this. Scott has Cuba on the brain and he's gone—"

"Viv, John McCone will not hear this from you. You will know why when you've heard the tape. Part of the operation is to implicate *you* in Soviet Russia Section activities in such a way as to fatally compromise you and the entire bloody desk. Viv, we're not talking about a dirty trick, we're discussing a *coup d'état,* nothing less—if it's true, and that's for you to find out. I mean it's not because they don't like his hair or accent, it's to effect a basic shift in U. S. power. It is—if you will forgive the lyric—to bring about a redistribution of wealth to what good old Ike's saved speech writer so memorably limned as the 'military-industrial complex.' More for them with JFK gone. I mean, of course they despise Jack Kennedy because he has balls—in the political sense as well—but the motive is no different from Iran or Congo or all the rest of it . . . if this is the real thing . . ."

It was as if the cold were congealing Vivian's thought processes. There was a sharp pain over his left eye, he tried to replay Philby's words in his mind as if they were on a tape . . . *coup d'état* . . . The cancer was in the DOD—the Domestic Operations Division— created only weeks ago, early in 1963, to conduct "clandestine operations against foreign targets within the United States." The offices of DOD were one block from the White House under the cover name "U. S. Army Element, Joint Operations Group" . . .

"We know about your new DOD," Philby was saying, as if reading his mind, "but the President doesn't, does he? Scott and those people who disgraced him in Cuba are now all stewing about in a boiling pot of intrigue, claiming to be tracking down Castro agents in the United States. You've got to put him out in front of this DOD strike force—I'm warning you, old chap, these are *your* colonels . . . And this is not the work of a single psychopath. This is a murder plot in whose wake a number of dominoes are meant to fall, including any plans you may have to become DCI. We are now talking about, as I say, a seizure of power."

Philby leaned toward him, neither stammering nor slurring in the least. "Viv, you've known for weeks that your Domestic Operations Division is completely Black. You've known that out at the Farm assassins from all over the earth are being trained to kill, blow up automobiles, provoke riots and destabilize governments

306

all over the world. So I say look in your own Domestic Operations Division, the filthy DOD, look out at the Farm . . . What I'm saying, Viv, is that the planners of this will be using money, men and material originally organized by you or Bobby Kennedy or the President himself to assassinate the president or leader of some other country. This is Hegelian tragedy—'even-handed justice returning to plague the inventor'."

Philby shook his head gloomily. "After all, Viv, during the war the United Kingdom and the United States operated under the rule of a kind of secret government in an all-or-nothing fight to the end against fascism. After V-E Day the British dismantled their secret government, virtually on the floor of Parliament. But you, dear boy, your country *never* did. So it's now or never."

Philby rose and began to pack up his case. "Scott is a middle level manager, De Mohrenschildt is a glorified errand boy, the Cubans are cannon fodder—you will have to find the top of this thing yourself, if you hope to stop it—"

"Kim, is there a mole high up here in our shop?"

"Would you believe me if I answered you?"

"I don't know."

"Well, Viv, given what I've just t-t-told you, perhaps we should h-h-hope there is." If the stutter was meant to distract Vivian, or even to generate some sympathy, it was not successful. This discussion was at an end. All that mattered was the tape. And the scary notion of Philby's that a Soviet mole in the Agency might be less dangerous than one of the Animals gone berserk.

It was almost nine when Vivian arrived at the Donahues' place. He parked and sat in thought. Philby's parting message to him had made the entire nightmare somehow more real . . .

"If they beat you and they kill him," Philby had said as they stood at the door, "the Soviet Union will have no choice but to intervene. I mean by that that unless the United States ruling circle can be absolutely convinced that your President did *not* die at the hands of a Soviet assassination plot, then we're all in for it. World War III. Armageddon. We will move at once to put proof of some kind in your hands that completely clears the Soviet Union. Depending on the circumstances, the proof may be true or manufactured to represent the truth. In either case, if you yourself are not compromised, then you *must* argue for the acceptance of the proof . . . and, Vivian, I beg you not to trust De Mohrenschildt. He's half mad, can't even remember which client he's informing on at what time. He doesn't know that he made the tape for us, we used a White Russian sleeper. De Mohrenschildt is a rabid anti-Communist. So if you hope to penetrate the conspiracy, you will have to go much higher than him, at least as high as Scott . . . but when you've heard the tape you'll realize all this. There's no one better than you, Viv. I should know. After all, I was one of your teachers—God bless, Viv." His pose seemed to evaporate and Philby seemed, at last, just a burnt out if very human case . . .

Vivian shivered. The windows of the old two-story Donahue home shone bright against the dark winter night. Philby, the Marxist's Marxist, had invoked the name of God at the end. For a moment Vivian considered driving away and flying to New York to tell it all to his father, who, for all his so-called progressive ideas, would also pray to God in the face of this terrifying development. No. Sam Prescott would pick up the telephone and call the President. Nothing on earth could stop him. Wait! Maybe he, himself, should call Jack Kennedy. They could attack together. After all, the campaign of 1960 had been a tremendously successful joint effort . . .

He and Senator Kennedy, the candidate, had relished the delicious irony of the fact that it was the excesses of the Animals—the hawks as they were now generally called—that had given Kennedy his razor-thin victory. The U-2 affair had undermined the last phase of the Eisenhower administration, leading to the general's lashing out at the "military-industrial complex" in his farewell address to the nation. Then there was the advance information on the Cuban invasion, provided to the candidate by Vivian, that allowed Kennedy to upstage and out-hawk Richard Nixon in the TV debates. Finally, Vivian's exposure of billionaire Howard Hughes's clumsy interference in the election had cost Nixon dearly where it hurt most—in his middle-class business base . . .

Vivian and his loyalists had come out of the U-2 humiliation looking good, the only ones in the Agency who had. Because Tim Donahue had been able to run half a dozen agents on the ground inside the Soviet Union, Vivian had been able to represent—in memo after memo to Allen Dulles—that there was no need to risk

308

the U-2 overflights as the time for the Eisenhower-Khrushchev Vienna summit approached. Wisner and Dulles had overruled the Prescott recommendations, and, with the U-2 affair, had come to grief.

Sherman Scott, Richard Helms and their fellow hawks had convinced Dulles that the Soviets could never bring down the super spy plane and that the Prescott agent network inside Russia was too insecure to trust during the summit year. Vivian had warned them. Candidate Jack Kennedy followed the game of the cover stories with fascination from the sidelines. And so the hawks prevailed, winning out for getting one last U-2 flight under their belts before the scheduled May summit. They were afraid the Paris meeting would result in putting a stop to the flights altogether, so when Eisenhower did not withdraw his approval, on May 1 the mission went off as scheduled . . .

Francis Gary Powers, a thirty-year-old CIA pilot from the hill country of Kentucky, had watched tensely for his "go" signal on an airstrip in Pakistan. This mission had already been postponed twice, and, Powers knew, the plane, number 360, had a history of a crash-landing the year before. The pilot was now hoping for another cancellation, he didn't have much confidence in this particular aircraft. But at 6:20 A.M. the authorization came through and he was cleared for takeoff . . .

Not until the fifth of May did the announcement come through, direct from Premier Khrushchev himself, that a plane had been downed. And the incredible period of chaos that followed at the highest levels of the United States government was what the young presidential candidate John F. Kennedy had observed so carefully.

The first story to come out of Washington was that the plane had been on a NASA "weather" mission when its pilot ran into trouble. After a significant two-day silence in order to let all the world hear this response, Khrushchev issued a second announcement: He had both plane and pilot in his possession. The State Department then rallied with an admission that the plane had in fact been on a spying mission but quickly added that no such mission had been authorized by Washington. Two days later, however, Eisenhower took this back, taking responsibility for the U-2 program and adding a statement that many thought was a declaration of his intent to continue such flights. This seemed to be the final straw, and when the summit came around Khrushchev stormed and demanded an apology. No more U-2s over Russia . . . and with that the Paris conference fell apart.

What Senator Kennedy and a few others knew was that the original cover story was issued because it was assumed that Powers had been acting under instructions to blow up his plane. Thus, the CIA thought the evidence would be destroyed. All U-2s contained a destructor unit with enough power to blow the plane apart, and all pilots were instructed to activate it and eject in the event of any trouble. Allen Dulles himself was aware, however, that many of the pilots were apprehensive about the timing of this delicate device —an apprehension that came from the pilots' uncertainty over just how much time they had to get out.

The real story that Senator Kennedy was privy to, thanks to Vivian, was that the apprehensive Powers, unable to use the automatic ejection, climbed out of the plane and then couldn't reach back to activate the destructor switches. No one was asking about whether he was under mandatory orders to destroy his plane because obviously the CIA didn't want too close a look taken at the unit. And only the CIA knew what would have happened had the device been activated.

Vivian knew that the Agency had planned for Powers inadvertently to destroy himself rather than be captured. The only question that still haunted the Director of Plans was: Had Scott and the Animals *deliberately* sabotaged the Eisenhower-Khrushchev summit, even as they had attempted to forestall the thaw following Khrushchev's denunciation of Stalin?

"It was the foreknowledge of the Cuban invasion that won the presidency for me," the President had told Vivian on the night of victory.

Cuba was the hawks' baby.

Perhaps Vivian's most important contribution to his old friend's presidential victory could be traced to the electronic listening device that the Director of Plans and Tim Donahue had been able to install in Vice-President Richard Nixon's capitol office. By early 1960 Senator Kennedy was being kept *au courant* of a series of sneak attack scenarios that were being drawn up by Nixon's team. The planning was much more aggressive than President Eisenhower was to know until the very end of his term. The scenario had three key authors: Nixon, his military aide General Payne, and representing the more Neanderthal elements within the Agency, F. Sherman Scott. Eisenhower was eventually given an anti-Castro project to sign off on. The plan contemplated the use of only thirty-three exiles, who were to set up a secret base for insurgency in the same mountain redoubt from which Castro himself had sprung in the 1950s.

The hawks' secret strategy was made known to Kennedy . . . "to maintain an invasion force on Cuban territory for at least seventy-two hours and then to proclaim the Free Government of Cuba." From there, they believed, the new president would have no choice but to announce a worldwide panoply of Free Cuba fronts. The OAS, the U.N., Geneva—all the stops would be out to move the "Cuban situation" to the Big Power level of war or Soviet capitulation. Kennedy read through the plans that Vivian's agent had stolen and shook his head grimly.

After Kennedy's election but before he had taken over the reins of power, Sherman Scott's forgers in the Agency had changed the *33*s to *3300*s. Kennedy received the news from Vivian with a cold fury, and it was then he decided that he would double-cross the double-crossers and hang them out to dry on the beach at Playa Giron.

Nixon's stake in the scheme had been, of course, based on the hope that the invasion of Cuba and the overthrow of Castro would take place before the November presidential elections and guarantee him the victory. But once again Eisenhower had frustrated his appetite for power. In fact, when Ike became aware that some sort of deception involving CIA and the Joint Chiefs was in the works, he took the decision to make his famous speech warning the nation of the rise of a "military-industrial complex" out of the control of the chief executive. He had not gone public with what he knew for the same reason that Jack Kennedy and Vivian Prescott would not: fear that the country would be torn apart by the exposure of a secret government that conceivably could reach over the head of the highest elected official to plunge the nation into war.

Vivian's advance information on the Cuban invasion had been parlayed by Kennedy into a successful string of speeches about the need to liberate the tiny island. Nixon, who dared not comment on the plans for secret war because of the deception involved, was actually upstaged on his right, so to speak, by JFK. Nixon, the consummate cold warrior, was obliged to stand by in silence while the shock-haired playboy, whom he despised, stole his thunder . . . "Now I'm stuck with it, Viv. I can't back down. All I can do is let the damn thing roll downhill and hope that it can be detained," Kennedy had said.

The price of Kennedy's electoral victory was, therefore, a feeling of absolute impotence in confronting the Agency hawks and the Joint Chiefs. Later he would tell Vivian that "the cost was too high."

CIA plots to murder Castro were an old story. In August of 1960 Sherman Scott for Richard Helms had contacted Robert A. Maheu, a former FBI agent and lieutenant of Howard Hughes, and asked him to aid in recruiting a mobster for the hit. The price the CIA was paying for the assassination of Castro was $150,000. Two top mafiosi were eventually brought in to do the job: Momo Salvatore (Sam) Giancana and Santos Trafficante. The mob's motives for wanting Castro out of the way were obvious: the Cuban Premier had taken away their lucrative gambling interests in Havana, and with him out of the way they might be able to get them back; $1,000,000 was added to the assassination kitty by syndicate chief Meyer Lansky.

The instruments of death were six pills prepared by the CIA that contained a toxin that would do away with Castro without leaving any trace to be found in an autopsy. The pills were delivered to Cuba, to be put in the Cuban leader's drink or food, but the plan ultimately failed. The plotting against Castro's life, however, continued, and more pills were passed to gangsters to be smuggled onto Castro's dinner table. Again, the plan failed, but even now another was under way, this time using a poison pen.

Vivian reflected on how by mid-1962 President John F. Kennedy, now well past the Cuban situation, had emerged as a leader with a fresh sense of his own competence. In the Cuban missile crisis he had faced down the Russians, and with new self-assurance reveled in the country's praise. Exceptions to this were the radical left, which thought he had risked too much for too little; and the radical right, which thought he had risked too little for so much. But what had most importantly emerged after the crisis had passed was a clear vision to the world of what the potential of nuclear death was really about. And the frightening reality behind the propaganda produced by both the United States and the Soviets gave way to the chance of a thaw in the geopolitical hostility. Possibilities were aired for the lessening of tensions that had not been heard since World War II days of alliance. In perhaps the best speech of his administration—Vivian listened with a respect he knew his father would share—the President called for an attempt to control and limit weapons of destruction, called for a review of U. S. attitudes toward the Soviet Union.

Because of their pipeline into Nixon's Cuban plans, Kennedy and Vivian had decided that they only needed to use the Howard Hughes section of the Nixon dossier that Vivian's team had put together. Tim Donahue had come up with a masterly overview, even the summary paragraphs relating to each rich increment of the man's career were provocative.

"Just sample the man's biography. It's worse than you think, Jack."

"It's filthy," the candidate said.

Campaign Supporters:

—MICKEY COHEN (successor to Bugsy Siegel for the national crime syndicate in California)
—HOWARD HUGHES (magnate with mob involvements in Las Vegas and the Bahamas)
—TRUJILLO (Dominican dictator, friend of Syndicate)

The list continued for three crowded pages. "There's a whole other government trying to take over this country," the candidate said.

"I know," said Vivian, "and they've been grooming Nixon since before World War II."

There was page after page of summary outline, plus a looseleaf volume of some 700 pages. Senator Kennedy was impressed. His eyes were filled with a kind of sad laughter. "The political Snopes family come to power."

"The man's a barnburner, a worldwide carpetbagger, a study in resentment," said Viv. "Deep, abiding, damn near paranoid."

"This man should never be President," said Jack. "Never mind whether I make it or not."

"He never will be," said Vivian. . . .

So Nixon was beaten. Barely. But at Playa Giron the hawks had taken their revenge. Once again Vivian had gone outside the Agency to act as the President's personal agent. The struggle had been vicious but in the showdown Dulles had fallen, Bissell had been forced to resign, and Vivian's superior, Frank Wisner, had blown his brains out. Wisner's suicide and Kennedy's influence combined to ensure Vivian's appointment as Director of Plans. Vivian had emerged a winner again—the new Deputy Director of Plans, and soon to be DCI.

The Bay of Pigs operation, the "Fiasco," as it would ever after be called, had been doomed from the moment that President Kennedy refused to permit the Bissell-Barnes-FitzGerald-Sherman Scott assassination of Fidel Castro to go forward. That, and the refusal to order full air cover, sealed the fate of the Agency's exile army on the beaches of Cuba.

The DCI, Allen Dulles, had arranged to be at a conference in Puerto Rico during the invasion, but Kennedy rejected this signal of disinvolvement from the old spymaster. In Vivian's presence the President lashed out at Dulles . . . "If this were a parliamentary system, the government would fall, but as it is *our* system, it is *you* who are through." The old man's face turned purple and his glare at Vivian said, "traitor." Dulles knew that Kennedy had been given information by Vivian about a plot by Barnes, FitzGerald and the other planners of the invasion to trap the President into ordering air cover. Kennedy, warned, had made the decision to go outside the Agency to impose an order of battle plan on the Joint Chiefs so that no disruption of the chain of command could take place and commit the United States to an all-out invasion.

"Mother" Angleton, Scott and the Animals knew that the President was being fed information from inside, knew that Vivian was JFK's agent in place. But the young Commander-in-Chief was also shrewd enough to hold out hope to the hawks until the last possible moment. When they heard that final telephonic rush of information from the Prescott home phone, they knew it doomed their effort. Reduced to cold print on Scott's internal counterintelligence logs the telephone call spelled out the stab in the back at Playa Giron:

314

"JACK. YOU'RE AWAKE?—NO, I KNOW, I'M NOT EITHER. ALL RIGHT, JACK, I HAVE THE DOCUMENTS IN FRONT OF ME. THEY'RE GOING BEHIND YOUR BACK. A CONTRAVENTION OF EXECUTIVE ORDER THAT NO U. S. PERSONNEL BE INVOLVED IN THE INVASION. AMERICANS *ARE,* REPEAT *ARE,* ATTACKING WITH CUBAN NATIONALS.

"ONE—AMERICAN PILOTS FROM THE ALABAMA AIR NATIONAL GUARD WILL FLY SUPPORT MISSIONS. TWO —AMERICAN CREWS WILL MAN LCI'S IN THE VANGUARD OF THE CUBANS' FLOTILLA. THREE—AMERICAN JETS FROM THE CARRIER *ESSEX* WILL FLY RECONNAISSANCE. FOUR—AGENCY OFFICERS WILL ACTUALLY DIRECT LANDING OPERATIONS. THERE WILL BE A DIRECT RADIO HOOKUP FROM LANGLEY, *BYPASSING* YOUR WHITE HOUSE SITUATION ROOM. FIVE—THE DESTROYERS *EATON* AND *HOUSTON* WILL ACTUALLY LEAD THE BRIGADE INTO THE BAY, AND EACH "SKUNK," OR CUBAN SHIP, WILL HAVE AN AMERICAN BABY-SITTER. ALL U. S. SHIPS WILL BE STRIPPED AND CAMOUFLAGED, BUT THEY WILL STILL BE, REPEAT *WILL* BE, EASILY RECOGNIZED . . ."

There was a charged silence from the President's end. The transcript resumed with Vivian's clinching argument:

"JACK? I KNOW IT'S UNPRECEDENTED . . . IT'S INTOLERABLE. JACK, IT'S BEEN A PART OF THE PLAN ALL ALONG . . . LISTEN, YOU FOUGHT IN THE SOUTH PACIFIC. YOU KNOW THE LOGISTICS REQUIRED TO TAKE A FORTIFIED ISLAND—THE SHIPS, THE PLANES, THE SHOCK TROOPS. WELL, JACK, THINK ABOUT IT— CUBA MAKES GUAM OR WAKE LOOK LIKE A SKIRMISH. DO YOU REALLY BELIEVE THAT THE WORLD WAR II VETERAN COMMAND OFFICERS AT LANGLEY AND THE JOINT CHIEFS DON'T *KNOW* THAT A COUPLE OF HUNDRED POORLY TRAINED CUBANS CAN'T EVEN *BEGIN* TO OVERTHROW CASTRO?"

That had done it. If the President had hesitated, Vivian was prepared to reveal to him that he had found out that Sherman

Scott, himself, was informing Castro—through double agents—about the impending invasion so that a humiliating defeat on the beaches would *force* the President to send in the flag. Vivian was genuinely sorry that there was no practical way that he could inform the Cuban fodder of this betrayal by their Agency masters . . .

After the shaken DCI had shuffled out, the President turned to his friend. "Viv, I have to appoint a Republican until after reelection. The clean-up in the Agency begins tomorrow, under the hand of the Attorney General. You wouldn't want to take over at Langley, wearing a bulletproof vest, would you, Viv?"

And thus began the interregnum of John McCone. Vivian was disappointed. McCone was the president of Bechtel Corporation, a multinational giant. Vivian worried that he would spend his time and energy in using the Agency to enhance Bechtel's vast interests. Worse, in Vivian's estimation, was his record of heavy financial support for Richard Nixon during some of his various campaigns.

"That's the *system.*" Pat was angry too when he told her. "Your friend Jack Kennedy is a perfectly charming Prince Charming and Camelot is a gossip columnist's dream, but it's the Bechtel Corporation and names like McCone that run the show. You know that. Your father taught you all about it. Viv, sometimes I think that you're the first and the last of the great American idealists."

He didn't answer her. His legs were numb with cold. Perhaps if he went in now the boy would be asleep.

The green yule wreath on the wooden double door jogged Vivian's memory. He had been invited to help decorate the Christmas tree and stay over for the holiday weekend. He stood in the cold listening to the laughter and music inside, not knowing if he could conceal his terrible information from the Donahues. Then he remembered that Pat's mother was visiting from Chicago. His head began to throb.

Inside decorations and wrapping paper were everywhere. Terry Donahue had not believed in the existence of Santa Claus since he was six years old. Now, at twelve, Christmas Eve was an occasion of yearly hilarity for the family. Before he could say much of anything, Vivian was handed a generous cup of eggnog by Pat's mother, and for the next two hours he avoided joining in the

316

merriment by meticulously hanging silver foil from top to bottom of the large ten-foot-high tree. At eleven o'clock Pat took him into the kitchen for a piece of homemade fruitcake. Just as he was about to speak, Mrs. McGuire came in to "put the kettle on." Rose McGuire was a heavyset woman, with a real Irish brogue and the indomitable cheerfulness and courage of a coal miner's wife. Vivian liked her, but at this moment he had to talk to Pat and Tim alone. He whispered in Pat's ear as she passed and took his tea and cake upstairs to the guest room.

Moments later he heard Pat running up the stairs. Below Terry was playing his Kingston Trio album for the third time. Pat looked radiant in a glen plaid slack suit and her modified Jackie Kennedy haircut was immensely attractive, but now Vivian needed her in a different way.

"What—"

"Pat, listen. Tell the others I'm coming down with a bad cold and I've gone to bed. Then as soon as you can, get up here with Tim and bring the tape recorder. Make it as soon as you can."

"That bad?"

"Worse, I'm afraid."

He stretched out on the bed, closed his eyes, waited. Slowly his breathing returned to near normal . . . A montage of scenes of himself and Jack Kennedy swam up before his eyes . . . He was exhausted, and gradually sank into an uneasy state between consciousness and sleep, at the threshold of nightmare . . . Sunlit memory flashes, like old snapshots, of Hyannis Port and Narragansett, pub crawling in London, football games in Cambridge and New Haven, weddings and family gatherings, walks on Fire Island, the great campaign of 1960, Bay of Pigs and after . . . These and other shapes of the past fell together like pieces of a dream puzzle. Jack had grown and changed. His avatars had encompassed playboy, war hero, conservative Democrat, crime-busting senator, cold warrior, and now, at last, a peacemaker . . . Vivian felt that it had all been worthwhile after all, when the President told him, "Yesterday negotiations were concluded in Moscow on a treaty to ban all nuclear tests in the atmosphere, in outer space, and under water. My revenge for the fiasco in Cuba is going to be peace, and I'm going to shove it down the throats of the diehards in the Pentagon and at Langley . . ." Vivian had seized his friend's hand, gripping

317

hard. Just months before, during the missile crisis (which the Kennedy brothers and Vivian considered a direct result of the Fiasco), Bob, on Vivian's advice, had had to send a message to Premier Khrushchev: "We are under very severe stress. In fact, we are under pressure from our military to use force against Cuba . . . If the situation continues much longer the President is not sure that the military will not overthrow him and seize power . . ." None of them would ever forget that day . . . "Peace is the best revenge, Jack," he had said, still gripping his hand . . . The yellow fire was licking at the periphery of his remembering. He could see himself sitting in the Sleepy Lagoon inferno as Jack Kennedy tried to call and signal to him through the flames. But he could not make out what it was his friend was calling, so in the dream he rose and fought his way forward into the choking smoke and fire toward Kennedy—"Jack! Jack!" he heard himself call. *I'll save you, Jack—*

He awoke, gasping and choking. Pat was bending over him in the dark. He was nearly panting, his body rigid. "God," he breathed. Pat bent closer. "Viv, what *is* it?" Wiping perspiration from his forehead, she cradled him in her arms and he relaxed. He rubbed his cheek against her sweater, feeling her nipples come erect through the soft wool.

"Did you have a bad dream, Viv? Why don't you wash up while I put the kettle on. Terry and mom are going to bed. We can use the kitchen to talk. The tape machine won't disturb anyone down there—are you all right?"

"Go ahead. I'll be right down. Let me use your toothbrush."

In the kitchen he found Pat, Tim and the new dog Pancho, a springer spaniel. Steaming mugs of tea were waiting. Tim and Pat looked expectantly at him. His face was pale, his eyes hot as if he were ill from the abrupt onset of some virus. He removed the boxed tape from his attaché case and handed it to Tim to thread into the machine.

He said: "I was told today that there is a conspiracy under way to assassinate Jack Kennedy. I suspect this tape, which I haven't heard, will tell us how credible it is. It's in Spanish. Go ahead, Tim. Pat, you're the best linguist, will you take some notes?"

They looked at him as if he were a figure of terror in one of *their* dreams. The dog sniffed around, begging for cookies. Tim, with-

318

out a word, reached to turn on the tape. Pat jumped up to get a tablet and pen. The quality of the recording was muffled, which was not unusual when an agent wore a "fargo" recorder taped to or secreted on his body. The poor fidelity of the sound was further complicated by the speakers being recorded . . . one man's Spanish was spoken with a heavy underlying European accent; a second man they recognized at once as F. Sherman Scott, who with his typical pseudo-elitism affected a classic Castilian accent; two other voices could be just made out speaking Spanish in the rapid Cuban manner.

Pat began to jot notes while Tim, whose grasp of Spanish was limited, bent over her shoulder. Vivian sat with his eyes closed, so pale that he could have been dead. The tape was short, no more than ten minutes. After it ended, abruptly, Pat rewound and began it again and typed a hurried transcript on the portable, Tim turning the machine on and off at her direction. She handed Vivian each page as she finished typing.

SPANISH TAPE–1–1–1   PAGE ONE
MAN #1: . . . *(unclear) (unclear . . . . . .)* . . . FROM EDUARDO
OR "MACHO" *(unclear)* . . . TAKE OUR ORDERS.
MAN #2: ABSOLUTELY. THE MONEY WILL BE RUN
THROUGH BEBE'S BANK. HE IS *(unclear . . .)* GEORGE CAN
YOU HANDLE *(unclear)* . . .
MAN #3: . . . *(unclear)* VERY UNSTABLE AND *(unclear)* . . . I
HAVE A, UH, RELATIONSHIP WITH HIS WIFE.
MAN #2: *(laughter)* . . . WATCH YOUR *(unclear)* . . . *(laughter).*
MAN #4: HE'S CRAZY. I THINK HE'S A COMMUNIST.
MAN #2: THAT'S THE POINT *(unclear . . .)* . . . TRAITORS
AROUND KENNEDY IN THE "COMPANY" *(unclear)* . . .
MAN #4: MIAMI IS *(unclear . . .)* I MEAN, YOU KNOW, I LIKE
NEW ORLEANS BUT *(unclear).*
Page one of four   *(-More-)*

Vivian, in a low, clear voice, put what they'd heard into the perspective of Philby's briefing. At his mention of Philby's name, some eyes widened perceptibly. Vivian had only hinted before to Pat and Tim that Philby was a double agent, whose heart was with the KGB. Well, now it was time to trust old and best-loved col-

319

leagues . . . "Man number two is pretty obviously Sherman Scott," Vivian said. "Number Three is a double agent named George De Mohrenschildt. Okay, let's go on . . . Tim, turn it on again, please . . .

PAGE TWO

SCOTT: LAKE PONTCHARTRAIN CAMP IS SECURE. *(unclear)* IS KNOWN THERE. DAVE IS THERE AND HE CAN WATCH HIM AND *(unclear)* . . . *(unclear)* IS THERE AND HE'S THE CONTACT FOR JACK AND JIMMY AND THE BOYS.

MAN #1: GEORGE WHERE'S THE TOILET . . . OH, YEAH.

MAN #4: BUT YOU KNOW, HE'S CRAZY. HE'S QUEER, YOU KNOW. WHY DO WE NEED HIM?

SCOTT: DON'T YOU COMPREHEND? MACHO, CAN YOU HEAR ME? *(unclear)* IS PERFECT. HE WORKED FOR PRESCOTT IN *(unclear)* AND IN RUSSIA FOR THE COMPANY FOR PRESCOTT. GET IT? THEN WHILE HE WAS THERE HE WORKED ON *(unclear)* TO WORK FOR THE RUSSIANS. NOW DAVE TIES HIM IN TO CUBA AND *(unclear)* EVERYBODY'S HANDS ARE TIED. *(unclear . . .)* THE POINT IS THAT THE SHOOTING WILL BE THE SIGNAL FOR A REAL INVASION OF CUBA . . . *(unclear . . .)* THEIR *(unclear)* IN IT IN THE COMPANY AND THE WHITE HOUSE *(unclear . . .)* THE USE OF DOING IT IF IT DOESN'T LEAD TO AN INVASION IN FORCE? *(unclear)* . . . THIS SHIT!

MAN #1: HOW YOU GOING TO GET HIM TO DO *(unclear . . .)*

DE MOHRENSCHILDT: ONE THING AT A TIME . . .

Second page of four   *(-More-)*

Most of the balance of the tape was unclear, but within an hour the spine of something began to emerge through Pat's rough draft, especially in the perspective of what Vivian said Philby had told him.

"Put this De Mohrenschildt at the top of your list, Tim. Keep going over the tape, with enhancement, at the shop—we'll go in tomorrow . . . What time is your Christmas dinner?" . . .

It was after three in the morning when they stacked the cups and dishes and turned out the light. In the morning Tim left for the

Agency and returned in time for the complete holiday meal at four in the afternoon. While Pat and her mother prepared the feast, Vivian had a walk with Terry and the new dog, Pancho, named in honor of Terry's tennis hero Pancho Gonzalez.

The day was bright and clear. The boy's red head came almost to Vivian's shoulder. They did not talk much. Vivian could not help recalling walks, years before, with his own father. Something deep in him wanted now to tell Terry that he was his father. Something about Philby's terrible communication had stirred the unexpressed but long smoldering need for kinship and continuity. But it was Terry who broke the silence to discuss again with his "godfather" the respective merits of Big Bill Tilden, Don Budge, and Pancho Gonzalez.

By nine o'clock that evening Vivian, Tim and Pat were seated around the breakfast table again. Tim's report was predictably concise and factual.

"I handled everything myself. Enhancement of the tape reveals the following names: Jack Ruby AKA Jake Rubinstein, David Ferrie, Guy Bannister and our own William A. Must, Jr. I couldn't clear up the reference to the man referred to as 'crazy,' 'queer' and 'working for the Company in Russia,' and 'possibly working' for Russian intelligence. There may be a reference to Jimmy Hoffa. As Viv said last night, the second and third men, respectively, are Sherman Scott and George De Mohrenschildt. Here's just a snap summary on the files of these six. I suggest we stop and read through them and then discuss our next move. Oh, and please take a look at page four. Right at the center of their plan seems to be some person or fact that compromises you, personally, Viv, and the Agency. I'm not sure, though . . ."

"I assume," Pat interjected as Tim passed out unmarked folders, "that by our next move you mean dumping this bombshell right in the President's lap."

"No, dear, I was assuming that the President's brother was the logical—"

"Let's just hold the assumptions," Vivian said softly as he flipped open his folder. Some of it was boiler-plate to him, like countless others he had read. Two were of special interest:

321

DAVID FERRIE:

Ferrie was key contract agent for Cuban Operations during period of Agency early support for Castro (when Agency still hoped to control him after his victory) and after in preparation for Bay of Pigs. Ferrie is Agency control for anti-Castro exile training camps in New Orleans area. Camps situated on land owned by Lansky Syndicate. He also acts as bodyguard and agent of New Orleans boss Carlos Marcello . . .

JAKE RUBINSTEIN AKA JACK RUBY AKA "PINKY":

Organized Crime payoff man in Dallas-Fort Worth area. FBI and Dallas P.D. informant. Gun runner for Cuban exile anti-Castro attacks. Involved with Lenny Patrick, Dave Yaras and Willie Block as part of Teamster murder squad in Chicago prior to relocation in Dallas. Visited Cuba twice in 1959 with Lewis J. McWillie to attempt release of crime boss Santos Trafficanti from Castro jail. Ruby was hit man for Chicago Teamster boss Paul Dorfman.

Vivian skimmed through the rest of the thin dossier. He was all too familiar with the other names and their violent biographies: George De Mohrenschildt, Guy Bannister, Carlos Marcello and F. Sherman Scott. He waited for Pat to finish reading, then said, *"Whoever* the Cubans are, this list boils down immediately to elements in the Agency and in the Syndicate."

"Mongoose," said Tim.

"Operation Mongoose," Vivian repeated, "the plans to execute Castro . . ." Then, agitated, "Those damn women of his—"

"Women. Of his? This is unbelievable . . ."

A melange of events—rumored widely but known to only a few including these three—since the inauguration spun through their minds. The Kennedy men, for better or worse, had the reputation of being womanizers. Jack Kennedy liked several different women, almost all of whom he seemed to find more exciting than his wife. Political realities and family religion, of course, prevented serious consideration of divorce. And so perhaps once a month, as Vivian well knew, the President partook of the favors of some eager, and interchangeably beautiful, sexual climber. A small problem was his penchant for having them on top of his oversized Oval Office desk. Pat was particularly critical of the film queen who had been delivered to the White House in a long crate marked RUG. Kennedy, a voracious reader too, had borrowed the idea from Shaw's *Caesar and Cleopatra.* The problem for Vivian and the CIA was the political fallout of these adventures. Certain Hollywood notables well-connected with organized crime had elected, in effect, to play pimp to the President. One in particular had been requested to serve up a series of starlets for the Kennedy brothers in general and the President in particular.

Kennedy had tried to keep the Hollywood people at arm's length after the election, but during the campaign he had, in effect, allowed himself to be set up in Las Vegas . . . The buxom young woman with whom he began an occasional two-year affair also just happened to be the mistress of Sam "Momo" Giancana and handsome Johnny Roselli. And it was these two gangsters who represented the mob in negotiations with Central Intelligence in preparation for the invasion of Cuba and the assassination of Fidel Castro.

It was Vivian, calling upon his long friendship with Jack Kennedy —and with a combination of wit and tact—who brought the bad news to Hyannis Port that first summer of the administration: Both the mob and J. Edgar Hoover's FBI were compiling a treasure trove of blackmail tape recordings. Kennedy was sobered by this, though not out of guilt . . . that wasn't Jack's style. At length he echoed Vivian's ironic tone: "Viv, you trying to tell me they don't love me for myself?" And together they had begun the program at least to contain the damage. . . .

"I want to tell you what I think," Pat said, her temper fraying. "I think that women, sex, are a major weapon in this thing. I mean, we used women against Castro, his ex-mistress was one, his sister was another, she even worked for the Agency. The Agency tried to set up Sukarno with women. In Iran, you told me, we set the Shah up with little boys. Correct? All right, now don't tell me that the golden voice wasn't acting as an agent for the mob when he began to push the President's famous buttons—"

"But, Patty, what's blackmail got to do with this—"

"We want to find the top of this thing, don't we? We need to find it, I gather, before we can ask the President or Bobby to act . . . because if the prime movers here are the same people who compromised John Kennedy with the Exner girl and poor Marilyn Monroe *and* Bill Must's wife, then the Agency and the Syndicate operation in Cuba were only the tip of the iceberg. And if that's so, then somebody, or somebodies, is coordinating an Agency-Syndicate coup, and *has* been since *1960,* since the election . . . Viv, you know a lot more about this Syndicate connection and you'll have to discuss it now. And simply cursing his women doesn't exactly provide an adequate analysis . . ."

With the mention of Judith Must, she'd convinced Vivian that she had the start of a handle on the implications of the tape. . . .

Judith Must was no Las Vegas chorus girl or starlet. Her father was in the Dulles law firm, and her alma mater was Bryn Mawr. A woman of horsy good looks and confident sensuality, she and the President became involved in rather more than a series of one-night stands. Judith Must was a match for Jack Kennedy—in nerve, and wit, and downright pride. She was also the separated wife of one of the Company's top agents, Bill Must. The previous September Judy Must had been found strangled to death outside her fashionable Washington brownstone. Vivian and his old Yale classmate James Jesus Angleton, now the famous "Mother" and head of counterintelligence, had been sent to tear her apartment apart "in search of love letters," Angleton said. And now Bill Must's name had been turned up, linked to Sherman Scott, in the conspiracy.

". . . so, Pat, your guess is that if Judith Must was silenced because she was going to blow some play of her husband's and the Scott bunch, then we're talking about the highest levels of the Company. On the other hand, if Judy was murdered because of her unfaithfulness, then we have a personal vendetta wrapped inside a *putsch* scenario . . ."

They continued to speculate, to "game" out the "lines of force" so as to have a clue about where to start to react. Here were three minds trained to penetrate appearances and the mundane surface of everyday life. Now they focused their imaginations on the conjunction of sex and death and potential assassination that had intruded on their Christmas holiday.

Great spies, Vivian had said to Pat just weeks before, like great artists have tragic imaginations. "And what," she had responded, "do the hacks that we've been working with—with damn few exceptions—what do *they* have?" She had told him that it was "B movies," that they, the Sherman Scotts and J. Edgar Hoovers, had "psychopathic personalities, every one of them. Trepper, when we met him in Paris, was great. Gehlen had flashes but he's a monomaniac on race and a megalomaniac on method. Dulles had style but little substance. Intrepid, I think, was tops. Wild Bill Donovan was very good. You, my love, will be, I predict, one of the very best—"

"In love or war?" He had reached for her hand to answer himself.

He reflected now that in their secret love life, over the years they had had as much and probably more erotic time together than if they had been married. What they had really lacked, were starved for, was time to talk. Time to just *be* with each other. To talk past the reasons and rationales to the stuff *beneath* the reasons, to the unspeakable language that grows up between lovers among their primary passions, out of the old hat of their courting gestures and the first true lies of love. Not that most couples, he knew, ever really made this use of each other, ever truly used each other in this way . . .

His throat was raw, head pounding. "All right," he said now. "Let's look at Mongoose." And once again they reviewed the long, weary increments of invasion and assassination attempts against Cuba and Castro. "It's an *idée fixe,*" Pat said. "An obsession. Day in and day out every CIA station in North and South America plots to wipe out that man . . . Will you tell me, Vivian, whether or not —Tim, you have a computer brain—will you two tell me whether or not the names of Howard Hughes, Richard Nixon and James Hoffa keep coming up and up and up?"

Again it was three in the morning. They had made basic preliminary decisions and delegations of responsibility. Pat would go to Texas, into the field after De Mohrenschildt, a notorious womanizer. "Don't say it," and she had laughed without humor. "In this little team of three I know who's the sex bomb." And then, soberly, "I'd guess it will take more, though, to penetrate this nightmare far enough to get the *hard* information to justify going to the President, or Bobby, or whomever we feel we can trust enough . . ."

Tim would go to New Orleans. New Orleans was key—Bannister, Ferrie, Marcello and the unknown man who had worked in Russia were all in Louisiana.

Vivian would go recruiting throughout the American, British and French intelligence community for help in gauging the conspiracy. He would also see his friend the President and, without revealing the alleged plot to him (Jack would simply have demanded more hard evidence, which was what they were after) at this point, try to call his attention to the inherent danger building up in the Cuban-exile-CIA community, would try to urge that a new policy be launched against the Cuban shock troops from the Bay of Pigs and their extremist American handlers.

And that is what he did.

President Kennedy was waiting for the Director of Plans in the Oval Office. Vivian chatted with JFK's secretary, Mrs. Lincoln, as she showed him in.

The office was cool and sunlit as Vivian entered. The beige sofas, the fireplace, the rocking chair, even the large mahogany desk that bore the Great Seal of the United States spoke of Jack Kennedy's quality of understatedness. The only really personal items were his collections of whales' teeth, ship models and naval paintings, and they seemed almost lost in this thirty-five foot long, twenty-eight foot wide nerve center of power. But lost they were not on the President's friend, who had always possessed an avid eye for detail.

"Hi, Viv." The President was seated reading in the rocking chair he used to favor his back, injured in the South Pacific during the war. "Just the man I wanted to see."

"Jack . . . Mr. President, how's the family?"

"Fine. Jackie's resting a lot, until it's time for the baby."

"How's the back?"

"I adjust."

They smiled at each other, then Vivian gestured to his old friend as he opened his briefcase and took out a pad and pen. In his neat hand he wrote: "Jack, I need to talk to you, but *not* here. Mrs. Lincoln's supply area would be safe." He held up the pad so that the President could scan the message. Kennedy raised his eyebrows and heaved himself to his feet. "Come on, I want to show you something my father sent me."

Wordlessly, the President led the way through a series of secretarial offices to an area of about ten feet by twenty, shelf-lined with supplies. "Shut the door. Viv, if my *office* is bugged, for God's sake, why haven't you told me? Is that what you came to tell me?" The President half sat on a rolling stepladder used to reach the higher shelves. Vivian stood with arms folded around his lean frame.

"Jack, I have reason to believe the Secret Service has been penetrated by a faction in the Agency that's been out of control since the Bay of Pigs, and—"

"Vivian, I want *names.* I'll put them in a federal prison so fast that they won't have time to pack." Kennedy paced furiously. His handsome face was flushed red.

Vivian's voice stayed cool and low. "There's more to it than that, Jack—McCone is simply not on top of the Agency, and there is a bunch of hard-liners, supergrades, together with some of the officers that you fired after the Bay of Pigs, who are preparing to start their own private war with Mr. Castro. They—"

"Good Lord, Viv, Bobby's supposed to be riding herd on the Agency and you're the goddamned director of Plans. How can anything like this have developed? Standing here and talking like a couple of truants in the supply room. It's intolerable!"

It was clear, as they talked, that the President was well aware that high-ranking career men like Tracy Barnes, Richard Helms, Desmond FitzGerald and William Must, because of their independent wealth and aristocratic backgrounds, felt they had a fiat to rule in what *they* considered the best interests of the nation.

John F. Kennedy was as shrewd as he was angry, and within ten minutes the two had come to a decision to verify the bugging of the White House by independent means under Vivian's direction, and second, to declare their own war on the all but out of control CIA officers, ex-officers and their Cuban "assets." Vivian would privately feed information to the President, who in turn would, Vivian hoped and urged, direct his brother to coordinate attacks using the FBI, Treasury Department, Coast Guard and Customs Service as a small army under his control. Vivian had not seen John Kennedy so serious since the missile crisis. Now Kennedy shook his head and intoned, "Cuber, Cuber, Cuber . . . God where will it end?"

Right then Vivian almost told him that it might end in assassination, but restrained himself. It would serve nothing, and in fact be counter-productive . . . Jack Kennedy would smile, look at him and suggest he had succumbed to the paranoia and melodrama of the Agency extremists. Better stay plausible, protect Jack as best he could in spite of his famous skepticism (fatalism?) . . . He suggested that they meet from then on in the small library of the Executive Office Building, across the way, or out at Bobby's Hickory Hill estate.

"Thanks, Viv. Let's clean this up, and as soon as the '64 campaign is over you'll go in as director at CIA and then we'll grab their nuts!"

By March first coordinated, lightning raids had the Cuban exile militants in a state of shock and disarray. For the first time in American history armed agents of federal law enforcement confronted agents of a rival intelligence agency—the CIA. Vivian and the White House were able to manage the news so that the public was unaware of CIA involvement in the raids on CIA arms depots and operations. In the opening skirmishes of the secret Kennedy-Prescott war, the Secret Service was used to smash counterfeiting operations in Maryland. These aborted the Scott cabal's plan to flood Cuba with bogus money in order to destabilize the island economy. Vivian's worry was that unless the raids continued and were intensified the conspirators would step up their timetable of execution. There were still large arms and explosives caches in Louisiana, as well as training camps run by anti-Castro extremists and supplied by the Scott network under cover of their illegal Domestic Operations Division in New Orleans, Dallas, Miami, as well as in the Bahamas under Howard Hughes's cover.

In this fashion the conspiracy was being hurt somewhat at the operational level, and the President and his brother were pleased at the progress and grateful to Vivian. But Vivian received the ominous news in mid-March, from both Pat and Tim, that the raids had mostly served to fire up the potential assassins of the President to a greater intensity of hate and desire for revenge. It was maddening to Vivian that they had as yet been unable to climb the conspiracy ladder any higher than Sherman Scott—and they had already known that much from Philby's tape.

Then in April Pat succeeded in striking up a relationship with George De Mohrenschildt, and they learned the name of the man who was intended to compromise, all at once, the Agency and the

Soviets and the Cubans. Strange and yet not so strange bedfellows. At the same time Tim, by exhaustive cross-checking, had narrowed the possibilities to the same man. . . .

Pat had contrived to secure employment with the *Journal of Petroleum Products*. It was there that she met George De Mohrenschildt, who would drop into the oil-industry subsidized journal offices to pick up mail, and new secretaries.

De Mohrenschildt was a husky man of well over six feet. He had the manner and bearing of an aristocrat, wavy hair and well-shaped features. Yet, Pat felt herself shrink from him. With time of the essence, she forced it down. She would do what she had to do. A job. And it could not be delegated.

Her approach: an interview with De Mohrenschildt, the geologist and world traveler, for the *Journal*. Her cover identity of a single, freelance journalist and editorial writer worked well with De Mohrenschildt. Dinner and drinks were the natural aftermath of the interview. The Russian was a glib and compulsive talker, so that Pat at least had very little verbal dissembling to do.

They dined in the luxuriously appointed Murchinson dining room of the elite Dallas Petro Chemical Club . . . "An impoverished aristocrat knows how to live better than anybody, Cindy." Calling her by her cover name, Cindy McNally, and adding pompously that "living well is the best revenge, you know."

"Against whom?

His laugh was a rich basso profundo, his accent still very slavic. "No, no, I bear no grudges. Life is too short. My religion is orthodox hedonism. What is yours? Have some more wine . . ."

"I believe in love—or money."

His laugh rolled across the almost empty clubroom. What a stupid man, she thought, for all his narcissistic old world charm. He proceeded to spin out a saga of travel and adventure stories. She indicated strong interest in the fact that he'd hinted broadly that, in his time, he had led the life of a secret agent . . . "Now, Cindy, off the record. Do you know Kuwait? Ah . . ."

By their second brandy she had steered his monologue around to his contacts in the American aristocracy in general, and the Kennedy clan in particular. "Poor Jackie, I'm afraid that she's married a hero *manqué*—he begins with great *panache* but never *finishes* anything. They say that he is a disappointing lover . . ." Now Pat/Cindy began a show of interest.

"Oh, yes, the President's love life is *tout à fait,* the thing. Very athletic but—do you understand French?—but, you know, *à la papa* . . ."

Pat seized the opportunity. "Oh, no, how disappointing. Not what I pictured at all."

"No? So. What does Cindy picture, tell me?" His hand, an obscene invasion, was on her leg as he signaled for more brandy. She felt nauseous.

The rich in Dallas dine early on heavy cuts of beef. The ornate room was empty by half past ten, but the Cuban waiter, who apparently was familiar with De Mohrenschildt's drinking and dating habits, stayed within a discreet distance. Two more brandies later Pat pretended to lean on her escort's arm for leverage as they rose, laughing, to go up to the fourth floor of the brick-and-glass building. The club maintained several handsome suites for members' occasional use, and De Mohrenschildt, as the director for public relations, kept a permanent penthouse facility in readiness.

Inside, the Naugahyde and other synthetic fabrics made the small one-bedroom spread a study in "motel modern," thought Pat, weaving her way to a bathroom that, predictably, sported a decor of cavorting nymphs and centaurs. She was not really inebriated at all, only needed time to prepare her approach so that she could find some clue to the identity of the man De Mohrenschildt was "baby-sitting"—the man referred to on Philby's original tape as the set-up for the plot against the President.

Having sex with a man like De Mohrenschildt, she decided, might never bring a word of truth, much less the name of the unknown man. The answer, short of a windfall, was eventually to get access to his papers or telephone or appointment book. With that goal in mind she swung out of the bathroom. Filling up the small sitting room was De Mohrenschildt, stark naked. In one hand he gripped his curving tumescence, in the other a sinister looking black leather whip. He motioned her into the small, almost antiseptically clean bedroom, pointed at the head of the bed and moved heavily toward the closet. He emerged at once holding a large leather box, the whip still in his hand. Light spilled in from the next room, but his face was in shadow when he spoke.

330

"Do you prefer to be the jockey or the horse?" and snapped his whip.

If he hits me with that, Pat thought, I'll kill him, Kennedy or no Kennedy.

He opened the leather container and handed it to her. She stared into the shallow shadow of the box, as if in a dream, unable to comprehend its contents. Then, in near-shock, she understood what it was that was expected of her, and now, when she stumbled back against the wall and slid down onto the bed, she was not faking disorientation.

The box contained a tube of Vaseline jelly and a six-inch hard rubber model of a penis attached to a thin leather belt. He handed her the whip as he vaulted onto the bed, the hard mattress giving under his weight, crawled up on all fours, supporting himself with his left arm and hand, commencing to masturbate with the other hand. He shot her a sidelong glare of such intensity that she knew with certainty that he was capable of murdering her on the spot if she refused to satisfy his need.

Her fingers trembled as she buckled the dildo belt around her waist . . .

And prayed she would not throw up.

Pat did not tell Tim or Vivian how she had managed to find an occasion to hurriedly scan De Mohrenschildt's appointment book after he had collapsed into a drunken stupor. Only that there were two references for the following weeks to meetings with an "M. Oswald."

"*Oswald . . .*" Tim's voice was high and tense in contrast to his habitual low key. The three were gathered in the crowded Donahue recreation room. Terry was sleeping at a neighbor's, the house was empty. The dossiers of the Cubans, Bannister and Jack Ruby were spread out on the Ping Pong table.

"Here it is." Tim pulled out a one-inch "20" Agency file from a stack in his briefcase. "Read it," Vivian said. Pat poured more tea, trying by an act of will to erase the awful pictures from the glue of her memory.

Tim scanned the document quickly, giving the two others only fragments of what he read. "There is a Fair Play for Cuba cover already started on him in New Orleans . . . The Chinaman's been

331

looking after him so far . . . He's had a really checkered career . . . highly trained . . . schizothymic personality, schizoid but able to function within normal-seeming bounds. Fits the profile—"

"*Wait* a minute," Vivian said. "Let's go back over this. What's this I see here about a drill out of Atsugi?"

"Well, we used Eurasian bar girls as agents, as you know. The Queen Bee was our major recruiting situation—it was one of the most expensive nightclubs in Tokyo and we had no trouble arranging for enlisted men like Oswald to get there as part of someone's "birthday" celebration. Once there, we made sure that some of our girls approached the men with offers to buy secrets, or trade favors to buy them. Step number two was to interview any of those who had been approached at the Queen Bee and who reported the contact to ONI. Oswald was one of those who reported in . . . There were about a dozen others over the period of our operation there. The next step was to ask those who reported in whether they would be willing to help out by selling some false information to the girls . . . whom we identified, naturally, as Russian agents. These records show that Oswald was gung-ho to play spy and did. He was pretty good. So along with four others—here are their files —we started giving him Russian language training and briefing him to infiltrate the Soviet Union. And eventually he did."

Vivian and Tim were standing as if squared off with each other.

"So inside the Soviet Union you paid him and ran him under Red Cross cover, I assume."

"That's it."

"Who told him to redefect and start screaming to come back?"

"I don't know, Viv."

"What happened to the other men we infiltrated?"

"KGB rolled up all but two of them."

"Tim, I think this Oswald could have been turned . . . what do you think? Is there any chance that he supplied the Soviets with information on the U-2 overflights?"

"I don't know. They rolled up almost our entire network after that insistence by the Animals on continuing those flights and wrecking the summit. It sure wrecked us at the same time."

"It sure did," muttered Vivian. His stare had turned into a glare. He did not trust himself to speak, and instead turned toward the big picture window in the Donahue house. He saw only his own

332

reflection glaring back at him. "The nights are dark in Virginia," he thought automatically, as if the figure looking at him out of the window's reflection were a complete stranger.

So Oswald had been *his* agent . . . Vivian thought of the Atsugi U-2 base, so secret that, where Oswald worked, anyone approaching the forbidden area at night had to kneel in the roadway while a powerful searchlight trapped the visitor in its beam and guards with automatic weapons approached to search—

Tim's methodical diction broke into Vivian's reverie. "But I don't see how Oswald could have even been anything but ours. When he returned to the United States after Russia, he was met in New York at the dock by a man named Raikin. Raikin's the secretary-general of the American Friends of the Anti-Bolshevist Block of Nations . . ."

Worse and worse. The Raikin group was housed in Taiwan but they had abiding ties to the WACL, the World Anti-Communist League, and that meant the Kuomintang in Taiwan and their agents and friends—such as Richard Nixon—in the United States. It also meant close ties to the Agency's assets in the WACL, *and* it meant an even closer connection to the Gehlen organization. Vivian writhed in his mind . . . like the Laocoön, the snakes of his past hissing up around his knees . . . He turned back to Tim. "What cover did we use to recruit him?"

"Well, the Agency was supporting Castro, a presumed winner, *against* Batista at that time in '58, and that support was the best tack to take with an adventurer type like Oswald . . ."

The tea was cold. Pat walked to the thermostat to turn the heat up against the March damp. From the living room, they silently counted as the clock struck eleven.

"The perfect patsy." Vivian's voice was as dry as the raking of leaves. "Somehow they implicate him, leak his files, after the fact, and tie him to us *and* the KGB with the same noose . . . Then, they take over the Agency and launch the real invasion of Cuba. The Soviets react—"

"And that's the end . . ." said Pat, her hand on the thermostat.

Vivian broke the following silence. "Pat, you have to go back to Dallas. Tim, you have to go to New Orleans." He pushed the Bannister file toward Tim.

"We have the low man on the totem pole, finally. What we *don't* have is the control above De Mohrenschildt. We have Sherman and Must above him but none of us can go anywhere near the two of them. I'm going to go laterally. I'm going to make contact, somehow, with Jack Ruby's syndicate *capo* and work back to find out how high this thing goes in the Agency.''

They stared at him. It had been almost twenty years since they had heard that tone of voice or seen his wide, gray eyes blaze with that look that was beyond hope, or fear.

Over the Easter holiday Vivian activated the Agency's Clandestine Section's key operative in the Chicago FBI office. Rob Garabedian was the assistant special agent in charge of the big Chicago office. He was still taciturn and tough and as hard to read as he had been during their training together at Camp X over two decades ago.

The CIA had over two hundred informants and "assets" inside the Bureau, but Garabedian was the best. There was a risk . . . Garabedian had been brought into play as a double agent by Kim Philby, and knowing what Vivian knew, there was at least the possibility, if remote, that Garabedian was also a Soviet asset. But Vivian knew that there was no one else he could trust for what he had in mind. Philby's defection had rocked the Americans and British, except those in the know who held back exposing him as a mole and admitting fifteen years of being outwitted by the Soviets— until, of course, he defected and there was no more covering up the enormous embarrassment. In any case not a hint of trouble had touched Garabedian.

The chubby Armenian listened impassively as Vivian gave him the cover story . . . "The point of all this, Rob, is that the mob intends to try to inhibit the President's war on organized crime with telephone-tap conversations between the White House and the Las Vegas woman . . . You get me a complete make on Tito Carbonara and his family—I mean right down to which mass they attend on Sunday—and I'll horsetrade from there." Outside the old Plaza Hotel room on Clark Street, that Garabedian employed for covert meetings such as this one with his old OSS buddy Prescott, the streetcars clanged and rattled. Once again, the gears of the OSS Old Boy network began to crank like the ancient red trolley cars rumbling in the street below. Before parting they walked across the avenue to the Old Heidelberg for one of its huge and famous apple pancakes.

Vivian spent the next thirty hours in a two-bedroom town house on a quiet street in Glencoe, forty-five minutes north of Chicago's Loop. The Agency maintained safe houses in every section of the country, a number of which were always available to him as the Director of Plans.

There was no way to know whether or not the plotters were aware of his penetration of the conspiracy. Tim and Pat were the best undercover operatives that there were, never an indiscretion or provocation, but now that he was activating FBI assets the chances of a leak had gone up by the numbers.

Just as he was about to go out for dinner on Tuesday, the telephone rang. It could only be Rob Garabedian. It was, saying, "I have the package," and hanging up.

They met in an upstairs corner dining area at the Old Heidelberg, the restaurant a maze of gleaming white table-clothed nooks and rooms. They shared a giant order of Hoppelpoppel. "You never put on a pound, you lucky bastard," Garabedian mourned as he shoveled in the delicious sausage-onion-egg pancake.

"I still play a little tennis, Rob. What about you?"

"Me? Oh, yeah, I get exercise. Once a day I smoke a cigar by an open window."

To Vivian's memory, this was the only unnecessary, not to say purposely humorous, remark that he had ever heard the gloomy, thick-set Armenian make. While they ate, Vivian studied the summary of John (AKA Juanito, AKA Tito) Carbonara. Tito had been raised and groomed by his Spanish bootlegger mother and had risen fast through the fat of the tail end of the Capone gang. Like Jack Ruby he had "made his bones" by executing a number of soldiers from other gangs. Vivian sipped the good coffee . . . Bones at Yale and bones in Chicago, a little different but a lot the same.

Now Tito lived in a twenty-room Tudor style country house near Northwestern University with his wife and two children. He kept his mistress in a suite at the Drake Towers on Lake Shore Drive. His son he sent to Camp Tuskora in Michigan. On Dad's Day he was there every summer for the softball game and minstrel show. Known as a perfect gentleman along the small whiteway of Chicago's Rush Street by the twenty-six girls and the headwaiters, and as a religious churchgoer in his parish, Tito Carbonara was a "made man." On those rare occasions when his name appeared in one of the columns, the explanatory title, "Rush Street restaurateur," always followed the appellation.

Garabedian lit a cheap cigar and groaned when Vivian suggested that they share an apple pancake. A revival of Charlie Chaplin's *City Lights* was playing next door at the Plaza Theater as they emerged from the old German *gasthaus*.

"Rob, thanks for everything. I'm going to use the Eagle River house for a while. I'll let you know when it's free."

"Anytime," nodded Robert M. (for Mugar) Garabedian, the double or triple agent whose goal in life had narrowed down to the undoing of John Edgar Hoover—whom Garabedian had once heard, he said, make a viciously unflattering comment about the Armenian people.

As Vivian turned onto the Outer Drive to return to his suburban safe house, he reviewed his options . . . An old-time killer like Tito Carbonara could be dealt with in only one fashion, and that was force, but a plan of force had to have exquisite balance factored into it. He needed Carbonara's cooperation not for an hour, for as long as he could hold a gun on him, but for several weeks at least. The point of pressure was, unavoidably, Anna Maria Carbonara, the thirteen-year-old daughter of the hit man-restauranteur.

Vivian could not possibly delegate a kidnapping inside the United States to a control agent or one of Garabedian's men. If anything went wrong the shock waves would crash all the way up to the Oval Office. This would be an op of behind-the-lines magnitude, only this time Mush and the rest of the Prescott team would not be there.

The memory of Mush made him take a deep breath. The wooded lakefront of Chicago's North Shore district merged in his mind with the stand of birch trees in the middle-distance into which Mush had melted that evening in Russia that had changed both their lives. In his heart Vivian was sure that Mush was dead. The more he'd thought of it, the more it was clear that the KGB had been aware of every step he and Mush had taken between Paris and Moscow.

The DCI at that time, Allen Dulles, had called it "the intelligence prize of the century." Vivian had received covert credit for securing the grand plum of western intelligence—the Khrushchev speech—and had, because of his coup, taken a giant step into the upper reaches of CIA. The truth was that since they had been supported along the way by Philby men in MI6 there was every possibility that the Russians had wanted the United States to have the speech, that the doves in the Politburo had *used* Vivian and Mush to achieve their own victory over the hard-liners and hawks, just as he and Mush had had to fight in Paris for their lives against Sherman Scott and his Animals under contract to the Agency . . . He wished that Mush were here now to help him. He desperately needed to talk to someone he trusted. It was impossible to call Tim in New Orleans or Pat in Dallas and risk blowing their covers.

He felt completely alone, remembering the receding back and broad shoulders of his friend as he disappeared into the Russian spring evening, and a phrase from somewhere ran through his mind . . . "O lost, and by the wind grieved . . ."

It was exactly three the next afternoon as Vivian alighted from the big green bus at the corner of Greenbay Road and Kent. Under his tan raincoat he wore a charcoal gray suit, in his attaché case was folded a black chauffeur's peaked cap. Two blocks west was the exclusive St. Monica School for Girls. In front of the ivy-covered red brick building several limousines waited each afternoon to collect the daughters of wealthy North Shore Chicago families. Toward one of these, a new black 1962 Cadillac, Vivian walked at a casual pace.

Three uniformed chauffeurs were smoking and talking next to a black Chrysler limousine about forty yards west of the Carbonara Cadillac. Vivian continued until he was abreast of the Chrysler, then stopped and addressed a short olive-skinned man in his mid-fifties. Vivian's Italian was more than effective enough for his limited purpose. . . . "Mr. D'Amico? I have a message for you from Mr. Carbonara." Vivian turned without waiting and walked back toward the Cadillac. The thin little man stood looking after the tall, handsome stranger in the raincoat. D'Amico's cigarette hand was suspended in mid-gesture, his brow furrowed. The other two drivers watched Vivian blankly. After this momentary hesitation, the

Carbonara driver dropped the cigarette to the street, adjusted his cap and followed Vivian toward the Cadillac. As he walked, he let his right elbow brush against the handgun he wore strapped inside his liveried tunic. From the school the first bell sounded. Late model automobiles driven by maids were pulling up to doublepark and wait for the second bell.

"Mr. D'Amico?" Speaking English now.

"Yeah?"

"Mr. Carbonara's secretary asked me to bring you a package to give to the Mother Superior." D'Amico's eyes narrowed. "Secretary?"

Vivian was already unzipping the cordovan attaché case and extending it for the chauffeur to see the contents. D'Amico moved a step closer and looked down into the angled receptacle. When he saw the Luger pointed up at his head, with the tall man's finger on the trigger, he froze. The second bell rang. More cars were arriving.

Vivian made his voice appropriately low and cold. "The boss says if you make one funny move I should let you have it. I don't know what the fuck you've done but Mr. Carbonara wants to see you right now. Get in the car and when Miss Carbonara comes out you drive where I tell you. Better get in right now. Drop your gun in here." D'Amico's eyes began to focus again, his face was white. Vivian nudged his arm with the case and, like a doll, the bantam-sized driver-bodyguard bent into the seat behind the wheel. Vivian slammed D'Amico's door and slipped into the jump seat immediately behind him, resting the gun case on the bolster against the driver's neck, reaching over to take away the bodyguard's weapon.

Prepubescent girls in green sweaters and skirts were trooping out of the wide iron ivy-decorated doors. From the photograph supplied by Garabedian, Vivian recognized Anna Maria as she approached. The girl was overweight and wore black-rimmed glasses that looked much too old for her. As she walked toward the limousine she pulled with her brace-wired teeth at a taffy bar while trying to balance four books and a looseleaf notebook with her other hand. Five feet from the Cadillac she dropped the books and as she bent to recover them, the notebook slipped sideways out of her hand and fell open into the gutter. Pencils, erasers, a compass and ruler all bounced into the street.

"Oh, *shit*," Anna Maria said, and then, "Eddie, will you please get out and help me pick up this junk."

As the driver leaned forward Vivian swung the briefcase into the base of his skull. "Sit still, Mr. D'Amico." With the case still pressing against the driver's neck, Vivian opened his door and put one foot into the street in order to angle himself free to call to the girl. "Miss Carbonara. Please get right in. Your father's been taken ill and you're needed at home. Please hurry, miss." The girl's eyes opened wide as she stood balanced on the curb, staring at the stranger, who had resumed his position in the jump seat. She gathered up the books. Vivian reached across to open the rear door for her. She usually sat in front next to Eddie and the change in routine and the strange man made her heart beat fast. She felt an asthma attack coming on. Her glasses were slipping down her nose as she fell into the backseat, her books again spilling to the floor.

"Go north on Alton Road. Stay within the speed limit at all times . . . Hello, Anna. My name is Richard Voss, I'm a friend of your father's." Vivian smiled.

"What's wrong with him?" The girl's voice had an adenoidal undertone.

Vivian shook his head. "We don't know. He drove up to Wisconsin this morning to look at some property and around noon he fainted. We're going right there now . . . Mr. D'Amico, I believe you want to turn right at the next corner." . . .

It was an hour later, after they had stopped at a service station to use the toilet—D'Amico and Vivian together every moment, silent, side by side at the urinal—that Vivian told them their destination. Eagle River, Wisconsin. The driver's eyes went to the rearview mirror searching for the stranger's face. Vivian's stare was empty when their eyes met in the glass.

D'Amico was truly worried now. The Teamsters had a secret resort-retreat on Lake Taylor just outside the town whose out-of-season population was fifteen hundred. During the short summer wealthy Chicagoans came in impressive numbers to relax in the north woods and enjoy superb fishing on the chain of lakes. Now, in the cold Wisconsin spring, the resorts and summer homes would still be shuttered and empty. . . .

It was near midnight when the long limousine left the highway

339

to follow a short dirt road to a two-story white farmhouse. There were no animals in the red barn and a handyman and his wife from the town, three miles away, were the only occasional visitors. A path from the house led down through a wooded area to a clear water lake. A motor launch was maintained in operating condition in the boat house. The lake connected to the larger Silver Lake, and one could motor by a roundabout route to the shore of the Jack-O-Lantern Resort, which the Teamsters had purchased and luxuriously refitted for their private gatherings and council meetings. Or a walker could set off in the other direction from the house, across fields and through more woods to the rendezvous spot, the old Jack-O-Lantern.

The Agency paid the caretakers' salaries through a Madison trade magazine, and the Zimplemans did not ask questions or broadcast to any friends or relatives in Eagle River or Rhinelander that they received $1,000 a month to look after a big country farmhouse that had been used once in ten years . . . That time, in 1958, Mrs. Zimpleman had cooked generous German dinners for the handsome Mr. Voss, as Vivian was known to them, and for his two friends, who were also, she was told, professors of geology who might indulge in a bit of deer hunting. She and Martin, her husband, had wondered why the other professor with the heavy foreign accent had seemed to disappear so suddenly after the third day, but they were not the kind to ask questions. Vivian, as Director of Plans, had had to make the decision to "terminate with extreme prejudice" a Soviet "defector" whom he had outwitted, inducing him to reveal the purpose behind his self-styled change of heart. The man, Boris Shatov, had been a KGB plant whose secret assignment was to convince the CIA's Directorate of Plans that the Prescott-Donahue network of infiltration into the Soviet Union had all been discovered and turned around to work for the KGB. Vivian remembered the man with bitterness because it was precisely one of these infiltrators, Oswald, who was now to be used as a dagger to stab him in the back and to participate in a plot against the President. Not for the first time, he was struck by how well the KGB hawks and the CIA Animals, Scott, for example, would get along, how terrifyingly alike they were—through the looking glass . . .

D'Amico inched the limousine forward in the dark over the rutted road toward the bulk of the house just coming into the

340

scope of the Cadillac's powerful bright beam. The driver was very tense, the girl had finally awakened and was rubbing her eyes and fumbling for her glasses.

"Just pull right in under that shed to the right—sharp right." Vivian removed an elongated flashlight with a specially designed wide beam from his briefcase and turned to Anna Carbonara.

"I don't see any lights, they must have taken your father to the hospital in the next town. We can go in and use the phone. You had better wait here until Mr. D'Amico and I go in and turn on the lights . . ." He nudged the chauffeur in the neck with the case and the man stepped out of the car into the dark. Vivian snapped on the inside light over his head, smiled at the bleary-eyed girl and joined the other man on the loose gravel of the yard area. The beam from his flashlight led them toward the house.

Vivian unlocked the rear door and snapped on the kitchen light. As he knew it would be, everything was clean and functional. He tried the locked basement door and turned to D'Amico, who was standing in the middle of the linoleum-covered floor, almost at attention with fear.

Vivian had learned long ago, in another farmhouse behind the lines, how to combine politeness and threat in order to produce optimum terror. "Mr. D'Amico, I'm going to tell you what I've been ordered to tell you. I'm a lawyer. I cannot tell you who I work for but I will say that *I* know that *you* know this area of Wisconsin very well, that this house is less than two miles from a certain resort with which you're familiar. Mr. Carbonara's orders are that until the war is over that—"

"What war?"

"The war between Mr. Carbonara and certain people in Miami. I think you know who I mean. Now, Mr. Carbonara wants you to stay safe *and* hidden here at least until tomorrow. Then you're to go to another place near here, you know what I mean, and from there Mr. Carbonara will take over himself."

"Whose place is this?"

"Mr. Carbonara's." Vivian unlocked the basement door. As it swung open D'Amico's small black eyes almost came out of his head. What appeared to be an ordinary wooden farmhouse basement door revealed that the closed side was heavy steel plate, that the plain white painted wood was a facade. Everything was a facade here. The basement—as D'Amico was about to find out—was a clean, comfortable apartmentlike prison—soundproof, fireproof, escape-proof.

In this maximum security cell the "defector" Boris Shatov had been interrogated. And here he had been given a tasteless poison in his evening meal. "You wait down here, Mr. D'Amico, I'll go get Miss Carbonara." The little man was rooted to the linoleum. "Mr. D'Amico, Mr. Carbonara believes that an FBI informer has infiltrated his personal household. I told him that I was sure that it wasn't you. But he told me that if you so much as hesitated to follow his orders I should do away with you and protect his daughter myself." Vivian showed him the Luger and D'Amico began a fast shuffle toward the basement stairs. Vivian pushed an electric light switch and locked the door after the man. Then he unlocked the door again and cracked it open. "Say nothing to upset Miss Carbonara. *Nothing.*" Then he closed and locked it again.

Outside the Wisconsin spring air was still chill. Vivian was annoyed because the expensive heating system that the Agency had installed had never functioned well and the old furnace had been torn out when the basement was transformed into a cozy prison chamber in the early '50s.

"Miss Carbonara. Please come with me. I called the hospital and your father is much better. He wants you to stay here tonight, then in the morning we'll drive over to see him . . . are you hungry?" The tense face stared at him, then she picked up her books and climbed out to follow him in.

"Get a good night's rest," he said as he escorted her down the stairs. D'Amico had turned on the lights below and was perched like a stuffed animal on an imitation Revere desk chair, vintage American revolution, more or less a few years.

Upstairs one of the bedrooms had been converted into a work area. Locked in the reinforced closet was a powerful shortwave radio. Vivian checked his watch, then wheeled the steel radio stand out into the middle of the room. Garabedian would not be expecting his call for almost an hour. He tried to adjust the thermostat, then stepped into the hall to use the toilet.

In the basement the Carbonara child curled up for warmth on the divan and tried to sleep. The driver sat on the early-American-style chair like a dead toy.

Upstairs Vivian dialed the Zimpleman home to tell them that he would be spending the night and part of the day tomorrow and that he was very sorry he could not stay "long enough for one of Mrs. Z's memorable entrees." He then addressed himself to the radio and Rob Garabedian. Garabedian understood that he was to pick up the Prescott signal and patch Vivian through to the Carbonara residence by telephone.

". . . Mr. Carbonara please."

"Who's calling?"

"I have a message from Anna Maria . . ."

"*Hello!* This is Carbonara. Where's—"

"Shut up. Meet me in room seven twelve of the Plaza Hotel at Clark and North Avenue at midnight tomorrow night. Come alone. Anna Maria is fine . . ."

He clicked the receiver down, cutting off the soft wail from the killer on the other end of the line.

He walked out the front door, down the path that led through the woods to the lake. The moon was at one quarter, cold and yellow. The air vibrated with frog booms and cricket sounds. In the morning he would walk out here again and watch the deer nibbling to the east in the clover field. The Soviet double agent was buried in these shallow woods under the ruins of an old fishing cabin. Someone else had dug the grave . . . "my *hands* were not dirty that day," Vivian thought. The chill air made his temples throb and his muscles contract under the light Spanish raincoat. He stopped in a copse of birch and was again reminded of the Russian countryside where Mush had said good-by at the edge of the woods.

He reached out to touch the dry, cracked whiteness of a tree. The bark was rough, scraping his fingers. A longing passed through him to put his mouth to the tree's tough coat, to taste with his tongue the acrid surface of nature. Anything to pierce the cold onionskin of despair that was wrapping itself around him. He tried again to think of an alternative to killing the chauffeur, D'Amico . . . and the Carbonara child? Unthinkable . . . but time was running out, the attempt on the President might come at any moment and all the Prescott team had so far was a handful of adventurers at the bottom and a clutch of top Agency officers who could never be taken without ironclad evidence.

Carbonara would do almost anything for his daughter. Vivian

needed him to do a number of things over a period of time. There was no one and no place to keep the girl for as long as it might take, much less the driver . . .

He tore at the white skin of the tree. Jack Kennedy was the President of the United States, Jack Kennedy had saved his life one night in Boston during the fire . . . and reminding himself—a junta of conspirators was once again trying, as they had in Roosevelt's day, to seize power, take over a nation . . . this was war, for real . . . Tito Carbonara was a murderous excrescence, no loss, and the driver D'Amico was a parasitic scum . . . the girl . . .

He raised his fist to smash it into the tree but did not follow through, instead stood there in the pale, cold light with head bowed and arm raised as if it, too, were the gnarled branch of a dying tree. The pulse of the crickets rang in his ears.

He walked to the edge of the black lake on the short sandy beach, thinking of the black, freezing water that had cut Camp X off from the main. That was war. He and Janet had crossed over the water of death, she to stay . . . *War.*

The word *death* he remembered from the Indo-European language base *dheu*—"to become senseless." Seeing the word spelled out on the flat black surface of the lake as if it were a schoolroom blackboard trying to distract or trick his mind . . . *"Janet . . ."* His whole self called out across the water.

Out in the blackness of the lake a muskie broke water, splashing. Vivian turned. The wet footprints leading to where he stood were his, he knew, and yet suddenly the woods throbbed, like cricket sound, with danger. He half ran to the trees and broke off a branch, returned to the water's edge, then walked backward toward the trees again, erasing his footsteps as he moved crabwise away from the lake and into the underbrush.

He stood in the impenetrable blackness of the woods. Above, the Milky Way spilled across the last quarter of the night. He could not kill this child. Could not do it even to save Jack Kennedy's life. But he also could not return her to Tito Carbonara either, unless he was ready to quit and let them destroy the President of the United States without doing everything possible to get to the top people . . .

If he poisoned D'Amico first the girl might by accident eat the same food. But if he fed her first and the food was drugged, then

344

she would be out while he took care of the chauffeur. And while Anna Maria was still unconscious he could deposit her at the Hughes Gateway Home and Clinic outside Rhinelander, forty minutes away . . . Behind him a forest bird gave a premature call and subsided. The volume of the frogs' boom went up as the night passed.

Vivian shook his head with a stubborn, throttled rage. He would have to turn her over to the clinic, and he hated the notion . . . The Hughes Gateway was one of two dozen experimental homes and clinics scattered around the country from Texas to New York State. Some were huge, as in Houston, others held less than twenty patients, like the Rhinelander unit. The facilities were all funded by a Howard Hughes front that the Agency had been using since 1955 . . . Vivian knew about the drug experiments conducted there, made no attempt to rationalize them . . . there *were* limits to that process . . .

The chorus of crickets and frogs drummed the question . . . "What to do, do, do?" He arched his neck to stare up at the glittering sky. No answer. The child would be drugged, deposited and, eventually . . . what? Well, if we can stop the Animals then the girl can be rehabilitated. This can't go on for more than a few months. I'll keep her off Thorazine, they can give her barbiturate-based compounds, less permanent in their effects . . . I'll be head of the Agency, I'll personally monitor her progress . . . and if I can't help her and they kill Jack then what difference will anything make —no, that's crazy . . . either way I am responsible for this child. If Jack lives—no, if *I* live, then *she* lives. That's all. That's *it.*

The stars were going out. Vivian turned toward the house. He could now begin to make out its outlines in the false dawn. Somewhere in the forest he heard the crash of a big buck moving.

Wearing the chauffeur's cap, Vivian sped along the highway in the long black limousine. D'Amico was buried in the woods next to the Russian, and Vivian's thoughts flew forward ahead of the hearselike Cadillac toward his meeting with Tito Carbonara. . . .

At one minute after midnight the elevator creaked open at the seventh floor of the Plaza. A huge man in an expensive gray topcoat rolled out into the corridor, trying to figure whether to go to the left or the right to find room 712. To the left.

The door to 712 was ajar. The man, who was built like a professional football lineman gone to fat, pushed the door in slowly. A chair had been moved into the middle of the room, an envelope was set conspicuously taped to the cushion. With ham-heavy hands the man tore it open and read the neatly printed note inside. GO NOW TO ROOM 204 OF THE MARK TWAIN HOTEL AT SURF AND DIVISION. The vast chest and shoulders rose and fell with a sigh. He turned his wrestler's face toward the wall for an instant, then stalked out, slamming the door with such force that plaster rained down like thick dust.

Across the corridor in 713 Rob Garabedian went to the telephone and put in a call to room 204 of the Mark Twain Hotel to tell Prescott that Carbonara was on his way, alone.

Vivian knew the drill with the likes of Carbonara. "Force and face." Begin from force, go to force, end with force. But always remember "face," leave your killer a face-saving way out. . . .

"Mr. Carbonara, thank you for coming alone. Let me talk first, please. Your daughter and Mr. D'Amico are quite safe. They are in another country. In no way will they be harmed. You have my word—"

"Who the hell are you?" The powerhouse of two hundred ninety pounds shook off the offer of a chair.

"You will never know that. Take your pick . . . from Meyer Lansky, the FBI, the CIA, the Howard Hughes group, the KGB . . . the *point* is we have your daughter and we want something from you in return for her."

"Keep talking." The Countess Roth tie rose and fell with his heaving chest.

"Mr. Carbonara, it seems some of your friends are in on a plan to murder the President of the United States. I can tell you that Jack Ruby in the Dallas-Fort Worth area is one of the cutoff men, Johnny Roselli in Vegas is another, and I'll give you more in a minute. If the President is murdered it means that a lot of people are going to die. Like you and me and your daughter. What do you say, Mr. Carbonara?"

"I don't know what in the *fuckin'* hell you're talkin' about . . . I never heard of no plan to kill no President—"

"No, I'm sure of that or you would tell me what you know and I would have your daughter home within thirty-six hours. Now, let's talk about Mr. Hoffa and Mr. Giancana . . ."

Within an hour Vivian had briefed the man on what information he needed and how contact would be initiated. Carbonara stood the entire time like a tree planted in the middle of the cheap hotel room. Finally Vivian got up. "Mr. Carbonara, if you are able to help us save President Kennedy's life you will not only be reunited with your daughter but you will . . . I have been asked to assure you . . . you will lead a charmed life in this country for the rest of your days. Thank you. Oh, yes, your black Cadillac is parked in the Surf Theater parking lot across the street. Here are the keys. The tank is full."

Pat, again in the persona of Cindy McNally, telephoned De Mohrenschildt from the Six Flags Motel on March 30. He turned instantly cozy . . . "Cindy, welcome back, just in time for the racing season, ah, ha . . . dinner tomorrow night?"

"Well, George, I'd like that, but I don't know if I'll be staying. My father is going to recover, they think, but I can't really take a full-time job. You know my . . . skills, and I was wondering if there were any part-time openings . . . with you. I mean, like personal secretary, and so forth . . ."

"We'll talk about it tomorrow. How would you like to be my personal agent?"

"Oh, I really would, George. That sounds very exciting." . . .

On March 31 Pat forced herself to play jockey again, but not before she drew out of him the most strange story of General Walker . . . De Mohrenschildt's characterization of Major General Edwin Walker was clever, and cruel. Walker, a World War II hero, had apparently gone around the bend some time in the mid-1950s. Thereafter he had become the center of a ragtag right-wing fringe army. The general had covered himself in glory by leading a charge against federal troops positioned in front of the University of Mississippi and, in reprisal, the Kennedy brothers had begun an ongoing campaign against him. That night and throughout the next week, Pat was able to piece together the critical elements in the Walker operation. De Mohrenschildt bragged to her about "the Walker farce . . ." It seemed that at about eight o'clock one evening two weeks earlier General Walker had been seated at a desk in his study, working on his income tax return. He was startled out of his concentration by a bullet that came screeching

347

through a window, past his head, to lodge itself in the wall behind him. Although he was sprayed with white pellets of plaster that had broken away from the wall, he was unhurt. Pat had to admit that the plan was pretty clever . . . Set Oswald up as the man who had shot at General Walker, make sure the press was fed tidbits, then later, after the President was dead, match up the bullets and the "motivation"—that Oswald was a psycho who got his kicks shooting up famous personalities . . . and a lousy Commie to boot . . . "I have to meet this clown Oswald." She laughed.

"We'll see," De Mohrenschildt said, and her heart jumped.

On the following Saturday afternoon Pat and De Mohrenschildt stopped by the Oswald apartment. Showing off, De Mohrenschildt tried to shock Oswald . . . "Lee, how did you manage to miss General Walker the other day?"

Oswald flashed a quick, stunned look toward his wife. Pat immediately picked up on the scrawny young man's condition. So nervous, in fact, did he appear that she felt he was truly now functioning with the bare minimum of control.

Her own nerves, she also realized, were none too good either. Thank God this was her last night in Dallas.

Pat and Vivian were lying in bed at the Maryland safe house. The clear, bright end of an April Saturday was completely theirs. They had made love with an almost primitive desperation, attempting to purge the secrets they carried inside them. Clinging, smothering each other, wrestling to climax yet still not free of what both felt they had to leave unspoken. Pat closed her eyes as Vivian tried to think through the maze of problems to a new set of options and decisions . . . On the drive over she had told him, "There's nothing more I can do in Dallas," and he had agreed. Besides, he knew that she needed to be at home with her son at least some of the time.

"What you've done is to give us a clock on the plot, Pat. This Walker provocation is more than a dress rehearsal. You can be sure there will be everything but a newsreel of the event produced at the propitious moment to establish the man's Communist credentials. You've really done a remarkable job. Did you ever think of a career in law enforcement, miss?" He touched the tip of a nipple and felt it rise, then began to tickle the whole of it counterclockwise.

348

"Umm, the old hand hasn't lost its cunning . . . I needed this. Dallas and De Mohrenschildt . . . I need to forget . . ."

But he was still too full of the awful implications of what they'd found out. "You know, I kept hoping that Philby's story would turn out to be some tabletalk of Scott and the Animals, one of their crackpot capers. Until Tim and you came up with this Oswald from two sources. Since that moment, it's been serious. A war. I just hope that whatever you had to do to get close to—"

"Let's not discuss it. What's next?"

He rolled onto his back and stared up at the ceiling. "I'm going to get results very soon from Chicago, I think. And—no, let's talk about Tim. He's sending in written reports. Let me get the latest one for you."

She watched him as he crossed the room in his lithe quick manner, bending to open his attaché case. She never tired of looking at the flat, tight buttocks, the long muscles of his arms and legs, his cock and balls with their sculpted cast—especially his cock, long, thick and slanted slightly to the right—and the light body covering of brown hair . . . "Will you get back in here . . ." she said with mock imperiousness.

Tim's letter was hand-written, neat and lucid like the man himself. The sight of the clear script made her sigh. If Vivian Prescott had been her whirlpool, Tim Donahue had been her rock.

"Read it out loud," Vivian said. "I want to think it over again, I'm not clear on every cover phrase he's using, except that he felt it necessary to write in that deep a cover and *never* use a telephone, say that he has penetrated some level of the conspiracy, that he's under either suspicion or scrutiny, and the people he's close to are sophisticated, with the resources to monitor telephone and or mail. In short, he's behind the lines."

He could see a pulse in her throat begin to throb against the rosy freckled skin as she read. No, he half prayed, don't let anything happen to Tim Donahue.

April 29, 1963

Dear Mom and Dad,
As you can see I had to change rooms again. The other place was not really clean. I am more attached than ever to this

349

beautiful city and really believe that whatever job decision I make after my "fling" here will be for the best. One thing I know is that I will never return to Montgomery Ward.

I have made a number of new friends and have had a chance to see some of the more picturesque and historic sights. *Incredible!* You two must try to get down here before my savings run out. I ran into a hometown man last week in the French Quarter, old Lars Anderson the druggist. I'll try to write more often, please give my love to *all.*

Your son,
Mike

"How do you read it, Pat? To me it says I've got to go down there right now. He had a close call of some kind at the other address but he's getting very close to something big. Let's see . . . 'picturesque' . . . he has some actual evidence for us to take to Jack or Bobby. Oh, here, '. . . ran into a hometown man,' that's a CIA officer, and I suspect he must mean Sherman Scott. Do you remember that I told you that years ago Mush and I ran into Scott in Le Drugstore in Paris? In '56? Well, I believe that's what Tim, with his total recall, has in mind here. But he can't mean that Scott saw *him* . . . And 'love to *all,*' well, that's obvious, isn't it?"

"He is really a beautiful person, Viv. I know that you appreciate him, but the Agency has always underrated his real talent . . . What about that reference about not returning to Montgomery Ward? I think he's referring to *this* Company . . . Anyway, I read the other parts of the letter to mean that he wants to change jobs, that he'd like to travel, that he's sick to death of the Monkey-Ward culture that too much of the country seems to be becoming. He addresses it to 'Mom and Dad!' His folks are dead, of course, and . . . wait a minute . . . his dad died at the end of the war . . . he went home with Mush, and you and I went after General Gehlen and then down to Juan-les-Pins for that glorious holiday. I still think of that immense sky, pink and blue, every night before I sleep. You remember?"

"I remember. Everything. Those perky tits begging to be kissed, this flat teenage tummy, this sweet tight cunt . . ."

350

"I thought then, and I think now that Tim knows about us. 'Love to *all*'—oh, *yes*, right there, Viv . . ."

But Tim's face hung over the rim of their consciousness as they tried to immolate themselves in each other. The guilt and the ineluctable sense of the guilt they felt over the betrayal of their friend did not diminish their fierce hunger . . . in fact, it sharpened the need to a cutting edge of pain. Somehow, as Pat said, Tim indeed had to have guessed. That he had said nothing—out of fear of losing her entirely? out of transcending love? out of both?—but had gone on and raised the child that he might also have perceived was not his . . . this was what was unspoken and unbearable between them, and at the same time formed a bond of complicit intimacy and guilt.

Vivian checked into the Bentley Hotel in Alexandria, Louisiana, some two hundred miles from New Orleans, and there Tim met him for the debriefing. The hotel was something of a freak in this quiet deep southern town of 50,000. Built by an eccentric millionaire in an act of revenge against the Lafayette Hotel for refusing him entry without a tie, the Bentley was a grand edifice that could have graced a much larger city.

"I've become accepted in the Bannister office," Tim reported, "and I've developed informants all around Oswald, *and* I've seen what I think might be the training site for the assassination, and I've got a line on Carlos Marcello and the mob component in this thing, and, somehow, Mexico City is going to figure in. Is the President planning a trip there?"

"I don't know. I'll find out. Oh, here's some money in big bills and twenty-five hundred dollars in traveler's checks. Let's start with Bannister."

"He's an ultra right wing militant . . . former FBI special agent in charge of the Chicago office. Don't you remember, Viv, we used him in '61 as a contact for funds and communications for Cuba? Now he's a licensed private investigator."

"Okay, Tim, exactly what story are Scott and his Animals feeding Oswald?"

"They're letting him find out—through another man, David Ferrie—that he's part of an 'executive action' aimed at Castro. They're telling him that it's official government stuff all the way—with the

351

attorney general himself running the show. This is just for the preparation period. It's supposed to be as if the original action against Castro had been revived. And if Oswald doesn't go for it, they're prepared to let him discover that it's domestic, and just a spectacular right wing simulation to, as they put it, scare the shit out of the country and alert the public to the Communist menace. They're also telling him that he and the others will be using blanks. The point is they intend to change the story as often as they have to. Oswald can hardly fire a gun, he's up in the clouds from all their double-talk and need-to-know song and dance. They've got him crazy with new stories every few days. Ferrie is a devil, and a very adroit hypnotist—we trained him . . ."

There was a short pause, and then Vivian pulled himself out of his thoughts. "Let's go down and see if we can find some southern fried chicken. Are you hungry? That's good stuff on Bannister, I can plug Rob Garabedian into that. Now, Oswald . . ."

"Let's see. We'll skip the Walker stuff . . . okay, Oswald arrived in New Orleans on April 25 with personal papers and the dismantled rifle. He set up his Fair Play for Cuba Committee out of Bannister's office about two weeks later. After that he started picking up media attention by passing out leaflets in front of Clay Shaw's office at the Trade Mart. In June he lectured on his Russian experiences to a group of Jesuit scholars at Spring Hill College in Mobile, Alabama. Then he tried to infiltrate an Agency-run anti-Castro group in New Orleans, and was temporarily appointed military adviser to the exiles. It was after that that he started meeting with FBI agents on a regular basis in Comeaux's Bar. Then . . ."

Tim concluded with descriptions of the anti-Castro Lake Pontchartrain training base. Vivian took careful notes on this portion of the information only because he was due to meet with JFK shortly and this was what he needed for the FBI to begin its raids. About Carlos Marcello, Tim could state that Jack Ruby had reportedly been in and out of his antebellum mansion outside New Orleans proper.

"But what we don't know," Vivian said, "is whether or not the New Orleans plan is the *same* plan as Scott's, or whether *several* plans are being drawn together by Scott and whoever is over *him*. Now, Tim, is it safe for you to stay any longer? No fooling around."

352

"Viv, I think that I'm very close to identifying the hit man. I'll tell you why. The Bannister office is all revved up about someone they call Carl, who's expected in a few days. And they're laying on end-of-the-world security for him . . . safe houses, armed escorts and on and on. I have to believe that this is the technician for the hit. Whenever they refer to Carl it usually includes something about Mexico City. So . . ."

Vivian wanted to reach out to the quiet redhead, half wanted to talk about Pat with him, and about the boy Terry. But all he said was, "Let's eat. And talk afterward."

"I wanna know, how's my little girl?" . . .

The breakthrough came for the Prescott team during the first week in June.

With Pat back at Langley covering for him, and DCI McCone on perpetual junkets, Vivian was able to travel extensively around the country without raising any more suspicions than always accrued to high officials in the Directorate of Plans. So strict was the compartmentalization of operations in Plans that Vivian could disappear for a week at a time with no one, including the DCI, having the remotest idea where he was. To Vivian's frustration, though, the same was true of Sherman Scott or Bill Must or Richard Helms or any of the supergrades and ex-OSS luminaries who were referred to bitingly by the officers in Estimates and ordinary intelligence gathering as the "all-star secret team in ops."

"How is she? You gotta tell me?"

"She misses her daddy, Mr. Carbonara. What do you have for *me?*" Carbonara's murderous weight drove the springs of the burgundy-colored chair into the threadbare carpet of the old Clark Hotel. Vivian was as immobile as the gangster, but his mind raced. At some point, he told himself, this man is going to go berserk over the loss of his daughter. And he knew that then he would have to kill him.

"I got somethin' for you. The man's gonna be hit sometime this year. Momo Giancana and Dandy Johnny Roselli is the paymasters. Lansky and Trafficanti is callin' the shots as far as the outfit's concerned. Some guy named Scott is in charge of the Cuban connection for the feds. That's it. Now where's my daughter?"

"One minute, Mr. Carbonara. Who actually has the contract?"

353

Carbonara could not be managed much longer. Tonight would have to be it.

"I tell you that after I get my daughter back. *Period.*"

"You just made yourself a deal, Mr. Carbonara. Let's go right now. She's in this country. We'll drive all night. You ready?"

"Let's go."

"Mr. Carbonara, you are a patriot and a great American."

"Your fuckin' *A.*"

As he followed the barndoor back down the corridor toward the elevator, Vivian thought venomously, Sure, they were all patriots, Carbonara, Giancana, Roselli. Hadn't they all worked for the U. S. government—the CIA? Weren't they descendants of that great American folk hero Al Capone? They were his *boys,* weren't they? What was it that Big Al had said that time in Miami at a press conference? "The American system of ours, call it Americanism, call it capitalism, call it what you like, gives each and every one of us a great opportunity if we only seize it with both hands and make the most of it." He remembered that gem from 1929 because his father had flung it in his face when the Agency had used mob money to help fund the Dewey campaign in '48. He tried not to think of his father now as they reached the elevator and Carbonara mashed the DOWN button into the wall.

Vivian turned his rented car off the highway at the Wisconsin farmhouse. It was not cold. Through their open windows they could hear the first cocks crowing at the nearby small farmsteads. Carbonara's bulging girth filled the entire space between the seat and the dashboard. His face was pale with tension. Silver streaks were bleeding through the gray dark as the '63 Oldsmobile two-door rolled to a stop in front of the still, white farmhouse.

The loose gravel complained under Carbonara's weight as he swung his mammoth shoulders sideways out of the car. Before Vivian stepped out to join him he freed the silencer-equipped Luger from the attaché case.

"Turn around, Carbonara. Your daughter's in there. She's just fine. You tell me the name of the hit man now and I'll drive the two of you home. If you say no I'll shoot you down here and then I'll shoot Anna Maria. You deliver and you're made for life. What's it to be, Tito?"

A cock's crow filled the mild June morning. Soon the summer people would be arriving, and the camps that catered to boys and girls the age of Carbonara's daughter would be coming to life. From the lake came the pulsing of frogs . . . "Tito . . ." Vivian barely formed the word as he lifted the Luger to point at the man's massive chest. Carbonara's little eyes were red in his wide face. "My daughter . . ." he breathed. Vivian waited. Carbonara's head drooped on the column of his neck.

"The trigger man's a guy named Carl Bender." . . .

The woods of the world, Vivian speculated as he drove back onto the highway and pulled around a hay wagon, the woods are filled with bodies under the ground. Not just the KGB "defector," and D'Amico the driver, and Tito Carbonara, loving father, practiced killer . . . And not just in Wisconsin, U.S.A.—though God knew farmers and their wives had been poisoning each other and their neighbors *and* their neighbor's animals for centuries—but all over the carnivorous world too. The poet Robert Frost, at Jack's inauguration, had written that the woods were silent and deep. They were, in more ways than one, Vivian thought, steering his way through the country road early morning traffic of wagons and jalopies.

So the man hired to kill Jack was "Carl Bender." The conspiracy went higher than he had guessed. By a perverse twist Bender led back to Jack and Bobby: "Carl Bender" had been the name assigned to QJ/WIN, the man who had murdered the African leader Patrice Lumumba for the Central Intelligence Agency.

"Sit down, Viv. I have some of that mint tea that you used to like so much and some cookies from Rumpelmayer's." Samuel Adams Prescott, in his mid-seventies now, had become the very model of the distinguished bachelor whom life has worn as clean as a hound's tooth. In his niche, surrounded by books and paintings, playing host at well-appointed small dinner parties for the remnant of the movers and shakers of the Roosevelt dynasty, Sam Prescott was a liberal exemplar that all sides of the domestic cold war struggle had come to respect.

Sam was especially keen about this rare visit of his son to his New York penthouse suite that overlooked Central Park. The park in June was busy with people, and Sam liked to watch them from his high vantage. This afternoon had been fine and clear, and with the narrow balcony window ajar the Prescott *père* and *fils* could hear a distant fraction of the full sound of children and horses . . . Why, the father wondered, had his son come on such short notice to pay a call? Sam was cutting a lemon into wedges, and from his position at the stove he could observe his son's straight strong back as he stood at the open window looking down on the shapeless moving life in the park below.

Sam Prescott had never quite believed that his son had become a powerful and, within his secret world, a famous spy. It did not add up. The boy he knew and remembered had been frank, open, curious. Spies, classically, were suspicious, devious, secretive. Viv still believed in world peace and democracy—in a different way, to be sure, than he himself, but then they were men from different generations and, more important, different wars. What happens between fathers and sons, *why* must there be an ordeal between the generations?

The tea was steeped. Vivian crushed a fat crumb from a Rumpelmayer chocolate chip cookie between his tense fingers and allowed his father to refill the teacup. "Dad, I want to talk to you, and to listen, even if I don't take your advice. Then, I think, I have to confront the President."

The late afternoon breeze brushed gently at his father's fine silver hair. Vivian looked at the long, lined face, now in shadow, looked as always for his own image there and the memory of his mother . . . "Let's begin with a man known to the Agency as Carl Bender" . . . telling him about Bender in the hope that by starting the story there it would somehow be easier to talk about the imminent murder attempt on the President, and especially feeling the pressure because he had to warn Tim immediately about who Bender was . . .

Vivian had known Carl Bender as QJ/WIN when Bissell, Scott and Helms had been charged by Dulles with setting up an "executive action" facility to assassinate foreign leaders. Vivian had been given the task of selecting the "action team." Carl Bender, or QJ/WIN, had been the weapon employed by the Agency to execute the African hero Patrice Lumumba, and the cable traffic to Léopoldville that passed across Vivian's desk every day was as regular as the reports of a hospital deathwatch. They told the whole grisly story . . . Shortly after the Congo had declared its independence from Belgium the CIA assigned a new officer to its Léopoldville station. There had been for some time growing concern among the policy makers in the Eisenhower administration about Lumumba's political strength. This concern was exaggerated by a series of intelligence reports encased in cable code which spoke repeatedly of the threat of Lumumba's Communist sympathies and of a resultant Communist takeover in the Congo. The cables further stated that the Agency objective in the Congo should be to replace Lumumba with a pro-western representative. Of course Sherman Scott and the Animals jumped at this opportunity for blood and replied to the station officer that they would apply for State Department approval for such an operation. Finally in August confirmation for the proposed project arrived in the Congo direct from DDP Richard Bissell . . . "You are authorized to proceed with the operation." The removal of Lumumba now becoming a prime objective of the Agency Covert Action staff.

Even though the following month Lumumba was ousted as premier, the U. S. Government felt concern about the strong power base he still held within the Congolese parliament. The flow of cabled communications continued at an ever-increasing rate, all revolving around the same theme: the struggle for power within the Congolese government was on, Lumumba in opposition almost as dangerous as in office, the United States would contribute any "technical" aid possible to relieve the tension . . . The overwhelming concern of Scott and his Animals was the dynamic power of Lumumba's personality, irrespective of his formal position in the government. Given the slightest exposure, his capacity to sway sympathy to his side seemed almost irresistible. Finally when Lumumba placed himself in UN custody, a place from which he could wield a safe base of power, the station officer cabled Washington that he was serving directly as a consultant in a Congolese effort to "terminate" Lumumba. The reply came back promptly from Langley: the former premier must be removed from the scene as soon as possible . . . The cables crossing the Atlantic now concerned the outright request for arms, the weapons now deemed necessary by the CIA station officer in Léopoldville to effect the "removal." Finally Dick Bissell had asked Sherman Scott to explore the possibility of terminating Lumumba directly. He had also asked a CIA scientist to make plans to assassinate or incacitate an unnamed Communist leader. Bissell was acting, he said, on the "highest authority," and so the scientist procured the toxic biological materials that were requested of him. He was then ordered by Scott personally to deliver these materials to Léopold-ville. It was then that Vivian Prescott came up with QJ/WIN, whose operational code names were "Carl Bender" and "Joe." The cable informed the station officer:

> (JOE) SHOULD ARRIVE APPROX 27 SEPT . . . WILL ANNOUNCE HIM-
> SELF AS "JOE FROM PARIS" . . . IT IS URGENT YOU SHOULD SEE (JOE)
> SOONEST POSSIBLE AFTER HE PHONES YOU. HE WILL FULLY IDEN-
> TIFY HIMSELF AND EXPLAIN HIS ASSIGNMENT TO YOU.

The cable bore the flagword PROP, which indicated extraordi-nary sensitivity and restricted circulation at CIA headquarters to Dulles, Bissell, Scott . . . and Prescott.

Vivian could still recall with the clarity of a walker in a nightmare the final series of Helms-Bissell cables.

> HAVE HIM TAKE REFUGE WITH BIG BROTHER. WOULD THUS ACT AS
> INSIDE MAN TO BRUSH UP DETAILS TO RAZOR EDGE.

> IF HQS BELIEVE CIRCUMSTANCES BAR HIS PARTICIPATION, WISH
> STRESS NECESSITY PROVIDE STATION WITH QUALIFIED THIRD
> COUNTRY NATIONAL.

> (JOE) LEFT CERTAIN ITEMS OF CONTINUING USEFULNESS. (STATION
> OFFICER) PLANS CONTINUE TRY IMPLEMENT OP.

> POSSIBILITY USE COMMANDO-TYPE GROUP FOR ABDUCTION
> (LUMUMBA). EITHER VIA ASSAULT ON HOUSE UP CLIFF FROM RIVER
> OR, MORE PROBABLY, IF (LUMUMBA) ATTEMPTS ANOTHER BREAK-
> OUT INTO TOWN . . . REQUEST YOUR VIEWS.

> IF CASE OFFICER SENT, RECOMMEND HQS POUCH SOONEST HIGH-
> POWERED FOREIGN MAKE RIFLE WITH TELESCOPIC SIGHT AND SI-
> LENCER. HUNTING GOOD HERE WHEN LIGHT RIGHT. HOWEVER AS
> HUNTING RIFLES NOW FORBIDDEN, WOULD KEEP RIFLE IN OFFICE
> PENDING OPENING OF HUNTING SEASON.

> VIEW CHANGE IN LOCATION TARGET, QJ/WIN ANXIOUS GO STANLEY-
> VILLE AND EXPRESSED DESIRE EXECUTE PLAN BY HIMSELF WITHOUT
> USING ANY APPARAT.

WILL MUTINY WITHIN TWO OR THREE DAYS UNLESS DRASTIC ACTION
TAKEN SATISFY COMPLAINTS.

STATION AND EMBASSY BELIEVE PRESENT GOVERNMENT MAY FALL
WITHIN FEW DAYS. RESULT WOULD ALMOST CERTAINLY BE CHAOS
AND RETURN (LUMUMBA) TO POWER.

THE COMBINATION OF (LUMUMBA) POWERS AS DEMAGOGUE, HIS
ABLE USE OF GOON SQUADS AND PROPAGANDA AND SPIRIT OF DE-
FEAT WITHIN (GOVERNMENT) COALITION WHICH WOULD INCREASE
RAPIDLY UNDER SUCH CONDITIONS WOULD ALMOST CERTAINLY EN-
SURE (LUMUMBA) VICTORY IN PARLIAMENT . . . REFUSAL TAKE DRAS-
TIC STEPS AT THIS TIME WILL LEAD TO DEFEAT OF (UNITED STATES)
POLICY IN CONGO.

The pressure on Vivian's Langley desk had become almost unbearable. At last, after weeks of mounting tension, Vivian's desk
flashed the signal to QJ/WIN. From the field came back Sherman
Scott's response:

THANKS FOR PATRICE. IF WE HAD KNOWN HE WAS COMING WE
WOULD HAVE BAKED A SNAKE.

So they had not used poison, or a third country national, or a
special forces team. They had used "Carl Bender" . . . "Your man
Bender" was the way Dulles had referred to the contract killer
when he congratulated Vivian. . . .
Sam Prescott refilled his curved-stem pipe from a faded soft
leather pouch and pulled the cup of wooden matches to within
striking distance. "Viv, I don't know exactly why you're telling me
this, but it confirms my worst fears. You told me in 1960 that your
policy and Jack Kennedy's policy of limited covert operations
would replace the infinitely more dangerous Dulles concept of
massive retaliation and that God-awful brinkmanship. And though
I believed—and *still* believe—that Adlai Stevenson was the better
man, I did agree that perhaps the limited covert policy would
prove to be the lesser of the two evils. But what you tell me now,
and what is common knowledge in my circle about the attempts on
Castro, what this means is that the lesser of two evils is still much

359

too evil, not to mention dangerously counter-productive." Sam struck a match and puffed, his eyes lowered.

In that instant Vivian decided that he really could not tell his father the rest, the point of the whole story. The silence lengthened—he could not . . . what kind of a spy was he getting to be? . . . concoct even a plausible lie. His father's eyes, fixed on him through the curling smoke, were sad and watchful. "Viv, are you working up to telling me that you are somehow involved with this man, that in some way you have lost control over him?" Vivian took the opening by lamely affirming that his father had guessed correctly and that now he wanted to urge JFK to modify the Agency's fiat and to cashier contract types like Bender.

He meant it, but was it already too late . . .?

Riding down alone in the elevator the director of Plans was aware that his palms were wet with perspiration, his temples pounding. The pattern of complicity was etched as if in blood. He could not tell the old man about Oswald because that would lead to the Agency's role—even if not his, at least not wittingly—in compromising the Eisenhower-Khrushchev summit. He could not mention Lansky or Trafficanti or any of the crime syndicate because *that* would have to expose the marriage of the Agency and Murder Incorporated in a host of unholy Caribbean assassination adventures, past and *present*. He could not face telling this good man about the poisoned cigars, and the shoe polish, and the vitamin pills, or the swine flu bacilli released to poison Cuban livestock or the poison that Langley had used to contaminate Cuban sugar. He could feel the shame and disgust seeping into his mouth. There was, in short, no language left by which he could confide in the man who, long ago on Deer Island, when life was so much simpler and cleaner, had taken his young son into his confidence. Then Sam Prescott had been able to talk about and do something about the plot against FDR. Sam Prescott, unlike Vivian Prescott, had not been compromised. He had not, perhaps, needed to take that chance . . . The times, after all, *were* different . . .

Slowly, feeling like an old man, Vivian crossed over into the darkening park and sat down heavily on an empty bench.

The official New Orleans coroner's report listed "suicide" as the cause of death of Raymond X. O'Connor. It had taken Vivian a frantic eleven hours to track down Tim Donahue under his assumed name. The police report described in the usual awful bureaucratese the end of his friend.

6/12/63

N.O.P.D.

MALE CAUC. I.D. RAYMOND XAVIER O'CONNOR. DISCOVERED AT
0800 HRS. ON 6/10/63. CAUSE OF DEATH: SUICIDE DUE TO LOSS
OF BLOOD.

The corkscrew English of the report went on to tell Vivian that a Mrs. Gladys Meyers, manager of a Magazine Street court of furnished apartments, had discovered Tim's decomposing body naked in the bathtub, slashed open at the wrists and throat.

As he walked back to the morgue to claim the body, Vivian saw it all as surely as if he had been a witness. Tim had stuck like glue to the Bannister Detective Agency office at Camp and Lafayette waiting for the hit man to arrive. Bender had walked in, with Bannister or maybe David Ferrie, had taken a good look at Tim. Then, or a few hours later, Bender—who was, after all, one of the top contract killers of the secret war—had tied Tim to Langley. Next, Bender would have contacted Sherman Scott to describe the slight, red-haired man, and Scott, recognizing Tim as a Prescott man from Plans, would promptly have given Bender the order to terminate Tim.

A light rain had begun. He was dead. Tim Donahue—son of Irish immigrants, acolyte at St. Bernard's, architect, spy, husband of Pat and unknowing stepfather of Terry, and *friend*—was no more.

Now he had to claim the body, though that meant taking a serious risk if any of Scott's people were staking out the morgue. And of course he must, somehow, tell Pat. To telephone her to fly down to New Orleans was to risk dragging her into the net. He needed time to think. He stepped under the marquee of a newsreel theater to avoid getting drenched, then on impulse bought a ticket and slipped into the noisy darkness to try to put himself together, try to sort out his next moves.

Ironic coincidence. The big screen throbbed with the vitality of the Kennedy clan frolicking at Hickory Hill. There was touch football, tennis, horseback riding . . . even group isometrics before breakfast. The stocky cigar-smoking profile of Pierre Salinger was the only blot on the scene, the President himself never giving up hope of reforming his press secretary by asking everyone on his staff to lose five pounds. After this happy abstraction of the First Family the news footage cut to triumphant scenes of that great Kennedy victory known to the world as the Cuban missile crisis. Vivian closed his eyes. He had watched these scenes over and over again on the news. For Vivian—who had been deeply involved, himself, in the crisis—these popular news versions of the events were like a comic book version of *Hamlet* to an English scholar. The screen held an aerial image of a Russian ship moving stealthily through the sparkling sea. The narrator's booming voice forced Vivian to open his eyes . . . "This is the tanker *Bucharest,* her only cargo petroleum, and is therefore allowed to proceed through the circle of American warships that surrounds her," and which the audience could now see as the camera pulled back to widen the view from above. The background music was ominous. The audience could see the crude images of men, hurriedly filmed, working rapidly to uncrate bombers at a missile site. The narration resumed with the story of Kennedy's continuing message to the Soviets: the missiles and bombers must be removed. Nothing short of that was acceptable. Next the screen spanned the grandeur of the United Nations Security Council, where Valerian Zorin was making the mistake of challenging Adlai Stevenson to produce evidence of the missiles. The audience sat hushed, awaiting Stevenson's response to the attack, beginning to stir excitedly only when he turned on the Soviet representative with his scorn. "Do you deny the missiles are there? Don't wait for the translation, *yes* or *no?*" And Zorin replied nervously, saying that he was not in an American courtroom. "You are in the courtroom of world opinion right now and you can answer *yes* or *no,*" Stevenson insisted. And Zorin's retreat: "You will have your answer in due course." Stevenson now had his moment . . . "I am prepared to wait for my answer until hell freezes over, if that's your decision. And I am also prepared to present the evidence in this courtroom." The half-filled newsreel house broke into spontaneous applause at the now familiar film of the haggard Kennedy brothers meeting with Congress

362

at the climax of the thirteen-day ordeal . . . Khrushchev had blinked first, but Kennedy had told intimates, including Vivian, that he would remove American missiles from some of the countries that bordered on the Soviet Union. "Gentlemen," he had said, "let there be no crowing or claims of victory. The clock of the world still stands at 11:59 P.M."

Vivian remembered all this now, the scenes behind the scenes that the American public would never view on any screen. He stared at the dirty floor, postponing for the moment decision about Tim, Pat. He would have to convince Kennedy to take some action without actually revealing to him the thrust of the conspiracy. Bobby, the Attorney General, would have to be brought into the picture. He clenched a fist. Hard blows would have to be struck against both Sherman Scott and his masters in the Agency, *and* the mob. The counterattack *must* convince the conspirators that he knew and had told the President everything and that JFK had decided to retaliate in force. The conspirators must receive a message at the highest level. At the same time Bender—whose name or role could not be mentioned to the Kennedys—had to be executed. That, Viv would do himself. It was peculiarly his job . . .

Still, how much simpler if he could now finally lay the entire tangled web before Jack Kennedy, with its considerable documentation. But then what? If the President acted he would have to go all the way. What Scott and the other conspirators were doing could lead to a firing squad. This was a death penalty matter, and the Animals would unload every media and legal gun to make Vivian and his people seem the traitors. The Animals' considerable media assets would polarize the country. Philby's name would be involved, and Tony Blunt's. Vivian and Blunt would be headlined around the world as Philby's "other men." Oswald and Bender were . . . actually *had* been . . . Vivian's men—the President would have no alternative except to get rid of Vivian. There would be false charges against him, fake documents. It would be either that or Jack would be obliged to order Vivian to kill the Animals before the plot went further. Except that was impossible, a sort of whole-sale execution . . . No, in a showdown Vivian felt he couldn't control the outcome, which could not only destroy him but also split the whole country, polarize the right and middle—never mind the left. He had to try to stop this assassination plan by acting on what he'd uncovered—by stopping Oswald and Bender, patsy and killer. Otherwise the price was to wreck the country . . .

The deep-voiced plea brought his attention back to the screen. Martin Luther King was speaking at the funeral of a murdered civil rights worker. "Truth crushed to earth," the marvelous voice rang out, "will rise again!"

"No!" Her voice rose. "Let him be buried in an unmarked grave or whatever they use in New Orleans in *place* of graves," and threw the glass with all her strength at the wall, the cut glass still not breaking.

She cursed Vivian for not warning Tim soon enough, then cursed herself for not insisting that the entire mess be thrown into Kennedy's lap from the first, and she cursed Tim for being a sweet, naive patsy in the whole filthy business.

Then she cursed him again. "You . . . you wouldn't go to Kennedy. Oh no, you had your *team* and you were going to drop behind the lines and singlehanded wipe out the fascists all over again. Stupid, vain—"

"That's not exactly fair. You damn well know that if I go to Jack with it he has to confront the Animals in the Agency. We're already raiding their camps, sinking their boats on the high seas. What the hell do you want? To shoot it out at Langley, *and* Miami, *and* New Orleans, *and*—"

"You coward, you vain, selfish—"

"What more do you want? Don't you think they'll shoot back? What makes you think we'll win? You want a showdown? The Joint Chiefs despise Kennedy. You want a goddamn civil war? I'm not exaggerating."

"You're tied to Oswald and you're tied to Bender and you can't face it—"

He could never hit her. Instead he grabbed and held her, as she sobbed in his arms.

Around nine o'clock he managed to convince her to go out for dinner. She couldn't eat, drank martinis and became violently ill. He was up most of the night with her, she could not stop vomiting. "You're white as a sheet. Let me call a doctor."

Near dawn she fell asleep. Not him. He sat in the armchair near the bed and watched the hot sun rise. Thinking, She will marry me,

364

she will have to marry me now. I will raise the boy as my stepson. I will tell Kennedy everything and resign and we will live abroad and never come back to America. And then he thought, No, we will marry and I will tell Kennedy no more than we had originally planned. We will stop the conspiracy and I will be made DCI and after the '64 election we will dismember the goddamn secret government. . . .

The next day they agreed to order the remains to be cremated and shipped home. They did not discuss their personal relationship. Pat, pale and shaky, left to pick Terry up at school to tell him, *by herself,* that his father had been killed in the line of duty.

The Agency would be tricky. "Suicide" could not go on the books, for Pat's and the boy's sake. "Murder"—by Bender—was equally unacceptable because then their entire operation to stymie the assassination would be blown . . . They'd merely recruit another assassin . . . He would have to tell McCone that Tim had been on the trail of an important Russian defector and that the KGB had gotten wind of it and sent in an assassination team from their base in Mexico City. That story would also explain why the Director of Plans would need leave-time to follow up the KGB murder of his personal deputy and old friend.

Taped behind the commode in the apartment bathroom Tim had secreted his last report. From past experience, Vivian had known to look there before leaving New Orleans. Again as he studied the rough jottings his body tensed like a spring. Oswald was being moved by the DOD, Scott's illegal Domestic Ops Division, with an ominous acceleration. Vivian knew he had to move and move now. He would tell JFK that the hawks were about to provoke a second Bay of Pigs. Which was true, except that what had to remain secret was the fact that the opening shots of the new war would be fired at the President. That, and the fact that both Oswald and Carl Bender had been, so to speak, "Vivian's men" in Russia and the Belgian Congo.

So, first the Kennedy brothers had to be unleashed against the hawks and then he had to go to Mexico City to kill Bender. He could only hope that neutralizing Bender would be sufficient. If Sherman Scott had to be taken out, then, he was convinced, civil war would break out in the Agency, and spread throughout the government, and then the whole country.

365

He had worried this one through too many times. He craved the opiate of action.

Bobby Kennedy squinted up from the ledge at the deep end of the pool at his brother Jack and Vivian Prescott. The water shone on his lithe body, the grin was a good-humored twist. "That's right, blame me. I always told you that I wasn't ruthless enough to purge those Ivy League heavyweights."

The three were alone at Hickory Hill. Ethel Kennedy had left with the children and dogs for the long July 4th holiday at Hyannis Port. The place now hung in unusual quiet, and except for the conversation of the three old friends, themselves comfortable enough with each other to tolerate some silences, there was nothing to disturb the tranquility. It occurred to Vivian, as he sat musing for a moment, that if one listened hard enough, the echoed laughter of young children and barking dogs could almost be heard reverberating across the rolling lawns and drifting in through the sparkling panes of the now shut French doors. But reality told him they were in fact gone, and he was left a guest in Camelot, without its accoutrements, and with only the company of the prince and his brother to host him. Reality . . .

The President and Vivian eased off the steps into the water. The day was warm and muggy. Bobby dog-paddled over. "Viv, can what you have to tell us about Old Boy hijinks at the Agency getting out of hand wait until after the two of us take you on for some bloodsport tennis? Please answer as you would to an equal."

"Get him, Jack!" They held the Attorney General under water for thirty seconds and then went off to the tennis court. An hour later, as they sat in the shade draped in towels, Bobby was serious enough as they listened to the President.

"Vivian, Bobby's done all he could. I simply can't fire everybody from Bay of Pigs until after the election. These crackpots have a base that cuts right across the middle levels of the Pentagon. Bobby, just how far can you go?"

"Jack, I believe that the operations with the Mafia against Castro have been stopped. I mean, these people lie *all* the time—they lie when they don't have to."

"Viv, tell Bobby what you told me yesterday."

Vivian laid out the rebellion at CIA, underscoring Miami and

366

New Orleans. He stressed the involvement of such old enemies as Howard Hughes and Richard Nixon in the Cuban plotting. At length the President slapped his thigh in anger. "Viv, what do you want?"

"Jack, I want marching orders. I want an inter-agency task force —Customs, Treasury, FBI. I want to move onto the docks in Miami, I want to drive the DOD teams off the high seas, I want to raid illegal training camps, bases and storage depots. I want Bobby to front for me, give the orders. I'll call the shots, supply you with the information. I want to hit them so hard they'll forget all about provoking another Bay of Pigs, they'll be so busy covering their ass."

"Viv, in the history of this country there has never been a case where armed federal agents were ordered to confront armed operatives of another branch of the government—"

"I know, Jack. And there's never been an underground government like this before."

Within thirty minutes the brothers had agreed to most of what their old friend had urged. It was time to get dressed. The President adjusted his towel as he rose. "Well, Prescott, now that you've lured us out here into the wilds of Virginia, may I inquire where the girls are?"

Pat said that she and Terry would spend two weeks at the Prescott place on Fire Island if Vivian's father was also included in the party.

She and the boy had gone home to her mother. Terry was so proud of his father—he had been told when he was ten that Tim was a colonel, assigned to the Pentagon, who wore civilian clothes and sometimes had to go on dangerous secret missions. All of which was pretty close to the truth. The sharing of such information was a clear violation of Agency regulations, but when Vivian and Tim had reminded her of the strict code she had given them the rough side of her tongue. The discussion came to a sudden halt when she drew her small, full lips together over the slightly buck teeth. "This isn't Skull and Bones, me boys, this is real life. You remember *real life*, don't you?" Vivian had muttered something about Mother Machree and subsided. The boy had been inspired to learn about his father, and he surmised that his Godfather Vivian enjoyed similar honorable employment.

Terry took the news "well." He was glad to walk and play tennis with Vivian after his return from Chicago. Then, sipping orange drinks, Vivian would tell him again the stories from behind the lines in World War II—stressing Tim's role—and the boy's eyes would fill with tears. Vivian felt something for the boy akin to what he had experienced years before with Janet. Something protective, and total . . .

"The three of us should live together," he told Pat. She nodded but continued to stare out the window.

Nor did they resume sexual relations during the month of July. Vivian spent hours at Hickory Hill briefing Bobby Kennedy. Now, as Director of Plans, he could bring enormous resources to bear on mindless anti-Castro ops in the Caribbean and, through his own agents, introduce and factor in all of Tim's New Orleans estimates of the Lake Pontchartrain bases. In August the Kennedy brothers lashed out at the DOD ops in a secret war that had explosive potential if it ever became public. (But, Vivian reminded himself, less explosive than the consequences of blowing open the actual assassination plot.)

Behind McCone's back the Agency was in turmoil. Crack treasury teams were wiretapping hundreds of Agency assets, disrupting counterfeit money operations. Customs was in the process of smashing the Agency's small armada of anti-Castro attack vessels in the Miami area. Immigration was confronting Langley's Cuban leadership with the choice of disarming or being deported. Federal narcotics enforcement had a scalpel into the mob-exile-DOD alliance at the root of the conspiracy. Timed to coincide with the lightning raids was the attorney general's ever widening purge of Plans in general and the DOD in particular. Vivian had asked specifically that men like Scott, FitzGerald, Angleton and other high ranking hawks *not* be fired. He feared that if the hard-line supergrade leadership was forced *out*side now there would then be absolutely no way to control their secret army from inside. "Keep them where we can watch them until after the election," he kept repeating to the President's hard-driving younger brother. "They're on the ropes," he told RFK. Scott, he had learned, was virtually in hiding in the bottomless pit of the Mexico City CIA station and that was where, Vivian was certain, he would find Carl Bender.

The Directorate of Plans was under siege. Vivian doubled his own contingent of bodyguards. Strict new measures were initiated to disrupt any in-house bugging of his work areas. At the same time he now felt able to begin wiretapping across the board. He knew that Scott and company were taking countermeasures of their own, and that he could hardly hope to learn so easily whether or not the planned assassination of the President had been completely disrupted. He was disturbed that a few senior Old Boys had quietly resigned under the pressure and had become, thereby, like Charles Cabell and Richard Bissell, immune to his intramural surveillance.

By late summer he felt reasonably certain that all that remained to shatter any remnants of the plot was the execution of Carl Bender. In their now seriously weakened state the hawks would hardly risk contracting for another top grade assassin out of fear of discovery. Without a killer of established caliber he felt no conspiracy or coup could go forward. He knew these men. They would not commit treason out of hate alone. Only for the *assurance of power* would they risk their lives. And they would be risking their lives. The penalty for what the hawks had been organizing was a firing squad, according to the law of the United States, and John F. Kennedy, he believed, was the President to invoke that law if he had to. He believed the hawks believed it too.

Fire Island had never been more crowded. The spirit of Jack Kennedy's New Frontier seemed to have melted the nervy grimness of the preceding witchhunt period almost completely. The beautiful people thronging to the island looked happier and healthier. Even that aging queen Red Russian Rose and his entourage seemed to have risen above their former relentless nihilism. The Prescott house, however, this year was at the far end of the island, well away from the density of the transient main drag.

It was good for Terry to have Sam Prescott as a companion. If the elder idealist had been a good father to Vivian, he was a superb grandfather for the boy. Pat and Vivian would watch the two of them strolling down the beach and smile at each other. Pat was, for the first time since Tim's death, unbending; she would swim far out into the cool ocean, then bake in the sun on the clean sand of their restricted portion of the beach. But except when she was with Terry, Pat was quieter than Vivian had ever known her to be.

Their first serious discussion of the future did not occur until the day before he was scheduled to leave the island to prepare for the trip to Mexico City.

"Pat. Hi." They were lying on the old blanket, drying off. Sam and Terry had set off on a long hike for groceries. "Listen, about Mexico City . . . can we talk about it? It's not too painful?"

"No. It's time."

"Scott's gone to ground there. The DOD is almost completely smashed. With Bender out they'll know that we—and that means the White House—that we know everything. And that we know that they know that we know—"

"That *they* know, that *we*—oh, Jesus, Viv, *I* don't know whether to laugh or cry," laughing openly for the first time in months. He rolled toward the sleek, tanned, blue bikini figure to nuzzle and hug her so hard that she almost cried out.

"My love," he said, leaning over her on one elbow, "we have to go on living. I'm going to roll up these madmen. I'm going to be the next DCI and when Jack finishes his last term in '68 I'm going to quit. Then—who knows? Jack will still be young. There's the real possibility that under the Robert Kennedy presidency Jack and you and I and some of the best of his braintrust can launch some kind of international peace foundation. I'm talking about an organization that would have *real* power, not like the old World Federalists, not an impotent front group. And my father and his people would come in too, with big money—"

"Viv, wait a minute . . . my God, I haven't seen you so full of hope in twenty years. Are you sure that the same thing wouldn't happen all over again, that—"

"No, listen, Pat. Jack plans to meet with the Soviets for discussions right after the election—you know, he's miles ahead of either Goldwater or Rockefeller in the polls. He's going to announce the pullout from Vietnam next month—"

"Thank *God.*"

"Amen. He told me in strict confidence. He's getting quite a few people riled up about a lot of things. But you know Jack . . . he's going to roll back prices and if that doesn't work he'll freeze the damn things. He is in the process now of really developing three

370

main thrusts for the administration: *lead* the black revolution instead of fighting it; set the wheels in motion for a verifiable test-ban treaty; and Pat, I promise you he *will* get out of Vietnam. Last week he told me, 'If I try to pull out completely now, we would have another McCarthy Red scare, but I can do it after I'm reelected. So we'd better make damn sure I'm reelected!' "

He knew how she felt about what had happened the week before. South Vietnamese Special Forces—trained at Michigan State by the Agency—had carried out midnight raids against Buddhist pagodas across the country. Two days later the CIA and dissident South Vietnamese generals began to plot a coup against the Diem regime. Diem and his brother would have to be eliminated in an executive action. The problem was that the President refused even to discuss the question of the further murders of heads of state. As Kennedy's friend and Director of Plans it was Vivian who had been ordered by McCone to secure a private, unofficial nod from the Commander-in-Chief so that the plotters in Saigon could go forward. Vivian knew his limits; he needed the complete backing of the President to wipe out the DOD, he could not harass him about Saigon, Kennedy was sick about the situation in Southeast Asia. Again and again he told intimates that the United States must get out of Vietnam. When the question of using tactical nuclear weapons against Hanoi arose—which the Nixon group had argued for in '54—Kennedy laid it on the line. "They're the same thing. There's no difference. Once you use them, you use everything else. You'll destroy Europe, everything." The President was afraid to say this aloud to the country—*he* knew that there was thunder on the right. Vivian agreed.

He told her what Jack had said at Hickory Hill: "They want a force of American troops. They say it's necessary in order to restore confidence and maintain morale. But it will be just like Berlin. The troops will march in; the bands will play; the crowds will cheer; and in four days everyone will have forgotten. Then we will be told we have to send in more troops. It's like taking a drink. The effect wears off, and you have to take another."

Vivian told Pat about these private sentiments of his friend, but not about the murder being planned against the Diem brothers. It was too complicated because they, the Prescott team, were now supposed to be trying to stop an executive action aimed at the

President of the United States. She had shaken him just after Tim's murder by saying that the guns and money and technicians now gunning for Kennedy were originally part of the killing machine assembled for the Bay of Pigs . . . "Chickens coming home to roost," she said.

It was best not to tell her everything until the assassination plot was stopped.

He was holding her close to him now. Their sun-warmed bodies melting away a deep layer of grief at the core. He stroked her forehead, touched her earlobes, bent to kiss the rising of her breasts. She tasted like the sea. "After the election will you marry me? I want to take care of you and Terry. I love you, Pat. I respect you. As a mother, a wife, a lover, you are a truly magnificent human being. That sounds so damned stilted. I love you, my love. What more can I say?"

Her mouth was open. They lay there, embracing, kissing like two fabled lovers washed ashore from the sea. His thighs thrust toward her with a force of their own. "Love me," she said. "Come inside and make love to me. Kiss me all over and let me love you and kiss you all over." In the blaze of the sun he seemed to merge, in her remembering, with the glorious youth she had loved on the Midi —young forever, never to die, tumescent with love and war.

And they rose as if from the sea and ran across the sand toward the house.

Vivian was sanguine about the situation. Besides, he couldn't stop the President from beginning his campaign tour. So, in late September, when Kennedy made his great speech in Billings, Montana, Vivian began to believe that, indeed, everything was possible.

So, too, did John Kennedy. Slowly, agonizingly, he was getting out in front of his hawks. With a man he could trust like Viv Prescott on top of CIA, after the election they could begin to step out of the deep freeze of the cold war, begin to return America to a stance of democracy instead of mindless so-called anti-Communism that did little to offset Soviet power and so much to drain our own strength. He felt a sense of growing clarity and leadership. With Vivian's help they had undercut McCone's plan at CIA to undercut the nuclear test-ban treaty. McCone and the hard-liners had been feeding the extremists in the Senate—especially John Stennis and the old guard of the powerful Senate Armed Services

Committee—selected classified information to make the case against the disarmament treaty. Forewarned, Kennedy had been able to rally the Senate to his side, and was now confident of winning in a showdown. In '64 he would go to the country against Goldwater to stand strongly on this issue . . .

Such were the President's thoughts, and Vivian's, on the windy day in Billings when he cast aside his set speech and spoke from the heart . . . "What we hope to do is lessen the chance of a military collision between the two great nuclear powers, which together have the power to kill three hundred million people in the space of a day. That is why we support the test-ban treaty. Not because things are going to be easier in our lives, but because we have a chance to avoid being burned."

The conservative, far-Western crowd on the small town square was silent. Then a low murmur began. Then a sound of frozen and long deferred hope building toward a roar of affirmation.

The clear air was vibrant with the sound. Autumn would forever be cut into Vivian's memory; that day when the leaves had begun to fall.

Phillip Daniels, the CIA station chief in Mexico City, was a compulsively conscientious Agency bureaucrat and it bothered him no end to have the Director of Plans on his hands for what seemed like an interminable stay. Vivian's cover story of a special assignment to assess KGB penetration of the United States from Mexico sounded plausible enough to Daniels's literal-minded way of playing the Agency game. Besides, Prescott was a good man to accept at face value. True, he did not have a deep base of power in the Agency, but he *was* Kennedy's fair-haired boy, a hero from the big war, and without question Kennedy's next DCI. The entire top level at Langley was marking time waiting for the McCone interregnum to pass. Under McCone's dull leadership all of the Old Boys had been tunneling away from within, building bigger and better niches of power against the day of the Prescott administration. Daniels, for his part, was sitting tight, making no waves. Then, too, Prescott was perfectly friendly and did not interfere at all with Daniels's low-keyed stewardship of the small Agency army contingent housed under State Department cover in the American embassy.

Prescott was sure to leave in another week or two at the most, so not to worry. If it weren't for the disquieting fact that Sherman Scott was somewhere around the city, too. Scott was bad news. His endless Cuban operations had compromised half a dozen stations from Chile to Guatemala. Daniels resented the fact that the gung-ho clandestine types like Scott considered him a weak station chief and perfectly suited to use like a piece of Swiss cheese to bait their various covert traps . . . Daniels made another double. He would be glad to see Prescott as DCI drive the Sherman Scotts away from the trough at Langley. The truth was that whatever the KBG was up to, it was Scott and the DOD that were running illegal Black ops into the United States from all over the perimeter of Central America. Maybe Prescott was really down here to check *that* out. He hoped so but, of course, did not choose to get involved. Heroes come and go, he often said to himself, I'll just wait them out until retirement rolls around. . . .

Daniels was no problem for Vivian, who kept his own counsel in a suite at the El Presidente Hotel. Perhaps once a day he would drop into the embassy code room to look over the cable traffic to and from Langley. Toward the end of the first week the information he had been waiting for turned up in the normal CIA routine. Thank God, he thought, that the left hand doesn't know what the right hand is doing. He had not, though, been prepared for one item in the first cable.

WARNING:
CENTRAL INTELLIGENCE AGENCY   SENSITIVE
Washington, D.C. 20505   SOURCES AND
10 Sept. 1963   METHODS

MEMORANDUM FOR: Distribution List

SUBJECT: CIA Dissemination of Information on Lee Harvey OSWALD,

    1. This department has been requested to furnish a copy of the dissemination on Lee Harvey OSWALD made to several Government agencies by CIA on 3 September 1963.

    2. An exact copy of this dissemination (Out Message No. 74673) by teletype is attached. It was transmitted to the Depart-

ment of State, Federal Bureau of Investigation and Department of the Navy. A copy was concurrently made available by hand to the Immigration and Naturalization Service.

3. Please note that OSWALD's middle name was erroneously given as "Henry" in the subject line and in paragraph two of the dissemination. (The same error occurs in the message to the Navy discussed in paragraph four, below.) The maiden surname of Mrs. OSWALD was mistakenly listed as "PUSAKOVA."

4. A teletyped message (Out No. 77978) was sent to the Department of the Navy referring to Out No. 74673, and requesting that the Navy furnish CIA as soon as possible two copies of the most recent photograph of OSWALD that was available, for use in checking the identity of the Lee OSWALD in Mexico City.

Subject: Lee Henry OSWALD

1. On 3 September 1963 a reliable and sensitive source in Mexico reported that an American male, who identified himself as Lee OSWALD, contacted the Soviet Embassy in Mexico City inquiring whether the Embassy had received any news concerning a telegram which had been sent to Washington. The American was described as approximately 35 years old, with an athletic build, about six feet tall, with a receding hairline.

2. It is believed that OSWALD may be identical to Lee Henry OSWALD, born on 18 October 1939 in New Orleans, Louisiana. A former U.S. Marine who defected to the Soviet Union in October 1959 and later made arrangement through the United States Embassy in Moscow to return to the United States with his Russian-born wife, Marina Nikolaevna Pusakova, and their child.

3. The information in paragraph one is being disseminated to your representatives in Mexico City. Any further information received on this subject will be furnished you.

Attachment B

OSWALD IS REPORTED MEETING WITH VALERIN KOSTIKOV KGB "DEPARTMENT 13." KOSTIKOV IN CHARGE OF TERROR AND ASSASSINATION FOR KGB IN WESTERN HEMISPHERE.

Subject: Lee Harvey OSWALD

Reference is made to CIA Out Teletype No. 74673, dated 3 September 1963, regarding possible presence of subject in

Mexico City. It is requested that you forward to this office as soon as possible two copies of the most recent photograph you have of subject. We will forward them to our representative in Mexico, who will attempt to determine if the Lee OSWALD in Mexico City and subject are the same indthe same individual.

This information is being made available to the Immigration and Naturalization Service.

Accompanying the memorandum was the photograph of the man who was, unmistakably, Carl Bender. The telescopic lens cameras located across from both the Soviet and Cuban embassies had snapped the bullet-headed assassination technician as he entered, obviously to stage a deception, in the name of Lee Oswald. It was clever, and it was madness . . . the Agency's intelligence section was picking up evidence of a killer being run by elements within that *same* Agency. The hunter, the footprints, and the hunted—whichever way you ran the film—were *all* extensions of the *Agency.* And Vivian was hunting them, but *they* were also hunting him. Wheels within wheels. The seed, the sower, the sown.

Vivian now had no choice but to stake out both the Russian and Cuban embassies as well as the Commercio Hotel, a favored meeting place for extreme anti-Castroites. He half expected at every moment suddenly to bump into the spare, hollow-chested, dapper conspirator Sherman Scott. With the hawks developing cable traffic that "Oswald" was meeting with Kostikov—the Soviet master spy in charge of terror and assassinations in the Western Hemisphere for the KGB's "Thirteenth Department"—there could be no stopping short of a war if by some chance the operation was still going forward. There was every probability, one reasoned, that the Bender deception was mostly a defensive ploy by the top plotters to cover themselves, to provide a blue chip to play in case Kennedy decided to expose their aborted coup plans. He *had* to hope that that was the extent of the implications of Bender's masquerade. But he *also* knew that he still had to eliminate Bender in case the thing had gone critical and even the hard-pressed masters of the conspiracy had lost control of their infernal machine. It had happened before—in Guatemala, Vietnam, the Bay of Pigs. An organized murder op, he knew, tended to take on a life, so to speak,

376

of its own. Besides, and over and above . . . he had to do it for Tim.

He felt adrenalin pump through his long body. Bender could kill a man with his hands or any of a variety of weapons—with anything rigid enough to pick up and hold. And Bender knew what the Director of Plans looked like.

In his hotel room Vivian prepared his own deception. The costume he had chosen was an ancient linen suit, yellow with wear and use. The battered sandals fit comfortably. His face was known to every intelligence service in the world. Two hours were required to transform the chiseled features even partially. If only he were in Langley, he could requisition everything he needed—wig, beard, dentures—from the Department of Technical Services. There was no time for that now. He was on the enemy's terrain, and he had to redress the relationship of forces and go on to the hunt.

First, he wrapped a large dirty handkerchief tightly around his head so that it covered his hair and forehead like a sweat band. He streaked his chest, neck and hands with grime so that on the street, without a shirt, he would appear to be a derelict. Against an agent of Bender's experience Vivian could not risk using theatrical makeup, so he rubbed grease into his face to darken his complexion. Two days' growth of beard helped to age him by at least ten years, especially with the stubble blackened by mascara. He applied clown white makeup selectively to create the illusion of gray whiskers among the black and to age the patches of sideburns that extended from under the linen band. Dirt was caked under his nails and rubbed into the backs of his hands, and his feet too became gray appendages. The process of deception was completed by washing his mouth out with wine and spitting it liberally over his costume. The remainder of the bottle bulged out of one sagging coat pocket, masking in the process the switchblade and the palm-sized Spanish Astra automatic. He practiced a staggering, shambling walk in front of the mirror. Not quite convincing enough. An eye patch. Too obvious? No. Cheap cigarettes held between the filthy, trembling fingers? Yes. Could he black out a tooth? No. But he could darken his strong white teeth down so as to give the impression of rot. Okay. He was ready. Wait. Into the bathroom, purposefully letting the remainder of urine seep into his pants. Minus his Yale class ring and any other identification, of course, he slipped out and down the service stairs to the alley behind the hotel, and within moments melted into the street crowd of Mexico City.

He moved through the stifling streets of this city of contrasts. At once he passed elegantly dressed natives, decked out in the finest of gold and leather, taking their stroll after a fine European meal in one of the city's magnificent courtyard gardens. Next, he was confronted by the other side of life, which sprang from the eyes of leering, hungry men who often would push forward a high-cheekboned Indian woman, infant strapped to her back, the young ones around her feet begging outright or offering a grubby handful of "Chicklets" to uncomfortable tourists who did their best to pretend the children did not exist. The beggars traveled in packs here, and Vivian felt especially conspicuous because he was alone. . . .

Bender's brawny bulk came striding out of the Commercio Hotel at the height of the one o'clock heat. Vivian picked him up from his position across the street in the park, among a group of four other drunks sitting on the grass, passing Vivian's wine bottle around the swaying circle. Vivian slipped the empty container into his pocket and staggered off, maintaining a block's distance behind Bender's ramrod back. Bizarrely, in spite of the heat, Bender was wearing a windbreaker; he was carrying a small canvas duffelbag. He strode now into the deserted Cuban embassy. Vivian ambled into a doorway and curled up. In his pocket was a thin sheaf of hundred dollar bills in case the police took an interest in him.

Twenty minutes later Bender emerged, walking fast. Vivian knew that the hidden CIA camera was taking Bender's picture. In fact, the powerfully built Bender was virtually posing for the camera on the walk in front of the building . . . the duffelbag—Vivian realized then that Bender was heading for the bus station, the one way out of Mexico City that would leave no trace. The bus station —he had four blocks in which to kill him, and the gun was useless in the open street. He scooped up a discarded newspaper from the vestibule and wrapped a sheet around the switchblade.

Bender was now a block away and walking fast when Vivian began his sprint. Because of the siesta hour and the heat, the street was much less crowded than previously. Sweat poured off Vivian as he burned up the space separating Bender and himself. At thirty-five yards Bender turned, a graceful animal ready for fight or flight. He squinted against the sun, trying to fathom the meaning of the ragged white dervish coming toward him.

As Bender turned, Vivian began to gesticulate wildly, call out incoherently. Bender's hand moved toward the zipper of the duffelbag and his shoulders hunched up around his bull neck, the bullet head pulling down for protection. At ten yards Vivian slowed, heaving for breath as if stopping. "Your passport, *su visa, su visa,*" he slurred drunkenly, "you dropped your *visa,* señor." Vivian started to unfold the newspaper concealing the knife. Bender relaxed his strained attention ever so slightly as the bum approached, and at that instant of minute shift in the relationship of forces between the beggar and the assassin, with Bender's hand pausing on the duffelbag zipper, Vivian, from out of his slowing run, kicked and sprang forward.

Bender, too late, was digging for the gun in the bag, then swinging it up at the last second in a vicious arc that would have snapped Vivian's neck had he not angled his body sharply to the left. Vivian hooked the switchblade in a low circular motion from right to left, while at the same time turning his own head and body away and down and to the left so that Bender's bag only scraped his right ear bloody.

As Bender drove the bag up toward Vivian's head, the effort stretched his abdomen and groin taut. Almost at right angles, Vivian's curving forearm drove with force into Bender's tight, impacted gut. Vivian let himself fall to the left, dragging his knife hand after. The blade was so deeply embedded in the intestine that Vivian could not drag it free, bringing the heavy Bender down on top of him, the wine bottle smashing. Bender lay face down now across Vivian's legs, his blood running out, soaking through pantlegs and spreading onto the sidewalk. Three little girls who were running an errand for a priest turned the corner and found themselves standing over the two blood-covered men.

Vivian tried to smile at the girls to reassure them; they understandably only became more frightened and ran. Across the street a small crowd was gathering. Vivian leveraged his legs out from under Bender's deadweight and stood, testing his bruised right knee, attempting to get his trembling under control, the blood running down his leg. He bent down again to drag the knife free, instead used the corner of his coat to wipe fingerprints off the handle. He scraped up the dead man's duffelbag and limped around the corner as fast as he could move, the little girls scattering and screaming as the bloody scarecrow loomed over them.

Skull and Bones.

Vivian lay soaking his bruised and lacerated body in the bathtub of the Maryland safe house. Pat perched on the closed commode, green eyes wide with concern as Vivian told her of Bender's death.

Vivian's long body lay limp in the water, his knee still black where he had taken Bender's weight. Pat moved to kneel by the tub, frowned at the discolored knee, then began to soap him lightly. Vivian was so exhausted that he breathed through his mouth and closed his eyes. His head was tilted back in the water and he seemed, to her, to have aged. The bones of the brow and the jawline were more pronounced, the Adam's apple more prominent, the smoky gray eyes circled and touched with darkness.

"Love," she murmured, "are you going to stay in bed here all weekend and let me take care of you? Terry's been asking about you but he'll understand. He knows that you're . . . investigating Tim's death."

The steam was draining him, his voice was soft and low. "Pat, Bender's duffelbag had a notebook with coded plans in it . . . I think I can make out some plan for something in November in Chicago . . . I'm going to have to spend time over the weekend on the phone with Garabedian . . ." His whole body rose and fell with a deep sigh.

She helped him out of the tub. He leaned against the wall as she toweled him, then dressed his torn hip. He opened his gray eyes to look at her as she slowly dried him. She looked lovely in a simple, lime-green shirtwaist, the buttons opening down the front to where he could just make out the lines of her rising breasts as she bent toward him.

"Do I detect a slight sign of recovery, Mr. Prescott?"

"What did you say your name was, nurse?"

She cupped him, his genitals overflowing her small hand.

"My name is Nurse Sex, sir. It's time now for your aspirin and—"

380

With his free arm he brought her to his chest, leaning on her as they walked slowly toward the bedroom.

Pat sat reading the new Gore Vidal novel while Vivian slept. He did not rest easy, jerking and twitching from some bruise of the spirit darker than the one on his knee. She knew that Mexico City had been a close call. You did not take on Carl Bender, and win, without stepping part way through death's door. Was it really over now, as Vivian said, or was there some new loose end in Chicago, something to do with the Mafia and Vivian? He was so sparing with details that her imaginings, on their own, actually came quite close to accurately assessing everything they had been doing since they had first begun last Christmas to try to save the President—*and* to save themselves, she thought.

When he awoke she refreshed him with just-squeezed orange juice, herb tea with lemon and honey and his favorite, a dish of French vanilla ice cream. "Talk to me," she said when he had finished.

"What would Terry's reaction be to my moving in so soon?"

"Positive, I think. I'm going to talk to him about it tomorrow. You know he's always been crazy about you . . ." She moved the dishes back to the tray and began to take off her clothes. The day was overcast and getting cold, she hopped into bed and rubbed her feet against him.

"Ow!"

"God, I'm sorry, Viv. Shall I kiss it and make it better?"

"Did you say bigger or better?"

"Viv, you intend to be faithful after we're married?"

"Do you?"

"In theory, no, in practice, yes. More or less."

"*That*, I believe, was the most completely quivocal answer ever given to that time dishonored question. Well, would you tell me about any outside affairs?"

"Would you?"

They were both shaking with laughter.

"Who wrote this dialogue? Pat, I couldn't tell you about any juicy indiscretions, I'd be laughing too hard. Come here. Here, feel how warm this sweet pussy feels." He put his fingers to her lips for her to wet them so that he could reach down and lubricate her clitoris, and move her fingers in to touch herself in concert with

381

his hands as they explored her vagina and around her smooth anus, including at the end of his strokes the firm muscles of her buttocks.

"You *are* an old hand," she said. "Did I ever tell you that I love your hands?"

"I believe you mentioned it—hey, watch the knee," and he pulled her over on top of him, continuing to touch her to the end of her passion as they both rose and fell, she as if impaled on him. She knew herself through him, felt the hard "man" identity in her rising along with the opening of all of herself for him. This alone could cancel and obliterate the memory of the terrible moments with De Mohrenschildt in Dallas. She was shaking, possessed with their togetherness. "So good!" She sighed deeply. "So good to be together, oh, Viv . . ."

"So good, so good . . ." He took up the refrain. "No," she called out, "no." Then, "Viv, Viv, Viv . . . *ahhh* . . ." her thighs fluttering out of control, the juices pouring out of her. And then he came. Like electric shocks driving the pain from his leg and from his mind. Vaulting, his sperm jetting up into her, then running down again and out of her.

The little death that gives birth, together at rest in the eye of the hurricane. They clung to the moment, out of time, floating in the ocean of their flesh, blotting out any thought of the death of the President, toward which the tides of time were washing them.

Rob Garabedian flew into the Baltimore airport on Monday and taxied to the safe house. There he showed Vivian a copy of the raw FBI teletype:

URGENT   1:45 AM EST 10-17-63 HLF   1 PAGE

TO   ALL SACS
FROM   DIRECTOR

THREAT TO ASSASSINATE PRESIDENT KENNEDY IN DALLAS TEXAS NOVEMBER TWENTYTWO DASH TWENTYTHREE NINETEEN SIXTY-THREE. MISC INFORMATION CONCERNING.
INFO HAS BEEN RECEIVED BY THE BUREAU. BUREAU HAS DETERMINED THAT A MILITANT REVOLUTIONARY GROUP MAY ATTEMPT TO ASSASSINATE PRESIDENT KENNEDY ON HIS PROPOSED TRIP TO DALLAS TEXAS NOVEMBER TWENTYTWO DASH TWENTYTHREE NINETEEN

SIXTYTHREE. ALL RECEIVING OFFICES SHOULD IMMEDIATELY CON-
TACT ALL CIS; PCIS LOGICAL RACIAL AND HATE GROUP INFORMANTS
AND DETERMINE IF ANY BASIS FOR THREAT. BUREAU SHOULD BE
KEPT ADVISED OF ALL DEVELOPMENTS BY TELETYPE.

SUBMIY FD THREE ZERO TWOS AND LHM
OTHER OFFICES HAVE BEEN ADVISED
END AND ACK PLS
MO. . . .
CO . . . . .
NO. . . . .
KT TI TU CLR . . @

"So I know now what you've been working on."

"Rob, give me background on this before I say anything." The
saturnine Armenian had not yet taken off his hat or out-of-style
gabardine topcoat. Vivian limped into the kitchen to pour coffee.
He wore an old tennis sweater and khakis.

"Hurt your leg?"

"Yeah."

"Well, there're two criminal informants, I found out. One's a
guy in New Orleans named Oswald, and the other's an old friend
in Dallas named Jack Ruby. Ruby's Tito Carbonara's man and
you're Kennedy's man so I put two and two together about what
you were up to. By the way, the mob is going nuts looking for
Carbonara. The word is that the Giancana family rubbed out Tito
and his daughter too—she's been missing for months—as part of
the gang war for control of the North Side. The Chicago families
are going to the mat and all hell is supposed to break loose. Lucky
for me, none of this means shit because Mr. Hoover, as you know,
says that there is no Mafia in America." It was a long speech for
the normally taciturn Garabedian, waiting for his coffee to cool,
then flooding it in milk and sugar.

"Rob, take off your hat and coat or at least your hat, will
you? I have to *talk* to you." He had to talk to someone. Tim
and Mush were no more and he could not drag Pat back into
this nightmare just when she was beginning to function again.
Besides, she had made it plain that she was sick to death of
these "cold war games," as she called them. So it would have
to be the irascible FBI special agent, whether or not he was or
had been Philby's man . . .

383

They sat at the small breakfast table. Vivian told him enough, then gave him the notes to study that he had found in Bender's bag. They couldn't get anywhere with them today, so they turned to Jack Ruby. "Rob, my approach now is to neutralize the operational cutouts. The President and the Attorney General are putting maximum heat on the DOD and the Cubans. Bender's gone, leaving Ruby in Dallas and David Ferrie in New Orleans. But Ruby's worked for the Bureau for years, so I have to believe that he'll never go through with his end of this thing. You agree? That leaves Ferrie—I don't have many options left. De Mohrenschildt has disappeared, Ruby and Oswald are informing on the plot, Bannister and Scott have gone to ground under the pressure from the White House, the weapon—Bender—is out. This's why I was so *positive* that the thing had been derailed. What's keeping it moving? We've scotched the snake . . ."

"Huh?"

"I'd say we've hacked the plot to pieces and it keeps coming together again. What can the FBI do? Can you go and see the director personally?"

"Well, you know how—"

"I mean today. *Now,* Rob."

"Now?"

"Right. Why not? You haven't taken your coat off yet. Bad joke. I'll wait here for your call before I fly out to New Orleans." . . .

Shortly after four that afternoon Vivian listened to Garabedian's report of his meeting with the Director.

"Prescott? Garabedian . . . the great man has taken it under advisement. He just got back from the races in California and didn't even know anything was in the wind, and no one from the SOG wanted to disturb his . . . 'working field trip' to Del Mar for anything as *chicken* shit as a plot against the President—"

"What will he *do,* Rob?"

"Don't know. He said it was the same thing as the Dillinger case. Then he said it was just like the Rosenberg case, that you couldn't move too soon, that you had to have all your ducks in a row. Then he said that I appeared to be over the Bureau weight limit."

"He *what?*"

"Oh, yeah. First things first. I know him, he'll wait until the last minute and then come charging in on a white horse. Then—I'm

384

telling you, I know how his mind works—then he can tell Bobby Kennedy to go screw himself and JFK can forget about making him take his mandatory retirement after the election. He'll outlive us all."

"Rob, I have to go. Try and get me a fast reading on Tim's Bender notes. Thanks. And do what you can with Ruby. Find out what's happening in Dallas. I have to know if the whole thing is dependent on Oswald being set up as the patsy and decoy, because if it is—"

"Yeah, okay, see ya." . . .

Pat's voice was tense on the telephone. "Will you call me every night? . . . All right, have a good trip. Wait a minute, there's a young tennis type here who has a news flash about Tony Trabert's new spin serve that he has to tell you . . . Viv . . . take care of yourself . . . here's Terry . . ."

Vivian pried open David Ferrie's apartment door and sat waiting in the dark for the man who was strange even by clandestine standards.

Everything was in disarray. Through the filthy window an eerie spray of moonlight illuminated the scene: books on subjects from medicine to law to the occult and intelligence were strewn about everywhere; handguns, rifles and automatic weapons lay fixed and propped against an oversized cross mounted on a homemade altar.

The smell of something unknown made Vivian's stomach lurch, and then he became aware of another equally unfamiliar sensation of motion and sound: the screech and scuttle about his feet were due to what seemed to be a floor undulating with perhaps fifty squirming white mice.

Paralyzed for a moment, Vivian's first impulse was to run. Through the doorway to his left he could see an extension of the world he had just walked into. A set of scarlet-and-white falseteeth grinned at him from their place on a sideboard, more books on cancer research, more guns, an American flag, a college pennant. Where, he thought, were the whips, chains, hoods and exotic instruments? All here, no doubt, if somehow hidden. "Discipline" and "correction" were the euphemisms used in the sexual underworld for Ferrie's habits, and the inventory Vivian now encountered certainly provided more than adequate evidence for the man's weird ritual behavior.

But Vivian knew the other side of David Ferrie, that of the accomplished pianist, the hypnotist, the chemist, a queer kind of Mephistophelian renaissance man. Most important, he knew him to be a fearless and versatile operative. At the clandestine level his outlandish homosexual and religious practices were an asset for both cover and recruitment work. Ferrie, in his orange monkey hair wig, was running informants, provocateurs and penetration agents for them now as "Fairy" in the homosexual clubs; as "Father Ferette" in the Apostolic Order of the Orthodox Old Catholic Church and a dozen sectarian offshoots, including magic and witchcraft cults; as "Captain Ferrie," Civil Air Patrol and Air National Guard; and he was the prime mover in those circles of contract agents working out of New Orleans who constituted the dagger's point at Cuba. . . .

The sun was beginning to come up. He was stiff with sitting for four hours. His bladder was protesting again. His leg throbbed. He stood awkwardly, in no condition to overcome a sophisticated karate practitioner like Ferrie. He began to limp toward the bathroom when he heard the giggling sibilance of Ferrie's voice on the stairs and that of someone with him.

Naturally the spy queen would bring some trade he had picked up in the quarter home with him for a late night snack. Vivian kicked dirty linen out of the way in order to secrete himself in the closet. Closing the door after him, backing behind the clothes and pulling out his automatic, waiting, trying not to breathe in the heavy perfume of the air that seemed to radiate out of the cheap and gaudy slacks and shirts hanging crazily around him on wire hangers. He could hear clearly as the apartment door banged open and Ferrie's sharp sibilance slipped like a snake under the closet door.

"Ssh. The landlady's such a cunt. Get the ice while I piss. Jesusss, Mary, did you see how Big Marie coldcocked the sailor? Jesusss— rough trade!"

In the silence Vivian heard a mouse squeak at his feet. That could bring Ferrie in. Slowly he crouched. As the flushing of the commode roared, he scooped up the tiny animal and broke its neck.

He could hear them drinking. One of them had put a recording of *Madame Butterfly* on the machine at a low volume, and Ferrie sang along with what Vivian knew must be an impression of Kathryn Grayson, the movie soubrette from the 40s.

"Oh, David, these fucking mice."

"You be Nelson Eddy, I'll be Jeanette MacDonald. Ooo, my dear. Why, Mr. Eddy, what big meat you have, oops, sorry, I thought that was your trusty .44 . . ."

Vivian's knee was screaming with pain and his need to urinate was becoming irresistible. He bit into his lip. There was an ominous silence. Then Ferrie was speaking in a quiet, serious voice . . . "What's the matter? Listen, Ronnie, I'm not crazy—"

"I don't want to get mixed up in this thing with Clay. I'm not —"

"My poor baby, listen to mother. Screw Clay Shaw, he's just a rat . . . you just play along for now, I'll give you the word, and then thee and me will be long gone."

"Well . . ."

"And there'll be plenty of *moneeey*. The most I would do is fly them around *before* and get the *moneeey*. They're so full of shit they'll never go through with it. Okay. Have I ever lied to you?"

"Oh, Jesus."

In the darkness Vivian dared to sigh with relief. So it had fallen apart. He could hear them drinking, they had to fall asleep soon. Even the mice had settled down again. He felt strangely, inappropriately grateful that he would not have to kill Ferrie.

"Mmm. Let's dance."

He could hear them undressing. Finally he heard them stagger out of the room toward, he assumed, the bedroom.

In the dark Vivian removed his shoes, cracked the closet door and picked his way noiselessly through the few visible mice to the door.

He had no choice but to relieve himself in the gutter before hurrying down the block to his rented car. Thinking, thank God. It's over. It *must* be over now.

Garabedian met his plane at Midway. The Chicago winds were blowing and the flight was a half hour late. They sat in the coffee shop. The FBI man had deciphered the Bender notes. There was to be an executive action, the murder of the President, on November 2 in Chicago during the halftime of the Army-Air Force football game. "You tell the President," Garabedian growled. "I don't know if this is the Oswald-Ruby thing down south or not. You better tell the President."

"I will," said Vivian.

The Kennedy brothers and Vivian sat around the fireplace in Bobby's Hickory Hill den. The President's reaction to the Chicago situation was unexpected. He did not rage or threaten. Very quietly he said, "Bobby, late next Friday we'll pass the word that I have a heavy cold, can't travel. Regrets. Same excuse as Bay of Pigs. Some of the same madmen too, probably."

Vivian had only given them a rough sketch of the Chicago threat. They had debated whether or not the Secret Service could be trusted to take charge. "I believe so, I'll suggest some agents, but in any case when the news breaks that you aren't going I imagine that it will all melt away. In any case, I'll stay after it all the way . . . Jack, do you *have* to travel for the next few months?"

Romping children and dogs crashed against the locked door to the den, then subsided. The fire was bright and cheerful.

"I have to, Viv. I'm scheduled for a western states tour. I must go to Dallas. The party is tearing itself to pieces down there."

"Dallas?"

"Look, Viv, if someone or some group wants to eliminate a leader there isn't all that much anyone can do."

The younger brother broke in. "I don't completely agree, Jack. Look at de Gaulle. *That's* security. There've been a dozen attempts but they cahn't get close enough through the flying squads. I'd like to have a crack at shaping up Secret Service security."

"Why not? You're running everything else. Sure, after the election you can bring in the Notre Dame front line to lead the motorcade." They laughed and sipped their tea. ". . . Sometimes I feel like quitting after this term."

Had he been hit harder than they knew by the recent death of his infant son? They looked at the President with concern. He rocked, staring into the flames. "Vivian, you'd remember—what was it that Churchill said about, ah, 'plots and deceit' . . . ?"

" 'Plot and counterplot, deceit and treachery, double-dealing and triple-dealing, real agents, fake agents, gold and steel, the bomb and the dagger' . . ."

"Viv, the joint chiefs and their pals in the Agency are after me and after me to order assassinations—Castro, Diem. After Lumumba, I said never again and I mean it. Bobby, you know. Gawd, they really want to sow the wind." . . .

On Saturday the Air Force Academy shaded the Army team at Soldiers Field. Vivian watched the game in Virginia with Terry. The crowd of some 76,000 fans included high government officials, but not the President, who, Press Secretary Salinger had announced, was suffering from a head cold. The halftime pistol sounded without incident. Terry jumped up from the rug. "Viv, let's toss the ball around." Somewhere a telephone jangled.

"Well, I still can't run on this leg—"

Pat burst in from the kitchen. "Viv, you're wanted at Langley. The Diem government has been overthrown in a coup in Saigon. Diem and the head of the secret police, his brother, have been assassinated. Go on, I'll get your topcoat."

He leaned on her shoulder trying to hurry down the stone steps on his injured leg. "The Diem brothers murdered, Viv, the Seventh Fleet is going in. *Brothers*, Viv—"

"I know." The Kennedy brothers . . .

"Viv, did you know this was coming?"

"I swear to you, the President has little or no control over the elite agents in the field, the hard-liners are still calling the shots there . . ." More than he'd thought, apparently.

He stumbled into the Buick and sped north to Langley. He had sat in with the DCI on any number of game theory sessions of contingency planning for the so-called dirty little war in Southeast Asia. The assassination of Diem had been discussed frequently but the green light had never been given in Vivian's presence. And the President, unless he was lying, had not given the order. Who *was* running the country? Who? Who was Philby's control? Tony Blunt. Or was Philby Blunt's control? Of course there were still spymasters hidden throughout the secret empire . . . Christ, if Tony Blunt could be a mole, who couldn't?

And who was he, Vivian T. J. Prescott? For the first time in months Vivian felt that he could let down a notch and just think. Who was calling the shots? Could it be that the whole operation had been Philby's last audacious gesture against the West, either to kill Jack and set up Vivian or to fake the conspiracy in order to drive the Department of Plans into starting a civil war in the United States? But if Philby was the master, then Sherman Scott, Must, De Mohrenschildt and the other Animals must *all* be Soviet agents, parts in a network that reached to the top of the Agency . . . But how could Philby possibly control a thing like this? Slow down . . . The hawks and the mob . . . the prime movers the *capos* in Las Vegas, Miami, New York, Chicago. And as for the Scott cabal . . . could they be self-starters, a spontaneous combustion of conspiracy and murder? How high is their backing? High enough to execute the President in an American city, they thought, but not powerful enough to stop him from winning reelection? . . . All right, then the stealth and violence are in a way a sign of weakness as well as of power. Real power doesn't have to work with killers like Bender and patsies like Oswald—not in the continental United States it doesn't . . . that's for Katanga or Guatemala or . . . so the odds are that the Scott-Must axis of the Agency reaches up to, even includes some of the brass in . . . the Joint Chiefs, but at least probably not anyone at the highest level in the cabinet . . . he hoped . . . *"Cui bono?* Who would profit—Lyndon Johnson, but there isn't a scintilla of evidence involving him. The oil barons of Texas, of course, but that's taken for granted with Dallas and De Mohrenschildt . . ."* Enough.*

His head ached worse than his leg as he drove. It was almost dawn. The trees along the parkway were clumps of shadows. The face of Carbonara's daughter came into his thoughts so that the car swerved across the empty traffic lane. He spun and recovered control of the vehicle, the sweat pouring off him in the chill early autumn morning.

On November 21 Vivian talked on a clean telephone to Dallas. Garabedian's hoarse staccato was music to his ears.

"Prescott. Unless some nut pulls something here, we're in good shape. Oswald is still working . . . his informant number is S-179 . . . and so is Ruby. The Bureau knows everything and Mr. Hoover's brilliant plan is to arrest a pack of Cubans right after JFK leaves."

"Rob, you're the best. Will you stay until he leaves Dallas?"

"Why not? This town is murder. They got big posters up all over the place sayin' KENNEDY—WANTED FOR TREASON, for Christ's sake. They—"

"I know, Rob. You'll stay?"

"Yeah, sure, sure. Mr. Hoover wouldn't have it any other way."

"Thanks, Rob. I—"

"It's okay, Prescott. I'll see ya."

Garabedian walked over to the pharmacy section of the drugstore and began comparing prices for remedies for athlete's foot. The parking lot was dark. As he climbed into his car a man lying on the floor of the backseat rose and jammed a tiny .22 automatic, fitted with a silencer, behind Garabedian's big right ear.

Secret Service agents Freeman and Hendricks tested the private switchboard that linked the Dallas Sheraton Hotel and Washington, ate breakfast, left the hotel and arrived at Love Field by 9:00 A.M.

With the White House communications office they began their checkout of the presidential limousine, code name "Lancer," and the Secret Service follow-up car, code name "Halfback." They examined both from top to bottom, checking out all of their mechanical functioning and removing the seats to search for detonating devices.

Lee Harvey Oswald huddled inside a phone booth at the Texas School Book Depository. He was talking in low tones as he stood making a long-distance collect call . . . "I can't go to the Bureau, I told you, because they want me to stay with it, to keep the whole thing under control. This is what they're telling me." He fidgeted nervously as he listened to the voice on the other end.

"It's political, what else could it be?" he said. "They just want to scare the shit out of the public so they'll . . . what? yes, that's the point, he's supposed to be in on it himself . . . what? No, I'm just supposed to set up a distraction." He listened again to the man in Washington . . .

Jack Ruby hung over the teletype machine at the Dallas *Morning News,* but no one paid any attention to this familiar figure, who had just placed his usual weekly nightclub advertisement at the paper.

391

"Stock prices plunge. Prices on the New York Stock Exchange dropped sharply yesterday, triggered apparently by investors' reaction to the brokerage house suspensions . . ."

Ruby, the fat little hit man, went sweating to a pay phone and tried once more to call David Ferrie in Galveston. No answer. He then settled into a swivel chair, and positioned himself to gaze out of the window and across the street, giving him a perfect view of the Texas School Book Depository.

The big green Marine helicopter circled over Dallas's Love Field. The sun was glistening and a crowd of more than five thousand was beginning to gather. As if in total synchronization, television sets all over the city began to be switched on, while rooftops, porches and windows started to fill up with curious onlookers. The airfield began to swarm with officers armed with crowd control ropes, and streets were blocked off by police who had under surveillance every window and rooftop along the presidential route. There were four hundred officers alone waiting at the airport and another two hundred at the Trade Mart, the President's destination.

Rows of cars lined the airport fence, each bearing a sign labeled PRESIDENTIAL MOTORCADE. As Air Force One loomed into view the field intercom repeated, "D.V. arriving. D.V. arriving. Attention, Distinguished Visitor arriving." And because of fine weather, maintenance crews were busily finishing the dismantling of the heavy plastic bubble that was to cover the President's limousine in case of rain.

The roar of Air Force One drowned out all other sounds at the airport. In the cockpit, its pilots braced themselves for landing in a nasty cross-wind. Finally the wheels hit with a puff of smoke, bounced and came to a jerky halt, settling down in one of the many puddles of water that dotted the field.

There were thirty-six aboard the President's jet, some of whom were Secret Service men, now busying themselves as they downed one last Alka-Seltzer to stave off the remains of last night's hangovers. Jacqueline Kennedy sat stiffly staring out the window, and thinking with annoyance that her pink suit was too heavy for the Dallas sunshine. She had not slept well the night before, still suffering from frequent nightmares about the loss of her baby.

392

As the door of Air Force One opened, the crowd cheered and began to surge forward. Mrs. Kennedy emerged and soberly accepted the bunch of red roses offered to her. The President, in contrast, smiled warmly as he followed his wife, shaking hands and ignoring the placards that called him TRAITOR. And once again, as the Kennedy motorcade inched away, a multitude of portable radios snapped on in sync with the disappearing heads of the ruling couple of Camelot.

Robert Kennedy and Vivian Prescott sat in the late afternoon around the Kennedy pool. They were discussing "purging the Agency of everybody who'd ever touched a Cuban or a gangster. I'm talking about five hundred senior officers and five *thousand* field grade men." The poolside telephone buzzed. Vivian breathed in the sweet air, rested his eyes in the symmetry of the trees. Bobby reached over to pick up the official telephone.

It was J. Edgar Hoover calling. They hurried to the teletype machine in the mansion's electronics area.

UPI—207

HANOVER, GERMAN. NOV.WW(UPI)—

THE STATE PROSECUTOR

BUST

BUST

QMVVV

UPI—207

BULLET NESS

PRECEDE KENNEDY

X DALLAS. NTEXAS, NOV. 22 (708 LAS THREE

SHOTS WERE FIRED AT PRESIDENT KENNEDY'S

MOTORCADE TODAY IN DOWNTOWN DALLAS

HSZETPEST

VVUPLF208

HANOVER, GERMANY NOV WWKVUPI)—

THE STATE PROSECUTOR TODAY DEMANDEJ

AMQIAMONTH PRISON TERM FOR WEST

GERMANY SJS ZSTZRILIZATION DOCTOR."

THREE JU THAT HANDSOME DR. ALEL DOHRN.

%%WAS N IDEALIST BUT BROKE THE LAW IN

AT LEAST IP OF THE QXEEP STERILIZATION

```
OPERATIONS H J HAS PERFORME ON LOCAL
WOMEN
            MORE
               HS137PEST
RV
SSSSSSS
FLASH
        KENNEDY SERIOUSLY WOUNDED
PESTSSSSSSSSSS
            HS 138/
SSSSSSSSSSSSSSSSSSSSSSS
    GJ      OWHL       W WOUNDED BY
          HQ139PESTXXXXXXXXXXXXXXXXXXXXXXX
KENNEDY WOUNDED PERHAPS FATALLY BY
ASSASSINS BULLET
            HS139PESTSSSSSSSSSSSSSSSSSSSSS
```

Vivian saw the moment that he had not been able to stop over
and over again. Running through his brain like an endless loop of
film . . . the familiar face and head of his boyhood friend . . . the
eyes with their special vulnerability, the jaw with its stubborn stamina, the electric energy of the shock of hair and head . . . all of it
exploding into a red blur . . . They had, god*damn* them—God help
him—found someone as good as Bender for the job . . .

He swayed, the injured knee giving under him, staggered back
and fell. The attorney general and the others hunched over the
teletype machine did not take notice.

All of the telephones in the D.C. area were out so he drove
toward Pat's. Terry was already home from school, sitting in front
of the television set with his mother, holding her hand. As Vivian
half-stumbled through the door they both ran to throw themselves
into his arms. Staggering, crying they made for the television set.
Walter Cronkite was choking out the news ". . . is dead. John
Fitzgerald Kennedy died today at—" He pounded the off button
and hobbled as fast as he could toward the bar on the enclosed side
porch. Behind him he could hear Terry turning on the set again.
The dog Pancho was under the couch.

"Don't drink, Viv. *Viv.* You have to go to Langley. Or don't go.
Quit! Quit, quit *now*, Viv."

394

He drank straight from the bottle of scotch. Wiped his chin, "Oh, no. I'm going to have a talk with the Vice-President. I *will* be the new DCI and I *will* hunt down *and exterminate every goddamn one of them!*"

From the livingroom he could hear the sound of his son crying.

It was dark. Vivian continued to stare at the photograph on his desk, or at where he knew it was. Was it actually there if he could not see it? It was engraved in his mind's eye for as long as his cortex would function . . . himself at twenty standing in front of the graveyard under the arch in his senior year at Yale. Then, as he had posed for the picture, his back had been to the dead. Now, thirty years later, he faced toward those whom he had lost. In the dark he swiveled his desk chair to look out the office window. The only illumination in the long room was the dim glow of the electric desk-calendar clock: 7:27—November 22.

Outside, below his office, the grounds of the Central Intelligence Agency were cold and still. In the shadowy woods that surrounded the gray-white building complex, even the cricket sound was reduced to its bare winter minimum. The sliver of moon was blue-white like an old scar against the black sky.

Another sky, black and star-flecked, Wisconsin, now superimposed itself before his gaze, and on that screen of memory the frightened face, as it was then, of the girl Anna Marie Carbonara.

Christmas week 1963 he had telephoned the clinic where the child was being held. The director's words told him where the power now lay: "Mr. Prescott, this ten-year-old female, admitted by yourself under the name Ann Carbo on 4/16/63, was released, in satisfactory condition, into the custody of her uncle on 11/28/63. I assumed that you had been informed, since he specifically mentioned your name and produced a release form marked U. S. Government bearing *your* signature—"

"Dr. Wintersole, stop there. My signature?"

"That is correct."

"What was the uncle's name, doctor?"

"One moment. Ah, a Mr. Carl Bender of Dallas, Texas."

Oh God . . . "Forwarding address?"

"No. He said they would be traveling."

So they'd dared to use the name "Bender" and to forge my name. The animals. Well-named. *Maybe* I can keep the DCI's office

395

out of their hands, but as far as the covert control, they've now got it, it's theirs . . . Jesus . . . where is she? Did they kill her? No— they're holding her to use in case I decide to go public about the assassination. They'll hold her somewhere, until needed . . . The nearsighted vulnerability of the child's face filled the entire sky.

Vivian turned back, away from the woods below. He stared at the clock and the date. In the seven years since the assassination of his best friend Jack Kennedy, no day had passed that was not in some way colored by that political murder, the lives destroyed because of it . . . The carnage in Dallas continued to bleed through the thin-spread surface of his life.

First of all it had seeped into his marriage. . . .

Langley, Virginia, 1970

On November 22, 1963, Vivian had run out of Pat Donahue's
Virginia home, heading for the White House. He had holed up at
the Mayflower and waited for the call from the new President. The
message had been delivered in person by a Johnson aide during
the funeral rites for the slain President . . . "LBJ wants you to get
your ass over to his office on Friday."

The new President sat on the commode. The door to the Oval
Office's small toilet was wide open so that the chief executive could

conduct business with his visitors. One of Johnson's younger aides ushered him in for his 10 A.M. appointment.

"Good morning, Mr. Prescott. Uh, nature calls. Bill, give Mr. Prescott whatever he wants to drink. Uh . . . Mr. Prescott, my spies tell me that you were the closest man at Central Intelligence with President Kennedy. Is that right?" The quiet flush of the toilet was the only sound in the room for a moment. Vivian stared out the window toward the frozen rose garden. "Is that right?"

"He was my friend. Yes."

"Now, you're the chief of the Agency's secret operations, and you were one of his best friends, so I'm going to ask you and I'm only going to ask you once—was this dirty little sonofabitch Oswald working for the Cubans or the Russians?" The two men were now alone.

"No." Philby's creased face floated behind his eyes.

"You *know* that?"

"Yes."

"In other words, Prescott, you're saying to me that there was no conspiracy at all in this thing?"

"I don't believe I said that, Mr. President."

The big Texan stood frowning down on Vivian. Johnson was always ill at ease with "aristocratic types" like Vivian Prescott. To him they seemed to look right through him. Which was why he had staged the toilet scene, hoping the encounter would throw Prescott off-balance, undermine his poise. But it never worked . . . not with the late Jack Kennedy and not with his friend Prescott. They were two of a kind. Now he stood here, glowering at Prescott, feeling like a clumsy ox.

"Have you had your coffee?"

It was tea.

"Yes, I have. Thank you, sir."

The President hunched his shoulders and lumbered for the security of the big desk. "Mr. Prescott, as you know, I'm just a country boy. I don't intend to play any chickenshit games with you. President Kennedy told me that you were his choice to direct the Agency after the election. I would like to honor that wish of his. I would like to be able to count on you as he counted on you . . ."

"Yes, sir."

The President massaged his hands as if they were arthritic as he leaned far over the desk. His shrewd, small red-rimmed eyes studied Vivian. "I see that you've noticed that the furniture's been changed already."

"Yes, sir."

"Prescott, I'm going to tell you the truth. I'd give anything, *anything* not to be sitting here. I've been Commander-in-Chief of these United States less than a week and the military brass, the son-of-a-bitchin' Joint Chiefs, have already put a hook with a fat worm on it, called *Vietnam,* down my gullet. I just have to know if there was a conspiracy in Dallas. Well?"

"Mr. President, I see by the paper that you've commissioned a blue-ribbon panel headed by the Chief Justice to look into—"

"Prescott, that stuff makes the grass grow green!" Johnson rolled up and began to pace like a sick bear. "Judge Warren sat right where you're sitting now with the *tears* streaming down his face. It was pitiful! Do you know *why* he accepted the appointment after the *third* meeting? Because we could be on the edge of a nuclear war." The Texan was a huge ball of raw energy. He did not quite pull at Vivian's tailored lapels, but Vivian was beginning to feel the force of the pressure. The emotion-charged nasal twang was cutting into him.

"John Hoover has given me a commitment that this Oswald acted alone, and *that's* what the Warren panel is going to find. Because, Mr. Prescott, if anyone should find that this was a Soviet conspiracy, then there are people in this country, powerful people, who would move into a confrontation with the Soviet. You know that, don't ya?"

"Yes, sir."

"All right, then. I'm telling you that I don't give a shit about all the signs that point to a Cuban or a Russian plot. I don't even give a shit if there *was* one. How do you like that? I'm not going to give these goddamn so-called hawks the excuse to steal this government, my goddamn government, and start World War III. Now, I'm asking you to tell me that *there was no plot.*" The President threw himself down, as if for ultimate emphasis, in his desk chair, the springs complaining to the floor.

"Sir, I believe I can tell you that there was no Soviet conspiracy in Dallas." Vivian felt for the man. Within seventy-two hours of

Dallas the hawks that JFK had banished had closed in again on Johnson with Vietnam escalation scenarios. Vivian knew that Curtis LeMay, Chief of Staff for the Air Force, along with General Powers, had descended on Johnson.

"Godamighty, it's more than a man can stand . . . They want to pulverize North Vietnam with B-52s, they want to stop swatting flies and go after the whole manure pile . . ."

He's going to have another stroke, Vivian thought. Rostow and the Bunday brothers are going to kill the man with their "can do" Ivy League macho . . .

"They've got a hard-on for big bombs." The President's nasal sound rose almost to a scream.

In the following silence Vivian's brooding resumed as he again looked down at the rug. The Pentagon's repeated think-tank phrase about a "viable society following a nuclear war" had almost driven Jack Kennedy mad. Through the rhetoric Kennedy had seen the flames of the thermonuclear fire storm burning his children and Vivian's children and everybody's children to death. Jack had finally gotten out in front of the war-lovers, and now, like the fates, they were back buzzing around the man from Texas with the same old death's head song and dance.

Lyndon Johnson's small eyes narrowed dangerously, seemed almost to merge into one red orb of burning suspicion. His face drained. He gripped his hands together to stop, Vivian now knew, their trembling.

"No damn *Communist* conspiracy . . . but you can't tell me that there was no . . ." He'd pronounced the word as if it were "Commonist." The penetrating nasal tension of the voice sank and died.

Within ten minutes the two men had reached their understanding. Lyndon Johnson did not want to hear *any* details. What he craved was Vivian Prescott's assurance that after Prescott was appointed DCI that he, the new director, would personally protect the new President from whoever it was—Prescott *had* hinted—whoever it was who had killed John Fitzgerald Kennedy.

The President squeezed Vivian's long, cool hand in his own wet ones. He looked on the very ragged edge.

"Mr. President," murmured the DCI-to-be, "I will do everything for you that I would have done for Jack Kennedy." . . .

"What exactly does *that* mean?" Pat asked softly as she lay next

400

to him in bed in the Maryland apartment that night and listened to his account of the meeting with LBJ.

He did not, or could not, answer.

"Viv, I'm worried about you. What are you planning?" (No answer.) "Do you hold yourself responsible? After all we did? After . . . Tim?"

"Yes."

"Christ, what vanity! I've just about had it. My husband is dead—murdered. My son is on the verge of a breakdown. My son's father—my lover—is lying here refusing to so much as touch me, conjuring up some hideous revenge scheme to clear his magisterial conscience . . . oh, I know you, Vivian Prescott, how I know you . . ."

And he knew that she was crying silently, and he could not even touch her. Could not lift his leaden arms to hold her. In the dark the tears, finally, came.

"He's dead," and she was sobbing, "he's dead," and he knew that she meant the President and Tim and, perhaps, himself.

Still, he could not tell her that Moscow Center's agent, one Uri Nosenko, had appeared as predicted by Philby, at their last treff. Nosenko's pose as a KGB defector was for the single purpose of reassuring Langley that Oswald, while in the Soviet Union, had never been the KGB's man, that Russia had no responsibility for the assassination of President Kennedy. Vivian, as the new DCI, had given his blessing to the "defector's" credibility as a legitimate defector. But the Animals had guessed as much and did their sadistic damndest to break Nosenko, to try to force him to implicate Russia or Cuba or both. After all, the American people must never know what, at their highest levels, they knew . . . that the conspiracy that cut down Jack Kennedy in the streets of Dallas was home-grown, made-in-America. Not that the Russians had any love for Kennedy . . . they simply preferred the devil they knew to the wild men they feared would replace him.

No, Vivian did not want to tell his wife about a bank vault covered by what appeared to be a simple single-dwelling house in the Maryland countryside, where since his "defection" in '64 Nosenko had been tortured by the Animals. Well, he had not cracked, had not implicated Russia or Cuba, and Vivian could now at last order the KGB man's release on the seventh anniversary of Jack's mur-

401

der. He had, in fact, signed the order and handed it to his man Vic Korcuska on the previous day. . . .

The desk clock clicked to 8:10. Vivian leaned forward and slowly unlocked a drawer. His hands moved in the dark like crepuscular animals. The long fingers found the portable tape recorder and the Luger. He lifted them up onto the desk and laid them on the message sheet reminding him to call his wife, his father and a Miss Buchanan. The grip of the Luger was worn and cold. The Gestapo officer to whom the gun had belonged was dead these twenty-seven years, his ashes mingled in the coarse grass of the Czechoslovakian countryside.

Vivian had killed the Nazi with an assured audacity then. Why could he not now, he asked himself for the thousandth time, kill the men who had killed his President and stabbed his country in the back? His reflexes were, if anything, more subtle and tempered now, his power, authority, inestimably greater, his passion for revenge as personal and profound. Some of them, a few of them, were, he was certain, even now in the building, waiting for him. Stronger than the Gestapo, but he could at least make a beginning.

The answer was always the same. He could not shoot it out single-handedly with the traitors in the Agency. He could not mount and lead an execution squad composed of aides and secretaries. He could not have his son—who still did not know that he was his son—and his wife see him on the front page of the Washington *Post* or on the evening news as a rabid animal who had gone berserk at Central Intelligence. In short, Vivian knew that he could not play God, as once he and all of the young heroes had been allowed to play God. That was in Europe, in the age of heroes, an age that was past.

Vivian felt for the frames of the photographs on the desk. His hand brushed past the recorder and the Luger, paused at the paper with the messages. He should call Pat, she would be worried.

They had been married on Easter Sunday, 1964, by a justice of the peace in Vienna, Virginia. The only witness was their son, Terence Donahue, who thought that Vivian was only his godfather and now thought of him as his stepfather. But the boy loved him, admired him as he had his dead father. He was grateful for that. The three of them were never far apart. They withdrew into themselves, more like a small clan than a family. Though Vivian's name was, for the first time, comparatively well-known, they did not talk much about politics or the secret world of intelligence. Instead they read aloud together and played strenuous tennis on the Agency courts or, in bad weather, inside at the nearby U. S. armory. Terry was a national merit scholar and the captain of his high school tennis team. Almost as tall and rangy as Vivian, and with dark red hair, he resembled the Vivian of thirty years earlier. But there were differences . . . Terry was interested in mathematics and astronomy, not so much in the Greek and English classics as Vivian had been. He was less romantic, not nearly so obsessed with sex. He wanted, he said, to take a doctorate and then work in the space program, but first he would try Yale for a year.

For months after the murder Vivian and Pat did not make love. Late into the night, in the privacy of their bedroom, Pat let Vivian work through his hidden grief and rage over his failed attempt to abort the Dallas assassination. Until she could stand it no longer, putting her fingers gently over his lips.

"Viv, Viv. Stop a minute, let me say something. Darling, you're gnawing on a stone. You believed—Rob Garabedian *assured* you that the FBI would move. They *knew*. You knew that then, you know that now. You had every right to count on Hoover's passion for publicity and survival. And Hoover *did* move—"

"He moved. To eliminate Oswald after—"

"But, Viv, Garabedian, at the end, was the Bureau's man *too*. He was your agent, but for once in his life he was working for the FBI *too*. In the last days you and the FBI were on the *same* track. We had won. Oswald and Ruby were *both* informing on the conspiracy to the Bureau, and Garabedian was in the field and—"

"But Pat, they didn't move *after* Garabedian was murdered. They knew that he had disappeared and they didn't act . . . and then it was too late, and Scott's people had Oswald fingered and tied to *both* us and the Bureau, so Hoover had to let Scott send Ruby in to kill Oswald so that the goddamn Bureau wouldn't be embarrassed after the fact by the Oswald connection. Then I had to cover up the whole rotten thing so that the Agency—let's be honest, so that *my* connections to Bender and Oswald—wouldn't be . . ."

And on and on like a new and bloodier Homeric saga of murder and deceit. But there was no god from the machine to descend

403

from the wings of history to mete out justice and bring catharsis. Sometimes she would come to his side of the bed, turn out the light and try to comfort him, taking him in her mouth . . . part nurse, part lover. Nothing, no orgasm to make him clean. No catharsis. It was many months before he could do anything but lie there in his bed of unexpressible grief. . . .

The whole nation had been wounded that day, the American people sitting numb, huddled around the bright television sets that awful weekend as the endless loop of film programmed the slaughter and its aftermath into their consciousness, then stumbling into their cold beds to relive the blood and terror all night in their ever repeating nightmares.

Many had not been able to wake up from that national nightmare, and Vivian Prescott was one of them. As the new Director of Central Intelligence he was making Langley hum with the best intelligence estimates—on Vietnam, especially—in the Agency's history. The hawks had been stalemated after Dallas by the Prescott-Johnson strategy. The President and the new Director had depoliticized the murder. Oswald had been stripped of almost every vestige of intelligence garb, reduced to a loner acting out of a mindless apolitical resentment. There had been a few independent muckrakers who had seen through the shock and subterfuge and said conspiracy, but the Agency had ordered its "assets" in the media worldwide, to "debunk" the critics of the official assassination report with innuendos and charges about the so-called assassination buffs' financial exploitation and political motives.

Still, the ghost of the fallen President hovered in the consciousness of the average man and woman, as it did in Vivian's, and a new generation of young people seemed to perceive in the murder the beginning of the soul-destroying war in Southeast Asia. But the media, the opinion-makers, the wise men of the syndicated columns and the doyens of university political science departments repeated the official line with near religious fealty. Except that by 1968 more and more had ceased to believe. Vivian had almost ceased to care any more if it all came out, began to think about forcing it out, burying, exorcising the ghost.

The public's trauma was also Vivian's, except he could not be consoled by the official myths. For Vivian there were still only the mourners walking in procession from St. Matthew's Cathedral to

404

the Capitol Building Rotunda, the coffin draped in flags, the honor guard from the combined services, the Navy Hymn broken by the guttural beat of the drums . . . the midnight horse Blackjack, riderless, stirrups backward, rearing behind the caisson of the slain leader. And the family, the children, the brothers Robert and Edward. The widow in black. . . .

The clock on the desk stood at 8:52. The walls of the dark office held half a dozen pictures of Vivian Prescott and Jack Kennedy: at Yale and Harvard, in London before and during the war, at Hyannis Port and Fire Island.

Again, as he stared into the gloom, the funeral procession unfolded in his memory, the widow and her children came into the focus of his recall . . . Jacqueline Kennedy was now Jacqueline Onassis, and Richard Nixon was the President. Vivian was one of the few who had learned that in 1953 the then Vice-President Nixon had connived with Sherman Scott and the Animals at CIA to wreck Onassis's oil tanker fleet so that an Anglo-American consortium could pick up a slice of the multimillion-dollar tanker trade. There had been an agent in the Department of Justice running interference for the Nixon front group's operations against Onassis's tankers, and that agent, he'd been told, was Warren Burger, now Nixon's appointee as Chief Justice of the Supreme Court of the United States. And Sherman Scott had left the Agency to head up a special team already preparing for Nixon's 1972 reelection campaign.

Quid pro quo, Vivian thought, the long and continuing godawful payoff. His gray eyes squinted tight. Well, you all have a payoff still to come. His jaw clenched as he reached for the tape recorder. His fingers felt for the control buttons. Snap. "Tape Four. Side two. November twenty-second, 1970. Continuation of the report by the Director of Central Intelligence concerning the illegal, unconstitutional executive apparatus: code name Operation Gemstone . . ." Snap. The echo of his low, resonant voice hung for a fraction of a second in the dark.

Vivian's hand rested momentarily on the sheet of paper that listed the telephone calls that he was supposed to return. He would have to dial at once if he wanted to speak to his father before the octogenarian retired for the night. Without seeing, he touched the Manhattan telephone number on the keys, then hung up after six rings. It was unusual for his father to be out in the evening. Where was the nurse-secretary, Mrs. Regas? Could the old man be ill, dead? Could that be why Pat had called—to tell him? He felt nothing, blank. His father had been failing since 1968. He'd attended the Democratic convention in Chicago with Terry Donahue (the boy had not taken Vivian's name), and both of them had been overcome by police riot control gas in the street in front of the Hilton Hotel. Sam Prescott had had to be hospitalized. Later, when it was plain that Richard Nixon would be President, Sam had told Vivian, "I wish I had just passed away that afternoon in the streets of Chicago." Vivian had gripped his father's thin hand. "The war will bring Nixon down, too, dad. Nothing lasts forever." A slight smile had creased the long, sad face. "Thank God." Then before closing his eyes to sleep, he had quoted a few of his favorite lines of Shakespeare's John of Gaunt . . . "Methinks, I am a prophet new inspired/and thus expiring do foretell of him:/His rash, fierce blaze of riot cannot last,/for violent fires soon burn out themselves . . ."

Vivian had left the penthouse suite quietly that day and crossed over to Central Park to be alone for a while. Sitting, staring at the young lovers and the adolescent muggers moving fatefully toward each other in the gathering dark, he had completed the dying John of Gaunt's prophecy of the fall of England, except Vivian had America on his mind. ". . . is now bound in with shame/with inky blots and rotten parchment bonds. That England that was wont to conquer others/Hath made a shameful conquest of itself . . ."

Vivian brushed the message sheet to the floor. He could not face Pat tonight, even by phone. He reached instead for the tape recorder, thinking, "Rotten. Rotten to the core," and snapped it on. The director of Central Intelligence bent his head close to the machine and dictated, without notes, for the balance of the tape's forty-five minutes. His voice was low, urgent, he did not pause until the warning whirr of the expended cassette emitted its mechanical signal. Concluding, ". . . provocation and paramilitary violence timed to coincide with the Republican convention in San Diego in 1972 leading to the declaration of a state of national emergency. This, together with the quotes, neutralization, close quotes, of Governor Wallace is . . ."

In the dark he ejected the filled cassette, fitted in a fresh one

406

from the desk drawer, stacked the used tape in a box with half a dozen others. The desk clock clicked to 9:19. His fingers brushed the Luger and flinched away. A bead of perspiration rolled down from the close-cropped curly hairline. Vivian leaned back in the swivel chair and opened the top button of the soft white cotton button-down shirt, one of two dozen made up for him each year by his New York tailor. He massaged his sharp Adam's apple, then stood up to go into the office lavatory. He felt light, relieved that he had at last made up his mind not to return Kathy Buchanan's call either. . . .

Katherine Buchanan, at first, had been just another coltishly handsome classmate of Terry's that Vivian sometimes saw around the house on weekends or driving up in a car full of high school seniors to pick up Terry.

It was in late '67 that he had actually talked with her alone for the first time. Pat was in the kitchen preparing supper and Terry was laboriously shaving when Vivian responded to the front door chimes. Hushing the spaniel, he had opened the door to find Kathy Buchanan standing there in the brisk November night. He had brought her in to the fire and offered her a glass of white wine. Her color was high, her fair skin rosy from the cold. As she took off her tweed blazer, her cashmere turtleneck sweater tightened across the firm, thrusting buds of her young breasts. Did he vaguely remember that she had run for the girls' track team? Yes. They talked about that for a moment. As they chatted, waiting for Terry, Vivian realized that her father was Joseph "Bucky" Buchanan, an influential and wealthy Washington lawyer whose firm contained a number of CIA "assets." Terry came down the stairs, apologizing for his lateness, mumbling that he had been detained at the armory by a five-set match with someone named Jay Marshall.

Vivian admired the two of them as they stood in front of the fireplace. Pure and yet at the same time nubile and sensuous. Vivian smiled at his son. The shock of red hair reminded him painfully of Jack Kennedy at the same age. Terry had his mother's hazel eyes and strong teeth, but the forehead and lean body were Vivian's contributions to this new gene pool that he and Pat had conceived in one night of love; a night, like so many others, both innocent and forbidden. Did the boy, now almost eighteen, ever suspect that Vivian was his real father? Vivian still thought not. As far as Terry Donahue was concerned his real father, Tim Donahue, had died a hero during a secret mission for the United States government.

Kathy was tall, almost reaching to Terry's shoulder. She was telling the two men about Bob Dylan, whose concert she was about to escort the young Mr. Donahue to. Pat came in time to give them both a kiss good-by. The dog tried and failed to get out with them in the general confusion.

It was quiet after they had left. "Steak's ready," Pat said.

They ate by themselves in the dinette. "Aren't they beautiful young people? Viv? What are you looking like that for? Is the steak too fat?"

"I never really noticed her before. Do you think that, ah . . ."

"You know, my darling, for all your famous philandering, you really are an ass-aching puritan. Of course they're making love. This isn't the forties or God help us, the fifties. You and Terry talk about sports and Democratic party politics, but I think there's a sort of mutual shyness, on both your parts, to talk about, uh . . ."

"Now who's searching for words? The sharpest tongue in the East all tied up in knots over a little word like sex."

"The sharpest *teeth*, not tongue . . ."

"How would you like me to eat you for dinner, Miss Smart Ass?"

"Mmm." It was as if the young couple had liberated some residual store of youthful love energy in them. Not since the assassination had they spontaneously reached for each other with such need. As they ran up the stairs for the bedroom it was as if their bodies themselves remembered all of the times over all of the years in Europe and America when they had explored and learned each other, so that now they could come together again, even after the long hiatus of grief when he had shrunk from her intimacy. Now his body responded to all the secret calls of the flesh. Wanting to immolate himself in her, sinking to his knees, dragging the skin-tight blue jeans down off her hips. He was in her . . . his tongue, his fingers, his cock . . . both of them in a fit of bursting, insatiable need . . .

Some ten minutes later, still in each other's arms, she spoke first. "My God, that was incredible. What came over you? . . . did the idea of Kathy and Terry—?"

408

"I don't know. Maybe. Is there any ice cream? Jesus, I feel good . . ."

Back in the kitchen drinking coffee with ice cream in it, talking as if they had been separated from each other for a long time . . . "Pat, what do you think? Does he feel completely at ease with me? He's candid with you, isn't he?"

"He is. I think that until about a year ago he was very proud of you and Tim, your war records and so forth. But I think that he began to realize that as DCI you were a national figure. There's a lot of anti-war feeling now, even in the high school, and a lot of the kids have parents who have taken them to marches and demonstrations and, as you know, CIA is fast becoming a very dirty word. And . . . I think that he's read one of the books that argues that the Agency may have been involved in the assassination. It disturbed him. I told him to bring any questions he has directly to you."

"What did he say?"

"Um, noncommittal . . . what would you tell him?"

"I don't know . . ."

The talk with Terry came a month later, during the Christmas holidays. Terry and Kathy Buchanan had, without telling anyone, arranged to join an accredited special project that would allow the two of them to spend some three weeks with the McCarthy for President campaign.

"Mom, I know that you're a Bobby Kennedy lady, but Gene McCarthy is terrific. He's a poet and he was the first senator to denounce *Joe* McCarthy, he's even a Catholic, too."

"I know, I know"—Pat laughed—"two cheers." The four of them lounged in front of the fireplace, sipping mugs of cider with cinnamon sticks. Vivian again took in the young beauty of the two. Both wore jeans and heavy flannel shirts. Kathy's hair was a warm brown full of blonde highlights reaching well down her back, Terry was just beginning to let his red hair grow. Both of them sat with their long legs stretched out, unselfconsciously sensuous. Terry's question made its way into his reverie.

". . . my going cause you any problem?"

"Problem . . . ?"

"Well, there's lots of stories on all the kids going clean for Gene and, you know, you're the head of the CIA and, you know . . ."

Kathy picked up the ball. "You know, would we be getting you in any trouble?"

"Oh, no, of course not. I'm a free agent, so to speak, when it comes to personal—"

"Is that true, Mr. Prescott?"

Vivian flushed as they all looked at him. Pat was watching him over the rim of her mug. "I beg your pardon, Kathy?"

There was a glint of irony in the girl's round green eyes. Terry was looking at the two of them out of the corner of his eye. Kathy was more mature than her boyfriend, that was clear, though they were both seventeen. Kathy's voice was clear and, it seemed to Vivian, just a bit taunting.

"You know, you signed that petition of Terry's calling for at least negotiations between the United States and Hanoi but—"

"But *what?* Come on, out with it."

Her poise was remarkable. She was talking to the Director of Central Intelligence as if he were any old slightly superannuated upper-class liberal uncle. Vivian couldn't help grinning at the same time he was trying to frown. "You know, Mr. Prescott, the Gulf of Tonkin incident—"

"Yes."

Now Kathy's porcelain skin was starting to flush too. "Well, I mean, you know, it was a hoax and the CIA was part of the lie." The last word cut into the cheery holiday ambience and drew blood. Vivian sensed that this delightful young woman was about to say something irrevocable. Secrets came crowding to the surface of his consciousness. It had been a long time since anyone had spoken to him in a language stripped of the obligatory Washington doubletalk that reduced everything to probabilities and estimates of political success . . . "Kathy, you sound as if you've been reading the—"

"New York *Times* and I. F. Stone. I mean, every kid in school knows that LBJ faked the whole thing in order to escalate the war . . . and, uh, what about the Saigon secret police?"

"What about *them?*"

Her voice was sweet and penetrating at the same time. "Terry, go get that Bertrand Russell pamphlet that details the CIA training of torture techniques in Saigon, *and* South Korea *and* Iran, *and* Bolivia, *and* Guatemala."

Vivian stood up. "Bertrand Russell?"

410

"Yes, you know, Mr. Prescott. The world's greatest living—"
The mug rang as Vivian tried to place it carefully on the mantel.
Terry had not moved. Vivian's back was to all of them now. He
could feel their eyes on him. The telephone ringing in the kitchen
broke the silence.

Pat jumped up. "Saved by the bell," but there was a clear edge
of tension in her laugh as she left the room.

Vivian swung back, the two young people were looking up at him
with curiosity and, perhaps, something else in their eyes. He
managed a half-smile. "Well, Kathy, anyone as well-read as you
seem to be must know that the political decision-making process
in *our* system allows for a wide diversity and—"

"You sound like my father," she said as Pat came back into the
room and asked who wanted a grilled cheese.

"Don't change the subject, mom." Vivian and Pat looked at
Terry as if he had blurted out a phrase in some exotic language.
They were getting a taste of the scene that was being played out
in holiday livingrooms across much of America.

Vivian guessed at what Pat must be thinking. She knew that
President Johnson had demanded that the CIA prepare a secret
report that would expose foreign Communist manipulation of the
young people's peace and protest movement that was going up by
the numbers from day to day—the movement that had launched
the McCarthy challenge against a sitting President who had been
elected by the largest majority in American history. Johnson had
cursed bitterly at what Vivian, as DCI, had personally presented
him. Entitled "Rebellious Youth," the study had said that the
youth movement was essentially an indigenous phenomenon of
dissent. The core of the movement, Vivian had written in his introduction, was made up of intelligent, idealistic young people who
for the most part came from affluent families. "The Communist
influence is small but will grow if the war continues to escalate,"
had been Vivian's final statement to a very angry President . . .
Now, sprawled on the Indian rug in front of his own fireplace were
two statistics from his report come to life, and he was shaken.

"Go ahead," Pat said, "get it out in the open."

"I think you two are oversimplifying." Vivian sat down again.
"Were you aware that the good Senator McCarthy himself has
been a friend of the CIA, and that his campaign manager, Blair
Clark, was actually with the Agency? So you see—"

"McCarthy!" Terry and Kathy spoke at the same time, rolling up from the rug.

"That's correct." The two young people looked at each other. Terry's mouth was open and he looked like a little boy.

Vivian pressed his advantage gently. "I support what you want to do. That's our system. My father is contributing a lot of money for the New Hampshire campaign. You have my vote, I think you're both terrific."

Kathy's eyes were misted. She bounced to her feet and hugged Vivian, then kissed Pat. Terry grinned like a big Charlie Brown, his favorite cartoon character. The aroma of Kathy, her hair and fresh skin, as she touched him, stirred Vivian. Somehow he wished he could chuck everything and go with them. Then, as they ran to get their coats—to go and try to persuade Kathy's parents—Vivian remembered who he was and where he had been and that he could no more go to New Hampshire than he could go back in time. The New Hampshire primary campaign was a search for lost innocence. But Vivian Prescott's innocence, he felt, as he stared into the flames, had not only been lost. It had also, face it, been traded—traded for power. Power that he somehow had to use in order to justify and vindicate that moral bargain that had come to define his life . . .

Terry had returned from the grand adventure in New Hampshire a very politicized young man. From January through March the legions of upper and upper-middle-class young men and women had sustained a crusade against the war that would bring down Lyndon Johnson. Vivian knew that the Johnson government would fall in the spring, but he did not have the heart to tell Kathy or Terry that much more than the electoral results in the snows of New Hampshire had forced the Agency and LBJ administration hawks to the wall.

There was no American vocabulary—outside of Langley or the Oval Office—to describe the covert struggle for power that raged behind the rhetoric of the popular press reports that ordinary citizens read. Neither highschool nor college courses in government prepared even such bright youngsters as Terry and Kathy to grapple with the realities of power in the infrastructure of America. Other nations had "ruling circles," "purges," "class struggle," "parliamentary crises" and "coups," but *not* America.

412

Except that she did.

Vivian had advance notice of Secretary of Defense McNamara's resignation before Terry and Kathy returned from campaigning. A decisive coalition of center forces and their media outlets were massing to end the war in Vietnam before the American dollar and spirit were destroyed. Both Vivian and his father were meeting privately with separate groups whose aim was to open the door for a Robert F. Kennedy presidential peace campaign. Johnson knew that his DCI was feeding facts to the old JFK—now RFK—team. By the beginning of March it was clear that McNamara had lost his backing even in the big business community that had formed him. Vivian stood in the rain as LBJ bade farewell to the ex-Ford Motor Company whiz kid, and knew that the raw-boned Texan's days were numbered as well. . . .

April 2: Pat laid on corned beef and cabbage for Terry's eighteenth birthday. Terry and Kathy told about how they had tasted victory in the snow. They had both mastered an enormous amount of information and data on the actual logistics of "the dirty little war." Terry had become an effective advocate. Wearing a shirt and tie, he would speak to Rotarians and Kiwanians about what the war was "doing to our economy." And Pat and Vivian applauded as, at the table, he gave them a sample of the speech. Pat obviously was enormously proud of her son. If only, Vivian thought, he could have revealed, on the spot, that Terry was *his* son too . . .

After dinner Kathy teased Vivian until he finally told her that there had actually been a secret anti-war demonstration at CIA. It was true, but they were dubious. "It's true, honey," Pat assured her son, "not in Plans, of course, but in the Intelligence section." Kathy wanted to know the difference; Vivian hedged.

Then, unexpectedly as had happened before, there was steel in her laughing voice. "What section was it that murdered Che Guevara?"

Vivian's face tightened.

Pat's rejoinder was immediate. "Kathy, don't you think that you're just a little impertinent? You know, I think you're an extraordinary young woman, but occasionally the brat shows through the breeding."

"Mrs. Prescott, I apologize for coming on so heavy to your

413

husband, but he can't—Mr. Prescott, you can't have it both ways. Well, can you?"

Terry was quiet, watching. His manner reminded Vivian of Tim's.

No one spoke. Only a Virginia nightingale opened up in the early April evening . . .

Ernesto Che Guevara, he filled up Vivian's mind's eye like a poster. He remembered the day, right after LBJ had made him DCI, when Bill Breem of the Latin American desk had run through the secretarial pool calling out, "Mr. Prescott, sir, we've found him!"

Johnson had kept his promise by appointing Vivian, but with his usual ambivalence the President had vetoed the Prescott plan to purge the Directorate of Plans of its Animals. Frank Wisner had blown his brains out after Bay of Pigs—after learning that his deputy, V. T. J. P. on the memo, had exposed the inner workings of the fiasco to President Kennedy, thus guaranteeing that he, Wisner, would be fired along with Dulles. Wisner was gone, Dick Bissell had been allowed to resign and was hiding out somewhere in the Ivy League licking his wounds. Tracy Barnes was at Yale fishing in the troubled waters of black ghetto politics, but still reporting to Dick Helms. And Helms and Sherman Scott were hiding behind "Mother's" skirts in the depths of Plans. Mother—James Jesus Angleton—Helms, Scott and their shock troops in the DOD were active again against Cuba. In their spare time they worked on a master plan that would once and for all link V. T. J. Prescott to H. A. R. Philby. This dream of Mother's had become an article of religious faith to the hard-liners. They could see it now: the handsome, arrogant DCI exposed as the supermole of history, followed by his disgrace, destruction and a grateful nation . . .

After November 22, 1963, Scott's man Howard Hunt had removed to Madrid to prepare launching plans for a new invasion. The assassination plots against Castro were once again operational. Vivian had had a showdown with LBJ . . . "You know, Mr. President, that President Kennedy did everything he could to break up these provocative adventures. Now you're sitting by while men who were disgraced on the beach at Playa Girón tempt disaster in Cuba again. And again in conjunction with organized crime."

414

The President pulled morosely at his dewlapped jowls. "Shit. You don't have to tell me that we're running a goddamned Murder Incorporated in the Caribbean. What the hell can I do? I can't tear the Agency apart and still keep a congressional majority or a *minimum* war policy. I got people crawling up my ass with atomic bombs to drop on Hanoi. Christ, Vivian, I need your help. You're the DCI—get these crazies involved somewhere where they won't blow us all up. Find something else for them to play with besides Cuba."

And so they had thrown Che Guevera to the wolves at Central Intelligence. Che stood for the Cuban and the entire "Third World" revolution, but he was a freelance. Killing *him* was not killing Castro and forcing a response from the Soviet. Che was a handsome, audacious doctor, symbol of the "new socialist man" that haunted the nightmares of the Ivy League tough guys at Langley. These "action intellectuals," as they liked to be called, were preoccupied with maleness in a way that, by turns, amused and disgusted Vivian. Rostow, Helms, Scott and Hunt would be up and out every morning playing their clumsy desperate style of tennis, trying to remain fifty-three years old forever.

"I'd say," Pat had told him, "they've got galloping homosexual panic. These frantic asses, misnamed hawks, are so damned insecure they have to prove that they can bomb as many people and train as many torturers as any KGB op. You, my stud, were a tennis champion, otherwise you'd be just another closet Bonesman sucking up to the big boys in the Pentagon. And that's one reason that they hate you so, just like they hated Jack . . ." She held him in her arms as she always did when he was hurt . . .

Breem's Latin desk had identified a photograph from Bolivia of a balding gray-haired man with glasses as none other than Che in heavy disguise. This was what Vivian needed, the lure to draw the Agency wild men away from the Caribbean.

By running SIX teams (sabotage, intelligence, experiment) from the special forces based in Panama, Helms and Scott were able to blanket Bolivia with counterinsurgency troops. Technology fresh from Vietnam could identify human beings and their waste matter from a low flying aircraft above the jungle canopy. Che's hemispheric revolutionary scenario was never to unfold . . . before the Cuban advance guard could build its base they were betrayed by informers competing for Langley gold. The rebels were soon surrounded in the highlands. Che was wounded. Scott, from La Paz, flashed the signal to Langley, THE LION IS DOWN.

Vivian flew out in an Air Force jet that night. He knew that Che would meet an "accident" at Scott's hands unless the DCI was on the scene, and Vivian wanted a chance to talk to Che, to tell him the truth—that the Soviets were as much an enemy of any honest Latin American reform or revolution as the most cynical of Yankees. He had made clear that Guevara was to be kept alive if captured, but he had no illusions about that order being adhered to for very long, if at all.

Across primitive roads and through tropical downpour, Vivian's jeep spun and slid toward the makeshift provincial prison house. The slime and mud made the unpaved path to the guardhouse an obstacle course. Vivian fell back in the mud, cursing as he heard the .44 go off. He scrabbled to his feet and lurched forward to the wooden piling that led to the house.

In a burst of furious Spanish Sherman Scott and Dick Helms came through the door. Scott, immaculate in starched tans, held the smoking .44 in front of him as he lectured the Guardia Nacional colonel and his two aides. A sense of *déjà vu* swept over Vivian as he reached the wooden walk and stood there, dripping from the humidity, watching the spectacle. Scott, of course, was speaking in the Castilian accent.

". . . talk about trial? La Paz is not secure. In no way is it secure. What? Are you insane? The man was *not* a martyr, the man was one of the great criminals of our time. You will report that he was shot while trying to escape. We've just bailed your lousy little country out again and you—come back here, Colonel Garcia, how dare you walk away from me when I—oh, hello, there, Mr. Director . . ."

They stared at each other across the mud yard. For a moment Vivian thought that Scott might lift the heavy automatic and shoot him down in the mud where he stood. Vivian's temples were pounding . . . Scott's voice, that damn accent the same as on the Dallas tape that Philby had given him, the voice planning in Spanish for the execution of President Kennedy . . . Vivian turned his head away from Scott's blank sun-glassed face to speak to Helms, now the Director of Plans. Helms, who—but for Vivian's special relationship with JFK—would have been DCI, and who never forgot. Helms: OSS, Ivy League, Skull and Bones. An Old Boy who never forgot, or forgave . . . His overbred face pursed as he focused on the DCI's large gray eyes, the skinny shoulders arched up for protection. But Helms knew that if Prescott should pick this time and jungle site to have it out and square accounts, he and Scott would be at a disadvantage . . . the Guardia would hardly come to their aid. Just the opposite, in fact . . .

"Dick,"—Vivian's voice was dry as hay—"I'm holding you responsible if there should be a reaction in the capital. The situation is volatile. You can't bring Guevara in. Bury the body in secret, away from this place. Don't confide in the Guardia or anyone else."

He turned and walked slowly back to the jeep. His deputy, Vic Korcuska, was standing by the open door, waiting with an automatic weapon in his hand.

Scott waited until the jeep had gone to cut off Guevara's head and hands, which he would bring back to Langley. . . .

"The CIA killed him after he'd been wounded and disarmed. Mutilated his body. Do you deny it?" Kathy's tone was no longer taunting, only questioning.

"No."

"And what did it accomplish? Today I have a poster with his picture on my wall and so do half the people my age."

Vivian looked into her green eyes and nodded. How could he tell her the reason he had turned the Animals lose on Che? . . . He said nothing. Kathy was sprawled across the ottoman, her jeans hugged her flat belly and long legs.

"You're a regular Tania, aren't you?" Vivian finally said.

"Who's that?" Terry asked.

"Tania was a beautiful young woman and Che's lover. She was killed when his vanguard was ambushed. What I don't think you know, Kathy, is that Tania was also a Soviet agent. You see, the KGB watched Major Guevara as closely as we did. They were very wary of a grass fire that could ignite a world war."

"Is that true?" He had surprised—and impressed—her again.

"Yes." . . .

She called him Vivian for the first time four days later. The four were gathered for a farewell dinner. Kathy and Terry were leaving early the next morning by car for Oregon and California to continue their campaign work for Eugene McCarthy. Vivian and Pat's

417

support for their Virginia neighbor Bobby Kennedy in no way dimmed their enthusiasm for what the young people were doing. It was good to be able to go to the American people in open dialogue instead . . . the Prescotts could not help reflect . . . instead of, as in their day, setting out across the cold dark water for Camp X and its school for deadly games.

At 7:05 P.M., just as Pat was proposing a toast to the Democratic party's victory in 1968, the red telephone rang. The instrument connected Vivian to the White House and to Langley. Vic Korcuska was on the line to tell the DCI that Dr. Martin Luther King, Jr., had just been shot to death in Memphis.

"I'll be right in." He hung up and stood alone in the den. In the past he would have called out to Pat and Terry, told them, then left for Langley. But now, their new almost-family member Kathy, and Terry too, would not be able to accept an announcement that Martin Luther King had been gunned down. They had met the rights leader in New York, where his support for McCarthy was critical, and they simply would not let Vivian leave for Langley, if they knew, without a scene. He did not know what he was going to do until he turned to see Pat in the doorway.

"You have to tell them," she said quietly. "You can stay in Langley all night. Who did it?"

"Yes . . . all right . . . I don't know . . ."

Vivian was not prepared for Terry's collapse. Kathy, after an outburst of heartfelt profanity, ran to turn on the television in the den. Pat went quickly up the stairs to comfort her son, Vivian walked to the den doorway to watch the coverage. CBS was cutting from Chicago to Washington, D.C. The ghettos were erupting.

"Burn it down!" Kathy said, not knowing that he was standing in the doorway behind her.

"I beg your pardon?" The look in her eyes as she turned was a mature woman's. "I said, let it burn, Vivian."

"That's what I thought you said." He nodded, turned and walked to the foot of the stairs. "I have to go, Pat."

She came down to the first landing to meet him. "Viv, he's terribly upset. He didn't even take Tim's death this way."

"Should I go up?"

"No, I don't think so. He admires you tremendously, but . . . well, I don't think he feels totally open. He's shy, you know. And

418

Kathy has him sort of organized to protest and rebel. It's good for him, as far as it goes, don't you think?"

"If it doesn't go too far . . . I have to go, I'll call you at midnight." . . .

On the Sunday, the four of them watched the huge funeral procession on television. More than two hundred thousand moving out in the grueling Georgia heat. The mule-drawn coffin leading the five miles of marching humanity from Ebenezer Baptist Church to Morehouse College. The network kept cutting to Chicago and Washington as the burning and the uprising continued across the nation, more than one hundred cities were in flames. Then back to Atlanta ". . . deep in my heart I do believe . . ."

"May I speak to you alone, please?" The low voice startled Vivian. It was Terry leaning down by his chair. Vivian called the spaniel and they walked out into the warm spring weather.

"Vivian, you know I'm not much of a talker, except in a place like New Hampshire, and my dad taught me to respect the government and I . . . well, I never asked you anything about your job, you know . . ."

"Go ahead, Terry." Maybe because Terry believed he was only his stepfather he would be able to say more, reveal more than he'd been able to with his own father. Not that Sam Prescott hadn't always tried, but Vivian had never been able to develop a vocabulary much beyond liberal platitudes with his father. Now, walking here next to him in blue cords and one of his old Yale letter sweaters, was this six-foot-three redhead. Quiet, shy, idealistic—in search of a father.

"Mom wants me to make up credits in summer school so that I can start at Yale in the fall . . . But I want to stick with the McCarthy campaign right through the election in November and then start college in the winter semester."

"Can you talk her into it?" They turned and began to walk back toward the house. The street was empty, Americans were inside watching funeral rites again.

"What do you think?"

Vivian stopped and sighed. Here was a chance to share something with his son—not on a "man to man" basis, as it was always put at Skull and Bones (Terry had made it clear that he would join no secret fraternity). He wanted to open himself to his son, and though he seemed, as he began to talk, to be sharing details of national estimates with Terry, he was really speaking his own grammar of love to his only son and offspring . . . "Well, let's try to project the next few months. In government we work with estimates, Tim—your dad was one of the best in the field. We're much better at estimates—evaluation and prediction—than we are at some of the things that you and Kathy are so upset about. So let's look at what's happening in the country and how your particular situation is affected by it. The gold outflow crises in January and February while you were in New Hampshire . . . Secretary McNamara resigning in March . . . the Tet offensive shattering the light at the end of the tunnel—the military says that our side gained a victory during Tet, the Agency has told the President that Tet was the last hurrah for the United States in Southeast Asia—next you all claim your victory in the primary, and *then* Johnson resigns, and then Dr. King is assassinated . . ." The spaniel nudged at their legs and they began to walk again, past the house . . . "Question: is there a common denominator that we can find to give us an angle from which to predict? I think so. Our National Estimates finds that it is the war in Vietnam. Now, I see you're smiling and you may wonder why it should take ten billion dollars a year and eighteen thousand employees at CIA to come up with what is perfectly obvious to any highschool student. Well, the point is that CIA is part of the same system that's prosecuting the war, so that the contradiction, when we say 'get out,' when it comes from *us,* is considered fact. When it comes from *you,* from a placard in a march, some people see it as treason. So, the war is bleeding the economy, a ruinous inflation is coming, and our international monetary credibility is going down by the numbers. The big banks and bond houses don't want their children protesting in the streets and the dollar discounted against the yen and the deutsche mark by the Swiss gnomes, and it's *they*—I hate to say it, the Establishment—that gave McNamara and Johnson their marching orders. Now, wait, I don't mean it cynically, don't pull a Kathy on me. I simply mean that we're losing the war and the administration, the government is wobbly . . . Forget all the rhetoric . . . we are *losing* this war. Not just Tet. The hawks say it's because we have one arm tied behind us, the doves say because it's immoral. That's all talk. We are simply losing."

420

Terry stopped, was looking at him seriously and, Vivian thought —hoped—with a kind of respect. "You're saying that the anti-war movement, McCarthy and—"

"Exactly. You're on the right side, not just *morally* but in terms of saving the *system*—like Roosevelt in the Depression. But . . ."

"But what?"

"Catch 22. Here's where the game or probability theory, the Estimates figure in. If black people and young people are encouraged by powerful interests to take to the streets, then power can change hands, *but* how do you turn it off? The tides start running —there's a reaction. Those who've staked their power and their credibility on the war *react.* And *they* send out signals too, and a leader like Dr. King, the symbol of the peace and the rights movement, is caught in the crossfire. The—"

Terry reached out to grip his shoulder. "Do you know who killed him?" His hazel eyes, so like Pat's, were wide. Vivian chewed his lip. How far should he, *could* he go with this youth who was growing into a man almost before his eyes. What was the good of any of it if he couldn't share something with his own son?

"You truly care, don't you, Terry?"

"Don't you?"

He had told Johnson to his face that these young people were intelligent and decent—the best part of the nation. It was the lying about the war, about everything that was driving them, the whole country into a nervous breakdown. The strong young hand was an irresistible pressure on his shoulder. On Deer Island that summer Sam Prescott had shared the threat against Roosevelt and the country with Vivian, could he do less now with his own son?

"Terry, we *think* it might be some sort of conspiracy." The words were out, his heart was racing. The boy's eyes flinched involuntarily, then returned.

"But the Attorney General said—"

"Terry, there are one hundred and sixty-eight towns and cities in flames. Washington is burning. He had to say that—"

"No. No, he didn't. God, do you think we're children?"

It was Vivian who dropped his eyes. The dog was disappearing around the corner. The break in the boy's adolescent voice was a kind of judgment, he felt, on his whole generation. "Vivian, what are *you* going to do?"

Vivian stared at the new spring grass at his feet. Someone had dropped a penny. "What do you think I should do?"

"Tell the truth. That's all."

"Terry, you know that CIA doesn't involve itself in domestic affairs. The FBI's in charge of—"

"Bullshit! Excuse me, but bullshit."

Vivian raised his eyes to Terry's level. The man of action . . . he was swept with the irony of it . . . the big hero behind the lines, the Director of Central Intelligence, of the most powerful secret force in the world, was morally checkmated by the simple question of an eighteen-year-old. Tell the truth, that was *all* that his son was asking. All that the government was being asked to tell a nation's children. And they could not do it. But somebody *had* to do it.

"Terry, you want me to find out and then do what—hold a press conference?"

"I didn't say that."

"What, then?"

"Well . . . well, first you have to find out before you know what to do next, don't you?"

"That's logical."

"Okay."

"Okay, but officially I can't—"

"Okay. *Un*officially then."

"You'd like me to go to Memphis . . ." He was thinking aloud.

"Why not? We'll go with you."

"Who's 'we'?"

"Kathy and I."

So there it was. Vivian smiled and looked up at the cloudy spring sky. Remembering London in '40 and himself and Janet, and Jack Kennedy and his father, and Kim Philby and Mush Hollander. He laughed softly and looked into Terry's puzzled eyes . . . "Let's go in now and talk about it later."

Inside, the television continued to spin out its saga. The four-mile funeral march was passing along a line of helmeted Georgia state troopers armed with machine guns. Robert Kennedy led the contingent of notables. The mourners were filling the Morehouse College quadrangle. Only 100,000 could press in to hear Dr. King's old college president deliver the last eulogy.

Vivian's eyes were like stone as the camera panned the crowds.

Terry, Kathy and Pat were all weeping silently. The camera came back to the old black professor at the microphone . . . "Too bad, you say, Martin Luther King, Jr., died so young. Jesus died at thirty-three, Joan of Arc at nineteen, Byron and Burns at thirty-six. And Martin Luther King at thirty-nine. It isn't how long but how well." Then the throng was singing the old Negro spiritual again.

By instant replay the network now began to rerun the tape of the funeral service in the hot and crowded church that had preceded the march, the camera roving from the Kennedys to Hubert Humphrey to Richard Nixon to the chairman of the Black Panthers. All of them wet with perspiration, listening to a tape recording of Dr. King's last sermon, as requested by his wife, the booming passion overwhelming them all, and the millions watching at home:

"If any of you are around when I have met my day, I don't want a long funeral. Tell them not to mention that I have a Nobel Peace Prize. That isn't important. I'd like somebody to mention that Martin Luther King Junior tried to *love* somebody. That I *did* try to feed the hungry, that I *did* try in my life to clothe those who were naked . . ."

Terry and Kathy were sobbing in each other's arms. Pat sat on the floor, bowed, silent, covering her face with her hands. Vivian stared out the picture window at the high clouds, praying, "In the name of Christ, don't let there be a conspiracy."

He didn't expect his prayer to be answered. . . .

In Memphis at the Holiday Inn—Rivermont—they ate their dinner in Vivian's suite. Terry and Kathy had been as quiet as schoolchildren since their flight from Dulles that afternoon. They were in awe of traveling with Vivian in his official capacity of DCI.

They had not been able to leave until three days after the funeral. Sixteen thousand troops had been required to restore order in the nation's capital, and Vivian had been on emergency standby at Langley. As DCI his estimate of foreign reaction to the murder of Dr. King, and its fiery aftermath, had been blunt and simple. When Bill Moyers had called, asking for "input for the President's course of action," Vivian had told him coldly, "Tell the President that the official estimate of Central Intelligence is, quote, Instruct all troops not, repeat *not*, to shoot to kill. Trade goods and appliances for human lives. Bad European reaction to the assassination and related violence. Neutral and Communist bloc countries are reaping propaganda harvest based on conspiracy rumors, close quotes."

Vivian now pushed his steak away. Terry and Kathy picked at the hotel fare and watched him. They didn't know just how but he did seem different. He had not removed his jacket or tie. The coffee was cold and he pushed that away too. When he spoke his voice was resonant and much lower than at home in Virginia.

"A man will be here in a few minutes. I will introduce him to you as Jack Armstrong." Kathy smiled for the first time that day. "Not exactly the all-American boy. He will give me a report and leave. I will not introduce you to him. It would be best if you didn't say anything. He'll go and we can talk. That's all."

Vivian got up, switched on the TV news and pushed the table and uneaten food out into the corridor, then they all stood around the set watching the coverage of the Kennedy campaign, which had resumed after the days of mourning. They were struck by a new and stinging intensity as Bobby Kennedy threw caution to the winds in Indiana. He stood in his shirtsleeves on the red leather backseat of a convertible, his voice hoarse and embattled . . . "If our colleges and universities do not breed men who riot, who rebel, who attack life with all the youthful vision and vigor, then there is something wrong with our colleges. The more riots that come on college campuses, the better the world of tomorrow. I am concerned that at the end of it all, there will only be more Americans killed. More of our treasure spilled out . . . so that they may say, as Tacitus said of Rome: 'They made a desert and called it peace.' I don't think that is satisfactory for the United States of America. I am willing to bear my share of the responsibility, before history and before my fellow citizens. But past error is no excuse for its own perpetuation. Tragedy is a tool for the living to gain wisdom, not a guide by which to live. Now, as ever, we do ourselves best justice when we measure ourselves against ancient tests, as in the *Antigone* of Sophocles: 'All men make mistakes, but a good man yields when he knows his course is wrong, and repairs the evil. The only sin is pride' . . ."

They continued to stare at the screen as the commercial came on—a sharp rap on the door cut through the announcer's words. Vivian punched the "off" button and motioned for them to sit, then disappeared momentarily into the small entrance area. Out

424

of their line of vision they could hear him say, "Hello, Jack," and then something else too low to make out.

The man who accompanied Vivian into the room looked to be in his late forties. He was well-dressed, in the southwestern style —low highly polished boots, string tie, Neiman-Marcus wash-and-wear suit.

"Jack, these are some friends of mine. This is Mr. Armstrong." The man nodded and sat. Terry was surprised that Vivian, always so polite, did not offer to send down for coffee or a drink for the visitor.

Armstrong was built like a good light heavyweight. He had thinning blond hair, slicked-down, his features angular, his fair skin sunburned. There was a soft Texan twang in his voice. He began talking directly to Vivian, without preamble—the two young people could have been pieces of furniture.

"Fifty thousand dollar contract run through the New South Industrial Conference. Security was stripped two hours before the hit. The MPD was penetrated at the top. Police radio was jammed. The riot on the twenty-eighth was started by APs. The order to move him to the motel came from the SOG." He spun the combination lock and fished a manila folder out of his shiny black attaché case, handed it over to Vivian as he stood up. Without looking at the young people he followed Vivian out of their sight to the suite door. They could hear the two men say something in lowered voices, then the door slammed and Vivian reappeared, already skimming through the thin folder. He sat and continued to read for a minute, then looked up at the two faces, filled with questions. "All right. I'll trust you. Why not? It's time. I'll try to translate. Our informant tells us that there was fifty thousand dollars offered to kill Dr. King by an ultra-conservative, deep south business group. The top of the Memphis Police Department may be involved. Dr. King was in Memphis on the day of his death because a sanitation workers' strike march on March twenty-eighth erupted into violence. But this violence, we're told, was caused by agents provocateurs posing as black militants in leather jackets. Then a series of leaks to the press was ordered by Mr. Hoover himself from the SOG—the Seat of Government, as he likes to call the Bureau headquarters in Washington. The FBI and the usual Memphis

425

surveillance of Dr. King were called off two hours before the murder. That's it so far."

They sat staring at him, shaking their heads. Kathy spoke first. "Who is 'Jack Armstrong'?"

"Jack Armstrong, the all-American spy, is a contract agent of ours whose job was to watch Dr. King and his entourage in case of violence."

"To spy on him?" Her voice had returned to its normal irreverence.

"No, Kathy. So that he could do just what he did today."

No one thought to turn on a light.

"But what did he *say?* Who did it?" Terry asked.

Vivian was struck by how much younger Terry seemed than Kathy. "Terry, we don't know that yet."

"The Memphis police did it." Kathy was looking straight at him. He wanted to say to her that political murders were not crimes of passion; not done out of hate, but for *power.* Then he thought, what if she asks me about the hate generated in the drive for power . . . ?

"We don't know that, Kathy. Let's not get paranoid." The DCI tried not to sound like her father. . . .

He waited with them at the airport until their Los Angeles flight left. They had decided against taking the time to drive to Oregon to catch up with the McCarthy campaign advance team. The fiery enthusiasm of New Hampshire had now become a steely resolve.

"Good luck," he said as their flight was called, and promised a long talk after the California primary. "Thanks, Vivian," Terry said softly, and Vivian felt a rush of tenderness, wanting to hug his son rather than just shake his hand. As he turned to embrace Kathy, his lips touched hers. Was it his imagination that hers lingered for a split second before she ran off to board?

He walked across the Delta concourse to the terminal bar. His agent, "Armstrong," was sitting in a corner booth with his back to the wall. Vivian sat and ordered a vodka martini on the rocks. He was drained, had been for a week. "What happened, Bill?"

"They used a mixed black-and-white team. I told you a year ago it was coming, didn't I? After they sent him the letter telling him to kill himself they upped the stakes. They hired a black actor that looked a little like King and two white whores and they shot a little bullshit film in a warehouse in Tampa. Put curtains in front of the camera so that it would look like it was hand held outside a motel window. Then they took the film and started peddling it around the country, to the media and anyone else they could interest. That didn't work and King found out about it. Then their informers found out that he was going to take a half hour on national TV and say, 'I'm a human being, I like women, what's that got to do with the civil rights movement?' Something like that. So that's all she wrote. They set him up on the twenty-eighth, then maneuvered him into that shooting gallery, the Lorraine, and stripped the security. They've got some ex-con they've been moving around that they'll pin it on. But I don't think they'll ever catch him. He's going out on a red carpet . . . signed, sealed and delivered."

"Bill . . . this New South Industrial Conference, the money . . . is it the FBI all the way?"

"All the way."

"DELTA AIRLINES FLIGHT 152 FOR CHICAGO AND WASHINGTON NOW BOARDING AT GATE 15A. ALL ABOARD PLEASE." . . .

On the night five weeks later that Senator Robert Kennedy was assassinated in Los Angeles Terry called home to talk to his mother at 1:30 in the morning. Vivian was on the red phone to Vic Korcuska, ordering an 8:00 A.M. extraordinary meeting at Langley. He rang off and turned the TV back on and started water boiling for tea. Pat joined him.

"He's taking it differently than when Dr. King . . . Viv, what's happening to this country? Did you see the TV? People are going crazy. Terry says he and Kathy are going over to the Kennedy headquarters to help if they can. Then they're going on to Chicago to organize for the convention, for McCarthy . . . he sends his regards to you . . . Viv, what's . . . is there a connection between . . . ?"

"Jack and Martin Luther King and Bobby? . . . I don't know. I'm going in to the office in a couple of hours. I'll—"

"You don't know what's happening either, do you? There aren't any reliable *estimates* for tragedy, are there?" The telephone rang, it was Sam Prescott calling from New York. "Hello, dad. How are you? No, Viv's right here. I don't think so. Hold on . . . he's upset, wants to know what's happening to this country . . . talk to him, Viv. See if you can tell him."

In the bedroom the picture tube sent image after image of disorder and shock, like a radioactive pile, or a bomb, and all the commentators were asking, "What is happening to America?" And not a damn one had the ghost of an answer. . . .

The electronic clock clicked to 10:11 P.M. In less than two hours there would be a tiny click and the date would change to November 23, 1970. The DCI, without seeing it, held the photograph of his son in front of him. He could have been suspended in fluid at body temperature, deprived of all sensory feedback . . . a victim of one of the Agency's psychological warfare experiments. The pressure of his fingers on the cool metal frame of the photograph of Terry was the only existential proof Vivian had that he was actually there.

He thought of his enemies somewhere in the complex, and the wormwood of that burning trace of memory made his body flow to life again and know that *it,* the secret infrastructure, was there in the dark too—as real as the photographs in the shadows, as the past. When he thought of, remembered his enemies, then he knew that he existed. He was defined, now, by them. He had ceased to exist once before, way back after Janet's murder . . . His memory turned back, down another path, to New Haven. What were Professor Mann's words . . . ? "In the political realm hostility becomes spiritual. The new state needs enemies more than friends; in opposition alone does it feel itself necessary, only in opposition does it *become* necessary. And it is the same for the internal enemy . . ."

The need for revenge was like the craving for a narcotic. Vivian felt for the tape recorder in the dark. His mind scurried away from the photograph in his hand, and in his memory, of his son. Onto the field of his mind came the contending vanguards of Yankees and Bonesmen, princes and pretenders. All of them looked so much like each other . . . the Prescotts, Kennedys, Helmses, Scotts, Barneses, Angletons—all of them "cousins" like the murderous clans that contended against each other on the flat earth of *Macbeth.* In his mind's eye he had to keep them facing each other . . . that way they could not mask their true intentions under a familiar face.

He pushed the "on" button. "Operation Gemstone: Tape five, side one. The use of the Central Intelligence Agency by the Committee to Reelect the President . . .". . . .

The Director had reviewed his situation, "put his ducks in a row," as Philby used to say. Since Nixon's election in '68, the most out-of-control of the Animals had begun to migrate to the newly formed Committee to Reelect the President in 1972. CREEP had been set up with a skeleton staff under Sherman Scott even before the inauguration in January of '69. Scott, in turn, set up a cover in a public relations firm, the Blanton Company, down Pennsylvania Avenue from the White House. Blanton's only client, the only one they needed, was the Howard Hughes Organization. Scott had hired Agency castoffs and rogues as fast as Vivian could purge them. Scott, of course, had resigned after a face-saving interval in late '66. From then on he had worked openly for Nixon, seeding his "10/2" boys throughout the campaign. Since '68, Scott's army of mercenaries had been building a paramilitary machine unlike anything seen before in presidential politics; even the tight Kennedy clan was nothing beside it.

Vivian had been right behind his enemy's well-tailored jacket, walking in the wake of the aroma of Latakia Number One, as Scott observed his brogans being polished. The DCI's men were watching too. Vivian knew too much that was stewing under the well-barbered, dyed blond hair, and he didn't like it . . . Scott had established a school for spies at Blanton, and the Nixon legions came to him and his iron guard as if to train for a *putsch* in 1972 rather than an election. Haldeman, Erlichman and the California Old Boy group were already setting up an agent network on the West Coast. Under Scott and E. Howard Hunt's tutelage Charles "Tex" Colson was enlisting an extended East coast squad of ex-police and private detectives. Nixon's boyish-looking lawyer, John Dean, had a posse of Arrow-collar killers running legal and public relations interference for Colson's and Scott's strong-arms.

Why? It had to be for more than an election. The only possible challenge to a Nixon reelection was Ted Kennedy, and Chappaquiddick had put an end to that . . . Always the Kennedys, Vivian thought, as he spun his chair toward the window to look out over his secret kingdom in the woods . . . And how had Hunt and his spooks known to be at Edgartown *before* the death by drowning of Mary Jo Kopechne? Before! That, Vivian had discovered when his own investigation turned the spooks up after the incident scavenging for damaging statements among the islanders. Of course one of Scott's obligatory ops was to follow Ted Kennedy everywhere as part of a "sexpionage" master plan, a ridiculous buzz word invented by himself. Vivian was satisfied that Ted Kennedy really couldn't remember what had happened that night after he had parked the car in the bushes. Anyway, there would be no Kennedy candidacy, now until 1976 at the earliest, so . . . *why* the paramilitary buildup for a '72 campaign whose only slogan could be "Four More Years." *Four,* not *forty*. And still they were after Kennedy's wife Joan, who had a drinking problem; Scott had schemed so as to addict by heroin one of the secretaries from the Chappaquiddick party. Why? Why the continuing blind fear and hatred of the Kennedys when Nixon himself was busy with secret big power deals that went well beyond anything Jack Kennedy could have proposed in '64 or '65, if they *had* let him live. So what were these Nixon people so afraid of? If, indeed, they were afraid at all. Not bloody likely . . .

Vivian hated to admit it, but he knew that it wasn't really Nixon himself who was spearheading a secret takeover of the country. He began to speak into the still-turning tape, enunciating carefully, striving to make credible what he knew or believed was true . . . "Paramount to any clandestine operation is the chain of command and the compartmentalization, as it is called . . ." he knew he sounded didactic, stiff, but it was the only way he could manage this now . . . "In Gemstone, the President's Special Counsel Charles W. 'Tex' Colson plays the role of a station chief in foreign intelligence work. His job is to oversee the spymasters, who in turn control and run the secret agents. Colson's operations chief is F. Sherman Scott of CIA. I believe John Mitchell and the two presidential assistants, Robert Haldeman and John Ehrlichman, are equivalent to diplomatic heads of an American mission. Together with their secret force, headed, it appears, by Assistant Attorney General Robert Mardian, they are to handle the cover-up to the operations, as well as the undermining of the Justice Department, the FBI, the CIA.

"As of November 1970, there are basically three covert operations. One is under the aegis of Haldeman's 'November group' and will be called political propaganda/espionage. This group's field controls are former New York City policemen John Caulfield and Anthony J. Ulasewicz on the east coast and a Donald Segretti on the west coast. A second team of amateur political agents work out

of the Committee to Reelect the President, appropriately designated CREEP. It was these young middle-level bureaucrats who
began to panic when Nixon slipped behind Edmund Muskie and
George Wallace in some of the early 1970 polls. The third operation is the Colson-Scott attack group or black advance. This includes, I believe, the Hunt network, the Gemstone axis of the
conspiracy. This paramilitary, unofficial Gemstone net not only
controls the other political efforts of the presidential campaign but
seems to have penetrated and is beginning to use and compromise
the FBI, CIA, Treasury, Office of Economic Opportunity, Internal
Revenue Service, Department of Justice, Bureau of Narcotics and
Dangerous Drugs and perhaps a dozen other federal agencies, plus
local squads set up across the country. Such appears to be the
magnitude of Operation Gemstone.

"Colson and Scott, as special counsels, are supposedly liaison
between the White House and various sympathetic political group-
ings. Covertly, they are liaisons *to* the White House *from* the secret
network with primary responsibility for Operation Gemstone.
Their plan is:

"1. Prepare to reelect the President. Eliminate Wallace. Isolate
the left.

"2. Seize the government. Disrupt the GOP convention. Blame
the left *and* the center. Declare a state of national emergency. Rule
with Nixon, or without him.

"3. Cover up. Eliminate anyone who could 'talk.' Scott is an
expert.

"4. Build a new mass base. Use American Bicentennial celebration to drown dissent in patriotism.

"Ever since his days in the wartime Office of Strategic Services,
through two decades in the CIA, Scott has been known as an
assassin. Scott's aides include former CIA sharpshooters who have
figured in a number of known assassination plots, including the
one that killed John F. Kennedy. Gordon Liddy, James McCord,
Bernard Barker and their squad of Cuban exiles all bring particular
skills to the Scott team, but they are all specialists, paramilitary
professionals, who I believe will inexorably gain a stranglehold
over their "civilian" superiors. Richard Nixon and John Mitchell
will protest that they never intended Gemstone to go so far. By
then it will be very late. Put another way, Haldeman, Ehrlichman

and the political "November Group" are being taken over by Scott's "Attack Group" and its paramilitary arm, Operation Gemstone.

"Richard Nixon set the tone. He appeared in Burlington, Vermont, early in the 1970 congressional elections, and as Air Force One taxied in officials allowed a group of protestors onto the landing strip. One of the protestors threw a single stone about the size of a fifty-cent piece, which landed approximately eighty feet from the President. Striding ahead, Charles Colson picked up the stone and turned to Mr. Nixon. 'These rocks will mean ten thousand votes,' he said. Such is the executive mentality of America's leaders . . ."

Vivian came to a stop. He strained to hear the silence, tried to catch the eyes of those in the photographs . . . Behind his closed eyes the Yale-Harvard tennis championship match of more than 30 years ago unwound in the rich sunshine of his remembering . . . the sky above Cambridge was high and blue, he was arching and twisting in mid-air, and in the bleachers Jack Kennedy and Janet Hammersmith rose to applaud . . .

The Director started. The tape had been turning for minutes in the silence. He had lost his place again. Where was he? . . . Terry, no. Bobby, yes, 1968 . . .

He wheeled past the guard gate. The cool morning dew glistened from the surrounding woods. The vast parking areas were empty. He went in "black," still hearing the bird song as the tunnel closed around him, the song cueing the images of the Kennedy brothers to life—condemned to live on in his mind, shock-haired, running, swimming, climbing, screwing. He hunched his shoulders as he hurried down the secret entrance corridor, as if he half expected a bullet in the back.

But *why?* This fresh bloodletting in Los Angeles had made the question urgent.

Vic Korcuska and two aides from Security were electronically sweeping the DCI conference room when the Director arrived a few minutes after 6:00 A.M. With all his wiry intensity, Korcuska pursued the dead mouse, the bug, the KGB device that must one day be found, but never had, at Langley. What Vivian and his deputy *had* found—three times since his appointment in 1964— was a listening device that had been implanted by his historic

432

rivals. "Mother" Angleton, Helms, Sherman Scott and their super-grade legions only wanted the bugs, when discovered, to signify to the DCI that the hawks and their hosts in the Agency were out there, waiting . . .

Korcuska, the Director's "prole" or "slav" as the Old Boys sneeringly referred to him, had a cup of English tea sitting at the head of the long oak conference table. At every place the tireless aide had placed a summary from the scene in Los Angeles. Vivian scanned the thin abstract of violence: ". . . single assassin apprehended . . . six others wounded . . . senator removed to . . ." He looked up, Korcuska was standing over him.

"He's dead. They're going to announce it in the morning. Our asset with Life magazine says the suspect is a Palestinian Arab named Sirhan Vishara, or Bishara Sirhan. We're running him now."

Vivian led the way toward the DCI Situation Room at the fork of the executive corridor. Sleepy-eyed men with guns strapped under their summer suits were already circulating in the outer offices, in the corridor and around the elevators.

The clerks in the map-lined military situation room stepped away from the racing teletypes to let the Director read the copy as it came off the electronic keys. The clocks reflecting the major time zones of the world looked down on the taut body of the Director as he bent over the billowing paper of the printouts. The pulsing hum of the electric oracles was the only sound in the room. Vivian held the edges of the unfolding copy in his tapered fingers as he scanned up and down, back and forth. No wire service in the world ever scooped CONDUIT, the Agency's own telex.

SSSSSSSSSS
. . . repeat, three through and through gun shot wounds back to front . . . six others wounded by suspect front to back . . . fatal shot point blank behind right ear . . . HSQWV fatal bullet was a special long rifle .22 slug, repeat . . .
+ * % % % VVVVVVVVVV
. . . suspect under influence of controlled substance . . . unidentified controlled substance . . . six one hundred dollar bills found on suspect . . . several numbers follow . . . QQQQVVVVV G-MFLLLLL . . . several numbers follow . . .

ten, repeat ten rounds accounted for . . . suspects weapon
Iver-Johnson model 55SA capable of only eight, repeat, eight,
repeat, eight, repeat, eight rounds . . .
                    RSSSSSSSSSSSSSSSSSSSS
. . . serial number of suspects weapon follows . . . more, more,
more, more, more, more

. . . source says that columnist Jack Anderson will release state-
ment of Senator Kennedy to New Orleans District Attorney Jim
Garrison . . . quote, there are guns between me and the White
House, close quotes . . .

   A half hour later in the conference room the directors and their
deputies sat smoking and waiting for the appearance of the DCI:
Morgan, from the Directorate of Intelligence, Bones '39, Vivian's
sports editor on the old Yale *Daily*, a friend; Lafitte, from the
Directorate of Science and Technology, OSS, Camp X, a friend;
Lee, of the Directorate of Management and Services, Wolf's Head,
Yale '38, a timeserver, a question mark; Duff Douglass and James
Jesus Angleton, Bones '39, from the Directorate of Plans, the
spook chiefs of the Clandestine Services, fronting for Dick Helms
and Sherman Scott—enemies so powerful as to offset the friends
of the DCI.
   The clock crawled to 8:00 A.M. Angleton and Douglass had their
heads together in the cloud of smoke erupting from Angleton's
chain of Pall Malls. Cigarette ash sprayed in a penumbra about the
Chief of Counterintelligence's patrician head.
   The Director entered on the stroke with Vic Korcuska at his heel.
   "Gentlemen, Mr. Korcuska is distributing an update to the
agenda. I have just spoken to President Johnson and I think it
would be well if we first discussed the party line."
   Angleton barked a cigarette laugh and showered Douglass with
ash. Douglass's heavy body fought for air.
   In the gray smoke, it seemed to Vivian, Mother's long gray face
seemed to fade in and out of sight like Banquo's ghost. Mother was
all gray, dressed in gray, only his fingers, yellow from nicotine,
were starkly visible. Once, thirty years ago at Yale, he had been a
most handsome fellow, when they were fellow spooks in Bones
. . . "The FBI has determined that the rumors of foreign or Arab

434

involvement with the assassin are unfounded. The assassin, acting alone, was a malcontent with a Palestinian heritage of hatred toward friends of Israel . . ."

Down the table a match exploded in the poet-hands of Jim Angleton as he tried to light his twentieth cigarette since his breakfast of orange juice and scotch two hours earlier. The burning sulphur sizzled past Douglass like a flame-tipped arrow and buried itself in Conrad J. Lee III's soft white thatch. The smell of the singed hair spread out along the table. Connie Lee ducked as if he expected a second and more deadly missile to follow instantaneously.

Vivian allowed himself a smile from the nose down at Angleton. Mother, as head of the Israeli desk as well as Counterintelligence, had been surgically removed from the fiat to take over that Sirhan's Arab connection had promised until that very moment. All the other chiefs smiled knowingly back at the Director.

"Our elite media assets are to be instructed that the U. S. government views this as one single fanatic's act, taken on his own, unconnected to any other . . ."

Pat had watched the funeral on television alone. As she sat in front of the set, she kept trying to get through to Berkeley, where Terry and Kathy had gone to stay with other young people until the presidential campaigning began again after the week of suspension for mourning.

The NBC camera panned the dark vault of St. Patrick's. There were the heads once again: Johnson, Nixon, Humphrey, McCarthy, Goldwater, Rusk, Harriman, Sam Prescott and, for an instant, she was sure she had spotted Vivian's long, pale profile. Then the remainder of the Kennedy family. Rose, the matriarch, in black, and all the children in white. From the pulpit high up in the nave the youngest and last surviving son, Edward, struggled to speak the last words.

". . . Those who loved him and take him to his rest today pray that what he was to us, and what he wished for others, will some day come to pass for all the world. As he said many times, in many parts of this nation, to those he touched and who sought to touch him: 'Some men see things as they are and say why. I dream things that never were and say why not.' "

The mourners flowed out of the magnificent church to merge with the thousands waiting in the streets. Andy Williams's voice carried the "Battle Hymn of the Republic" out to the grieving throng. The crowds picked up the old anthem and echoed it as the hearse moved onto the train bound for Washington. Vivian would be heading for the Washington shuttle. He would not see the thousands of Americans all along the line of the lonesome train that, like Lincoln's, cut through the heart of the nation.

The train chugged slowly down the miles and ranks of pale and frightened faces. Suddenly an unfamiliar visage was superimposed on the screen over the pathetic scene, and an announcer's voice cut in to state that the "Director of the FBI, J. Edgar Hoover, has just announced in Washington that James Earl Ray, the fugitive sought in the assassination of Dr. Martin Luther King, Jr., has been apprehended at London's Heathrow Airport. We repeat . . ."

Pat swore aloud, thinking of Hoover, who had obviously timed his announcement to upstage the rites for Robert Kennedy, whom he hated. Pat's redheaded temper was further stirred by her knowledge that by this time the FBI undoubtedly had one of its KA (Key Activist) COINTELPRO files opened on her own son. Working for Gene McCarthy was definitely subversive, as far as J. Edgar and his aging coven were concerned. And Kathy too would now be listed in the freeze-dried files as a target for COINTELPRO, the Bureau's counterintelligence program, the successor to that old favorite—COMINFIL. Inevitably, her son would also be listed in the Bureau's RABBLE ROUSER INDEX . . . "It rouses *me*," she had snapped to Vivian when he told her about it. "I come from a long line of rabble, Irish on both sides . . ."

"Oh, the miserable s.o.b.," she crooned as Hoover's face hung suspended over the anguished people massed along the railroad tracks. She tried dialing Berkeley again. Somehow, as long as Terry and Kathy were together she did not feel quite as concerned about him going to Chicago for the Democratic party's national convention. She knew the Windy City and its finest too well to do anything but hope that McCarthy would quit before August. But then, she worried, the two young people might join the campsite known as "Resurrection City," the shantytown in the center of official Washington that had been planned by Martin Luther King as the arena for nonviolent struggle in his Poor People's Campaign.

When Vivian returned after nightfall she was still sitting there watching. The TV cameras were now following the caravan along the lamp-lit streets and the walls of sad, frightened faces through the city, across the Potomac to the Virginia side and Arlington. It was eleven o'clock. Vivian knelt down beside her just as the candle-lit procession passed the eternal flame marking the grave of John Kennedy. At Arlington the moonlight filtered down on the family, the friends and the rest as Vivian asked softly, "Have you heard from the kids?" . . .

The summer, the waiting for Chicago, stretched out flat and drear. Dr. Spock and certain of America's clergy were indicted for counseling draft resistance. Terry called from Berkeley in late July to announce that he had burned his draft card. American casualties in Vietnam were now in the hundreds of thousands and student radicals were mobilizing to confront the Democratic convention in Chicago. The night before leaving to organize in Chicago, Terry and Kathy called. Terry did not say much to Vivian except that he could not make his arrangements to attend Yale in the fall "until I find out if the system really works in Chicago."

When Kathy came on, Vivian said, "Kathy, don't either of you overplay your hand in Chicago. I want to tell you that there is an army of undercover agents waiting for all of you there. Military Intelligence, police, so-called Red Squads, FBI—"

"CIA?" she asked.

He wondered if Terry was listening on an extension. His answer stopped her. The wire hummed. "Yes. So be careful."

Finally . . . "In that case, we'll be sure to carry pictures of you posing with the President." . . .

In August, hell broke loose in Chicago. On the first day of the convention both Terry and Kathy were roughed up when patrol-men blundered into the Hilton Hotel's fifteenth floor McCarthy headquarters to roust them and their colleagues.

Vivian was made aware by Vic Korcuska that Helms's and Sherman Scott's moles in Plans were running an illegal DOD operation under Montgomery Ward cover during the convention. Their further cover was the Agency's Operation CHAOS, set up to infiltrate the peace movement in order to determine whether or not any Moscow gold was swelling the coffers of Another Mother for Peace or Clergy and Laymen Concerned. Predictably, somewhere along the way, Mother's and Scott's Animals had taken over, and legal intelligence gathering aimed at foreign sources had been transformed, by Scott's clandestine alchemy, into provocation against domestic, First Amendment-protected political activity inside the Democratic party.

Now, Vivian and Pat watched their set as the police began to beat newsmen as well as long-haired protestors. Inside the convention, Vivian actually caught a glimpse of his father in the New York delegation.

The site of the convention, the International Amphitheater, was ringed by a seven-foot, barbed-wire-topped chain-link fence. Armed National Guard and troopers were everywhere. The networks, angered at the apparent hostility of Mayor Daley's people, were busy cutting from the Soviet occupation of Prague to the police-state scenario unfolding in Chicago. Pat and Vivian watched. They knew Chicago and they knew Prague. And the similarity at this particular moment terrified them.

Vivian flew out to Chicago on the eve of the debate over the wording of the Vietnam plank in the Democratic party platform. The police were out of hand, beating and gassing. The war plank was McCarthy's last hope to split the convention. The bosses of the Democratic machine ordered the police to disrupt the building demonstrations that were demanding an end to the Vietnam bombing and gaining momentum almost by the hour. "The whole world is watching!" they chanted, and the networks carried the scenes of demonstration to the delegates being pushed around inside the convention hall. The coverage truly pictured the situation as getting out of hand. Vivian was debating calling an emergency meeting at Langley when Kathy called from Michael Reese Hospital on Chicago's South Side to report that Terry and Sam Prescott had been both maced and gassed on the street in front of the hotel housing the heavily pro-peace New York delegation. Terry was recovering, but the elder Prescott was in an oxygen tent. Kathy ended, weeping bitterly. Vivian cut her off—"I'll meet you in the visitors' lounge sometime before midnight." He felt sick. . . .

The smell of riot gas hung acrid in the August night. A wind off the lake had dispersed the suffocating substance south so that as Vivian got out of his Checker cab in the hospital driveway he inhaled the noxious smells of the turmoil. As he hurried in under the canopy he remembered Mush Hollander saying, in some long forgotten connection, that he had been born at Michael Reese on

438

April Fool's Day. Mush, he thought, Mush would have known what to say about these Chicago police . . . Vivian had flown out of Baltimore without contacting any of the Agency assets in the Chicago PD. He was, he hoped as he approached the crowded information desk, still capable in his own country of looking after the interests of his own father and son.

The New York delegation had secured a private room for Sam Prescott. When Vivian tiptoed in, it was dark. He at once heard his father's labored breathing, but the oxygen tent had been taken away. He made out a figure asleep in a chair next to the window. As he turned to go and look for the floor nurse, Kathy stirred. "Vivian?" her voice was hoarse, flat.

He looked closely at her as she joined him in the corridor. "Kathy, are *you* all right?" Her jeans and thin short-sleeved sweater were frayed and dirty, her honey-colored hair mussed and tangled. Her face was drawn, pale with slashes of sunburn on her high cheekbones and across her wide forehead.

"Your father's condition is improved. Here's the doctor's number—no, that's something else—here it is. Dr. Lerman. He said that you can call no matter how late."

Her green eyes were washed out by the late night illumination of the hospital corridor. Any moment a nurse was bound to discover and protest their presence. He noticed a bruise on her forehead at the hairline. "Where's Terry?" he asked as the tall floor nurse approached. "Later," she whispered, and slipped back into the room to get her bulging leather tote bag. . . .

It was almost two in the morning before the taxi delivered them to the windswept entrance of the elegant Drake Hotel. Even miles north of downtown there were contingents of police and Guard in evidence. The tall, distinguished-looking man in the lightweight blue suit of expensive London cut and the willowy young woman in torn jeans immediately excited the close-eyed stare of two rumpled plainclothesmen standing flat-footed and protective in front of the revolving door. One sniggered something out of the side of his mouth to his partner, who coughed and spat near Kathy's foot. Vivian, leaning in to tip the driver, was fairly certain that he had overheard the word "pickup" pass between the detectives.

"Let's see some I.D."

Vivian was tired; the faint fumes of the gas irritated his nose and throat; the wind had turned hot; the doctor had been gloomy about his father's general condition; his son, he had just been told, was somewhere outside the city sitting in on an all-night meeting of a radical political contingent; the two policemen were looking at Kathy as if she were a hippy-creep who had picked up an effete New Yorker and had brought him to one of the country's most exclusive hotels to take dope and commit God knew *what* acts of sexual outrage. His voice in reply was high New England.

"I beg your pardon, officer."

"She's under age. Have to show I.D."

"She's with me. We're stopping here—"

"You ain't 'stopping' here, mister. This is the Drake Towers. You don't get in here without a reservation." Both men were in their early forties and both were muscle gone to fat.

Vivian shifted the duffelbag to his left hand. "Please don't concern yourselves about our accommodations." The hot wind seemed to sprinkle his cool words in their faces.

"Let's go, let's see the I.D."

Vivian took note of their large hands—two good and loyal sons of Chicago's working class committed to the sanctity of gangsters' and machine politicians' mistresses stowed away in the Drake. Mush would probably have called it "the ultimate debauchery of the proletariat."

"Something funny, mister?"

"Perhaps . . . I think I had better ask you gentlemen to see *your* I.D. first. I mean, with all these dangerous Yippies in town you could be *anybody,* couldn't you?"

The detectives made sure that Vivian saw their bulging police special holsters with the .357 magnums as they felt around for their wallets.

"Well, Mr. Kercelik and Mr. O'Bannion, it appears that you are the real thing. Now you say that—"

"Okay, let's take her in." They moved on Kathy, pushing hard past Vivian.

He shifted to a new tone of voice. "I suggest you take a look at my I.D. first. Now."

They stopped, unsure of the conflicting signals. Could this guy be a big shot? Vivian's card said DEPARTMENT OF STATE in impressive black official lettering.

440

"Yeah, so what?" A hundred-dollar-a-night whore and a beefy faced man in a woven Palm Beach hat brushed past them; the officers faintly nodded and touched at where the bills of their caps would have been, then crowded against Vivian and Kathy again.

"Gentlemen, if you will step into the lobby, I will put a man on the telephone to you, a man very close to the mayor." The invocation of Mayor Daley had its effect. Vivian plunged into the slight hesitation, pushed the revolving door, and was inside the dimly lit lobby. Kathy stood outside, along with the two representatives of the Internal Security Section of the C.P.D. They stood like that, looking at each other through the heavy waves of glass. The policemen made the choice that Vivian had gambled on, they followed him in. He would either win or lose in a matter of seconds. He stood at the cusp of the rubber-tipped revolving door. As the two men pushed in to their respective revolving compartments, Vivian hit the nearest door edge with the hard heel of his hand, which caused the rate of revolution to increase sufficiently to throw the two detectives slightly off balance. As Kercelik appeared a split second later he was defenseless before the same straight-armed heel, now going into his jaw. Vivian's arm shot back again like a piston, then forward to heel O'Bannion's face into the heavy glass.

Three times in two seconds he had moved his arm and hand into the door and the faces of the two men. As the lurching dead weight of them slammed the doors around, Vivian leaped in to be spun out into the entranceway, ordering Kathy to "get inside" as he rushed the disoriented detectives into the marble siding of the opening.

Not ten seconds had elapsed since the revolving door had first moved. Vivian drove in low and fast with angled chops low down on the groin, both men doubling over. With a hand on each man's throat, he slammed their backs against the marble, their heads cracking.

"She's my daughter. I'm an official of the United States Government." Crack went the heads again. "If I ever see your faces again I'll give you to the Justice Department for prosecution of civil rights violations." He stepped back until he could slip into the revolving door.

Inside, he took Kathy's arm and headed for the elevator and the suite that Central Intelligence maintained at the Drake. In the elevator she stared at him and shook her head. His breathing was returning to normal as he stared at the lighted buttons on the wall.

In the suite she asked him, "Couldn't you have explained who you were to them? I mean, my God . . ." He half-smiled at her. Why had he done it? There was the chance that they would call out to one of the cruising green-and-blue police vehicles. Had he been trying to prove something to this young woman standing there now, smudged and worn, asking him why he had played soldier with those two men? "You better take a bath," he said.

"How original." She laughed but went off into the luxurious bathroom.

Was it the gas in the air, the armed camp of the streets, the building impact of the whole assassination summer? *Something* was triggering him toward war again . . .

She emerged twenty minutes later, wrapped in a batiste robe that Vivian kept in the suite. "Are you hungry?" he said, looking at her now glistening hair as she continued to towel.

"I've got some fruit in my sack. I'm just on fruit and vegetables anyway."

"You are? You're not in the clutches of that dangerous dietitian Dick Gregory, are you?"

"Did you see the march he led last night? He's a great man."

"I saw it on TV . . . So you think Terry'll be in touch with the McCarthy headquarters tomorrow?"

"Well, Vivian, unless they start machinegunning people. Who knows what's going to happen?" He took the proffered orange. Her green eyes were circled with fatigue, but she kept talking. "You know your son—"

"My stepson."

"Your *stepson* . . . God, you're so uptight . . . well, Terry was panicked when your father fell down . . . McCarthy doesn't have a chance against the machine, does he . . . ?"

"Kathy, how is it that you didn't go with Terry to the meeting?" He loosened his tie and reached for a tissue to wipe the orange juice from his fingers.

"Oh, I really don't agree with the tactics they're going to discuss. I don't believe in force, that's all."

"What tactics?"

"Oh, I don't know. Fighting back against the police."

"Terry's talking about fighting the *police?*"

"I said *they.* He just went to observe . . . I think."

"God, Kathy, that meeting tonight is bound to be infiltrated. There're going to be indictments coming out of this. Violence would be totally self-defeating—"

"Tell it to the police. You don't have to convince me. I'm a Gandhi disciple, I believe in his 'weapons of the brave' . . . But if people like you don't do something, a lot of people like Terry are just going to give up on the whole system. I mean, why is it that people in power always carry on about nonviolence after *they've* called out the armed troops?" Her eyes were hot again. One long leg showed free of the robe. "Vivian, you're part of the government, aren't you? A very top part. The damn war is illegal, isn't it? Special Forces are torturing, burning, bombing women and children, aren't they? The CIA is there, isn't it, doing their dirty things . . . I mean, who violated the Geneva Accords? Who staged the fake Tonkin Gulf provocation? Who backed the French collaborators against Ho Chi Minh in the first place, *after* he had taken on the Japanese?" A thousand anti-war teach-ins rang in her words. Still, her indictment was not out of line, and to the DCI a judgment.

He was sorry the moment he opened his mouth to answer. "Kathy, it's gotten out of hand, we didn't intend—"

"Don't give me that bull, Vivian. This is not a freak, any more than Korea, or Iran, or Guatemala, or wherever were exceptions to the rule. This is U. S. policy since Hiroshima. And God or history, whichever you believe in, will never forgive you . . ." She stood up, the bruise on her forehead was turning purple against the pink of her scrubbed skin . . . "Well, I'm beat," she said, "I'll see you in the morning."

"Good night, Kathy." He sat alone, without moving. "The weapons of the brave" . . . she had spoken Gandhi's phrase to him. What, then, were his? The weapons of cowardice? of the fearful?

He got up to undress. A hot bath, that might relax him. His cheek burned where he had scraped it on the revolving door. Stupid of him. But those detectives had brought back the Gestapo, pushed a nerve button.

Janet. His wife, no, his dead wife, came back to him as he stretched out in the steaming water. He would have a long talk with Terry. Maybe they could take a trip, all of them, and postpone starting Yale until the next semester. He closed his eyes. The fat, hate-filled faces of the detectives swam through his mind.

The faucet dripped. Kathy's scream drove him up out of the tub. Trailing water, he ran into the darkened bedroom. She was sitting up in bed, he realized, as he felt for the table lamp.

"My God, Vivian, I'm sorry. I had a terrible nightmare . . . I dreamed that the police had shot Terry . . ." She started to shake, crying, reaching for him, pulling him away from the night table. He felt her tears on his chest as he held her. "It's all right, Kathy. This whole thing has been a nightmare . . . I know . . ." She shook silently now.

He got up from his knee to sit on the edge of the king-size bed and realized, as Kathy shifted in his arms, that she was uncovered, at least from the waist up. "You're all wet," she said, sniffling.

"I was in the bath . . ." His eyes were accustomed enough to the dark to see the broad outlines of her neck and shoulders . . . could she see his sudden excitement?

"Here," she said, trying to pull the blanket toward him to dry himself. "Oh"—her hand brushed past and paused at his arching erection. He shrank back, her hand was on his thigh now. Her voice was low. "There was more to the dream . . . in the dream they killed Terry because of something you and I had done . . ." Her hand jerked involuntarily on his thigh. It jumped again, the fingertips catching in his pubic hair. Then she arched, took a deep, shuddering breath. As she let it out he felt her fingers uncoil and slip loosely around the base of his penis. And, no longer able to resist, he leaned toward her. Her lips and tongue were pliant and tender on his mouth. He shifted his position and kicked the covers back and away. As he touched the tips of her breasts she whispered, "Is this—sick?" Vivian's throat was tight with desire. Instead of speaking he slowly kissed her nipples. She groaned. "You're a woman," he whispered, as much to himself as to her. . . .

There wasn't enough of Terry's body found to cremate.

In the middle of the late-September heat wave Vivian had been informed by a grim-voiced Vic Korcuska that a Weatherman "bomb factory" had blown up in a Greenwich Village town house and that "Your stepson is being listed as one of the missing, Mr. Prescott . . . a car is waiting to take you to the shuttle."

The luxurious brownstone was nothing but a smoking shell

444

when he arrived. The crowd was being held back by New York police. Vivian spotted Ernie Heidt and waved him over. Heidt was an Agency asset in the FBI.

"Vivian . . . I hate to tell you . . . two lived, but your boy and the Shawn girl and the Gold girl were in the basement when it blew up—"

"Ernie, I have to know. Is there a positive I.D.?"

"Yes."

"What is it?"

"An informant."

"Ernie, did your 'informant' blow them up?"

The skinny FBI man mopped his neck and spat into the street.

Vivian grimaced, trying to focus his vision, the thought screaming like a shell through his mind . . . Don't say it was a provocateur from the Agency's CHAOS operation or I'll kill you on the spot with my hands . . .

"That's all I know now, Vivian." The FBI Special Agent went back into the crowd of fire and police officials.

On the telephone Pat refused to talk to Vivian. Not hating him, simply unable to form any words to speak the unspeakable. To accept or even hear the unacceptable.

The next day as they walked for miles into the Virginia country-side she said, "No grave, my son has no grave in this country." Her voice was strangled. Vivian clenched his fists, his throat felt as if it were bursting. "Terry's crumbs," she sobbed, her knees starting to give way. The two of them clung to each other by the side of the road.

"He's just disintegrated, Viv." They tried to walk again. The air signaled the coming rain. "He's just . . . disappeared . . ." Through the film of tears Vivian searched the sky, then the trees and the low hills beyond, thinking, my son is vanished into the air.

She would not, she said, have any mass said for him as she had for Tim for her mother's sake. Now she was the mother. "Oh, my God, it's so obscene . . . for him to go before me . . . Like all those boys in Vietnam . . . No, I think God has turned his back on this country . . ."

Kathy and her father stopped by the next day for a few minutes. Pat was unable to see anyone so Vivian stood on the front steps. He and Kathy did not look directly at each other. Buck Buchanan could only shake his head and mumble, "Where will it end?" and "What's happening to us?" and grip his daughter's thin hand as if he were afraid that she, too, might disintegrate and vanish before his very eyes.

Sam Prescott was too ill to come down, so Vivian went up to New York. The old man was shattered. He had come to love the boy as if he had been his own. In Chicago they had laughed and cried together. He felt betrayed by the land that he had loved like his life for some eighty years. How to love now?

Across the street in Central Park Vivian sat in the dark imagining that Terry's essence was somehow all around him, merged with Janet and Mush and Tim, and he longed to be part of them. He was so lost in his reverie that he did not for a minute even notice the man who sat down on the other end of the bench. When some noise did cause him to turn in the dark, to look at whoever it was, he knew that he had finally gone around the bend. Because the man staring at him in the pale moonlight appeared to be death himself. He could see the ghastly countenance as pale as an apparition. Where the eyes should have been were small dark tunnel openings with eyes at the ends of them. Vivian could only stare. Very slowly his perception widened to include the mundane details of the man's loose wool suit, blue-gray in the moonlight. The jacket hung loose from the bony shoulders . . . Something about the shoulders sent a signal echoing through Vivian's brain—beyond anything so simple as memory—into his very being.

The other man on the bench was Mush Hollander.

The voice was the same, or rather a low hoarse abstraction of itself. "Don't have a heart attack, Viv." Two lovers walked in and out of the perimeter of moonlight around the bench.

"*Mush?*"

"Hello, Viv."

"You're *alive?*"

"More or less." The voice belonged to a very sick man, a dying man. "I knew you would be coming up to see your father. I waited." He muffled a cough.

"Mush . . . are you . . . ?"

"I'm not working for Moscow Center. I've been teaching for more than ten years. I've not been unhappy, Viv . . . I *do* have a few friends in the center. I kept up with you. I've seen Philby. I

446

know about Tim, and now Terry. I'm sorry as hell." His breathing was shallow, through his mouth.

Vivian could see in the moonlight that he was glistening with moisture. He could have been a man of seventy. His hair was thinned to a smudged gray, eyes black hollows and dim embers, his large-muscled frame seeming to have fallen in on itself, lost now in the folds of the Russian wool suit. Mush lifted a shaky hand to wipe at his face . . . Mush, Vivian thought, so many years, he wanted to kiss him, to hold him . . . As always, the moment passed.

"Viv, Moscow Center has its sane people too. I'm full of pain-killer now, so let me get to the point. The cancer is terminal, anytime. So my friends at the Center asked me to bring a message to you . . . I'm going on to Chicago. I want to be buried in the Jewish cemetery, you know, next to my parents." The labored breathing seemed to tear through his throat, forcing him to stop. Vivian looked down to see that Mush was hanging onto the side of the bench with a near-skeletal hand.

"Rest, Mush, take it easy—"

"No. Moscow Center has penetrated a network of Asian fronts that have drawn together behind Nixon's candidacy. It's the old Taiwan bunch plus the whole adventurist net in Vientiane and Bangkok. They're pouring millions into the Nixon campaign, but that's not the problem. Working through Anna Chennault and other agents the Nixon people are going to sabotage the Paris peace talks that Johnson set in motion when he resigned . . . They've convinced Thieu and Ky that a President Nixon will esca-late and finally win the war. So the South will stall the peace talks and Nixon will win. They've worked out a four-year plan with the South"—the sweat was pouring off his gaunt face—"the plan is to escalate arms and aid and the South in turn will funnel back cash to Nixon through secret bank accounts already set up by his people in Hong Kong, Rangoon and Geneva. We're talking about hun-dreds and millions of dollars. The deal includes the Howard Hughes organization and other war industries that are cleaning up from the war. It's a massive operation and it includes Agency people and assets. You know . . . Scott, Hunt, Chennault—" He began coughing again.

"Mush, you're saying that Moscow Center has proof that Nixon's agents are undermining the peace negotiations between the

447

United States government and the government of the South and the North Vietnamese and the NLF in Paris?"

He nodded, slipped a tablet into his mouth. "That's it, old buddy."

"So Nixon is taking money for prolonging the war. It comes to that, Mush?"

"It comes to that."

"This is set to go, correct? And Agency assets are being used . . . All right, if they go ahead then it's treason. Nixon, too, he could be impeached—"

"There's more, Viv. Unless something is done to expose this before the escalation reaches the point of no return, unless the Paris peace conferences continue under a Nixon presidency the Russians—" A fresh paroxysm of coughing shook him. Vivian could barely stand to watch him.

"What, Mush? The Russians *what?* Will come in?" The contorted body rocked back and forth in assent, like an old Jew *davening* in the *shule*.

"But where? How?"

Mush was gasping for breath. "Three stages . . . Middle East—Suez—give Hanoi rockets to hit Saigon—Berlin for the showdown. *Their* hawks're ready . . ."

Vivian stared past the figure of his friend toward the relief of the tall hotels of Central Park South. It sounded convincing, too damn terribly convincing . . . Since Mush's defection millions of uncommitted people in the unindustrialized countries, the so-called third world, had been taken over by the Russians or the Chinese and not a single Soviet soldier had been used or sacrificed in any contest from Korea to Vietnam. Now Mush was telling him that the Russians were going to react to American escalation if the Nixon scheme to use the Paris peace talks as a screen for more war went forward . . . Except what, he thought, if Mush had been sent by the KGB to plant this harrowing scenario on the American DCI, his old friend? But Mush was *admitting* as much, he was speaking for the moderates. They had sent a dead man to deliver a signal. Of course it was a plant, but it was also true . . .

Mush tried to get up, fell back, pushed himself up the side of the heavy iron bench, stood there stooped and swaying, trying to speak. Vivian quickly stood to catch him if he collapsed. He reached for Vivian's lapel, pulled him close.

448

"Get out, Viv. Expose it and get *out . . .*" The sound struggled out of his throat. "Tell Pat I love her, always loved her. Don't follow me . . . good-by, Viv . . ."

Vivian stood and watched him stagger, shamble like some kind of wounded beast into the shadows; disappearing, merging into the park foliage and its shadow. His eyes blurred again so that the retreating outline of the wounded man was superimposed in his mind's eye by the strong, straight back of a dozen years past when his friend had walked off into the Russian forest, in hindsight a sort of rehearsal for tonight—

He did not see the mugger until almost too late. The scrawny kid seemed to materialize out of the night to Vivian's right. The switchblade caught a dull reflection of the moon.

"Give me your money, motherfucker."

Vivian's hair-trigger reaction system came into play automatically. He noted the knife hand trembling, heard the voice shake, saw that the kid was no more than about eighteen . . . Terry's age. A junkie too.

"Take it easy, son," feeling no measurable fear. Death had too many faces tonight in the park. Maybe if he had had more fear in his life he would have been better off. Remembering that Philby used to refer snidely to him as "Captain America," implying that a man without sufficient fear was a man without good sense . . . "Son," he said to the boy, "put that away."

The kid mumbled and lifted the blade a little higher.

"Listen," Vivian said slowly, "I'm trained. I could maim you with one kick."

"Kill me," said the kid. "I ain't leaving without some money. I got to have money . . ."

"Yes," Vivian said calmly. "Here's fifty dollars." Reaching for his wallet and fingering out bills. The boy reached out with the other hand, really trembling now.

"Okay," he mumbled, and then he too disappeared, and Vivian Prescott the spymaster was left alone in the dark park, thinking, "Motherfucker. What's in a name . . . ? Too much, in this case, Vivian Prescott . . ." And then he tried to shake it off and walked briskly out of the park. . . .

After his victory Richard Nixon established temporary headquarters in Manhattan's Hotel Pierre. Vivian's was one of the first appointments. He met alone with the President-elect at nine in the

449

morning. Nixon, with his insatiable relish for intrigue, had scheduled a private meeting with the DCI. For some reason Nixon had the air conditioning on.

The man from nowhere was flushed with victory, literally jumping with energy in a new blue suit and a conservative hand-painted tie. Jack Kennedy's epithet . . . "the one hundred percent unexamined life" . . . came back to Vivian as he shook the cold hand.

Over coffee and tea the two men chatted about the state of the world, Nixon talking about "dealing from strength," sawing the air with his characteristic gestures.

A stray bit of intelligence from the Nixon dossier drifted across Vivian's thoughts as he tried to tune out the breathy resonance of the figure who had gotten so caught up in his geopolitical disquisitions that he'd launched into a kind of jitterbug-ramble around the suite. (In private, with his close associates, Vivian had heard, Nixon favored a bright red dinnerjacket. The man was a treasure trove of bad taste, right down the line.)

As Nixon moved about, it occurred to Vivian that here was a man who every night dreamed not of success but of *failure* . . . that was why he had outlasted men like Sam Prescott . . . they died of broken hearts . . . Nixon, with nothing to lose, broke them . . . Vivian remembered the ad in the California paper that had brought Nixon onto the political stage.

> WANTED: Congressman candidate with no previous political experience to defeat a man who has represented the district in the House for ten years. Any young man resident of the district, preferably a veteran, fair education . . . may apply for the job. Applicants will be reviewed by 100 interested citizens . . .

"I, myself, trapped Hiss . . ." Nixon was saying, and without realizing what he was doing, the eternal candidate pulled at his crotch.

Now, after a quarter of an hour, Nixon began to unveil his "secret plan for peace" in Vietnam. "The Communists understand only force," he confided to the director. There then ensued a commentary on his "big-power poker strategy to mate their domino theory." The geopolitical word salad, prescribed by Kissinger, tossed by Nixon, continued until Vivian interrupted to point out

450

that "the Russians still have a range of options to bring into play if we continue to escalate."

Nixon flushed. "No, they, uh . . . see, they're chicken in the crunch. They'll blink first. Now, the Russians respect strength. They'll, uh, back down before an ultimatum. Eisenhower proved that in Korea. I was the one who . . ."

Vivian's irritation built. "That's two Soviet weapons systems ago, Mr. Nixon. Our Estimates Directory has hard evidence that if we invade across the DMZ, our best Marine units are likely to float back in their own blood. Soviet-equipped North Vietnamese elite units are at one million strength, they're as yet uncommitted but they're ready . . ."

In the silence Nixon pulled at his pants and stared at the DCI. Then—he spat it out—"Shit!" and relapsed into a moody silence. When he stirred himself it was to begin a rehash of his triumph in exposing Alger Hiss and the "Communist conspiracy in the fifties."

Vivian stared at his trouser cuffs while Nixon recalled how he had "fooled them before" and how he "was not about to preside over the dismemberment of the free world" and how he hated "defeatism" and those "who would reduce America to the condition of a helpless giant." Then he fell into still another morose silence.

At length, Vivian looked up from the study of his cuffs. "Mr. President, have you read former Secretary McNamara's rather pessimistic secret study of the Vietnam conflict?"

"That pansy!" But the tone was a little frightened. "That punk and his bleeding hearts. This administration is going to play *hard* ball, Mr. Prescott. This is the first team." He pulled at his pants, not looking at the DCI. "I have my own sources," he said.

Vivian decided that he had to make his move now, or not at all. "Mr. President, our intelligence is that Saigon will not fight. We have evidence that they're in it for American money, that they're willing to trade off American lives and huge casualties for *money* . . . that Saigon is rotten to the core. The Thieu regime, sir, are gangsters, corrupted root and branch. The scandal is so massive that when it breaks it could backlash all the way to Washington."

Nixon's scurrying eyes narrowed. He had, Vivian knew, understood the message, and the threat in the use of the word "gangsters."

"Listen, Prescott, I don't want to hear that stuff. I don't want to hear the goddamn Communist line from *my* Director of Central Intelligence. President Thieu is a statesman—an Asian Churchill. We don't need to hear the Moscow line from Langley. The days of Kim Philby and the traitors are *over.*" . . . So Sherman Scott had briefed Nixon on Philby *and* Oswald, and tied them to the DCI. He waited for the rabbit punch . . . "I tell you, Prescott, that kind of talk from Langley will draw a signal from the White House. The American people have been through hell since Dallas. I warn you not to tear this country apart. If the bleeding hearts at your shop try to pull their backstabbing defeatist shit on us, we can dig up every rotting corpse since the Cuban thing."

The gall of Nixon to threaten him with Dallas. Nixon had to know that Vivian Prescott was aware that he, Nixon, had flown into Dallas on November 21, 1963, on government business. Vivian knew about the small party on the evening of the twenty-first at the estate of Texas oil magnate Rafe Hutchinson at which J. Edgar Hoover had been one of the guests and George De Mohrenschildt another, and H. L. Hunt, the billionaire, another . . . and that one Jack Ruby had visited the estate less than an hour before the festivities, and that after Ruby shot Oswald to death in the basement of the Dallas Police and Courts Building Nixon had stated to the press—"two wrongs don't make a right." One more word about Dallas from Nixon, Vivian told himself, and there would be some blood spilled in the elegant hotel suite.

Vivian stared at the rich carpet. His fingers ached to choke the life out of Nixon's lying throat. Instead he shrugged. The code words hung in the artificial air: money, gangsters, Philby, Dallas . . .

"I have *my* sources," Nixon repeated after the long pause as he shuffled to the door and walked out on the DCI. . . .

Pat spent the month of October with her family in Chicago. Once again, the McGuire women were closing the circle of fortitude and protection. She would, she said, begin full-time teaching after the first of the year at the junior college five minutes from their house. She appeared to be adjusting to the loss, but when they were alone they did not talk. Somehow, after all the deaths, it seemed a scandal that they were still alive, and this may have explained why they were now, for the first time, somewhat embarrassed with each other, as if ashamed of their lives, of being alive.

While she was gone Vivian began to have the same dream every night. He would wake up paralyzed by a sense of dread. By the second week Vic Korcuska and his secretaries were insisting that he had returned to the office too soon. He refused to talk to any of the psychological counselors cleared by the Agency. He had nothing but contempt for them. They were, he believed, to psychology what Henry Kissinger was to political science—aberrants.

Somehow, though, he remembered a man who used to live in the old southwest ghetto section of Washington. He found the name still listed—Isador Sookerman. Mush Hollander had delighted him with stories about this ex-Freudian, ex-Marxist psychotherapist that Mush had gone to when the pain over his divorce became too intense. Black men in Goodwill overcoats sat on the steps of the building, drinking wine and talking about what Cassius Clay would do when he got out of jail. They looked suspiciously at the lean white man who asked if Dr. Sookerman lived here. "The old Jew? Yeah, he's here. He a bad old man . . ."

Vivian understood enough ghettoese to know that the therapist was considered "bad"—which was to say, by their lights, *good.*

Vivian walked past the entrance to the tiny furrier's shop and up two flights. At the head of the stairs was a door with a very dirty index card tacked to it: ISADOR SOOKERMAN—COUNSELING, DAY OR NIGHT. Vivian almost turned back, but just at that moment the door was flung open and there was Sookerman.

"You're not Miss Glass . . . you're not her father, are you?"

"Dr. Sookerman?"

"Mr. Sookerman. I'm an old-timer."

Behind him Vivian could see a tiny apartment that could have come out of a time capsule of the '30s: fringe lamps, overstuffed chairs, crystal radio, Persian throw rugs, grilled icebox.

The little man was bundled up in two sweaters and a bright checked shirt. "Come in," he said warmly, and Vivian followed after him. "It's a great honor to have the head of the secret police drop in for a personal visit. You look surprised. I read the paper, I watch TV, *every* news show. I saw you on 'Meet the Press'—quite a performance. So, I'm very happy to meet you in the flesh.

Though I don't look it, we're in the same racket—but yes. You look surprised, again. Sure, a good therapist is God's spy . . . You're thinking of leaving for Georgetown? What a pity. Am I lacking in charisma? My lack of professional dignity, does that put you off? I am excited to meet a great spy and celebrity . . . I'm trying hard to keep calm but it's no use, my demon is joyful. Do not worry, sir, it is not necessary for the psychoanalyst to be above the patient or to be a superior person . . . not at all. You see, it is not with my intellect I work, it is with my memory. Yes, I can remember off the record, as they say, and my work is to help others to remember. Wait . . . do not speak yet. Tell me whether I am right: have you come concerning a problem of your own or for another person, and how did you choose me for your purpose?"

"Mr. Sookerman, I've come on my own account, and to you because I had your address from a man named Mush Hollander. Marshall, you may—"

"So? Is that possible? A wonderful boy, where is he now?"

The round little man had plumped down in a chair and was pointing to the sagging divan. For some reason Vivian liked it here in this unlikely den. There was an ancient yellow photo of Freud on the wall. It seemed to go with the territory. He wanted to talk about Mush. He found himself being almost frank about Russia and Lieberman . . . "Ah, Lieberman," the therapist intoned . . . When Vivian described Mush's disappearance into the forest, Sookerman's eyes seemed to mist, which moved Vivian so much that he almost told him that Mush was still alive. Barely . . .

". . . so, so. Mush Hollander. Yeah . . . yeah, and I'm still here, over the furrier—the second one. Ahh, you should have seen this neighborhood in Mush's day, 1951, '52 . . ."

The old clock ticked. Vivian finally took off his topcoat.

"So Mush—that's why you came to me . . . what is it, a divorce?"

"No."

"No. Divorce is a kind of dark comedy suited for those who have failed at romanticism but continue to hope. But you, tell me if I'm right, are a classicist, a man if irony. Do I read you correctly?"

"You read me pretty well, if too kindly."

The old man fished a cough drop out of a cardboard container, then threw the box on the cluttered coffee table for his guest. "Please continue, Mr. Prescott."

454

"Well, quite recently I suffered a loss—my stepson. I began to dream . . . not be able to sleep . . ."

"What's the dream?"

"All I remember when I wake up is a hanging on the New Haven Green. But the tone of the dream is mockery, somehow."

"So at the eleventh hour you thought—'Sookerman!' "

Vivian smiled. "I know you know the Faust legend . . ." Sookerman was nodding his head, chuckling. Vivian was actually, he told himself, feeling like a human being. He was right to have come, and the thought of the confusion of the inevitable KGB surveillance of him added good measure to the unlikely encounter. "I seem condemned, Mr. Sookerman, to speak in rather ponderous metaphors—it's my background, I guess. We don't employ many straight lines."

"Well, there are many ways, I've found, to tell the truth, even grammatically."

Vivian felt like a student again, trading insights with Professor Mann back on William Street. Sookerman, he now realized, meant "searcher" in German . . . "To pursue a metaphor," Vivian went on, "will you go along with me if I say a devil's bargain in reverse?"

"Reverse? In reverse?" The old man was rocking. "This may be psychologically impossible, but sure, I haven't had so much fun in years. Pardon my levity. I know you are serious. A bargain with the devil in *reverse*. A new version of the legendary deal . . . you want to trade, to sell your *life* in order to preserve your *soul*. Instead of soul for *life*, by *you* it's life for *soul*. Have I understood your metaphor?"

"Exactly. More romantic than classical, I'm afraid. Still, I feel sort of better, for no good reason . . ."

"You don't need good reasons. You have no good reason to die, so you certainly don't need one to feel an intimation of hope."

"I wouldn't go so far as to say hope." Vivian felt torn between the need to reveal himself to this strange therapist and, as always, to hide his thoughts, as he'd been trained to do so much of his life.

"No, you wouldn't, but *I* would. I haven't got your style, but I think I smell a little hope."

Vivian just stared, unable to answer. What an agent, he thought, Sookerman would have made.

"You smile. You are a big man, Mr. Prescott, head of the secret

455

police, but you are not ashamed of suffering, are you? . . . I ask you also not to be ashamed to hope."

"From the very bottom of Pandora's box . . ."

"Yeah, that's a good quote, but the box has been opened, hasn't it?"

"Perhaps."

"Hah! I got inside one of your metaphors, didn't I?"

Which made Vivian laugh softly.

"Wait a minute—here we are having a good time, the interview is over, and we haven't even talked money, time, nothing. Forty-five years, I still don't do nothing right. Nothing! But you feel hope —that ain't borscht, Mr. Prescott. Who knows? If I knew what the game was, maybe I could remember the rules. Never mind, we'll discuss all that tomorrow, same time. Yes?"

"Well, I don't know, I—"

"Wait a minute. What time is it? This lousy watch has stopped again."

"Just four."

"Four? Where is Miss Glass? She's ten minutes late. She's never late . . . me, yes, but never Miss Glass. A wonderful girl, an actress, a little on the heavy side. Oh boy, maybe she's got a job. So, take a few minutes more. Wait a minute, I want to hear the news, okay?" Without waiting for a reply he scrambled up to turn on the ancient radio.

The man, Vivian told himself, is playing me like a musical instrument.

Sookerman fiddled with the dial, then sat expectantly.

". . . so when you hear this voice, 'Ho, Ho, ho,' then, ladies, you know you have a giant just where you need him, just *when* you need him. In your kitchen on blue Monday. If you are not satisfied . . ."

Sookerman heaved himself out of the chair to turn the dial.

". . . bringing the body count to five thousand enemy dead so far this month, according to military intelligence. At the White House a highly placed source expressed guarded optimism, saying, 'Our selected, pinpoint bombing of the enemy's major industries is responsible for bringing him to the peace table.' The source stressed that pilots were instructed not to bomb civilians in the densely populated areas surrounding the targets . . ."

456

Sookerman shut off the radio. "Son-of-a-bitch! What a theater it is! What a theater. Jolly giants come through the air, ho ho ho, and drop detergent, ho ho ho. Then a high source tells me that fire bombs wouldn't kill any civilians, ho ho ho. Yesterday I shut it off in the middle. Some Casanova tells me I should promise them anything but give them French perfume instead and another highly placed source tells me promise them everything but give them American perfume instead, but not on civilians, ho ho ho! Then a cowboy assures me only real he-men smoke mint cigarettes, and my leader, the tricky *vilde chaye* from California, informs me that he wouldn't preside over the dismemberment of a helpless giant, meaning the U.S. of A. Dismemberment of a helpless giant! This is a *meshygener,* you understand Yiddish? No. You understand psychoanalysis? Yes. A psychopathic personality, also a nut . . . I'm giving you an objective, scientific diagnosis, you understand. Meanwhile bisexual singing groups tell me yeah, yeah, yeah, and the civil rights movement has burned out the block twice except for Orloff downstairs, the furrier. Why not Orloff too? Because the movement likes me for some crazy reason. But don't worry, it's getting worse . . . the whole building is going up in flames and me with it. Orloff the furrier wants to give me rent free so I'll stay and protect him. The insurance is canceled, but from the ghetto I ain't moving. I'm a hostage, see? Sookerman the ransom. Light up, boys, instant sainthood, whoopee. Oii, yi, yi, ho ho ho, what a theater. Please, forgive me, forgive me. The radio gets me *crazy,* the papers worse. I had a TV. When my wife died I put it away for a while. Until it got too lonely. We used to like the Cagney movies. The TV ran out of old movies, and my wife died. You smile? My wife died, I went a little crazy. Yeah, and as far as my great colleagues are concerned, I'm Sookerman the scandal. A logical positivist I'm not—positive I'm *definitely* not—but crazy altogether I'm not also. I've been through the wringer, that's what I am. So continue, forgive the slight interruption, please. So your dream, Mr. Spy?"

The old man's manic energy was irresistible. "Mr. Sookerman, I hate to spoil this interlude."

"You have some little bad dreams up your sleeve, huh?"

"Just one. Very bad."

"Where did you get such a bad one? You're smiling again."

"Well . . ."

" 'Responsibility begins . . .' "

" 'In dreams.' "

"Marvelous, Mr. Prescott, perfect. Yeats, my favorite poet." The therapist now glared at the yellowing photograph of Sigmund Freud on the wall. *"You,* great one, should have said that . . . how did *you* say that? Never mind . . . So, back to work."

Vivian sighed and without meaning to began to talk in a low voice. "I am standing in a shadowed but open place. It reminds me of a university corridor at Yale. Time passes, I remain standing in this silent, shadowy place. Waiting. Then in the stillness, *out* of the stillness, like an extension of the silence itself, I hear my name called. Once, and very lightly, gently. A curious paradox . . . the tone and manner of this call are gentle, delicate, almost caressing. But despite this, or perversely because of it, this call of my name somehow freezes me with fear . . . On the Green a silent crowd waits for the hanging to begin . . ."

The clock ticked. Sookerman stared at him as if he were dreaming the same dream. "This dream commenced after your stepson died?"

"Yes."

"Do I remember Mush telling me that your wife died in the war?"

"Yes."

"Were you happily married—the first time? If that question makes any sense."

"Well . . . there was a lack in the matter of, ah, ecstasy, if you'll forgive the word."

"Ah, ecstasy. It is a pleasure to use the old words with you, Mr. Prescott. Please pursue, in these last few minutes before the news, the topic of you, your first wife, and ecstasy."

"Well . . . the ecstasy wasn't available, except—"

"Except through secular intercourse, huh?"

"Yes, and only, well, sporadically . . ."

For some reason the old man's voice seemed younger than his own. "Yeah, it is so common—this attitude of failure, I mean. A man and woman, or any two lovers, same thing, can do so much, are needed by the world, need each other if they knew it, but they don't have a certified vaginal orgasm and right away it's, 'How *do*

458

you do, Mr. and Mrs. Nonentity!' The man does the whole multiplication table or he thinks about Theda Bara or whoever they're thinking about these days—and this he does only *if* he's still trying. And the woman . . . she runs to a therapist, Dr. Quack, next she buys a love manual for Mr. Outraged who's sulking at home dreaming of Theda Bara, then God knows what she does next. Listen, this is a pet peeve with me. You make sex the way you do everything else in your life. You have a little freedom to grow, to try, to understand. But this orgasm collecting, this amateur gynecology, this definition by mutual explosion and colored lights and seeing God *every* time, or at least two out of three, or any crazy statistic made up by someone who don't know you, this is nuts! You're right, no ecstasy any more. Politics? Forget it. The Communists are to the right of the chamber of commerce. And you don't want no drugs. You want a *catharsis,* not a frontal lobotomy. It's all the same now, no ecstasy anywhere, any more—except in that king-sized bed during the commercials. Listen, sex never could, never would, never will be the only door to *meaning.* Who, *what* could stand that strain? Sex . . . it's wonderful, especially for children . . . all they can get . . . and once in a while, whenever you can, you work it in. You know, 'In a real man a child is hidden— and wants to play.' You got a problem? Okay, you talk it over. You come to me, you lay your cards on the table. Fine. But you have to learn about miracles . . . how to recognize them. 'I was in *love,* doctor, I got married, then the miracle ended.' That's so crazy. The miracle's just *begun.* Now it *begins.* How? The point is you weren't *in* love when you got married—not at all. That was just a little trick of your nervous system to force a decision, to force the issue—the *issue,* get it? Now you're stuck. Now it begins. You see, it don't matter. Anything that gets you started, gets you involved is okay. Love from any source, any fiction, any daydream, any swamp. You're *started.* That's all that counts. Yeah, I know—how do you *program* hot pants into a life?" Sookerman was almost singing now. His eyes seemed to shine in the later afternoon gloom.

"The miracle is in the *trying.* For the first time in two million years we really want to do it. What do these divorce statistics that everybody quotes mean? *What do they mean?* Hedonism, cynicism, nihilism? Rubbish! This is the age of *ideals,* the age of *love.* We want

459

the whole shooting match: companionship, partnership, love *and* ecstasy! And for the first time in history, if we don't get it, good-by. For two million *years* nobody had illusions like this. Love *and* marriage? Love and marriage *and* ecstasy for *life?* Never in a million, in two million years. This is very big *hubris,* Mr. Spy, it's *chutzpah!* Some people—the lucky triers—pull it off, sometimes. Off and on, there it is. And what's the secret? Love from any source. That's the ticket. You felt it once? Then, gamble you'll feel it again. But why change people? Doesn't the stranger you live with have enough faces for one lifetime? So, you let yourself be swindled by love, you play the rube at the fair, you let your body con you. Why blow the whistle—it's the only game in town? Get me? So, the experts keep yelling, There is no substitute for orgasm ho ho ho. Well, I, the only failed ghetto psychoanalyst in the world, I, Mr. 'Yehudi' Sookerman, got news for them . . . there may be no substitute for an orgasm, but an orgasm ain't no substitute for life!"

He subsided. The flat was almost dark now. Vivian stood up. Was the old man asleep?

"I guess Miss Glass ain't coming," he mumbled, not looking up. Then, "No charge, Mr. Prescott. For old time's sake . . . for Mush's sake . . . we didn't get a chance to talk about your dream, did we? . . . Well, maybe next time."

Vivian waited for a moment, then turned toward the door.

"I won't see you again," he thought he heard the old man mutter. Then, "Take it easy, my boy, remember—no one can control their thoughts . . ."

Downstairs the drunks glared at him. The temperature was dropping.

Richard Nixon—the DCI's jaw tightened as he waded through the trash—Richard Nixon, the *meshuganuh,* the *vilde chaye* . . . or however you said it . . . would, finally, pay. . . .

It came down to who had more guns. Nixon had his forces *and* the Black supergrade units at Plans as well. Vivian could and would leak the Vietnam war estimates, the secret bombing of Cambodia and Laos—the Gemstone plan. But that was not the same as going public for a finish fight. He would have to rely on stealth if he was going to bring down every tree in the forest.

By early '69 Vivian had an agent taping Nixon's Oval Office meetings. The rough draft of the plan to set up what amounted to an American Gestapo was in his hands by late spring.

RECOMMENDATIONS

TOP SECRET

Handle via Comint Channels

Only

Operational Restraints
on Intelligence Collection

A. *Interpretive Restraints on Communications Intelligence.* RECOMMENDATION: Present interpretation should be broadened to permit and program for coverage by NSA of the communications of U. S. citizens using international facilities.

B. *Electronic Surveillance and Penetrations.* RECOMMENDATION: Present procedures should be *(unclear)* changed to permit intensification of coverage of individuals and groups in the United States of interest to the intelligence community.

At the present time, less than *(unclear)* electronic penetrations are operative, with only a few authorized against subjects of pressing internal security interest.

Mr. Hoover's statement that the FBI would not oppose other agencies seeking approval for the operating electronic surveillances is gratuitous since no other agencies have the capability.

Everyone knowledgeable in the field, with the exception of Mr. Hoover, concurs that existing coverage is grossly inadequate. CIA and NSA note that this is particularly true of diplomatic establishments, and we have learned at the White House that it is also true of new left groups.

C. *Mail Coverage.* RECOMMENDATION: Restrictions on legal coverage should be removed.

Also, present restrictions on covert coverage should be relaxed on selected targets of priority foreign intelligence *and* internal security interest.

D. *Surreptitious Entry.* RECOMMENDATION: Present restrictions should be modified to permit selective use of this technique against security targets.

E. *Development of Campus Sources.* RECOMMENDATION: Present restrictions should be relaxed to permit expanded coverage of violence-prone campus and student-related groups.

Also, CIA coverage of American students (and others) traveling or living abroad should be increased.

Budget and Manpower Restrictions

RECOMMENDATION: Each agency should submit a detailed estimate as to projected manpower needs and other costs in the event the various investigative restraints herein are lifted.

Measures to Improve Domestic Intelligence Operations

RECOMMENDATION: A permanent committee consisting of the FBI, CIA, NSA, DIA and the military counterintelligence agencies should be appointed to provide evaluations of domestic intelligence estimates, and carry out the other objectives in the report.

The need for increased cooperation, joint estimates and responsiveness to the White House is obvious. There are a number of operational problems which need to be worked out, since Mr. Hoover is fearful of any mechanism which might jeopardize his autonomy. CIA would prefer an *ad hoc* committee to see how the system works, but other members believe that this would merely delay the establishment of effective coordination and joint operations. The value of lifting intelligence collection restraints is proportional to the availability of joint operations and evaluation, and the establishment of this interagency group is considered imperative.

The desk clock stood at 11:41. They would still be there in the bowels of the building monitoring the taping system they had installed somewhere in the DCI's office. Suddenly, almost as if in a vision, Vivian was certain that there was a remote microphone embedded in the desk clock.

What did it matter anyway? Intelligence—the *word* as applied to what he did was a gross impropriety, the notion a black farce. Stalin had not believed Leopold Trepper when he sent in firm information that Hitler would attack Russia. Philby's and Tony Blunt's massive penetration had substantially compromised Anglo-American intelligence efforts. So much so that, in a real sense, it would have been better if there had been *no* British or American intelligence at all. Nearly everything since World War II had been compromised and turned around. And Philby's moles—some of them . . . at least two of them—were still in place in the Circus, at MI6, and at Langley in Plans. Operations blown, lives wasted . . . Penkovsky had compromised Moscow Center as well. And he and all the other major defectors had been walk-ins in any case, no thanks to Plans. And he had heard years ago from his father that Hoover had *intelligence* about Pearl Harbor and ignored it. The latest irony, delicious to him, was Vic Korcuska's flash that Berlin operatives had just confirmed that East German Communist agents had thoroughly penetrated the Gehlen organization. Gehlen, the old fox, his meal ticket, would have worked, finally, for Stalin himself if the price had been right. Another great man—whores, all of them . . .

The tape in his head turned and turned. His sigh was more like the pant of a long distance runner. There were so many tapes to make and no time left. A record must be released of the businesses and proprietaries that had been purchased with the Agency's Asian opium traffic proceeds. The key "agents of influence" of the mass media must be exposed . . . the Nixonian-Scott op to murder the President of Panama under a narcotics enforcement cover . . .

Shame rose on the surface of his skin like sweat. He pressed his wide forehead as if to stop his winding thoughts. But Sookerman had said, "No one can control their thoughts" . . . Tracy Barnes had left Langley to return to Yale, there to test a new "urban affairs" plan for control of the black ghetto under a cover of enlightened liberal sociology. Barnes's informants had told him that an FBI agent provocateur was setting up the Black Panther chapter in New Haven on torture-murder charges. Barnes, with support from Old Boys at CIA, instead of alerting authorities had ordered his plants in the Panthers to carry out the provocation. A young Panther, Alex Rackley, had been mutilated and killed. Now Barnes was feeding the details—with the FBI provocation hidden—to former agents of his who had run Black propaganda disinformation ops in Division Ten in Western Europe. As the case came to trial, Barnes's media network began their attack under liberal cover . . . There were famous names and Vivian intended that they be blown: the editor of *Gotham Magazine*, Goldstein of *Manhattan* . . .

"No time, no time . . ." His lips parted mechanically. The tape in his head was speeding up, faster and faster. "Intelligence," "Plans" . . . as if this feral scheming had anything to do with the human intellect or capacity to plan. His eyes blurred in the darkness. Hadn't the KGB handed him the Khrushchev speech on a silver platter? He was a designated agent . . . delicious thought . . . of Moscow's so-called enlightened moderates . . . He, the great spymaster, had risen to the top—or sunk to the bottom?—because he could scheme so that other men could pretend that their hands were clean.

His father's and Pat's faces seemed to hang like photographs. The old man's eyes were sad. Had he passed away? Pat's expression was gentle. He wanted to reach out to touch the thick hair, the delicate freckles. What were they trying to say to him? It was like that night at Skull and Bones when, blindfolded, he had heard the deep tones ring through the vault. Now other words reverberated in his head . . . "You have become what you set out to destroy. You came sprinting out of the Ivory Tower and have at last reached the rim of the abyss . . ." The voice was not quite his father's. It was a composite of sounds of the people whose lives had touched him, whose lives he had touched, a rising, grieving composite voice . . . "In your blind alley, your cabinet of secrets—you cannot hide from who you are. You are haunted by who you are not, who you were meant to be. Waste. You were given everything and you traded it for power. Freedom for power. Rationalized, prettified, but in the end, never mind your good intentions, power without conscious responsibility. That is what's unforgivable in you . . . you had the authority to say no and you refused. You said yes, to murder, the romanticizing of murder. You have been caught, ho ho ho, red-handed."

He jerked his head around to look out the window, the chair swiveling. His father had never talked to him like that, no one had, or would. Pat would never talk to him like that. Where was she? He needed her . . . her voice, her breasts, her mouth with the slightly buck teeth and full lips, all the openings and byways of her body, and her mind and her soul too . . . "Pat," he said softly into the dark night. The thought of her focused his thoughts . . . forget Bones, what are the Estimates and the "back-channels" of information in the case of one Vivian Thomas Jefferson Prescott?

464

So he had, he thought with savage irony, escaped the reductive clutch of Skull and Bones only to finish as bloody harbinger for the Rockefeller-Morgan circle that his father had fought for so long in New York and London. Call it Bilderberg Group, or Council on Foreign Relations, or the Trilateral Commission, or the Round Table group: he knew that he, the spymaster, more a sleepwalker, had been their creature and their creation—the rest was largely rhetoric. He had been a cog in a great wheel crashing downhill. He'd thought to control it, had been controlled instead. By an elite, collective dream of power as old as Skull and Bones. He had written *War against War* when all along he had known that Rudolph Mann had the answer when he said, "There is no way to peace, peace *is* the way."

His brain was racing now. The only people who really could be trusted with the truth were the people. What a discovery! . . . rediscovery . . . Let Scott and Mother listen to the tapes as he made them. And read them when printed, thanks to Pat. McNamara's classified Pentagon study of the Vietnam debacle would reach the people. He had seen to that. And so would the information about Nixon's private Gestapo. He had awakened from the dream of a lifetime. All through the decades he had soothed himself with the heroic-sounding words, and all along he had been hanging in pipedreams on the back of a tiger.

Oh yes, it was the military-industrial complex that fueled the murders in Dallas, Memphis, Los Angeles—the other horrors— but what *was* the military-industrial complex if not the bone, brain and blood of an army of secret warriors of which he, Vivian T. J. Prescott, was the *head*? Wasn't he the DCI? He had tried to save Jack Kennedy's life with one hand, while the other, belonging to the company of men who plotted its end, was numbed, unable to warn. The Hoovers and the Howard Hugheses and the juntas and their generals and the munitions makers, the Nixons and their palace guard, the Meyer Lanskys and their bought cops and politicians—all of these a mere handful in a nation of two hundred million people. And what could these animals do without the brains of the brightest? Like me, he thought, catching an angle of reflection in the dark window.

As he stared, the woods around the secret fortress appeared to mass, and then move. He closed his eyes against the moving trees,

465

as in his mind's eye he could see Pat striding in her brisk way ahead into the future. Yes, she would make the truth public for him . . . She kept going, disappeared and, suddenly, in the near ground was Janet, radiant as she had been in the clear winter at Camp X, now holding him with her dark eyes, and beckoning to him to come to her at last.

Pat had promised him that when . . . that if . . . the time came she would contact her good friend at the Washington *Post* . . . if, for some reason, he himself was unable to go public. "Just promise me," he had said to her. "We have Nixon." "I promise," she had said quietly . . . His left hand crawled like a living thing across the surface of the white telephone, the fingers stuttered on the face of the digits. "Vic. Report in now for an urgent hand delivery. Tapes. Come in black." Breaking off the connection, the right hand engaging the tape machine again.

He pushed the ON button. In the bowels of the complex the Animals' machine would pick up the click and the endless reels would begin to turn. "Tape Five: Operation CHAOS and the neutralization of the radicals, blacks, students . . ." He swung the chair away from the desk to face the window again. The moon was down. The dark bulk of the woods was a bulge across the night.

What was it Professor Mann had told him on William Street? Beware when you look into the abyss, the abyss looks into you.

He swiveled back around to face the desk. 11:54. A bead of perspiration rolled down from his hairline. The unseen photographs stared down at him from the walls. He could feel their eyes looking into him. Janet, Mush, Jack, Bobby, Terry, Tim, Pat, Trepper . . . Sam Prescott, FDR, Kim Philby . . . the silence was louder now . . . Dulles, Gehlen, Intrepid, Bill Donovan . . . Vivian Thomas Jefferson Prescott who at age twenty declined to look at the graveyard, but at a later age looked again, and again.

The tape spun silently in the cassette. He remembered, Einstein had said that whatever reflected the passage of time was a clock. 11:56. In the bowels of Langley Scott would be watching the silent tape turn. Raw time was being recorded. The tape in his head turned in time with the other tape in the machine.

A mechanical record of words, abstractions. Not the idea, not the deed, just the words. Like recorded history itself. A recording. Bloodless and frozen on tape. But if I were to pull the trigger of the old Luger, if I were to pull the trigger, the sound would register on the tapes somewhere beneath the level of mere language. The transcript of the tape, later, would merely reflect a space, a gap in history. But below . . .

Silence, raw time poured into the microphone. He could hear the nothingness of the silence roaring in the room, in his head.

The tapered fingers of the championship hand inched forward in the darkness. The clenched digits of the hand pulled it toward the Luger like a crab. Digging into the hardwood desktop like a crab digging into the everlasting, ever shifting sands of time. . . .